To Beryl,

On your 90th B

This is not a

something we hope you may

enjoy.

<u>Mary Knighton</u>

Love from,

Duncan, Eli, Sophia and Amelia

Thomas Richard Brown

Thomas Richard Brown

22·05·18

1st Edition Published by Second Child Ltd

ISBN: 978-0-9956709-0-7

Mary Knighton copyright © Second Child Ltd 2017

Proofread by Julia Gibbs
juliaproofreader@gmail.com

Cover design by SilverWood Books
(www.silverwoodbooks.co.uk)

Cover image supplied by the author

British Library Cataloguing in Publication Data

A CIP catalogue record for this book is available from the British Library.

Table of Contents

Dedication

For my grandfather, William Brown

Prologue
March 1961

It is half past twelve by the time I hop off the school bus. It is Saturday morning and I am going to Grandfather's for lunch. A car toots from behind.

"Do you want a lift, then?" calls John, a farmer from up in the village.

"Yes please," I reply and jump in.

John chatters away about teachers at my school – he was there once too and always likes to know what's going on there – before dropping me at Grandfather's house.

The smell of boiled neck of mutton greets me as I amble in through the scullery; one of Grandfather's favourites – not one of mine. Margaret, who has been Grandfather's housekeeper since Grandmother died, greets me with a smile. She is in her mid-sixties – tall and thin, with very white hair held round the back in a bun. She tells me to go into the dining room where Grandfather is reading the paper – his normal pre-lunch ritual.

"Well, Peter boy, what have you been up to this morning?" he asks as I enter, folding up his paper.

"Not much," I answer – this tends to be my usual reply.

"And what are you doing this afternoon?"

"Nothing much," I reply again, unsure why he is asking.

"That's good. I want you to drive me to Northampton. I want to go and see Cousin Mary."

I have never heard of Cousin Mary and rack my brains to remember any time that she has been mentioned.

"I will go and ring her before I forget," he says, making his way off towards the phone, turning in the doorway to ask, "You did pass your test?"

I nod and watch him stride out to the phone. When he has finished he calls me into the kitchen for lunch. No sooner have we sat down than a small dark blue Morris Minor van drives up into the yard.

"Here comes George," Margaret says. "Shall I put the lunch back in the oven?"

"No, he won't be long," Grampy replies.

We hear the door of the car slam and in walks George with a large butcher's basket under his arm. Silently, he pulls out a joint of beef from the basket, puts it on a plate on the dresser, and hands a black bag to Grandfather with a smile. Grampy takes the bag from him with a nod and tips the contents of the bag onto the table – notes and coins as well as a small cash book. He quickly counts the money and checks it off in the book. Finally, he adds up the columns of pounds, shillings and pence, running his finger from top to bottom very quickly.

"Well done, George; that's all correct."

George smiles again and leaves.

After lunch, Grampy puts on his trilby hat and a long straight mackintosh without a belt. I look at him carefully; he is still very fit despite his seventy-five years but with his white hair and lined face he looks an old man. He stands in the hall and consults his watch, which hangs from a chain in the pocket of his waistcoat. A red handkerchief pokes from the top pocket of his light-grey suit jacket; and I think how smart he looks.

"Well, Peter boy, it's about time we went," Grampy says. "Go and get the car. I think the keys are in it."

I rush to the garage – I have not driven the car before but have been in it plenty of times. The leather seats are cold to the touch as I slide into the driver's seat – pulling out the choke and slotting the key into the middle of the burr walnut dashboard. I turn the key and it starts first time; the thrum of the engine very quiet compared to my father's car. I engage reverse and back slowly out of the garage. In the light the dark green of the inside trim gleams - subtly matching the green of the leather seats. I pull round to the front door and wait for Grampy to say goodbye to Margaret.

Grampy gets in and we drive down the lane from Covington, turning up the hill onto the A45 in the direction of Northampton. The car is majestic; it has plenty of power to pull away quickly but without any fuss or noise and glides along the road like a ship on a millpond. At Wellingborough we are held up at the level crossing; as we wait I watch the ironworks in the distance belching out steam and smoke. The ore for this works comes from a pit that has been dug on one of Grandfather's farms at Little Irchester. The train pulls past us at the level crossing and I ease the accelerator forward again. We continue through Wilby and on to Northampton. Grampy directs me to a rather select area where we turn down an avenue lined with trees and pull up at the first house. The house is imposing and large – a red brick creation surrounded by a sizeable garden. I bring the car to a stop and we make our way to the porch. Grampy rings the bell.

Chapter One
Slaughtering the Beast
January 1898

The morning was cold. Ground frost crusted the grass of the field at the back of the butcher's shop, where a lone beast stood grazing in the farthest corner. The animal had been bought at Thrapston market the day before and walked back to Dean by Herbert, a labourer for the butcher Thomas Dunmore.

The squeak of the pump could be heard from the back of the house where Sarah Fisher, the housemaid, was filling buckets of water from the well. A bib apron with a small flowery pattern covered her long dark blue skirt and heavy cotton shirt; her sleeves were rolled up to the elbow showing her strong, deeply tanned arms. Her face was thin, but tanned and rosy, framed by short hair which stuck out in all directions despite all her attempts to smooth it down, and when she smiled her teeth, although still white, grew in all directions except up and down. With the bucket full, she moved back across the cobbled yard, leaning to her left to compensate for the weight of the bucket, which she set down by the sink in the scullery. She moved to the range in the kitchen; after cleaning out the grate, she would black the front and light the fire with the sticks and coal she had collected earlier.

Thomas was sitting at the table, readying himself to deal with the slaughter of the beast.

"Morning, Sarah. Anybody here yet?" he asked.

Sarah went to reply, but no sooner had the question been asked than the sound of hobnail boots on the cobbles announced the arrival of Herbert. He had worked for Thomas Dunmore all his life and lived next door in a small cottage with his wife and two children; a jack of all trades, he worked on the farm and in the butcher's shop as required.

"Well," said Herbert, with a lopsided smile, "what are we up to today, then?"

"We're going to kill that beast I bought yesterday," replied Thomas.

"Oh yes," said Herbert, pulling his pipe out of one pocket and his shut knife out of the other and scraping round the inside of the pipe bowl.

"We can't kill that beast on our own," frowned Herbert. "Who's coming to help?"

"Fred and Harold are coming up directly, we should manage with them."

A door slammed upstairs and the sound of feet clattering down the uncarpeted wooden stairs was heard before William burst into the kitchen. Thomas's only son was a tall boy for his eleven years, with fair hair and a slim figure and as an only child was the apple of his parents' eyes. You couldn't say he was spoilt, but he had every attention from everyone in the household and certainly knew his own mind.

William was followed closely by Charlotte, his mother.

"Now, William Dunmore, you're not to go into the slaughterhouse and get your clothes dirty before school; I spent all day Monday washing and ironing them," she chided.

"Can't I help?" William begged, turning to his father.

"You heard what your mother said so do as you're told. You can help get it in and then watch from the door."

"Thomas, don't let him get any blood on himself, for goodness' sake," implored Charlotte. "I can never get the stains out."

"All right, Mother, I'll make him stand out the way," chuckled Thomas.

"And you make sure you're not late either, William," she continued, "I told you that you've got to take George and Reuben with you to school. It's their first day and they want someone to go with."

"Do I have to?" William protested. "They're a couple of squirts."

"Yes you do, my boy, it's the least you can do for good neighbours."

Sensing it was pointless to argue, William glowered and stomped out of the back door to stand with Herbert who winked at him over the bowl of his pipe,

"Mother knows best, Master William," he chuckled. "Sooner you learn that the better."

William scowled and scuffed his feet on the door mat.

"Here they are," said Thomas, rising from his chair as the imposing figure of Harold strode into the yard, the smaller framed Fred scuttling along beside him. Harold wore a waistcoat and shirtsleeves which barely contained his

5

muscular body; he had worked for a blacksmith all his life and was as strong as an ox. Fred, by comparison was much older; his watery bloodshot eyes were sunk deep in his head and he was a good foot shorter than his companion. Evidently he had just finished milking at his small dairy farm, as he smelt of cow dung which was spattered over his boots and leather gaiters. He wore a jacket and a dirty cap, whose peak he would turn to the back when he milked the cows so that the muck would rub off the cows away from his face.

Thomas put his bowler hat on and walked into the back yard, grabbing a hazel stick which leant against the wall on his way to the slaughterhouse. Everyone followed, the noise of the hobnail boots on the cobbles ringing around the courtyard.

"Now," said Thomas, "poleaxe, rope, buckets for blood, knives, axe, saw – what else do we need?"

"That's about it," said Herbert. "Are the knives sharp?"

"Yes, I did that last night," replied Thomas. "Let's get on with it then."

He turned to his son.

"William, you stand here by the gate and turn the bullock in when we drive it up, and don't get yourself dirty or I'll never hear the end of it."

The four men walked out of the gate, over to where the animal stood in the corner of the field below the huge elm trees. At four years old, it was well grown, a dusky red splotching the white on it coat. It had large, almost straight horns, which it raised as the men opened the gate, sensing that something was happening; it lowered its head again, flicked its tail and looked at the approaching men with suspicion.

"He'll be all right," Herbert said. "He was tame as tame when I drove him back; he must have been hand reared, I reckon."

Sure enough, the beast allowed itself to be driven calmly around the edge of the field against the hedge and under the trees, from which crows sounded out their warning from the heights of the elm tree branches. The gate into the yard in front of the shed was open and William stood back to allow the animal to come forward. Coming level with the gate, the beast stopped; this was the point of no return. Someone whistled but the animal flicked its tail and stood its ground. Thomas tapped his stick on the ground and waited; if the beast

6

turned round and ran back into the field they would have to start again. The cold morning made everyone's breath steam and the bullock blew out what looked like smoke in two directions from its nostrils as it appeared to decide whether or not to move forward.

"Shoo, get on there," Herbert shouted finally, and with a toss of its head, the beast moved into the yard. William quickly grabbed the gate, latching it behind the men as they drove the animal towards the slaughterhouse.

This part of the butcher's shop consisted of brick walls and a thatched roof, and ran from the shop in a single storey rather than two, as the shop was. The floor was tiled with hard blue bricks which had grooves in them for drainage; in the middle of the expanse of blue, lay a huge ring held to the floor by a metal bolt sunk deep into the ground. Against the walls were the tools they needed: the buckets for the blood, knives, an axe and a saw and propped up next to them, the brutal looking poleaxe.

Thomas took off his jacket and bowler hat, hanging them on a nail in the wall. He rolled his shirt sleeves above his elbows before undoing the top button of his shirt; it had no collar but was a rather smart striped one. Clearly it had once been his Sunday best, but had seen better times. He took a steel and quickly put an edge on two of the knives, his hands moving so quickly that the blades were lost in a blur; he ran his thumb along the blade, daring it to cut him. Satisfied, he nodded to Herbert who was checking the noose on the rope; he had also taken off his jacket, as had Fred. Thomas looked across at Harold, who was undoing his belt – he unbuttoned the top of his trousers, tucked his shirt well down, before redoing the buttons on his trousers and rebuckling his belt one more notch tighter than usual. He looked up to Thomas and nodded sheepishly.

William stood at the open gate of the slaughterhouse watching the bullock, which stood quietly under the big beam that ran across to the wall alongside the road. Attached to the beam was a thick rope attached to a block and tackle, from which a rope joined to a small length of chain dangled.

"Right, Herbert, put the rope on him," Thomas instructed.

"Right you are, master," replied Hubert, opening the door. He threaded the end of the rope through the ring on the floor, opening out the noose into a big circle. Harold and Fred held the other end, paying out more rope as Herbert approached the beast. It was not going to be easy to get the noose over the head; its horns were long. Gauging the distance, Herbert launched the rope, which hit the nearest horn with a dull thud and fell limply onto the ground. The animal lowered its head and pawed the ground with its front foot, eyeing the rope warily. Herbert snatched back the rope and flung the noose with lightning speed towards the downcast head of the animal. The rope spun in the air and fell perfectly over the bullock's head and horns. Momentarily uncertain, the animal looked up sharply as Herbert scrabbled back to join Harold, Fred and Thomas who had rushed to grab the other end of the rope, which tightened mercilessly around the animal's neck. Its eyes widened in terror as the four men heaved on the rope. The beast backed into the corner, pulling the rope even tighter, and began to bellow in alarm. The strength of the men on the rope was gradually bringing the animal forward, the noose tightening more around the animal's neck, which was damp with sweat – veins standing proud on its thick neck. Everyone was puffing and sweating; steam streamed from the mouths of men and beast alike.

All of a sudden the beast, seeing the gate behind the men standing open, rushed to make its escape. The unexpected charge forwards slackened the rope; the men tumbled over, all of them losing their grip on the rope, which started to run back loose through the ring in the ground. William, who had been waiting for his chance to participate, launched himself towards the snaking end of the rope, seized it and looped it twice round the top of the gatepost, pulling it as tight as he could. The beast continued to surge forward, but as it neared the middle of the shed the re-secured rope started to tighten again. Finally it could tighten no further – the gatepost lurched angrily to the side, but did not come out of the ground; the bullock grunted and was brought with a sudden jolt to the ground. It gave a mournful bellow as the men, who had managed to grab the rope again, heaved it flat to the floor; panting, it lay with its face tight to the cold blue bricks, fight draining from its eyes, its sides heaving. Thomas grabbed the poleaxe and positioned himself behind the animal's head. He brought the poleaxe slowly up above his head and with one carefully aimed blow, struck the animal between the ears. The rope went slack in the men's hands; as they straightened up, blood spotting their faces.

"Come on, then, quickly let's get it bled," Thomas ordered. "Bring them buckets quickly. William, give me that knife."

Thomas made a clean cut in the neck of the beast; blood spurted out, steaming and boiling violently into the bucket that Herbert was holding. The animal was completely lifeless – its big round eyes had closed; the whole process had only taken a minute. When the blood had ceased running, the butchering started. The head was cut off and thrown to one side, the front legs were removed from the knee joint and Herbert started to skin the animal down from the legs. The chain that hung from the roof was looped round one of the animal's back legs, which had also been taken off to the knee joint. Harold and Fred heaved on the block and tackle, pulling the animal off the ground from its back end. Once part of it was in the air, it could be rolled one way and then the other to remove the skin from underneath until it was completely skinned. There was no way that the beam in the roof was strong enough to take the weight of the whole animal but there was enough height to gut it. Thomas made a cut right down the middle of the carcass, being careful not to cut into the gut itself which would make an awful mess of everything. The stomach and guts came out like a huge python, slipping and sliding across the brick floor. The usable organs were separated from the mass of intestines, which were thrown to the side, leaving the beast carcass hanging emptily in the middle of the shed.

"Time for breakfast," Thomas said, turning to William to add, "and it'll soon be time for you to go to school, my boy."

He examined the small bloodstains on his son's shirt.

"That'll be my guts for garters," he groaned. "Come on, boy, let's try and get those stains out before your mother sees them."

Chapter Two
School Boys Fighting

Sarah was stoking the fire and Charlotte was setting the table when William and Thomas came in from the yard.

"Now look at you, William, I thought I told you not to get dirty," Charlotte scolded.

"It's only a few spots of blood, Mother, they will wipe off," said Thomas reassuringly.

"Come here, let me have a look," sighed Charlotte, throwing a disapproving look at Thomas.

She eyed William's jacket critically, shook her head and started to busy herself dabbing at the spots on William's clothes with a cloth rinsed out in cold water, tutting and muttering under her breath as she did so. William stood still and looked at his mother as she continued to mutter and tut. William thought she looked old at forty-four; her hair was completely white and the lines on her face made her look older than her years. Her expression was careworn and she rarely appeared happy with life. Her hair was long, but always rolled and pinned at the back of her head and her clothes were immaculately clean and pressed, if on the dowdy side; she had no interest in fashion.

The main driving force in Charlotte Dunmore's life was Christianity. She worshipped at the Congregational Chapel in Upper Dean every Sunday and twice if she could manage it. She had numerous Bibles positioned strategically about the house and read from at least one of them every day. She made every effort to influence those around her in the same way she had been influenced as a child, but neither Thomas nor William had the same convictions, and it was Sarah that took the brunt of Charlotte's religious zeal – which took the form of regular sermonising and strict instructions to say her prayers before she went to bed.

Having tried her best to get the spots of blood out of William's jacket, Charlotte turned to supervise the cooking of the breakfast, which was the same every day; bacon, bread and butter. Sarah stood on a chair and reached down a small piece of bacon that hung by a bit of string from the beam in the ceiling.

She tapped it with the flat of the knife to knock any maggots out and cut several thick slices. It was the belly bacon and mostly fat; all the better cuts were sold in the shop and they ate what would not sell. The slabs of bacon were laid in a big frying pan on the range, which spat back darts of fat as the bacon began to cook.

There was a faint knock on the door.

"See who that is, Sarah," instructed Charlotte, turning her attention back to the bacon.

Sarah pulled open the door to reveal two small boys, George Lowe and Reuben Heighton.

"Come in, come in," Charlotte said, looking up at the pint sized boys. "Let's have a look at these two on their first day at school."

The boys came in. George, the shorter one, appeared very shy; he was rather plump with a round face and small eyes and mouth.

"And how are you today, George Lowe?"

"Very well thank you, Mrs Dunmore," came the quiet reply as George sidled down the wall trying to shrink into the background.

Reuben on the other hand was taller with dark hair and a broad grin on his face. He was not at all intimidated and looked around at all those in the room.

"And, Reuben, how are you?" said Charlotte.

"Very well, thank you," he replied in a confident clear voice.

"Now, who would like a biscuit then?" she said, reaching for the barrel on the sideboard, which she always kept full for these occasions.

"Yes please," chorused the boys, stretching out their hands for the biscuits before retreating to the chairs by the door to wait for William to finish his bacon.

There was a jingle from the door of the butcher's shop.

"Go and see who that is, Sarah, there's a dear," Charlotte said.

Sarah obediently rose to attend to the customer; a murmur of conversation could be heard through the door before Sarah popped her head back in.

"It's Mrs Webb. She wants a pound of lard but she ain't got any money, she says she will pay next week."

Charlotte frowned towards Thomas, who raised his eyes to the ceiling before replying.

"Yes, that'll be fine!"

Thomas was a man of few words but a kind disposition. He was not rich but came from a yeoman background and had the enterprise to run and expand his small butcher's business. He was a man of principle, discipline and habit. He was tall and slim and had a tidy short beard. He always wore the same old bowler hat which only came off indoors or in church and only wore a tie and collar on Sundays or special occasions. Above his hobnail boots he wore leather gaiters which came up to just below his knee, and were polished when he went to market at Thrapston, or St Ives. Across the front of his waistcoat hung a chain which secured his gold Swiss watch, which he would pull out and check at regular intervals.

"Come on, William, time you went to school," he said after consulting the timepiece.

All three boys got up.

"Now wait a minute, William," Charlotte said. "I want you to take this note for your Uncle John and give it to Mary to take home. Don't give it to Henry – he will forget it."

"Yes, Mother," William replied, pulling on his cap and moving out of the door.

Charlotte's brother, John, was a farmer and lived at Cold Harbour with his wife Ann. They had four children and three of them, Henry, Mary and Lucy, went to school with William. The eldest, Bessie, was already married and had moved away. However, John was in poor health and the farm suffered as a consequence.

The three boys set off with William in the lead carrying a bundle of books bound by a leather strap. Reuben followed close behind and George brought up the rear, having to run every few yards to keep up. All down the road there were groups of children of all ages walking to school. There was no uniform at the school and everyone wore clothes according to what their parents could afford; some had no shoes or top coats but others, like William, were quite smart.

They followed the road round to the left and through a deep cutting lined with tall elm trees; the rooks rose, cawing, from the trees, their voices echoing down to the boys and girls as they walked along chattering to each other. Out of the cutting the road rose up and bent round to a straight stretch between the two villages. Along this road they could see a flock of sheep approaching, driven by two old chaps with a dog; this was going to hold them up and they would all be late for school. The children bundled together on one side of the road so the sheep could pass on the other. The sheep pottered towards them, and then stopped, the front ewes unwilling to pass the gaggle of noisy children.

"Shut up, you buggers, or they won't go past," shouted one of the men, as the sheep started to bunch and eye up the bushes for a quick escape.

"Goo on, get up," shouted the man, startling one sheep into a bold dash forward, which the rest of the flock took as their cue to follow.

With the sheep gone, everyone started to run to catch up time. The throng of children surged through Upper Dean, passing the big farm, Dean Hall Farm, and Dean Hall– the home of Mr Watson-Foster, one of the gentry of the village. They passed the tailor Mr Lilley, sitting cross-legged on a table in the window of his shop sewing a jacket: past the baker's shop where wonderful smells made empty stomachs rumble and past the blacksmith's forge where Art had just started shoeing a carthorse.

Opposite the church was a small turn up to the school past the post office. The bell on top of the school had started ringing to tell the children to go into the class.

"Come on, George, I'll show you where to go," urged William, grabbing George's hand and pulling him towards the door. As he did so William felt a tap on the back of his head and his cap was flipped off. He whirled round angrily to see his cousin Henry Knighton standing, hands on hips, with a big grin on his face.

"Come on, William, pick it up then," chided Henry. William retrieved his cap, stuck his tongue out at his cousin and hurried towards the school door with George and Reuben in tow. At the door of the school stood Henry's sister, Mary Knighton, whom William worshipped; she was nearly four years older than him and would soon be leaving school. She had been made a monitor and was the last to go in. She wore a cream pinafore dress with a dark blue long-sleeved shirt underneath. Her dress was calf-length with black stockings and lace-up boots. She was tall with golden shoulder length hair, which she pulled up into a topknot. As William walked past she darted out her hand and ruffled his hair.

"Don't do that, Mary," he snapped.

"Serves you right," she replied. "Who are these little squirts, then?" she enquired looking at George and Reuben. George ducked in case Mary did the same thing to him but Reuben smiled and winked up at her, before following William into the school hall.

Absolute silence descended as the headmaster, Mr Sparks, strode into the large hall in which the hundred or so pupils had assembled. He was accompanied by another teacher – Mrs Warby. Every day started with assembly, which consisted of prayers and a hymn and once a week, on Fridays, a pupil was selected to give a Bible reading. There was a piano at the back of the room which Mrs Warby played for the hymns. There were no hymn books; the children had to learn them off by heart, but as Mrs Warby's repertoire didn't stretch further than ten hymns, this was quite easy.

After assembly, the children were divided into two classes; Mr Sparks took the older pupils and Mrs Warby the younger group. There were not many books and most of the work was done on slates with white chalk. The roll call was done for each class before work started and each child stood up and said, "Present, sir", or "Present, miss," when their name was called out.

William usually sat next to his cousin Henry, which suited them both; Henry was older than William but he was not as bright so he relied on William to help him out with the class work. In return, there was some protection afforded by Henry if William got into trouble with the older boys.

"There's going to be a fight, you know," Henry whispered to William.

"When?" William whispered back.

"Lunchtime," said Henry.

"Who?" William enquired.

Henry, aware of the eyes of Mr Sparks on him, shook his head and said nothing.

Fights were common between the boys and most weeks there was a scrap;

but this fight was to be between two of the biggest and oldest boys and everyone knew well in advance.

"What's it all about?" William asked Henry as they filed out into the playground for lunchbreak.

"Don't know. I don't think it's about anything; they just don't like each other."

At the top end of the playground above the lavatories was a gap in the hedge leading to a grass field that was out for hay and had no cattle in it. The two boys involved, Fred Nicholson and George Fox, went through first followed by about twenty others. None of the girls went and the younger boys were prevented from watching by a sentry of older boys. No sooner had the spectators made their way through the hedge than the fight started.

Both boys threw their jackets to the ground and started to square up to each other. Whispers around the circle spread the information of the grounds of the fight. George had walked part of the way home on Friday with Mary Knighton and Fred was not going to allow this. Of the two, Fred was a lot bigger although clumsier in his fighting, and his first few punches were ducked by the smaller boy, who skirted around to Fred's left. Fred stumbled slightly and wheeled around to see George barrelling towards him. The force of the tackle knocked George to the ground, upon which the two boys continued to wrestle, rolling over and over, throwing punches when their hands were free. All those standing around were shouting their support for one of the pair and by now some of the girls had come through the hedge to see what was happening.

Lucy, Mary's sister, came up to William.

"Who's winning?" she said. "I can't see a thing."

"It looks like Fred is; he's much bigger."

Fred was now on top of George, who was on his back, trying to fend off the rain of blows to his face; his lip was swollen and split and his nose had started to bleed. Suddenly, his arms dropped to the ground; his eyes rolling up in his head to stare straight up into the sky as if fixed on an imaginary object. Fred continued to pummel blows down as George's limbs started to jerk. The smaller boy's body started to thrash violently about, throwing Fred to the ground. Fred leapt up and moved in to hit him again, but Henry and two others held him back.

"Leave him, you sod, there's something wrong with him," Henry shouted angrily.

But Fred's blood was up; he tore himself loose, aimed a boot at George's wide-eyed face and kicked him a glancing blow on the side of the head. For a few moments George continued to thrash about, then as quick as it had started, his limbs went loose and he lay prone, as if completely lifeless. His face was turned to his left side; blood poured from his cut lip and nose; his shirt was torn open and he looked a mess.

"You've killed him," Harry said.

"No, I ain't," Fred replied. "He's just pretending."

Henry knelt down and shook George by the shoulders.

"Come on, wake up, George, we'll soon have to go back to class."

There was no reply. George didn't move; his eyes were half open but showed no signs of life.

"Is he breathing?" someone asked.

"Can't tell," Henry replied.

The children looked from one to the other in shock. No one had seen a dead body before.

"You've killed him," Lucy whispered. "You've killed him, Fred, what are you going to do now?"

Everyone turned to Fred; the colour had drained from his face and he picked up his jacket and started to put it on.

"He's only pretending to be out so I won't hit him anymore. I know what he's up to. You wait and see he'll be up in a minute."

He wiped a hand over his face, licked his lips and once again knelt down to shake the small form on the ground. There was no reaction; the body was completely lifeless, pale and cold.

"What are we going to do, then?" whispered Fred, rising and turning to the other boys, as the awful truth began to sink in. Horrified faces stared back at him.

"What do you mean, what are we going to do? You mean, what are *you* going to do? You hit him," said Henry.

One of the girls started to whimper. Mary, who had only just heard about the fight, pushed herself to the front of the circle. Seeing George's motionless body lying on the floor, she put her hand over her mouth to contain the shriek, which did not come and tears ran down from her eyes. Lucy moved to her and held her hand.

"I don't think he's dead; I think I know what's wrong with him."

"Shut up, Lucy," Mary snapped. "Look at him, he must be dead."

The sound of the bell summoned the assembled crowd to action.

"What are we going to do?" said Fred desperately, his eyes flicking from the dumbfounded crowd to the lifeless body on the grass.

No one answered; instead they turned and one by one went back through the hole in the hedge and down to the playground. Left on his own, with the body and helpless, Fred turned to follow the rest of the crowd back to the school building.

Mr Sparks sat at his desk at the front of the class as they made their way to their places. Each desk had a bench behind it and two children sat at each. They all stood at their place until they were told to be seated by Mr Sparks, who moved to the blackboard, which had been cleaned by Mary. He took a piece of chalk and started to write.

"This afternoon, we will have a mathematics test. I am about to put ten calculations on the board and you have half an hour to complete them."

The chalk squeaked its way slowly across the board, punctuated every so often by a tap as Mr Sparks put a full stop after each question.

"Are we all clear?"

"Yes, Mr Sparks," the class chanted back.

"Well, get on with it then," he said, sitting down in his chair, putting his feet on the table and continuing to read the paper in front of him.

There was silence; no one could concentrate, their minds absorbed by what had happened up in the hayfield. Worried faces looked one to the other, fear and concern lining their faces. Henry sat rolling his pencil between his fingers, unable to focus enough to copy William's work – which William had completed. Lucy, glancing up to check that Mr Sparks was occupied, scrawled a note on the corner of her book and passed it to Mary. It read:

I think he had a fit

Mary shook her head, unable to read Lucy's hurried scrawl, and rustled the book away. Someone dropped a pencil.

"Silence," Mr Sparks shouted, rising from his chair and walking towards the back of the room. He reached the place where George normally sat.

"Where has this boy gone?" he shouted.

He turned to Robert Tuffnail who sat at the same desk.

"Where is George Fox? He was here this morning."

"Don't know, sir, I ain't seen 'im," muttered Robert.

"Well *someone* must know where he is."

The motionless class were frozen by his gaze, which finally alighted on Fred's grazed knuckles. He strode towards the quaking boy and grabbed the offending hand.

"What do we have here then, eh? I suspect we may have been fighting." He looked Fred straight in the eye and pulled him closer.

"No, I ain't, sir," Fred insisted, "I fell over playing football."

"A likely story. Where is George Fox?" he shouted.

"I ain't seen 'im, sir, honest," Fred moaned, cringing in anticipation of being struck.

"Now," he roared, "someone is going to tell me where he is. Lucy Knighton, stand up!"

His voice lowered dangerously, as he prowled towards Lucy and demanded,

"Where is George Fox?"

"He's up the field, sir," Lucy replied, shaking in terror.

"Up which field?"

"The hayfield at the back, sir," she stuttered.

"And what's he doing in the hayfield?" His voice was now reaching a crescendo.

"He's lying down, sir."

"Lying down! Lucy Knighton, come with me and show me where George Fox is 'lying down'. The rest of you – not a sound."

He turned and yelled towards the adjoining classroom.

"Mrs Warby, I am out for two minutes. Make sure this lot keep quiet."

He marched out of the door followed by Lucy.

"Now come on, girl, show me where George Fox is lying down," he demanded.

Lucy showed him the gap in the hedge and led him to where the fight had taken place. There was no one there; just an area of flattened grass where the fight had happened.

"He was here, sir," said Lucy, bowing her head, "I'm sure he was."

"Follow me then," he snapped and marched off back to the class.

"Now, I am going to get to the bottom of this," growled Sparks as he stormed back into the classroom. "Sit down, Lucy Knighton. Something has been going on and I am going to find out what."

Mr Sparks began walking up and down the rows of desks, looking intently at the pupils one by one.

"Aha! What do we have here then?" he exclaimed gleefully.

"Stand up, William Dunmore. What is that on your shirt? It's blood, if I'm not mistaken. Open your jacket!"

William complied to reveal the dark brown stains down his front; his mother had got the blood from his jacket but not from his shirt.

"Well then," he shouted in William's ear, "you've been fighting, haven't you!"

"No, sir, we killed a bullock this morning and I got some blood on me from that, sir."

"Another likely story. My, my, we're telling fibs today."

At that moment there was a click from the latch of the classroom door; it opened slowly to reveal George Fox; his face was swollen, his lip had an open cut and his hair was wet.

"Aha!" Mr Sparks shouted triumphantly. "The traveller returns! And where have you been and with whom have you been fighting?"

"I've been down the pump, to wash me face," George stuttered, his teeth chattering and his small frame shaking.

"And how did your face get in such a state? Or rather, who put it in that

19

state then, George Fox?"

"No one, sir, I did it myself."

"You did it yourself."

"Yes, sir, I had a fit and fell over; I've got hepilepsy."

"You've got what?"

"Hepilepsy."

"You mean *epilepsy*, don't you? And what about your lip?"

"I must 'ave bit it, sir; I do that when I get a fit. My mum puts a bit of stick in my mowf when I 'ave a fit to stop me biting my tongue or lips."

"And what about your face?"

"I bashed it when I fell, sir."

There was silence. Mr Sparks walked up and down the class looking first at George, then at Fred then at William. He went down to the front of the class, picked up the cane which lay on his desk and banged it down in frustration.

"Sit down, George," he snarled. "Come on then, finish off the test. I will give you another ten minutes."

There was a collective but silent sigh of relief – most notably from Fred, who managed a feeble wave from his desk towards George in the middle of the room. George shrugged and looked blearily at the blackboard.

"See," whispered Lucy to Mary, "told you he was all right."

Chapter Three
A Letter from the Headmaster

Life at the butcher's shop was always busy; everyone had a job to do and Sundays were the only part of the week when there was any time for relaxation. As the shop led out of the kitchen there were always people going backwards and forwards. The shop had a big window at the front and a marble top to display the meat. A butcher's block stood in the middle of the shop, and a bench along the back wall, with a small drawer at one end where the money was kept. Above the bench a long rail was fixed to the wall, from which many hooks hung, laden with various joints of meat. A door at the end of the shop led to another large room where the sides of beef hung alongside the carcasses of sheep and pigs, waiting to be cut up. In the middle of this room stood 'the Lead'– a big bath of brine and saltpetre where the bacon was cured. Most of the meat was not sold from the shop but delivered in a pony and trap. Thomas had the custom of the two big houses in Upper Dean; The Watson-Fosters and the Fitz-Allens, as well as the St Johns at Melchbourne who took between them a large quantity of meat. Thomas would deliver in the week, but on Saturdays William was sent out.

Charlotte would manage the shop while Thomas was out and also kept the account books. The big houses would settle their bill every eighteen months and everyone else when they had some money. The books were always open on the kitchen table as it was rare that anyone paid for an item as they took it.

The one regular caller at the shop was Albert Muskett the postman, who not only brought the post but also Thomas's paper, *The Standard*, which he read avidly every day. On the morning of April the twelfth he called with a single envelope addressed to "Mr Thomas Dunmore" and a card. He came into the shop as usual – leaving his bike propped against the wall of the house – on his way back from the villages of Lower and Upper Dean and those from Covington to Kimbolton.

"Come on in, Albert," Charlotte called out, as Albert made his way through the shop. "Sarah, get a cup and saucer for Mr Muskett, he'll have one as usual."

Albert laid the post on the table and sat down in one of the ladder-back chairs, putting his battered panama hat on the table in front of him. He lifted his satchel over his head, dropping it to the floor and pulled *The Standard* from his inside pocket, putting it on the table, before sitting back in the chair and undoing the bottom button of his waistcoat, exposing the enormous silver buckle on his belt. The belt did not hold his trousers up— that job was performed by his braces; but the belt was necessary to hold everything together in the middle. He reached down to adjust his leather gaiters which had moved round on his bicycle journey to Dean; they had to sit so that the buckles faced backwards to stop his trousers getting caught in the chain of his bicycle, something he had overlooked once and wouldn't again.

Sarah busied herself laying out the cup and saucer as Charlotte sat herself down on the other side of the table and picked up the two items of post. The card showed a hand-sketched picture of Upper Dean Post Office and written on the other side was a handwritten note, which she read out.

"Dear Mr Dunmore,

Would you be able to come and kill my pig which is now about fat? The next day or so will do.

Yours Sincerely,

Harry Rawlins."

"Well, that's a bit more work for Thomas," said Charlotte handing the card to Muskett. He held it up to the light and read it again. With his other hand out of sight of Charlotte and behind Sarah, who was pouring milk into his cup, he ran his hand up the back of her dress touching it lightly with his fingers until he reached her bottom. He gave a couple of quick squeezes and dropped his arm to his side.

Sarah jumped.

"Oh!" she exclaimed, standing up quickly to her full height and spilling the milk into the saucer.

Charlotte looked up.

"Sarah, what *do* you think you are doing? Go and clean that saucer up, or go and get another one."

"Yes, Mrs Dunmore," Sarah replied, scowling at Muskett as she went to fetch a cloth.

"I wonder what this one is," Charlotte said holding up the other envelope. The copperplate handwriting was in jet black ink.

"I know what it is," Muskett said, deigning to speak for the first time.

"Oh, you do then, do you, Albert. Opened it already, have you?" asked Charlotte.

"No, I ain't," sniffed Muskett, "but I can tell the writing. It's from the headmaster at the Grammar School, I'm sure it is."

"What's he want with us, do you think?" Charlotte enquired.

"I know," said Albert.

"You know everything and a deal too much for your own good, Albert Muskett! Well, what does he want then?"

"He wants your William to go to his school. I bet that's what it's about; you see if I'm not right."

"Well, I can't open it; it's addressed to Thomas, so we will have to wait until he comes in. I suppose as he went to the Grammar School himself, they expect William to carry on the tradition."

Charlotte put the letter and the card on the mantelpiece next to the clock ready for Thomas at lunchtime.

"Good Lord, is that the time!" said Muskett looking at the clock on the side. He pulled his own pocket watch out of his waistcoat and flicked open the case.

"Ohhh." He sucked his teeth and shook his watch, before holding it to his ear.

"Your clock's fast, Mrs Dunmore, but I'll have to go all the same."

He put two spoons of sugar in his tea and stirred it noisily before pouring as much tea as he could from his cup into the saucer. Then taking the saucer with both hands he brought it to his mouth and blew on the liquid to cool it before guzzling it down with the most dreadful sucking and slurping noise. He repeated this process twice more under Charlotte's disapproving gaze and with a satisfied final slurp, banged the cup down in the saucer.

"Must go, must go," he said, rising and making towards the shop. "Many thanks for the tea, Mrs Dunmore; see you tomorrow."

23

Lunchtime came and Thomas returned from sorting out the sheep. He picked up the card by the clock, read the back and then turned to the letter.

"What's this then?" he said, turning to Charlotte.

"It's from the headmaster at the Grammar School or that's what Albert Muskett reckoned," she replied.

"Let's have a look then," Thomas said, opening the envelope with a penknife he pulled from his pocket.

'Dear Mr Dunmore. It has come to my attention that your son William has just turned the age of eleven and I was wondering if you wished to enter him for a place at Kimbolton Grammar School.'

"How did he know William's age, then?" Charlotte enquired.

"Don't know, but I expect Muskett told him! Anyway he goes on: *'I will be in Dean on Thursday and would like to call at 3 o'clock to discuss the issue and also interview William. I understand that you were a pupil at the school yourself and he would thus be able to keep up a family tradition. I remain your obedient servant, Reverend Belpeel'.* Well, there we go then; Muskett was right –I suppose he must be a scout for the school. What do you think, Charlotte?"

"I think if the boy passes the interview and we have the money to pay the bills, we should send him. After all he's our only one and what else have we got to spend the money on? A good education would give him a good start in life."

So it was agreed – Reverend Belpeel was to come and interview William on Thursday.

When the day arrived, Thomas put on his frock coat and for once put a collar on his shirt and a tie and Charlotte put on her Sunday outfit. William had a tie on today with his jacket and breeches and his boots were polished so they shone.

The appointed hour of three o'clock came and went; Reverend Belpeel still hadn't arrived by a quarter past three or by half past three. It wasn't until five minutes to four that they heard a knock on the door. Thomas opened the door to hear an enormous crash; Reverend Belpeel's bicycle had fallen into the road from where he had propped it against the small piece of fence between the front door and the shop door. He recovered the bicycle with some difficulty and once again propped it against the fence before rushing over to shake Thomas's hand.

"Good afternoon," he said in a very deep, ponderous voice. "I'm sorry I am a little late but I had another call in Tilbrook which delayed me somewhat."

He ducked his head as he came through the low door and trotted into the kitchen where he was introduced to Charlotte and then William. Sarah came and took his coat and hat – a large dark grey homburg – both of which smelt of mothballs.

"Shall we go this way," said Charlotte, leading Belpeel into the front room. The Reverend nodded enthusiastically and followed Charlotte, forgetting to duck as he went through the door, and banging his head hard on the lintel.

"My goodness," he groaned, "I didn't notice that, I must put my glasses on."

He rubbed his forehead, went in and took a seat in the big armchair. Sitting there he looked rather comical as he had forgotten to take off his bicycle clips. He took his glasses from the top pocket of his jacket and carefully threaded each arm of the specs over and around his ear. His face was long and drawn; his hair grey and cut very short. He had no colour in his face at all, even though he had just cycled four miles, and his dog collar seemed two or three sizes too big, dangling around his neck like a hoop thrown over a coconut at the fair.

"Could I offer you some tea and a piece of cake?" Charlotte enquired.

"That would be very nice," intoned Reverend Belpeel, forcing his mouth into what he probably thought was a smile.

"Sarah dear, could you, please?" said Charlotte.

Sarah, who had been standing at the door, bobbed and went into the kitchen.

Charlotte and Thomas sat on the sofa, letting William take his place on an upright chair against the back wall. They all sat nervously, waiting for something to happen.

Reverend Belpeel cleared his throat and started:

"It gives me great pleasure to be with you this afternoon," he sermonised, looking not at the assembled family, but at an imaginary spot high up on the wall. "This day has come about with the guidance of the Great Almighty who loves us and watches over us all the time. And I have no doubt it is He who has inspired you into the considerations of educating your son at our school in Kimbolton. Might I add that this is, without doubt, a very wise decision that you have made, and one I am sure that you will never come to regret. We must give thanks for the guidance that God has bestowed upon you and ponder the greatness of His wisdom."

With that, Reverend Belpeel sucked in a lungful of air, opened his leather briefcase which was sitting on his lap and pulled out a small booklet. Brandishing the booklet before him, he continued doggedly to pursue his prospective parent patter:

"It now gives me great pleasure to be able to present you with a prospectus of the school, which includes photographs of our magnificent building and facilities."

"We know about the school," interjected Charlotte. "Thomas was a pupil there himself."

"Ah ha. I'm sorry, I did not remember. What a wonderful event for the son to follow in the father's footsteps."

He frowned slightly, pushed his glasses up his nose and looked carefully at William.

"That is, assuming that the son is of the required standard to enter the school. The governors are very strict regarding qualifications of the pupils who enter our establishment and in no way will we let the standard drop. His Grace the Duke of Manchester, our chairman, is very insistent on this."

He paused as Sarah came in with a tray of tea things, put them down on the table, bobbed and went out. Charlotte poured the tea, cut the cake and handed Reverend Belpeel and Thomas a plate. The Reverend Belpeel was a messy feeder and for every crumb he managed to ram into his mouth, the same number of crumbs migrated down his front and into his lap. Pausing in his hurried efforts to inhale his cake, he swallowed noisily and grasped at his tea cup, which made its way shakily towards his mouth, tea splashing about like the rough seas. William watched in fascination, but Reverend Belpeel seemed unconcerned and unembarrassed by his feeding display; he replaced the cup and plate on the table and leant back in his chair, before continuing.

"Our school at Kimbolton provides the finest education in the area. No efforts are spared in raising our boys up to the standard that the good Lord permits. Our religious education is based on annotated editions of the Old and New Testament and is directed by myself under the guidance of God to whom we all owe our existence and deliverance. We also teach reading, writing and spelling, English grammar and composition, English history, arithmetic and geography. These are our basic subjects. In addition and according to the ability of the pupil, we offer Latin, Greek, French and German, shorthand, book-keeping, natural science, drawing, gymnastics, music and carpentry."

Charlotte and Thomas looked at each other; Belpeel was not a good salesman and his reputation as a headmaster was not a favourable one. The school had under thirty pupils which brought the finances under severe pressure. However, they both knew that there were many good teachers there, some of whom they knew and they had decided in their own minds that they wanted William to go, if possible.

"Would you like another piece of cake, Reverend Belpeel?" Charlotte enquired.

"That would be most kind," he replied, proffering his plate for another slice and attacking it with as much enthusiasm as he had the first.

"Perhaps it might be as well before we go any further, that I interview the boy to assess his qualities." He turned to William and on seeing no movement from Charlotte and Thomas, added, "it would be preferable if I could do that on my own."

"Of course," replied Charlotte with some nerviness, chivvying Thomas hurriedly into the kitchen.

"Now, boy, what's your name, again?" he said, looking over his glasses directly at William.

"William Dunmore, sir."

"Now, William Dunmore, tell me the first ten books in the Old Testament."

This was easy for William as his mother had schooled him in the contents of the Bible since he had been able to read and he quickly went through them.

27

"Now, my boy, here's a copy of the Bible, find in it St Luke, Chapter 10 and read me the first ten verses."

William once again had no trouble with this; he was a regular at the Sunday school at the chapel and was often asked to read aloud to the groups.

"Do you say your prayers at night, William Dunmore?"

"Yes, sir, every night," William replied quickly.

"I hope you shut your eyes, my boy."

"Yes, sir, I do."

"Now, we must try some arithmetic. What are twelve nines?"

"One hundred and eight, sir," replied William without hesitation.

"Four sevens?"

"Twenty-eight, sir."

"Forty-nine minus twenty-seven?"

William looked to the ceiling for a moment.

"Twenty-two, sir."

"Divide fourteen into seventy-two."

William once again looked at the ceiling and was a little longer.

"It goes five times, sir, and two over."

"Now, have you done fractions and decimals?"

"Yes, sir."

"And percentages?"

"Yes, sir."

"And what about geography?"

"Yes, sir, we have done some."

"What is the capital of France, then?"

"Paris, sir."

William stood still waiting for another question, which did not come. Reverend Belpeel put his briefcase on the floor and stood up. He pulled a watch from the pocket of his waistcoat and flicked open the cover.

"Hmm," he said looking critically at the carpet which was strewn with crumbs from his cake. He sighed gently, suddenly noticed that he had not taken off his bicycle clips and in one swift movement bent down, pulled them off and thrust them hastily in his pocket.

"Well, my boy, I think it's time that we had another word with your parents, so I would be obliged if you would go and call them in."

William went into the kitchen to fetch Thomas and Charlotte, returning to find the Reverend warming his legs by the fire and gazing absently at the ceiling. When Charlotte and Thomas had sat down he started again in the same slow ponderous tone.

"Well, I am pleased to say that I feel that William just makes the standard required for our Grammar School and I feel that he will benefit greatly from the education that we have to offer. We do have a place for him to enter the school in September."

In fact there were a lot of places available in September, and William would have gone to the school however he had performed in the interview; Thomas and Charlotte knew this as well as Belpeel did, but said nothing.

"I would recommend that he comes as a weekly boarder; all the details of the cost are in the prospectus together with the required clothing towards the back. I hope that is all clear."

"Yes, we are familiar with the requirements and would like him to come," Charlotte replied.

"Very well then, we are all agreed. I would be grateful if you could confirm your acceptance of a place in writing and I will make the necessary arrangements at the school."

He picked up his briefcase decisively and tried another lip-cracking smile.

"Can I thank you for your hospitality and bid you good day." Belpeel bowed to Charlotte and made his way out, ducking carefully through the doorways as he did so. In the kitchen, Sarah handed him his coat and hat and watched him trot back through the shop to his bicycle.

William peered out of the window to watch him go; he was clearly very unathletic and unmechanical. He strapped his briefcase onto a small rack behind the saddle and with his left foot he pushed the left pedal to its lowest point. Then, putting his foot on the pedal he started to scoot along the road, gradually building up speed before hoisting his right foot over the saddle to get going. His right leg was halfway over when he clearly thought better of it, returning his right foot to the ground and dismounting. Once again, he brought the left pedal to its lowest point and started the whole procedure again. This time he had more success and eventually got astride the bike and started vigorously pedalling. He only gone a few yards when the bike screeched to an abrupt halt and both feet were returned to the ground. Reverend Belpeel stood astride the crossbar but could not move. His trouser leg had caught in the chain and was trapped between the chain and the cog on the pedal spindle; he had forgotten to put his bicycle clips on.

"Come away from that window, William, and you, Sarah, he'll see you," chided Charlotte as William and Sarah howled with laughter, watching Reverend Belpeel looking dejectedly down at his trapped trouser leg.

After a moment or two it seemed he had decided that the only way to get out of his predicament was to go backwards. He started shuffling in reverse but the chain would not relinquish its hold on the trouser leg. With an ineffectual windmilling of his right hand, he lost his balance, letting go of the handle bars completely as the front wheel swung round, giving Reverend Belpeel nothing to balance on. Arms flailing, he tumbled backwards and fell down hard on the grass verge; the back wheel spun, turning the pedals and releasing his ensnared trousers. After a cursory look around, he pulled his bicycle clips from his pocket, as if this was the task he had always been intending to do when he landed on the ground, and fastened the clips securely around his calves. Gingerly, he picked up the bicycle and pushed it off towards Kimbolton.

Chapter Four
Mary's Last Term

William and Mary were soon into their last term at Dean School and this was to be announced on the first day by Mr Sparks. William left the shop to walk to school; George and Reuben were waiting for him in the road – despite the age difference they had all become friends. George was clearly bright, as was William, and Reuben was a very capable sportsman. It was a lovely spring day and the road was dry after a very wet winter; there was chattering from the trees as the rooks were nesting. Reuben was collecting birds' eggs, leaving the road every so often to peer through the hedge and scout for a nest.

"Got one!" he shouted, pushing his hands through the thorns to fumble for the eggs. He pulled one out and looked at it.

"Bloomin' blackbird," he said, turning the mottled blue shell over in his palm. "I've got no end of them," and he thrust his hand back through the hedge to replace the egg.

Another nest further down the hedgerow yielded a better result:

"Hedge sparrow, haven't got one of them. I'll blow one. Anyone got a pin?" he shouted looking up and down the road at the crocodile of children threading their way to school. No one had, so he pulled a thorn from the hedge and carefully made a hole in each end of the egg, before blowing into one end. After two or three attempts the yolk and white of the egg poured out the hole and splashed messily onto the ground. He carefully put the egg in a match box with some cotton wool and scurried up the road to catch up with George and William.

Mary and Lucy were approaching from the other direction. The farm where they lived, Cold Harbour, was on the very top of the hill about a mile and half south of Dean. Their older brother Henry had now left school and was working on the farm helping their father. Since no one else lived in this direction they walked alone until they reached Dean and then it was only a short distance to the school. Most of the fields they walked through were grass, either left for hay or dotted with grazing cattle and sheep. The sun was warm as it beat down on their faces; their mother made them take straw hats to wear for school but

31

neither of them put them on, preferring to feel the warmth of the spring sun on their heads. The spinney they passed was a mass of bluebells, now all in flower and covering the ground with their vibrant colour.

Mary, the elder of the two, was now fourteen and leaving school in the summer; she was planning to work in a dress shop in the small town of Raunds, where she would stay with relations and come home at the weekends. Although she had been brought up as a regular churchgoer, there was a strong rebellious streak in Mary and her parents were struggling to control her as she grew older. With her long golden hair and grey blue penetrating eyes she was growing into an extremely attractive young woman. She was very particular about her clothes and would never have anything out of place; for school she always wore a pinafore dress pinched in at the waist, with a shirt underneath, which showed off her developing figure. The laced boots she wore had a higher heel than most, which made her taller than the other girls of her age.

Lucy, on the other hand, was eighteen months younger and much slighter in build. She wore a similar pinafore dress, but hers hung on her like a sack, being one of Mary's hand-me-downs. She had shorter mousy coloured hair, small delicate features and a perpetual drip at the end of her nose, leading her to sniff and wipe her nose every two or three minutes; summer and winter she seemed to have a permanent cold.

Mary looked on Lucy as the younger sister she could really do without, and thus they did not speak much as they walked through a field of bullocks that had just been turned out.

Suddenly Mary yelped.

"Damn and blast! Damn, damn, damn; look what I have done! Trodden in cow muck."

Blood rushed into Mary's face, which was contorted with rage.

"Look at it, just look at it; it's right up and there's some on my stocking."

She stamped her foot.

"Hold still a minute, I'll wipe it off," said Lucy pulling some grass to do the job and kneeling down to wipe it off the shoe.

"Careful, *careful*, Lucy; you'll wipe it all over the place."

"Stand still, can't you, or I'll never get it off," said Lucy, pulling out another handful of grass and continuing to scrub at the boot.

By now the cattle had heard the commotion and ambled over to see what was happening. It wasn't long before they had surrounded the girls, sniffing the ground and edging nearer and nearer.

"Get away, you buggers," Mary shouted angrily.

The cows moved tentatively back a pace or two.

"Mary, don't swear," Lucy said. "You know what Mother says."

"I don't care what Mother says," snarled Mary. "Just get on and get that muck off."

"All done," said Lucy, rising from the grass, "or at least, that's the best I can do with grass."

Mary examined her boot, sighed and stomped off across the field, her attention firmly on the passage of her boots.

Before long, they arrived in the High Street where they could see throngs of children from Lower Dean or Shelton straggling back as far as the Marquis of Bute pub. Among them were William, George and Reuben, and they walked up the road to the school altogether.

"Gor, Mary, you smell a bit of cow muck; I'm glad I'm not sitting near you," William said.

"Don't you dare say that, William Dunmore, or I'll never speak to you again," scolded Mary, raising her hand to tip his cap over his eyes.

"Now, now, don't lose your temper, Mary; it's not becoming of a lady."

"Oh, shut up," she snarled and stalked off to talk to some of the other girls.

The bell rang, summoning the children into the school for the first assembly of the term. The children stood in rows, smallest at the front and biggest at the back. They sang one of the small selection of hymns and, after the usual prayers, Mr Sparks rose to make an announcement.

"Now at the end of this term the following will be leaving the school to pursue careers in the outside world: Mary Knighton, Thomas Drage, George Fox, John Goodge, Elizabeth May, Fred Nicholson, Mabel Cox. Finally, William Dunmore leaves to take a place at Kimbolton Grammar School."

An audible murmur rippled round the assembled children, some swivelling to take a look at William.

"We wish all these pupils the best of luck in their new positions. Now everyone go to their desks."

The children rose and turned to one another to chatter.

"Silence!" Mr Sparks roared, slamming his cane on the table, provoking each child to scurry to their allotted desk, and stand there until he shouted,

"Sit down."

Obediently, the class sat and waited in silence. After pausing a moment for a controlling effect, Mr Sparks continued.

"This morning we will do a composition. Everyone has a piece of paper. You are to write a composition on the following…"

He paused, moving to the blackboard to chalk the words as he spoke them:

"…Human beings are merely well-developed animals. Discuss."

He banged the blackboard with the chalk to mark the full stop and threw the chalk on his desk, blowing the chalk dust from his fingers as he turned round to the class.

"Well then, get on with it! Don't just sit there like dummies," and with that he sat down, hoisted his feet onto the desk, crossed his legs, picked up the daily paper and started reading.

Everyone looked round at each other, not knowing what to put down on the paper. Some grinned, some poked their tongues out at one another, some grimaced, and the odd one started writing. After ten minutes, Mr Sparks put down his paper and stood up.

"Come on, get on with it, George Fox; don't just sit there looking at the ceiling."

He put a finger in his waistcoat pocket, pulled out his watch to consult the time and sighed heavily. Then, tucking both thumbs behind his braces he started to walk up and down the rows of desks. His shoes had a metal plate on the heel and every time his foot hit the floor, there was a click. He continued slowly up and down the lines, prompting the children to hurriedly lower their heads to shield their blank pieces of paper as he passed them by. Coming level with Mary who was sitting at a desk with Alice Cowper, he stopped and sniffed.

"What is that smell? Who smells, then?" He looked round. "We can't have this, who is it, come on now. Who is it, I said?"

Mary put her hand up.

"Please, sir, I trod in cow muck on the way to school and it must be on the bottom of my boots," she cringed, lowering her head.

"Well, you must be more careful, Mary Knighton, look where you are putting your feet and stop daydreaming, eh?"

He leant on her desk and spoke quietly into her ear:

"Go and take them off, put them outside the door and clean them at break time."

Mary moved shamefacedly out the door and through the porch, putting her boots down around the corner. A voice behind her made her start.

"Hello, Mary."

She whirled round to see Ellen Webb grinning at her. The Webbs lived in a small thatched cottage next to the church in Melchbourne.

"What are you doing here?" Mary asked curiously.

"I want to see the headmaster about the children coming to school," said Ellen, pointing to two small boys and a taller girl who were standing behind her.

"I'll tell him when I go back in," Mary said, smiling at the children and moving back into the classroom. She sat down and raised her hand.

"Mary Knighton, what is it now?" Mr Sparks snapped.

"Please, sir; there is someone outside to see you. Mrs Webb."

"Very well, go outside, Mary, and tell her I will see her at break time."

She retraced her steps to the playground where Ellen was waiting with the three children.

"He says he will see you at break time which is in about two minutes," said Mary, noting how exhausted the woman in front of her looked.

"Isn't it a long way for them to come to school – I thought you lived in Melchbourne?"

"We got thrown out of our house 'cos we couldn't pay the rent. My old chap has been short of work. Mr Watson-Foster has given us one of the houses in Chapel Row."

Ellen looked haggard and grey. Her hair fell straight down to her shoulder, she was painfully thin and her clothes hung on her like they might on a scarecrow, and clearly had not been washed for ages. The children had no shoes on and their clothes were in the same condition. The eldest, a girl, Molly, had short black hair that stuck out in all directions in tight curls. She had a short-sleeved dress on but no shirt underneath and she looked cold even on the warm day. She, like the boys, looked thin but not in the same way as the mother. Her feet and legs were dirty but tanned, as were her face and arms. Despite her appearance she was quite a pretty girl and when she smiled she revealed a gap between her front teeth, which gave her a slightly comical air. The two boys, Colin and Brian, were twins but not identical. They stood holding hands and were much younger than Molly. They had dark grey shorts on, held up by braces and long-sleeved shirts which were far too big for them. They both jumped as the bell sounded and Mr Sparks came speeding out of the classroom.

"Well, Mrs Webb, I thought you lived in Melchbourne," he said.

"We used to, but got thrown out the house and came to live in Chapel Row. Mr Watson-Foster let us 'ave one of them; we got to see if the old chap can get more work."

Ellen's husband Ray was a cobbler and made uppers for shoes as an out-worker from the factories in Raunds. The cut leather would be brought round by horse and cart and Ray would then sew them up and send them back two or three days later. Pay was on a piecework basis; the rates were competitive and it was hard to make ends meet if the work dried up for a while.

"I assume that you want the children to come to school here, Mrs Webb," said Mr Sparks.

"Yes, if there's room," she replied.

"I'm sure we can fit them in somewhere. Let me take some details. Now, you," he peered at Molly over his glasses, "what's your name?"

"Molly, sir," she replied.

"And can you read and write, Molly?"

"Just a little, sir."

"And you, boys, what's your names?"

"That's Colin, and I'm Brian, sir."

"And what's your age?" demanded Sparks, staring down on Colin.

"I'm nine," said Colin shyly.

"And I'm nine too," chirped Brian.

"Very well, Mrs Webb. Now, the children have no shoes; will they be getting any?"

"Don't know, sir," Ellen shrugged, "hope to soon if Ray gets some work."

"Well, send them along tomorrow; Molly will be in my class and the boys will be with Mrs Warby."

The sad little group left and made their way up past the pub to their new home, passing Albert Muskett on his bike who was making his way to the school. He leant his bike against the wall, took one letter out of his bag in the pannier and walked up to Mr Sparks, who was standing at the doorway critically observing the children as they milled about in front of him.

"Looks like an official communication, Mr Sparks," said Albert, examining the letter before he gave it to Mr Sparks.

"I'm surprised you've not already steamed it open and read it," he said in a sarcastic tone.

Mr Sparks did not like Muskett – a sentiment returned with interest by Muskett, and with a scowl he returned to his bicycle.

Sparks took a penknife out of his pocket, cut the letter open and began to read it. A smile started to spread across his face, and he turned on his heel and made his way to see Mrs Warby.

"Mrs Warby, my dear, we are saved! They have agreed to supply another teacher. Listen to this…" and he read from the letter.

"Dear Sir, I am pleased to inform you that after long consideration and having taken into account your concerns as to the numbers in your school, we have made arrangements for you to be allocated another classroom teacher. Her name is Miss Ethel Standish and she will start as soon as suitable accommodation can be found for her.

Yours etc."

"Well, that is good news, Mr Sparks," said Mrs Warby cheerily.

"I will announce it to the whole school before they go home."

Accordingly, at exactly half past three, the whole school was assembled for the announcement.

"It gives me great pleasure," Mr Sparks said, "to be able to tell you that today I have received a letter from the Education Authority informing me that they have allocated us an extra classroom teacher. Her name is..."

But the assembly did not hear the name of their new teacher – for Sparks's voice was overshadowed by the sound of a clear, shrill whistle. Eyes started to light up around the room – this wasn't a sound that had been heard in the village for months – the traction engine had arrived.

Chapter Five
Rats

As soon as Mr Sparks had let them leave, William, George and Reuben sped down to the road to wait for a glimpse of the engine, and Mary and Lucy weren't far behind them.

"What is this about you going to Kimbolton Grammar School, William Dunmore?" said Lucy, having not had a chance to speak to her cousin since assembly that morning.

"Well, I've got a place to go in September," he shrugged.

"You're spoilt, you know, William; just because there's one of you, you're spoilt rotten."

"It's not that," he stammered, "it's just that Mother and Father think I will learn more there."

"Why can't *I* go then?" she demanded.

"They don't take girls there, stupid," Reuben laughed.

"Don't you call me stupid, Reuben Heighton, because I ain't," Lucy huffed, crossing her arms and standing back to scowl at Reuben. "I bet you won't go there either, will you? You're no good at reading and writing like George is, so there."

She sniffed, angrily dabbed at her nose with her hankie and looked down at the ground.

"William is spoilt rotten. Your parents couldn't send you, Reuben, even if you could get into the school, and neither could our parents send us even if they did take girls 'cos there's four of us and only one of William."

William stood frozen in indignation, opening and shutting his mouth in an attempt to try and find something to say to defend himself; Mary came to his rescue.

"Don't be mean, Lucy, it's not William's fault that Aunt Charlotte and Uncle Thomas want him to go. She's only jealous, William, ignore her – I think it's good that you have a place. Now tell us what it's going to be like."

"I don't know much," William said, smiling gratefully at his cousin. "I'm going as a weekly boarder and they teach all sorts of things including French and German and Latin and Greek and all those sorts of things."

"Well, I'm sure they will all be very useful for a butcher's boy to know," Lucy scowled. "Mary, I'm going home, are you coming?"

"Aren't you going to watch the engine?" William asked.

"What for? I've seen them lots of times when they come up our end to do the stacks. Anyway, it's boys' stuff – engines! Are you coming, then, Mary?"

"I s'pose I'll have to," sighed Mary.

"Well don't rush then, will you!" sniffed Lucy, stomping off away from the group. Mary rolled her eyes, ruffled Reuben's hair and set off after her sister.

The boys could now see the smoke from the engine, which was rounding the bend by the chapel at the other end of the street. It tooted its whistle and after a few minutes they caught sight of the machine lumbering past the baker's shop. It was going slowly, pulling both the threshing drum and an elevator behind it. The engine itself was black, with brass lettering on the front of the firebox which read 'Fowler of Leeds'; the driver on the engine, and another man perched on the drawbar of the threshing drum. The driver was tall and stood bolt upright, standing sideways to the direction of the engine's travel so he was facing the boys as he went past. His dirty cap, shining with grease and oil, was jammed onto his head, partially obscuring his rosy face. He sported a large bushy moustache and in his mouth was a long pipe with a very small bowl on the end which he clutched with one hand, his other on the steering wheel. He had taken his jacket off to reveal a tight fitting waistcoat which left a gap between the bottom of the waistcoat and trousers, exposing his braces. The button of his trousers was not done up to allow his stomach room for manoeuvre.

As it drew nearer, the boys could see the mechanism that drove the engine. The green painted flywheel was spinning fast like a big metal grind stone, and the pistons from the cylinder reached backwards and forwards like a boxer punching. They could see the governor on top spinning vertically, revealing the two small metal balls shooting in and out according to how much power was needed. They could now smell the smoke, which gushed brownish-black against the white of the steam that leaked from various other places.

"Woo up!" the driver called.

"Woo up!" the boys echoed, as the driver turned forward, pulling the regulator back and stopping the engine as he threw the lever into neutral. The clatter from the wheels of the drum and elevator were silenced; all that could be heard was the hiss of the steam-release valve.

"Need some water, Bill," the driver shouted over his shoulder and both men hopped down from the engine. The driver unhooked a bucket from the back of the machine and ambled over to the village pump at the side of the road.

"You boys there," he hollered at William, George and Reuben, "come and work the handle; we won't get there if we don't put some water in."

The two younger boys not being tall enough, William scuttled over to work the pump. Up and down he heaved until the water came gurgling up the pipe and tumbled into the coal-stained bucket at his feet. When the bucket was full, the driver poured the contents into a small hopper on the back of the engine where it ran into the water reservoir. He gave the bucket to Bill and jumped back onto the engine to examine the water gauge.

"Quite a bit more yet," he said tapping the gauge and nodding at Bill to give the bucket back to William, who trotted back to the pump.

"That'll do," he shouted fifteen buckets later, leaving his seat to make sure the drum and elevator were still attached properly.

Reuben approached him eagerly.

"Is that a compound engine, mister?" he asked.

"Yes, me boy, one of the best, how did you know that, then?" he asked.

"Well, it's got two cylinders, ain't it?" Reuben replied.

"Well there, yes it does," chuckled the driver, shifting his cap further back on his head to take a better look at Reuben. "And what are you going to be when you grow up, me boy?"

"An engine driver, of course."

"Well done, well done," he said, "and what are you going to be?" he said to William.

"A butcher."

"And you?" he enquired of George.

"A butcher," George squeaked.

"Well done, well done," he smiled. "Right, we must be getting on."

With a wink to the boys, he climbed back onto the footplate, pushed the gear forwards and slowly applied pressure to the regulator. The engine growled into life; the flywheel started to revolve, the governor spun, the pistons moved backwards and forwards, the crank revolved and off they went down the road.

At the end of the street was a very sharp right-hand corner; Reuben nudged George in anticipation; it was going to be difficult to manoeuvre everything round as the whole train was so long. The driver slowed right down to let the engine round, the drum dutifully following the path set by the engine. The elevator, however, seemed to have a mind of its own and after hitting a pothole, it swung to the inside of the bend, coming perilously close to the garden wall of the house on the corner. Bill had leapt down and was standing by the wall, directing the driver by shouting and waving his arms. The front wheels of the elevator passed with inches to spare but the back wheel was going to catch the wall.

"Woo up!" Bill shouted, but it was too late.

With a crunch, the wheel caught the wall. The drawbar of the elevator pulled tight forcing the draw bar of the drum to pull tighter also; the driver pulled the regulator back and everything stopped. There was a hiss as the engines let off steam.

"Bugger, damn and blast the sodding thing; that sodding elevator never follows properly," swore the driver, taking off his cap and wiping his forehead.

"Let's try backing it a bit, Bill," he shouted, pulling the gear backwards and easing down on the regulator.

Slowly, the drawbar of the drum tightened towards the elevator and they both started to move backwards.

"A bit more," Bill shouted, watching the back wheel of the elevator come away from the wall.

"A bit more – No! Stop! *Stop*!" Bill yelled, as the front wheel turned on its turntable and jammed itself closer to the wall.

"Sod it," cursed the driver, coming to inspect the damage. "Nothing for it but we've got to unhitch."

Bill pushed a wooden block under the elevator's back wheels and then pulled the pin out of the coupling before towing the drum one hundred yards up the road where it was left. The engine came back to retrieve the elevator.

"Come on, you boys, you'll have to give us a hand we're going to push it straight. Is there anyone else about?"

By now, two or three others had turned up to see what was happening.

"Right, everyone on the drawbar and see if we can pull it round," yelled the driver.

Everyone heaved at the drawbar until the wheels came round on the other lock.

"Now let's see if we can push the bloody thing straight," grumbled the driver, wiping a hand over his forehead and removing the blocks.

The assembled crowd pushed the elevator, some pulling on the spokes of the wheels. Gradually it moved forward three yards, straightening up away from the wall as it did so. The men pulled the front wheels straight again, hitched the elevator on to the engine and away it went up the road to be reattached to the end of the train.

The driver came up to the boys.

"Well done," he said. "Thanks for the push and all that."

"Where are you going, mister?" asked Reuben.

"Up to Henry Knighton's at Cold Harbour. I think there's about four stacks left to do."

"Can we come and have a look, mister?" Reuben asked.

"Well I don't 'spect anyone will mind that, boy, but we must get on or we won't get there tonight."

He hopped back onto the footplate and tapped the latch to open the firebox before shovelling a few lumps of coal on.

"You better sit on the elevator, Bill, and bang the shovel so I can hear if it ain't going to get round the corner by the pub."

Bill nodded his assent, climbed up onto the elevator and gave the boys a wave as they moved off.

"You know what I'm going to do when I grow up?" Reuben said as the boys watched the engine recede down the lane.

"No, but I'm sure you're going to tell us," replied William.

"I'm going to have the biggest Fowler ploughing engine there is, so there."

"You ain't sharp enough for that," said George, "you can't even write properly yet."

"Yes, I can."

"Well I ain't going to be an engine driver and get all black and mucky all day. I'm going to be a butcher like William and have my own shop," George stated.

Reuben shrugged and skipped on ahead to follow the engines, William and George following behind.

The farmhouse at Cold Harbour was large with a long drive up to it from the road. The front door was flanked by two floor-length windows – both arched at the top – and the window on the right opened onto the lawn. On the east side of the house was a glass conservatory with another French window that opened onto the lawn. The house was on the highest point in the area and had views all around only blocked at the back by the cattle sheds and stack yard. At the back of the house were the scullery, pantry, dairy and kitchen. The well was just next to the door to the scullery and across the path was the cattle yard. All the animals had been turned out weeks ago except one cow, which was lame, and stood chomping hay in the cavernous barn, a calf suckling happily by its side. At the back of the cattle yard was the hay barn which was now empty – this was where they were going to put the wheat and barley when it had been thrashed.

Mary and Lucy had had some tea and bread and butter, before going out to see the engine arrive. John stood by the gate, leaning on a stick, wheezing; he had been in poor health for years and suffered from a bad heart. As a consequence, the farm had gone downhill over the years and if it had not been for Henry coming into the business after leaving school, the farm would have been sold. At two hundred acres it was much bigger than most in the area and much of the farming was arable.

Mary and Lucy had been told that they would not go to school the next morning until the stacks were finished, which did not please Mary. She did not like getting dirty and thought that work on the farm was beneath her. Neither did she like working with the older men whose raucous banter and wandering eyes made her feel uncomfortable. Lucy, on the other hand, did not mind and quite happily joined the gang.

Within minutes, Lucy spotted the engine trundling up the drive into the stack yard where it was backed alongside the first stack. Henry supervised while John sat on a chair that had been brought out for him. It took a long time to get the drum into the right position and make it level by jacking up the corners and putting blocks under the wheels. The engine went off to the bottom of the hill to collect the elevator and bring it to the stack yard. This was manoeuvred to the back of the drum to take away the straw. By six o'clock all was prepared for the early start the next morning and the belts from the flywheel of the engine had been attached as had the belt from the drum to the elevator. The driver banked up the fire to ensure it would still be hot in the morning, and left for home on his bike.

In the morning everyone gradually arrived; the engine driver first to stoke the fire and then the five men who worked on the farm. The sunshine had been replaced by low lying dull clouds, gusted through the sky by a strong breeze from the southwest. Henry had cycled to Dean with a note for Mr Sparks to say that the girls were not coming to school and after breakfast they were all out waiting for the men to take the thatch off the stack; they were going to pass the sheaves to Henry, who in turn would fork them onto the drum. The driver stayed with the engine and Bill stood on top to cut the bands and feed the sheaves into the drum. Two men were going to build the straw stack, two would deal with the wheat as it went into the sacks and one would take away the chaff that was blown out.

"Are we all ready?" the driver shouted.

"Yes!" Bill shouted and the driver slowly pushed the regulator forwards.

As the drum gradually started turning so did the belt to the elevator, the slats started to move up and the other belts and pulleys on the machine kicked into motion as speed picked up. The straw walkers at the back started to dance

45

up and down like horses on a fairground ride and the sieve boat at the bottom shook backwards and forwards. The fan which sucked the air in to blow the chaff away started to hiss as the smoke was sent skywards and away; turning slowly whiter as the engine warmed up. As the speed of the drum built up the hum of the whole machine increased with it like a spinning top until it reached the required speed. Faces looked expectantly towards Bill, waiting for him to feed in the first sheaf.

"All right, then," he shouted finally.

To start with there was only room for Henry on the stack but as soon as he had thrown the first two or three feet to Bill the two girls were sent up. Their job was to pass the sheaves from the far side of the stack so that Henry could fork them to Bill. Gradually the sacks on the spout on the opposite end of the machine filled up with wheat; the sacks were then put on a sack barrow and wheeled to the scales where they were weighed off at eighteen stone, tied up and lugged into the barn. The chaff went into lighter sacks and was put to one side.

As the day went on, the stack of sheaves gradually reduced as the stack of straw rose. Although the smoke from the engine was blowing away, the strong wind made the dust and chaff swirl about, creeping into everyone's eyes. Mary, who really did not like the work, was sulking and refused to talk. Lucy, however, enjoyed being part of the team and was always chatting to Henry and Bill. As the day went on they all began to sweat in their heavy clothes and the straw scratched the legs of the two girls through their stockings.

"When are we going to have a break?" Mary complained. "Look at my hands."

"Just get on with it and stop moaning," Henry snapped back. "The quicker you work, the sooner we will be finished."

No sooner had he said this than Bill shouted out that the fans needed adjustment and the engine more water. Mary sat down where she was, high on the stack but Lucy made her way to the ladder.

"Where do you think you're going?" Mary snapped.

"Down the end," she replied.

"You should have gone before we started," she sniped, but Lucy did not hear; she was already off across the yard. Mary lay back on the straw and stared at the sky as the clouds scurried past; the wind cooling her face. She could hear the slow 'click click click' of the sack winder as it hoisted the sacks high enough for the men to get them on their backs to carry into the barn to join those that had already been wheeled in. The engine hissed as it slowly let off steam and the smoke and smell of the coal tar wafted up to the stack. She looked at her hands which were now red and rough; two of the nails were broken. Her hair – usually brushed straight – was straggly and full of bits of straw and chaff, and the drying sweat on her forehead had mixed with the dust and made dirty streaks from where she had dragged her hand across it. Her boots were full of bits of chaff and straw and were very uncomfortable. She sat up, undid the lace of one, pulled the boot off and hauled her foot onto her other knee so that she could brush off the offending chaff and straw. She looked round to check no one was in view, pulled up her skirt and untied the garter which held up her stocking. Quickly, she rolled the stocking down to reveal the white skin of her calves laced with angry red scratches from the sharp ends of the straw; she spat on her hand and rubbed it gently against the small red spots and scratches that had appeared on her legs. Then, checking once again that nobody was watching, she started to roll her other stocking down. Suddenly the ends of the ladder started to shake and wobble; she quickly pulled her skirt down as a face appeared between the rungs. It was Lucy.

"Oh, it's only you."

"Well, who else is it going to be?" Lucy replied.

"I don't know, it might have been one of those smelly old men."

"Don't be nasty, Mary, they're all good people. You shouldn't say things like that."

"Why not, they do smell, don't they?"

"Everyone smells, even you."

"No I don't."

"Yes, you do, so there," Lucy sniffed, sticking her tongue out at Mary and rubbing her fist across her nose.

"Don't sniff like that, Lucy," Mary hissed, "it really gets on my nerves," and she flung herself back on the sheaves and stared at the sky. The rooks swung round above their heads, dipping up and down beneath the backdrop of scudding clouds which moved swiftly across the sky.

"'Bout time we started, ain't it?" Henry's voice came up from below.

The ladder started to dance again as Henry climbed up – Mary hurriedly pulled up her stockings.

The stack was not a big one and should be finished by the end of the day, but there were still about ten feet to go.

"Right, we'll stop at one for lunch, then," Henry shouted to the driver, climbing back down the ladder.

The fire door on the engine clanked shut having just been re-stoked. The buckets stood at the back where they had been used to fill up with water and the yoke for the buckets lay on the straw next to the back wheel. The driver pushed the regulator forwards and everything reluctantly started to turn. The girls stood up and prepared for Henry to fork the first sheaf up; waiting for the drum to pick up speed. Gradually it started to hum; Bill fed in the first sheaf and there was a singing noise as the wheat was drawn in and the grain was stripped from the ears by the beater bars. The grain fell down onto the shaking sieves, which took out the pieces of straw that had broken off. The wind from the fans blew the chaff out as the clean grain fell into the sacks. Mary and Lucy took it in turns to pass sheaves to Henry and gradually the stack diminished. Lunchtime came and the girls and Henry went into the house to report to their father. John did not come out during threshing – the dust got on his chest and made him wheeze more than usual.

The engine driver Bill and the five men on the farm took an empty bag each from the heap waiting to be filled and laying them against the straw stack, sat down to eat their lunch. This consisted of half a loaf of bread and a lump of cheese; some of them had a slice of bacon as well, the whole lot being wrapped in a page of an old newspaper. The engine driver washed his hands at the pump but no one else bothered. Each man got his penknife out to cut his bread and cheese, wiping their knives on their trousers before starting. As they sat, one rat, then another and another scampered across the yard to the last stack at the end of the row.

"Come on, boy, get your catty out and 'ave a go at them," Bill said to James, the youngest of the farm men.

"I ain't got any stuns," he said.

"Go on with you, there's a heap of gravel over there," laughed Bill, pointing across the yard.

James rose and selected an assortment of stones before sitting back on his sack and laying the ammunition out in front of him. He pulled out his catapult – a branch of hazel with a leather sling held by two pieces of black elastic out of his jacket pocket. He loaded a stone into the sling and pulled it back a couple of times.

"Quiet, you buggers, or they won't come out," he whispered.

The men fell silent. Sure enough, another rat emerged from the cattle yard and started to run to the end stack. About halfway it stopped and looked up; James had his catty fully extended and as the rat stopped he released the stone. It hit the ground just in front of the rat, rising up in front of its nose and bowling it over. It scuttled to its feet and started to run back; but by this time Bill had leapt to his feet, armed with a stick – the rat fled for cover, but to no avail – the stick came crushing down on its skull. The men laughed and Bill sat down again to wait for another one. This time James had a direct hit and killed it first time.

"I know," he said, "I've got an idea."

He rose and moved over to the rat, picking it up by the tail and bringing it back to his sack where he wrapped it in the piece of newspaper he had eaten his lunch from and waited.

Five minutes later Henry followed by his two sisters emerged from the house and everyone rose to make a start again.

"Hey, Lucy, do you want a piece of my mum's cake?" said James. "She gave me a big bit and I can't eat it all."

He handed her the newspaper parcel. Lucy looked dubious, but James's mother was a notoriously good cook, so she opened the newspaper, revealing the prone rat.

"You nasty boy, James!" she shrieked, throwing the rat at him. "I'll get my own back one day, you wait and see."

The men all laughed as Lucy rushed to climb the ladder – a single tear rolling down her cheek, she sniffed and rubbed her nose with her fist.

Work continued all afternoon and they were nearly finished at four o'clock when William arrived with Reuben and George.

"Come on, we'll give you a hand to finish," said William; rolling up his sleeves and wandering over to the stack to help get the last sheaves to Henry, who by now was having to work very hard to pitch the sheaves eight feet high to Bill on the top of the drum.

"What are you all doing here?" Mary asked.

"Well, we all wanted to see the engine. Reuben is mad about them; he wants to be a driver or so he says," said William.

Reuben smiled.

"Come on, you boys, you might as well help me get ready for the morning," said the driver, "while Bill gets the drum sorted out."

"Right – you – what's your name?"

"William, mister."

"Right, William, you look big enough to fetch the water so get that yoke and two buckets and make a start."

"And you, what's your name?" he said bending down.

"George, sir."

"Well, George sir, you go and work the pump for William."

"And you, what's your name?"

"Reuben, mister," grinned Reuben.

"Reuben what?" demanded Bill in a jocular tone.

"Reuben Heighton, mister," Reuben looked confused and hesitated and quickly added, "sir."

"Right, Reuben, you hold my oil can for me while I open all the oilers on the old engine."

William was still a bit short for the yoke so they shortened the chain and he and George went across the yard to the pump. William got it going and once the water started to gush from the spout, George took over, his face soon red with exertion. When the buckets were full William could only just manage to carry them to the engine – the yoke bore down on his small shoulders, and the buckets felt like leaden weights as he poured them into the sump at the back of the engine, before trotting back to fill two more buckets. George continued to give the pump a crank as William was filling up the engine so that the water remained in the cylinder. As soon as William returned and placed the bucket beneath the spout, George would enthusiastically heave on the lever again. It took ten trips to fill the engine and by the time they had finished William was completely beat and sat down, his face flushed. The driver and Reuben had finished the oiling and the smoke box door was open – Reuben was helping the driver brush out the boiler tubes. When this was done the driver filled the bunker with coal which Reuben stacked up, blackening his face and hands in the process. The driver then emptied the ash pan underneath, damped the fire down and put enough coal on to keep it hot overnight. Bill had done all the oilers and greasers on the drum so they were all ready for the morning.

"Come on, you two," said William, "let's go and see if we can get a biscuit or something."

George and Reuben grinned and followed William towards the house. They entered via the scullery, and added their boots to the neat line that stood against the wall.

"Is that you, William?" a voice shouted from the kitchen.

"Yes, Auntie Ann, there's George and Reuben as well."

"Come on in then. I expect you want a biscuit or a piece of cake or summut."

William marched in with Reuben and George in tow.

"What do you bring these two squirts with you for, William?" said Mary. "They're still in short trousers."

Mary and Lucy were sitting at the table eating bread and jam and drinking tea. There was a plateful of buns on the table as well, which Reuben and George eyed eagerly.

"Come on then, sit down," Aunt Ann said. "Have one of those buns each."

"What about us, then?" Mary said in a resentful voice.

"Come on with you, Mary, there's enough for everyone. Father, what about you?"

John, who was sitting in a rocking chair next to the range, turned to his wife. His breathing was laboured; every inhalation crackled as though the air was struggling to get into his lungs.

"Not just right now, thank you," he replied. "What about Henry, isn't he going to have one?"

"Don't worry, there'll be enough."

The boys all sat down and tucked in to the buns, gratefully accepting a cup of tea from Ann.

"What about Kimbolton Grammar School, William?" said Lucy, sniffing and wiping the dew drop from the end of her nose with her fist.

"Do you have to sniff like that, Lucy? Use a hankie," Mary snapped.

Everyone smiled except Mary who grimaced, and William hastily answered his cousin's question.

"Well, I don't know much, I haven't even been there, only been past it. Mother says I am to be a weekly boarder and we will learn Latin and Greek."

"You're spoilt, you know that, don't you, William?" Lucy scowled. "I told you that before. I wish I could go to a school like that, but there isn't one for girls, it's unfair."

"So what are you going to do, Mary, when you leave school?" William asked hurriedly.

"Well there's a thing," said Mary with a smile. "I'm going to work in the dress shop in the High Street in Raunds and I'm going to live with Aunt Sarah during the week. It's a very smart shop, even for Raunds. *And,*" she said with excitement and great emphasis, "I get paid twelve and six per week which I don't get paid here, do I, Father?"

She shot a sly glance towards her father, who winked at his daughter, before looking back towards the fire.

"Don't say it like that," her mother reprimanded. "You work here to help your father out and you know there's not much money in farming."

"Well, how much longer will it take to thresh all the stacks?" Lucy asked.

"Oh, about another three days," John replied. "But I don't know about the last one; I've seen a lot of rats running about it. I rather suspect they may have done some damage."

The clock on the wall struck five. William looked up at it and then down at the two smaller boys.

"We better get going, it will take us three quarters of an hour to get home across the fields. We'll come and help tomorrow, if that's all right?"

"I'm sure it is, William," Ann replied. "And tell your mother that we will see them in chapel on Sunday."

With this the three boys pulled on their boots and caps and left the house.

The threshing continued on for another three days as John had predicted and it looked as if all would be done by the Friday night. William and the two others came up every night to help with the clearing up and Mary and Lucy remained off school until the job was finished.

On the Friday they started the last stack of wheat; Henry opened the top as usual and the girls went up the ladder as soon as there was enough room for them. Although Bill kept feeding the sheaves in the top there was very little grain coming into the waiting sacks and at lunch time they had only half of what had yielded from the other wheat stack.

"I bet it's the rats had the grain," Henry complained.

The straw stack at the other end of the drum had grown enormously and by manoeuvring the drum and elevator all the wheat straw had been put into one towering stack. The two men doing the stacking were forming the top into a point so it could be thatched ready to be used next winter.

After lunch Henry, Mary and Lucy returned to the top of the stack to start again; but as the stack decreased, rat muck was more and more in evidence.

"They're here all right," said Henry. "We must get the dogs out to catch them as they come out the bottom."

Simon, the man who was on the chaff bags, went to the scullery door and let out the terrier and two big collies who were in a pen round the corner. The collies bounded over, running backwards and forwards around the stack. The terrier, Gip, thrust his nose deep into the stack sniffing fiercely, his short tail wagging furiously. He sniffed again, backed off and started to bark at the stack, his head cocked to the side.

Mary and Lucy continued pitching the sheaves to Henry. Suddenly there was a scream from Mary – she had picked up a sheaf to reveal a rat, hiding underneath.

"Ow!" she shrieked. "I hate rats, do something, Henry; do something!"

"Throw us that stick up, Simon," yelled Henry. "Now, Mary, you pitch the sheaves and I'll lift them up."

Mary gratefully switched jobs with her brother, she could pitch the sheaves without much trouble as they were so light. Henry stood ready with his stick.

"Lucy, you lift up the sheaves and I will have a go at the rats," he instructed.

Nearly every sheaf they lifted had rats lurking under them. Many of them were fully grown, but a lot were young and there were even nests of babies under some of the sheaves.

"Henry, I'm not staying here," said Lucy with a shudder. "It's horrid. They'll go up my skirt soon."

"Nor am I," agreed Mary. "It's not safe."

She handed the fork to Henry, and she and Lucy made their way back down the ladder. Henry shrugged and followed his sisters. He started to tie round the bottom of his trousers, instructing Simon to do the same.

"Right, you two girls, have a stick each and stand one each side of the stack and bash them as they come out. Simon, you come up with me and we'll take Gip on top of the stack. Mary, you keep the collies with you and Lucy."

The rats continued to be revealed throughout the stack; the lower the stack fell, the more the straw had been chewed up and the sheaves did not hold together. Every now and again a grey shape would come scurrying out from the bottom of the stack, the dogs had some of them and Mary and Lucy hit the odd one, but if they escaped they simply rounded the stack and shot back into it another way.

Gip had jumped down from the stack; he had killed a lot of rats but had been bitten and was frightened of Henry's stick which had caught him several times in Henry's frenzy to get to the rats. The two collies had both been bitten on the nose and would only go after the rats as they ran.

It wasn't long before the driver stopped the engine; the sheaves were falling to bits before they could be thrown up.

Henry jumped down from the stack.

"It's no good, we're not getting anything out of it," he called to Bill.

They had not had a sack of wheat in the last half hour.

"What we'll have to do is burn it. There's no wheat in it and the straw's no good; it's the only way to get rid of the rats. "

John had come out; he walked around with his stick, poking the stack every now and again.

"Nothing you can do, boy," he wheezed, turning to Henry. "I've seen it before, it's a plague; you'll have to burn the stack and take the loss. Nothing else for it."

"This is not going to be easy with all the straw about but the wind's in the right direction so let's have a go."

Everything had to be packed up; the belt taken off the engine and elevator and the engine turned round and hooked to the drum. Mary and Lucy were sent to get rakes and raked the loose straw towards the stack, where it was piled up to be used for thatch.

"Simon, go and get an axe and chop some of those ash poles down, just the thin ones. We can use them to beat out the fire if it gets away."

By this time, William, Reuben and George had arrived.

"Come on, William," shouted Henry, "get the buckets and wet the straw round the bottom of the straw stack."

William sighed and returned to the yoke and buckets, as George scurried to work the pump – the pair ferrying the water to Reuben who threw the water round the stack. Gradually everything was prepared; a heap of ash saplings – their leaves on – was piled to one side. Everyone was given a stick – even George – and stood round the remnants of the stack which had been isolated from the big straw stack as best they could manage.

Henry turned to his father.

"What do you think, Father, is it going to be all right?"

"I don't know, boy; it looks all right but there's nothing else you can do, you can't let them rats stay there."

The remaining bit of the stack was now only about four feet high and had collapsed from the rats chewing it. Occasionally a rat would sprint out of the scraggly pile and dogs would rush after them, seize them in their jaws, and with a quick shake of the head, kill them. Gip was much quicker at this than the collies, but by now was showing signs of tiredness.

"Right, everyone get their trousers tied up," shouted Henry.

"What about us then?" Mary complained.

"I don't know. Just stand back or summat and see what happens."

"Right, who's got a match?" Henry asked, turning to the engine driver who had just lit his pipe.

"Here you are, boy, only use one, mind you."

Henry took the matches and pulling some straw together, he turned his back to the wind and struck the match.

"Damn," he said, as the wind blew the first one out. He tried again and a whisper of white smoke turned to a flame which started to flare in the straw in his hand, dancing above it like a genie. Henry threw the handful of straw into the stack and they all watched as the flame spread quickly, leaping through the sunken stack. The straw began to crackle, the smoke blowing towards Kimbolton Woods. The heat of the fire could be felt on the faces of those who were closest, forcing them to take a step back. Mary and Lucy had turned two buckets upside down and stood on them next to their father who was leaning on his stick. Rats could be seen on top of the stack jumping up and down in confusion, but none had risked leaving the stack yet.

Suddenly the wind changed direction and picked up; some of the ash and straw blew off the top of the inferno and set light to straw in front of the big stack. Everyone dashed to the heap of ash saplings, grabbed one and went to beat the fire out as William and George rushed to the well with the buckets. It was now very hot; the smoke and heat was blowing towards all those beating out the fire – it was difficult to see as their eyes smarted in the smoke. Within a couple of minutes, with everyone beating out the fire, the flames by the big stack subsided; William rushed up with more buckets of water and finally put out the embers.

Suddenly the dogs started barking; the rats had started to emerge from the burning rick like a heaving sea of undulating grey waves. The dogs, three together, turned the stampede in the direction of the fire fighters and as they stood there the rats ran through them. They ran over everyone's boots and round their legs and Mary and Lucy – their faces black from the ash – shut their eyes and screamed. No one had a stick with them and the rats ran past unhindered, away from the stack and down the hedge line. As they ran they made no sound; the dogs kept barking but backed off, totally outnumbered by the seething mass of escaping creatures. Mary and Lucy opened their eyes and looked down at the ocean of grey dashing away from the fiery furnace dragging their tails behind them. It dawned on Mary that they were in no danger as long as they did not move; the fear evaporated from her face and she looked down in amazement at the sea of grey migrating away towards the hedge. As suddenly as it had started, the rush of rats stopped, leaving only the pungent smell of small grey bodies that had not escaped the furnace.

Chapter Six
An Invitation from On High

"Come on, Mary! Lucy! For goodness' sake hurry up or we'll never get there."

Ann was getting ready to go out to tea at Charlotte and Thomas's in Lower Dean. They would take the pony and trap but there was only room for John, Ann and the two girls, so Henry had been detailed to walk over the fields.

"Come on, Lucy, move out the way, I can't see myself in the mirror," complained Mary.

"All right," snapped Lucy, "for goodness' sake, you never stop looking in the mirror, I was just combing my hair."

Mary did up the buttons on her long-sleeved white blouse, smoothing the brocade down the front and tucking it into her long dark blue skirt. She stood in front of the mirror and combed her hair vigorously back over her ears. Then putting the comb in her mouth, she deftly pinned her hair back so it fell down to her neck.

"Now, where's that damn hat?" she hissed.

Her eyes swept the room, alighting accusingly on her sister.

"I don't know! Don't look at me like that," said Lucy.

"There it is on the hook on the back of the door; give it here, Lucy," ordered Mary.

The hat was small and rounded – like a bowler – with a fat rim and a red ribbon over the dark blue. She put it on and pushed it to the back of her head.

"What's that look like?" she demanded, turning to Lucy.

"Absolutely wonderful!" came the sarcastic reply. "Come on, we better go."

"Just a minute!"

Mary stood back and looked at herself in the mirror again, brushing down her skirt and straightening the buttons down the front of her blouse by slightly turning the waist of the skirt. Mary at fourteen, had a figure envied by all the girls around.

"Right, we're ready to go. Come on then, Lucy."

Lucy sniffed and wiped her nose on her fist.

"Don't sniff like that, will you!" Mary insisted but Lucy took no notice.

She was wearing a flower patterned pinafore dress with a plain blue blouse and carried her boater rather than wearing it. They clattered down the wooden stairs and the latch clicked on the door at the bottom before they reached it, to reveal Ann's pinched face glaring up at them.

"Come on, come on, what on earth have you been doing? Now have you both been down the end before we go?"

"Mother," said Mary, rolling her eyes to the ceiling.

"Don't they look smart, John, aren't you proud of them?" said Ann wonderingly.

John smiled at his two daughters.

"Yes, they look a picture," he said, bending down to pick up his panama hat.

He stood up, leaning heavily on his stick and walked to the door. He was wearing his frock coat and breeches, highly polished leather gaiters and brown boots. His collar was very stiff, held together by a tightly tied tie with an extremely small knot, meaning that he had to turn his whole body when he looked round. Across his waistcoat – from pocket to pocket – hung a gold chain; a gold watch on one end and a match box on the other and from the middle hung a small compass.

John went out the door first followed by the girls and Ann at the rear, wearing a black dress with a jacket and black straw hat. She also had a fox fur draped round her neck, which Mary and Lucy both thought looked out of place for a summer's day.

"We're just going, Freda," Ann shouted as she went out the door. "Don't let the fire go out will you."

"No, Mrs Knighton," shouted back a voice from the scullery.

"And don't forget to milk the cow if we're not back by five."

"No, Mrs Knighton."

"And don't eat all that cheese; Henry will want some when he gets back."

"No, Mrs Knighton," the voice repeated resignedly.

"Bye, then."

"Bye."

The pony – trap attached – was out in the yard tied to the gate. John, Ann and Mary got in.

"Untie the pony can you, Lucy, and open the gate."

"Why do I always have to do it? Just because I'm the youngest!" she complained.

"Mary can do it on the way back," her father said calmly as Lucy slumped out of the trap.

The gate shut, Lucy skipped along and jumped in the back of the trap, closing the little door on the back of the trap behind her.

The pony's hooves clattered over the stones as they made their way down the drive away from Cold Harbour. It was a hot early summer afternoon and cattle stood grazing as they passed; lambs jumped and skipped and raised the back legs of the ewes off the ground as they suckled. As they reached the gate at the end of the drive, Lucy got out and ran round to open it.

"Don't tread in any cow muck," her mother shouted.

She could only just manage to pull back the spring on the gate hook before pulling the gate open. She stood back to allow the pony and trap to pass through and swung the gate hard to shut it, jumping on the lowest bar as the gate closed. As the gate hit the post and the latch clicked shut, Lucy was jolted against the top rail and green mould from the wood rubbed off onto her dress and hands. She quickly climbed the gate and ran to get in the trap.

"Now look at you, Lucy Knighton, look at your dress and hands," scolded Ann.

Lucy looked down at her front and then at her hands and went to brush one off with the other.

"No, no don't do that!" her mother screamed. "Spit on your hands and go and wipe them on the grass. We will get the stuff off your dress when we get to Aunt Charlotte's."

Lucy wiped her hands on the grass and got back in as the pony turned down the hill towards the butcher's shop at Lower Dean.

A mile away, coming in the other direction from Kimbolton in a very splendid four-wheel open carriage drawn by two well-groomed bay horses, was John

William Watson-Foster accompanied by his daughter Verity, and his sister-in-law Lettice. He sat at one end of the carriage looking forwards, Verity and Lettice sat at the other and the driver, Walter Snellgrove, was perched on the seat behind their heads.

John was originally from Yorkshire but had settled in Dean at The Hall; before buying a good deal of land in the area, which he was surveying this afternoon. Life had dealt him some heavy blows – his wife had died soon after Verity's birth and he had suffered from polio in his mid-twenties, which had left his legs paralysed; he had been confined to a wheelchair ever since. However, these setbacks had not dulled his spirit and he had never let his disability curtail his life. He continued to run his estate and although he could not ride, he had had a wheelchair constructed that could be pulled across the fields by a pony, and was thus able to enjoy shooting. Verity had been brought up by a series of nannies, with some additional help from John's sisters and sisters-in-law; and now attended boarding school. The afternoon trip had taken them through Dean, Hargrave, Covington, and on to Catworth and they were now on their way back. A quarter of a mile along the road they came to the first house, a thatched cottage, where the Heighton family lived. The house was tiny.

"I don't know how all those people live in a house as small as that," John said. "There must be seven or eight of them crammed in there."

"They are not poor though, are they, Father?" Verity asked.

"No, my dear, they had some land with the house, which they farm so they must have more income than most."

"Now, Walter, I want you to stop at the butcher's shop. I need a word with Dunmore."

They passed the farmstead and cattle yard that Thomas owned and pulled up outside the shop.

"Now, Walter, go and knock the door of the house and see if anyone is in," instructed John.

Walter tied the reins to the fence to secure the horses and went to the door and knocked. After a few moments Sarah came to the door, wiping her hands on her apron.

"Hello, Walter," she said, "fancy *you* coming to see us."

"Hello, Sarah, don't you look a picture!" Sarah blushed. "I've got Mr Watson-Foster here to see Mr Dunmore."

Sarah turned round in the doorway and shouted:

"William, is your mother or father about?"

"I don't know," shouted back William. "Who wants them?"

Sarah smiled at her visitor and turned to move slightly into the house, out of earshot:

"It's Mr Watson-what's-it," she said in a loud whisper.

"Oh! Hold on, I'd better come; you go and see if they are out the back somewhere."

William smoothed his hair down and confidently strode up to the carriage.

"Good afternoon, sir, I'm not sure where my parents are but Sarah has gone out the back to find them."

"Well," said John, peering down from his seat, "you must be William. How are you?"

"Very well, sir."

"Verity, Lettice, do you know William Dunmore? Say hello, Verity."

"Hello, William."

"Hello, Miss Watson-Foster, hello, ma'am," William said, addressing Verity and her aunt.

Verity smiled; she was not at all shy.

"Now, William," John said confidentially, "a little bird told me that you are going to Kimbolton Grammar School next year; is that right?"

"Yes, sir, I'm going as a weekly boarder from September after harvest."

"Well done, well done, that's splendid," John said, stroking his beard a couple of times before bringing his hands to rest on his chest.

"Now, William Dunmore, I was going to ask your mother this but in the meantime I will ask you. Verity here," – he smiled at his daughter – "has no brothers and sisters and spends her holidays in our great big house with only old people such as Lettice and me to talk to. I am proposing to invite you and your cousins for the afternoon to The Hall sometime next week so she can meet people nearer her own age. How would you like that?"

"Very much, sir, thank you."

"You didn't tell me that, Father," said Verity abruptly. "You might have asked me first."

"Come, come, Verity," soothed Lettice, "I'm sure William is a very nice boy."

"Now, Verity," said her father, "I did not say anything before because the idea has only just revealed itself to me at this moment. I am sure, however, that it is a very good idea and I will confirm it with Mrs Dunmore directly."

No sooner had he said this, than Charlotte came bustling out of the house followed by Sarah. She walked up behind William and rested her hands on his shoulders.

John turned and raised his hat.

"Good afternoon, dear lady, what a pleasure to see you again."

"Good afternoon, Mr Watson-Foster, the pleasure is ours; and what can we do for you this afternoon? I'm sorry I was not here when you arrived, but we are having my brother and his family for tea and I was getting ready."

"Aha, that's Mr and Mrs Knighton if I'm not mistaken; well I won't keep you long. I've just been talking to William – what a splendid chap he is – he tells me he's going to Kimbolton Grammar School, a fine place. Anyway, let me get to the point: I have invited William to attend The Hall next week in the afternoon to be a companion for Verity, if that meets with your approval."

"Yes," Charlotte said, "I'm sure William would enjoy that."

"Well, I intend to invite his cousins as well and we will send you a card to confirm the date when we have consulted the diary."

He smiled gently, then clasped a hand suddenly to his head.

"Oh dear, I'm sorry, Mrs Dunmore, I did not introduce you. This is Verity and this is my sister-in-law Lettice. Say hello, Verity."

"Hello, Mrs Dunmore," Verity said with very little grace.

"Pleased to meet you Miss Watson-Foster and you too, ma'am."

Thomas had now arrived, having put on his best clothes in readiness for the visitors.

"Aha, Dunmore, just the chap. I would like a quick word."

"Yes, sir, how can I help?" said Thomas, drawing closer to the carriage as

John lowered his voice.

"Now, Dunmore, just to let you know that Dean Way Post Farm will be up for let before long. Old Joe is coming to the end of his days and I will need someone to farm it. You are, after all, right next door and William is growing up – what do you think?"

"Well, I'm not sure," said Thomas slowly. "It's a big farm; over four hundred acres and it will need a lot of financing."

"How about the first year for nothing, so no rent until the second year?" shot John with a smile.

"Well, that sounds tempting," Thomas nodded. "We will think it over and thank you very much for the offer."

"No, thank you, Dunmore, and also you Mrs Dunmore for letting William come; you will get a card shortly. Good day to you all."

He raised his hat and smiled.

"Drive on, Walter," he instructed.

Walter shook the reins and off they went, down through the cutting and on their way to Upper Dean and The Hall. As they turned the corner by the cricket field, they noticed that John and Ann's trap had stopped to let the Watson-Fosters pass. John Watson-Foster looked up.

"Aha, just the very people; that's Mr and Mrs Knighton and daughters if I am not mistaken. Walter, draw up, can you? I want to have a word."

The carriage came to a halt adjacent to the Knighton's trap.

"Good afternoon, Knighton and Mrs Knighton," John Watson-Foster shouted across, raising his hat to Ann. "Just the people I wanted a word with."

"Lucy, jump out and hold the horse, we will have to get out and see him, he can't come to us," John Knighton said, pulling the pony to a standstill. Lucy quickly opened the little door and ran round to the pony to hold onto its bridle. Mary got out, followed by Ann and John, manoeuvring himself awkwardly with his stick. They moved to the side of the carriage.

"Now, Mrs Knighton, can I introduce my daughter Verity and my sister-in-law Lettice."

"Pleased to meet you," Ann replied with a smile.

"We were wondering if you would permit your two daughters to accept an invitation to spend an afternoon at The Hall next week to be a companion for Verity. It will be a great change for her to have someone of her own age in the house."

"I'm sure they would love to come," Ann said turning to Mary, "wouldn't you, Mary?"

"Yes, Mother," the unconvincing reply came.

"I can see Mary's quite the young lady now and Lucy is growing up fast as well. We will send a card to confirm the date and time and will look forward to seeing you both. Good day, Mr and Mrs Knighton; drive on, Walter."

He raised his hat once again and made his way off along the road.

"That Mary's a lot older than me, Father," Verity sighed.

"No, no, not that much: maybe two or three years, that's all."

"She's very pretty, isn't she?"

"Yes, she is," said Lettice, "and she dresses very well too."

"Well I'm not pretty and I don't care what I wear, so there," said Verity, turning to catch a glimpse of the Knighton trap as it moved off again round the corner.

The Knightons got back into the trap, John cracked the whip and they continued to Lower Dean.

"What was that he said, Mother?" said Lucy. "I couldn't hear it all."

"He wants you and Mary to go to The Hall one afternoon next week to be a companion for Verity."

"Oh, that'll be nice," said Lucy with a smile.

"No it won't," Mary said. "She's much younger than I am. What am I supposed to do when I get there?"

"I thought she looked a nice girl," said Lucy. "Anyway they've got pots of money and I bet we get a good tea."

"Now stop talking about it and tie up the pony, Lucy," instructed Ann, as John brought the trap to a stop outside the butcher's shop.

Lucy leapt down, tied up the pony for Henry to unhitch when he arrived on foot and followed her family into the house, where Charlotte had laid on sandwiches, cakes and tea. They took their places around the kitchen table.

"Now it's Sunday so, William, say grace, will you?"

Everyone shut their eyes while William rushed through the shortest grace he could remember. The plates were handed round, Sarah filled the teapot and the sandwiches were eaten before anyone was allowed cake.

"William, you won't ever guess where we're going next week, will he, Mary?"

"No, you'll never guess, William."

"If I can't guess you'll have to tell me," said William speaking through a mouthful of ham sandwich. He looked expectantly at Lucy.

"We're going to The Hall to spend the afternoon with Verity Watson-Foster! See, you would never have guessed, would you?"

"Well," William said, "you'll never guess where I'm going next week then, will you?"

"No, we won't so tell us," Mary said with waning interest.

"I'm going to The Hall to spend the afternoon with Verity Watson-Foster," smirked William.

"You're not!" said Lucy.

"Yes I am, aren't I, Mother?"

"Yes you are, William," nodded Charlotte importantly.

"Do we have to go?" sighed Mary. "They're very posh, aren't they?"

"Why should that make any difference?" said Charlotte. "You will all enjoy it, I'm sure. I think it's very kind of them to ask you; they haven't asked anyone else in the village."

"Now," said Ann turning back to Charlotte, "did I tell you about Bessie?"

The children turned their attention back to the sandwiches, which they polished off quickly, not wanting to hear the gossip, before addressing the cakes.

"Well," said Charlotte, when the table had been cleared, "we're all going into the other room to hear Mary play the harmonium. She's the only one I know who can play and it's such a waste if it's never used.

"I bag I pump it," said William rushing through to make sure that he got there before Lucy. The harmonium was ceremoniously uncovered and they all sat down, Mary on a stool at the keyboard.

"What shall I play then? I've got no music. Oh I know; get pumping,

66

William."

She opened with a shaky rendition of *God Save the Queen*. Everyone stood up and sang the first verse before bursting out laughing.

"Come on, Mary, you must be able to play some hymns."

"Yes, Aunt Charlotte, but I haven't got any music; there must be a hymn book somewhere with the music in as well as the words. Come on, William, you help look for one."

When it was found, along with several others, all the books were passed round and shared and they continued to sing for half an hour.

"Time to go," John said looking at his watch. "We must get back in the light. Can you go and fetch the pony, William? Lucy will come and hold it while you put the trap on. Henry, you had better get going; I'm afraid you will have to walk again."

"I bet I'm back before you are," he said, rushing to say goodbye to his aunt and uncle before yanking open the door and heading off at a trot up the road.

William brought the pony from the stable, took the halter off and put the bridle on before attaching the rest of the harness and the trap to that. Lucy then led the horse to the side gate and round to the front of the house where everyone stood outside the front door. One by one the Knightons hopped in.

"See you next week at The Hall," called Mary to William as they made their way onto the road.

William waved at the trap as it departed and followed his parents back into the house.

Chapter Seven
The Hall

"William, come here, let me have a look at you; have you brushed your hair?"

"Yes, Mother."

"And have you got a hankie in your pocket?"

"Yes, Mother."

"Now, William, you make sure you remember your pleases and thank-yous, and if they say grace when you have tea you make sure you shut your eyes."

"What time did it say on the invitation?" William asked.

Charlotte moved to the clock to check the visiting card for what must have been the tenth time.

"Let me have a look. Half past two. Yes, half past two; you've got plenty of time."

"Which door shall I go to, Mother; the back or the front?"

"I'm not sure," said Charlotte with a small frown.

"I'll go to the front door. Guests don't go to the back door, do they?"

He kissed his mother on the cheek and walked off in the direction of Upper Dean.

William was not sure about Verity Watson-Foster; you could never tell with the posh people whether they were snobs or not. William thought that Verity did not appear to be a snob, but he couldn't be sure; since she had been away at school, she had not been seen much in Dean.

It was another fine day; the barley in the field running down the side of the road was now in ear and waved in the wind like a green sea. In the next field over, two old chaps had taken a pause from cutting the hay to sharpen their scythes. William could hear the scrape of metal as the stone was moved up and down the blades, gradually giving an edge to their tools.

"Where are you off to, William Dunmore?" hollered one of the men who went by the name of Simon. "All dressed up like a dog's dinner. You must be going to see a fancy lady, I've no doubt."

William blushed and looked at his feet.

"I'm going to The Hall for the afternoon."

"Aha," said Simon, looking round to his companion, "didn't I tell you! Didn't I tell you, Moses? He's got a fancy lady; it must be that Verity – yes that must be who it is. And how did you get an invite there, me boy? She's not your clan."

"I don't know," shrugged William. "They just invited me, that's all I know; and anyway Mary and Lucy are going as well."

"Ah, Mary, now there's a fine looking lass if there ever was one," smiled Simon, turning to wink at Moses.

He pulled a pouch out of one of his jacket pockets and a short clay pipe from the other, shrugging the jacket off his shoulders and hanging it on the hedge. He began to fill the bowl of the pipe with tobacco from the pouch, pushing it in with his index finger, before fumbling for a match in his waistcoat pocket. He looked around for something to strike it on, deciding that the blade of the scythe was easier than the hobnails on his boots. He lit the match and held it to the tobacco, sucking at the end of the pipe as hard as he could at the same time as pressing the tobacco into the bowl with his finger. William watched as a thin stream of spit dribbled down the length of the pipe and dripped off the end. The pipe now alight, Simon surveyed William over the bowl.

"Well, I suppose we had better do a bit more work, Moses; this young man's got to get on or he will be late for his appointment."

With a sharp laugh, he hoisted his scythe and they turned to start cutting again, the blades whipping through the grass with a swish as they worked through the field.

William moved on along the road to the drive of the Watson-Fosters' imposing house. He straightened his waistcoat and made his way up the drive around to the front of the house, where the carriage stood.

"Hello, William, have you rung the bell yet?" came Lucy's voice behind him. He swung round.

"No, I thought I would wait for you."

"Go on, ring it," said Mary, "let's get this over with."

"Don't say that, Mary," whispered Lucy, "they'll hear you."

William rang the bell and stood back and waited.

Nothing happened.

"Ring it again, William," instructed Mary.

They still couldn't hear anything.

"There's obviously nobody here," sighed Mary. "We might as well go home."

"I can hear footsteps," insisted William, and sure enough a heavy footfall could be heard inside the house. They could hear the lock being turned and then the bolt at the top followed by the bolt at the bottom being drawn back. The door swung open.

A middle-aged plump woman with a white bonnet tied under her chin stood before them. She had a long white apron over her black dress. She looked them up and down but said nothing.

"I'm William Dunmore and these are my cousins, Mary and Lucy, and we have been invited for the afternoon," said William nervously.

"Yes, I know who you are. I know your dad, boy, he's the butcher, ain't he? The likes of you should come to the back door, not the front."

She turned and started off down the hall; halfway down the length of it she turned again.

"Well, don't just stand there, come in and follow me."

Verity suddenly appeared at the other end of the hall.

"Dorcas, is that our guests?"

"If you call 'em that, miss, yes, it is."

"Thank you, Dorcas," Verity said. "That will be all."

"I don't know why you have to have the likes of them here," Dorcas said under her breath. "And coming to the front door as well, I don't know what things are coming to!"

"That will be all, Dorcas," Verity said again in a much firmer voice, and Dorcas stomped away.

"Do come," said Verity, "we will go in the drawing room."

It was clear from her demeanour that Verity was very accomplished for her age; she acted as though she were in charge of the whole house but in the absence of a mother she had had to grow up very quickly. She wore a dark three-quarter length plain red dress over black shoes and black stockings. Her hair was fair but cut quite short and her features were fine and precise. She was pale, unlike the rest of them who were tanned from being out in all weathers, and her hand felt very soft as she offered it to each of them in turn, smiling as they shook it very delicately.

"I'm so sorry," she explained, "I bet none of you wanted to come today especially you, Mary. I was so embarrassed when Father asked you but he would not take no for an answer. He was right about one thing, it is a bit lonely here on my own with all these old people. Father is often out and that leaves an occasional aunt and the servants for company – and you can see what Dorcas is like. I hope she wasn't too rude, she can be really dreadful at times."

She stopped and looked at them, drawing breath.

"Please don't be sorry," said William quickly. "We were very pleased to be invited."

There was silence.

"Yes," said Lucy, "it was very kind of your father."

"Yes it was," added Mary.

"Well, what shall we do then? What would you like to do? I thought we could play cards as there are four of us and I've got the table laid out."

The others nodded and followed Verity down the corridor towards the drawing room.

The room was large with a fireplace at one end, surrounded by sofas and chairs. At the other end was a bay window with doors out onto the garden, and to one side was a grand piano. The walls were hung with portraits and tapestries and either side of the fireplace were big bookcases that stretched to the ceiling.

"Do you play whist?" Verity enquired.

The three cousins smiled at each other.

"Yes," said Lucy with a sigh of relief, "we all know how to play that."

"William, you're the only boy, you deal," instructed Verity.

They played for about half an hour; William was the best player and dominated the game, much to Mary's annoyance. Verity sensed this and after a while announced:

71

"I think that's enough of that, what about some music? We have a wind-up gramophone or we can play the piano. Well I mean I can't play the piano, I can't get hold of it. Can any of you play?"

"Yes, Mary can," piped up Lucy. "She's very good."

"Can you really, Mary?" said Verity. "Could we hear you? There's some music in the piano stool if you need it," and opening the stool, she let Mary rifle through the selection of dog-eared music books, alighting in the end on *HMS Pinafore*.

After four years of lessons from Miss Poynter, Mary had become quite proficient and had a natural ability and ear for music.

"Shall we sing the words?" said Lucy enthusiastically. "You can take the Admiral part, William."

"No, I refuse; you know I can't sing two notes together," grumbled William, with an angry glare at Lucy.

"Oh, go on, William," pleaded Verity.

"Come on, William, just for me," Mary said with a wink.

"All right then, but only one song," he insisted.

So they all sang, giggling at William who sang his words towards his feet with a very red face. After two or three attempts they made a passable rendering of *In the Queen's Navy*; Verity applauded gleefully.

"Well done, well done, Mary, I've never heard the piano played so well, in fact, I've hardly ever heard it played. Now that's enough of that, we ought to have some fresh air, let's go and play croquet."

"What's that?" asked Lucy with a small frown.

"You know," William said, "they've got it at the Rectory, you have to knock balls through hoops on the lawn."

Lucy shrugged and followed William out through the French doors, where they found the box with the balls and mallets under a veranda. Verity cautiously opened the box; the hinges were very rusty, the inside full of cobwebs and the mice had eaten the instruction book.

"Right," Verity said, "we'll play doubles. I will play with Lucy and Mary play with William."

"But we don't know the rules," Lucy protested.

"Well, we will have to make them up, I can remember a bit about it."

She proceeded to give an account of the rules she could remember and the four started to play. Halfway round Lucy sidled up to Mary and asked,

"I want to go down the end. Do you know where it is?"

"No idea. I can't see anything that looks like one out here. Hold on, I'll ask William."

Checking to see that Verity was occupied, Mary beckoned William over to her.

"William, Lucy wants to go down the end; do you know where it is?"

"No idea, I've just been behind that bush." Mary went back to Lucy. "We don't know, can't you wait?"

"No, I can't. I'll wet my drawers if I don't go soon."

Mary bit her lip and looked around.

"Look, I'll knock the ball over there in the hedge and get Verity to help me look for it; you can go behind that bush."

"I can't do that, not here anyway."

"Yes, you can, you've been behind plenty of bushes in the past."

"Yes, but not in people's gardens."

"Well, just get on with it," Mary hissed, lining up her ball and hitting it with all the strength she could towards the hedge. "Sorry about that," Mary tittered. "Can you help me find it, Verity? It must be here somewhere."

With a pointed look towards Lucy, Mary dragged Verity towards the hedge.

"You stand there, William, and shout if someone comes; and don't look either," said Lucy in a loud whisper as she dashed round the back of the bush.

"Here it is," called Mary loudly, falling to her knees to crawl into the hedge to retrieve the ball.

"No, no, don't do that, Mary, you will get your white blouse dirty. Come here, let me do it," and Verity pushed in front of her and scrabbled for the ball.

"Here it is; we didn't want to spoil your clothes – they look so lovely on you," said Verity. "I think you are the prettiest girl I know, much more than any of the girls at my school and you choose your clothes so well."

Mary did not know what to say.

"I don't *have* many clothes," she stammered, "just what mother gets in Raunds."

"Well, whoever does it you look wonderful. Anyway it must be time for tea."

Verity led the way back into the house through the kitchen where Dorcas sat with the cook.

"Do you want to wash your hands?" Verity said, offering them soap and a towel. "There's hot water at the sink, it comes much quicker here than in the bathroom."

Mary looked at Lucy then at William, none of them had *running* water in their houses let alone running hot water; everything came from the pump and was heated on the range and they washed in a bowl.

"Is that all right?" asked Verity uncertainly.

"It's fine," laughed William, "we just don't have taps in our house."

"Serve tea in the drawing room will you, Dorcas," Verity ordered and she led the way down the corridor and into the hall.

"If anyone wants the WC it's down there," said Verity, pointing to a door at the end of the corridor.

"The what?" asked William.

"The lavatory."

"Oh no, I'm fine."

"So am I," said Lucy with an eye roll towards Mary.

"I'll go," said Mary. "Don't wait for me."

Verity led the others into the drawing room, Dorcas following them with a trolley which rattled and clanked as it moved over the stone flags and the worn Persian rugs. William and Lucy sat down and Verity handed round the plates and the sandwiches and sat to pour the tea.

Next to the drawing room, they could see a library through the open door, and on the middle of the table there were two or three daily papers.

"Did you want to look in the library?" Verity asked, noticing William looking in that direction.

"Yes please," he replied. "It's the papers I like reading."

"So do I," said Lucy, and the two of them rose to explore the room, passing

74

Mary in the door as they left.

"Now, Mary," said Verity, "I was wondering."

She stopped for a moment and chewed her lip nervously.

"I was wondering if you could help me. Since I have no mother it's not easy for me – only having aunts and the like. I would really like someone to help me shop for clothes and I was wondering if you could come with me? You look so smart, Mary, and you're so pretty and you wear your clothes so well and you're a bit older than me and you would know what to choose. I'm hopeless at that and don't know what's in fashion. Would you come with me?"

"Do you think I'm the right person?" asked Mary, surprised. "Haven't you got other friends from school? I'm sure they would be much more useful than I would be."

"No, Mary, I'm sure you're the right person and anyway you live much closer than any of them. We could go to Northampton. Father has an account at most of the big shops there, we could catch the train from Rushden."

"Very well," shrugged Mary, "but I must ask Mother first."

"Splendid," said Verity. "I expect Father will insist that we take Dorcas with us but that can't be helped. I will persuade him that Harriet should come, she's much easier to get on with."

The tea party then concluded and after saying their thank-yous William and his two cousins walked down the drive to the road.

"What about that?" said William. "What did you think of Verity?"

"I think she's lovely," said Lucy. "And it's so sad she hasn't got a mother."

"I think she's nice," said Mary. "And guess what, she asked me while you were in the library, to go shopping with her. Dress chooser for Verity Watson-Foster – what about that!"

Chapter Eight
Delivering the Meat

The last day of term arrived and it would be the last time both William Dunmore and Mary Knighton would attend the school. At the morning assembly, after the hymn, Mr Sparks read out the names of all those leaving and wished them all well, before handing each leaver a Bible donated by Mr Fitz-Allen who lived at Dean House; he had written in each one. Mary was glad to be leaving, she had outgrown the place and was desperate to start work and earn some money for the first time.

William on the other hand was sad. He was a very good pupil and came top in most of the subjects he took. He had some good friends among the boys and although glad to be going to Kimbolton, he would miss the school at Dean, so it was with mixed emotions that he wandered out of the school gates that morning.

"Give us a look at your Bible then," sounded a voice behind him as he ambled from the school.

William swung round to see Molly Webb smiling impishly up at him. She was in better circumstances now and had a clean dress on and even shoes. Her father had been in work ever since they had arrived in Dean and her mother worked in the kitchens at The Hall. Her shoes had come from Verity who had insisted that her father do something to help the family that lived in one of his houses.

"Here you are then," shrugged William, handing over his gift from Mr Fitz-Allen.

"That's smart, ain't it? Ooh, look here it says: '*To William Dunmore with best wishes for the future from.... Malcolm Fitz-Allen*': ain't that nice?"

Molly grinned. Her curly hair hung down to her shoulders and her face was tanned, as were her arms and legs. She handed the Bible back to William and smiled.

"Ain't you going home?" William said as they passed Chapel Row, where Molly lived.

"Ain't no point. There ain't no one there; Mother's at work and Father's walked to Raunds to get more leather. I'm going to walk along with you for a bit."

"All right," said William dubiously.

He was not sure about girls, and tried as hard as he could to avoid them, with the exception of Mary and Lucy.

"Don't say it like that then," said Molly, poking William in the ribs with a bony finger. "Sound a bit more enfusiastic. Not everyone's got someone to walk along with them."

William said nothing, but kept walking as she skipped along beside him. He increased his pace.

"Can you spit, William? I mean can you spit and hit things with it?"

"Don't know, I've never tried," shrugged William.

"I can. Look at me, William; see this gap in my teeth." She turned her head towards him and grinned. She had perfect white teeth and the top two 'tombstones' as she called them had a big gap between them.

"What shall I spit at then, what do you think?"

"I don't know. Whatever you like," mumbled William noncommittally.

"Look there," she said, nodding in the direction of Hall Farm House. This was the farm owned by Mr Watson-Foster, Verity's father, and where Mr Milligan and his family lived. The farmhouse was right on the side of the road and had a big front door with a large brass door knocker in the middle of it.

"I'll get that door knocker."

She squeezed her cheeks and a dimple appeared each side as she sucked to assemble the spit in her mouth; she stretched her neck forward and spat, hitting the knocker from four or five yards away with a large globule of bubbly spit which ran down the shiny knocker and dripped slowly off the end. She turned to William and grinned.

"There you are. Bet you couldn't do that, William Dunmore," she laughed, and with a toss of her hair she skipped on along the road.

"What did you want to do that for? The knock'll be all gooey now when someone gets hold of it."

"Serve 'em right. Anyway they'll only be posh people; only posh people go to that house – I've seen 'em."

"Ain't you going home yet?" William insisted with a bit more urgency.

"No I ain't. I told you, there's no one there and I'm walking along with you, William."

There was an uncomfortable silence. Molly turned coyly to William.

"Do you want to hold my hand, Williyum? I wouldn't mind if you did."

"No, I don't, so there," William said, blushing and turning away.

"Look! William, 'ave you got your catty with you? There's a rabbit just over the hedge in that field."

"No."

"Shame! I'm good with a catty; I could hit that rabbit any road. I'm sure I could, I've got a stone as well." William shook his head, and once again increased his pace, marching on passed the lane to the woods.

"Are you coming for a walk with me up the woods?" cooed Molly.

William stopped and turned angrily to Molly.

"No, I'm not, so there, why don't you sod off?"

"Temper, temper! You've gone all red in the face, William! Well if you don't want to come up the woods I'll walk to the butcher's shop with you and see your mum; I bet she'll give me a biscuit out the barrel of the kitchen table, she all'as does."

"Just go home, won't you," groaned William.

"I'll go home if you promise to come for a walk up the woods with me another day," persisted Molly.

"No."

"All right then, I'm coming along with you."

"Fine! I promise as long as you go," hissed William.

A smile spread across Molly's face and before William could do anything she grabbed his arm and quickly pecked his cheek.

"Bye bye, William," she laughed, swinging her dress from side to side with her hips as she walked back in the direction of Upper Dean. Shaking his head in bemusement, William turned and stomped home.

He now had five weeks to help with the harvest and the butcher's shop before he went to school in September. He was old enough to take the pony and trap on the butcher's round, and the arithmetic he had learnt from Mr

Sparks made it easy for him to deal with the cash. The big houses and some of the famers had accounts with his father and only paid once a year, or more, but the poorer people paid with cash if they had any.

The next morning – Saturday – he fetched the pony from the field, fed and groomed it and put the harness on before backing it into the shafts of the trap.

"Now, William, let me show you the order," said Charlotte, moving to the marble slab in the shop where the three baskets of orders for the big houses sat.

"Now here they are; this is Mr Watson-Foster's; this is for the Reverend Packham and the Fitz-Allens. There's only eggs for the St Johns as they sent for their meat yesterday."

She pointed to the items as she spoke.

"Here's the rest to sell; I marked the weights on them. That big joint of beef will do for Mr Hartford and the rest you know what they usually have."

There was a timid knock at the door; it was George.

"Can I come, William? I can open the gates for you," he squeaked.

Although only six years old, George was always eager to be involved, especially if it meant spending time with William.

"All right then," said William, "but go and tell your mother first and get some bread and cheese for your lunch; it'll be four o'clock before we get back from Knotting."

George dashed off in the direction of his house, which stood fifty yards away from the butcher's shop and was back again in a few minutes with his bread and cheese wrapped in a piece of newspaper. He grinned up at William who was sitting in the trap, and scampered up to join him.

For late July, the weather was not hot. It was overcast and there was an occasional spot of rain in the wind which blew down the valley from Shelton. As yet the harvest had not started, although the first swathe of wheat around Freeholds, the biggest field, had been cut by scythe to allow the horses to get round with the binder without trampling through the crop. Bright red poppies stuck through the top of the corn in the fields, fighting for sunlight with the wheat. On the other side of the road running down to the brook at the bottom, were grass fields that had been cut for hay. The weather had not been good for raking and it had all been forked up onto haycocks to keep it dry, but the grey colour of the stacks belied its poor quality. The trap moved on – past the cricket pitch where someone was busy taking the fence down from around the wicket ready for the match that afternoon.

The first call was at The Hall; William turned the pony into the back yard and up to the back door. George jumped down and ran round to hold the pony while William picked up the basket with the order for Mr Watson-Foster. He knocked at the door and walked into the scullery where one of the maids was washing the breakfast dishes in the sink. Through the door into the main kitchen he could see Dorcas stirring a large saucepan on the stove. She looked up.

"Well, William Dunmore, you've come to the wrong door. Thought you all'as come in the front door now."

William blushed and did not answer, quietly emptying his basket onto the kitchen table, checking each item off against a list in the order book.

"Come here," ordered Dorcas, moving from the stove into the scullery. "Let's have a look at that beef." She turned the meat critically this way and that.

"How old was this animal, William? I bet it was an old cow, not a bullock; look at all this gristle! How am I going to cook that? I'll have to boil it first."

"That's good meat, Dorcas," insisted William firmly, "It's from one of our bullocks and it's been hung for two weeks: can't be any longer in this weather."

"Well, I bet it was an old cow," she insisted, turning to Verity who had just walked into the kitchen with the order book for next week.

"Now, Miss Verity, you look at this beef that William 'as brought. I say it's an old cow, what do you think, shall I send it back?"

Verity looked helplessly at the joint, unable to make any sort of adequate judgement.

"That looks all right to me, Dorcas, you're just making a fuss; I'm sure it will do."

Dorcas raised her eyes to the ceiling, tut-tutted under her breath, and with a murderous glance at William, moved back to the stove and her saucepan.

"Now, William," said Verity, "I've been reading about the slaughtering of cattle in a magazine and it seems absolutely barbaric. It said the cows were pulled to the ground, and then hit on the head with a hammer called a poleaxe. Is that true, William?"

She turned anxiously towards him.

"Yes, that's how it's done," said William smiling. "It doesn't take long; it's all over in a flash."

"Do you mean that's how your father does it?" said Verity, her forehead furrowed in concern.

"Yes," said William, surprised at Verity's distress. "Everyone does it that way around here."

"But in this article it says it should be done by shooting them with a humane killer; surely you've heard of them."

"I know," said William, "but we don't kill enough to have one."

"But that's not the point; it's cruel!" Verity was now getting insistent. "I must have a word with your father about it, it can't go on you know, I mean it, it can't go on."

She frowned and turned her attention to the order book.

"Dorcas, have you made out the order?"

"Yes, miss, it's all there."

Verity looked down the list and held it out to William.

"Very good, here you are, William; here's the order for next week."

He took the book from her and turned to leave.

"By the way, William, are you going up to Cold Harbour today? I've got a note for Mary."

"Sorry, no, we're on our way to Knotting today, it'll take us all our time to get there."

"Very well then, I'll send Walter up with it. Thank you, William."

She turned and left the room, leaving William to pick up his basket and make his way back to the trap.

The next stop was The Manse, where Reverend Packham lived. The boys could see him through the large window at his desk, no doubt writing his sermon for the service tomorrow. William walked round to the back door past the window, and on seeing him the Reverend raised his hand in acknowledgement and rose to meet William in the kitchen.

"Well, William Dunmore, and what have you brought us today?" boomed Reverend Packham, peering at William over the top of his glasses.

"Mother thought you would like a leg of mutton."

"Ah, your mother! What a wonderful lady, a truly wonderful lady! A dedicated follower of our Lord and His good works."

He looked sharply at William.

"The Lord always provides, William; for those that believe; the Lord *always* provides. Look on His works, William and admire the words of the Lord. Admire them day and night and be in awe of what He achieves."

He paused, looking critically down at William to assess the impact of his words.

"Tell your mother I will pay next week," he murmured, turning back into the room from which he had come and calling back over his shoulder,

"Make sure I see you in chapel tomorrow, William."

The next houses on the street were in Chapel Row where Molly Webb lived.

"George, just run down to the Webbs with this; don't bother about the money today, I'm sure they won't pay," said William, handing George the pound of lard and piece of neck of mutton which was the Webbs' weekly order.

No sooner had George started to knock than the door was yanked open.

"Oh, it's you, George; where's Williyum? I was waiting for 'im," said Molly peevishly.

"He's round at the pub taking the meat."

"I'm coming to see 'im, "said Molly. "What did he send you for, you little squirt?"

"Don't know," said George as he followed Molly up the path and round into the street.

William had tied the pony to the post that held the sign for the pub and was nowhere to be seen, so Molly stroked the pony and waited. William came back with his empty basket.

"Hello, Williyum, don't you look smart this morning? Don't he look smart,

George, in that smock?" William always wore a brown smock buttoned down the front for doing the deliveries.

"Yes, yes," William said, untying the pony and jumping in the back. "Jump in, George, we must go, we've got a lot to deliver."

He shook the reins at the pony, urging it away as fast as he could.

"'Member what you promised yesterday," Molly shouted after them, "Williyum Dunmore, did you 'ear me?"

William did not look back.

"William," insisted George, tugging at William's sleeve, "we've missed four houses already."

"We'll come back to them," William insisted. "We'll go to Dean House first and then come back, I can't stop here with her about."

At Dean House, George jumped out to open the back gate and then skipped up the drive after the trap, running to hold the pony's head while William took the meat in. As he came out George had bad news.

"William, the pony's thrown a shoe."

"Oh no," moaned William, moving to the pony to check. "We'll have to go back to Art and get him to make another; we can't go to Knotting like that."

So they retraced their journey back to the blacksmith who had his forge in a building close to the church. The blacksmith – Art Tuffnail – was in his early thirties and had taken over the business from his father who had in turn taken over from his father. The forge was alight six days a week and kept the whole community supplied with anything they needed in iron. His main task was shoeing horses but he was also a wheelwright, a nail and hinge-maker and anything else that could be hammered into shape.

"Well, William Dunmore, what can I do for you?" smiled Art as William directed the cart into the yard. "In fact, I can see what I can do for you; that pony'll be needing a shoe, won't it?"

"Yes, and quickly if possible, Mr Tuffnail; we want to get on the round again as soon as possible."

"Well, me boy, you're going to have to wait a bit, I'm just putting a tyre on that cart wheel for Hubert Hartford and it's just hotting up so I can't leave it for the moment."

William sighed.

"Well, we'll just have to wait, won't we?"

"You can get the horse apart from the trap so she's ready," said Art.

William undid the harness and George walked the pony to the side of the road, tying him to the post next to the forge. William sat down on the verge.

"Might as well eat our lunch now, George. We'll have to get a move on when the shoe is on."

George moved to sit next to William, and together they ate their bread and cheese, washing it down with cold tea from an old whisky bottle.

"Right, come here, William, you can give me a hand," Art shouted. "Grab a pair of these tongs and help me lift the tyre on the wheel."

There was a lot of smoke from the circular fire that had been lit to heat up the tyre enough to get it over the wheel which lay on the ground.

"Right, you grip that side and I'll have this one and when I say so, lift it over the wheel. As for you, George Lowe, get that watering can and fill it up at the pump."

George grabbed the can and ran down the street to the pump.

William was getting very hot in front of the fire.

"Are you ready, boys?"

"Yup."

"Well, lift then."

It was heavier than William expected, and an awkward job as the wheel had to be lifted at arm's length to avoid the heat of the fire, but they managed – hoisting the metal the two yards to the right until it was over the wooden wheel. They lowered it slowly but it would not fit over the wood.

"Bugger, bugger, bugger, it's not round," Art cursed. "Lift it again, boy, let's move it round a bit and see if it'll go over."

They lifted it again, moving the metal a quarter way round the wheel.

"No, not enough yet," Art cursed, "round a bit more."

Still it would not go over.

"Nothing for it," Art shouted, grabbing a nearby sledge hammer and giving the metal an almighty wallop, so that it slid grudgingly over one side of the wheel. Another wallop to the other side set the metal in place, before Art tapped it into the exact position.

"Come on, George Lowe," hollered Art. "Where's the water?" He looked up to see George staggering the twenty yards up the street, leaning heavily one way to balance the weight of the watering can.

"Give it here then, boy," laughed Art, grabbing the can and pouring water around the tyre. The metal hissed and steamed, shrinking resentfully onto the wheel.

"There we go, good job done, thank you, William, thank you, young George."

Mopping his brow with a dirty brown handkerchief, Art sat down heavily on the anvil.

"Now, William Dunmore, I ain't starting that old nag of yours before I have a cup of tea, what do you think?"

"If you say so, Mr Tuffnail."

Art turned and shouted to the door of his house.

"Is the kettle on, Mrs Tuffnail?"

"What do you want now then?" came a shrill voice from inside the house.

"Come on, there's folks out 'ere want a cup of tea."

Ruby Tuffnail came to the door. She was a big woman with wide hips and a huge bust; her sleeves were rolled up revealing her powerful forearms and a round rosy face splodged with white from the flour she was baking with.

"What are you bawling about, Tuffnail?" she shouted back in a voice nearly as loud as his.

"We would like a cup of tea."

"Oh yes, and who's 'we'? Aha! I can see who 'we' is; it's young William Dunmore the Master Butcher of Lower Dean, and if I'm not mistaken, it's George Lowe as well."

She bent down to pat George on the head, her bosom inches away from his face. The blouse looked in danger of bursting open and George coloured and looked away.

"Very well then, since we've got guests I'll see what we can do."

And she turned her back, revealing an equally large bottom which swung her skirt as she walked back to the door.

"Tea, William?"

"Yes please, Mrs Tuffnail."

"Tea, George?"

"Yes please, Mrs Tuffnail."

"Biscuit, William?"

"Yes please, Mrs Tuffnail."

"Biscuit, George?"

"Yes please, Mrs Tuffnail."

"What about me then?" Art demanded.

"You'll get what you're given, Art Tuffnail, so there," laughed Ruby, returning through the door. Two or three minutes later she was back, bearing a tray with the teapot, cups, a milk jug, sugar bowl and a biscuit barrel; she perched the tray on the bench by the forge and started to pour out the tea. From his position sitting on the anvil Art pulled up the hem of Ruby's mid-calf length skirt, sliding his hand up until he had reached her mid-thigh and squeezing. For a moment, Ruby froze before turning, placing the teapot calmly on the bench and swinging her left arm round in a circular motion until her clenched fist came in contact with Art's cheek and then nose. The blow was of substantial force and knocked him off the anvil, where he rolled over in the dust.

"What did she do that for?" Art asked William.

"No idea," said William looking particularly vacant.

Art got up and dusted himself down, smiling at the two boys.

"Just keep your hands to yourself, see," Ruby shouted, glaring at Tuffnail.

"Come on, you boys, have a biscuit but only one, mind, we ain't made of money."

She opened the barrel and handed it to the two boys.

"Now, William Dunmore, have you got any sausages in that cart of yours? I was wanting to ask you when I saw you earlier but you sailed on straight past us."

"We just did things in a different order today," said William hastily, rising

86

to move to the cart. "I have got some sausages for you, I'll go dig them out."

William walked across the road, and drew out the sausages, wrapped in greaseproof paper.

"Hello, Williyum, fancy seeing you again," called Molly, skipping up to the forge with her two brothers in tow. "You went off in such a hurry I couldn't say goodbye."

"Well, Molly Webb, and what you want?" demanded Ruby.

"Dad sent me up."

"Sent you up for what?"

"He says 'ave you got any hobnails you could spare as he's got to do a pair of Hubert's boots."

"Well, 'e ain't paid for the last lot of nails he had nor the lot before that," frowned Ruby.

Molly reddened and looked at the ground.

"Please, mister," she whispered, turning to Art, "my dad's trying very hard, I'm sure he *will* pay, soon."

Her mouth lifted slightly at one side and an alluring smile spread across her face.

"Very well then, go on with you," growled Art, tossing her a small bag of nails from the shelf on the wall of the forge. "And you tell your dad to come down and settle his bill."

"You weak-willed fool," snapped Ruby as Molly snatched the nails from Art's outstretched hand.

"And be off with you, Molly Webb, and don't come back without any money!"

"Now, William Dunmore, don't you have anything to do with that girl, she's far too pretty for her own good," grumbled Ruby. "She's trouble, you mark my words. Only twelve years old and she can twist that poor fool round her little finger."

With that Ruby turned on her heel and stomped back in the house.

"Come on then; drink your tea, you boys, let's get on with this old hoss," said Art, draining the rest of his tea and rising.

"George, you hold the hoss; William, get on the bellows and bring the fire up. I'll see if we've got a shoe to fit."

With his back to the pump head, Art grabbed some pinchers and picked the pony's foot up, wiggling the remaining nails from the hoof, and examining the shape of the foot with a frown.

"I've not got a shoe to fit. I'll need to start afresh," he muttered, dropping the pony's foot and moving to select the iron he needed to fashion a new shoe.

The fire now glowed red; Art cut the piece of iron to length and put it in the fire to heat up. When it glowed red he used a pair of tongs to remove the iron from the furnace and on the pointed end of the anvil, he gradually bent the length of iron round into the shape of the horse's foot. Satisfied with the shape, he picked up the horse's hoof and gently pressed the livid red shoe to the hoof. The hoof smoked and hissed as the acrid smell of burning hair filled the forge.

"Near enough," he mused, turning to make the holes in the shoe for the nails with a sharp spike. He turned once more to check the dimension on the pony's foot, nodded and moved to the water trough to plunge the shoe in the murky water, where it hissed and bubbled. He rose, collected a selection of nails and set about hammering the shoe into place.

"There we are, William, all's done," smiled Art, rising slowly and pushing his hands into his back as if to shove himself upright. "I'll settle up with your father when I see him."

George led the horse into the middle of the road and they pulled the trap from the hedge and attached it to the animal.

"Thank you very much, Mr Tuffnail," William said. "And thank Mrs Tuffnail for the tea."

Art waved a hand in acknowledgement and moved back into the house.

William shook the pony's reins, and steered it down the hill. The shrill whistle of a steam engine could be heard from the direction of Melchbourne on the next hill.

"Did you hear that, George?"

"Yup, must be a ploughing set on the move."

"Sounds like they're near the The Grape Vine; let's get a move on and we'll see them."

Chapter Nine
Roland Cumber

As they came up the hill towards the pub, William and George could see the two engines and tackle parked in a line along the road. The gang had gone into the pub for some beer and were just coming out as they drew up.

"I better lead the horse past them," said William. "You sit tight, George, in case it bolts."

The engines seemed huge compared to the ones used for the threshing; they had great, big barrels under the boilers, around which was coiled the wire rope which was used to pull the plough. Behind the first engine the plough was coupled, attached to a cultivator; the second engine drew the living-van and the water cart. As they drew closer they could hear the engines hissing slightly as small amounts of steam escaped from the leaky joints and a wisp of smoke coiled from the chimneys. Both engines were black with brass name plates announcing one engine as 'William' and the other 'Mary'.

"Whoa, steady," cooed William as the pony shied and reared at the hissing valves, eyeing the contraptions with fear.

"Come on now, will you," he insisted, tugging the harness; the pony gave a snort and rushed forward, almost knocking William off his feet. Once past the engines, he quietened and George leapt down from the cart to hold the reins whilst William rummaged through the remaining orders to find the basket of meat for the pub.

Blocking his way at the front door of the pub stood Roland Cumber, the foreman of the ploughing team. He was a tall, powerfully built man with long whiskers straggling down the side of his face. His hands were black and his face smeared with coal dust. He wore a dirty white shirt under his waistcoat, with no collar and the sleeves rolled up to his elbows. A wide brown leather belt with a huge brass buckle held up his dark woollen trousers. From a trouser pocket he pulled a yellow packet of Capstan cigarettes, pushed the cigarettes up through the sleeve of the packet with a grimy finger and selected one. Tapping the end of the cigarette on the packet, he raised the end to his mouth, rolled the cigarette against his moist tongue and gripped it between his lips.

From a small pocket in his waistcoat he pulled a box of matches, struck one and lit the cigarette. He took a deep draw and glowered at William who was waiting patiently for Roland to unbar his entrance to the pub. He blew a stream of smoke slowly and deliberately into William's face.

"Where do you think you're going, boy?" growled Roland, his voice laced with menace.

"Going to deliver the meat, sir," said William nervously.

"No, you ain't, boy, not while I'm stood 'ere," he sneered, lowering his face towards William, who took a step backwards.

"What yer got in that basket then, boy?" he demanded.

"Just the meat, sir."

"Give it 'ere then," scowled Roland, grabbing the basket and turning over the joints in his filthy hands until he came to some ribs of beef.

"That looks the piece for us," he said, removing the ribs from the basket.

"Cook boy!" he yelled. "Cook boy, where the bloody 'ell are you, you stupid bugger?"

"Here, Roland," came a small voice from the back of the gang standing assembled in the doorway behind Roland.

'Boy' was the wrong term for Bernard Thorp the cook; he was at least thirty-five but looked fifty. He walked with a severe limp due to a club foot and his face was puffy. His eyes were small and his ears flapped forward, compressed down by his oversized cap and he had no teeth at the front of his mouth as a result of a fall.

Bernard rocked his way down the steps past the other three members of the gang and presented himself to Roland.

"Here, boy, take this back to the van, we'll 'ave it for dinner tonight and bring the money tin back, I 'spose we'll 'ave to pay for it."

"There ain't no money in the tin, Roland."

"There ain't no money?" growled Roland, grabbing Bernard by the ear and pulling him forward so the two men stood nose to nose. "There ain't no money? *Why* ain't there no money? You had your hand in the tin, 'ave you?"

"No, Roland, no, there ain't no money 'cos we ain't bin paid," squeaked Bernard, turning his head to one side to relieve the pain to his ear.

"So we ain't, I forgot that," sneered Roland, releasing Bernard's ear, "Well go and cover that meat up so the flies don't get it. Christ, where they found such a stupid bugger as you to send with us I don't know."

He turned to William.

"Well, Mr Butcher boy, I ain't going to pay you 'cos I ain't got no money 'cos they ain't paid us." William stood frozen to the spot.

"Don't just stand there looking stupid, boy, get on about your business! Go on with you."

He stepped onto the gravel and made towards the engine.

"Wha – what do I tell Father?" stuttered William

"You tell your father what you bloody well like, boy," chuckled Roland. "Who is your father anyway?"

"Thomas Dunmore."

"Ah yes, I know that old sod, well tell 'im we'll pay when we come past. If we've got any money."

Roland turned on his heel and marched off towards the engine, the rest of the gang trailing behind him. Shaking slightly, William made his way into the pub to explain to the landlady that her joint had already been sold.

"Don't worry, William, that man's a nasty piece of work, make no mistake about that; I saw what happened. I'll take some sausages off you if you have any and that will be enough for this week."

"Where are the ploughing gang going?" asked William.

"Only just down the road to Hubert's; they're going to plough that big field running down to the brook. You'll pass them on your way back."

So William and George went in one direction and the engines went in the other. Having finally made it to Knotting and back the round was completed and they turned the horse for home. The animal, glad to be on the way home, upped its pace and William slackened the rein and sat back – the pony knew its way. George, lulled by the steady pace of the cart, had fallen asleep and didn't wake until the trap approached the field where the engines were working.

"Can we stop and have a look?" said George. "I love to see them working. I'll walk home if you like. I can see that Reuben's in there watching."

"All right, we'll stop," said William. "Old Roland is on the engine the other side of the field so we won't get into trouble."

William pulled the horse up next to the living-van where Bernard was lighting the fire ready to cook the joint of beef.

"Woo up, you boys, you made it back then," Bernard said.

He had taken his jacket and cap off and they could see an angry looking boil on the back of his neck. "You ain't got any dripping or lard in your trap to go with these tatters, 'ave you?" he enquired of William.

"No, we've got nothing left at all," replied William pointedly.

"Ah well, they'll have to do then, 'spect I'll be in trouble whatever I do. I can pour some fat from the joint on them," he said, and he hobbled over to the back of the water cart and ran some water into a bucket, before sitting down on the drawbar of the van to peel the potatoes with a shut-knife from his pocket.

"'Spect 'e'll go up the pub any road, so when 'e comes back 'e'll be drunk and won't know what 'e's eatin', so bugger him that's what I say."

William tied the reins of the harness to a fence and the two boys moved away down the field towards Reuben who was standing in the headland of the field chatting to Joseph. The wire rope which paid out the plough was being pulled to the other side of the field by Roland's engine 'William'.

"Out the way, you boys, I'm coming back in a bit ready for the pull; watch you don't stand anywhere near the rope – it'll chop your legs off if it breaks."

The boys all moved back along the headland, as a whistle sounded from the other side of the field to signal for the pull to start. They could see the two men on the plough pulling it down into the ground as it started to edge across the field, jumping down as the contraption moved away from Roland's engine.

"Right," said William, "I'm going to set off home, the horse needs a rest. Are you coming, George, or are you going to walk back?"

"I'll stay here and watch a bit, then come back with Reuben," said George, transfixed on the sight of the plough's progress across the field.

William set off to untie the pony, hopped up onto the trap and made his way back through Upper Dean, keeping a wary eye out for Molly, who was luckily nowhere to be seen. Before long he was back at the butcher's shop. He unhooked the trap, took the harness off the horse and led it out into the adjacent field before heading into the house.

"William," said his mother, looking up from her seat at the kitchen table and gesturing to a sheaf of papers in front of her, "we have a letter from the school with a list of the clothes you need; isn't it exciting? We must see Ernest at chapel tomorrow and make arrangements to get you fitted out."

She handed William the list.

"Bible and prayer book; well I've got them so they won't be needed. Eton suit (for best) or black and waistcoat. What's an Eton suit, Mother?"

"I'm not exactly sure, dear, but you can have a black coat and waistcoat instead; I'm sure that will do."

Thomas looked over the top of the paper he was reading.

"Are you sure, dear? Ernest would be able to make an Eton suit; he doesn't want to be the only one without one."

"I'm sure he won't be, we will ask Ernest; he will know what to do."

William turned back to the list.

"Two suits for everyday wear (Norfolk style). What's Norfolk style?"

There was silence.

"Ernest will know," repeated Charlotte.

"One overcoat, one pair of kid gloves. Kid gloves! I never wear gloves, why do I need them?"

"Well, dear, it gets cold in the winter and they're to keep your hands warm."

"Three flannel nightshirts, three flannel day shirts, three vests (if worn) and three pairs of pants (if worn). I don't wear pants, Mother!"

"Well, William, this is the time to start," sniggered Sarah, who had been sitting at the table mending a pair of socks.

"Sarah, if you please," said Charlotte, looking disapprovingly at Sarah over her glasses.

"Twelve Eton collars, three shirt fronts, four pairs of linen cuffs. Ernest won't have any of them, Mother."

"Well, we will have to go to Raunds or perhaps we could go to Northampton. What do you think, Thomas?"

"Yes, dear, we could," replied Thomas absently.

William read on.

"Two pairs of boots, one pair of house slippers, a dressing gown, twelve pocket handkerchiefs, two suits of cricket flannels; he said we played cricket, didn't he?" said William excitedly. "We didn't tell him I played for Dean."

"William, you don't play for Dean," said his mother sharply.

"Yes I do; I played long stop last week in that evening match."

"That was only because the Drage brothers had to tend to their haymaking; you don't normally play. What else is on the list?"

"One football jersey and knickers, sponge bag with sponge, wash glove, tooth and nail brush, one clothes brush, a linen bag for soils, towels and that's all."

He lowered the list to the table.

"There's a timetable in there too," said Thomas, gesturing to the bundle of papers. "I went through it – very interesting."

William rifled through the papers to find the right piece.

"Come on, William, read it out; we all want to know what you are going to do there," said Sarah.

"Yes, read it out, William," agreed his mother.

"Very well. Seven am: dressing bell; Seven-thirty, run before breakfast! Eight am: breakfast."

William lowered the piece of paper – looking incredulously at his mother.

"*Run* before breakfast; run where?"

"It can't be far if it's only half an hour; it's to keep you fit, William," said Charlotte.

"Nine am: morning prayers; Nine fifteen to nine forty-five: farm work; Nine forty-five: farm work; Ten fifteen: third period; Ten forty-five: Interval; Eleven am: fourth period; Twelve to one: school games; One pm: dinner."

He stopped.

"That's a long morning, William," said Charlotte.

"It's no longer than we do with Mr Sparks and we don't have any games at Dean," he said.

"Very good, go on then, what happens in the rest of the day?"

"More lessons, it looks like. And then six pm: preparation under the supervision of a Master. What's preparation? I've never heard of that."

"It's homework," said Thomas, "we had it when I went there."

"Eight pm: house prayers and supper."

"I'm glad to see that they make you say prayers," said Charlotte gravely. "I think it's most important to do that and read your Bible regularly; you will do that when you get there, William, won't you?"

"Yes, Mother," William sighed.

"Eight-fifteen: boys under twelve go to bed. There, that means I can stay up later as I'm over twelve now. Nine forty-five, seniors go to bed."

"That's very late, don't you think, Thomas?"

"It does seem a bit late," agreed Thomas.

"I go to bed a lot earlier than that and I'm sixteen," said Sarah from the end of the table.

"Yes, Sarah, but it's not quite the same is it, dear?"

"No, Mrs Dunmore."

The next day was Sunday, and the evening brought the weekly pilgrimage to chapel. Thomas, Charlotte and William were close enough to walk, but the Knightons came in the pony trap as John could not walk that far. Mary and Lucy rode in the trap with their parents, but Henry had to walk. Everyone arrived early, standing outside in the cooling sun, chatting.

"Have you seen Ernest anywhere?" Charlotte enquired of the assembled group. "I've got this list for William's clothes for the new school and I want to know what he can make."

"List of clothes for the school," chirped Mary, turning to smile at her aunt. "How grand; do let me have a look, Aunt Charlotte, you know I'm interested in clothes."

Charlotte handed the somewhat crumpled list to her niece:

"Here we are, and don't you dare lose it, Mary. Give me a shout if you see Ernest."

Mary seized the list and snorted, moving across to William as she read:

"An Eton suit! William, what about that! You'll be dressed up like a dog's dinner – very smart! You'll be too grand to talk to us then, won't he, Lucy?"

Lucy sniffed.

"Lucy, do you have to sniff? You know it gets on my nerves."

"I'm sure you'll look very nice, William; don't listen to her," said Lucy, scowling at her sister, who stuck her tongue out and continued to read.

"*Two* suits. My – you will be a lucky boy, William. Overcoat, kid gloves, shirts, vests if worn." She paused at the next item and then burst out laughing. "Look, Lucy – I can't read this bit out."

She offered the sheet to her sister, pointing to the next item on the list.

"Pants, if worn," Lucy read, looking up at William's reddening face and starting to giggle.

"Give me that," snapped William, snatching the list from Mary and shoving it back in his pocket.

"Now, you girls, can we share the joke?" boomed Reverend Packham, who was moving out from the chapel to welcome everyone to the service.

"It's nothing," insisted William.

"Just having a bit of a laugh," said Lucy quickly. "Isn't it a loverly day?"

"I suppose it is," said Reverend Packham, turning away to talk to their parents.

Coming from the direction of the pub, the three could see Miss Poynter, the organist and Mary's piano teacher, scuttling towards the chapel. Miss Poynter had never married and was now in her early forties; she was short and round with a rosy face and a huge bosom, which strained against a very tightly fitting white blouse and jacket. A black straw hat perched on her greying hair and she carried a bundle of music under her arm. Her extremities wobbled as she took quick short steps towards the chapel.

"Hello, Miss Poynter," said Mary, who knew her well. "Why are you in such a hurry?"

"Mary darling, how are you? I'm in such a state," she gasped, trying to catch her breath.

"I'm so sorry," said Mary, "is there anything we can do?"

"No, no, my dear, I will be fine, but I've just had a bit of a shock. It's those men, you know."

"What men?"

"Those men sitting outside the pub. I think they're the ploughing gang working for Hubert."

"What about them?" Mary enquired.

"They are *drunk*," whispered Miss Poynter, conspiratorially. "I'm sure they are drunk; and at this time in the afternoon! What is the world coming to?"

"What happened?" Mary said, pursuing the issue.

"It was the big one; I heard the others call him Roland – what an oaf he is. He shouted at me, all sorts of—" She broke off, and shook her head as if to free herself of the memory. "It was embarrassing; I really can't tell you how embarrassing it was. I am all of a quiver, all of a quiver."

"How horrid, Miss Poynter," said Lucy sympathetically.

"It was, my dear, it really was," said Miss Poynter emphatically, bustling on into the chapel to prepare for the service.

"What do you think he said?" Mary asked Lucy and William.

"I've no idea," said William. "But I know he's a scoundrel. He stole some meat off me yesterday when we were on the rounds at the The Grape Vine; he's not a nice man at all."

"Hadn't we better go in soon?" said Lucy.

"No, let's wait a bit longer; look, here comes Verity."

Verity was walking beside her father's heavy wheelchair which was being pushed with some effort up the slope by Walter. John Watson-Foster was dressed in a tweed suit and tie and had a homburg hat on; they were on their way to church as well, but they went to All Hallows at the other end of the village. As the trio passed the chapel John raised his hat to the ladies he knew and acknowledged the men.

"Dunmore, are you well? Did you give some thought to what we discussed?"

"Yes, sir," replied Thomas. "I did I—"

"Can't stop, can't stop, my boy. Walter will never get me going again if we do; come on, Walter," and he waved cheerily at the assembled crowd and moved on.

Verity lagged behind – rushing to say to Mary, "I've talked to Father about going to Northampton and he says yes, if you still want to come."

"Yes, I'd like to," replied Mary.

"I'll send Walter up with a note when I have got a date but I must dash now," and she turned to follow her father. "Oh sorry – hello Lucy, hello William, I've got to go," she added hurriedly, skipping off after her father.

Everyone was now going into chapel. Mary, Lucy and William followed them in with an overwhelming sense of dread: they knew they ought to like the service but in reality they all found it very boring. The Reverend Packham was a dogmatist and followed the Bible and its teaching to the letter. His sermons normally consisted of his stringent views on sin and the shortcomings of the congregation.

The chapel was plain and unadorned with the exception of an inscription on the far wall which read *PRAISE Thee O God of Sion*. In front of this was a small dais from which the Reverend conducted the service and to the right stood the organ, where Miss Poynter sat perched on the rather narrow bench. The pews lined the aisle, halfway down which stood a large tortoise stove that heated the place in the winter. When full it would seat over one hundred people and most Sundays over half the seats were taken. The congregation generally consisted of the middle and lower classes of the village; most of the gentry went to All Hallows.

William, Mary and Lucy trooped in and found their seats, surveying the congregation in front of them. Everyone had their best clothes on and an air of mothballs pervaded the rather drab scene. The suits the men wore were shabby, the shirt collars tight, the cuffs of the jackets frayed and the trousers baggy at the knees. The women's dresses were all dark in colour and hung limply off the tired bodies. All the faces seemed to express the common feeling: "guilty as charged" as they awaited their sentence to be handed down by Reverend Packham.

Lucy sat against the wall with Henry between her and Mary. The evening sunlight slanted in from the high windows and shone on Mary's golden hair as it fell onto her shoulders. Henry leant on the pew and whispered to William in the row in front. The doors at the back clattered closed as Reverend Packham made his way solemnly to his dais.

"We will start out service this evening with hymn number two hundred and sixty," he said in a very sombre voice: "Hark my soul, it is the Lord."

There was a clank from the back of the organ, where Len, Reuben's brother, stood pumping the organ with a lever that he pushed backwards and forwards. Those sitting on the right-hand side of the church could see him clearly; Henry stuck his tongue out at him when their eyes met and Len did the same in return.

"Did you see that?" Charlotte whispered to Thomas. "I don't know what things are coming to when boys do that."

Miss Poynter pressed the first key and the organ burst into life as the congregation staggered to their feet; coughs started in one pew and were echoed in another across the chapel. Boots scraped the floor, dresses rustled, hats were adjusted, trousers pulled up, sleeves pulled down, bosoms brushed, skirts straightened and hymn books thumbed. Miss Poynter bent her head towards the music, craning her neck slightly to see the notes. The congregation collectively cleared its throat and began to sing; for some the hymns were the highlight of the week and the only time they heard any music. They stood up straight, stretched their necks and threw their heads back as the notes tripped out, one after another. Others just mouthed the words and pretended to sing, and a few stood looking vaguely embarrassed. Amongst the congregation there was a lack of good singers with the exception of Grace Phillpot whose clear and polished soprano voice could clearly be heard above all the others, pronouncing the words as they should be and hitting all the right notes with great ease and confidence. Grace was the cook for the Fitz-Allens and lived in a cottage at the back of Dean House with her seven children, her husband having died two years ago.

The hymn ended and prayers followed. The congregation then sat for a Bible reading. Claude Tickner, the small dairy farmer from Lower Dean, walked slowly towards the dais from the back of the chapel, his hobnail boots scuffing the wooden boards of the floor as he went, the noise echoing around the building. As he moved down, those sitting nearest the aisle could smell a faint odour of cow dung mixed with the whiff of spilt milk. He walked up the two steps to the dais and placed his Bible on the lectern. Claude was not a good reader but a willing one; his main problem was his failing eyesight, which he insisted was perfect. He opened the Bible to his marker on which was written the text he was going to read. The announcement of the reading was followed by a prolonged pause as he desperately sought the place on the page at which he needed to start. With an audible sigh of relief, he found it, looked up and began to read very slowly, following the text carefully across the page with his index finger. In between sentences, his tongue flicked from one corner of his mouth to the other in concentration and every so often when he felt he should emphasise part of the passage, he raised his head and looked pointedly at the congregation. They mostly looked back rather blankly, some smiled, some lowered their heads and others looked at the ceiling. A faint snore could be heard at the back of the aisle, where Thomas Clarage sat fast asleep, his chin on his chest. The reading drew to a close and Claude looked round to the Reverend Packham, soliciting approval for his efforts, and being rewarded with an insincere smile.

Another hymn followed and then came the address by the Reverend, the highlight of his week. He stood ceremoniously, with the air of an ancient warrior doing battle with the devil, and looked down critically at his flock. A sea of apprehensive faces looked back at him – some with admiration, most with an air of foreboding, as Reverend Packham began his half-hour long rant on the failings of the miserable people of Dean.

Chapter Ten
Shopping with Verity

It was now mid-August at Cold Harbour Farm and the wheat was ready for cutting. Henry had hired a team of four shires to pull the binder and Lucy had been detailed to lead the team while Henry sat on the machine. It was mid-morning and the sun was high in the sky – a few clouds drifting lazily over the field to the left of the driveway.

Everything was ready; the canvasses on the binder had been tightened up, the string to tie the sheaves was in its holder and the knotter had been threaded. Henry lowered the table ready to cut the wheat while Lucy held the lead horse; she would guide them round the field the first time and after that Henry could manage. As the horses were led towards the crop, he engaged the gear that would drive the mechanism; the knife chattered as it moved backwards and forwards, the points and canvases banging at the buckle, which held them together and wound round the rollers at each end. As the team moved into the crop, the knives shivered through the wheat, which fell back onto the canvas like soldiers being machine-gunned. The weight of the binder increased as they moved through the crop, and Henry had to urge the horses on with a long whip.

As Lucy and Henry moved down the field they caught sight of Walter Snellgrove coming along the road towards them on his bicycle. He had taken his jacket off and stuffed it into the bicycle basket and had rolled up the sleeves of his striped shirt. He waved as he passed Henry and Lucy and pedalled on, swerving to avoid the potholes in the track. When he arrived at the farmhouse, he leant his bike against the wall of the scullery, banged on the door and went in.

It was wash day and Freda was pouring buckets of water into the copper, which was alight in the corner of the low room.

"Mornin', Freda; is Mrs Knighton about?" he enquired.

"In the kitchen," she replied sharply, inclining her head to the kitchen door.

In the kitchen Ann was sorting out the washing into piles ready for the copper.

"Hello, Walter, what brings you all the way up here?"

"Got a letter for Miss Mary from Miss Verity and I've got to wait for a reply," he said, pulling a chair out from the table and sitting down.

"I'll give her a shout then, she's up doing the beds," said Ann, moving to the bottom of the stairs and calling up to Mary.

Since she had left school, Mary had been helping her mother in the house, preferring that to having to work on the farm as Lucy did. Her shoes could be heard clattering along the boards of the top landing, down the first stairs two steps at a time, along the next landing and down the last flight of stairs. In her haste she caught her heel in the hem of her dress, sliding down the last five or six steps on her bottom. She got up from the floor, laughed and brushed her skirt down.

"What a silly girl," she said, looking at her mother who was about to say the very same thing.

"What a silly girl," Ann agreed. "You'll break your neck one of these days rushing about like that."

"Hello, Walter, have you got a letter for me?" smiled Mary.

"Yes, me duck, and I've got to wait for a reply an' all," he said, looking meaningfully at Ann.

"I expect you would like a cup of tea then while you wait, eh, Walter?" said Ann with a smile.

"Well that wouldn't go amiss, Mrs Knighton; only three sugars, mind you."

"And a piece of cake?" Ann asked.

"Well, that would be very nice, an' all," Walter agreed, stretching back in his chair with his thumbs in his waistcoat pockets.

"You said you had a letter," Mary prompted.

"Ah, yes, yes, nearly forgot – it's in my jacket pocket. I'll just go and get it, it's on the bike."

He rose and clomped out, his hobnail boots banging on the flagstones of the scullery. In a few moments he returned, letter in hand, and gave it to Mary.

"Here we are, Miss Mary, hope you can read."

The letter was addressed: "*Miss Mary Knighton, Cold Harbour Farm*" and in the top corner was written '*By Hand*'. Mary took a knife from the drawer in the table, slit the envelope open and sat down at the other end of the table from Walter. Her mother sat down next to her and Freda came in from the scullery and sat on a chair against the wall. Mary began to read, mouthing the words as she did so.

"Well then," her mother said, "what does she say?"

"Well, she wants to arrange a trip to Northampton next week before she goes back to school and she wants me to go with her; she says she wants me to be her guest. What's that mean, Mother?"

"That means, she'll pay," said Walter. "They've got plenty of money, you know; yes, they're not short of a bob or two."

"Go on then," said Ann.

"Just wait, Mother, let me read it first," said Mary – reading the final sentences as the others sat in silence.

"Well," said Ann, "tell us all."

"She wants to go next Wednesday on the train from Rushden at ten o'clock. She says Walter will take us to the station if I can be at The Hall by a quarter to nine."

Mary frowned slightly.

"It says 'Afternoon wear'. What's afternoon wear, Mother?"

"I'm not really sure, dear. Do you know, Walter?"

"No idea, they all look the same to me, morning or afternoon; who knows the difference?"

"What a stupid thing to say: 'Afternoon wear'. I don't know!" huffed Freda disapprovingly.

"Well, you must reply, dear, and Walter will take it back with him. Now let's make the tea and get Walter a piece of cake, will you, Freda?"

"Yes, Mrs Knighton."

Mary collected the writing paper, ink and pen from the drawer in the sideboard in the front room and sat at the kitchen table, composing her reply in large, stylish handwriting; very slowly but very deliberately. When she had finished, she showed the letter to her mother.

"That's very nice, dear."

"Are there any spelling mistakes, Mother?"

"None that I can see, dear."

Mary put the letter in an envelope, addressed it to "*Miss Verity Watson-Foster, The Hall, Upper Dean,*" licked the envelope, put it on her chair and sat on it.

"What are you doing that for, stupid girl?" her mother demanded.

"William says you have to sit on them and then they stick down better," insisted Mary. "Don't you believe all your cousin says. Look, you'll get the ink all over your dress."

"No I won't and see, it's stuck down really well now."

"All right," her mother groaned, "go on with you. Just give it to Walter and then he can get on."

Wednesday morning arrived, bringing chaos with it to Cold Harbour. One of the old shire horses had trodden on Lucy's foot the day before and she was in a lot of pain. They had sent one of the men to call the doctor but he had not come until eight o'clock that morning.

Doctor Roberts walked into the house without knocking and went straight into the kitchen.

"Morning, Knighton," he said to John. "How are you today?"

"Well as can be expected, Doctor," John wheezed, taking a rasping breath. "But it's not me we called you for, it's Lucy; the old horse trod on her foot."

He pointed to Lucy who was sitting shivering in a chair next to the range; her foot in a bowl of warm water and witch-hazel in her hand. There was a clattering down the stairs and the latch on the door at the bottom clicked; Mary put her head round the door, looking at the assembled company in turn, her gaze settling on the doctor.

"Hello, Dr Roberts, sorry to butt in. Mother, could you give me a hand for a moment?"

"Directly, my dear, go back upstairs and I will be there in a moment when Dr Roberts has seen to Lucy."

"Now, Lucy, let's have a look at this foot of yours," said Dr Roberts, drawing up a chair and lifting Lucy's foot out of the water, resting it on a towel on his knee. Lucy winced but said nothing. The doctor felt it all over, pressing his thumb and fingers this way and that at various points on Lucy's swollen foot, twisting it gently from side to side. Lucy whimpered and tears came to her eyes.

"How did it happen, young lady?" the doctor asked.

"It was Sharper; I was leading him into the stack yard with a cart full of sheaves and he trod on my foot."

Lucy sniffed and wiped her nose with her fist.

"Can you use your hankie, Lucy?" scolded her mother.

"Well," said the doctor, "you'll be glad to hear there's nothing broken, but it's badly bruised; you must put some witch-hazel on it, bandage it up and keep your weight off it, Lucy. She'll need a crutch or a stick, Mrs Knighton, until the swelling goes down."

He stood up, picked up his bag and top hat and said,

"I'll say good day then, Mrs Knighton; I'll send my account in due course."

He nodded to Ann and John and went out the door.

"Now sit still of a minute, Lucy, while I see to your sister," said Ann, rushing out up the stairs to Mary.

"Now, dear, what is it?"

"The hat, Mother, the hat! Which one do I wear? Do you think I look smart enough? What about this dress? Is it creased at the back? Do you think my hair is right?"

"Now, Mary, just hold on, your dress is fine. Just turn round for me. Yes, and your hair looks lovely."

"And what about the hat?"

"I think the black one will be best."

"Are you sure? Don't you think the blue one, Mother?"

"No, dear, the black one is best. Now get ready quickly, you'll soon have to go."

"Can Henry drive me down in the trap? I'll muck my dress up if I walk."

"No he can't, he's off across the field already with the binder and there's no one else."

Ann turned pre-emptively to her daughter.

"And your father certainly can't, so don't ask," she warned.

"Do I *have* to walk?"

"Yes, you do," snapped Ann. "It'll do you good and there will be plenty of time if you get a move on." She rose and left Mary to finish getting ready, bustling back to check on Lucy in the kitchen.

"Now, Lucy dear, let's see to you. Freda, where are you? Come and give me a hand."

She sat down in front of Lucy, lifted the damaged foot into her lap and gently rubbed the witch-hazel into the swollen area.

"Freda, come here will you and find me a bandage from the bottom drawer and a safety pin as well, can you?"

Freda slouched in, lips pursed in annoyance and rummaged in the drawer until she found what she wanted.

"This it?" she asked Ann, holding up the bandage and pin.

"Yes, give them here," instructed Ann, taking the bandage and carefully wrapping the foot; first round the ankle and then under the sole until only Lucy's big toe was showing. She pinned the bandage and put the foot down on the floor.

"Now, what can we use for a crutch?"

"I know," said Freda. "Let's use that small sweepin' brush and wrap a duster round it. That's what we did for my brother when he broke his leg."

Once again steps could be heard on the stairs and Mary burst into the room.

"How do I look?" she exclaimed, twirling round in front of her family.

"You look lovely, dear. Now, John, give Mary some money, can you, she must have some money with her."

John stood up and dug his hand into his pocket, bringing out what change he had and surveying it carefully in his palm.

"Not enough here," he said, moving to the drawer and taking a sovereign from the tin.

He gave it to Mary with the handful of change.

"Now look here, Mary; the sovereign's not for spending, it's just in case, you know what I mean, don't you?"

"Yes, Father," sighed Mary.

"Mary, have you been down the end before you go?" Ann enquired.

"Do you have to ask me that, Mother?" Mary snapped. "I'm not at school anymore."

Lucy lowered her head quickly to hide the smirk on her face.

"Don't you say anything either, Lucy Knighton," Mary said in as superior a voice as she could manage.

"Time to go, dear," clucked Ann. "Have a nice time, won't you."

"I'm sure I will," smiled Mary, pecking her mother on the cheek, and rushing out the door.

"Don't tread in any cow muck, will you, Mary!" called Lucy after her.

Mary's head popped back round the door; she scowled and stuck her tongue out at her sister and left before her parents could say anything.

Mary arrived at The Hall to find the carriage waiting. A groom was holding the two horses and Walter was sitting on the garden bench by the door. Mary rang the bell and heard footsteps moving across the flagstones of the hall. The door opened.

"Oh, it's you then," Dorcas said disapprovingly. She was already wearing her hat and a light coat over her dress.

"Might've known it was – using the front door as you do. S'pose you better come in then."

She sniffed haughtily and turned to lead the way.

"Miss Verity, Mary Knighton's here," she shouted up the stairs.

"Just coming," a voice could be heard in the distance.

A door banged and Verity ran along the landing, appearing at the top of the stairs. She bounded down the stairs two at a time, pulling up in front of Mary to exclaim:

"Oh, Mary, how pretty you look! We are going to have such a nice time, I know we are; I haven't been out of Dean for weeks."

She trotted to the large mirror, put the hat on she was carrying and turned to Dorcas.

"Now, Dorcas, have you got the money Father gave you?"

"Yes, Miss Verity."

"You know he wants receipts for what you spend."

"Yes, Miss Verity."

"Dorcas is to come with us, Mary. Harriet couldn't; it's her day off."

Dorcas eyed Mary critically; she thought her far too common to be a companion for Verity. Verity on the other hand felt the opposite. She admired Mary's free spirit and thought her a kind person, who knew her own mind and would not bow down to what she did not want to do as directed by others. Despite the difference in age, Verity found Mary's company stimulating and thought her someone who she could emulate in terms of style. Verity's friends at school and the daughters of the other gentry in the area were all very sociable and interested in fashion and things that she felt uncomfortable with. Verity liked to read the paper and busy herself with social issues and, in particular, votes for women: Verity Watson-Foster wanted to change the world.

"Now, what's the time? We have to catch a train at eleven o'clock," gabbled Verity. "Dorcas, have you got the time?"

"Yes, Miss Verity. It's twenty minutes before nine and here's your watch for you to put on."

"I suppose I must but you know I don't like wearing it," she sighed, putting on the small golden wristwatch her father had given her for her thirteenth birthday.

"Now, miss, I told you that I will be meeting my brother at one o'clock, if that meets with your approval."

"Yes, Dorcas, that will be fine. Mary and I should be having our lunch then. Now come, Mary, we must go or we will miss the train."

She swept out the door towards the carriage.

The journey to Rushden station took an hour through the lanes; everywhere they looked people were gathering the harvest, loading the sheaves onto carts and wagons and taking them to stack yards at various farms. As the carriage passed, the men would touch their caps when they saw who it was and Verity would nod grandly. Mary blushed and lowered her head, feeling intense embarrassment every time she saw people she knew.

They arrived at the station in good time; Walter dropped them off and took the carriage to the livery at the back to the station hotel where he could get the horses fed and stabled for the day while he awaited the girls' return. In the meantime, much to his liking, the day was his; he could visit one or two of the pubs in the High Street and go to the barber's for a shave.

"Now, Walter," Verity said, with the assurance of someone ten years older, "can you meet the train at half past four and if we are not on that one, we will be on the five o'clock. Dorcas, could you get the tickets? First class, remember. Oh – and see if you can get them all the way through so we don't have to buy more tickets when we get to Wellingborough."

"Very well, Miss Verity," she muttered, stomping off in the direction of the ticket office.

Rushden was on a short branch line from Wellingborough; the trains shuttled back and forwards all day and the journey only took ten minutes. Dorcas took charge of the tickets and it wasn't long before the train arrived.

Verity moved down the train, looking into the windows of the first class carriages on tip-toe to find an empty one; when she found one they all climbed in.

Mary had only been on a train once before, but did her very best to appear as though she did it every day. At Wellingborough, the trio changed platforms to wait ten minutes for the Northampton train. Sitting on one of the seats, waiting for the same train was Ethel Standish, the new teacher at the school in Dean.

"Hello, Mary," she smiled. "And you must be Miss Watson-Foster; I don't believe we have been introduced. I'm Ethel Standish and I teach at the school in Dean."

She offered her hand towards Verity, standing as she did so.

"Very pleased to meet you," said Verity, smiling back. "How are you enjoying teaching at Dean?"

"It's a challenge, Miss Watson-Foster," sighed Ethel, "a real challenge. So many of the children come from poor families and only come to school if the parents have nothing for them to do."

"We must not discriminate against the poor, Miss Standish," replied Verity forcefully. "It's not their fault, you know; we must make every effort to look after everyone in the parish as best we can."

"Quite so, quite so, Miss Watson-Foster, I am sure we don't discriminate. Mr Sparks is very understanding."

"Yes I'm sure he is. Father tells me he is a very good head teacher and a good disciplinarian."

"He is, Miss Watson-Foster, and he needs to be with some of the children. That Molly Webb is one of the worst and some of the boys are no better."

"I know Molly Webb," said Verity. "Their family live in one of Father's cottages. She's got plenty of spirit, I'll give you that."

Verity looked up sharply to see the train pulling into the station.

"And here's the train. Lovely to meet you, Miss Standish, I hope you have a good day."

The trio moved away from Miss Standish to find a carriage. This time there weren't any free, so Verity chose one in which she felt there were the most acceptable fellow travellers. This turned out to be a carriage with one smartly dressed man in his early twenties. As they entered, the man raised his cap and half stood up; he wore a dark grey suit and white shirt with a winged collar and a striped tie. Dorcas sat on the same side as the man and Mary and Verity sat the other. The train started with a jerk and the smoke from the engine blew back into the window of the compartment where the girls were sitting.

"Dear me, we can't have this all the way to Northampton," Dorcas complained.

"Well shut the window, Dorcas, and quickly, before we all get asphyxiated," instructed Verity.

"I'll do it," said Mary. "I'm the tallest."

She jumped up.

"Do allow me," the young man said, reaching for the window and flicking it shut with a loud click.

"Thank you," said Mary, smiling.

"It's my pleasure," said the man, inclining his head towards her, and sitting down again.

The train gradually picked up speed, Mary sat back in her seat watching the countryside fly past the window. The young man took three pencils from his inside jacket pocket and a pencil sharpener from his other pocket; he laid out a newspaper on his lap and began to sharpen the pencils into the newspaper until he had a small heap of wood and pencil lead.

"What you goin' to do with that then?" Dorcas enquired, nodding at the heap.

"I was going to put it in the ash tray if that's all right with you, Madam."

"No, it ain't all right, 'cos the ashtray's full up. Anyway, what do you want all those pencils for and on a train as well?"

"I need them to make notes."

"A lot of blimmin' notes," Dorcas sneered, deciding then and there she did not like this man.

"I'm a reporter, you see."

"A reporter for a newspaper you mean?" said Mary. "How exciting."

"Which paper?" demanded Verity her face lighting up like Mary's.

Dorcas tut-tutted and returned her attention to the view.

"It's the *Northampton Echo*. It's really not very exciting, I can assure you."

"Well, what are you going to report on today then?" Mary asked.

"Well, first of all I had to go to the morgue in Wellingborough to see if there were any unexplained deaths today—"

"Ooh, were there any?" interrupted Mary.

"No," smiled the man. "Then I went to the magistrates' court to study the list of cases to see if there was anything exciting at court – but there was nothing of note so I am now on my way back to Northampton to the office."

"Well, what will you do when you get back?" said Verity.

"Well, if it's like every other day; I will be sent to the morgue in Northampton and then to the court to take over from the senior reporter, who by that time will be wanting to go for his lunch. Then I'll be packed off to the cattle market to get the report on prices and numbers of cattle that were sold, and if there is time I have to go and interview a Mrs Skelton to make a list of the presents given to her daughter last weekend for her marriage. So as you can see, it really isn't that glamorous."

"But don't you ever report on murders, or train crashes, or fires or anything like that?" Mary probed.

"I saw the body of a boy who was drowned in the river last week; but if it's a murder they send someone more important."

"So have we seen any of your reports in the paper? I know Father brings back the *Echo* sometimes. What's your name?" Verity demanded, looking keenly at him.

"My name is Rupert Nelson, miss, and no, you won't have seen it in the paper; they only put the names of the important reporters in."

"That's not fair," said Mary. "Surely you should talk to the editor!"

"Yes, miss," smiled Rupert, "but the editor also happens to be my father, and he is very strict about that sort of thing. Must get a lot of experience first, that's what he always says."

"Well, what you goin' to do with all that mess? That's what I want to know," Dorcas interrupted, glaring down at the pencil shavings.

"It will go in my pocket, don't worry," assured Rupert, and as if to prove it he folded the paper, funnelled the sharpenings into his hand and tipped them into his jacket pocket.

"Now you know my name may I enquire to whom I am talking?" Rupert asked, looking at Verity.

"I am Verity Watson-Foster and this is my good friend Mary Knighton," said Verity politely.

Dorcas coughed.

"Oh, and this is Dorcas who is accompanying us."

"I'm delighted to make your acquaintance; I think I have had the pleasure of meeting your father, Miss Watson-Foster. It's not often that I get the pleasure to accompany two such attractive young ladies." He smiled at Mary who blushed slightly, Verity looked at the floor and Dorcas rolled her eyes to the ceiling.

"Where are you wanting to go shopping, Miss Verity?" Dorcas enquired. "We're just about to get to the station."

"Well, I'm not sure but I expect we will head for Tibbitts; Father has an account there so we can use that. What do you think, Mary?"

"Oh, I don't know Northampton," insisted Mary. "I will follow where you go."

The train pulled up and the three women hopped down from the carriage; Verity turned to say goodbye to Rupert Nelson.

"Goodbye, Mr Nelson, it has been a pleasure to meet you," she smiled, nodding to him in her strange adult way.

"The pleasure is mine, Miss Watson-Foster," said Rupert, raising his hat to her. "My journey is in the same direction as yours so perhaps I could walk with your party?"

"That would be pleasant," she smiled and they set off, Rupert walking in between the two girls and Dorcas following grumpily behind. The three chatted as they walked up the street and Dorcas found the conversation not to her taste; she did not enjoy these days out. Verity was always on about causes, if it wasn't votes for women or the possible cures for tuberculosis, it was fox hunting or the inhumane killing of meat animals. As they walked up the pavement, cattle were being driven the other way from the cattle market, no doubt on their way to a slaughterhouse.

Dorcas knew what was coming.

"Mr Nelson," Verity started, "what is your view on the way they slaughter?" She stopped and watched the animals go past. "I think it's so dreadfully cruel to think of them being killed with a poleaxe, don't you?" She turned sharply to Rupert.

"I have never really given it much thought and I certainly have never seen it being done so I'm afraid I cannot comment," replied Rupert. "Have you seen a cow being slaughtered, Miss Watson-Foster?"

"Well not exactly; but Mary's uncle is a butcher and he slaughters his cattle with a poleaxe and I think it's barbaric!" she turned and looked apologetically at Mary as they walked on.

"I'm sorry, Mary, I don't want to criticise your uncle; I know he's a good man and I like William as well, but I feel strongly about the method of slaughter and if you feel strongly about something you should express your views."

Dorcas shook her head, plodding on behind her campaigning mistress. Verity turned sharply to look at her.

"Dorcas, you know my views, don't you? You must agree it's cruel."

"Yes," sighed Dorcas, "I know your views, Miss Verity, but they have to be killed one way or another. And besides, you eat beef, don't you? Thomas Dunmore's beef, an' all."

"Well I suppose I do," concurred Verity with a small frown.

"Are you going to the morgue, Mr Nelson?" Mary interjected hurriedly, turning to Rupert.

"I thought I would go to the office first to see if Father had any other orders," replied Rupert, lowering his voice to add, "You never know, there might have been a murder."

He winked at Mary; Dorcas rolled her eyes again and shook her head.

"Well, this is where we must leave you," said Verity, stopping outside the brightly lit entrance to Tibbitts. She offered her hand to Rupert, who swiftly took it, kissed it, then to Mary and did the same, giving her hand a quick squeeze before he released it.

"Goodbye, Miss Watson-Foster, goodbye, Miss Knighton," and he lifted his cap as he turned and strode off in the direction of the newspaper's office.

Verity and Mary watched him go.

"Well I never," said Dorcas, shooing the girls into the shop.

For the next hour they went from department to department trying to find outfits for Verity for the winter; some were just patterns to be made, others she tried on. She really had no idea how to dress herself, but with Mary there to guide her, they were able to choose some suitable items.

"Miss Verity, it's lunch time," said Dorcas pointedly at half past twelve.

"I know it is, Dorcas," said Verity, turning this way and that for Mary to check the suitability of a grey woollen coat she was modelling.

"Well, I was wonderin' where you were goin' to 'ave your lunch, miss," persisted Dorcas.

"I expect we will go to The County Hotel."

"Yes, miss, well I was wonderin', if that's the case I might slip away to see my brother Edwin. 'E don't live far away."

"Very well then, Dorcas," said Verity, slipping off the coat and handing it with an imperious nod to a member of staff. "When and where shall we meet after lunch?"

"Well, Miss Verity, if I come to the hotel with you and make sure you are settled and all that we can fix a time then and I will come back and find you."

"Very well then," agreed Verity, turning to make arrangements for her clothes to be packaged, before leaving for lunch.

Mary had not been in a hotel before, nor had she eaten in a restaurant, but she was a quick learner and followed Verity's lead. The restaurant was large with four enormous columns supporting the ceiling which was hung with sparkling chandeliers. There was a large marble fireplace on one side of the room with a huge portrait of a bespectacled man hanging above it and on the other were two sideboards on which various bottles and cutlery items were standing ready for use. At the end of the room was a big bay window looking out onto a small garden and at the other end two doors led into the kitchen. Despite the size of the room, there were very few people having lunch and there were certainly no other unaccompanied women. Any conversation bubbled quietly over the clink of spoons against china and echoed clearly around the room.

"Where would madam like to sit?" the waiter enquired of Verity, looking suspiciously at the two girls in front of him.

"We will go over there in that corner near the window," instructed Verity, pointing to the table she wanted.

The waiter led the way; he was wearing a tailcoat and black tie and had a thin very pale face and a pointed nose. His trousers were too long and crumpled about his ankles, like a half empty potato sack. He smelt of tobacco, mingled with the faint aroma of a chemist shop, as though he had an ointment smeared on some sore outpost of his undisclosed body. He pulled the chair back for Verity to sit down with his white-gloved hands and then did the same for Mary.

"Would madam like to see the menu?"

"Yes please," replied Verity as the waiter turned to collect two from the sideboard, his nose in the air. He returned with two menus and handed them one each without saying a word, all the while eyeing them disapprovingly, his mouth drawn into an inverted 'U' shape, his lips tightly shut. He turned to Verity, her small frame dwarfed by the large, high-winged chair:

"Would madam like a cushion to sit on?"

"No I would not," hissed Verity angrily, seething with indignation.

"Very well," smirked the waiter, sashaying back across the floor.

Dorcas meanwhile, was nearly at her destination; she had written a card to Edwin two days ago warning of her probable visit and was wondering if he had received it. The sky had clouded over, but it was still very warm and Dorcas had taken her jacket off and slung it over her arm for the uphill climb. The Griffin was just out of the main shopping area of the town and drew its clientele from the rows of terraced houses that had been built off Wellingborough Road; the occupants of which worked in the many boot and shoe factories that were dotted about the area. This time was usually busy as men came from the factories to have a pint or two in their lunch break.

When Dorcas arrived the main rush was over; she went to the door and cautiously pushed it open to see if she could see her brother behind the bar. She was ready to make a quick exit if he was not there as she did not like going in on her own. It was with some relief that she noticed him at the other end of the bar talking to some customers. The bar lined the left-hand side of the room, the shelves behind crammed with an assortment of bottles. On the right-hand side of the room, under the windows, was a long wooden bench which stretched the length of the pub and in the front of this, at regular intervals, were wooden topped tables. A skittle table and dartboard dominated the back end of the room, from which led a door into the back yard where the toilets were.

The air was heavy with tobacco smoke from the pipes and cigarettes of the men at the bar and at first Edwin did not notice Dorcas. He was nearly bald except for a fringe which wound from one ear round the back of his head to the other ear and his head shone as if it had been wax polished. He had a fat face with rosy cheeks and a large thick moustache that hung down each side of his mouth. He wore a striped shirt with no collar, and his sleeves were rolled up above his elbows. Over this a waistcoat incapable of containing his considerable paunch, which burst out from the bottom and was only just being contained by a wide leather belt round his waist which assisted his braces in holding his trousers up.

Dorcas moved up behind the man that Edwin was serving and waved.

"Well, well, look who we've got here. Dorcas, me duck, how are you?" chuckled Edwin, leaning over the bar and pulling his sister towards him, giving her a peck on the cheek.

"Did you get me card?" Dorcas enquired.

"Yes, dear, it came this very morning and very pleased to get it we were too. Now what you going to have to drink?"

"Well, I don't know," said Dorcas, examining the taps that lined the bar. "Maybe I'll 'ave an 'arf of bitter."

"Course you will and I'll give you a tot of rum with it, it goes down much better. Now what about somefing to eat? We've got some salt beef sandwiches."

"That'll be nice, but I must just nip down the end first, it's out there, ain't it?" she said, pointing towards the door at the back.

Edwin nodded and Dorcas made her way past the skittle players to the door out into the yard. As she passed the men stopped playing, looking her up and down but saying nothing; Dorcas lowered her head and quickened her pace. When she came back the men were still there, but this time did not move for her.

"'Scuse me," she said, turning sideways to get past.

"Do you want a game of skittles, missus?" leered one, offering her a cheese to throw.

"Not today thank you,"

"Come on, 'ave a go, you can't be worse than us."

"Come, come," said Edwin's voice from the bar, "that's my sister you're talking to; let her past please."

The men backed off to let Dorcas through and she moved to a table where Edwin was waiting with their drinks.

"Come on, Lizzie, where's them sandwiches and bring some pickled onions; Dorcas all'as liked pickled onions, didn't you, me duck?"

A figure appeared from the bar, carrying the food with her.

Lizzie was the only other woman in the pub and looked as though she had come off the stage of a burlesque show. She, like Edwin, was plump, and wore a flouncy red skirt topped with a tight white low-cut blouse and a very tight black bodice which shoved the rolls of fat upward towards her bust. Her hair was blonde and rolled up on top of her head, revealing dark brown roots. Her face was white with powder and her eyes were emphasised above and below with black lines of kohl. Her eyebrows were heavily drawn in and her cheeks had a large blob of rouge in the middle of each. Her black boots clomped against the wooden floor as she moved towards them, a plate of sandwiches in one hand and a jar of pickled onions in the other, a cigarette dripping from the corner of her mouth. As she walked the smoke from the cigarette wafted into her eyes, forcing her to momentarily flinch and clench them shut, dislodging the ash of the cigarette, which tumbled down her bosom and scattered over the sandwiches. She put the plate down, brushed her bosom clean and nonchalantly blew the ash from the plate of sandwiches. She smiled lopsidedly at Dorcas, pulled up a chair and sat down.

"Well, Dorcas, what's it like working for the nobs then?" she cackled.

"Don't you worry," Dorcas said grandly. "They look after me all right. If you treat 'em right you do all right."

She drained her half of beer and started to tuck into the sandwiches.

"Cor, this salt beef's good," she said through a mouthful, "and these onions; but it don't 'arf make you thirsty."

Edwin smiled indulgently and rose to pull her another beer, pouring a tot of rum to go with it.

"Yes, the nobs ain't bad if you treat 'em right," she said again, "'cept Miss Verity's taken up with one of them Knighton girls from Cold Harbour. You remember 'em, don't you, Edwin?"

"Well I don't remember the girls, but I can remember the parents. Always in the old chapel, ain't they, got God on their side if nobody else. What's wrong with the girl then?"

"Nothing's wrong with 'er, she's a nice girl but she ain't the right class for Miss Verity if you know what I mean."

"S'pose so," shrugged Edwin. "How is Miss Verity anyways?"

"Oh, she's all'as got these mad ideas about somethin' or other. She was on about slaughtering cattle this morning; gets on your wick a bit I can tell you."

Edwin smiled, and his eyes flicked to the door as it opened and a man wearing a bowler hat strode in and walked down towards them. As he passed, he looked at Edwin and tapped his nose with his index finger; Edwin in turn tapped the table with his knuckle. Lizzie looked up sharply, rose from her seat and lifted the bar flap, making her way through the door at the back of the bar. The man continued to walk straight through the pub and out the door leading to the yard at the back.

"Where's Lizzie gone?" Dorcas asked.

"Oh just out the back for a bit. Come on, Dorcas, let's 'ave another one. When do you 'ave to be back?"

"Not before half past two I guess and I bet they're not ready afore quarter to if I know Miss Verity. Then we'll 'ave to go back to the shop for the parcels no doubt."

"Well you've got time for one more, I'm sure of that," winked Edwin, moving back behind the bar to pour another half pint and tot of rum for his sister.

Ten minutes later, the man in the bowler hat returned through the door from the yard; he marched back down past the two of them; dropping two half-crowns into Edwin's outstretched hand as he passed and walking on out the main door.

Dorcas looked up at the clock by the door.

"Time I was off, Edwin," she said, rising to her feet.

She felt decidedly unsteady on her legs, as the rum was beginning to take its revenge. Lizzie appeared at the bar flap and helped Dorcas on with her jacket, and the three said their goodbyes before Dorcas made her way back to The County Hotel.

The menu in the restaurant at The County Hotel was not very inspiring.

"What shall we have to eat?" said Verity.

"I really don't mind," replied Mary. "You order what you think; I eat most things and you know what would be good."

"Very well then, we will have the soup and the lamb cutlets. Oh, where's that waiter gone?"

She looked round impatiently, but he was nowhere to be seen. At the other end of the room two elderly men were just rising from their table; Verity recognised one as Mortimer Allibone – a friend of her father's who came shooting at Dean at least twice a year and stayed at The Hall. As he passed through the dining room he caught sight of Verity and immediately came over.

"Verity my dear, how are you? How lovely to see you and on your own too! Or, I mean without your aunt."

"Yes! Mary and I have come shopping. Can I introduce my good friend Mary Knighton? Mary, this is Mr Mortimer Allibone."

"My, my, what a pretty young friend you have, Verity," smiled Mortimer, offering Mary his hand to shake. "In fact I would say quite a beauty, wouldn't you, Peveril?"

He turned to his friend as Mary looked down and blushed.

"I'm sorry, Verity; can I introduce Peveril Tibbitt? Peveril, this is Miss Verity Watson-Foster and her friend Mary Knighton. Peveril owns the shop, you know."

"Pleased to meet you, Mr Tibbitt; we have just been in your shop," said Verity.

"Well, I'm pleased to hear that. Was everything to your satisfaction?"

"Yes, it was fine, thank you. I brought Mary with me as my adviser; she knows everything about clothes."

"I can see that, my dear, from the way she dresses. Can I say what delightful taste you have in friends, Verity!"

Mary blushed again, a smile creeping over her face.

"I know," said Verity proudly, "she's so helpful. I have no idea what to buy."

"Well, Miss Knighton, if you ever want a job you must let me know. I am always on the lookout for talented assistants."

"Well we must be trotting along," interjected Mortimer. "Give my best regards to your father, Verity. I hope you have a better lunch than we had; this place is really going downhill and the staff are extremely rude, don't you know."

There was a loud throat clearing noise behind the two men from where the waiter stood – a smile stiffly in place – holding out their coats and hats. The men took their things from him, waved at the girls and left.

"Would madam like to order now?" said the waiter, drawing a pad and pencil from his pocket.

"Yes, we will have the soup followed by the lamb cutlets," said Verity imperiously.

"Very well, miss," said the waiter, adding with a sneer. "Would you like to see the wine list?"

"No, we would not, the thought of such a thing! We will have lemonade to drink, is that all right with you, Mary?"

Mary nodded and the waiter stalked off, returning a few minutes later with two soup spoons, which he exchanged for a knife in each place. Stretching across to change Mary's cutlery, the gloved hand parted from the cuff of his shirt, exposing a wrist covered in open scabs lathered in a sticky brown ointment. Verity winced and turned her nose up, before resuming the conversation with Mary.

"Mary, did you hear what Mr Tibbitt said about a job?"

"Yes," smiled Mary.

"Surely a job here would be better than helping on the farm or in the house?" said Verity excitedly.

"Yes," mused Mary, "it would be."

"Well what are you going to do? It's a chance not to miss, surely?"

"You're right, Verity, but what about my mother? She has been under the weather lately and with Father so frail, I just don't know. Besides, where would I live if I came here? It's all a bit difficult."

The waiter came out of the kitchen door with a tray on which stood two soup plates, a silver soup tureen and a ladle. He put the tray on the sideboard and walked over with the two plates, placing one in front of each of the girls. Verity gently touched the edge of the plate.

"Waiter, these plates are cold. We can't eat soup off cold plates. Go and get some warm ones."

The waiter said nothing but picked up the plates and slowly walked to the kitchen door. Some minutes later he returned with warmed plates and placed them once again in front of the girls, moving back to the sideboard to fetch the soup. With his back to them he took the lid of the tureen, quickly looked to check that he was unobserved and spat into the soup. He put the ladle in, gave it a stir and carried it over to the girls. Placing the tureen on the table, he started to ladle it into the soup plates.

"That soup's cold, I'm sure it is," said Verity, feeling the tureen. "Yes, stone cold. Don't eat it, Mary, we must send it back. Take it away, will you? We can't eat that; we will just have the lamb and make sure the plates *and* the food are hot this time."

"Yes, miss."

"And, waiter?"

"Yes, miss?"

"Do you know who my father is?"

"No, miss."

"He's John Watson-Foster; he eats here regularly as a guest of his best friend, Henry Lovitt, the owner of this hotel. If we do not get some better service soon I will make sure he knows about it!"

"Yes, miss," simpered the waiter, retreating with the soup and plates to the kitchen.

"Verity, you are brave," whispered Mary admiringly. "I could never do anything like that and tell that man off."

"Yes, you could Mary, all you need is confidence. I just copy what Father does when he doesn't like something."

She giggled and they returned to chatting whilst they waited for their food, all of which was delivered uneventfully. When they had finished, Verity signed the bill and put it on her father's account and they waited in the lobby for Dorcas to return.

Dorcas arrived five minutes later, a little red in the face and her hat at a slight angle; she bustled up the stone steps, tripping slightly on the top one.

"Miss Verity," she panted, "sorry I'm a bit late; I've come as fast as I could."

"Did you meet your brother, Dorcas?"

"Yes, miss, he was in the best of health."

"He keeps a pub, doesn't he?"

"Yes, miss. The Griffin, miss, and a most respectable establishment."

"I've no doubt it is," said Verity. "Have you been drinking, Dorcas?"

"Just had one with me lunch, miss, there ain't no 'arm in that. It ain't against the law for a woman to 'ave a drink with her brother of a lunch time I'm sure."

"No, Dorcas," said Verity hurriedly, "I'm not being critical; did you have a good lunch?"

"Very good, miss. Salt beef and pickled onions, couldn't do better than that. And you, miss? Did you and Miss Mary 'ave a good lunch?"

"No we did not, Dorcas; the waiter was rude and the soup was cold."

"'Spect you sorted that out, Miss Verity," said Dorcas with a smile.

"Yes, Dorcas, I did. Now, I don't think we will carry the parcels back to the station very easily so we will get a carrier to take them. Dorcas, you must go with the carrier to Tibbitts and collect all we bought and Mary and I will walk back across the park; the exercise will do us good."

She scanned the roads carefully.

"Now, can we see anyone to help us?"

"There," said Dorcas, pointing down the street towards a pony and small cart, where the driver sat asleep on the seat. Verity clapped her hands and waved but he did not hear.

"I'll go and fetch him, miss."

"Shall I whistle?" said Mary and before they could answer, she put her thumb and her index finger in her mouth and blew a sharp shrill whistle.

Everyone around immediately looked at them; Verity pretended not to notice but her disapproval was distilled somewhat when she realised the carrier had woken up and had started to make his way towards where Mary was standing waving.

"You've got the money to pay the man, Dorcas?" said Verity as Dorcas climbed up to sit next to the carrier.

"Yes, miss, in my purse."

"And you've got the return tickets, Dorcas?"

"Yes, miss, in my purse."

"Very well then. We will see you in about twenty minutes."

Verity and Mary walked across the park, arriving at almost exactly the same time as Dorcas and the numerous boxes. The boxes stowed in their carriage, Dorcas, Mary and Verity found their seats, and watched Northampton recede as the train pulled out of the station to take them home.

Chapter Eleven
Tibbitts

The harvest was drawing to a close; all the wheat and barley had been cut and only one small field of beans remained to be carted on Thomas Dunmore's small farm. William was preparing for his first term at Kimbolton Grammar School, his clothes had been made (a size too big with room for him to grow into them, on his mother's instructions) and he was looking forward to his new school. Mary on the other hand was not settled. Ever since her trip to Northampton with Verity, she had pestered her mother about going to work at Tibbitts. It had been arranged that she could work at the draper's shop in Raunds, but a position in Northampton was to her, much more attractive. However, Ann had not been well and Mary felt under pressure to stay at home and help look after the house.

"Mary, you never stop," her mother would complain. "I wish I'd never let you go with Verity. You have done nothing since but go on about it. Always thinking of yourself! What about me, and the help I need? And your poor father; his chest is so bad he can hardly walk across the yard."

"I know, I know," sighed Mary. "But Lucy will soon leave school and she can help, can't she?"

Ann looked up at her headstrong daughter, trapped by the imploring look on her young face, and softened.

"I'll have another word with your father and we'll see. Just keep quiet about it for five minutes, can you?"

Mary had decided that it would be possible for her to live with her Aunt Sarah in Rushden if she could manage to secure a job at Tibbitts. Sarah had married George Henry Chambers – a very successful shoe maker who had a large factory just outside Rushden. They lived in a spacious house on the edge of Rushden and only had two children – both much younger than Mary – and she believed that they would be able to make room for her and she would be able to go on the train every day to work in Northampton. After a week of pestering, Ann and John finally agreed that Mary could write to Peveril Tibbitt to see if his offer of a job was a genuine one. She contacted Verity for the address and between them they penned the letter to Mr Tibbitt, with John Watson-Foster agreeing to act as a reference. She also wrote to her aunt in Rushden to see if it would be possible to live with her.

Within a week Mary had a reply from Mr Tibbitt, calling her to an interview on the eleventh of October at ten o'clock, which meant an early start to catch the train from Rushden. This time her mother went with her and Henry drove them to the station. The sky was dark and as they walked from the station there was a heavy shower and by the time they arrived at Mr Tibbitt's office they were wet and bedraggled.

"Look at me, Mother," groaned Mary. "I can't go in for an interview looking like this. I'm all wet and my shoes are splashed."

"Just take off your hat for a minute, dear, and we can comb your hair straight while we are waiting," fussed Ann. "Here, clean your shoes with my hankie quickly now before they call you in."

Mary busied herself combing out the tangles in her long hair and her mother brushed the wet from her jacket the best she could. Satisfied that nothing more could be done to right the damage the rain had done, they sat down again and waited. Ten minutes went by and still no one appeared.

"Are you sure this is the right day, Mary? No one has come."

"Of course I'm sure, Mother; here's the letter – check for yourself," said Mary pushing the letter into Ann's hand.

"Perhaps they are busy. After all the effort we made to get here by ten o'clock!" Mary sighed. "I wish something would happen, the suspense is killing me."

"Just sit still, dear; read a magazine or something."

Mary surveyed the room impatiently; it was dingy and panelled in a dark oak that managed to create a claustrophobic atmosphere and there were no pictures on the walls. In the middle stood a table strewn with some old copies of the *Illustrated London News* and *The Tatler*; the room was lined with tatty, leather chairs that had seen better days. The sash window was open a little way at the top allowing the smells of smoke, town gas and horse dung to waft in at regular intervals. There was a small fireplace; but the fire had not been lit and on the mantelpiece was a clock that had read ten past two for the last fifteen minutes. The door on the opposite side of the room had "Peveril Tibbitt" written on it, and underneath "Managing Director"; both in gold letters.

Mary tapped the leg of her chair impatiently with her fingernails and shifted in her seat.

"Perhaps we'd better go and tell the girl that we are here again?" Mary said.

"Don't be silly, dear, she showed us up – she knows we're here; you will just have to be patient for a change."

"Look at my shoes, Mother, they've dried all patchy. What can I do?"

"Here we are, dear, take my hankie again, spit on it and give them a rub."

Mary took the hankie and did as she was instructed; it did the trick – they looked black again rather than a splodgy sort of grey. She stood up, brushed her skirt down back and front and tried to look at her reflection in the window pane.

"Sit down, dear; he'll be here in a minute," whispered Ann, exasperated.

"I bet he won't," hissed Mary. "I wish we had never come; I wish I had never written. It's all a waste of time and money; he must just be a stuck-up old faggot!"

"Mary!" scolded Ann, shocked. "Don't say such things, someone will hear you."

Mary sighed angrily, slumped in her chair and twiddled her thumbs, one chasing the other in never-ending circles.

Suddenly the door of the office opened and Peveril Tibbitt appeared. He was dressed in a frock coat, pinstriped trousers and a high wing collar with a red and yellow striped tie. He was wearing patent leather shoes, with grey spats. He looked to be in his late fifties and in remarkably good condition for a man of his age; he appeared younger than Mary had remembered him, and a good deal more dashing. In his right hand he held a cigarette in a black and ivory holder and over the smell of tobacco there was a definite odour of cologne which drifted its way towards the two women as Peveril pulled the handkerchief from his breast pocket, flapped it in the air and dabbed it delicately over his forehead.

Such a dramatic entrance took Mary and her mother aback; and Mary wondered whether he had been practising behind the door before he had flung it open.

"Ah, the lovely Miss Knighton, how are you today, my dear, and this must be your good mother Mrs Knighton?"

With a flourish, Peveril grabbed Ann's gloved hand and delicately kissed it, before turning to Mary and repeating the process.

"Pleased to meet you, Mr Tibbitt," said Ann, smiling at Peveril as he took a long draw on his cigarette and blew the smoke towards the ceiling.

"Now I must apologise," Peveril said. "I think I am all behind this morning; I came over a bit queer all of a sudden, down the corridor there," he gestured grandly to the door the women had entered by, "and just had to have a lie down for forty winks, so I suspect I must be a little late, but there we go. Better late than never, that's what I say, what!"

And with a smile he flicked a gold repeater from his waistcoat pocket and peered at the dial as it sprang open.

"Oh my goodness, it's half past ten, must be time for some coffee or tea. Now, my dear," he said turning to Mary," what are you here for?"

"I've come for an interview, sir."

"Interview? Interview for what?"

"A job, sir. You suggested I write when we met in The County Hotel a couple of months ago with Verity Watson-Foster."

Peveril peered at Mary myopically for a moment, before the memory sprang a smile onto his face.

"Oh yes! Yes! I remember; I was with my good old friend Allibone – splendid chap, you know; splendid chap."

He took another puff of the cigarette.

"I said to Allibone, yes I told him at the time: *that's* the sort of girl we need! I could tell, I could tell," he grinned.

"Well, if you want an interview, you shall have one and then you can have a job and that will be capital. Capital."

He strode towards the door of his office and shouted,

"Frisby! Where are you? Come on, don't hide, man!"

"Here, sir," a small voice squeaked from Mr Tibbitt's office.

"Now, Mrs Knighton, can I introduce Frisby my assistant. Now, Frisby, I want you to look after Mrs Knighton while I interview her lovely daughter Mary."

He turned and once again kissed Mary's hand.

"Frisby, get coffee, tea, cakes or anything Mrs Knighton wants while I see Mary. Mrs Gumley will get you what you want from the kitchen and Frisby, if Mrs Knighton wishes to look around the shop you escort her. Oh, and Frisby, get a message to Mrs Stevens to come to my office at her earliest convenience."

He turned to Mary and in a loud whisper he said, "Follow me, my dear," and ushered Mary into his office.

This was a much bigger room, with tall windows which invited in more light. To one side there was a desk behind which stood a large winged chair. On the wall behind the desk were portraits of various men and women who Mary supposed were family members. At the far end was a fireplace with a large marble surround, topped with a mantelpiece on which stood a splendid ormolu clock. The wall at the other end of the room was lined from floor to ceiling with glass-fronted bookcases.

"Now, my dear," said Peveril, "let's draw up a chair for you and one for Mrs Stevens when she comes. Now, Mary, would you like any refreshment?"

"No, sir, thank you very much."

There was a knock at the door.

"Enter," shouted Peveril, making his way round to his chair. "Ah, Mrs. Stevens, come in, come in and let me introduce Mary Knighton. I hope you agree, Mrs Stevens, that she will be a great asset to our staff. Mary, Mrs Stevens is our most senior floor manager and has been with us for many years now."

Peveril grabbed the tails of his frock coat and swept them lavishly to the side before plonking himself down in the chair behind the desk. Mary and Mrs Stevens took their seats opposite him.

"Now, Mary. Questions."

He took a pen from his pocket and a notebook from the drawer.

"Mrs Stevens, you must ask questions. I have forgotten what questions I should ask."

"Yes, Mr Tibbitt."

"Right," continued Peveril, as Mrs Stevens turned towards Mary. "Here we go. Mary, how old are you?"

"I'll be sixteen next March, sir," said Mary answering Peveril.

"You look older than that; don't you think so, Mrs Stevens?"

"Yes, Mr Peveril, she does look older than that."

"Mary, what education have you had?"

"Well, sir, I attended the local school in Dean until last summer; I'm good at reading and writing and also good at arithmetic."

"Can you sew, Mary?" interjected Mrs Stevens.

"Yes, miss, my mother has taught me."

"And can you measure people for their clothes?"

"Well I've never done it, but I am sure I could learn very quickly."

"Now, Mary," rejoined Peveril with a pointed look at Mrs Stevens, "can you add up pounds, shillings and pence?"

"Yes, sir, I'm not very fast but I can do it."

Peveril pulled a sheet from his desk with columns of figures lining the page.

"Right, Mary; add up that for us, could you?" he instructed, handing her the sheet.

Mary's heart sank, she knew she could do it but she was very slow and she really needed a pencil to carry forward the numbers from one column to the next. She frowned slightly and started on the right-hand column to deal with the farthings and half-pennies; she had watched William do it lots of times, he could just run his finger down one column, straight to the top of the next and get it right every time.

"Would you like a pencil, Mary, to carry the numbers forward?"

"Yes please, sir," she said gratefully, taking the proffered pencil and starting again.

Still it seemed to take forever – and even when she had finished, Mary was not convinced she had got it right.

"Mrs Stevens, you check it for us please, you will be much quicker than I am."

Mrs Stevens took the paper and surveyed it quickly.

"It's not correct, Mr Peveril," said Mrs Stevens, handing him the paper. "I've put the correct answer below Mary's."

"Hmm," said Peveril, gripping his chin.

"Mary, I have here a reference from John Watson-Foster who my friend Allibone tells me is a fine gentleman; and Allibone knows a good man if anyone did. The reference is very good; he says you come from a good family and you are friendly with his daughter Verity."

"Yes, sir," said Mary quietly.

"Do you have brothers and sisters, Mary"?

"Yes, sir; one brother and three sisters, sir – one of them is married."

"And your brother, Mary; he's a strapping chap I bet."

"Yes, sir, he helps Father on the farm."

"And, Mary, do you go to church?"

"Yes, sir, we all go to the chapel in Dean."

"Very good, splendid! Do you have any more questions, Mrs Stevens?"

"Yes. Mr Peveril – Mary, how will you get here? You live a long way off."

"Yes, miss, I hope to live with my uncle and aunt, Mr and Mrs Chambers, in Rushden, and travel here by train."

"You don't mean George Henry Chambers, do you?"

"Yes, sir; he's my uncle."

"Well, well, you *do* come from good stock, my dear," smiled Peveril, snapping open his silver cigarette case and selecting a cigarette.

"George Henry Chambers, indeed; he has one of the most advanced boot factories in the country. Fancy him being your uncle."

He smoothed the cigarette into the holder, lit it and sat back in his chair; looking intently at Mary before continuing.

"Yes, if you wait outside with your mother, Mary, I can have a word with Mrs Stevens."

Mary rose and smiled.

"Thank you, Mr Tibbitt," she said and left the room.

"Well, Mrs Stevens, what do you think, eh?" mused Peveril as the door closed gently behind Mary. "I made up my mind when I met her with dear old Allibone, but what do you think?"

"I think she's fine, Mr Peveril. I think we can work with her and get her into shape as an assistant."

"She'll do better than that, Mrs Stevens, you mark my word; she'll do better than a shop assistant or my name's not Peveril Tibbitt. Well let's have her in again and tell her she has a job, Mrs Stevens. If you would oblige and bring her mother in as well, will you – oh and Frisby as well – if you can find him."

Mrs Stevens went out and within a few moments all five were back in Peveril's office.

"Now, Mary, I am pleased to say that we will be able to offer you a position as assistant starting as soon as things can be arranged. Frisby will type the letter of appointment before you go, won't you Frisby?"

"Yes, Mr Tibbitt," squeaked Frisby.

"Yes, Mrs Knighton – what a lovely daughter you have, you must be very proud of her."

"Yes, Mr Tibbitt, we are indeed."

"Now, Mary, do you have any questions?"

"Yes, sir, what remuneration does the job of assistant attract?"

"Remuneration, remuneration, you mean pay, do you?"

"Yes, sir."

"Pay! No one has ever asked that question before. Mrs Stevens, do we pay our shop assistants?"

"Yes, Mr Peveril, we do; but we don't discuss such things in public; they are confidential."

"Quite right, quite right," mused Peveril, rising from his chair and moving towards a decanter brimful with Madeira.

"Now will anyone join me? Mrs Knighton?"

"No thank you, Mr Tibbitt," replied Ann, a touch more vehemently than she had intended.

"Mary?"

"No thank you, sir."

"Well that leaves just me!" he said gleefully, walking back to his chair with a generous glassful.

"Where were we? Yes! Pay! Pay, Mary; what are you going to do with your pay?"

"Well, I will have to pay my aunt for my board and lodging, sir, and I want to save up for a bicycle to get backwards and forwards from the station and to cycle home when I am not at work."

"Well, well," smiled Peveril, "Frisby good fellow, go and type the letter for Mary, can you – you know what to put and I will sign it."

He raised his glass.

"Cheers! My first today and let's hope there's plenty more, eh, Mrs Knighton?"

Ann managed a weak smile and looked down at her hands.

"A bicycle, eh? Well I suppose women do ride bicycles these days. Do you have a bicycle, Mrs Stevens?"

"Yes, Mr Peveril; I come to work on it every day."

"Well I never, how extraordinary. Can't ride one myself, can't ride a horse either come to that. I got on one once don't you know; a terribly frightening experience I can tell you – the ground was so far away! So I got off before I fell off, what!"

He took another cigarette from the silver case on the desk.

"Oh I'm so sorry! Do you smoke, Mrs Knighton, some ladies do these days I believe?"

"Oh no, I don't smoke, thank you, Mr Tibbitt," said Ann, recoiling from the open box in horror.

Peveril snapped the box closed, threaded the cigarette into the holder, lit it and took a deep draw, an expression of intoxication spreading across his face. He opened his mouth slightly, pushed his lower jaw forward and inhaled the escaping smoke from his mouth up his nostrils. Ann winced and momentarily shut her eyes; Mary, however, was amazed; she had never seen such a thing done before.

"My old friend Allibone," continued Peveril, "he rides, you know, goes hunting twice a week in the winter and rides all over the farm in the summer. Even went point-to-pointing when he was younger – can't understand it, can't understand it. Hunting eh, what a sport! Getting cold and wet when you could be sitting in front of the fire with a nice drink."

There was a knock at the door, as Frisby returned with the typed letter and handed it to Peveril, who pulled a monocle from his top pocket and quickly read the letter through.

"Very good, Frisby! Not one spelling mistake – you are improving."

He picked up a pen from the desk, dipped it in the inkwell, signed it and handed it back to Frisby who put it in an envelope.

"Well, my dear, we are complete! You can start on Monday week and we all look forward to seeing you."

"Thank you, sir," Mary replied, taking the letter from his outstretched hand with a grin.

"Thank you, Mr Tibbitt," said Ann. "I hope she comes up to expectations."

"I'm sure she will, Mrs Knighton, and thank you for bringing her. Frisby will show you out."

"Well I never," muttered Ann as they walked away down the street toward the station. "I don't know what to think of him; he's a real rum 'un, don't you think, Mary? Drinking in the morning! And all that smoking! I don't know if I like the idea of you working for him."

"I thought he was wonderful, Mother, a real character," said Mary wistfully.

"Well, if that's what you call it! I don't know – you wait till I tell your father about him."

She sighed heavily.

"Mother?" said Mary tentatively.

"Yes, Mary."

"Can we go for lunch? I know a place – I went there with Verity."

Ann stopped in her tracks and turned bad-temperedly to Mary.

"No, we can't, my girl, do you think we are made of money? No, we are going straight back to Rushden to see your Aunt Sarah. Are you sure she said you could stay with her? She's awfully posh, you know, in that great big house; it's not like living on the farm, you know."

"Yes, Mother, she said it would be all right," sighed Mary.

"Well, when we get back to Rushden and find Henry with the trap, we will go round to Hazelwood and see Aunt Sarah and make sure. I know she won't be expecting us but that can't be helped."

Chapter Twelve
Following the Hunt

The autumn of 1898 in Dean brought with it many changes. The school had a new teacher, Miss Standish, which allowed Mr Sparks to divide the school into three classes for the first time. George and Reuben were no longer the youngest in the school and had established themselves as a team; George could do the academic part of life at school, Reuben did the sport and threw the odd punch when it was needed.

The two boys were always together; they walked to school together and sat together in class. Reuben's fascination with steam engines intensified and if there was a set anywhere in the area he would go and watch, whether it was the ploughing engines or the engine and threshing set it did not matter. The ploughing sets were usually Blinkhorn's and Roland Cumber was the foreman. When he was there they would make sure to stand and watch the engine at the opposite end of the field to him and talk to Joe Bradshaw. Often they would run errands for him – going back to the village to fetch bread from the baker or meat from the butcher's shop and sometimes even beer from the pub.

Mary had started work at Tibbitts ten days after the interview. She worked Monday to Saturday and had Wednesday afternoon off. On Sundays she would walk home to Cold Harbour to see her parents, go to chapel and walk back to Rushden. To get to work at half past eight in Northampton, she had to catch the seven o' clock train from Rushden, which meant she had to leave her aunt's house by half past six. Gladys, the maid, would always be up by then to get her breakfast – bread, jam and a cup of tea – before she set off. She loved the work, and very quickly got into the routine.

Her job was to help in the women's department of the shop and she began to meet all the society ladies that lived in the area. At lunchtimes the shop closed for an hour and after eating at the canteen, she would walk about the town looking in all the shop windows or meander around the parks that surrounded the centre of the town. When the shop closed at half past five, she would make her way back to Rushden and was usually back at her Aunt

Sarah's house by a quarter past seven if she caught the right train. If she got home on time she ate with the family, otherwise she would have her tea in the kitchen with Gladys.

Lucy was now the only one of the Knighton family left at Dean School and was in the top class, which was taken by Miss Standish. Ethel Standish was forty-five and had taught all her life in a number of schools. She had only got the job at Dean because it was far enough from Bedford for her not to worry the education authorities. She had a reputation as a tough disciplinarian; to the extent that there had been complaints, not so much from the children and parents, but from other members of staff. Ethel's disciplinary code was not confined to school hours; she took it on herself to correct the children whenever or wherever she saw them about the village. Her reign of terror extended to the parents as well as the children and they were as much in awe of her as the pupils were. She used the cane – which always lay threateningly across her desk – liberally; the girls were administered on the palm of their hands or knuckles and the boys on their backsides. She would beat not only for misdemeanours and misbehaviour, but also for poor class work, which gave her plenty of trade; anyone who could not get half marks in a spelling test got the cane.

She was a tall, very thin woman and was always dressed the same – in a dark grey dress with long sleeves. The only addition was a plain black jacket, which she wore on her walk to and from school. Her face was thin and her hair, which hung down lankily about her head, was prematurely grey. She clearly smoked a lot as the index and second finger on her left hand were stained dark yellow with tar and the wisp of a fringe that hung over her forehead had a slight tinge of yellow.

Every morning she would take the roll call, which started with Lucy Knighton and ended with George Wilmott. Lucy could mostly keep out of trouble; she was the form monitor, like Mary had been before her and her main tasks were to clean the blackboard and fill the inkwells. Although she would not have been Miss Standish's favourite, she managed to avoid the levels of caning dished out to those that Miss Standish didn't like. Two members of the class were caned nearly every day; George Fox was one and Molly Webb was the other. George Fox with his small stature and was always picked on; Molly was a tougher character and would not bow down to Ethel Standish however much she hit her.

"I'll knock that expression off your face if it's the last thing I ever do," Miss Standish would say to her as Molly glowered defiantly at her. It infuriated Miss Standish that no matter how hard she beat Molly, the expression on her face didn't change – she didn't even cry when she was caned like most of the others did, even the boys.

The Wednesday before Christmas heralded the arrival of the hunt at Dean House and lots of people arrived to enjoy a small glass of port and some food before they set off for the hunt. Henry Knighton was one of the first to turn up, and William went eagerly to greet his cousin.

"Well, Henry, how's everything at Cold Harbour?" he smiled

"Not so good, William, not so good I'm afraid. We're struggling to make ends meet this year; the old bank balance goes down and down and what with Father not doing any work anymore, I've got a lot on my plate. Not like you, William, eh?"

"What do you mean, Henry?" said William sharply.

"That butcher's business always keeps the cash coming in, don't it? I bet your bank ain't going down."

Henry ran his eyes angrily over the buildings surrounding him and scuffed the ground with his boot.

"Well, we're keeping our heads above water," said William hurriedly. "Anyway, how is your father? I haven't been up lately."

"He's not too bad but he's all the while out of puff, only just gets across the yard. The doctor says it's TB but that seems to be what they say to everyone isn't it? And Mother ain't so well either. Doctor says she's got a weak heart." He gave a sharp laugh. "They're a right royal pair, if you ask me."

William shifted uncomfortably and was relieved to see George and Reuben approaching across the yard.

"What are you two doing here?" William asked. "Aren't you supposed to be at school, you haven't broken up yet, have you?"

"No we ain't," replied Reuben, "but they won't miss us, I'm sure; anyway Mrs Warby's all right – she won't mind, not like that old Miss Standish."

"Yup, we goin' to follow the hunt," said George, grinning hard enough to split his face.

"We're goin' to run with 'em," said Reuben, looking around at the assembled horses and people milling to and fro.

The huntsmen and whippers-in were mounted in their red coats and the master in his top hat was sitting astride his big bay mare, sipping some port. He walked his horse about the assembled company, chatting as he did so; looking up, he waved towards Henry and William.

"Come here, boy," he shouted at William. "Hold this animal, can you, and look sharp about it. And you, boy," pointing at Henry. "Come here and take a couple of notches out me girth for me."

He put his foot forward and lifted up the flap of his saddle.

William and Henry made their way over to the master and did as instructed, Henry having to stand on tiptoes to pull the girth up to the next holes; he replaced the saddle flap and stepped away from the horse. The master readjusted his seat, sniffed and without a word, rode off.

"That's gratitude for you," grumbled Henry. "Never said a word of thanks, and then he's going to ride all over our fields and push down all the hedges. As soon as some of these sods get high up on an 'oss they think they're God's gift."

"Well, I suppose they kill a few foxes," shrugged William, looking at the portly huntsman as they moved towards a maid who had just exited the house bearing a plate of food.

"Come on, Reuben," said George, spotting her, "there's a plate of cheese straws over there; let's have one."

"They won't let us."

"Yes they will; that's Martha holding the plate – she'll slip us one."

The boys made their way towards the house, just as the hounds were let out of their pen to mingle with the crowds. It wasn't long before they smelt the cheese straws and made a beeline for Martha. Seeing the advance, she held the plate in the air as high as she could, whilst shooing them away with her other hand. Not to be put off, one of the smaller hounds stood up on its back legs and knocked the flustered Martha over, plate and all, and the cheese straws were gone. The master, who had been watching the proceedings, laughed.

"Look at that, William," said Henry angrily. "I told you what they get like when they get up on a horse."

He moved over to Martha, who was red with embarrassment, and picked her up.

"Are you all right, girl?" Henry enquired.

"Yup," she smiled. "No bones broken and the plate's still in one piece."

"Are you sure?" said Henry. "You went down with quite a bump."

"Yes, honestly, I'm fine," she insisted, brushing the leaves off her skirt and smiling at Henry.

"You're not from around here, are you?" Henry said, looking hard at the short, pretty girl before him.

"No. I moved down from Derbyshire to live with my aunt in Melchbourne when I got the job here."

"And what's your name?"

"Martha How. Why, what's yours?"

"I'm Henry Knighton, this is my cousin William. And how do you know George Lowe?"

"You've got a lot of questions, haven't you?" Martha laughed, adjusting the clips which held the little hat on her head. "I know George Lowe because he comes on the butcher's cart and I know William as well, so there!"

She smiled at Henry.

"Now, I must go and get some more cheese straws or I'll be in trouble."

And with that, she ran off back to the house. Henry stood watching her go.

"Nice girl that, William, very pretty, don't you think?"

"If you say so, Henry," said William, who didn't think that any girls were particularly pretty.

There were about twenty mounted at the meet milling around, the horses impatient to get off; most of them were local gentry and some of them had brought a groom with them to ride after the hunt leading a second horse. There were only two women, both riding side-saddle and a girl of about fifteen who was also riding side-saddle on a large piebald pony that was being led on a leading rein by the girl's father. She was also very pretty as far as they could see behind the veil that hung down from her top hat over her face.

"Father, can't you unclip the leading rein, I feel so stupid. I'm not a baby," William heard her say.

"I told you I will unclip it when we move off and not before," said her father sternly.

"I'm the only one on a leading rein, it's not fair," she huffed, crossing her arms and looking about her grumpily.

There was a hush as the master took off his top hat, stood up in his stirrups and prepared to address the field. The whippers-in cracked their long whips and hollered at the hounds to bring them all back on to the lawn in front of the house. The master shouted orders to the field as to what they should do and where they were going and thanked the Fitz-Allens for hosting the meet. He then raised the horn to his lips and blew as the hounds assembled around him ready to move off. As soon as the horses heard the sound of the horn they pricked up their ears, knowing they would soon be off. The huntsman raised his cap to Mr Fitz-Allen and moved off up to the fox cover at the top of the hill.

"Well, that's them gone," said Henry watching the horses trotting off up the lane.

"Yes, it's a lovely sight they make, I like to see them," said William wistfully.

"Thought you'd be hunting too, William. It would be up your street with all them gentry," said Henry cattily.

"No, I'm getting a bicycle! That will be much more reliable than a horse and it doesn't need grooming or feeding."

"S'pose you're right," laughed Henry. "Now, William, I nearly forgot. Mother says to tell you that we will be coming to the butcher's shop on Sunday afternoon after chapel; that's me and Lucy and Mary. Our parents are all going to tea with Reverend Packham with a lot of others and we're to have our tea at your house. Can you pass the message to your mother that we'd be pleased to come?"

"But it will be too dark to go home, how will you see?" asked William.

"Well, we decided that it should be a full moon; but if it's cloudy I will have to lead the pony back with Mother and Father and the girls in the trap."

"Are you going to follow them, William?" said George excitedly, trotting up to William and Henry at the same time as cramming the last of a handful of cheese straws into his pockets.

"I'll walk back home that way and see them draw the first cover," nodded William before turning to his cousin, "are you coming?"

"No, I've got better things to do. I've got to litter up all the yards and that'll take me the rest of the day," said Henry, before saying his goodbyes and leaving in the opposite direction.

William walked up the lane after the hunt; by the time he got to the cover, the hounds were drawing it, around the outside, as the hunt stood patiently, spaced at intervals listening for the hounds. George and Reuben stood fifty yards back along the hedge and William stood with them to watch. Everyone was silent; a kestrel hovered over the wood and the crows circled over the valley having been driven off by the hunt. A single pheasant flew out of the cover; its wings flapping like a pack of cards being flicked, stopping as it glided into the valley. The master took his cigarette case from his pocket, extracted one and lit it, waiting expectantly.

"There's nothing in there," whispered Reuben.

"I bet there is," said George. "Dad said one was trying to get in our hen run last night."

"Shh, you two – just listen," hissed William, putting his finger to his mouth.

The kestrel dropped suddenly down at the edge of the trees, scrabbling on the ground for a moment before rising up again with a mouse in its talons. The church clock in the village could just be heard striking midday and a hush descended again. The huntsman came into view, riding round the woodland to see if the hounds were coming out; he approached the Master.

"Better pull them out, Sid; there ain't nothing in there."

"Give it two minutes," insisted the Master, taking a small flask from his

142

pocket on the other side of his jacket and unscrewing the lid. No sooner had the flask reached his lips, than the hounds - almost in unison – started to call. Hearing the sound, his horse frighted and reared enough for the master to spill the contents of his flask down his chin, soaking his stock.

"Damnation!" he shouted, pulling hard on the rein. "Stand still, you bugger."

The horse took a step or two backwards and stood still. There was a shout from the corner of the cover to the right.

"Gone away," came the call.

"I seen it," said George excitedly. "Did you see it, Reuben? Did you see it, William?"

"No! Where is it, then? You didn't see nothing!" said Reuben.

"Yes I did, I'm sure I did. It went down towards the woods. You saw it, William, didn't you?"

"I'm not sure; but they are on the scent and they're making towards the woods like you said."

The hounds kept up their barking and emerged from the corner of the cover, pelting across the ploughed field towards Kimbolton Woods. The huntsman came rushing from the other direction, jumped the hedge by which they were standing and blew his horn as he galloped off after the hounds. The Master followed, and behind the Master – from either side of the cover – streamed the rest of the hunt, galloping after the hound pack.

Bringing up the rear was the girl that they had seen at the meet; she could clearly ride well, and she now put her horse at the hedge where William, George and Reuben stood on the other side. She lined her pony up to take the hedge and kicked hard with the one heel she could use; the horse responded and was about to take off when it changed its mind. It raised its head, and straightened its front legs. The girl was dislodged from the saddle, the reins slipping from her grip as – with her arms outstretched in front of her – she went sailing over the horse's head. She hit the top of the hedge and somersaulted down the other side, her skirt rising to show her long knickers and a bit of bare leg above her boots. She rolled over a couple of times and ended up kneeling on the ground, her top hat in the dirt in front of her.

"Reuben, go and catch that horse quick before we lose it! Go and help him, George," shouted William; and the three boys ran down the hedge, climbing the small piece of fence that blocked up the gap to where the rider lay on the ground.

"Are you all right, miss?" said William, rushing up to help.

"No, I'm bloody not. What does it look like?" cursed the girl.

William held out his hand to her, which she grudgingly took, before pulling herself up and hobbling round in a circle, screwing her eyes up and pursing her lips as tight as she could. A tear ran down each cheek, which she dashed away with the back of her hand. She turned angrily to William, drew her head down a little and bawled at him.

"What did you have to stand there for, you stupid boy? It was going to jump fine until it saw you, why couldn't you keep out the bloody way!"

William had not heard a woman swear before and certainly not a girl and did not know what to say. The girl shook her head and continued to limp round in front of him.

"Are you hurt, miss?" said William tentatively.

"Of course I'm bloody hurt. What does it look like?"

A small amount of blood had started to run down from her nose, there was a deep scratch down her left cheek and her ear was scratched on the other. She pulled her glove off and wiped her nose with her fist, surprised when she noticed the blood.

"Bugger, my nose is bleeding," she exclaimed, wiping the blood on the grass at her feet.

William pulled a handkerchief from his pocket and offered it to her.

"I don't want that filthy thing," she sneered, pulling a small white handkerchief from her sleeve and dabbing her nose. Within a minute, it was saturated.

"Give that here," she demanded, grabbing William's handkerchief, holding it against her nose and tipping her head back. William picked up her top hat, which lay on the ground and brushed off the worst of the mud – inside the hat on the leather band, he could see the words *Tibbitts of Northampton* printed.

"William, you're going to have to give us an 'and," shouted George from

144

the other side of the hedge. "We can get it in the corner but we can't catch it."

"Just a minute," William said, turning to the girl.

"Are you going to be all right?" he asked.

"Of course I am, you stupid boy; go and catch the horse – and give that here," she snarled, grabbing the top hat.

William ran down the hedge and vaulted back over the rails to join the other two boys. They drove the pony into the corner of the field, where it turned and faced them warily. Lowering its head, it charged down the hedge line – William tried to grab the flapping rein, but missed and instead managed to seize hold of one of the pommels on the saddle, using all his weight to slow the pony down. The animal faltered, and William was able to grab the reins and pull it to a stop. He led the panting horse up to the end of the hedge, let it through the wooden fence and handed it back to the girl. Her nose had stopped bleeding; she had wiped the blood from her face and replaced her hat, although the veil had detached and was still lying on the floor

"How am I going to get back on?" she fumed. "There's no mounting block and nothing to stand on."

"Well, you could stand on those rails, miss, if we lead the pony up there," suggested William.

"Very well then, there's nowhere else," she said grudgingly.

William led the horse to the rails and the girl climbed up to the second highest rung, turning and balancing precariously. The horse, however, had other ideas, and refused to be led close enough for its rider to remount.

"Bloody horse," she shouted, jumping down to the ground, and shaking the pony's reins angrily. "Why don't we turn the horse round and put it against the rails," said William calmly, "Then we can lift you on."

"Don't be silly, you can't lift me; I wouldn't allow it."

"No, miss," explained Reuben. "All you do is bend your left knee and we lift your foot, you press down with your left leg and up you go into the saddle."

The girl looked at them suspiciously.

"Well, I suppose it's worth a go," she conceded. "But you just make sure you hold my foot and that's all."

The boys brought the horse round; George held its head and Reuben leant on it so it was tight to the rails. The girl held onto the two pommels and raised her left foot, letting William take hold of it.

"Now push down," William shouted as the girl pushed her weight into his hand, allowing William to raise her up into the saddle. He put her foot into the stirrup and looked up at her as she readjusted her reins. For the first time, she smiled.

"Thank you, boy; I've never done it that way before – it's easy, isn't it?"

"Yes, miss," said William.

"What's your name then, boy?"

"William Dunmore, miss."

"And you?" she said looking at Reuben and George.

"Reuben Heighton, miss,"

"George Lowe, miss."

"Well, thank you all. Right, I must be off. William – if you see a groom on the road, tell him which way we have gone."

"Who shall I say, miss?"

"Oh! Who am I, you mean? Rebecca – Rebecca Harding."

And with a smile she dug her heel into her horse's flank and rode off.

Chapter Thirteen
Fire at the Chapel

It was early spring 1899. Sunday arrived and Mary came home from her aunt's at Rushden, having got a lift most of the way with Walter, who had taken a visitor from The Hall back the station. She was dropped at the park gates and had only to walk the last mile. Her life had dramatically changed since she had left home and started work at Tibbitts. She had made lots of new friends in the shop, girls of her own age. She also was getting to know the customers who came from all over the county to shop there, Tibbitts being the best draper and ladies' outfitter in the town. With the money she was earning she was able to pay her aunt for board and lodging and she had saved some of the rest to buy a bicycle for herself. For the first time she had money to buy new clothes, perfume and cosmetics, which she put on when she got to work, but dared not wear at home or in Aunt Sarah's house.

The one thing that niggled at her was her parents; they were not getting any younger and were both in poor health. Lucy was still at school and was able to help a lot and as long as things got no worse they could manage; but the unsaid implication that Mary should give up her job and come home to help in the house always lurked in every conversation.

When she finally got home, Lucy was preparing lunch. Henry had just come in from a morning feeding the cattle in the yards and milking the cow. They had help on the farm but not as much as they would have liked and since John could not work, Henry had to do more than his fair share. Their housemaid Freda had been with them for years but she was awkward and difficult to manage at times. The farm, although quite big compared with some, had a big mortgage on it, making it difficult to make ends meet financially, which put even more pressure on Henry who was not the best of businessmen. All these problems conspired to make Mary feel guilty, but she was determined not to come home until things became desperate.

"Hello? Hello, everyone," she called, bouncing in the door and banging her valise full of dirty washing on the table.

"Lucy, what's for lunch? It smells lovely!"

"Don't put your bag there, Mary, we're about to have lunch," snapped Ann. "I suppose you want us to wash all that lot, don't you?"

"And iron it," said Lucy under her breath. "And it's beef for lunch. It's always beef for lunch; we never have anything else for lunch on Sunday, do we?"

"Well, that's not a very nice welcome is it?" said Mary quietly, removing her bag from the table and laying it on the floor.

"No, dear, I mean yes, dear," sighed her mother, turning to look properly at her daughter. "Well how are you, anyway; have you had a good week? And how's Aunt Sarah and Uncle George and those girls?"

"Yes, I have had a good week; all the weeks are good and the shop is very busy. Aunt Sarah and Uncle George are well – they send their love and the girls are well."

Ann picked up Mary's bag and took it to the scullery to put the dirty clothes in the wash basket ready for tomorrow.

"Mary," her mother said sharply, reappearing in the kitchen, "those clothes smell of tobacco."

"Yes, Mother, they probably do. It's all the people that come into the shop smoking."

"Well as long as you're not smoking, Mary Knighton! I would not be pleased if you were."

Mary said nothing but went over and lifted the lid of the saucepan bubbling gently on the range. Her father sat on his rocking chair reading a copy of the *Bedfordshire Times* which he put down to say,

"Now come on, my girl, help your mother get the dinner ready," before picking it up again and burying his nose in it.

"Well, what can I do, Mother?" Mary said looking round aimlessly.

"You can lay the table and when you've done that you can go and get another bucket of water from the pump to do the washing up so we are ready to go to chapel for three o'clock."

"Your father and I are going to tea with Reverend Packham and you are all going to have your tea at the butcher's shop; Aunt Charlotte and Uncle Thomas are coming with us and it will just be William there."

"Whoopee," said Mary.

"Just you make sure you behave," Ann chided.

"We always do, don't we, Lucy?" said Mary, winking at her sister, who sniffed and continued to stir the gravy.

After lunch the family got ready for chapel.

"Who's going to walk, then?" said Henry. "It's not going to be me because I'm sure I will have to lead the horse home. It's Mary's turn; Lucy cooked the lunch."

"Yes," said John, "Mary, you walk today, you'll get there at the same time as us if you set off now."

"I'll get my boots all muddy going across the fields!" protested Mary.

"No you won't, not if you look where you're treading and don't do any daydreaming."

"It's not fair," Mary whined, scowling at Henry.

"Yes, it is! You just get going and don't argue."

There was no alternative; Mary put on her hat and coat and set off. It was a cold day and there was still snow lying under the hedges. As she walked past the cattle in the yard; their breath steamed in the cold air as they stood chewing the hay out of the rack. Along the ridge towards Dean the path was dry and the grass short, and the crows rose up out of the trees as she passed, cawing noisily before circling back again to roost. The wind in her face stung her cheeks and the grey sky made it a very dark and dreary day. When she reached the bridleway down into the village there was a lot of mud from where carts had been up and down, and where the cattle had been driven. She picked her way down the side, sometimes leaping to the middle of the path to find a dry spot and avoid getting her boots too dirty. Eventually she reached the village street and made her way up past the church and towards the chapel. In the distance she could see Walter pushing John Watson-Foster in his wheelchair with Verity walking alongside. Mary had not seen Verity since the summer and sped up to meet the trio.

"Ah ha!" said John. "The lovely Miss Knighton – what a picture! Doesn't she look lovely? How are you, my dear?"

"Very well thank you, sir," smiled Mary.

"I've heard all about you from my old friend Allibone, what! Doesn't she look a picture, Verity?"

"Yes, Father," said Verity earnestly, "Mary's the prettiest girl I know."

Mary blushed and smiled at her friend.

"Going to chapel, Mary?" said John.

"Yes, sir. We're going to chapel at three o'clock and then we are going to William's for tea."

"How is William, Mary?" said Verity. "He's such a clever boy."

"Why don't you come to tea and find out? I'm sure Aunt Charlotte won't mind."

"Well, I don't know; we are expecting my aunt to arrive after we have come back from our walk."

"Verity you go if you want to," insisted John, "that is if Mrs Dunmore agrees."

He turned to Mary.

"Now, my dear, you ask your aunt if that is all right and come to our door after chapel and we will see how the land lies then."

"Very well, sir," said Mary, grinning at Verity.

"Come on, Walter – push! We've got to get round the block."

He lifted his hat and the three of them moved on.

Mary hurried on to the chapel, arriving at the same time as the trap bearing the rest of her family. As they passed her to tie up the trap, Lucy stuck her tongue out and Henry flicked the long whip at her.

"You beast, Henry, don't do that, it hurts!" exclaimed Mary.

"Stop that, Henry, just grow up, can't you," said John, looking nervously around at the assembling chapelgoers who had turned to see where the noise was coming from.

"Yes, Father," said Henry, laughing at the angry expression on his sister's face, and steering the horse towards the stables at the back of the pub, from where they would walk the last hundred yards.

As they rounded the corner from the stables, a great crowd greeted them, all shouting and staring up at the chimney of the chapel, from where a huge plume of smoke, laced with sharp red sparks, shot straight up into the grey sky and intermittently across the road towards The Hall. The air hung with the smell of burning soot and wood.

Lucy ran straight up to William, who was standing watching with his parents.

"William, William, what's happening? What's all the smoke from? The smell is awful!"

"Someone left the bottom of the stove open after they filled it up and it's overheated the chimney – look through there, you can see it."

Lucy stood on tiptoe, and through the open door she caught sight of the chimney, glowing red as far up as Lucy could see. Inside the chapel she could make out Art Tuffnail and Willy Lowe looking from the stove to the chimney, deep in earnest conversation. Art moved to the door to confer with Reverend Packham, who was hopping from foot to foot, deep concern lining his brow.

"I think that the chimney might be in danger of setting the roof timbers alight," said Art worriedly. "We can't put the fire out – it might explode if we put water on it, it's just got to burn itself out now I'm afraid, Reverend."

"I knew it, I knew it," the Reverend Packham lamented. "It's retribution on all of us dreadful sinners. It's a message from God."

"I don't know how to put them timbers out," said Art, ignoring the dramatics of the Reverend. "We can't get a ladder up on the inside; how do we get water up there on the outside? I'm afraid it's going to burn."

"What's up, then? Why's everyone out here?" exclaimed Henry, rushing up beside William and tipping his cousin's cap down over his eyes. William righted his cap with a sigh and explained what was going on.

"It's going to go up," insisted Art. "There's nothing we can do; we can't get up there."

"Yes we can," insisted Henry. "We can do it from the outside."

"How do you reckon we're goin' to do that, then?" Art said doubtfully.

"Put a couple of ladders up and take the tiles off. We can get at the fire with buckets of water, it will work if we're quick, Art, I promise."

"You're right, boy," nodded Art. "Well done, quick – now – where's the nearest ladders? It's goin' to be difficult to get the second ladder up, the roof is so high."

"We can throw a rope right over the top and pull it up," said Henry.

"Good idea, boy. Right; you go and get the ladders from Milligan's Barn, I know there's two or three there and someone go and get the long rope from the forge. Even better – get two, we'll have to throw a light one over first."

"I'll go," shouted Mary and William together, hurtling off in the direction of the forge.

"Bring a shackle as well, William," yelled Art, "to put on the end of the rope."

The forge was about three hundred yards away and Mary – a faster runner than William – got there first. She could see ropes hanging in great loops from a nail on the wall and grabbed the first one she came to before looking round for a shackle.

"What's a shackle, William?" she said, looking desperately at the objects hung about the wall. "He said bring a shackle; I don't know what one is."

"Here we are," said William, locating the device on another nail on the wall and turning to his cousin, "here you go, Mary; take the shackle and this light rope and I will bring the heavy one."

Mary took the rope off her cousin, hoisted it over her shoulder, hitched up her skirt with one hand and with the shackle in the other ran back as fast as she could.

"Good girl," said Art as she sprinted back towards him. "Give it 'ere."

He took the rope off Mary and tied the shackle to it, just as Henry and Willy Lowe were spotted running up the road with a long rick ladder, followed by two other young members of the congregation with a shorter one.

"We're going to have to go in the garden of The Manse, Reverend," shouted Henry.

"Oh, do as you think fit," muttered the Reverend, mopping anxiously at his brow with a dirty white handkerchief. "I am completely overcome."

He sank dramatically to his knees, his handkerchief clutched to his brow.

Henry, ignoring this, made his way into the garden of The Manse. Willy Lowe stood on the bottom of the ladder in the grounds of the chapel, his back to the chimney, which was still spewing out sparks and smoke, although not in such great quantities. Art was the other side of the building with the lighter rope, trying to throw it over the top of the chapel without a lot of success; the coils of rope had become tangled and would not pay out as he threw the shackle up towards the height of the roof.

"Let's put the coils over my arm, it should pay out then," said William.

Art nodded and started to coil the rope over William's arm. William stood back, swung the shackle backwards and forwards two or three times and threw the line as hard as he could. The shackle scudded its way into the air, just making it over the apex of the roof, from where William was able to flick at the end of the rope and send the shackle gradually down the other side to Henry, who was now up the bigger ladder, waiting at the eave. Henry grabbed the end of the small rope and climbed back to the ground, where he tied one end of the heavier rope to the end of the light rope, and the other to the small ladder. It was agreed that Art would pull the rope from the other side of the chapel to hoist the small ladder and Henry would help guide it into place from the bigger ladder, while Willy Lowe footed it. Art rushed back to the other side of the chapel and the ladder started to make its way up the roof – halfway up, the rope caught on the top of the bigger ladder, which started to wobble perilously. Art continued to tug on the rope, unaware of the snag the other side, and Henry's ladder shook violently.

"Stop!" yelled Henry.

"Stop!"

"Stop!"

"Stop, Art!" the shouts echoed round the building.

Art stopped; everyone was quiet. Henry's ladder stood five foot proud of the eave of the building, and the rope had become hooked over the top of it.

"Can you hear me, Art?" Henry shouted over the roof.

"Yes."

"Let the rope back a bit, could you?" hollered Henry.

The rope slackened, and Henry shook at it vigorously, trying to free it from the top of the ladder – there was no way it was going to budge.

"Hang on!" shouted Henry. "I'll have to climb up and lift it over."

Henry made his way slowly up the ladder – ten rungs up he looked back at William.

"Don't you dare move, William; get someone else – someone heavy – to stand with you on the bottom rung."

"I will, I will, I'm heavy!" squeaked Miss Poynter, rushing to fulfil her duty as ballast and squashing William uncomfortably to the ladder at the same time. Henry proceeded on upwards well above the level of the eave until he was high enough to lift the rope over the end. The smaller ladder was heavy, and Henry, from his precarious position, could not hold the weight of it on the rope –the rope pulled out of his hand, sending the second ladder sliding back down the roof. The rope jerked suddenly at Art's hand as the crowd gasped; Art grimaced but didn't let go. The smaller ladder dangled threateningly over the eave.

"Hang on a minute, Art," shouted Henry, "while I get into position."

He climbed down to eave level.

"Right, pull, Art, until I say," ordered Henry, easing the ladder up the roof.

"Woo up, let it back a foot, Art; we're there," yelled Henry, readjusting the position of the small ladder and securing both ladders together with an increasing sense of urgency. Smoke had started to seep gently between the roof tiles and Henry could feel the heat of the fire beating against the tiles under him.

"Good Lord, Mary, what on earth is going on; what's happening?" cried Verity, running up to her friend, who was staring nervously up at the roof.

"What's happening, who's that on the roof?"

"It's Henry," said Mary, not taking her eyes off her brother. "He's trying to put the fire out."

"Art?" hollered Henry. "We're going to need some water; get someone to get some buckets and go to the well at the back of The Manse."

Art turned swiftly to some of the small children who were gaping up at the activity on the roof.

"Well you heard the man, boys – you go and grab yourself a bucket each – quick as you can and fill it up from the well."

Delighted to be involved in the dramatic scenes, three of the boys scuttled off as fast as they could, one of them nearly tripping up over Reverend Packham who was kneeling on the ground with his hands clasped together, an expression of abject misery lining his face as he prayed for his beloved chapel.

A few minutes later the boys were back, buckets slopping water, as they sought to be the first person back to Henry, who had climbed down and was waiting for the buckets. With the first in his hand, he made his way slowly up the ladder; the iron chimney pipe was now nearly red hot, the lead flashing had already melted away and the tiles were almost too hot to touch. Fortunately for Henry they were pan tiles; held on to the laths by a nib, not nails, so they would come off easily. He lifted a tile far enough away from the heat of the flue to be able to handle and turned to throw it on the ground below

"Heads!" he yelled, throwing the tile as far as he could away from the mob below him.

Smoke gushed out of the newly made hole, directly into his face, stinging his eyes and making him splutter.

"Tell them to shut all the doors of the chapel to stop the draught," he shouted, covering his eyes with his arm and turning away from the plume of smoke. Lucy rushed to pull both doors of the chapel shut, running round the back to shut the door linking the school house to the chapel. The draught cut off, the smoke began to thin and Henry could see again; he continued to peel away the tiles. He could see that some of the timbers had started to burn around the chimney pipe but he had not removed enough tiles yet to expose all the fire. The closer that he moved to the chimney the hotter the tiles became; he searched his pockets for something to handle the red hot pieces of ceramic with, deciding in the end to use his cloth cap as a glove.

The crowd had swollen by now – curious faces turned towards the activity of Henry on the roof. Reverend Packham continued to pray but he was the only one; even Miss Poynter could not tear herself away from watching Henry fight the fire.

"Is it going to burn, Dunmore?" John Watson-Foster mused, turning to Thomas. "What do you think?"

"Well, if he can get a few more tiles off and put some water on the timbers it won't," said Thomas.

"He looks mighty precarious up there; I wouldn't want to do that even if I could," John continued, "he's a good boy that nephew of yours, Dunmore, he's got some guts – I'll give him that."

"Let's have some more water, then," shouted Henry. "William Dunmore, is that you down there?"

"Yes, Henry."

"Art, get William to bring the buckets up to Willy Lowe and he can pass them to me," instructed Henry, taking hold of the bucket he'd brought up the ladder and aiming it towards the hole he had made in the roof around the chimney. Flames had started to lick the beams and as Henry threw the bucket of water towards the flue it hissed angrily and the flames ebbed for a few minutes. Henry turned to collect his next bucket – Willy had made his way gingerly to the top of the ladder and was clinging desperately to the top rung, his knuckles white on the handle of the bucket.

"Pass it here then, Willy," said Henry, stretching his hand out for the bucket. But Willy, his eyes fixed straight ahead, couldn't bring himself to extend his arm to Henry; who was forced to crawl towards him and prise the bucket from his shaking hand.

"Maybe get someone else to bring up the next one," suggested Henry kindly. Willy swallowed hard and nodded, before making his way slowly back down the ladder.

"Are you all right?" Art yelled up to Henry. "Is it working at all?"

"Yup, I'm fine, just get us some more water, can you, and quick."

"Your cousin William is just on the way with another," yelled Art, as William appeared grinning, a full bucket in his hand.

"How many more, Henry?" he asked, handing over the bucket and making his way down again.

"I'd say three to be safe, William; she's not burning anymore but better to be safe than sorry."

Three buckets later, Henry made his way down the ladder to rapturous applause.

"That was a close run thing, Dunmore," said John, clapping Henry's return with the rest of the crowd.

"Yes, we were lucky not to have the whole thing go up in smoke," agreed Thomas, watching the crowd in front of him milling about discussing the event.

The doors of the chapel were opened and Art Tuffnail and a few others went in to examine the damage. The tortoise stove had ceased to glow; it stood benign and stoic, as if nothing had happened at all. Water dripped off the pews onto the floor, where lath and plaster lay scattered about the aisle. The roof timbers were blackened but not burnt through and the hole in the roof exposed the hard grey sky above.

"Did you see Henry, Uncle Thomas?" cried Mary, rushing up to her uncle. "Don't you think he was brave?"

"Yes he was, he was very brave," said Charlotte, butting in, "thank the Lord."

"Aunt Charlotte, I've got something to ask," said Mary hurriedly.

"Yes, dear, and what's that?"

"Would it be all right if Verity came for tea tonight to the butcher's shop?"

"Well yes, dear," said Charlotte, somewhat taken aback. "Are you sure she *wants* to come and will she be allowed?"

She turned expectantly to John Watson-Foster in his wheelchair beside her.

"My dear Mrs Dunmore, I know Verity wants to come and I am very happy for her to do so," insisted John, smiling.

"Yes, well that's fine then. We will leave Henry in charge."

"Ah yes," smiled John. "The hero of the hour. Now, Mary, just run and fetch that brother of yours. I would like to congratulate him."

Mary made to leave.

"Oh, and Mary," continued John, "if you see Walter tell him to come and help me. Verity is not strong enough to push me home."

Chapter Fourteen
Misbehaving

"What have you been doing, Master William?" scolded Sarah, as the young ones all trooped home from the chapel "Getting so filthy and all, and you, Master Henry, are even worse! All that black! Where did it come from?"

"Don't chide Henry now, Sarah," grinned Mary. "He's a local hero."

And the lot of them fell to filling in Sarah about the events of the afternoon.

"Well I never, whoever 'eard of such a thing!" exclaimed Sarah. "Well, come and get yourselves clean in the scullery and I'll get some hot water, the kettle is on."

In the kitchen the tea – sandwiches, pies and cakes – was laid out on the table, and the kettle chattered on the range where the fire glowed crimson between the bars. Sarah brought the kettle to where the boys were washing in the sink and poured it into the bowl, before refilling it and taking it back to the range.

"Miss Mary, would you like to come into the sitting room?" asked Sarah. "I'm sure Mrs Dunmore would want you in there, the fire is lit and it's nice and warm."

"Thank you, Sarah, that'd be lovely," said Mary, following Sarah through into the room beyond the kitchen and taking a seat beside Verity.

"I'll get some tea for you all but Mrs Dunmore said not to 'ave the food until she comes back," said Sarah, turning to leave the room.

"Shall we have a game of whist?" said William, walking into the room followed by Henry, both looking a lot less sooty than before.

"Do we have to?" complained Mary. "I'm no good at whist."

"Yes, good idea," said Henry to his cousin. "Don't take any notice of Mary, she can't have her own way all the time. Do you like playing whist, Verity?"

"Yes," smiled Verity. "It's a good game."

"Yes," said Lucy, moving to the sideboard to get a deck of cards. "It is a good game; and anyway, you only need four people for whist so, Mary, you don't have to play after all."

She stuck her tongue out at her sister and moved with the others to the table in the middle of the room. A lamp with a dark red glass shade threw light down onto the cards where they played and the shade glowed red like the stove pipe in the chapel.

Sarah moved into the room to sit and watch the game of cards. It wasn't long before William and Henry started to beat the girls; Verity, naturally competitive, was trying hard to be sporting about it, and was staring at her cards with grim determination.

"Aren't you bored with this game, Verity? I would be," said Mary from the armchair she was sitting in.

"No, it's a good game," insisted Verity, looking up from her cards to smile at her friend.

"Aren't you bored, William?"

"No, Mary, are you bored?"

"Yes, William. I am."

There was silence as the four card players concentrated on their hands.

"Can anyone guess what I've got?" said Mary loudly.

"No, Mary, I can't," said Verity, aware that none of the other card players were going to acknowledge her friend.

"Lucy?" said Mary.

"No, Mary, just keep quiet, won't you; I'm trying to concentrate."

"William? Henry?" she enquired again.

"No," sighed Henry. "I have no idea; but I'm sure you're going to tell us."

"Go on, Miss Mary; what have you got?" said Sarah eagerly.

"Well this is what I've got," declared Mary triumphantly, pulling a packet of cigarettes from the pocket of her skirt and waving them above her head.

"Mary! Where did you get those?" scolded Lucy, turning from her cards to reprimand her sister. "You know Mother doesn't approve, she would have a fit if she knew."

"Well she doesn't know, does she?"

"But where did you get them?"

"I got them from Mr Peveril."

"You mean Mr Tibbitt?"

"Yes."

"And what's he doing giving you cigarettes?"

"Well, I was in his office with the stock lists and I was watching him smoke; he draws the smoke out of his mouth and up his nose," she laughed. "It's fascinating."

"Sounds revolting to me," said Verity under her breath.

"Well, what's that got to do with him giving you a packet of cigarettes?" said Lucy.

"Well, he noticed me looking at the way he smoked and he said, 'what are you looking at?' and I said, 'nothing' and he said, 'Do you smoke, Mary?' and I said, 'No,' and he said ,'Quite right, don't start,' and he said, 'Here you are, have one of these and it will make you very sick and then you will never start,' and then he gave me this packet."

"Does it make you sick?" asked William curiously.

"No," said Mary in a very superior tone. "They don't make me sick and I have been practising how he blows out smoke and I can do it."

"Do what?" said Lucy.

"I can take a puff and draw the smoke from my mouth up my nose."

"I bet you can't," said Henry.

"I bet I can."

"Well, show us then!"

"I will," Mary said contemptuously.

"You can't smoke in here, Miss Mary, Mrs Dunmore won't like it," said Sarah quietly.

"Oh don't worry, Sarah, she'll never know," said Mary, pushing up the bottom of the packet with her thumb, "the smell will have gone by the time they are back."

She looked around the room.

"Anyone want one?"

Everyone shook their heads.

"Not even you, Henry?" asked Mary, surprised.

Henry looked a bit sheepish.

"I did try them once but it made me awfully sick like your Mr Tibbitt said, and I vowed never to have another one."

"Suit yourself," shrugged Mary, taking a cigarette between her fingers.

"I haven't got a light," she complained, looking around the room.

"There's some matches in the kitchen, shall I get them?" asked Sarah.

"No, I'll light it like Mr Peveril does sometimes. Come on, move those cards, William."

"Why do I have to move the cards?" he asked.

"Just move them and I'll show you," laughed Mary.

William picked up the pack, grumbling all the while.

"You're not really going to light it are you?" said Verity disapprovingly.

"Yes, I am – just you see."

Mary climbed onto a chair and stepped onto the table, which was covered with a thick brown cloth, making sure to duck a little to stop her head brushing the ceiling. She lowered herself gracefully – her arms outstretched and the cigarette in her right hand – until she was sitting cross-legged in front of the lamp; the light reflecting on the sequins sewn round the bottom of her skirt.

"How are you going to light it then?" asked Lucy, sniffing.

"Don't be so impatient, Lucy, and don't sniff like that, you get on my nerves."

She scowled at her sister and moved herself a little nearer the lamp, placing the cigarette delicately between her lips. She stretched both arms backward with her fingers spread and leant her torso slowly towards the lamp. As she bent forwards, the light of the lamp illuminated her face from below giving her an enchanted appearance; her eyes sparkled and her hair shone. She pursed her lips, sucking in on the cigarette as it came to an inch above the glass chimney of the lamp. The others all watched as the end of the cigarette began to glow. Mary pulled back, her face falling into shadow as she took the cigarette from her lips and blew out a thin blue stream of smoke.

"There," she said, "now watch, this is how Mr Peveril does it."

She put the cigarette in her mouth and took a deep draw. Her cheeks dimpled as she removed the cigarette, opened her mouth a little and jutted her jaw out, breathing in through her nose. The smoke rose from her mouth and slowly was drawn up her nostrils. Unable to contain herself any longer; she started to giggle, coughing the last of the smoke out of her mouth.

Everybody laughed.

"Do it again, Miss Mary," begged Sarah.

Mary smiled, wriggled back from the lamp a little and took another drag before repeating the performance.

"I think that's disgusting," said Lucy and sniffed.

"You would, wouldn't you, goody-goody," Mary snapped.

"I'm sure I couldn't do that," said Verity. "But it looked very sophisticated, don't you think so, William?"

"Suppose so," said William, unconvinced.

Verity looked up at her friend – full of sparkle and determination. She did not approve of smoking but her father did it so she accepted it; she wished that she could be as daring as Mary – she was unlike anyone else Verity knew.

"Miss Mary," said Sarah, "watch out you don't put the ash on the tablecloth. Mrs Dunmore will see it and you will be in trouble for sure."

"Thank you, Sarah," said Mary, jumping off the table to flick her ash into the fire.

"You better hurry up and finish that," said Lucy. "They will be back from tea with the Reverend soon."

"No, they won't," said Mary. "They will be saying what a hero our dear brother Henry is and how he saved the chapel from being burnt down."

"Well, Henry was a hero," interjected Verity, "I saw it as well as everyone else. I thought he was magnificent and he did save the chapel. Who was it that left the stove open in the first place, did anyone say?"

"I didn't hear," said William.

"Anyway, it was much more exciting than a boring old sermon from Reverend Packham," said Mary scathingly. "Did you see him kneeling down praying? He would have done a lot more good if he had helped carry the water."

"You shouldn't say that," said William sharply.

"No, you shouldn't," said Lucy. "He's a nice man. I bet you don't even say your prayers when you are at Aunt Sarah's."

"Yes I do actually, so there. All I'm saying is that his sermons go on forever and all he talks about is sin, sin and more sin. I think it's boring."

"Does he say that smoking's a sin?" chipped in Verity as Mary took another puff of her cigarette.

"Well said, Verity," laughed Henry, pointing at his sister.

"Well, he said going to see girls is a sin, Henry Knighton," chided Mary. "And that's what you do!"

"Who said I do?"

"Don't look so innocent, Henry, I know you go down to see Martha at Dean House; you've been twice this week, Lucy told me."

"What if I did? He didn't say visiting people was a sin."

"He said fornication's a sin," said Lucy thoughtfully, before turning to her sister. "What's fornication then, Mary?"

"I don't know, do you know, Henry?"

"No."

"Do you know, William? You know everything now you go to the grammar school."

"No."

"Verity, you must know what it is."

"No I don't," said Verity. "Our vicar said it was a sin so I asked Dorcas about it and she went all red and said it wasn't a thing that nice young girls should know about and that was that."

"Well, whatever it is we shouldn't do it," said Mary determinedly.

There was a noise of hooves and people chattering on the road outside.

"They're back! Quick, Mary, put that on the fire," said William. "Put the cards round the table again, come on, quickly before they come. Sarah put the kettle on ready."

"It is on, Master William. I'll go and open the door for them and take their coats."

There was a long pause as they listened to the adults get out of the trap and move into the house. William heard his mother move towards the sitting room just as he noticed that Mary had left the packet of cigarettes on the table; he snatched them up and thrust them into his jacket pocket.

"Hello, everyone, and hello, Verity, it's very nice to see you here," said Charlotte with much enthusiasm as she bustled into the drawing room, up to the table where they were sitting.

She stopped, and sniffed once, tipping her head back and sniffed again.

"Who's been smoking? I can smell smoke. What are you all looking so guilty about?"

"Oh, it was Mr Muskett, Mrs Dunmore," said Sarah from the door, "he called in on his way past while I was lighting the fire in here and he was smoking. He wants Mr Dunmore to go over and kill his pig sometime this week if that's all right."

"Well I suppose that's it," said Charlotte rushing out to supervise the preparation of the tea, "But next time do ask him to smoke outdoors, Sarah, it really is a most revolting habit."

Chapter Fifteen
Lizzie

Winter turned into spring; spring to early summer. The roof of the chapel had been mended and services had started again, much to the disappointment of the younger members of the congregation. The spring barley had been drilled, thrusting small shoots of green above the brown of the fields and the beans would soon be in flower. The ploughing engines of Percy Blinkhorn had returned and were moving slowly from one farm to the other, cultivating the fallow land. Roland Cumber was in charge of the gang again. He was a man that very few people liked – a bully and a thief – a reputation that he cared very little about. He bullied all the men in his gang, especially Bernard who came in for the most punishment. Every night Roland would go to the nearest pub, or if it was too far, he would send Bernard to fetch in the beer in a big stone jar. The publicans detested him – he would swagger into the pub, get drunk and normally end the evening by touching up any girl that wasn't quick enough to get away from him.

It was around this time, that Dorcas invited her brother and his wife to stay for a week; Edwin hadn't been back to Dean for some years – most of Dorcas' family had moved away years ago. Mr Watson-Foster was away much of the time and as Verity was still away at school there was plenty of time for her to entertain her brother. The first night after they arrived in Dean; Lizzie and Edwin decided to walk to the Marquis of Bute and have a drink. There was a bench outside the pub from where you could sit and watch the world go by, and Lizzie sat herself here, enjoying the evening sunshine, whilst Edwin went in to get the drinks. Inside the pub it was dark – the windows were small and the curtains half closed – allowing the late day sun only enough access to stutter about the tiled floor and half way up the opposite wall. The fireplace on the right-hand wall still bore the remains of ash and burnt-out coals and on the mantelpiece stood a broken clock smothered in dust; above it a faded picture of Queen Victoria in a gilt frame stared gloomily down, her face dotted with thunder flies from previous summers. A stained door in the left-hand corner led to the scullery and a scuffed wooden bench lined the other three walls, the green distemper back rubbed clean where the bodies of thirsty men had leant against the wall. The ceiling had started off white, but after many years it had dulled to a brownish yellow from ingrained tobacco smoke. A single oil lamp with a white glass shade and chimney hung from the beam in the middle of the room, throwing its meagre light tentatively about the darkened room. The floor was tiled with red brick, a path worn down from the door to the bar by the years of hobnail boots traipsing across it. A potent mixture of odours hung in the air; the bitter tang of tobacco laced with the stench of cow muck and unwashed bodies.

A black and white mongrel – its head lying across outstretched front legs – lazily opened its eyes as Edwin came in and followed his progress to the bar. In the big chair next to the fire sat Roland Cumber, a pewter mug in his hand and cigarette in his mouth. He had not shaved for some days; his hair and whiskers were long, sticking out from under his greasy hat. On the bench opposite the door sat the other engine driver and two ploughmen – Joe, and Ron and Jeff. Minnie Chettle, the wife of the landlord, stood by the door to the scullery, rubbing an old tea towel round the rims of the dusty glasses – her daughter Sally on the bench beside her, legs swinging backwards and forwards showing her dirty bare feet. On the bench by the window sat Art Tuffnail and Martin Schole, chatting to Oswald Chettle the landlord, who leant against the wall surveying the customers.

A hush fell as Edwin walked in – his waistcoat and bowler hat starkly marking him out as an outsider in the musty room.

"What do you want then?" Oswald sneered, moving slowly towards the bar.

"I'll have a pint of beer and a tot of rum if you please, landlord," said Edwin merrily, trying to break the aggressive look on Oswald's face.

"We don't sell rum; only beer in 'ere," growled Oswald.

"A pint and a half then thank you, landlord," he replied, as Oswald scowled and moved to behind the bar without another word.

"The beer ain't no good, you know that don't you?" piped up Roland, leaning forward and pointing at Edwin.

"Well, we'll try it and see how we like it," said Edwin, shifting his weight from foot to foot uncomfortably.

"You ain't from round 'ere are you?" Roland enquired.

"Used to be, I used to be! I was born here, I'm Dorcas's brother."

"Are you now!" said Roland, markedly lacking any interest.

"Yes, we keep a pub in Northampton now and are here for a week's holiday."

"Well I never," said Roland, with a sneer to his companions.

"I remember you!" said Art, with a vigorous nod of his head. "Yes I remember you! Cor, it's been years, you ain't 'arf changed. It's Edwin, ain't it? You used to be in the same 'ouse as Dorcas is in now."

"Yes, that's where I was born," said Edwin enthusiastically as Oswald moved over with his beer.

"Nother pint, landlord," ordered Roland, irritated to have been cut out of a conversation he had initiated, "but we'll 'ave it from a new barrel; I'm not drinking any more of that muck."

"What do you mean? This beer's good, I ain't openin' a new one and you ain't paid for what you've 'ad anyway," complained Oswald.

"I ain't paid 'cos no one's paid me and until they do I can't pay you; so put it on the slate and open a new barrel."

"No!" said Oswald, the quaver in his voice belying his confidence.

Roland leant forward and pointed at him aggressively.

"Now look 'ere," Roland growled, "you do what I say or I'll fetch you one."

"Oh, do as he says, Oswald," said Minnie. "It ain't worth arguing with 'im; he always causes trouble when he comes in 'ere."

"What am I going' to do with the rest of the beer, then?" insisted Oswald.

"The others'll drink it and that trouble maker'll be gawn by the end of next week," said Minnie, scowling at Roland.

"You keep your mouth shut, you old hag, I'll smack you one if you don't shut up," snarled Roland, making to rise from the bench.

"Sit down, Roland," said Art authoritatively, raising his huge frame from his seat and staring angrily at the engine driver. Roland shrugged and sat down, as Edwin scuttled – beers in hand – from the room, bowing comically at Oswald on his way out.

"I'm goin'," snapped Minnie, throwing her tea towel to the bar. "I'm not sittin' 'ere with the likes of 'im."

And with a glare at Roland she slammed out the scullery door.

"Who's for a game of crib, then?" said Roland looking round to the others with a smile on his face.

"I ain't playing you, Roland, you all'as wins," grumbled Art, turning back to his beer. There was a murmur of consent in the room.

"I wonder if that bloke outside wants a game, I could beat 'im, couldn't I; what's 'is name, Art?"

"'is name's Edwin," said Art, as Roland moved out of the door of the pub.

"Well, well, what 'ave we 'ere; this must be Mrs Edwin," said Roland with a disingenuous smile as he presented himself in front of Edwin and Lizzie outside. Lizzie was wearing her Sunday clothes and a black straw hat; she looked very smart and, to Roland, more inviting than the other women of Dean. Roland made a low whistle and lifted his cap.

"Pleased to meet you," Lizzie said quietly, turning herself away from the persistent gaze of the man in front of her.

"I come to see if you'd like a game of crib," Roland asked with a leer.

"Yes, I'll give you a game," shrugged Edwin.

"What about you then, Mrs?" Roland said, his eyes roaming over Lizzie.

"No, I don't play."

"Well come inside and watch."

"No! I spend my life in pubs and I'm on holiday."

"Go on, then," Roland laughed, "only one game."

"No," said Lizzie, "I'm going back to chat with Dorcas, Edwin; you have a game if you wish."

She rose and left. Edwin shrugged and followed Roland into the pub.

"Where's that card table, landlord?" boomed Roland. "Let's 'ave it quick as you like; draw up that other chair, Edwin, bring the cards and the crib board, Oswald."

They sat as Oswald placed the rickety card table between them.

Edwin was good at crib and it wasn't long before the matchsticks were piled

168

heavily in his favour. The more the game wore on, the more the beer started to take a toll on Roland's playing ability and an hour and a half later he was beaten.

"Do you want another game?" asked Edwin with a smile.

"No I don't," growled Roland, throwing his cards down on the table.

A snigger rippled round the room.

"Come on, you lot, we're going," said Roland, downing the last of his pint and stomping out the room. The rest of his gang hurriedly finished their drinks and rushed out behind him.

Edwin rose from the table and smiled at Oswald.

"Thanks very much, landlord, I'd best be going."

"No thank *you*," said Oswald, breaking a smile for the first time that afternoon. "It's about time someone showed that bugger up; he won't be back for a while. The next pint's on the house when you come through."

Three days later the ploughing gang had moved to the other side of the village to one of the biggest fields in the parish and were ploughing for Mr Milligan. Roland was sitting on his engine at the top of the field and at times was out of sight of the other engine which sat at the bottom by the road. George and Reuben as usual were glued to the scene and stood at the bottom of the field talking to Joe. They could just see the top of the funnel of Roland's engine and any communication between the two drivers was carried out by coded blasts on the whistle. The plough had made its way down to within a foot of Joe's engine boiler – Ron and Jeff then leapt off, grabbed the mould boards at the end of the plough and Joe gave two blasts on the whistle. This was the signal for Roland to engage the drum under his engine and the rope then started to make its way back up the field. When the slack had been taken up the plough started to move; Ron and Jeff – assisted by the two boys – pulled the plough down and as the shears touched the ground they began to sink into the earth, turning the soil over as they did so. Ron jumped onto the seat – a wooden board with a sack wound round it – and grabbed the steering wheel of the plough. Jeff sat on the very back of the plough, his weight securing it in the ground, as the plough made back across the field.

The day was hot and the sun high in the sky; the men had taken their waistcoats off as well as their jackets. As the plough went up the field, flocks of crows, jackdaws, rooks, plovers and starlings screamed above it – fighting for the worms and grubs that the plough turned up as it went up the field. Once the plough had moved away from the engines, the only sound that could be heard was the scraping of the odd stone against the mould boards and the occasional bump as they hit bigger ones. Ron kept the furrow as straight as possible as they went up the field; Jeff sometimes walked beside the machine, or sat on the back and pushed the trash through the plough when it became blocked. There was no whistle on the plough so the only way of communicating a problem was by waving. Jeff had a catty and a handful of stones in his pocket, which every so often he would extract and aim at one of the wheeling birds following the plough. If he shot enough rooks they could have rook pie, which everyone liked; but they would have to find someone other than Bernard to cook it – pastry was beyond his culinary capabilities.

At the bottom of the field against the road the boys were helping fill the coal bunker; the living-van parked next to them.

"What 'ave we got for dinner then, Bernard?" asked Joe. "You been gone a long while."

"We've got a bit a pork belly I'm just got from ol' Thomas at the butcher's shop and I'm bin up the baker's and got some nice new bread."

"That'll never be cooked, me old mate," said Joe. "You've only just lit the fire; I can see by the smoke."

"What's the time then, Joe?" asked Bernard; he didn't have a watch and couldn't have read the time even if he had had one. Joe pulled his watch from the pocket of his waistcoat hanging on the side of the coal bunker and offered it to George.

"What's the time, boy?"

"Half past eleven, Joe," said George.

"We've got plenty of time then; that'll be cooked by one o'clock dinner time, sure it will," assured Bernard, bustling back towards the living-van.

He waved at Edwin and Lizzie, who were headed in the other direction, taking a walk.

"Mornin', Edwin, mornin', Lizzie," shouted Joe, "Are you going to beat Roland at crib again tonight?"

"No he ain't," said Lizzie, "He's keepin' out the way of that Roland. He ain't no good; I can feel it in my bones."

"Where are you off to all dressed up then?"

"We're just takin' the air. I'm showin' Lizzie round where I were brought up and all."

"Well, it's a nice day for it."

"Yup, we're going along to Lower Dean then up the track by the cherry orchard; can we still get up there?"

"Yes," said George. "The muck's all gone now, you can walk up there."

"Very good," smiled Edwin, taking Lizzie's hand and walking on past them.

The plough was now just over halfway up the field and Joe had moved his engine on a little, ready to pull it back again when it reached the top. Suddenly the plough stopped dead; Ron was thrown forward, his face smacked the steering wheel, cutting his lip. Jeff was thrown off the back of the plough and lay sprawled on the ground. The rope had broken ten yards from the plough and snaked angrily up the field; the broken end whipping from side to side before coming to rest on the ground. Roland's engine changed its note immediately; its low "chuff chuff" replaced by a high-pitched rattle until Roland pulled the regulator back and disengaged the winding drum.

"Bugger!" he spat, squeezing his eyes tight shut, throwing his cap onto the footplate and stamping on it. He peered over the side of the engine at the cocking gear to make sure nothing was broken and moved off down the field towards the plough. Joe and the two boys met him in the middle.

"Did we hit summut?"

"No, it just broke," said Ron, holding a hankie to his bleeding lip.

"Come on then, everyone up to the top; you boys can come too – help – pull the rope out."

They moved back to Roland's engine and started to pay out the rope, which got heavier and heavier the further they pulled it.

"That'll be enough," shouted Roland. "Go and get the other end and we'll splice it together."

The two ends of the rope were brought together, but there wasn't going to be enough length to splice the two.

"Damn," said Roland, "not enough slack. Goo on, Joe and let a bit more out. I'll stop 'ere and open out the ends; bring them wire snips back with you, they're in my bag on the engine. Goo on the rest, on you go and help 'im."

Splicing the rope was skilled work; Roland was the only one who could do it well enough to ensure that the join would not snag on the drum as it wound in. He stood up, pulled a packet of cigarettes from his pocket and put one in his mouth. He tapped his pockets again.

"No bloody matches! Who's got a light?" he growled.

Nobody had.

"I'm got some matches in the van," said Bernard, turning and hobbling in that direction.

"Don't you go, you stupid bugger; you'll be all day then you'll forget what you've gone for when you get there. You, boy," he turned to Reuben, "run up to the engine and get the matches out my waistcoat; it hangs on the coal bunker; and don't you touch nothing else, see."

Roland made a start on the rope, whilst Reuben ran to get the matches. He returned panting two minutes later.

"Now, boys, another job fer you. Go down to the pub and fetch me another packet of cigarettes – you'll 'ave to go to The World's End; the one down 'ere don't 'ave 'em. A packet of Capstan Full Strength, can you remember that?"

"Yes, Roland," said George eagerly.

"What about the money?" demanded Reuben.

"Money? I ain't got no money, tell 'em they're for me and I'll pay 'em when I'm paid, all right?"

"Yes, Roland," said Reuben, turning with George and rushing off towards the pub.

Roland continued to splice the rope; after twenty minutes he stood up.

"What's the time, then?"

"It must be about half past twelve; I heard the clock strike on the church a bit back," said Joe.

"What's for dinner, then?" Roland demanded of Bernard, who was standing day dreaming – his eyes slightly closed to avoid the bright sun and a small bubble of spittle oozing from the corner of his mouth.

"Bernard, you silly bugger, what's for dinner?" shouted Roland.

Bernard jumped, wiping the back of his fist one way across his nose, then back over his mouth, smearing saliva over his chin.

"We've got a nice piece of belly pork, Roland, it's in the oven now. We've got some nice fresh bread too, been' as we're near the bakers."

"Right you get back there then and make sure it ain't burnt," ordered Roland. "Joe, I'll pull up to the top and we'll do one more down the field then go and 'ave our dinner, all right?"

"Right you are, Roland," said Joe, walking with Bernard back down the field towards his engine.

As Roland approached, he noticed Edwin and Lizzie standing admiring it.

"Hello, Roland, how are you keeping?" said Edwin with a smile, sensing it was unwise to bring up the crib match.

"Not too bad," said Roland. "And what brings you up 'ere?"

"Oh, just out for a walk showin' Lizzie where I were brought up and all that. We're goin' to watch the plough come up if you don't mind.

"Please yerself," said Roland, eyeing Lizzie up and down as he got on the engine.

"I don't like that man one little bit," murmured Lizzie to Edwin under her breath.

Roland engaged the drum gear, pushing the regulator forward as the piston rods started their progress backwards and forwards. The rope drum began to turn, then the plough appeared over the rise in the ground and made its way slowly towards them.

"I'm going to have a ride down on the plough, Lizzie," said Edwin as the plough neared them. "I ain't done that for years! You walk along here to the bridleway and I'll meet you along the road at the bottom. That all right, Roland?"

"All right, suit yourself," said Roland as Edwin ran and plonked himself on the back of the frame of the plough as it went off down the field. Lizzie stood for a moment watching Edwin and the plough disappearing over the ridge, unaware of the eyes on the back of her dress. Roland watched the plough go, before scanning the headland of the field. He could see for a quarter of a mile – there was not anyone about. From his position up on the engine he could see over the hedge – there was no one that way either; as far as he could see.

Roland leapt off the engine and positioned himself behind the back wheel of the drum, which rattled and wheezed. Lizzie rounded the engine and made to walk along the headland to the bridleway to meet Edwin. As Lizzie drew level with Roland he stepped out and blocked her path.

"Let me get past will you, Roland," she said.

"Not so fast, Lizzie, I thought we may be able to do a bit of business."

He smiled toothily.

"What business is that, then?"

"Well I heard a little whisper of what you get up to in that pub of yours in Northampton and I thought – well, you know—"

He spread his hands out in front of him.

"What business I do in my pub in Northampton is my affair and that's that; so let me past," said Lizzie angrily, making to move past.

"No," said Roland quietly, standing his ground.

"Let me past, I told you or I'll shout," snarled Lizzie.

"Shout all you like, Lizzie," laughed Roland. "There's no one out there to hear; go on, shout."

"Let me past," she shouted, bringing her right hand up hard across his cheek.

Roland, unfazed, looked back at her and laughed.

"We've got a bit of spirit, then, have we?" sneered Roland as Lizzie raised her hand to hit him again. But Roland was quick; with one hand he grabbed her flailing fist, pulled her towards him and held her tight.

"There's nice big tits you've got, my dear; perhaps we should 'ave a look at them. What do you think?"

"Let go of me, you rotten bastard," shouted Lizzie, writhing in Roland's vice-like grip.

"I said we've got a bit of business to do."

"I do business with who I choose and not rotten sods like you; so let me go."

Around the corner of the hedge, Reuben and George were returning with the cigarettes – Roland had not been able to see them over the hedge.

"What was that noise, George? Sounded like a crack," frowned Reuben.

"Don't know," said George, "I can hear the rope drum clanking, but that's all."

They rounded the bend in the hedge; catching sight of Roland with his back to them, Lizzie struggling as he manhandled her.

"What are they doing?" hissed Reuben.

"Don't know; but I don't think we're s'posed to be here," whispered George, drawing back towards the hedgeline where they wouldn't be seen.

"Now, Lizzie," whispered Roland, his breath hot on her face, "I'm goin' to turn you round and you grab one of them spokes of the wheel when I do."

He wrenched her shoulders round – pulling her hands towards the spokes and squashing them to the wheel with his own hands.

"You won't get away with this, you bastard, you wait till Edwin hears," sobbed Lizzie, tears of rage coursing down her cheeks.

"Edwin ain't going' to hear, Lizzie," hissed Roland in her ear, "cos you ain't going to tell him, see."

Lizzie struggled in his grip, trying desperately to escape.

"And don't you dare move or I'll thump you one you'll never forget."

He grabbed her hair as it fell down her neck, knocking her straw hat off and pulling her head back. He reached down and roughly tugged up her skirt.

"You can't afford drawers, then, Lizzie," he laughed. "You're just like us then after all; it's only real ladies that wears drawers and you ain't a lady, are you, Lizzie?"

George and Reuben stood frozen against the hedge.

"What's he doin', George?" whispered Reuben.

"Don't know," trembled George.

"What shall we do; he's hurtin' her, ain't he?"

"Don't know, just keep quiet," implored George.

Lizzie, her hands briefly freed by Roland's hands in her hair, let go of the spoke, trying to turn around.

"Just you put your hands back or you'll be on the floor and that won't do your dress any good, will it," snarled Roland, pushing her back against the wheel.

"Just get on with it, then," she screamed. "You bastard, I'll get my own back one day, you see if I don't."

Roland laughed, undoing his belt and slipping his braces off his shoulders – his trousers fell to the floor, his long shirt falling to just above his knees.

"I know what they're doin'," said Reuben, watching Roland spit on the fingers of his right hand before fumbling around in front of himself and clamping his hands around Lizzie's trembling body.

"So do I," said George. "The old boar does it when we take the sow up to Milligan's. I don't think it's right, Reuben; I think we shoulda done somethin'."

The boys stood indecisively, looking from each other back to the violent scene in front of them. At this moment Roland, who had finished and was reaching for his belt, turned and spotted the boys.

"You little..." he snarled, pulling up his braces and running towards the hedge. Reuben made to sprint away, but George, in his panic turned and tripped over a tree root. Hearing his friend squeal, Reuben turned, giving Roland time to grab his shoulder and throw him to the ground.

"You little sod," he hissed, picking Reuben up by his shirt collar and dragging him back to where George lay. "I'll teach you a lesson."

He wrapped his belt around the fist of his hand and started to rain down blows upon the cowering pair.

"I'll teach you little sods to spy on people," he bellowed, lashing his belt down as hard as he could.

"Don't you hit them poor boys like that, you great brute," screamed Lizzie, grabbing his arms.

Blood had started to run down the boys' faces and arms, although Reuben was shielding his friend as best he could.

The shrill scream of the whistle halted the progress of Roland's arm.

"That'll be dinner," he said with a nasty smile, lowering his belt and glaring at Reuben. "Where are my fags?"

Reuben fumbled in his pocket, pulling out the crumpled packet and handing it over.

"Now, you," he said pointing at the boys, "if you so much as mention one word of this I'll put a knife through your hearts; do you understand?"

He glowered at the shaking boys.

"Do you understand?" he yelled.

"Yes, Roland," said George, tears running down his cheeks.

"Yes, Roland," said Reuben, hatred etched over his young face.

"I'm off then," he said, turning to Lizzie. "Nice to do business with you, missus."

He winked at Lizzie and walked off across the field in the direction of the living-van, doing his belt up as he went.

Chapter Sixteen
Adelaide takes Rebecca Shopping

By the autumn of 1900 Mary had been at Tibbitts for two years, establishing herself as a valuable member of staff. She had worked in all the departments of the big drapery store, but had finally settled into the women's fashion department. Her life had been transformed by the purchase of a bicycle at the end of September. This allowed her to cycle backwards and forwards from Hazelwood to the station every day; and home to Melchbourne every weekend. The first weekend after she had bought it she went to the butcher's shop to show her new purchase off to her cousin.

After the service on Sunday, Mary collected her bag of clean clothes from her mother, which had been stowed in the trap, put it in the basket on her bike and prepared to cycle back to Rushden for work the next day.

"Now, Mary, I have a note for Aunt Sarah," said Ann, handing over a rumpled piece of paper.

"Yes, Mother."

"And, Mary, be sure to send my best wishes to Uncle George."

"Yes, Mother."

"And Mary, do you want to go down the end before you go? I'm sure you could go to The Manse if you want to."

"Mother!" hissed Mary. "Don't ask me that! I told you before."

"Mary, we don't want you going behind the hedge now you're the age you are."

"No, Mother."

"Mary?"

"Yes, Lucy."

"Martha and I are coming to your shop next Friday; Mother says I can have a day off school. Martha wants to have a look for a new pair of shoes; she's seventeen now. Mother says we can go together as it's her day off."

"Only if you promise you won't embarrass me, Lucy, if I'm with a customer. How are you going to get there? You will never walk both ways to

Rushden and back in a day."

"The butler is going to give us a lift in the carriage; he's got to go and fetch Mr Fitz-Allen from the station," shrugged Lucy, before looking at Mary indignantly. "What makes you think we would embarrass you? Well I hope we don't see you at all, so there."

"I didn't mean it like that, you silly girl; but you just can't butt in if I'm busy. And don't sniff like that." Mary swung her leg onto her bicycle, did a figure of eight in the road and waved at her family before heading off in the direction of Rushden.

The evening was sunny, but cool; a breeze from the south-west caught in Mary's hair and made her eyes water. From the chapel she turned towards Yielden, pushing her feet hard into the pedals as the road began to curve upwards. She was determined not to get off, standing up to put more pressure on the pedals to make it to the crest of the hill, where the road levelled out by the The Grape Vine pub. From the top of the hill she could see the ploughing gang's living-van; being Sunday, the men were not at work, but she could see them milling about around the van, making the most of the evening sun. Bernard was walking up the road towards the van carrying a large stone flagon, two fingers looped through the small handle, his other hand supporting the bottom. He was limping as always, his large body swaying from side to side as he tried to take the weight off his bad leg. She could hear him humming to himself as she drew up level with him, and rang her bell. Bernard jumped, took two steps to his right, and swung round, the speed of this movement throwing him off balance, causing him to fall backwards onto the grass verge.

"Cor blimey, you give me a frit; I didn't 'ear you comin', not a sound," gasped Bernard, clutching the flagon to his heaving chest.

"Are you all right?" asked Mary, stepping off the bike and standing astride it.

"Yer, I'm fine," he said. "Didn't spill none of the beer, no 'arm done."

He squinted blearily into the top of the flagon.

"Yer, it's all there, can't spill none or Roland'll want to know where it's gawn. He'll say I drunk it, but I never."

He turned round, rested the flagon on the verge and pushed down hard on it, heaving himself onto his feet. He turned to look at Mary.

"Where you goin?" he asked.

"Just to Rushden."

"Where you come from then?"

"I live at Cold Harbour."

"Oh, we've bin there. Ol' John Knighton, ain't it?"

"Yes, he's my father," nodded Mary. "Sorry I scared you, I had better be getting on if you will excuse me."

She remounted her bike, smiling at Bernard, who touched his cap as she biked on. Approaching the living-van she could see Jeff perched on a barrel, talking to Roland who sat on the bottom step of the van steps, leaning back, his elbows resting on the top step. A cigarette dripped from his mouth as he followed Mary's progress up the road.

"Who's this, Jeff?" he said, not taking his eyes off her.

"Looks like John Knighton's girl, I think," said Jeff, looking up. "We see 'er when we went up threshing last year."

"She looks stuck up to me," said Roland loudly, as Mary approached, eyes to the ground, her face reddening with the effort of passing the men as quickly as she could.

"Yer, she looks stuck up all right," Roland continued at the top of his voice, "tryin' to be summut she ain't with her new bike and posh clothes. She's the sort that thinks her shit don't stink, I know that sort."

Still Roland's eyes remained glued to Mary, who stared straight ahead, trying not to listen; although she knew he meant her to hear. She shivered, feeling the force of his eyes on her back as she rode away from him. The road dropped downhill from here; she could freewheel down into the village and rest her calves, which burned from the exertion of getting away from the hateful Roland Cumber.

Half a mile from the town, she overtook Edwin and Lizzie on their way to the station to catch a train back to Northampton. Edwin carried a small suitcase and they waved as she went past.

"Hey, Miss Mary, your tyre's going flat," Edwin shouted.

"Oh no," said Mary, squeezing the brakes, "and now I'm nearly home!"
"'Ave you got a pump, then?" said Edwin.

Mary nodded, looking back at the tyre which, sure enough, was nearly flat.
"Come on, give it 'ere, I'll pump it up and you hold the bike."

He knelt to affix the pump, the air hissing into the deflated tyre.
"Listen," he said, tipping his head to the side.

A sharp hissing could be heard from the wheel.

"You've got a puncture, Miss Mary; you're gonna have to push it from here or ruin the tyre," said Edwin sagely.

Mary sighed and walked along next to the couple.

"Have you walked all the way from Dean, then?" Mary asked, pushing her bike alongside her.

"No fear!" said Lizzie, "You wouldn't catch me walkin' that far. No, we got a lift as far as the turn back there so it's not far now. Have you cycled all the way?"

"Oh yeah; it's easy on this bike – except I had to pass the ploughing gang, which wasn't very nice."

"You mean that Roland?" said Edwin. "He's a nasty piece of work if there ever was one."

"Don't speak to me about 'im," mumbled Lizzie, lowering her eyes to the ground and tightening her grip on Edwin's arm.

"Why don't they go home on Sundays?" asked Mary.

"I don't expect he's got anywhere to go since he got out of prison. His wife's left 'im and I don't think he's got anywhere to live, or that's what I'm told," said Edwin.

"What's he been in prison for?" Mary asked.

"Well I don't rightly know; my informant didn't go as far as to know about that."

They walked on in amicable silence – Edwin and Lizzie leaving Mary at the station, where she caught the train to Rushden.

The next day Mary walked to the station to get to work. She was now in the ladies' outfitting department; Mrs Stevens was in charge but she would let

Mary deal directly with customers. At half past ten on the dot, Mrs Harding came into the shop, her daughter Rebecca in tow. Mary looked round desperately in the hope she could get someone else to deal with her. Mrs Harding had a fearsome reputation; they would rather she take her business elsewhere, but she was friendly with Mr Tibbitt and thus had preferential treatment.

"Good morning, madam," said Mary politely.

There was no reaction; Mrs Harding did not look up or show any sign that she had heard what Mary had said. The daughter looked at Mary and shrugged, before looking away. She was a pretty girl of about sixteen, wearing a thick military style woollen coat, with no hat. Mrs Harding was slim with a featureless figure; her face was spikey – the lines of her face sharp and her lips pursed into a thin angry gesture. She wore a tight jacket over a high-necked white blouse; a matching long skirt hanging above highly polished ankle-length boots. On her arm she carried a petite crocodile skin bag, in her hand a lightly rolled black umbrella with black lace trim. Round her neck a fox fur hung, the head and front leg hanging forlornly down her front, its tail and back legs draped limply over her shoulder. On her head sat a wide-brimmed dark grey hat circled with a band of leaves and fruit, perched at a slight angle.

She turned and walked up and down the aisles, before sitting down in the chair against the counter.

"Can I be of any assistance, madam?" said Mary timidly.

"*You* can't!" Mrs Harding sneered, "I want to speak to someone who knows what they are talking about. Where's Mrs Stevens?"

"I'll go and fetch her, madam."

"Do you know who to say it is, girl?"

"Yes, madam. Mrs Harding, madam."

"At least you've got that right," sniffed the woman, as Mary hurried off to find Mrs Stevens.

"Please, Mrs Stevens, Mrs Harding wants to see you," said Mary, knocking on the open door of the office, where Mrs Stevens sat at her desk checking a list of inventories. She put her head in her hands, before rolling her eyes up to the ceiling.

"Oh no, God give me strength," she sighed, standing up from her chair.

"Mary – go and tell Mr Peveril she's here, perhaps he will handle her; she's always better when he's about."

Mary hurried off to his office and knocked on the door.

"Enter," boomed Peveril.

Mary tentatively opened the door; Peveril sat in his chair, his feet on the table, dictating a letter to his secretary, who sat opposite him scribbling into a notebook. He was smoking a cigarette in its long silver holder, blowing smoke rings toward the ceiling, trying to skewer each ring with his index finger as it meandered lazily towards the ceiling

"Mary Knighton, what is it, girl? Can't you see I'm busy?"

"Please, sir, Mrs Stevens sent me to tell you Mrs Harding is in the Ladies' Fashion Department," whispered Mary.

"Oh no," groaned Peveril, shutting his eyes and lifting his feet from his desk.

"Is she on her own, Mary?"

"No, sir; she has a young lady with her; I think it must be her daughter, sir."

"I'm going to need a drink. Mary, pour me a glass of port and bring it here," he said, pointing at his sideboard.

Mary moved over to the assortment of decanters and glasses; she had no idea which one held port or which glass she was meant to pour it into.

"In the *decanter,* girl, that tall decanter," snapped Peveril, sensing her hesitation and waving impatiently towards the bottles.

Mary took out the glass stopper, tipping the ruby liquid into the first glass she could find.

"No, no, no, no, no!" shouted Peveril. "Not that glass, you ninny, one of the ones at the back. No, no, not that one; no, nor that, yes, that one! Come along, be quick about it!"

Mary poured out the port, carrying it to her boss on a small silver tray that had stood ready on the table.

"Now, Mary, go and find out what she wants and come back and report; quick now," ordered Peveril, waving Mary out the room at the same time as draining his port.

Mary rushed from the room towards the Ladies' Fashion Department, where Mrs Harding stood in full flow.

"I really don't know what the world is coming to! Aren't I a good customer of this shop?"

"Yes, madam," nodded Mrs Stevens.

"And haven't I been coming here for many years?"

"Yes, madam."

"Well why am I left with a slip of a girl to serve me, eh? What's the meaning of it?"

"I'm sorry, madam, I was busy with stocktaking and did not realise you were on the premises," simpered Mrs Stevens.

"Very well," sniffed Mrs Harding, momentarily mollified. "But make sure it doesn't happen again."

Mrs Stevens smiled stiffly, before clearing her throat and starting again:

"Well, madam, what can we assist you with today?"

"It's not me, it's Rebecca here. She needs a ballgown; we want to have one made so we will need to look at styles and patterns."

"Very good, madam; we have books of the very latest fashions, which we can match with patterns and materials to make a gown. Mary, quickly fetch all the books, will you."

Mary moved to the shelves at the back of the counter, carrying back the necessary books.

"I hope you are up to date with these designs, Mrs Stevens," tutted Mrs Harding. "I really don't want to have to drag myself all the way to London for this. Now come on, Rebecca; show a bit of interest; this is your first ballgown you know."

Mrs Harding snatched the top book from Mary's hand and started to leaf through the designs.

"Where's Mr Peveril?" Mrs Stevens whispered to Mary.

"He said I had to find out what she wanted and report back."

"Go on then; get him down here as soon as possible," hissed Mrs Stevens.

Mary discreetly made her exit, returning to the office and knocking on the door.

"Enter!"

"Please, sir, Mrs Stevens says come as soon as possible, if you please, sir."

"Yes, yes, she always says that when Mrs Harding comes in! But what does the infernal woman want, girl?"

"She's come for a ballgown for the young lady, sir."

"Ah ha, that's not so bad; is this girl's name Rebecca?"

"Yes, sir."

"Go and tell Mrs Stevens I'll be down in five minutes; but let them stew a bit that's what I say, eh!"

"Yes, sir," said Mary uncertainly, closing the door and making her way once again back to the shop.

Mrs Harding was removing a silver cigarette case from her bag; she took one out and tapped it on the counter. She then coaxed it into an ivory cigarette holder, before lighting it with a small silver lighter. She inhaled deeply and blew a stream of smoke towards the ceiling.

"Now what do you think, Rebecca? Can you see anything you like?"

"No I can't! I don't want to go to the stupid ball."

"There's no need to be like that, my girl," Mrs Harding retorted sharply. "There are some very nice gowns in these books and you *are* going to that 'stupid ball'. You may be able to wind your father round your little finger, but you're not going to do the same with me."

"But I'm not old enough to go to balls yet! I can't dance and I hate it," Rebecca moaned, throwing herself down on a chair at the other end of the counter.

"Now look here, my girl; if you don't go to the ball I will ban all your hunting this winter – what do you think of that?"

"You wouldn't!" Rebecca cried. "You couldn't."

"Yes I could, and I will! Your father and I are going to the ball and you are coming with us. Now get looking through these books and when you have found something you like we will choose the material." She turned to Mrs Stevens. "Mrs Stevens, do you have some we can get her to try on to get the size right."

"Yes, Mrs Harding, I'm sure we have."

"And we'll need some shoes and a coat or cape."

"Yes, madam."

"Now, come on, Rebecca, lots of girls would have no choice as to what to wear; at least I have given you that!"

She smiled insincerely at the scowling girl, whose frown deepened.

Peveril Tibbitt emerged from his office with a flourish, his dark hair shining with Brilliantine and brushed as close to his scalp as was possible.

"My dear Mrs Harding – Adelaide! How are you? How wonderful to see you."

He clicked his heels together, glided across the room towards Mrs Harding and grabbed her hand, which he kissed with a low bow before embracing her, bringing their two bodies together with the lightest of touches.

"Darling Peveril," simpered Mrs Harding, "how nice to see you – how well you look and how beautiful you smell."

They laughed.

"Just cologne, my dear, just cologne – to keep me nice and fresh."

He smiled kindly at Rebecca, who was staring moodily at the pair.

"And who do we have here? I don't believe I've had the pleasure," he turned to Mrs Harding, "do introduce me, darling."

"Peveril, this is my daughter Rebecca. Say hello, Rebecca."

Rebecca said nothing. Undeterred, Peveril grabbed her hand and kissed it ostentatiously. Rebecca snatched her hand away and thrust it into the pocket of her coat.

"What an absolutely charming young lady, don't you think so, Mrs Stevens?" smiled Peveril, turning to the others in the room.

"Now, dear Adelaide, I hope we are able to help you this morning; what exactly do you require?"

"Well we came for a gown for Rebecca, so she can go to a ball. Most girls of her age would give their right arm to go to a ball and meet boys."

"Oh, that will be nice, won't it," said Peveril, glancing once more at Rebecca.

"But her – no!" continued Adelaide. "*She* doesn't want to go; all she wants to do is to ride horses and go hunting."

"Ah ha, she must know my dear friend Allibone; what a lovely chap. Do you know him, my dear?"

Rebecca looked up, and for the first time smiled.

"You mean Mortimer Allibone?" she asked.

"Yes."

"Yes I know him; he's lovely. I've met him a lot out hunting."

"I can't understand it myself," sighed Peveril, with a shake of his head. "I hate horses; but we won't go into that."

He pulled a handkerchief from his cuff, mopped his brow delicately and turned to Mrs Harding.

"Now, my dear, I wonder if I can offer you a little refreshment?"

"I thought you would never ask," Adelaide replied conspiratorially.

"We could retire to my office while Rebecca consults the designs in the books? Mrs Stevens could help her – and Mary; she has very good taste."

"Who?"

"Mary! She is up with all the fashions, you know and she is Rebecca's age. I think we can safely say we can recommend her – can't we, Mrs Stevens?"

"Yes, sir," said Mrs Stevens, smiling at Mary.

"Well if you say so, Peveril," said Adelaide snootily, slipping her arm through his and marching him in the direction of his office.

"Now come on – let's leave them to it," she sighed, calling over her shoulder: "Make sure she tries something on, Mrs Stevens!"

Rebecca stuck her tongue out at Adelaide's retreating back and crossed her arms angrily.

"Now, Miss Harding, what should we do?" said Mrs Stevens cheerily. "First choose a design and material; or try one on for size? We could get it all done before your mother comes back."

"She's not my mother, she's my stepmother!" snapped Rebecca. "My mother died of diphtheria three years ago."

"Oh I'm sorry to hear that," said Mrs Stevens uncertainly, looking towards Mary.

"Perhaps Mary could help you choose a design."

"Very well," huffed Rebecca. "Let's get on with it then if you think you know which book is best."

Mary sat in the chair vacated by Adelaide, selected one of the books and started to thumb the pages. She came to one and opened it on the counter.

"I think this might suit."

"I suppose so," sniffed Rebecca, looking at the picture and then back at Mary. "It's not too bad, is it?"

"It's very nice, Miss Harding; I'm sure you will be pleased with it."

"Where did you get to know about dresses, Mary?"

"Well I've worked here for two years now; I suppose I've just picked it up in that time."

"Do you come from Northampton, then?"

"Oh no, I live in the country – at a place called Melchbourne, near Dean."

"I know that; I went there hunting last season."

"Yes, miss, the hunt does meet there; I think it was at Dean House last time."

"Yes it was," Rebecca smiled. "Do you ride, Mary?"

"Well, miss, I can ride – I ride my brother's horse – but only round the farm. I don't go hunting."

"Do you ride side-saddle, Mary?"

"No, miss, we haven't got one; I usually ride bareback but it's not very ladylike, miss."

"No, I imagine it's not; but how exciting! But what does your father say?"

"Nothing, miss, I don't know if he knows; he's not very well at the moment."

"When I went hunting at Dean last time I fell off," said Rebecca with a laugh. "It was most embarrassing! My horse refused at a hedge and threw me over the top. I blamed it on three boys standing near the hedge, but it wasn't their fault really; they didn't know I was coming. In the end the biggest boy caught the horse and got me back on it."

"Yes I know, miss," said Mary, with a shy smile.

"You know? How do you know?"

"Well, miss, the older boy was William, my cousin – and the two others were Reuben and George. William told me what happened."

"Did they say anything else about what happened?"

"No, Miss Harding, he just said you fell off, but weren't hurt and that they helped you catch the horse."

"They didn't say that I used bad language?"

"No, Miss Harding."

"Well I did and they looked quite shocked. I think William did not approve, in fact I'm sure he didn't."

"Yes, miss – that sounds like William."

"Do you ever swear, Mary?" asked Rebecca with a wink.

"I try not to, miss."

"Please don't call me miss – call me Rebecca," she insisted.

"No I couldn't do that, miss," said Mary, looking up sharply. "I'd get the sack, miss; Mr Peveril is very particular."

Rebecca shrugged and pointed to one of the dresses in the book.

"Well let's get on with this job; have you got a pattern for this gown?"

"Yes, Miss Harding."

"Well, what about the material then?"

"We really only have to choose the colour; the pattern dictates the type of material to use," said Mary.

"Well you choose the colour, Mary, you know what would be best,"

"Perhaps we should have hunting pink as the main colour," suggested Mary with a smile, "and coordinate the rest with it."

"What a good idea! How appropriate for someone like me; let's do it."

Mary turned to Mrs Stevens.

"Do you think that is satisfactory, Mrs Stevens?"

"Yes, yes, Mary, keep going – you are doing very well."

"Well, all we have to do now, Miss Harding, is to get your size; we can either measure you or try you in another dress."

"Well, whatever you say," said Rebecca cheerily, surrendering herself to the situation.

"I would suggest we do both to be sure," said Mary carefully. "We don't want any mistakes."

Adelaide, meanwhile, was settling herself into Peveril's office.

"Frisby; where are you hiding?" Peveril bellowed.

"Here, Mr Peveril," squeaked Frisby, scuttling into the room.

"Quickly, man, take Mrs Harding's coat and hang it up."

Adelaide unwound the fox from her neck, took her jacket off and handed both to Frisby.

"Now a drink, Adelaide, what can we get you?" asked Peveril.

"Well it's a bit early but you know what I would really like? A couple of fingers of gin in a glass with a little soda," replied Adelaide.

"Frisby, you heard what Mrs Harding said, get on with it."

Frisby beetled to the table, picking up the bottle of gin and a tumbler before turning with a bewildered look on his face to Peveril.

"He doesn't know what a couple of fingers are, Peveril," Adelaide sneered, throwing herself down in the nearest chair.

"Keep pouring, Frisby, I'll say when," said Peveril. "I'll have a glass of port."

Frisby poured the drinks and delivered them on the silver tray.

"That will be all, Frisby," ordered Peveril, ushering the small man from the room and raising his glass to Adelaide.

"Well, here's to old times, Adelaide; you've come a long way since I first knew you."

"Yes, old times, Peveril, and you've done the same. Think what a poky old place this was when your father died."

"Now how many times have you been married?" said Peveril, his eyes glinting mischievously.

"Only three; it's not a record, you know! They keep on dying on me and I don't even poison them."

She threw back her head and laughed throatily, before taking a sip of gin.

"This is the best one though; got the most money, boot and shoe through and through! Got the tanneries as well – there's no end to it. Only problem is that damn daughter of his, I can't do anything with her."

"Well, you will soon be able to marry her off," said Peveril with a wink.

"Yes, that's the plan; that's why we're here. She should brush up all right, if we can get her in the right gown."

Peveril eyed the woman in front of him, a smile playing at the edge of his mouth as he watched her raise her glass to her lips once again.

"Your accent's changed, Adelaide."

"Yer, it ain't 'arf," she said with another bark of laughter. "Needs must, Peveril. I'm no fool."

"And what about that brother of yours, what happened to him?"

Adelaide shrugged.

"I haven't spoken to him in years! I think he's driving ploughing engines somewhere," she sighed. "Roland always was trouble, even when we were children. He was lucky to get off that last time; if it hadn't been for the girl dying and not being able to testify—"

She took another large gulp from her glass.

"Even so, I hear he was in for at least a year."

Adelaide shook her head as if to dismiss the subject and raised her eyes to survey Peveril.

"And what about you, Peveril? Who's going to run this place in years to come; you have no family, have you?"

"Well no, but there's a nephew who is showing some very good signs; I'm sure we'll carry on."

He drained his glass, placing it back on the sideboard and offering Adelaide his arm.

"Shall we go and see how they are getting on?"

They left the room and made their way back towards the shop floor.

"How have we been getting on then, Mrs Stevens?" enquired Peveril.

"All done, sir; Miss Rebecca has chosen a gown and the material; all we need now is a date for a fitting from Mrs Harding."

"My word, that was quick. Let's see what you've chosen then," said Adelaide, moving towards the open book on the counter. "Well that's not bad I have to say, not bad at all. What colour is it going to be?"

"Red," said Rebecca.

"Well I suppose it'll be all right; but there are places *I* wouldn't walk in

Northampton in that colour."

She turned and winked at Mrs Stevens who smiled weakly, before adding, "What about a date for the fitting?"

"I don't need to come to that, do I?" said Adelaide sharply.

"No, madam, I'm sure we can manage."

"Well, fix it with her then; she will know when she can come, better than me! Mrs Cubitt can come with her."

Rebecca grimaced and turned to Mrs Stevens to fix a date. Five minutes later, they were gone.

"Thank God," said Peveril, sinking into the nearest chair. "What a dreadful woman! We must be thankful there are not many like her."

Mary giggled. Peveril smiled back and hoisted himself from the chair.

"Tell anyone who needs me I'm busy for the afternoon," he said, moving swiftly towards his office to seek solace in his decanters.

Chapter Seventeen
Funeral Procession on the Isle of Wight

The death of Queen Victoria on the 22nd January 1901 was a momentous occasion for the whole country; its effect reaching even down to Lower Dean. The Queen had died at Osborne House on the Isle of Wight where William had two great uncles who were tenants on the Osborne Estate. They immediately wrote to Thomas and Charlotte suggesting that William should be sent down to see the funeral procession, the funeral having been set for the 4th of February.

As soon as they received the letter, Thomas and Charlotte went down to see the Reverend Belpeel, who immediately agreed to let him off school for the period.

William had never been on a train before and had certainly never been to London. The weekend before he left, all his clothes were washed, a black tie was purchased and a small suitcase packed for the trip.

"William, you're a lucky boy then," said Henry, who had come with Mary and Lucy to see him before he left. "Going all that way and across London too! I wouldn't want to do it."

"I would," said Mary with a heavy sigh, "I wish I could go, it's not fair! Girls never get the chance; it's only the boys. They're *our* uncles as well; why didn't they write and ask if I would like to go?"

"Well I don't expect you would be able to – you will be at work, so maybe that's why," said Charlotte curtly. "You mustn't be jealous, Mary."

"I'm not really, Aunt Charlotte," Mary mumbled. "I hope William has a good time, but girls just don't get the chances that boys do; you must agree, Aunt Charlotte?"

"Well you're not a girl any more, Mary; look at you – you're a woman; you're old enough to get married now."

"I suppose I am," sighed Mary. "Aunt Charlotte, Verity says that women should have the vote at elections, she's very keen on it; she's joined some society or something. So if I'm a woman, I will be able to vote!"

"Men don't vote till they are twenty-one," said Charlotte, "so whatever happens, you won't have the vote yet. I don't think I agree with it anyway – I don't think Reverend Packham does either."

"He would call it a sin if women had the vote," laughed Mary. "He thinks everything is a sin."

"He won't be talking about sin today, I'm sure. It'll be the dear old Queen. Sixty-four years on the throne – long before I was born; such a long time. I'm sure her funeral will be a great spectacle."

"Have you ever been to a funeral before, William?" asked Lucy. "I don't think I would want to go; it's going to be awfully sad, don't you think?"

"No," William said thoughtfully, "I've never been to one before; but I'm not going to the funeral – only the procession. Uncle Henry and Uncle George are going to be in it as they are tenants on the Osborne Estate."

"We've never met them," said Lucy, "and I don't remember them ever coming to our house."

"No, I haven't met them either," said William wistfully. "Mother says they can't afford to come back."

"How are you going to get across London?" asked Lucy.

"He's just got to use his common sense," said Mary sharply. "He's got a tongue in his head; he'll have to ask if he doesn't know. And he's got to get to the Isle of Wight so he'll have to cross the sea; you've never seen the sea have you, William?"

"No," agreed William. "Although we are supposed to be going this summer on a school trip."

"So are we," said Lucy. "We're going to Hunstanton on the train for the day."

"How much does all this cost then, William?" cut in Henry. "There and back?"

"I don't know," said William. "Father's given me a five-pound note, which he thinks will cover it all."

"Five pounds, William! You lucky boy! Now you must send us a card or we won't believe you went," said Mary.

"Look," said Lucy excitedly," look what it says here in Uncle Thomas's paper; it says that the Kaiser of Germany is going and the Tsar of Russia *and* the kings of Denmark, Sweden and Norway. There's a whole list of other people too; do you think you are going to see them all, William?"

"I really don't know, Lucy, until I get there," laughed William. "I'll tell you in my postcard!"

After the long train journey and crossing London, William waited in anticipation for the ferry from Portsmouth to Cowes; this was the first time he had seen the sea and the first time he had ever been on a boat. Finally, it arrived, puffing out vast columns of smoke as it manoeuvred into the dock. The sun was setting in the west and the surface of the sea shone in the dwindling light. The engine engaged the paddles and the deck started to vibrate, the sound of rushing water echoing from both sides. The boat reversed out of its mooring and once in the middle of the channel, slowly turned until it was pointing out to sea. Everywhere William looked he could see boats – warships, sailing ships and cargo steamers, all rushing in and out of Portsmouth Harbour. Within an hour, the boat was pulling into the dock at Cowes. Just as William was wondering how he would get to his uncles he noticed two old grey-haired men standing by the edge of the jetty. Disembarking, he made his way towards them; smiles of recognition spread across their faces.

"William Dunmore, my goodness, what a fine chap you are! Don't you look just like your mother – don't you think so, Henry?" said the taller of the two men.

"The spitting image, George!" agreed Henry. "I could tell who he was by just looking at him! Well I never, there's a real likeness."

"Now," said George, "the trap is round the back so we better get going or it will be dark before we know where we are."

Henry lived with his wife Aunt Maud and had a small farm on the Osborne Estate; George lived further away but still on the estate. William was welcomed by Maud who had prepared a meal for him. He handed over the presents his mother had sent over with him, and after a long evening chatting was sent to bed. He was asleep as soon as his head hit the pillow.

There were still two days before the procession, which gave William a chance to explore the town of Cowes. Evidence of preparation for the big state occasion could be seen everywhere; seating was being put out at strategic points along the roads and the gun carriage for the procession was seen practising the route time and time again. Every so often a member of the Royal Family would arrive, escorted to Osborne House by a troop of cavalry in their splendid uniform. Up and down the streets bands marched, playing sombre music while the muffled church bells tolled. Flags hung at half-mast and many of the townsfolk wore black armbands. Back at the farm Henry's clothes were being pressed; he and George would be walking in the procession as would all the tenants of the estate.

On the day everyone was up very early. Henry dressed and made his way to Osborne House with Maud in tow and William put on his black tie and left in the other direction. William made his way to the entrance of East Cowes Town Hall where his reserved seat was and waited. Gradually people started to trickle into the streets, either taking a seat or lining the pavement. Soldiers moved to line the route at regular intervals, marching in groups to their allotted positions. A man in a bowler hat raced up to William from the other side of the street.

"Is that seat taken?" he asked eagerly.

"I don't know, sir, mine was booked; no one has come to claim it yet," replied William.

"Very well then, I'll take it," said the man, sitting down.

He was a man of about twenty; smartly dressed and with a small, neat moustache. His coat hung open revealing his jacket and waistcoat, across which was slung a gold watch chain. His shoes were patent leather and shone in the dull light of the cold morning. He flicked open his watch.

"Another hour yet," he said to William. "I hope it's all worth it."

He replaced the watch and buttoned his coat.

"You got a black tie, young man; I suppose I should – but can't be helped. If I wrap my scarf round no one will see."

William looked closely at the man – he thought he had seen him somewhere before. He was quite a striking individual; handsome and quite a bit taller than William. The man stood up again, turning to rake his eyes through the crowd behind him as though he might see someone he knew. Sitting down, he stamped his feet and rubbed his hands together.

"Have you got anything to eat, young man?" the stranger said. "I didn't get any breakfast before I came out."

"No, sir, my aunt said I wasn't to eat, it would be disrespectful to the old Queen."

"My, my, we are being correct today, aren't we!" chuckled the man.

"What's your name then, boy?" he said after a moment's pause.

"William Dunmore, sir," William answered, unwilling to continue the conversation.

"And where does William Dunmore come from then?"

"I'm staying with my aunt and uncle who live in East Cowes, but I live in Lower Dean."

"Well I never," the man laughed. "You mean Lower Dean near Kimbolton?"

"Yes, sir."

"Well I never," he said again, "I come all this way and sit down next to a near-neighbour. There's someone in Lower Dean who has a butcher's shop called Dunmore, I'm sure there is."

"Yes, sir, that's my father."

"What a coincidence; it's a small world, don't you think, young Dunmore?"

"Yes, sir, but where do you live?" asked William.

"Bythorn, my boy, Bythorn; not five miles away from you – what about that?"

"Yes, sir, that is a coincidence," replied William politely. "Have you just come for the funeral, sir?"

"God bless my soul, no! Funerals are not my favourite occasions. No, I've come buying horses but while I was here I decided to have a look, as nobody will do any business today – that's why I'm here."

He looked around again before turning his attention back to William.

"So your father has the land behind the butcher's shop, does he?"

"Yes, sir, and some on the way to Upper Dean. He's going to take on Dean Way Post Farm next Michaelmas."

"That will be a big farm, William – if he has all that lot," said the man admiringly.

"Yes, sir. Do you have a farm?"

"I farm it with my brother at Elgin Farm, do you know it?" the man asked.

"I know where it is but I've never been to the farm," admitted William.

"Not good land, very heavy and sticky. We have it nearly all pasture; you can't plough it with horses if you have any sense, so we keep it all grazing and I breed and deal in horses. Sell them mainly to the army – good trade at the moment as well."

He chuckled and nudged William.

"There! Fancy you coming from Lower Dean; I will have to call and see your father. If he's taking on more land he will need some more horseflesh to plough all that lot."

"He has the steam plough mostly, sir and I know he's booked it for next autumn; the hills need ploughing up as well."

"And what do your brothers and sisters do, William?"

"I don't have any, sir; I'm the only one."

"Well that's a nice position to be in, boy, with all that land and only you to have any of it," the man said with a wink.

"I suppose so, sir."

"So which are you, William, are you the butcher or are you the farmer then?"

"Well, sir, I'm still at school, so I help to do both on my holidays."

"Where at school, William? Wait I know! I can tell by the way you act – I bet you are at Kimbolton Grammar School, aren't I right."

"Yes, sir," said William, growing increasingly irritated with the man next to him.

"Old Belpeel! He's a bumbling old fool if there ever was, what do you think, William?"

"Well, sir, I enjoy being at the school and I have learnt a lot, even some French."

198

"French, why do you want to learn French for? Butchers don't need to speak French!"

"I have heard people speaking French in Cowes, sir," said William indignantly. "Quite a few people."

The man gave a harsh laugh and pulled a card from his pocket. He handed it to William.

"Now, William, this is not in French," he winked. "When you get home I want you to give it to your father and tell him that I will make a visit in the next little while, particularly as he is taking on more land. By the way, William, who's the landlord at Way Post Farm?"

"Mr Watson-Foster, sir," said William, taking the card and reading the engraved writing:

NOBLE THOMAS WILLIAM LADDS
ELGIN FARM
BYTHORN
HUNTINGDON
Supplier of Superior Draught and Saddle Horses

William put the card into his pocket and looked warily at the man.

"Excuse me, I think that's one of our seats," came a voice from behind them; William turned to see a family of four – parents and two daughters both dressed in black. He stood up.

"I'm sorry, sir; I think I am in the correct seat."

"Yes, young man, I can see you are by the numbers; but I think this gentleman is in the wrong one."

He tapped Noble Ladds on the shoulder.

"Excuse me, sir, I think you are in one of our seats."

Noble whipped round and glared at the man.

"I was here first," he grunted, turning back to the front.

"But these seats are booked," insisted the man.

"So what?" he snapped. "I'm sitting with my friend William here."

He folded his arms, refusing to move.

"I really must insist that you move," the man in black said, with more force. There was a moment's silence.

"Go on then, have your damn seat," Noble snarled, jumping up and stalking off along the pavement.

"I'm sorry, sir," said William quietly. "He's not a friend of mine, I've only just met him."

"Don't worry, my boy," said the man, patting William's shoulder. "All's well that ends well, eh?"

They took their seats, the eldest of the two girls sitting next to William. She unfurled a copy of the local paper from her pocket and started to read through the list of royalty and dignitaries that were attending and in what order they would walk in the procession.

"Would you like to have a look at our list?" she said suddenly, turning to William, who blushed and with a shy smile, took the copy.

"Thank you," he said, quickly reading down the list and handing it back with another "Thank you." The girl smiled.

"Thank *you*. William isn't it – that's what that horrid man said? I'm Hannah and this is my sister Rosie but she doesn't say much, she's only twelve."

"Yes I do," said Rosie indignantly. "Hello, William."

William, not knowing quite what to do, touched his cap, smiled and murmured, "Hello."

"Have you seen the Queen before, William?" said Hannah.

"That's a stupid question," hissed Rosie. "He's not going to see her *now*; she's in the coffin."

"I know that, stupid," snapped Hannah. "But have you, William?"

"No, I'm afraid I haven't."

"Well we have, lots of times, when she drives about in her carriage; we live in Cowes, you see."

"Now, no arguing you two," said the mother. "Just sit and be quiet."

There were a few moments silence, then Hannah whispered,

"Do you live here, William?"

"No, I live in Lower Dean – that's in Bedfordshire; but I've come down to stay with my Uncle Henry Dunmore as he's in the funeral procession."

Hannah looked impressed.

"He lives on the estate," explained William, "and he has the butcher's shop."

"We know that shop, it's just in the town. I'm sure that Mother has meat from him," said Rosie.

"Listen," said Hannah, putting her finger to her lips.

In the distance they could hear a band playing solemn music. William thought it must be coming from Osborne House; it wasn't far away and the procession was meant to move from there to the harbour where it would be loaded onto a warship to be taken over to the mainland for the trip by train to London.

The road was now clear; people had stopped rushing from side to side to pick the best vantage place, and the soldiers who lined the route stood at ease with their heads bowed.

"Are you getting cold, William?" asked Hannah.

"Yes, I'm frozen," admitted William, "it's just sitting here and doing nothing to keep warm."

"Shh," said Rosie, "something is happening."

As she spoke they heard a shouted order in the distance; all the soldiers along the route came to attention and they could hear the boots of the troops marching along the road. A hush fell and everyone stood, the men in the crowd taking their hats off and holding them to their chests. The procession was led by a troop dressed in long great coats; this was followed by the coffin on a gun carriage, draped in the Union Jack and pulled by six black horses with outriders. The coffin was escorted by the Household Cavalry, their plumed helmets bobbing with the motion of their mounts. Following the coffin were the Royal Family led by the new king, Edward VII. William peered to identify them; he recognised the king from photographs in the paper but he was a lot shorter than William had imagined. He could also make out the Tsar of Russia with his pointed beard, and the Kaiser of Germany was recognisable from the cap he wore, but thereafter he faltered. He could not tell the King of Denmark from the King of Sweden and by the time he had tried, they were gone. The European heads of state were all in uniform; those from the Empire wore traditional dress with long flowing robes and large head dresses. Following the heads of state were the politicians, led by the Prime Minister, Lord Salisbury, and after them the local dignitaries. At the very end of the procession came the tenants of the Osborne Estate, led by William's two great-uncles. Hannah nudged William and smiled.

After the procession had passed, the chatter of voices started to fill the silence; the troops that had lined the road formed up into squads and marched off.

"I'm frozen," shivered Rosie.

"I can't feel my feet, they are so cold," Hannah complained.

"Come on, you two, we'll go home and warm up; there's no more to see now," said their mother.

"Goodbye, William, I hope you have a safe trip home," said Hannah, smiling shyly.

William blushed and smiled, before making his way back to his uncle's house.

Two days later, with his bag packed, Henry took him back to the port to catch his ferry home. This time the sea was rough and the crossing bumpy; and it was with some relief that he stood on solid ground waiting for the train at Portsmouth station. Whilst he was waiting he noticed Noble Ladds leaping from a hansom cab to catch the same train. Pulling his cap over his eyes he made his way down the platform and stood behind a pillar. Ladds was one person William hoped he would never have to set eyes on again.

Chapter Eighteen
Dress Fitting

"Now, William," said Mary excitedly, who had rushed down to the butcher's shop with Lucy to see her cousin, "we want to know all about it, who did you see? What were they wearing?"

Questions were fired solidly for ten minutes – the number of royals that William recognised, the people he had met, what their uncles were like, and finally Charlotte interrupted.

"How are your mother and father?" she asked Mary.

Mary sighed and shrugged her shoulders.

"Not very well I'm afraid; they are not going to come to chapel – they say that they might catch a chill."

"Don't you think that you should stay at home and help your mother, Mary?" said Charlotte, eyeing her niece severely.

"Don't say that, Aunt Charlotte! That would mean I would have to give up my job and I really don't want to do that. Anyway, Lucy is leaving school in the summer and she can stay and help."

"But Lucy says she wants to train to be a nurse; didn't you say that, Lucy?"

Lucy sniffed and rubbed at her nose with the back of her hand:

"Yes, I am going to train at Bedford; but I can't start until I am sixteen, so not till next year."

"There, Aunt Charlotte," said Mary triumphantly, "Lucy can do it until she's sixteen."

"I know you don't want to leave your job," said Charlotte firmly, "but I still think it's your duty to your parents to look after them when they're as unwell as they are; after all you *are* the oldest."

"No, I'm not!" said Mary angrily. "What about Bessie? She's older than me – and Henry."

"I know that, dear," said Charlotte kindly. "But Bessie's married; she has a family now so she can't come."

"Well Mother says she can manage; didn't Mother tell you, Aunt Charlotte?"

"Yes she did," agreed Charlotte, "but—"

"There we are then," said Mary.

She turned imploringly to her aunt.

"Please, *please* don't tell me I've got to leave my job; I would die if I had to go back to live at Cold Harbour, just doing housework and cooking – I would really die."

Charlotte looked at her niece and decided to hold her peace, thinking it probably wasn't her business to interfere any further.

The next day Mary left for the train as usual; it had snowed overnight so she decided that she would walk to the station. When she arrived at Northampton, Rupert was waiting to walk her into town, as he had taken to doing whenever he could get away.

"Rupert! I haven't seen you for a week; what's in the news this week?" asked Mary.

"The Queen's funeral is all that has been in the paper; Father sent me to London to report on it at the weekend. Luckily, because of the funeral, they had to cancel that damn ball so I didn't have to go!"

"Don't you like balls then, Rupert?" said Mary curiously. "I've never been to one."

"Oh, I like them, but not when my mother comes as well to organise who I have to dance with; it's a nightmare, a real nightmare."

He turned to Mary.

"I would like it if *you* came too, Mary; I would go then like a shot."

Mary laughed.

"Don't be so silly, Rupert; your mother would never let you take a shop girl to a ball! Anyway I don't have a dress."

"Mother says they have rearranged for two months' time; say you'll come, Mary? I can fix it."

"No, Rupert," said Mary with a shake of her head. "Your mother would not approve; you're much older than me."

"Only four years, Mary!" laughed Rupert. "And it doesn't seem like that much."

"I'm not coming, Rupert," said Mary firmly. "I've met some of the people who go to that sort of thing; they're very posh, talk all 'hoity toity' and act as though they own the world."

They trudged on up the hill in silence for a while.

"Who do you know who's like that, Mary?" asked Rupert tentatively. "They're not all bad people."

"I know that Mrs Harding; she's dreadful," said Mary, as she recollected Mrs Harding's behaviour in Tibbitts.

"Yes she is; but Rebecca's nice, although she does only talk about horses."

"Yes, Rebecca's lovely," agreed Mary. "I think she's coming in today for her dress fitting."

They had reached the door of Tibbitts – Rupert turned earnestly to Mary and grasped her hand.

"When can I see you again?"

"Rupert, you're never here!" exclaimed Mary. "You're always being sent off to report on things."

"I'm always here on Thursdays," insisted Rupert, "to go down to the market."

"All right then," laughed Mary, "I will see you at lunch time on Thursday."

"Where?"

"Come here at half past twelve," said Mary over her shoulder as she moved into the shop, "that's my lunchtime."

"Super," called Rupert after her, "I'll be here."

Mary entered the shop, took off her hat and coat, changed her shoes and reported to the Ladies' Fashion Department. At the desk, there was a message to report to Mrs Stevens straight away.

"Ah, Mary, come in quickly," said Mrs Stevens as Mary poked her head around the door.

Mary moved into the room and sat down on the chair indicated.

"Mary, I need your help this morning," said Mrs Stevens confidentially. "That dreadful Mrs Harding is coming in for a fitting for Rebecca."

She looked anxiously around the office and lowered her voice.

"Mary; now this is between you and me – Mr Peveril would dismiss me if he knew what I was saying to you but—"

She hesitated, licked her lips nervously, and continued:

"I was brought up in the same area of Northampton as Mrs Harding, you know; I know about her background: all her husbands, that dreadful brother – he's been in jail, you know. Common as muck they are, common as muck! Now you got on well with Rebecca so I'll rely on you to deal with her today. Mr Peveril is not here so we'll have to do the best we can with dear Adelaide. I really can't stand her."

Mrs Stevens put her head in her hands and shook her head vigorously.

"Don't worry, Mrs Stevens," said Mary, with a good deal more confidence than she felt, "I can cope; Rebecca is very easy and I am used to difficult people. Mrs Harding doesn't frighten me."

"I know, dear, but her husband is so important in the town; we cannot afford to make mistakes."

"But, Mrs Stevens," said Mary earnestly, "Rebecca isn't her actual daughter; I'm sure she probably dislikes her stepmother as much as we do, if their behaviour last time was anything to go by. I don't think we should worry so much about Mrs Harding."

"I hope so, dear, I hope so," said Mrs Stevens, rubbing her hands together anxiously. "Anyway run along; they'll be coming in at about ten o'clock, so be ready."

At half past ten on the dot, Mrs Harding arrived with Rebecca.

"Oh, it's you again," she said, sneering at Mary. "Where's that Stevens woman?"

"Mrs Stevens is in her office, Mrs Harding, did you want me to fetch her?"

"No I don't; leave her where she is – you will do."

"Is Mr Peveril in?"

"No, Mrs Harding, he's in London for the day."

"Damn! So what am I going to do now?"

She glared at Mary.

"What's he doing in London? On second thoughts," she sniggered, "I don't want to know."

She sat at the counter and slammed her bag down; Rebecca didn't say a word.

"Now, whatever-your-name-is—" started Adelaide.

"Mary, Mrs Harding," Mary interrupted.

"*Mary*," she drawled, as if it might have been a name that she had never said before, "there's no hurry for this dress now. The damn ball has been put off thanks to this funeral – God rest her soul –the ball now won't be until late April."

She took a sideways glance at Rebecca and sneered.

"Make sure you don't make it too small; she'll be a size or two bigger by the time we get there."

She took out her cigarette case and lit a cigarette.

"I suppose the dressmaker is here with it?"

"Yes, Mrs Harding."

"Let's get on with it then," chivvied Adelaide. "While you do that, I have to pay a visit to old George Brummitt; do you have a telephone in this place?"

"Yes, madam, there is one in Mrs Stevens' office and another in Mr Peveril's," said Mary.

"Well, Mary – or whatever your name is; go and tell Stevens to telephone Brummitt and tell Mr George to expect me in five minutes'."

"Very well, Mrs Harding."

"And then you can fit this dress," she said as she turned to her stepdaughter. "Rebecca, is that all right with you?" "Yes," Rebecca replied sulkily.

"Yes what?" Adelaide said icily.

"Yes, Mother."

"That's better," said Adelaide with a grimace, turning and leaving the shop.

"Thank goodness she's gone," sighed Rebecca, turning to Mary with a smile. "I can't think *why* Father married her; she's so common."

"Yes, miss, oh – I mean no, miss," stammered Mary, reddening and looking at the floor.

"Mary, let's get this dress fitted and then we can talk. How's that cousin of yours? William – wasn't that his name?"

"William is very well, miss; he has just been down to the Isle of Wight to see the Queen's funeral procession."

"That must have been magnificent – all those kings! Just think! The Kaiser and the Tsar of Russia."

"Yes, miss."

"Now, the dress – this is it, I assume," said Rebecca pointing at a shop assistant who had just entered with a dress over her arm.

"Yes, miss. This is Julia; she's the dressmaker."

"Hello, Julia," smiled Rebecca. "Now where are the fitting rooms? I hope they're warm; it's very cold this morning."

"If you would like to come this way, miss," said Julia, "I'll hang the dress on the peg and you can put it on. Will you need any help, miss?"

"No, I'll manage; you just wait outside and we will see what it looks like."

Julia put the lights on, hung up the dress and retreated with Mary to the shop to wait. After a couple of minutes there was a shout.

"I'm stuck, you will have to come and help; Mary, are you there?"

"Yes, miss, I'm coming," called Mary, rushing to the room where she found Rebecca standing in her underwear; the dress over her outstretched arms and head, falling to just below her shoulders.

"I think the pins are catching somewhere!" she exclaimed. "Just get it on, can you!"

Mary fumbled through the folds on the dress, finally finding and removing the offending pin. The dress slipped down, covering Rebecca's long lacy white drawers; the straps of the dress came to rest on her white shoulders, the hem just brushing the carpet. Rebecca turned to look in the mirror and gasped, putting her hand to her mouth and staring intently at her reflection.

"I can't wear this, look at me! I look naked! Isn't there anything to go underneath? And look at these!" She pulled at the straps of her vest. "How can I walk about like this? It's not right, is it, Mary?"

"I think it looks lovely, miss; it's very fashionable. The top needs taking in around the waist a little and you will have to have something different underneath; but we can arrange that."

"What do you think, Julia?" said Rebecca, chewing her lip nervously, seeking out Julia's gaze in the mirror.

"I think it's the best dress I have ever made," exclaimed Julia with a smile.

"You look lovely in it, miss."

"But look at me, I look stupid! It touches the ground! Oh I don't know; I just don't like wearing things like this."

"Well, Miss Harding, let's—"

"Don't call me Miss Harding, Mary, call me Rebecca," interrupted Rebecca.

"I can't do that, miss, Mr Pev—"

"Mr Peveril's not here," said Rebecca firmly. "Anyway, if I'm paying, or rather if Father's paying you have to do what I say, so there!"

Mary looked at Julia and raised her eyebrows, believing that Rebecca couldn't see her.

"Don't do that, Mary, I just want to be friends," said Rebecca quietly. "If you had a stepmother like mine you'd need friends too."

Mary looked searchingly at the girl sitting in front of her, fiddling with the fabric of her dress.

"Miss, if you—"

"Rebecca!"

"*Rebecca*," said Mary – Rebecca smiled. "If you would stand up, Julia will pin the top tighter and you will see how lovely it's going to look."

Rebecca sighed and stood, looking dejectedly at Mary – suddenly her eyes brightened.

"I know! *You* put it on, Mary! Then I can see what it's really like; yes you put it on – you're about the same size as me."

"I couldn't do that," said Mary with a quick frown.

"Why not?"

"If Mrs Stevens comes in, I will be dismissed."

"No, you won't; I'll make sure of that. Julia go and ask Mrs. Stevens to come here."

"Very well, miss," said Julia, scuttling off and returning a few moments later with Mrs Stevens.

"Now, Mrs Stevens, I have asked Mary to put this dress on so I can see properly how it looks but she says she won't because you will dismiss her. I really cannot tell whether I like the dress and would like to see it on someone the same size as me. Is that satisfactory?"

"Yes, Miss Harding," said Mrs Stevens, evidently nonplussed.

"Very well then, Mary, get on with it."

"What now? With everyone looking?" exclaimed Mary.

"Mary it's only me, Julia and Mrs Stevens! Come on, Julia, help me with this and please find me a dressing gown; it's cold."

"I'll get the dressing gown," said Mrs Stevens. "You carry on, Julia."

Julia helped Rebecca to remove the dress, before turning to help dress Mary in it.

"Now you need some shoes, Mary," said Rebecca, sending Julia off to find some.

"Mary get rid of the straps of your vest, so I can see properly."

Mary obediently slipped the straps of her vest over her shoulders and tucked them into the dress.

"Julia – you stand behind Mary and pull the bodice in tight so we can see what it will be like."

Mrs Stevens and Rebecca stood back, surveying Mary critically.

"What do you think now?" said Mrs Stevens turning to Rebecca.

"It's lovely, isn't it? I'm being stupid! But Mary is a lot prettier than I am – she's got a better figure – turn round Mary."

Mary twirled round twice on the spot and Rebecca smiled.

"Very well then; you look really lovely, Mary. I had better put it on again so Julia can pin it."

Mrs Stevens went back to her office as Rebecca once more put the dress on for Julia to pin. When they had finished, Rebecca sat contentedly down to wait for her stepmother.

"Mary, I have just thought of the most brilliant plan," she said suddenly, her eyes sparkling.

"And what is that Rebecca?"

"You are going to come to this ball with me!"

"I can't do that," laughed Mary.

"Why not?"

"I don't have a dress for a start," said Mary.

"Well, I will get two and you can have the other one; we are the same size more or less!"

"I can't dance," insisted Mary.

"Neither can any of the boys," Rebecca tittered. "And you've got three months to learn!"

"Your mother would never allow it, Rebecca," said Mary gently. "I'm only a shop girl after all."

"*She* may not, but Father will; I can work him round. You must come, Mary, you are so pretty; I would really love you to come."

She looked expectantly at Mary, who was shifting from foot to foot, the idea of the ball playing over the features of her face. Rupert was going after all, and she was sure that Verity would be able to teach her how to dance.

"I don't know what to say! I'm only a farmer's daughter, you know. I would love to, but can I let you know next week when you come back for the final fitting?"

"Very well, we'll wait until next week." She lowered her voice and looked beadily at Mary "But the answer had better be yes."

Chapter Nineteen
Noble Ladds Calls

The fortunes of the Knighton family at Cold Harbour continued to decline. The mortgage on such a large farm weighed heavily on the business and they continued to lose money, no matter how well Henry worked the land. Lucy was due to finish school in the summer of 1901, so she would be able to help for a year before she was hoping to go into training to be a nurse. John's younger brother Edgar, who had recently given up a small farm near Raunds, had come to help Henry on the farm. He was unmarried and not in the best of health, so was something of a mixed blessing; being one more mouth to feed.

Henry continued to see Martha regularly and it wasn't long before they started to make plans to be married. Henry, realising that the farm at Cold Harbour would have to be sold to pay off the mounting debts, started to look for other farms that he could rent to start his new life with Martha. The sale of the farm should leave enough money to look after his parents in their old age, but he said nothing to them at the time, confiding only in William. Before long, he found a farm in Brington– a village six miles away – which was owned by the Church and would be coming up for rent in a year's time on the retirement of the present tenant. The land covered almost one hundred and ten acres, which he thought he could manage if he was able to borrow some money for the first year. William's father was the trustee of the land and would be the one who would choose the tenant, which Henry was sure must be to his advantage.

Mary in the meantime had written to Verity, asking if Verity could teach her to dance. Verity had replied with her customary enthusiasm that she would love to teach Mary when she was back at Easter; so Mary had confirmed with Rebecca at the next dress fitting that she would love to accompany her to the ball. Rebecca had agreed with her father that they would buy Mary a dress to wear and that Mary would come and stay in Northampton with them on the night of the ball.

The dancing lessons were organised for Mary's day off each week, which left them only three sessions. They needed a partner for Mary to learn with and as Henry flatly refused to cooperate, William was pressed into service, cycling down with Mary to The Hall every Thursday so that they could dance to the music of John Watson-Foster's gramophone.

"I don't know why I agreed to this," William moaned, as they cycled down to Verity's for their first lesson.

"Don't worry, William – you'll probably enjoy it and your mother said it would be very good for you to learn to dance."

"But it's a girl's thing, isn't it? When am I ever going to go to a dance? My mother and father have never been to one in their lives."

"I didn't think I would ever go to one either," agreed Mary, "But here I am going to a ball with Rebecca Harding of all people. You've met Rebecca, haven't you?"

"Yes, I liked her," said William thoughtfully, before lowering his voice confidentially. "Did you know she swears?"

"How do you know she swears?" said Mary.

"I heard her when she fell off her horse; she swore and blamed us for falling off."

Mary shrugged.

"I'd probably swear too if I fell off a horse – and blame you too come to think of it."

She stuck her tongue out at William and pedalled down into the back yard of The Hall, where they parked their bikes and were led through into the kitchen.

"Miss Verity's in the drawing room, you can find your way," said Dorcas, with something dangerously near to a smile.

"Yes, we'll find her," Mary said. "Thank you, Dorcas."

Dorcas nodded and went back to stirring a pot of bubbling stew on the range.

"Mary, William, how lovely to see you," said Verity as they walked into the drawing room. "Now we've got to get on, Mary; we only have three lessons to teach you everything – well not everything – but enough to get round the dance floor."

She moved authoritatively into the middle of the room.

"Now, Mary – you stand here and William you stand in front of her. Come on – closer. *Closer,* William!"

"Do I have to do this?" William moaned.

"Yes you do, William! Just try, will you! It's not going to hurt."

William moved grudgingly closer to her cousin, who grinned at him.

"Oh wait, a problem! You're taller than William, Mary – so take your shoes off for the moment and we'll see how we get on."

Mary kicked off her shoes, returning to stand in front of William who was scuffing the carpet with his shoes.

"Don't look like that, William!" scolded Verity. "Take Mary's right hand in your left hand and then put your right hand round Mary's waist; come on, you've got to get closer!"

She pushed William closer to Mary, who puckered her lips and blew him a kiss – William frowned angrily and stepped back.

"Come here!" grumbled Verity. "Let me show you! I will pretend I'm a man."

She shoved William out of the way and demonstrated the correct hold with Mary; William watched moodily and at Verity's bidding, returned to his cousin's side to try again. He could only be prevailed upon to dance for an hour, after which he insisted that he must return to the butcher's shop, but both the girls noticed that he had started to enjoy himself a bit.

"Mary, you must tell me all about this ball," said Verity, after William had left. "I've never been to one before. Who invited you?"

Mary explained about how she had met Rebecca at the shop.

"And are there any boys going with you?" Verity asked curiously.

"No, it's just Rebecca and her father and stepmother; but I do know a boy that is going. Do you remember we met a boy on the train who was a reporter? I met him again and he will be there."

"Oh Mary, how exciting! What's he like and where did you meet him?"

"I see quite a lot of him actually," said Mary coyly. "He works in an office near the shop."

"He was quite handsome, wasn't he?" said Verity slyly. "Didn't his father own the newspaper?"

Mary reddened and looked at the floor.

"Mary, you're blushing!" squealed Verity delightedly, clapping her hands.

Mary's hands rushed to her cheeks as she smiled at her friend.

"Well," said Verity, "we will have to work twice as hard at our next lesson so we can impress the man from the train."

On his way home, William met George and Reuben walking up the lane leading to Dean.

"Where are you off to then?" he enquired.

"We're bird nesting," Reuben replied. "It's just about the right time."

"What have you found then?"

"Just got a jackdaw's egg," said Reuben, opening his hand to reveal a speckled egg about half the size of a hen's.

"Had to climb all the way up that tree to get it," enjoined George, pointing to a nest high up in a nearby elm tree.

"We left three. Plan is we goin' to come back just before they fly, get one of them, grow it up and learn it to talk; they say you can, don't they?"

"Yes, I'm sure you can – but they don't *all* talk," said William reasonably.

Reuben shrugged and took a blackthorn out his pocket, making two holes in the egg and starting to blow out the contents, his face reddening with the effort.

"Has it been sitting? You've got one that's half grown in there I bet," said William.

"Give it 'ere, Reuben, you ain't no good at blowing them; let me 'ave a go," said George, taking the egg from his friend and blowing hard. The contents of the egg started to ooze from the other end, forming a long drip and pouring out in a rush.

"There," said George triumphantly, "I knew I could do it! That's one more for the collection."

"I must get home," said William, mounting his bike and leaving the young boys peering into the hedgerow.

At the butcher's shop, an unfamiliar gelding was tied to the fence outside.

"Your father's got a visitor, William," said Sarah, as William moved into the shop to identify the owner of the horse.

"Who's that, then?"

"I don't know; I think he's a horse dealer – he looks like one anyway."

William had a pretty good idea who the visitor might be, and it was with a sense of dread that he made his way to the kitchen.

"William, I believe you know our visitor?" said his father as he entered.

"Yes, hello Mr Ladds, pleased to meet you again," said William, shaking Noble's hand.

"Master William Dunmore, what a pleasant surprise to meet you again! I told you that I would pay a call to see if I could do any business with your father."

Noble Ladds, unlike the last time they had met, was dressed for riding; he wore high leather boots with spurs, a jacket and loud-check waistcoat. The stock around his neck was secured with a gold tie pin in the shape of a horse shoe, inlaid with small sparkling stones. His moustache was immaculately trimmed and his hair brushed close to his head.

"Mr Ladds wants to sell us horses, William, for when we take over the extra land," said Thomas.

"Some more tea, Mr Ladds?" asked Charlotte. "Or another piece of cake? William, if you want a cup of tea, go and tell Sarah and she will bring one."

William, delighted for an excuse to leave, went out to see Sarah.

"Who's that man, William?" whispered Sarah. "I don't like the look of 'im! All dressed up like a dog's dinner and talking the legs off a donkey."

"He's Noble Ladds; I don't like him either," grumbled William.

He sat down at the kitchen table.

"Can I have a cup of tea please, Sarah?"

"Coming up, William; but hadn't you better go back in there? They will want to know what you're up to soon. I will bring your tea."

"Suppose I'd better," sighed William, getting up and making his way back to the sitting room.

"Mr Ladds has asked us to go up to Bythorn to look at some draught animals, William," said Thomas as William re-entered the room. "What do you think? We'll need more when we get that extra land."

"Well I don't think we need to buy any until after Joe has had his sale," said William coldly. "We should be able to buy some of his; he has some good horses, I've had a look."

"Well I don't think it will do any harm to have a look at what Mr Ladds has to offer," insisted Thomas. "I can call in on the way back from Thrapston next week if that's all right, Mr Ladds?"

"Very good, Mr Dunmore! Young William here is a good deal more cautious by the looks of it, but I would be pleased to show you what we have to offer next week."

Noble Ladds stood up, thanked Charlotte for the tea and left the house, escorted by William.

Henry was just riding into the yard, crossing paths with Ladds as he trotted off on his hunter.

"Who was that dandy then?" he said to William. "What was his business here?"

"Mr Noble Ladds Esquire, horse dealer," said William through gritted teeth. "I wouldn't trust him further than I could throw him."

"How do you know he's that bad, William; you met him before?"

"I met him on the Isle of Wight when I went to the funeral; he was a nasty piece of work then and he's done nothing to change my opinion of him."

"Are you going to do any business with him then?"

"Father's going to look at his horses next week so we will have to wait and see," grumbled William, stroking the nose of Henry's horse, who pushed its head into William's hand, eager for more attention.

"Now, William, I want some advice about this farm at Brington; I want you to come and have a look at it with me and give me your opinion."

"Why don't you ask your father to have a look?" William asked, surprised. "He's been farming much longer than I have."

"I haven't told him yet," said Henry quietly. "I can't tell him – it would upset him if he thought I was going to leave. I'm sure we can't go on at Cold Harbour; the mortgage is crippling us and I want to get married and move.

There should be enough left over if we sell to see Mother and Father in their retirement."

"But what would they do? Where would they go?" asked William.

"I don't know quite," admitted Henry.

He looked earnestly at his cousin.

"Just come with me and look at this place, will you? You've got your head screwed on, William; you know about money and all that and you'll tell me if you think it would work."

William nodded and patted the horse's neck. Henry smiled, relieved:

"Two o'clock tomorrow then, William? I'll meet you here."

Henry and William travelled the next day to the outskirts of Brington.

"Where's the farm then, Henry?" said William, bringing his bike to a stop and looking around at the houses.

"I don't know, William," admitted Henry guiltily. "I've never been here before."

"But I thought you had everything sorted out!" exclaimed William.

"Well I have and I haven't," said Henry with a shrug. "I know the farm's coming up for rent and I know your father's the trustee – but I haven't looked at it yet."

"What's it called then?" said William, exasperated.

"Church Farm it's called; it's a hundred and ten acres and nearly all pasture so I'm told."

"Right, Henry," said William, exasperated, "Church Farm must be near the church – I can see a steeple from here, so let's go and look."

He pushed his bike off in the direction of the church, Henry leading his horse behind.

"There it is, William, look! It says it on the gate."

A big old farmhouse stood set slightly back from the road. The front was thatched, and the back, which must have been a later addition, tiled. In places they could see the plaster clinging desperately to the walls, and in many areas it had fallen off completely – exposing the mud between the beams. The buildings behind the house showed signs of neglect and in the big cattle yard the muck was piled up so high that the bullocks banged their heads on the roof timbers as they went in and out. A bigger stone barn, presumably for the hay and fodder, looked in slightly better repair.

"Go on, Henry, go and ask if we can have a look round," said William, taking hold of his cousin's horse and shooing Henry in the direction of the farm door. William watched as Henry knocked and started chatting to the man who opened the door – he had a peg leg and leant heavily on the door frame for support.

"What did he say then?" said William as Henry came back.

"He said we could go where we liked 'cos he was fed up with it. He said there's no money in farming, only work, and the sooner he got out of it, the better off he would be, so long as he didn't die first."

"That sounds encouraging, Henry," chuckled William, leaning his bike against the railing and tying up Henry's horse.

They made their way around the farm and all the fields, ending up once more in the yard. Henry turned to his cousin.

"Well what do you think, William?"

"Do you want my honest opinion?" said William with a sigh.

"Yes. That's why I asked you to come with me."

"It's a real mess, Henry; the buildings are rubbish, the fields are wet and need draining and the house looks in a state as well. It all needs money and I don't think that the landlord's going to spend any; so where's that cash coming from?"

Henry looked over at the cattle and shifted uneasily.

"That's what I was going to say, William; I was going to ask your father for a loan to get started. I can't do it otherwise – I've got no money, neither's Martha."

"But what are you going to stock it with, Henry?" said William. "It's all very well getting the farm, but you've got to have stock."

"Well I thought – well no, I *hoped* I could bring some from Cold Harbour; some cows and calves and I could borrow a bull, I'm sure of that. And if I brought some ewe lambs and a tup we could get the sheep going; it's much nearer Thrapston here to sell them?"

Henry looked at his cousin desperately, imploring him for some sign of encouragement that this could work.

"Would you help, William, if we came?" he begged. "I just want someone to add up the columns every now and again and that sort of thing; you know I'm not much good at that."

William ran his eyes over the dilapidated buildings, seeing months and years of hard work ahead. He looked back to his cousin who was so sure that he could make this work if only somebody believed in it strongly enough.

"Of course I'll help, Henry; I think that if you can get the farm you should have a good chance. The farm's a mess but there's nothing wrong with it that hard work can't cure and if Father gives you a loan you should be able to get going."

He smiled at his cousin.

"Now while we are this way, let's go home via Bythorn, it's only two miles up the road; we can see what Mr Noble Ladds' farm looks like."

Henry nodded and they made their way away from the farm towards the residence of Noble Ladds. On their approach to the village stood the pub, The Stags Head. From the street, four stone steps led to a big green front door, which stood open, and framed in the doorway they could see Noble Ladds. He tottered forward and began to descend the steps one at a time, desperately clutching the handrail with one hand, a cigarette in the other. The last step into the street was deeper than the preceding ones, which seemed to take Noble Ladds by surprise. He stumbled, losing his cigarette as he did so and falling hard on his face into the road. He rolled over and started to giggle.

"Come on, Henry," said William nervously, "we don't want to meet him in that state."

They took a left turn through the backyard of the pub, past the blacksmith's shop and onto the bridleway.

"Thank goodness we didn't have to talk to him," sighed William.

"What about his farm, I thought you wanted to look at the horses?" said Henry.

William laughed mirthlessly.

"Father won't buy anything from him if he knows he drinks like that; I'll make sure of it."

The Friday of the ball had finally arrived. After work, Mary walked to the Harding's house on the outskirts of Northampton, carrying only an overnight bag, her dress having already been delivered. No sooner had the front door been opened by the maid than Rebecca came running up the hallway.

"I'm so pleased you're coming with us, Mary," she gushed, hugging Mary. "Come and meet Father."

She ushered Mary down the hall into the drawing room where a middle-aged man sat reading the paper. He wore a thick, light brown tweed suit, with matching waistcoat and wore his beard in a similar style to that of the new king.

"Father, Father, you must meet Mary –I told you about her," gabbled Rebecca happily.

Mr Harding lowered his paper and smiled indulgently at his daughter.

"Mary, how pleased I am to meet you," he said, standing and offering Mary his hand. "Rebecca has told me all about you; but she didn't say how pretty you are. Come, my dear, take a seat and tell me about yourself; Rebecca ring for some tea."

Mary took the proffered hand, shook it and sat down in the seat indicated. She found it hard not to stare at the opulence of her surroundings – the expensive furnishings, the beautiful rugs and paintings.

"Now, Mary, Rebecca tells me that you work at Tibbitts."

"Yes, Mr Harding, I have been there for over two years now."

"And you know Peveril, I'm sure."

"Yes, sir."

"And your uncle is George Henry Chambers no less."

"Yes, sir."

"Now there's a go-ahead man if ever there was one; yes, he's a good man, I've known him for years. But I can't remember; where is home for you, Mary?"

"I live on a farm, sir, in Melchbourne, but the farm's much nearer Dean in Bedfordshire."

"Of course! I know it! We went hunting there Rebecca, didn't we?" he mused, adding mischievously. "Wasn't that the one where you fell off?"

He winked at Mary.

"Yes it was, Father," said Rebecca grumpily, "you don't have to keep on reminding me."

"What's the name of the fellow who owns all the land – there, it's on the tip of my tongue—" he gesticulated wildly with his hands, "he can't walk and they push him about in a wheelchair."

"That's Mr Watson-Foster, sir," Mary replied.

"That's the fellow! Quite amazing – even goes shooting in his wheelchair! Just imagine! Didn't his wife die?"

"Yes, sir, she died shortly after their daughter was born," replied Mary.

"Yes, I seem to remember something about it," mused Mr Harding, as the slam of the front door was heard.

Adelaide swooped into the room, pulling off a long fur coat and large hat, which she handed without acknowledgement to the maid. She glanced quickly at Mary.

"Oh it's *you*," she sneered dismissively. "Finished work, then?"

"Don't you think she's the prettiest thing, Adelaide?" said Mr Harding lightly, smiling at Mary.

"Well I suppose so," conceded Adelaide grudgingly, "considering she's just a farmer's daughter."

She turned her back on them, waltzing over to a glass-fronted cabinet which stood in the corner of the room.

"I could do with a drink, what about you, Charles?"

"Bit early for me, dear, but sit down, I'll get you one."

This had evidently been what Adelaide had been waiting for; she turned, walked back and threw herself into a large armchair.

"Now, Charles, I want you to have a word with Rebecca," she said loudly.

Mary cringed as Rebecca turned her gaze resolutely to the carpet.

"You've got to tell her that when we introduce her and whatever her name is over there to our friends that she's to answer properly and not ignore them as she usually does. It's so embarrassing – anyone would think she doesn't know how to behave! And after all the money you've spent on her education."

"Don't worry, dear, I'm sure they will both behave impeccably, won't you, Rebecca?" said Mr Harding quietly.

"Yes, Father," said Rebecca dumbly.

"Now, you girls, you better go and get ready, we leave at half past seven sharp."

Rebecca got up but said nothing, so Mary followed suit, smiling as she left the room. Walking up the stairs, Rebecca turned fiercely to Mary.

"That woman is the most dreadful specimen imaginable; I cannot think why Father married her, he must have had a brainstorm or something. She's just trying to marry me off you know; you wait and see when we get there – she'll hawk me round to all the mothers with 'suitable' sons. It's like the cattle market; they look you up and down, add up how much you might be worth – it's dreadful."

She turned with a sigh to Mary.

"Thank goodness you're here this time, Mary; no one knows who you are – so it's going to be all right".

The Hardings had a big car; and it was in this that they made the chauffeur-driven trip through the town and out to Wiston Hall for the ball. The night ran just as Rebecca had predicted; Adelaide swanned about, organising who the two girls met and who they danced with. There was clearly one front-runner for the hand of Rebecca, whose mother seemed equally as anxious as Adelaide for the match. His name was Jimmy Brummitt.

"Who's Jimmy, then?" Mary enquired when they had a moment to themselves.

"He's the son of the big solicitor; they've got pots of money. Jimmy's all right but a bit odd if you know what I mean."

"In what way? He looks all right?" said Mary, looking over towards Jimmy who was hanging somewhat awkwardly at the fringes of a group of laughing men.

"He's just away with the fairies a bit," she laughed. "I don't know what I mean really."

Before Mary could enquire any further, a hand was placed lightly on her shoulder.

"Mary, I've found you at last, don't you look so lovely in that dress? I'm sure you are the prettiest one here," said Rupert delightedly.

"And who's this then?" Rebecca demanded.

Mary blushed.

"Sorry, Rebecca – this is Rupert Nelson; he's a reporter on the local paper."

"So how do you know each other, Mary, you didn't tell me?"

Rebecca raised her eyebrows enquiringly at Mary, who blushed.

"We met on the train and we meet sometimes on my way to work."

"How nice," smiled Rebecca, "well, Mary, you had better make sure that Rupert takes you for a dance – you don't want those dancing lessons to have been for nothing."

And with a wink to her friend, she moved off into the room, a weather eye on the location of her interfering stepmother.

Chapter Twenty
The Flower Show

The approach of summer 1901 meant the last few weeks at school for William. It had been decided by his parents that with all the extra land they were taking on, he must leave to help on the farm. Reverend Belpeel, desperate not to lose his model pupil, had made a pilgrimage three times to the farm to try to make Thomas change his mind, but all in vain. His parents were determined that he should come back and start work for them.

Verity, after exerting pressure on her father, was to move to a school in Bedford rather than staying at school on the south coast; she wanted to be nearer home to take a greater part in the life of Dean. Almost half of the people in the village were either tenants of, or worked for John Watson-Foster, and it was their well-being that Verity wanted to be more involved with. She was still determined to go to university, but knew that with hard work she would be able to go, no matter which school she attended.

The highlight of the year in Dean was the flower show. It was always held on the first Saturday in August; a big tent was erected next to the cricket pitch and everyone entered their flowers and vegetables in various classes. Stalls dotted the green, some offering games for the children, games such as bowling for a pig – a ten-week old weaner – which could then be raised by the winner and eaten when fat. The band came from Raunds and played during the afternoon events. The children were all expected to wear fancy dress, and in the evening the pub provided a bar for the dancing.

The entries for the flowers and vegetables had to be at the tent by ten o'clock in the morning and were laid out in all their glory on long trestle tables. There were cake competitions, classes for eggs, honey, jam, wine, embroidery, lace; prizes were allocated for first, second and third, with special prizes for those who won more than one class. At the end of the morning the judges would be given lunch and at two o'clock Lord St John would open the show and announce the winners. Lady St John was to judge the fancy dress and then the festivities could begin. The band would strike up; their cheerful melodies drifting down the valley as the day was still, and the noise of skittle cheeses charging through pins would be heard, punctuated by great cheers when a new challenger took the lead. Running races were organised for the children – the boys separated from the girls – finishing with a sack race, the prize for which was an atlas. John Watson-Foster judged the races, sitting serenely in his wheelchair at the finish holding one end of the tape, the other being secured to a post.

Most of the village came to the fete – the children took special pains to avoid Ethel Standish, who was to be seen patrolling the grounds, policing the behaviour of adults and children alike. Roland Cumber and three others from the ploughing gang had just finished work for the weekend and made straight for the beer tent – with the exception of Bernard who sat snoring gently in a deck chair in front of the cricket game. Mary and Verity were running a tombola stand; Verity was putting the proceeds towards helping the wounded from the war in South Africa.

Ruby Tuffnail was in charge of the teas, which were served in a tent next to the hedge; close enough to Hall Farm house for them to transport boiling water from the range in huge teapots across the road. Cakes and sandwiches were laid out on a long trestle table; the delicate smell of cucumber drifting through the tent, intermingled with the sharp tang of onion from the grated cheese and onion sandwiches. Pennies and halfpennies clattered into the large saucer as the plates of food and cups of tea were handed out.

At half past four, thirty overs had been played in the cricket and the players wandered into the tent from the field, followed by the two umpires bearing the bails and ball. Players – some in whites, some making a concession to the dress code with pairs of off-white trousers – swung into the tent, plonking themselves on the long benches, constructed from planks and milk churns.

The band also stopped for tea, sitting around in their shirts and braces and peaked caps, their thick red coats slung next to them on the ground, eager to be replaced by the evening band who had just arrived in a pony and trap, lugging their instruments into the tent to set up. Fancy dress costumes lay abandoned in little piles at intervals by the hedge; too hot or cumbersome to be of any interest to their weary owners. Mary and Verity sat on the table next to their tombola drum; most of the prizes had been taken now and the two friends chattered excitedly together, the afternoon sun beating down on their smiling faces. Lord St John's chauffeur sat snoozing on the running board of the car, back propped against the mudguard, whilst children ran their dirty fingers along the paintwork on the other side and groups of people moved languidly towards the big tent where Lord St John was about to present the prizes for the flowers and vegetables.

Lucy, who had been leading the donkey rides, tugged her charge past Mary and Verity, a small girl perched astride the unwilling beast. The remains of sandwiches on the table next to Mary caught the animal's eye and it strained against the rein to snaffle some – Lucy heaved against the stubborn beast to tear it away. She gave it a tap on the rump to move it, but the donkey was undeterred, sensing an easy meal.

"Don't do that, Lucy!" Verity shouted angrily. "It's cruel."

"No, it's not!" Lucy fired back, tugging at the rein and flicking the small length of willow again towards the animal. "It's got a skin as thick as a rhinoceros; I can hit it much harder and it takes no notice at all."

Verity, taking pity on the hungry creature, took the remains of the sandwich and offered it up to the eager donkey, who devoured the sandwich in a single mouthful.

"Now, come on, you greedy beast," shouted Lucy, moving behind the beast and hitting it again. "Lucy, I wish you wouldn't do that, it's so cruel," Verity pleaded.

"I don't care, it's going to do what I say and that's that."

"Do you want any help, Lucy?" called George, trotting up to the scene with Reuben who held a bright red rosette in his hand.

"Yes, give it a push can you and I'll pull," puffed Lucy, her whole weight straining against the resistant donkey.

George and Reuben leant against the backside of the donkey, pushing it forwards, but it would not budge.

"I know," said Reuben with a wink at George.

He unclasped the safety pin on the back of his rosette and jabbed it into the donkey's fleshy rump. The donkey started, tossed its head and set off at a gallop across the cricket wicket, pulling the rein out of Lucy's hand and throwing its mount to the ground. The child rolled over once, sat up and began to cry.

"Why did it do that, Reuben?" Verity asked, rushing to the small child to check she was all right.

"Don't know," said Reuben innocently.

"Now look, I have to go and catch it now," Lucy moaned, making off towards the donkey who had found a green patch of grass to graze on, and almost bumping into Roland Cumber, who was heading out of the beer tent to try his hand at winning the pig, as she went.

"Watch it, girl," he growled, as Lucy sped past, waving her hand in apology as she did so.

"Come on, Roland, twenty-two to beat to win the pig," called Walter, who was manning the stand.

"How much?" he said, throwing his jacket to the ground and straightening his cap so the peak faced forwards.

"Threepence for nine cheeses," answered Walter.

"'Ere you are then," said Roland, flicking the threepenny piece to Walter. He spat on his hand and rubbed it against the other, taking hold of the first cheese and eyeing the line-up. The skittles stood on a leather covered table, which was marked with positions for their starting points; a well caught them as they fell, backed by a net to catch the cheeses as they were thrown. Roland approached the painted white line, licked the fingers of his right hand, wiped them on his trousers, readjusted the position of the cheese in his hand and with a powerful underarm throw released it at the skittles. The cheese hit the front skittle, which in turn took four more with it. The second cheese took out two skittles and the third, one.

"Well done, Roland," said Walter, moving to set the skittles up again as Roland walked back to the line. He licked his fingers again and threw, taking all nine skittles in one go.

"Flora!" someone shouted, provoking cheers from the watching crowd. The skittles were reset; Roland, with more of a swagger now, launched the cheese – it hit the front of the table and bounced back, coming to rest at his feet. He licked his lips and tried again, launching the cheese over the top of the skittles where it clattered into the well. A snigger rippled around the sea of onlookers.

"Six to win, Roland," someone shouted, as Roland stooped and with a quick sharp movement threw the cheese.

It scythed through the middle row of skittles, leaving three standing on either side. Roland side-stepped to the left and threw again; two skittles on the right tumbled down.

"You're level, Roland; one more and you're in front," called Walter.

Roland moved to the right, aiming at the three skittles on the left. The throw was hard and level, but missed its target. Roland threw his hands in the air, pursed his lips in anger and with a clean quick motion wrenched his cap off and threw it to the ground.

"Want another go, Roland?" said Walter encouragingly.

"In a minute I will, you ain't stopping yet, are you?"

"No, not till six."

"Right, I'll go and 'ave another pint," said Roland decisively. "I'll do better after that."

He picked up his cap and barged through the onlookers on his way back to the beer tent.

Ethel Standish was on the warpath – she had noticed a steady stream of boys making their way through a hole in the hedge at the bottom of the field and returning a few minutes later. Smelling wrongdoing, she determined to investigate, and set off towards the hedge, stopping briefly at the tombola stand.

"Mary Knighton, do you know what all those boys are up to going through the hedge?" she demanded of Mary.

"No idea, Miss Standish, we noticed them going as well and–"

But Ethel had already gone, marching towards the gap in the hedge; to get through she had to hold the brambles back, turning sideways to avoid catching herself on the thorns. A short walk across the rough grass brought her to the brook; the bank was not very steep here, so she lifted her skirt, stepped down and picked her way across. The brook had been dry for some time– the only water lying in stagnant pools between the gravel and stones. Reaching the other side, she looked into the field as it rose up from the brook; it had recently been cut for hay, which had been picked up and raised onto cocks to dry. Through the stacks she could make out two figures walking up the hedge line – George and Reuben.

"How far up 'ave we got to go?" said George.

"Nearly to the top; he said it was the third row from the top and the third one into the field."

"'Ave you got any money left, Reuben?"

"I've got fourpence; what have you got, George?"

"I've only got a penny."

"Well you ain't goin' to see much are you?" scoffed Reuben.

"How much is it then?"

"'E said for a penny she'll show her tits and for tuppence you can look up her skirt," advised Reuben.

"She ain't got no tits," said George, puzzled.

"Well you won't know till you 'ave a look, will you?"

Up ahead they could see a young boy standing by the haycock, waiting impatiently as another boy, hands on his knees, thrust his head and shoulders into the small stack.

"What if someone sees us?" said George.

"No one's coming up 'ere," said Reuben, looking round the field.

His eyes alighted on Miss Standish striding purposefully up the headland.

"Hey up George, we've got to scarper, old Standish is coming," Reuben hissed, taking off up the field, George just behind him.

The other two boys, meanwhile, had swapped places, the other dropping to his knees and peering into the stack. Suddenly the boy standing caught sight of Miss Standish cutting through the haycocks; he kicked his friend, who reappeared, hair ruffled and face red. He looked to where his friend was pointing and they both galloped back to the village on the same path that Reuben and George had taken before them.

Miss Standish stood in front of the offending hay stack, watching the boys running off up the field. She lowered herself quietly to her knees and crawled forward to put her head through the hole in the hay. With a gasp she sharply retracted her head slightly. Inside the stack, Molly Webb reclined on a heap of hay, her flowery pinafore dress unbuttoned at the top and pulled open to expose two small, perfectly formed breasts. The skirt of her dress was pulled up to her waist, her legs spread wide open. She was reaching up, trying to catch a spider in the hay above her.

"No touching, and make sure you put your money down," she instructed, looking down to see Miss Standish's shocked face staring back at her. Ethel pulled back through the hay, getting it stuck in her long hair as she stood up. She looked round the field, putting her hand to her forehead before shouting at the top of her voice,

"Molly Webb, come out here at once!"

Molly crawled out the hole, buttoning her dress as she came; she had no shoes on and her hair was full of hay as was Ethel's.

"Molly, what on earth do you think you are doing?" Ethel screeched. "I've never in my whole life come across anything so disgraceful, and so degrading! What am I going to do with you?"

Molly looked back defiantly, her lips were pursed shut and she was shaking slightly. She screwed her eyes up, leant forward and glared angrily at her teacher.

"You ain't going to do nothing, you old hag," she shouted. "There's nothing you can do. They're my tits and it's my cunt and I'm going to do what I like with it and I ain't never goin' to come to your school again, not never. I'm fourteen now and I don't have to come and listen to your old rubbish ever again." She wiped her fist angrily across her face to catch a tear trickling down her cheek. "What would you do then if you had no money, eh?" she continued. "What would you do if you 'ad no shoes? What would you do if you 'ad only had bread and lard for your tea every day? There ain't no point in us goin' to the Flower Show with no money."

She glared furiously at Ethel, bending down to pick the pennies off the floor and thrusting them into her pocket. She ran her fingers through her hair, brushed down her dress and strode off, picking her feet high to avoid the sharp edges of stubble and leaving Ethel staring helplessly after her.

The cricket had started again up at the Flower Show.

"Did you find what the boys were up to, Miss Standish?" Mary asked, as Ethel wandered past.

Ethel looked up distractedly, the hay still lacing her hair.

"Yes," she said thoughtfully, "I mean no; there was no one there."

"What was up with her?" said Verity, watching Ethel meander off. "And how did she get in a state like that?"

Mary shrugged, bewildered, watching the teacher wander towards the cricket pitch, crossing paths with Roland who was making his way towards the tombola.

"Here's that horrid man," hissed Mary. "Verity, that man is evil, I'm sure of it. I can't even tell you what he shouted at me the other day; it was so embarrassing."

"Who is he?" Verity asked.

"He drives a ploughing engine, I think he's the foreman," Mary replied.

She turned her back on him, to see Molly skipping towards her from the hedgerow, occasionally throwing her purse into the air and catching it again.

"Are you packed up?" Molly asked.

"Yes," said Mary, "we've got no more prizes left."

"Pity, I thought I would 'ave a go; but that's that, ain't it?"

"Molly," said Verity reproachfully, "I thought I gave you some shoes; what's happened to them?"

"I'm grown out of 'em," said Molly with a shrug. "Mum's given 'em to what's 'er name at the pub, it were over a year ago you gi' me 'em."

"I supposed it was, doesn't time fly," Verity sighed. "Come on then, we've got to take all this back home; if you help I'll find you some more."

"I don't want wore out ones," said Molly ungraciously.

"I wasn't going to give you 'wore out ones', and that's not a very grateful thing to say," said Verity sharply.

"Sorry, I ain't a grateful sort of person," shrugged Molly.

"But you can't go about with no shoes on, so pick that up and follow me," said Verity sharply.

"Yes, Miss Verity," sighed Molly, lifting a box and following Verity and Mary back towards The Hall.

Noble Ladds had just bought a horse at Bedford market and was making his way into town when he spotted Ethel Standish making her way in the other direction. He pulled on the reins of his horse and lifted his bowler hat.

"Excuse me, madam, is there anywhere here I can lodge for the night?" he asked. "My horse is about done in and I don't think it will get home."

"I think the pub's got a room," said Ethel, glancing up at Noble without much interest, "and there are certainly stables at the back; you can ask there."

Noble smiled and booted his steed in the direction she had indicated – seeking stabling for the horses and a room for himself.

"Where are all the people coming from?" he enquired of Minnie, watching people streaming down the streets.

"Oh they 'ave all bin at the Flower Show up the road; the cricket's still goin' on and Oswald's took a barrel up there."

"Well I might have a look," smiled Noble, tipping his hat at Minnie and heading in the direction of the show.

The cricket was still ongoing and the skittles contest was getting to a crucial stage – a crowd pressed round the table, red-faced men aiming cheeses lopsidedly at the skittles. Roland Cumber was standing smugly by the side; he was still the highest scorer.

"Right, anyone else for a go?" shouted Walter. "We got twenty minutes before we pack up."

He turned to Noble Ladds:

"What about you, mister, do you play?"

"Oh yes, I play," said Noble Ladds with a wink. "What's the prize?"

"A pig."

"Course it is," sighed Noble. "It's always a pig! I don't want one of them; but I'll have a go, if you like."

He took off his jacket and passed his hat nonchalantly to a man standing next to him, handing threepence to Walter and taking the cheese. He spun it in the air, caught it and threw; it was obvious he had done this before. Eight skittles tumbled down with the first cheese and the remainder with the second. Roland stood grouchily at the side, hands thrust in his pocket, as John wiped out another full set of skittles with his next two cheeses. The bystanders fell silent – with the next cheese John took out four more skittles, pulling him level with Roland Cumber. Roland coughed and shifted position, as Noble Ladds launched the next cheese, striking the remaining skittles. A cheer erupted – Ladds smiled cockily and winked at Roland.

"Are you goin' to 'ave another go, Roland?" Walter asked innocently.

"No I ain't," he snapped back. "Who the 'ell's 'e, anyway? Where's 'e come from?"

"Are you talking about me?" Noble said, looking around at Roland.

"Who else would I be talking about then?" sneered Roland, pulling himself up straight to look directly at Noble.

"Do you always welcome people like that?" said Noble with an easy smile, meeting Roland's threatening gaze. "You don't seem to be a very good loser! Come on, let me buy you a pint; you can have the pig – I don't want it and I can't get it home anyway."

Roland, taken aback by this offer, was momentarily speechless and eyed Noble suspiciously. Finally, he conceded.

"Well I s'pose you did win," he shrugged. "I'll drink a pint with you if you insist on it."

Noble laughed and clapped Roland jovially on the shoulder, guiding him over to the beer tent. The crowd had gone, the preparations had begun for the dance and Oswald had loaded the beer barrel in a wheelbarrow, ready to take it back to the pub.

"What's up, then?" demanded Roland.

"Barrel's empty, you'll have to come up the pub if you want any beer," muttered Oswald.

"Well I don't know," said Roland looking at Noble.

"Come on; we'll go up there, it ain't far," said Noble to his companion, following Oswald out of the tent towards the village.

Mary and Verity were back at The Hall, sitting at the kitchen table with glasses of golden lemonade, counting the money they had made. Dorcas sat watching, a cup of tea clutched in her chubby fingers. Piles of farthings, halfpennies and pennies lay on the table, intermingled with the odd silver coin. Mary pulled the coins off the table into her hand, counting them quickly as she had learnt to at the shop, and relating the numbers to Verity, who noted the digits on a piece of paper. A knock at the door heralded the arrival of Lucy who sloped grumpily into the room and slumped into a chair.

"I've never met a more awkward animal in my life," she groaned. "The only thing that would make it move was the offer of food or Reuben sticking a pin in its backside."

She pulled a small bag of takings from her pocket and dropped it onto the table.

"Mary, can you count this for me?" she asked. "I always get it wrong when I do it."

Mary reached for the bag, tipped the change onto the table and started collecting the coins into heaps, her hand flashing backward and forwards as she sorted.

"Can you count the heaps, Verity?" requested Mary, sliding the heaps towards Verity.

"Would you like golden lemonade, Miss Lucy, or would you like a proper cup of tea?" said Dorcas, rising from the table.

"Oh tea please, Dorcas," said Lucy gratefully.

There was another knock at the door; it was William. He took his cap off, limped across the kitchen and sat down with the others.

"What's up with your leg, Master William?" asked Dorcas.

"Nothing much, I just got bashed with a ball on the knee and it's a bit painful."

"Come here then," said Dorcas. "Let's have a look; roll up that trouser leg and put your foot on this chair."

William did as he was told as Dorcas examined his wound.

"Not too bad," she assured him. "Just a big bruise; I'll put some witch hazel on it."

She bustled off to the cupboard, retrieved the bottle and dabbed some liquid on the bruise.

"Don't you wear pads, William?" asked Verity.

"Yes, but we've only got two pairs," explained William. "The wicket keeper has one and the batsmen have one each. The ball hit the one I didn't have a pad on."

"That's stupid; you should have enough pads for everyone, shouldn't you?" tutted Verity.

"That's right," said Dorcas, "you never know where the ball might hit you."

She started to giggle. William blushed deeply and the girls looked at each other, unsure of what they had missed.

"Master William, are you going to have golden lemonade or tea?" Dorcas said, amusement still dancing in her eyes.

"I don't think I'll have either, Dorcas, thank you very much. I'll have to go home and get changed out of these things and come back for the dance. Are you all going?"

"Yes, we're all going," said Verity. "Or, I think we are, isn't that right, Mary, Lucy?"

"Yes, we're going," said Lucy, looking to Mary, who nodded.

"Dorcas, are you going to come? Walter's going to push Father up there," said Verity.

"Well I don't know about that, I am not much cop at that sort of thing and someone's got to look after the 'ouse," said Dorcas.

"That won't matter for an hour or two. You could lock up if you're worried; but who's going to come here? They will all be up at the dance."

"Very well then, I will see what your father says," said Dorcas.

"Is Henry coming, Mary?" asked William.

"I expect so; it depends whether Martha goes, but I expect she will."

At seven o'clock the party from The Hall left for the dance; John Watson-Foster, pushed by Walter, in front, the three girls trotting excitedly beside him and Dorcas bringing up the rear. As they left the house they could hear the band playing; the fiddler, accordionist and drummer serenading the early arrivals. The beer for the evening was provided by the pub at the other end of the village, The World's End, which could supply spirits – the Marquis of Bute only had a beer licence. Along the road, groups of people made their way to the dance – whole families coming from the outlying lodges scattered around the parish.

"Right," shouted John Watson-Foster, as the group reached the tent, "who would like a drink?"

He looked round expectantly.

"Well don't all shout at once will you!" he grumbled.

He fumbled in his pocket, plucking out a gold sovereign.

"Now, Dorcas – you are in charge of the money; Walter, you go and bring me back a glass of whisky and the rest of you– and you, Henry Knighton, and your young lady– get yourselves a drink. Dorcas, Walter, have one yourselves and, Dorcas, keep the change in your pocket for the next one."

He beckoned Henry over.

"Henry, come here a minute, I have not met your young lady," he boomed, as Henry and Martha walked towards his chair. "Come on then, Henry, introduce me."

"Yes, sir, this is Martha," said Henry proudly, beaming at Martha.

John Watson-Foster extended his hand towards Martha, who edged forward and shook it.

"Pleased to meet you, my dear, and where do you come from?"

"I work at Dean House, sir, as a housemaid, but my home is in Derbyshire."

"Well done, well done, and do you like it down here?"

"Oh yes, sir."

"And Henry, how's the farm going at Cold Harbour?" asked John.

"Not too good, sir," admitted Henry. "I think Father will have a job to hang onto it; the mortgage is too big."

"Thought as much," mused John, eyeing Henry thoughtfully. "And what will you do, young man?"

"Well, sir, I've looked at a farm at Brington that will come up for rent soon; we'll have to wait and see what happens."

"And are you two going to tie the knot then?"

"Hope so, sir," Martha replied quickly.

"That's the way, that's the way," chuckled John happily. "Now, Henry, when and if you want to take that farm, you are going to need some help; you come and see me and I will see what I can do." He nodded decisively.

"Thank you very much, sir," said Henry gratefully. "It won't be easy; I think Uncle Thomas might help, but thank you."

"Go along with you then," said John, pulling a cigar from his pocket and watching Henry and Martha move into the tent. He lit his cigar and surveyed the scene; young and old organising themselves into groups ready for the dance.

"I think we ought to dance," said Lucy.

"Do we have to?" Henry groaned.

"Yes we do; here comes William; that makes six – so we only need two more boys and we will be eight."

The caller was shouting for groups of eight, but no one wanted to be the first to start.

"We're coming," shouted Lucy. "William! William – over here."

She waved.

"Who else can we get?" said Verity.

"I know," said Mary, "look over there; there's George and Reuben."

"Aren't they a bit young?"

"Well, who else is there? Come on, Lucy, you grab George and I'll get Reuben – they'll say no, but hard luck."

"Right, George, you're coming with me," said Lucy, grabbing the unsuspecting boy's arm and pulling him towards the dancers.

"Where are we goin' then?" he looked enquiringly at Lucy.

"Dancing."

"I ain't dancing, that's girls stuff," protested George.

"Yes you are, George, I'll go and get Miss Standish if you refuse; she will tell you that you have to learn to dance, so there."

Mary had just reached Reuben and took hold of his hand firmly.

"Come on then," she said.

"Come on where?" replied Reuben, looking around for George.

"Dancing."

"I ain't dancing, girls do that."

"Yes you are, Reuben."

"No I ain't."

"Reuben!" Mary smiled, turning the full force of her charm upon him and stroking his cheek. "For me?"

"Just for you then, Mary," said Reuben, blushing slightly and allowing himself be led off.

"Sets of eight," shouted the caller, "sets of eight in a circle – boy – girl – boy – girl; come on everyone."

"Come on then," said Mary pulling Reuben with her, "Reuben, Verity, William, Lucy, George, Martha, Henry and me – all complete."

The group stood holding hands as other sets were formed around them; eventually the band began and the dancing started. Round and round and back and back and in and out they went; one dance then another and another, until everyone wanted another drink.

Roland and Noble Ladds had returned from the pub and stood watching the dancing, clasping their beer to their chests. In the cool of the evening, Noble had replaced his jacket and in his riding boots and waistcoat he cut a dashing figure.

"Who's that man talking to Roland, William? He can't be much good if he speaks to him," Mary asked.

"He's a horse dealer from Bythorn," said William noncommittally.

"Do you know him then, William?"

"Yes I met him on the Isle of Wight."

"He looks nice," said Mary, looking interestedly at the man, "except he's talking to that dreadful Roland."

"I can't stand either of them, Mary," William said, turning away.

"He looks nice," repeated Mary quietly, her eyes returning time and again through the course of the evening to the handsome man at the bar.

Chapter Twenty-One
An Automobile Arrives

That autumn – the autumn of 1901 – Thomas took over Dean Way Post Farm. The steam ploughing gang had started before the official takeover day and were getting on well with the ploughing. The farm had a large set of buildings, a big house at the Way Post and another set of buildings and cattle yards at Hardwick's on the hill above Tillbrook, where there was a house for the stockman. Of the four hundred acres on the farm, under half were ploughed, the rest being pasture grazed by bullocks and sheep, which Thomas planned to put through the butcher's shop. The butcher's business had expanded and he now employed a full-time butcher: Roy Lowe, George's father. The expansion of the butcher's business and the accumulated savings from his farm had enabled him to take on the extra land without any borrowing from the bank.

The stacks of corn standing in the fields had been bought from the previous tenant – Joe Shadbolt – and Thomas decided to get some of the stacks at Hardwick's threshed so that there would be enough straw for the cattle over the winter. Thomas had asked Clive Morris to bring his set from Raunds to do the threshing when they had finished in Covington at Mr Milligan's. It was a Friday morning and the gang were on the move from Covington, aiming to get everything in place to start threshing at Hardwick's on Monday morning.

At the butcher's shop, business was booming – Roy had taken over the responsibility of cutting up the meat from Thomas, which in turn had given him time to concentrate on the farm, and Roy's constant presence in the shop meant that Charlotte no longer had to serve all the customers. That morning had been quiet, but at lunch time the sound of the door heralded a customer.

"There's someone in the shop, Mrs Dunmore, shall I go?" called Sarah from the scullery.

"Isn't Roy there?" replied Charlotte.

"No, 'e's gone for 'is lunch."

"I'll go then," said Charlotte, moving into the shop from the kitchen.

Molly stood awkwardly in the middle of the shop, gazing around at the displayed meats.

"Hello, Molly, aren't you at school then?" asked Charlotte.

"I'm finished school, I ain't never goin' back there again," said Molly moodily, thrusting her chin out defiantly.

"Doesn't time fly, you're that old! I didn't realise!" said Charlotte, with a shake of her head. She smiled at the girl in front of her. "And what can I do for you, Molly?"

"Mother says can she 'ave a pound of lard but we ain't got no money till next week." She looked hard at Charlotte, her sharp little face pre-emptively aggressive. "Dad ain't got no work; 'e's gone over to Raunds today round the shoe places but they're all cuttin' down. No one comes round anymore to bring 'im stuff to do."

"And aren't you working, Molly?" asked Charlotte.

"I was gleanin' and then tatterin', but them 'ave all stopped now – so I ain't."

"Very well, Molly, I'll write it in the book and there's half a dozen sausages, take them as well."

Molly's eyes lit up, her expression softening.

"Do you want a biscuit, Molly?"

"Yes please, Mrs Dunmore," she said eagerly.

"Come on in the kitchen then and sit down while you eat it," said Charlotte kindly.

Charlotte went into the kitchen, opened the biscuit barrel in the middle of the table and proffered it towards Molly. Molly peered eagerly into the barrel to select her favourite, her small, long fingered hand – nails bitten to the quick – snaking into the barrel to snatch out her chosen biscuit.

"There's nice shoes you've got on, Molly," said Charlotte as Molly started to nibble on the biscuit.

"Yup, Verity gi' me 'em."

"You mean Miss Watson-Foster, don't you, Molly?" said Charlotte, a note of reprimand creeping into her voice.

"Yes s'pose I do," shrugged Molly.

"And how's your mother; doesn't she work at Mr Watson-Foster's?"

"No, not at the minute; she can't, she got hurt," said Molly quietly.

"Oh, how's that? I didn't hear," said Charlotte.

"She got scalded. She were liftin' the boilin' water out the copper with one of them buckets with a rope 'andle and the 'andle broke and the water went all down 'er and scalded her between 'er legs." Molly sniffed, blinking rapidly, "She can 'ardly walk and it don't 'eal up very quick. She says we'll 'ave to go into the work 'ouse if Dad don't get any work."

Tears started to spring into her eyes; she put her fist to her nose and lowered her head, and her small body shook as she tried to repress the sobs threatening to overcome her. She sniffed twice and fell silent.

"Have another biscuit, Molly," said Charlotte quietly, moving the barrel closer to her.

Molly smiled a watery smile and carefully selected another biscuit.

"Didn't your father work on a farm, Molly?" asked Charlotte gently.

"Yeah, 'e were born at Dean Lodge all the way up that track; 'is dad used to keep all the cattle up there. 'E said 'e started on the farm but the wages weren't no good, so 'e left and went into the boot and shoe trade when it were good money."

She sniffed again and started to eat the biscuit.

"'E said he wished 'e 'ad never left the farm, 'e liked the cattle 'e said," Molly sighed, "any road that's a long time ago."

"Now, Molly, finish your biscuit and run along back home with that meat," said Charlotte decisively. "I'll have a word with Thomas; we will see if we might be able to help your father."

Molly looked up, surprised, and smiled freely at Charlotte.

"Thank you, Mrs Dunmore," she said earnestly, rising and moving out of the kitchen. "Thank you very much."

When Thomas had taken on the new farm, he had hired some of the labour from the previous owner, but Charlotte knew they were still down a stockman. That evening, she made her case for the employment of Ray Webb. Thomas and William agreed that it would be the right thing to do and that William would go and talk to Ray the following morning.

William's visit was met with a mixed reaction. Ray was extremely grateful to have been offered a job – he knew the work and realised he had very little in the way of options. The job would entail looking after around fifty bullocks, kept in straw-littered yards at Hardwick's. The yards were open in the middle, hedged by lean-tos on three sides, a trough running the length of walls, with hay racks mounted above them. Water needed to be pumped from the well for the beasts, which could take up to an hour every morning; the cattle drank a lot and the water supply depleted rapidly. The basic food – hay – would be cut out of the stack with a large, flat, three-foot-long knife, and then barrowed into the hay racks around the walls. The cattle were also fed chopped mangles, mixed with chaff, rolled oats or barley. Half a dozen pigs were stabled in a barn to the left of the house, and occasionally a draught horse was in one of the adjoining stables. There was also a house cow, that had to be milked and the milk sent down to the butcher's shop.

Ellen, however, although pleased with the prospect of employment for her husband, did not want to move out of the village to an area of such isolation. None of the children wanted to leave either – Molly would have to stay at home and help her mother and the two younger children would have a long walk to school. For the Webbs, however, there were no alternatives – there was no work in the village and despite the vehement protestations of the children, Ray and Ellen agreed to the move the coming week. William sent a cart to collect the Webbs and their possessions and Ellen, after loading their few meagre belongings, perched on it, whilst Ray walked behind as it left the village to make its way to Hardwick.

Molly was sent with the key of the old cottage to The Hall. She reached the back door, banging on the door with her hand. There was no reply. Molly knocked again; someone was usually in the kitchen, it was odd that nobody was answering. Once again, there was no answer; with a shrug, Molly turned from the door and moved down the drive. As she did so she could hear shrieks and chattering from towards the outbuilding; curious, she made her way towards the noise. Rounding the last yew bush she was presented with the amazing sight of two shimmering motor cars. Molly had seen cars before; but none as big and splendid as these – gleaming black paint fronted with shiny chrome bumpers and grills, which were being polished by a chauffeur in uniform. The entire household were there to admire the machines. Dorcas and the two housemaids were watching from the front porch as John circled the car in his wheelchair, pushed as ever by Walter. Verity tailed them, chattering excitedly to Walter. A man in a bowler hat and pinstriped suit strode officiously beside John, pointing out each feature of the car with an elegant flourish.

"What I need to know, young man, is can I get out of this wretched wheelchair contraption and into it," Molly could hear John saying, gesticulating furiously at the car.

"I don't see why not, sir," simpered the young man. "Perhaps you would like to have a try?"

"Very well then," said John with a satisfied nod, "come on, Walter, I'll get in the back seat if I can." The canvas roof of the motor car was folded back, and the back door stood open; John looked suspiciously at the gap between his wheelchair and the car.

"Not a chance," he said firmly, "there's got to be something in between before I can get in."

"I know," said Verity, "let's get a stool and put it there."

She pointed to the running board and called behind to the audience on the porch.

"Dorcas! Send Betty to go and get a stool" she ordered.

Betty scuttled off to get the stool, returning to replace it on the running board.

"Possible, possible," said John, with an approving smile at the stool, "Walter, come on, give me a hand."

Walter removed the sidearm of the wheelchair, moving to stand behind John who reached out, grasped the door column in one hand, a roof handle in the other and heaved. Although having no use of his legs, his upper body was very strong and he was able to pull himself up and across until he was sitting on the stool, and from there it was an easy shift into the vehicle.

"There, that wasn't too bad," grinned John. "We could soon make something better than that stool." He surveyed the interior of the car for a moment before announcing:

"Now we need a run in it! Come on, Verity, jump in; Walter you get in the front to see how to drive the wretched thing, I'm sure I will never be able to."

Verity made her way round to the other door, catching sight of Molly watching as she did so.

"Just a minute, Father," she said, running over to Molly.

"I've come with the key, Miss Verity."

"Yes, I want to have a word, Molly; just wait ten minutes can you while we try the car?"

Molly nodded, as Verity rushed back in the car to sit next to her father.

"Where shall we go, sir?" asked the salesman.

"Just round the block to Shelton and back I should think," said John.

The salesman hollered at the chauffeur, who trotted round to the front of the car and took hold of the starting handle.

"Ready," shouted the driver, as the chauffeur yanked the handle upwards.

Nothing happened.

"Again!"

Once more there was no response – Verity giggled.

"Again!" demanded the driver.

The engine growled into life, as smoked puffed from the exhaust. The driver engaged the gears, released the brake and the car crept forwards around the drive and out through the gates.

"Morning, Tuffnail," shouted John cheerily as they passed the blacksmith, who was shoeing a horse.

Art dropped the leg of the horse and straightened up in surprise; he just had time to raise his cap and shout, "Morning Mister Watson-Fos—" when the horse took fright, rearing and pulling the rein free of the post he was tied to.

Art lunged for the rope, but the horse skittered from his reach and cantered off up the road.

"Oh my, did you see that, Verity?" said John quietly, turning to watch the horse galloping away from Art. "We're not going to be very popular – I can see that."

They passed the church, up past the Rectory.

"I bet they haven't got a motor car," said John with a chuckle. "What do you think, Verity?"

"I don't know, Father," said Verity. "But it's not a competition, you know; we are lucky we can afford one."

"Yes, dear," John replied hastily, ever aware of his daughter's social conscience. "I don't know whether we *can* afford one, we will wait and see."

John leant back, glancing from side to side as they rolled along the road towards Shelton. He poked Walter on the shoulder with his cane jovially.

"Walter, are you paying attention? You're going to have to know how to drive if we get one of these contraptions."

"Well I don't know about that, master, I really don't know," muttered Walter, who was concentrating with all his might on the movements of the driver.

They came to the junction in Shelton and turned right back towards Lower Dean.

"How fast will it go then?" John demanded of the salesman as the car was turned back towards Lower Dean, scattering a gathering of chickens who were pecking for grubs at the side of the road.

"Thirty miles an hour, sir," said the driver proudly. "But this road is too rough for that; we are doing twenty now though."

They returned to The Hall, pulled up behind the other car and climbed from the car, Walter muttering to himself and shaking his head.

"Now, my man," John said, heaving himself back out of the car into his wheelchair, "how much do you want for it, then?"

Verity, sensible of the fact that financial matters were not becoming for a young lady to listen to, made her way up to Molly who was talking to Dorcas and the two maids.

"Molly, come into the kitchen, will you; I've got something for your mother."

She led the way into the house, through the front door towards the kitchen.

"Molly, I didn't realise what had happened to your mother until Dorcas told

246

me; I feel so guilty."

"Yes, Miss Verity," said Molly, slightly unsure of what Verity had done to feel responsible.

"How is she then, Molly?"

"She's very sore, Miss Verity; the scalds don't 'eal up very fast and she can't 'ardly walk on account of the scalds down 'er legs."

"It sounds awful," said Verity compassionately. "Now, here is some cream that she must put on; it will cool the scalds and help them heal. I will come and see you next weekend when I am home but I have to go back to school now."

"Yes, Miss Verity, thank you, oh – and 'ere's the key to the 'ouse, miss."

She handed Verity the key.

"Dorcas, I want to send Mrs Webb something from the kitchen; she's going into a new house and the fire won't be lit so she will not be able to bake."

"There's some buns I did yesterday," said Dorcas grudgingly – she did not approve of Molly, or want to give her the buns.

"They will be fine, wrap them up and send them back with Molly," she said, turning to Molly.

"I must go. Molly – take the buns that Dorcas gives you and I will be over to see you as soon as I get back from school".

And with that she rushed from the room – a whirlwind of social duty – leaving Molly standing looking bemusedly after her.

Chapter Twenty-Two
Verity visits Hardwick's

The next week Verity was on half term and decided to pay a visit to the Webbs at Hardwick Lodge. The new car would not be able to go up the muddy track, so she resolved to walk; if the smaller children had to walk to school that way surely she could manage. She took the bridleway up from the village, picking her way carefully through the sticky mud created by the recent rain. The wind was behind her, whipping at the hem of her skirt as she trudged up the hill. The first leaves were falling off the trees, the rosehips shining bright red in the hedges and the last of the blackberries provided a welcome snack on her journey. Rabbits stood curiously on their back legs as she approached, dashing for the cover of the hedge at the last minute. As she reached the top of the hill, she could see Henry Knighton riding towards her.

"Hello, Miss Verity," he said, lifting his cap, "don't often see you up here."

"No, I don't know why I don't come up more," said Verity smiling up at him. "It's beautiful, but I'm actually on my way to see the Webbs at Hardwick Lodge."

"Ah yes, William said that Ray's doing the cattle up there," nodded Henry. "It's a bit stuck in the middle of nowhere when you get up to Hardwick's."

"I've never actually been there so it will be a new experience," said Verity enthusiastically.

"Surveying all your father owns, I expect," said Henry, a touch wryly.

"I suppose I will," said Verity, surprised she had never thought of it like that and had forgotten that her father owned the farm that Thomas Dunmore had taken on.

"Where are you off to then, Henry? To see Martha, I expect! Does she have the day off on Saturdays?" Verity smiled.

"Well I will see her later, but I'm going down to see Aunt Charlotte; Mother's not so good, she's been in bed for a day or two and I'm going to see if Aunt Charlotte and Uncle Thomas will pop up and see her, she gets awfully bored in bed on her own all the while with only Lucy to talk to all day. Father can only get up and down once a day and he ain't much good to talk to."

"Well send your mother my regards, won't you, Henry? Did Father say you were thinking of moving to Brington?"

"Well, that's a long way off I'm sure but you never know what might happen," he said mysteriously, raising his cap again and nudging his horse onwards.

Verity walked onwards along the bridleway across the ridge of the hill to the wood which nestled just below the crest of the hill. She could see the roof of Hardwick's in the distance, smoke curling gently from the chimney. To her left she could see another farmstead – Harrowig, also owned by her father and rented by Mr Milligan. The houses were similar in size and appearance; a house and buildings backed with cattle yards and peppered with stacks of hay, straw and some unthreshed wheat. As she turned down the hill, the noise of a hunting horn reached her ears and before long the red coat of the huntsmen came into view, followed by a field of ten riders, the hounds trotting in front. It was early in the season and Verity thought – with some distaste – that they were probably cubbing. As the field passed, steam rose from the hounds trotting close to the huntsman; they were covered in mud and panting from a long chase; several had blood on their faces so they must have killed. The huntsman leant slightly forward as he rode along, raising his cap as he went passed.

"Miss Watson-Foster," he said, smiling.

Verity smiled back, standing back against the hedge to let them by: she had to admit it was a splendid sight. The field were mainly men and boys; there was one woman riding side-saddle and one girl who rode astride her horse accompanied by another man. All the men lifted their hats and nodded their acknowledgement to her, and the girl riding astride smiled and waved; Verity waved back and at the last minute remembered to smile, realising it must be Rebecca Harding – Mary's friend. At the junction of the bridleway, past the woods two boys emerged from the thicket and as they neared her she realised it was George and Reuben; she waited to have a word with them.

"'Ello, Miss Watson-Foster," said Reuben grinning broadly.

"Miss Watson-Foster," said George quietly.

"Where have you been?" Verity enquired.

"We've bin followin' the 'unt," said Reuben. "It were great – they just got one down there and look 'ere George 'as got the brush."

George smiled and held up the fox's tail, wiggling it in the air.

"I don't know if I approve of that," said Verity tartly. "Where are you off to now?"

"We've got to wait here," said George. "Noah is bringing his flock of sheep back and we've got to go in front down to the village, but it will be ages before he gets here; he hadn't even got them out the field when we saw him."

"Well I'm off to see Mrs Webb, so I'll have to leave you."

"No, we'll come for a bit," said Reuben. "We've got our catties wiv us and we can see if there's any rats round them stacks; better than waitin' 'ere."

"What's a catty, Reuben?" said Verity curiously as they made their way down the hill.

"A catapult, miss; I'm got new 'lacky in mine, it don't 'arf go now."

"What's lacky then, Reuben?" she asked.

"Elastic, miss; thick stuff."

He pulled out his catty and showed her.

"Are you going to see Colin and Brian when we get there?" Verity enquired, reckoning that the Webbs' two younger boys must be a similar age to Reuben and George.

"No we ain't goin' there!" said Reuben disgustedly. "You never get a biscuit at their 'ouse 'cos they ain't ever got any. Any road the old boys 'ave got ringworm; they ain't at school, we don't want to catch it, do we?"

Verity shuddered; she didn't know what ringworm was, but it didn't sound nice.

"Do you want a biscuit? I've got some in the basket to take to the Webbs."

Reuben and George turned to her, their eyes lighting up.

"You ain't got custard creams, 'ave you, Miss Verity?" said George eagerly.

"No, they're biscuits that Dorcas made."

She pulled back the cloth over the top of her basket and offered it towards the boys.

"Only one each, mind you," she said warningly, as their hands darted forwards.

"Thank you, miss," said George.

"Thank you, miss," echoed Reuben.

"You know the best place to go for a biscuit, Miss Verity?" said George quietly.

"No, George, tell me?"

"It's Mrs Dunmore's at the butcher's shop; she's always got some and she always gives us one."

Verity smiled and covered her basket again; they had arrived at the farmyard and the boys went off around the stacks in search of rats. Verity made her way to the backdoor, picking her way through the ruts and cow muck, to knock at the front door. There was no answer, so she moved round to the back of the house and entered through a small scullery where a stone sink stood on two brick piers near the door, a copper bubbling in the corner. In the kitchen she found Molly sewing at the fire; she leapt to her feet as soon as she saw Verity.

"Miss Verity, you've come to see us, isn't that kind. Come on take a seat – move out the way, Brian– let Miss Verity sit down."

Brian sulkily rose to his feet, took his thumb out of his mouth and wiped his runny nose with his sleeve. His hair had been cut short and his scalp was a mass of red scabby sores. Verity assumed this was the ringworm that Reuben had spoken of – she recognised it from other children in the village but had never seen it close up. The room was bare, with the exception of a table in the middle of the room, a rocking chair by the range and three chairs round the table. A lamp hung from a nail in the beam across the range and a length of twine was strung across this, from which hung a few pieces of washing. On the table a small loaf sat sadly on the breadboard, a lump of lard beside it. Brian scratched his head and winced.

"Don't do that, boy, you'll only make it worse," scolded Molly, cuffing her brother lightly across the back of his head. She turned to Verity.

"He's got ringworm, Miss Verity; a lot of 'em 'ave got it, 'e picked it up at school. Everyone says it's the cattle that give 'em it but the cattle ain't in the yards yet."

Verity looked at the boy again and turned away quickly; the sight of his head made her feel quite sick.

"We cut 'is hair off the best we could with the sheep clippers," said Molly, pinching his cheek. "'E'll get over it; they all'as do."

Molly went back to the fire, which was now just catching; she fed in some sticks and coal, turning happily to Verity.

"We've got some coal yesterday; William brought us five hundredweight up on the wagon when he brought the salt blocks up; so we can 'ave a decent fire and cook something proper for the first time for ages."

"I've brought a few little things for you, Molly," said Verity, putting the basket on the table and sitting down on the chair vacated by Brian; she eyed the sticky table dubiously.

"There are some biscuits and a piece of bacon," she said, taking them out of the basket and placing the objects onto the table. Molly was still poking the fire, a look of concentration on her face.

"Is your mother here, Molly?" asked Verity, a bit desperately. "I really came to see how she was."

"She's just gone down the end, Miss Verity; she'll be back in a tick, but that cream is doin' her a world of good."

Brian came up to the table, watching the biscuits hopefully; Verity noticed that he had no shoes or socks on.

"Don't you dare touch 'em, my boy," yelled Molly. "You wait till Mother's back and your bruvver is 'ere."

The boy backed off moodily, moving to the other side of the table, as Ellen entered through the back door.

"Miss Verity, 'ow loverly to see you," she exclaimed. "I've got to thank you for that cream, it really does work, you know."

She hobbled across the room with the help of a stick and sat heavily in the rocking chair.

"Ray's not 'ere today," she continued, "'e's gone down to 'elp Master William in the butcher's shop; they're killin' some beasts. We were so lucky that 'e got this job, Miss Verity – it saved us from the work 'ouse I'm sure. We've got coal and we can pay off all we owe and soon we'll 'ave enough for shoes for the boys an' all."

Ellen smiled contentedly at Verity who, unusually, felt embarrassed and looked down at the table.

"Miss Verity's brought us some biscuits and bacon," said Molly, sensing Verity's discomfort, "Isn't that nice of 'er."

"Miss Verity, I don't know 'ow to thank you," gabbled Ellen. "We never get anything sweet do we, Molly?"

"No, Mother."

"And look at that bacon, how loverly; but we won't 'ave any eggs I'm afraid; the ol' fox came last night and killed all the 'ens – every last one of 'em."

"Did you want a cup of tea, Miss Verity?" interrupted Molly. "The kettle will boil in about ten minutes, I 'spect."

"I think no," said Verity hurriedly. "I must be going shortly."

"I am so pleased with that cream, Miss Verity," Ellen said again, "it's doin' wonders; come an 'ave a look."

She beckoned to Verity as she leant forwards, grabbed the hem of her skirt and hoisted it up to above her waist, tipping the rocking chair back as she did so. The sight that greeted Verity was horrific; angry oozing sores scored the top of Ellen's legs and all the skin on her legs was red raw. Ellen peered happily down at the sight.

"Look – it's gettin' better already," she insisted. "I can tell it is – and it feels much easier."

Verity rose with a lurch from her chair.

"I must have a little air," she said hastily. "I'll be back in a minute."

She rushed to the door, staggered out across the yard and was violently sick over the wall, her stomach heaving at the joint sight of Ellen's legs and Brian's scalp. Across the field, Reuben and George observed this sight from their position against one of the stacks.

"Are you all right, Miss Verity?" called George, moving towards her, concern etched over his young face. Verity, unaware she was being watched, looked up hurriedly and reddened.

"Yes, I will be fine in a moment," she said with a wave of her hand, "I must have eaten something that did not agree with me."

"Have a drink of water, miss, it will do you good," said George. "The pump is over there."

"Just a little then," said Verity, moving gingerly towards the pump. George took the handle.

"Let me give it one or two pumps, miss, to clear the muck out the pipe," he said, working the handle up and down until the water ran clear. Verity looked round for a mug or some other receptacle to drink out of.

"In your hands, Miss Verity," said George, cupping his hands to demonstrate. Verity looked down at her hands; they were thick with grime from the Webb's house – she rinsed them vigorously, before cupping her hands as George had shown her, to drink.

"That's better, thank you, George," she said, splashing a bit of water on her face "I'd best go in again."

Verity walked back into the kitchen; the room was starting to warm up, accentuating the pungent smell of unwashed bodies.

"Are you feeling yourself again, Miss Verity?" asked Ellen.

"Yes thank you," Verity replied, taking another look around the room.

Brian had returned to sit in the chair she had been sitting in – she looked again at his head; this time the feeling of nausea didn't return – she moved towards the boy and looked harder at the sores on his scalp.

"Perhaps you could try some of the cream on his head?" she suggested.

"No!" said Ellen firmly. "I ain't going to waste that on 'im. 'E'll get better in a week or two; they all'as do."

She looked at Brian fondly and then up at Verity.

"Miss Verity," she said quietly "Do you think the master will let me have my job back when I'm better? I would be very willing – you know that, don't you?"

"I'll have a word with him, Ellen," replied Verity. "I'm sure he will; after all, that nasty scald came from working for him, didn't it?"

"Well I s'pose it did," she replied with a smile of relief.

The door swept open as Colin entered, carrying two dead chickens.

"I think we could eat these two, Mother," he said, holding up the limp fowls.

"That damn fox," said Molly vehemently, "I hope the 'unt killed it this mornin'; I don't know why it wants to kill all of 'em chickens, why don't it just take one?"

Molly took the chickens from Colin and threw them onto the table in front of Verity.

"Well we've got somefing to eat," said Ellen. "Even if we didn't want it."

Verity looked uneasily at the chickens and swallowed.

"Well, I think it's time to go," she said, rising from her chair. "I will come and see you again when I am home at Christmas."

She bid the family goodbye and hurried out.

As she crossed the yard, she could see the remains of the fox's work within the chicken pen; half-eaten carcasses and feathers littered the floor – she looked away. George and Reuben were a short way in front of her up the track; she called out to them and went to catch them up. In the distance they could see the shepherd Noah walking slowly up the bridleway in front of them; his flock of sheep masked by the hedge.

"George, come on, we better run if we're goin' to get in front of them sheep," said Reuben "We'll be here forever otherwise – are you coming, Miss Verity?"

"You go on," said Verity, "I don't think I feel up to running."

Reuben and George grinned at her, and dashed off to overtake the flock, which had begun to stream from the gap in the hedge. Verity watched as the sheep filed past her, waiting by the hedge till the flock had passed so that she could walk behind them with Noah. He had been a shepherd all his life and was now well over sixty, with grey hair and a grey beard. A grey smock– that had no doubt once been white – hung to his knees over a pair of tatty brown trousers which were loose on his slight frame. His hat was felt with no brim and he lifted it as he noticed Verity. He walked with a long stick of hazel, his calloused thumb curled over the yolk and a sack tied to his person with a length of twine slung over his back.

"Mornin', Miss Verity," he called, "ain't seen you up 'ere before."

"No I haven't been up here much; I've just been to see Mrs Webb," replied Verity.

Noah's collie came bounding up behind the flock and sniffed Verity eagerly. Verity took a step backwards.

"Don't worry, 'e ain't goin' to 'urt you," chuckled Noah.

She surveyed the flock trotting in front of them.

"Why are you bringing the sheep back then, Noah?"

"We goin' to tup 'em next week, it's about time now; any road they just about eaten all the grass where they were."

"Oh," said Verity, unsure of what tupping was, but unwilling to reveal her ignorance.

"What's that one waggling its tail for, Noah?" she asked, watching a ewe at the back of the flock shaking its tail and reaching desperately back behind itself as if it to reach something.

"It's got the fly, miss, I'm goin' to catch it in a minute when we get down there," he said, pointing ahead, "We can hold 'em up where the hedges are thick and it narrows up there."

Verity, not knowing what "the fly" was either, fell silent.

As the road narrowed, Noah shouted up towards Reuben and George to stop the flock, ordering Reuben to stand at the front whilst George made his way behind the flock to stand with Noah and Verity.

"Now just let them mill round a bit and when I see the ewe, I'll run in and catch it," said Noah, turning to George, "you make sure they don't go back, George me boy."

He tapped the ground with his stick as the sheep shifted around in the flock, unsure of what was expected of them; the ewe with the fly finally moved towards the back of the flock. Noah dropped his stick, darted into the flock with an agility that belied his age and seized the surprised ewe. He knelt next to it, examining its rear end.

"Miss Verity, could you pass me the bottle that's in my sack over there," he called to Verity.

Verity nodded and went to rummage in the sack, pulling out an old wine bottle filled with a dark brown liquid. She held it up.

"This one?"

"Yup, let's 'ave it 'ere," beckoned Noah.

Verity made her way carefully through the flock of sheep towards Noah.

"You couldn't pour it out for me then I'll rub it in; that'll be an 'elp," he asked.

She uncorked the bottle and lowered it towards Noah.

"Pour it over 'ere, look," said Noah, nodding to below the animal's tail.

Verity looked down; to one side of the animal's tail the wool was densely matted and amongst the matt, Verity could see a mass of wriggling maggots eating into the skin of the sheep. A small, sore-looking hole was visible and the maggots writhed through it. Verity gulped and took a deep breath, pouring the liquid where she was directed as Noah rubbed it in.

"Into the 'ole, miss," he directed.

Verity could see the maggots starting to fall to the ground as the liquid hit the skin; she kept pouring.

"Good job we caught it, miss, else they would 'ave eat it alive," said Noah, releasing the ewe and wiping his hands on his grimy trousers. "Never known it as late as this afore; mind you it 'as bin warm that's why."

"Will it get better?" said Verity anxiously.

"Yes, don't worry, miss, that'll 'eal up in no time now we've got them out."

"But what about that hole?"

"Yup, that'll 'eal too; I've seen 'em much worser than that."

"Where do the maggots come from, Noah?"

"From the flies, miss; blowflies lays their eggs there and they 'atch into maggots."

Noah pushed himself up slowly from the ground and stretched.

"Gor, I'm getting old, miss," he groaned, taking the bottle back from Verity and replacing it in his sack. He turned to George.

"Right, George, you get back in front with Reuben and turn them toward Lower Dean; they need to be in the meadow next to the brook."

He turned to Verity.

"Thank you for your help, Miss Verity; you 'ave a good day now."

And snatching his stick and bag from the ground, he made his way slowly after the flock – Verity gazing after them.

Chapter Twenty-Three
A Trip to Northampton

"Did you say we've got to go shoppin', Miss Verity?" asked Dorcas as Verity sat at the kitchen table examining a list in front of her.

"Yes, on Tuesday; that's tomorrow, isn't it?"

"Yes, miss."

"We're all going in the car, Father is coming as well; you can come with me to Tibbitts while he goes to see Allibone and then we are all going to have lunch and come home. I expect you will want to go and see Edwin, Dorcas."

"Yes, miss, that would be nice; 'e don't know I'm comin' but I don't 'spect that will matter; 'e's all'as there at the pub."

Tuesday morning was dull and overcast – rain hung threateningly in the dark clouds and a cold breeze rippled around the village. Walter, having been assisted in pushing the car out of the garage – he still hadn't mastered the art of reverse – had pulled the roof of the car over. He drove the car to the front door where John, Verity and Dorcas waited on the porch. Betty stood behind them all; eager to see the new car.

"Verity?" said John.

"Yes, Father."

"You and I will sit in the back seat," said John, "and Dorcas you sit in the front. Now come on, Walter, help me in; I'm going to enjoy this."

Walter positioned the stool – they had had one purpose-made – and manoeuvred the wheelchair, allowing John to hoist himself into the car. He folded down the wheelchair and strapped it to the carrier at the back of the car.

"Come on, Dorcas, get in," said Verity impatiently.

"I really don't know, Miss Verity, do I 'ave to?" said Dorcas, eyeing the car with suspicion.

"Yes, yes come on, you'll enjoy it!" insisted Verity.

Verity opened the passenger door for Dorcas, who dithered momentarily before finally folding herself onto the front seat.

The journey to Northampton was slow, but uneventful. Walter surpassed himself and managed to change gear on the flat twice, despite also managing to find reverse for the first time at a railway crossing – a moment that might have been disastrous had there been any traffic behind them. Once in Northampton, Walter parked the car outside The County Hotel.

"Well, my dear, I expect you will go and do the shopping you require and I will get Walter to push me to the solicitor's office," said John to his daughter. "We can meet back here for lunch; say half past twelve?"

"Very well, Father, we will be here. Dorcas likes to go and see her brother while we have lunch," she reminded her father. "I'm sure that will be all right; perhaps Walter will go with her?"

"Very well, dear," said John. "I will see you later."

Verity and Dorcas made their way towards Tibbitts.

"I don't know why your father wants me to come, Miss Verity," moaned Dorcas. "You are very capable of going on your own; I'm sure you don't want me with you."

"You know what Father is like, Dorcas," shrugged Verity, before adding limply, "and I do appreciate your company."

"I'm not sure you do, miss," mumbled Dorcas under her breath.

"I do hope Mary is at Tibbitts when we get there; it could be her day off."

"Well, miss, that's a risk we will 'ave to take," said Dorcas with a heavy sigh.

At Tibbitts, Verity made her way straight to Ladies' Fashions. They were in luck – Mary was there, although serving another customer when they walked in. Verity decided to wait until she had finished, finding two chairs for her and Dorcas to sit down on to the side of the shop.

"Are you being attended to, madam?" came a voice at Dorcas's elbow.

Peveril had entered the department to check that all was going smoothly.

Dorcas jumped and inclined her head towards Verity, unused to being addressed in those situations.

"Madam," said Peveril again, turning towards Verity with a smile.

"Yes thank you, we are waiting for Mary, thank you very much," said Verity politely.

Peveril bowed slightly and moved away towards the counter. Mrs Stevens, who had been watching his exchange with Verity, caught his elbow and whispered urgently in his ear.

"Ah, I'm so sorry, my dear Miss Watson-Foster," cooed Peveril, moving back to Verity, "I did not recognise you, but of course we have met before, haven't we? Now come along – let's go to my office and give you some refreshment while you wait for Mary. Do come this way."

He beckoned to Verity who rose uncertainly and looked at Dorcas.

"I'll stop 'ere, miss, I don't want no refreshment," said Dorcas firmly, staying where she was.

Verity was escorted by Peveril to his office.

"Now, my dear, do take a seat," said Peveril, pointing to a chair. "Frisby!"

Frisby scurried in through the opposite door.

"Yes, Mr Peveril?"

"We want some refreshment, Frisby." He turned to Verity. "What can we get you? Hot or cold drink? Some biscuits?"

"Do you have lemonade?"

"I'm sure we do! Lemonade for Miss Watson-Foster! Bring some biscuits too, Frisby, and I will have a glass of port – first today."

He saw Verity to her seat, before sitting down in his large chair at the other side of his desk.

"It's all coming back to me now! We met you and Mary in The County Hotel; I was with dear old Mortimer Allibone. That was a lucky day for me when you introduced me to Mary! One of the best you know, one of the very best; don't find girls like her every day, worth her weight in gold you know." He leant forward, took a cigarette from the silver box on the desk and lit it, just as Frisby entered with a silver tray loaded with the biscuits and lemonade. He placed the tray on the desk and moved to the table across the room to pour a large glass of port for Peveril, who took it and raised his glass towards Verity.

"Your good health, my dear, and tell me, how is your father? He's a good friend of old Allibone's, you know."

"He's very well, thank you," said Verity, trying to hide her distaste at the cigarette smoke curling across the room towards her. "He's with us today; we came in his new motor car."

"A motor car! You mean he's bought one?" exclaimed Peveril.

"Yes, we've had it a little while," said Verity. "Haven't you got one?"

"Not likely, my dear," said Peveril with a snort. "I can't even ride a horse, let alone drive a car! Maybe I should buy one and make Frisby learn to drive it."

He snorted again. Verity sipped her lemonade and took a small bite of her biscuit, willing Mary to hurry up. There was a knock at the door.

"Enter," shouted Peveril.

The door was opened by Mrs Stevens; Verity could see Mary standing behind her.

"Mary's free now, Mr Peveril," trilled Mrs Stevens.

"Very good, Mrs Stevens. Come in, Mary, and sit down whilst Miss Watson-Foster finishes her refreshments, eh, my dear?"

He smiled at Verity, who grimaced – she did not like being called 'my dear'; she thought it was patronising. She drained the rest of the drink, turning to Mary with a smile.

"Is Dorcas still there, Mary?"

"Yes, she's fine; we got her a cup of tea."

"Well run along then, my dear, Mary will look after you," said Peveril, standing up and shepherding them out the door towards Ladies' Fashions.

"It's so good to see you, Mary," said Verity. "We haven't been in touch since the summer."

"Well how can we help you today, Miss Watson-Foster?" Mary said with a bow.

Verity laughed, slightly self-consciously moving to the counter, which Mary went to stand behind. "I want underwear, Mary; you know my size, don't you?"

"Well I can guess," conceded Mary.

"Right, well I want half a dozen pairs of drawers and half a dozen vests; don't get them out – just choose some pretty ones; I'm sure you know what's in fashion."

She looked cautiously around the shop and lowered her voice.

"And, Mary, I want one of those other things to go underneath – I don't know what they're called but, well, you know everyone wears them now."

She blushed.

"You know, Mary," she repeated quietly.

"Yes I know, Verity," said Mary with a laugh. "But just one?"

"Well I supposed half a dozen; you know the size, don't you?"

Mary pursed her lips.

"Not this time, Verity – you will have to try one; the wrong size will be uncomfortable. I'll bring some to the fitting room over there."

"Very well then," said Verity, before adding hastily, "but don't let anyone see what you're bringing."

"Don't worry, Verity," said Mary, squeezing her friend's hand, "no one's looking and Dorcas has gone to sleep."

"Thank goodness that's over," said Verity half an hour later. "I don't know what I would have done if you weren't here, Mary."

"So half a dozen of them, then?" said Mary.

"No, five," said Verity, "I've kept one on."

"Now is there anything else, Verity?"

"Well it's difficult, Mary, I do want something for Christmas; I've grown so much, the old things don't fit but if I have anything made I won't have time to come back for the fittings. Do you have dresses ready to wear that I can take with me?"

"If we haven't got anything that fits we can alter it and send it to you," said Mary firmly. "And if you do want clothes made – we can send them to you at Dean and I can come and pin it when you are home and then bring it back."

"Can you, Mary? That would be such a relief! I want coats, dresses, shoes, hats, everything!"

Dorcas having just woken up, had started to pace up and down; she had had enough of shopping.

"Dorcas, you will just have to wait," said Verity, sitting down with Mary to work out what clothes she needed, "I'm not quite finished and I will need your help to carry everything."

"Very good, Miss Verity," said Dorcas with a sigh, sitting down and starting to tap the counter with her fingers. Verity looked at her irritably and deliberately took longer choosing her clothes with Mary. Having agreed everything, she signed the account and loaded Dorcas up with parcels, before turning hopefully to Mary.

"I don't suppose you would be allowed out for lunch with us, Mary?" Verity asked as they made to leave.

"Oh no, I dare not ask, Verity. Mr Peveril is a nice man but he's very strict and I don't want to upset him. Where are you going?"

"The old County Hotel again."

"Well I hope you don't have that waiter again"

"Don't worry about that," said Verity coolly, "I can deal with his type."

She picked up the remaining packages from the counter and left, Dorcas trailing in her wake.

At the County Hotel, they piled all the parcels into the car and Verity turned to Dorcas.

"Dorcas, you can go and see your brother now if you like; I think you should be back here by three."

"No, miss I must come in," said Dorcas firmly. "I will make sure the master is 'ere; 'e would never forgive me if I left you 'ere on yer own, miss."

She ushered Verity into the hotel before her, through the lounge past a tall straight-haired man of about twenty with a small moustache, who was sitting at the bar talking to the barman. He was dressed in a check waistcoat under a smart jacket with riding breeches and boots; Verity recognised him, but could not remember where she had seen him.

"Dorcas, who's that?" she whispered.

"Who's which, miss?" asked Dorcas, looking around the room absently.

"That man sitting at the bar," hissed Verity. "I've seen him before somewhere."

"I didn't see, miss."

"Go back, Dorcas and walk past again, you'll see him, go on."

Dorcas sighed wearily, walking back through the room and inspecting the man at the bar more thoroughly.

"'E was at the dance after the Flower Show," said Dorcas. "He's an 'orse dealer from Bythorn; name of Ladds I think."

"I knew I had seen him somewhere," said Verity triumphantly. "Thank you, Dorcas; let's go and find Father."

John was in the dining room smoking a cigar with Mortimer Allibone, a large glass of brandy in his hand. Verity's heart sank; Mortimer Allibone talked of nothing but hunting.

"There you are, my dear," said John, noticing her and waving her over. "Come and say hello to dear old Allibone; he's going to have lunch with us."

Verity came forward, smiled weakly and shook Mortimer's hand. There was a small cough behind her.

"Sorry, Dorcas," said Verity, turning to Dorcas who was waiting expectantly, "did you want to go and see Edwin now?"

"Yes, miss. Sir, if you don't mind?"

"That's fine, Dorcas," said John. "But be back here by three."

"Very good, sir," said Dorcas, bobbing to John and leaving the room.

A smartly dressed lady in a long red coat with black lapels and brass buttons down the front crossed paths with her at the door to the dining room, a young man scurrying behind her.

"Come along, Rupert," the woman scolded, sweeping grandly into the dining room, "you don't come out with your mother very often, the least you can do is show some enthusiasm."

She paused on her progress, her eyes raking the room expectantly. Noticing John's wheelchair, her eyes lit up and she sashayed towards him, bending to give him a peck on the cheek.

"Who's that then?" said John with a start.

He looked up expectantly, a smile crossing his face.

"Well I never! Christiana, my dear, how are you?" he declared. "It's such an age since I have seen you."

"John, I'm well, very well," said Christiana winningly. "And how are you?"

"Oh I'm fighting fit; except for those old legs of mine don't work."

He gestured to Rupert.

"And who's this young man?"

"Sorry, John, let me introduce my one and only son Rupert. Rupert – Mr John Watson-Foster."

Rupert stepped forward to shake hands with John.

"Pleased to meet you, sir," said Rupert, before stepping back and smiling at Verity.

John turned to Mortimer and Verity and gestured.

"My friend Mortimer Allibone – and my one and only daughter Verity."

Mortimer and Verity both stood to shake hands.

"Well," said John contentedly, "this is a pleasant surprise, after so long. We were going to have lunch, Christiana; I wonder if you would join us?"

"What a splendid idea," said Christiana. "We would love to join you, wouldn't we, Rupert?"

Rupert murmured his assent, pleased to have the opportunity to avoid the inevitable lecture he might otherwise have received from his mother over lunch.

"Waiter, waiter," shouted John, summoning the same listless waiter that Verity remembered from her last visit.

"Verity, you sit next to Rupert," ordered John, grinning at Christiana. "Don't you think we should sit these young things together, eh what, Christiana!"

Christiana smiled indulgently as the waiter readjusted chairs and placed down menus for the assembled company.

"And, my dear Christiana, sit next to me and tell me your news. Allibone can sit the other side of you – I will have to share!"

"We've met before, haven't we?" said Rupert, turning to Verity.

"Yes, we met on the train," smiled Verity. "I was with Mary; you've seen her since, haven't you?"

Rupert raised a finger to his lips and lowered his voice:

"I'm afraid Mother does not approve of Mary," he said quietly. "In her opinion she's just a shop girl and I should not see her anymore."

He looked round surreptitiously at his mother, but she was deep in conversation with John Watson-Foster and Allibone.

"Do you see Mary much, Verity?" said Rupert.

"Yes – I saw her this morning, we went shopping at Tibbitts and I see her sometimes in Dean when I am home. Do you see a lot of her, then?"

"Oh no," Rupert shrugged, unable to keep the disappointment from his voice. "We sometimes meet on the train, or at the station and I sometimes see her in her lunch break, but I don't see her a lot."

He sighed.

"I think she's lovely, absolutely lovely; I can't stop thinking of her."

Verity was momentarily speechless, not expecting Rupert to be quite so frank with her.

"I like Mary a lot as well," she managed after a moment. "She's so pretty and so confident; everything I'm not really. But there we are – we can't all be alike, can we?"

She smiled at Rupert.

"Now tell me about your paper, Rupert; do you have a position on votes for women?"

Rupert held up his hands and laughed gently.

"I'm just a reporter, Verity, I don't write any of the leading articles; Father does that. I know Father's against votes for women – so I suppose our position is against it, in a word."

"Oh," said Verity, disappointed, "well what about fox hunting and slaughtering beasts with a poleaxe?"

"I do report fox hunting, I have to put the reports in the paper, but I don't ride and I don't go hunting myself so I can't really comment. The slaughtering issue – I don't know. It's never come up in the paper that I can remember and I've never been to a slaughterhouse – so I don't know."

"Well you should," said Verity determinedly before realising that this might not be the friendliest line of conversation, and she changed the subject.

Dorcas had made her way to the Griffin in ten minutes. She had not written to say she was coming, but hoped Edwin would be there as she had not seen him since they had stayed last summer. She peered in at the window of the pub; through the grime she could make out Edwin behind the bar. Taking a deep breath, she opened the door and stepped into the smoky room. Edwin looked up at the sound and seeing his sister, waved heartily.

"Lizzie, look who's here!" Edwin shouted, rounding the bar to give his sister a peck on the cheek. "This is a surprise! We didn't know you were coming."

"I didn't know I was comin' till yesterday; so there was no time to write," explained Dorcas apologetically.

"Pru, come 'ere will you," Edwin shouted to a young girl in a big apron who was collecting mugs. "Pru, this is my sister Dorcas; find her a table and sit her down whilst I pour her a drink. Give us twenty minutes, Dorcas, and this lot'll be gone and I'll come over. Do you want a sandwich?"

"That would be nice," replied Dorcas, following Pru to a seat by the window.

"Are you new 'ere then, Pru; I didn't see you last time I come?" asked Dorcas as Pru wiped the table for her and fetched her drink from the bar.

"I'm bin 'ere free mumfs," said Pru quietly.

"You don't look very old," said Dorcas.

"Just seventeen, madam," Pru mumbled, moving away from Dorcas's table to clear more mugs.

Dorcas's sandwich arrived – salt beef with pickled onion; a real treat she thought, washing it down with half pint of beer and a tot of rum. A rumble of laughter echoed around the room from the skittle table, the smoke was thick and it made Dorcas's eyes smart. Edwin served the rest of his customers and came to sit with her, joined moments later by Lizzie. The door opened and a man swaggered in – Dorcas recognised him as the horse dealer Noble Ladds. He scanned the room, his eyes coming to rest on Edwin, and strode towards their table.

"A word with you, landlord, if you please," he said loudly.

Edwin rose and moved to the end of the bar, conversing with John in hushed whispers. A couple of minutes later Edwin beckoned over Pru, who stared at the two men, her face paling and made her way sluggishly towards them. She moved to the bar, lifting the flap and exiting through the half door, pursued purposefully by Noble Ladds. Edwin returned to the table.

"What's that bloke up to, Edwin? I know who 'e is; I'm seein' 'im in Dean at the dance after the Flower Show."

Edwin was silent.

"You ain't goin' to tell me, then? And where's that girl gone? She ain't very old, Edwin – come on, just tell me."

"He's just gone for a bit of relaxation, Dorcas, don't worry about it, will you; 'ave another drink." Dorcas, realising that her brother wasn't going to be any more forthcoming, accepted another half pint from Lizzie.

"Now, Dorcas," said Edwin, "how is John Watson-Foster Esquire and his la-di-da daughter?"

"'Er name's Verity," said Dorcas sharply. "You know that! And she ain't la-di- da! She's a good girl and so's her father and I won't 'ave a word said against them."

"Hold on, dear sister, there's no need to get like that! I know what they're like; I was brought up in Dean too. But they've got money and that 'elps, don't it."

"I 'spect he earnt it," said Dorcas indignantly, "or 'is father did afore him, so what's wrong with that? 'E don't pay me a bad wage and I'm got an 'ouse rent-free; you know that – you stayed there."

"And what 'ave you bin doin' 'ere in the town then, Dorcas?" said Edwin knowingly. "I bet they've bin spendin' money, ain't they?"

"I'm took Miss Verity shoppin' and they're now gawn for lunch," sniffed Dorcas. "I'm got to be back at the motor at three."

"Motor! You mean 'e's got a motor car as well?" said Edwin with a low whistle. "I bet them as work in their family's factories don't 'ave motor cars or go shoppin'; I bet they struggle to make ends meet even if they 'ave got a job."

"Well I don't know anything about that," said Dorcas shortly. "I only know that 'e treats me all right and Miss Verity's got a heart of gold."

She looked down at her drink, swirling it round in its glass.

"Dorcas, Dorcas don't take it to heart," Edwin laughed, patting her on the back. "I'm only pullin' your leg; I know they ain't a bad lot as far as the nobs go."

He gulped down the last of his beer and lit a cigarette.

"Right, let's 'ave another then, Lizzie. Dorcas, what about you?"

"No I ain't 'avin' no more – it made me feel all queer last time."

She hiccupped as Edwin rose to refill his glass at the bar. Most of the room had cleared now, the men having gone back to work. The door at the end of the room swung open and Noble Ladds sauntered towards the bar, had a brief conversation with Edwin, placed some money in his hand and left. Dorcas stared after him, muttering to herself, convinced that Noble Ladds was a man up to no good.

Chapter Twenty-Four
A Catastrophe for Molly

The winter that year at the Dunmores' was not a cold one; there had been a smattering of snow and the occasional frost, but no prolonged cold spell. The grass started to grow early in the spring of 1902 and by the middle of April all the cattle had been turned out into the fields. The spring seeding was going well as the land had dried up after the open winter. The lambing, which took place mainly in March was complete; the lambs gambolled alongside their mothers in the fields along the brook, grazing amongst the bullocks who stared balefully at the young frisking bundles of white as they flicked their tails and chased each other around the grassy banks. The stacks of wheat had now been threshed, the remaining straw having been stacked and thatched ready for next year's winter.

At Harrowig, some stacks were still to be threshed; Mr Milligan had arranged for Percy Blinkhorn to send an engine drum and elevator up to the farm for the last week of April to complete the remaining four stacks. Roland Cumber, Ron Seamarks and Bernard came as well, there being no ploughing to do at this time of the year. It took a day to get everything up to the farm and as Mr Milligan did not have enough labour for a threshing gang, Molly, Ruby Tuffnail and Lucy came to help. Ruby always liked to get away from the forge for a day or two to earn a little money of her own and for Lucy it was a release from the daily drudgery of looking after her parents.

On the Tuesday morning everything was ready to start; Roland had lined up the engine drum and elevator, and the belts connecting the three machines had been tensioned. A pile of sacks were set ready for the wheat, next to a set of scales and a sack winder. The stacks had been opened the day before and the thatch taken off. A long ladder stretched up the stack which would get Molly, Ruby and Lucy up to the top, where their job was to throw the sheaves to Ron, who would feed them into the drum. Two men helped Bernard bag up the wheat, whilst two others stacked the straw and another carted the water and the coal for the engine.

"Everyone ready?" shouted Roland, who was directing the gang – there was a general murmur of assent and Roland eased the regulator forwards. The fly wheel slowly started to turn – moving the long belt which drove the drum – and the straw-walkers started to march up and down and the shaker to sieve. Roland leapt off the engine, walking round to make sure the machinery was working, before returning to the engine to bring the mechanism up to the correct speed.

"Right, Ron, let's start," he instructed, cutting the band of the first sheaf and feeding it in through the hole in the top of the drum. There was a fizzing sound as the beater bars seized the ears of corn, sucking the sheaf into the depths of the machine, where the grains fell onto the pan, which shook backward and forwards.

Bernard, standing in the sacking area, thrust his hand into the bag, letting the wheat trickle through his fingers as it fell back into the sack.

"Let's 'ave a look then," said Roland, who had come to inspect the sample. He shoved Bernard out the way, grabbed a handful of wheat and moved it around in the palm of his hand.

"That'll do," he grunted, moving back to the engine.

The sun had risen higher in the sky, a cool breeze blowing the dust and chaff away from Lucy and Molly, who were forking the sheaves from the stack to Ruby, who in turn threw them to Ron on the drum.

When the first bag was full, Bernard hefted the sack onto the scales, where it was weighed and tied, before being taken to the barn for storage. One by one the sacks were filled; gradually the stack of sheaves lessened and the stack of straw grew. The heap of chaff was being scratched at by half a dozen hens seeking out small grains that had blown out with the chaff. The day grew hotter and the breeze dropped; the men took off their jackets, the women rolling their sleeves up and gently fanning their faces with their hands. At lunchtime the men and women – the genders sitting slightly apart –went to sit under the stack, everyone eating their bread and cheese before falling back for a snooze in the heat of the early afternoon.

"I must go down the end," said Ruby, sitting up with a jerk. "Are you comin', Lucy? Molly?"

"Yes, I'm coming," said Lucy. "Where is it?"

"Miles over there," said Ruby, pointing towards a point a fair way behind the house.

"Ain't you comin', Molly?"

"No, I ain't walkin' all that way; I'll go behind the hedge over there," said Molly, rising and setting off in the opposite direction.

A few minutes later, she was making her way back, when Roland stopped her in her tracks – stepping languidly in front of her to block her path. He had been kipping in the living-van.

"Where you bin', then?" he demanded of Molly.

"I'm bin for a piss; ain't that allowed, then?" Molly sneered.

"Where are them other bloody wimmin, then?" he growled.

"We're 'ere," said Ruby rounding the stack. "There's no need to talk like that!"

Roland glared at her and stalked off towards the engine.

The next day was even hotter than the first; by the time they had started the second stack the breeze had dropped off and the dust lingered in the air, creeping into clothes and making the workers itch. Engine smoke gusted back into Roland's face and he fanned himself impatiently with his cap.

"Oi, Ron," he shouted up, "come and do a turn on the engine, will you; I'll come up there and feed the drum."

Ron did not answer, but began to climb down from the drum – there was no point objecting.

"Gawd, look who we've got now," groaned Ruby, as Roland started to climb up the drum. "I can't stand that man."

"Come on then, give us one, then," shouted Roland, leering up at her.

Ruby threw down a sheaf as Roland stared at her, his eyes glued to her bosom; a shiver ran down her spine.

"That damn man," she muttered to Lucy.

"What's he done now?" whispered Lucy.

"'E keeps on lookin' at me and I don't like it."

"Don't worry, Ruby; he's too scared of Art to do you any harm."

"S'pose so," said Ruby with a sigh.

Half an hour later Roland called lunch. The men sat against the straw stack, Roland returned to the living-van and the women went to lie under the stack, lulled into sleep by the gentle clucking of the hens on the chaff heap.

"I'm goin' for a piss," Molly said, leaping to her feet.

Lucy winced at Molly's language, but said nothing, watching Molly move between the stacks until she was out of sight on the other side of the hedge.

Molly turned down the line of the wall, walking another ten yards before checking that there was nobody around; she gathered up her long skirt and squatted down, the air cold on her bare legs despite the warm sunshine. All of a sudden, a shadow loomed over her, the warmth of the sun on the back of her neck replaced with an absence that chilled her to the marrow. She turned and started to stand – Roland Cumber stood over her grinning. She snarled and made to run, but before she could, his hand seized her arm, the other snaking around her neck and clamping tight against her mouth.

"Now, Miss Molly, you're comin' with me for a few minutes and don't you dare make a sound or I'll thump you so 'ard you'll never know what 'it you, see."

Roland's face was so close to hers she could see every pore of his face and the stench of tobacco stung her eyes. She whimpered – he was holding her so tight she could hardly move and when he went to drag her off, her feet hardly touched the ground. Her eyes sought desperately for someone she might be able to call out to, for someone to witness what was happening; but the hedge shielded them and nobody in the yard would ever see. Roland threw her into the living-van, kicking the door shut behind them.

"What are you doin', Roland?" Molly pleaded – her voice shrill and trembling. "What are you doin'? Why I'm got to come in 'ere?"

"You mean you don't know?" sneered Roland.

"No, I don't," Molly whimpered. "Let me go, why am I 'ere?"

"Well I'm 'eard lots of things about a girl who lifts 'er skirts for the boys to see. Who was that, then?" leered Roland.

"What if I did? It don't matter, do it? They paid up; they all liked it."

She edged backwards into the van as Roland advanced, peeling his waistcoat off as he did.

"Girls who do that deserve to be shown a thing or two, don't they?" he whispered threateningly, throwing his waistcoat on the bunk.

"What you want, then?" shouted Molly, tears springing to her eyes and coursing down her cheeks.

"You really don't know?" Roland said, eyeing the trembling girl incredulously.

"No, I don't! I told you, didn't I?"

She put her face in her hands, sobs racking her tiny frame – she could hear Roland bearing down on her, but there was nowhere that she could go. The odour of sweat and oil mingled in her nostrils, and she fought the urge to be sick. Now she could smell him, could feel him looming over her. She lifted her foot and stamped out hard in his direction, feeling contact, as the nail on the bottom of her boot tore a hole through his trousers, scratching his leg. Roland looked down angrily.

"You little bastard," he yelled, grabbing both her arms and throwing her heavily onto the bunk. She could taste the sweat embedded in the wool as he pushed her face down into the grey blanket – she couldn't scream even if she had wanted to. Molly could hear Roland tugging at his clothes – the breath heaving out of his body in short shallow pants. She didn't know what was going to happen, but she knew it was going to be awful; the blanket was damp under her face, tears of terror stemmed by the filthy wool.

She felt her skirt being lifted, up to her waist – she wrested her arm out from underneath herself, trying desperately to push the skirt down again, but a hand in the middle of her back pushed her down on the bed. She heard him spit, felt the calluses on his fingers as he wrested her legs apart – and then she felt pain. Pain like she had never felt before – and before she had time to try and contemplate the agony, everything went blank.

When she came to a few minutes later Roland was standing over her; hooking his braces over his shoulders. He grinned wolfishly.

"Like that then, did you?" he sneered, pulling his waistcoat on and checking the time.

"Five minutes," he said, flipping the cover shut with a click and putting it back in his pocket. He leant towards Molly, who cowered back against the wall.

"Now my girl, if you so much as breathe a word to anyone; I'll give you such a leatherin' that you'll never forget – see."

Molly cast her eyes to the ground, a tremor of fear beating through her body.

"Look at, me girl," he growled. "Did you 'ear what I said?"

Molly raised her eyes, wiping her nose with her fist as tears threatened to overcome her again.

"Did you 'ear what I said?" he roared.

"Yes," she whimpered.

"Yes, who?"

"Yes, Roland."

The sound of footsteps could suddenly be heard outside – someone was coming up the steps. The door opened to reveal Bernard standing at the door – his eyes vacantly moved from Roland to Molly and back to Roland, a stream of spittle oozing from the corner of his mouth.

"What the bloody hell do you want? Can't you see I'm busy?" bellowed Roland.

"Sorry, Roland," simpered Bernard. "Just came to get me baccy."

"Well, bloody well get it and bugger off then – quick," Roland snarled.

Bernard scurried in, cowering under Roland's furious gaze and fumbled in the pocket of a jacket, removing a pipe and a pouch, before scuttling out the door again. Roland turned back to Molly, raising his hand threateningly as he did.

"Just you remember what I said, my girl, not a word! I'll be watchin' you, don't forget that. Now bugger off."

He nodded towards the door. Molly gingerly raised herself off the bunk and stumbled out the door, unsure of where to go, knowing only that she had to get away from the van, away from that evil man. She couldn't go home – there was no one there. If she didn't go back to the threshing, would Roland follow her? What if he did that awful thing again?

Molly whimpered and dragged her hand across her eyes, knowing that she would have to go back to the stacks. She turned her feet towards the farm and dragged herself back to the workers.

Chapter Twenty-Five
Roland is Injured

"Where 'ave you bin all this while?" asked Ruby. "We thought you was lost."

"Just bin for a piss I told you, didn't I," mumbled Molly, squeezing her eyes shut in an effort to stop the tears falling.

"What's up, Molly? What are you crying for?" asked Lucy rising and putting her arm round the younger girl.

"You don't look right," said Ruby. "What's happened to you? Come on, tell old Ruby."

"Nothin's happened so there," snapped Molly fiercely, wiping her eyes.

"What are these marks on your arms then?" said Lucy. "Ruby, look!"

Lucy pushed Molly's sleeves up, revealing angry red finger marks.

"Who did this, then?" Ruby demanded of Molly. "Someone's bin at you, who is it then?"

"It's no one, see," moaned Molly, shutting her eyes tight.

Lucy looked meaningfully at Ruby.

"There's only one person could a done this; tha's Roland, I know it is," said Ruby.

"No, it ain't," Molly hissed, snatching her arms away and desperately rolling down her sleeves.

"What are we going to do, then?" said Lucy.

"There's nothing we can do, not for the minute any road," shrugged Ruby. "She ain't goin' to tell us anythin', that's certain."

"Come on, you lot, look sharp," shouted Roland from the top of the drum, as the engine began to chug back into action. The women climbed the stack, ready to start passing sheaves across to Roland; the stack was now about level with the top of the drum, but Ruby did her best not to look at the man she was passing sheaves to – only too sure of what he had done to Molly. As the stack decreased, Ruby was forced to throw the sheaves upwards, aware of Roland's eyes on her cleavage.

"I can't stand that man," Ruby whispered to Lucy again. "'E keeps lookin' down my front; it ain't right, you know."

"Come on, Ruby, let me have a go at pitching," said Lucy, taking the fork from her. "He won't look down my front, I haven't got anything to look at."

The sun continued to beat down. Despite them changing places, Roland continued to look at Ruby's chest as he fed the sheaves into the drum. Finally fed up with this and to divert his attention, Lucy pitched the next sheaf as hard as she could. Roland, taken unawares, stumbled backwards and disappeared from view. There was a bang and the drum stopped dead. The belt from the engine started to screech as it tried to turn the pulley on the drum, slipping round until smoke started to pour from the pulley. Ron jumped back on the engine and pulled the regulator back just as the belt flew off the fly wheel and landed with a thud on the ground. There was quiet; a little steam hissed from the engine and in the distance an early cuckoo called. Bernard put his hand into the sack to feel if there was any grain falling and quickly pulled it out again.

"What's that, then?" he said quizzically, turning to Ron and showing him his hand.

"'Ave you cut yourself then, Bernard?"

"No *I* ain't; that's blood, ain't it Ron? It's in the sack – 'ave a look."

"Where's Roland?" Ron demanded suddenly.

"On the top," replied Bernard.

"Lucy, can you see Roland?" shouted Ron.

"No, he just disappeared and the drum stopped."

Ron covered his face with his hands.

"Oh God," he shouted, "'e's in the drum."

Ron grabbed the short ladder that lay on the ground, leant it against the side of the drum and climbed quickly to the top. He could see Roland; face white, eyes tight shut, propping himself up with his hands – one leg out in front of him – a small nick visible on his calf, the other swallowed by the beaters of the drum. Ron had heard of this happening before, but never had he seen it – the speed of the beater bars revolved so fast and the momentum was so strong that even though the gap for the sheaves was little more than an inch, the power had sucked in Roland's leg, to just below the knee.

"Are you all right, Roland?"

278

"Roland," said Ron again kneeling down beside him – he could see no blood.

"Ron," Roland whispered, "Ron – wind her back; that'll get me out! Wind it back, you know 'ow to do it."

He groaned.

"It was 'er you know! She stuck me with the fork; that's what did it – it were that Lucy Knighton."

"Don't mind about that now, Roland. We'll get you out; I'm just goin' down to wind 'er back."

Ron descended the ladder – everyone, with the exception of Molly, had gathered at the bottom.

"It's Roland," said Ron to the assembled company. "'E's got his leg in the drum; we've got to wind it back to let 'im out."

He pointed to two of the younger men.

"Round the other side and turn the drum pulley backwards; someone go up and be with 'im–" he looked at the women. "Ruby, you do it – 'e's goin' to be in pain."

"I ain't goin' to look after that bastard, serve 'im right if 'e did get 'is leg in the drum," snapped Ruby.

"I'll go," said Lucy.

"Best not you, Lucy," said Ron. "You go, Bernard."

"We'll both go," said Lucy, turning to make her way up the ladder.

The two started to turn the big pulley on which the beater bars were bolted – there was a bloodcurdling cry from Roland.

"No, you silly sods, you're turning it the wrong way!" yelled Ron. "The other way should wind 'im out."

They turned the other way – there was a little movement and the pulley stopped, refusing to give another inch.

"It's stuck," shouted one of the men.

"Well, we've still got the elevator connected," shouted Ron. "So, someone go and pull the belt off quick – go on."

On the top of the drum, Bernard crawled across to Roland on all fours – he did not like heights at the best of times.

"Roland," whispered Bernard.

"Roland," he said again, having received no reply the first time.

"What do you want, you stupid sod?" groaned Roland.

"Ron said I got to come up 'ere and 'elp you," explained Bernard. "Does it 'urt, Roland?"

"Look at me, you stupid bugger – what do you think, look!"

He nodded in the direction of his trapped leg; Bernard looked down the hole, his face whitened, his pupils rolled upwards and with a thud he collapsed against Roland's good leg – his head lolling into the hole.

"Get this stupid sod off me, will you?" Roland sighed, his eyes screwed shut, as Lucy crawled over to him.

She knelt down and rolled Bernard over as best she could. Roland opened his eyes and looked at her.

"It were you, weren't it?"

"What do you mean it was me?" Lucy snapped.

"You stuck me with that fork, that's what made me step in the drum."

"I did not stick you with the fork – that's a lie," Lucy hissed. "You stepped in the drum because you spent your time looking at Ruby's tits and not at what you were doing."

She stopped suddenly, surprised at her forthrightness; she had never spoken like this to anybody before, let alone a man.

"Now," she demanded, "do you want me to help you or not?"

She stared at Roland, daring him to accuse her again. Roland looked away and winced.

"Well there ain't no one else," he sneered.

"We're going to turn it back now, Roland, are you ready?" shouted Ron from the ground.

Lucy looked over the side.

"Turn it slowly, Ron, I'm here," she said.

"Are you all right, Lucy?" he shouted back.

"Yes go on, turn it."

Lucy knelt to watch, as the pulley started to turn, feeding out Roland's mangled leg; Roland's head started to loll, the little colour in his face draining once again.

"Are you there, Lucy?" he muttered.

"Yes, Roland."

"Tell Ron to let the adjustment off on the concave – quick now."

His voice was shaking. Lucy crawled to the edge and shouted.

"Ron! Roland says let the adjustment off the concave."

"All right, Lucy," called back Ron.

He turned to a young boy:

"Quick; you go and get the spanners! Run – go on!"

The boy sprinted off, returning moments later with an oily bag, the contents of which he tipped on the ground. Ron selected a spanner and quickly started undoing the nuts that held the concave tight to the beater bars, before running around to undo the other side.

"Lucy, are you there?"

"Yes, Ron."

"We're goin' to turn again; are you ready?"

"Yes, go on."

Roland's leg continued to inch out of the machine – a mass of flesh, trousers and bits of bone which no longer aligned in any way.

"It's stuck again," yelled the man on the pulley to Ron.

"Go back a bit and have another go," said Ron.

The men did as instructed. Ron looked at them worriedly, guessing what they were going to say.

"Ron it won't budge; it's stuck solid," one of the men said quietly.

Ron sighed and shook his head.

"Lucy, we can't turn it no more," he hollered.

"I think I can see what it is," said Lucy. "It's the heel of his boot jammed – it won't come out."

"What we goin' to do, then?" Ron said desperately.

"We will have to cut his leg off," Lucy said coolly.

There was silence.

"Ron?"

"I'm here."

"We want some scissors; big ones and little ones – Mrs Hobbs will have some in the house – and a very sharp knife or even better a razor. And Ron, bring the strop – we must make sure it's sharp."

She moved back to Roland who was barely conscious, sweat beading every surface of his face.

"Lucy?" shouted Ron. "Hadn't we better send for the doctor?"

"Yes we had; but how long's that going to take?"

"Could be hours before we find 'im," Ron admitted. "Hang on, I'm coming up."

Ron scaled the ladder and crawled across the drum; he took one look at Roland's leg, groaned and looked to the sky.

"We can't wait for the doctor, Ron, can we?" said Lucy calmly.

"No, we can't; we've got to do the best we can. I'll send someone off to fetch the doctor and if he comes he does and if he don't – well, he don't!"

"Ron?"

"Yes, Lucy."

"We need something to bind the stump with when we've cut it off and we need some way to get him down to the ground."

"Right, I'll ask Mrs Hobbs."

Ron returned after five minutes with scissors, a razor and some old sheets.

"Ron, we've got to take some of those boards up so we can get at the leg to cut it off properly; we've got to leave as much skin as possible for them to sew up the stump."

Ron blanched and swallowed twice.

"Don't, Lucy! Don't say that—" pleaded Ron. "Them boards will come up easy enough; we had them up the other day – I'll get the bar."

With the boards up, the full extent of what had happened could be seen.

"Who's goin' to do it then, Lucy?" Ron asked, staring at the ruined limb in horror.

"I am," she said with complete confidence. "But you will have to help me."

"No I ain't," said Ron desperately. "I can't stand the sight of it; someone else'll 'ave to."

"Who then? Ruby won't. Molly will have to – go and tell her, Ron."

"Molly," he shouted, waving furiously, "come 'ere, Lucy wants you."

He turned back to Lucy, who was examining Roland's leg.

"Lucy, I'm got an idea 'ow to get 'im down; we'll make a stretcher out of a couple of sacks and two poles and I'll get the elevator 'ooked up to the engine. We can back it up to the drum and let it down and carry 'im down on that."

He smiled at her, pleased with his plan.

"I'm goin' to get it started."

"Did you sharpen the razor, Ron?"

"Yes, as best I could," said Ron, waiting for Molly to reach the top of the ladder before descending himself.

Molly stood staring at Lucy, her face free from expression.

"Do you think it 'urts 'im, Lucy?"

"What do you think, Molly?" said Lucy impatiently.

"Yes," said Molly viciously. "I hope it really hurts, and hurts forever; he's the rottenest man that ever lived – you know that, Lucy, don't you?"

"I know, Molly," said Lucy gently. "Just pass me the scissors, the big pair over there."

Roland's eyes flicked open, his hand moving slowly to his ruined leg.

"What you doin' then?" he said shakily.

"I'm going to cut the bottom of your leg off."

"Good, cut the bugger off – it ain't no use now; thanks to you," spat Roland, sighing heavily.

Lucy cut through Roland's trouser leg, pulling it down gently over the mass of leg, muscle and bone.

"I've got to find where the end of the bone is, Molly," said Lucy, pushing her index finger into the wound just below Roland's knee, running it down the bone until she found where the beater bar had severed through. Roland winced, his body jerking violently, then he lay still again.

"Molly, pass me that razor," ordered Lucy, holding out her hand.

"Why don't you cut his throat with it, Lucy, that's what he deserves," snarled Molly, sitting back on her heels and watching.

Lucy ignored her.

"I read in a book once that they always need plenty of skin left when they amputate so they can sew it over the stump."

She looked critically at the leg and muttered to herself.

"So now I know where the bone is; I should cut further down."

She grasped the razor and started to cut through the skin. She then continued cutting through to the muscle – until the lower leg and what remained of the foot hung limply from a tendon.

"Pass me the little scissors, Molly," she instructed, taking the scissors and snipping gently until the lower leg fell away.

"We've got to pull him back now, Molly; so he's out the way of that hole. You grab one arm and I'll get the other."

Roland groaned as the two girls yanked him onto the flat boards.

Lucy took the sheet, tore off some strips and folded the remainder into the shape she thought that she would need to bandage the leg.

"I'll lift the leg, Molly, you push it under," she said, raising the mangled stump for Molly to put the sheet under. Lucy started to wind the sheet round and over the stump.

"We've got to stop any more bleeding if we can," explained Lucy. "He's lost a lot of blood already."

"I don't know why you're botherin', Lucy; why don't you let 'im die like 'e ort to," grumbled Molly. "And what did 'e mean when 'e said 'thanks to you'; what did 'e mean by that the old sod?"

"He said that I stuck him with the fork when I put the sheaf up and that's why he trod in the drum."

"No, you never, Lucy, no you never!" hissed Molly, trembling with indignation. "I saw it! 'E were lookin' all the while at Ruby's tits; that's why 'e stood in the drum and serve 'im right. I hope 'e dies, so there."

Lucy had finished tying up the stump – her hands were covered in blood, her skirt splattered with red.

"There we are; that's the best I can do."

"What's happenin' then?" called Ron. "'Ave you got 'im out, Lucy?"

"Yes, he's out."

"William's here now, Lucy, he 'eard about the accident; 'e's helping get the elevator round, we'll soon be ready to get 'im down and we've got a cart ready to take 'im down the surgery."

"You stay here with him then, Ron, I'm going down to wash my hands," said Lucy, climbing back to the ground and making her way to the pump, Molly close behind.

"I'll work the 'andle, Lucy," said Molly as the two girls stood at the pump. "You wash your 'ands – and you've got some on your face an' all, 'ere look, let me."

Molly pulled up a corner of her skirt and ran a spurt of water from the pump over it; she delicately dabbed at Lucy's face, removing the blood. Lucy's eyes were bright with the exhilaration of what she had achieved, her face flushed.

More people from the village had arrived, having heard about the accident, and were eagerly watching Ron and William carry Roland from the drum. Molly looked over to the assembled group –she recognised the policeman from Riseley, pushing his bicycle towards Roland's prone body and tutted.

"He'll be wanting to speak to us too, Lucy," she whispered, watching the policeman pull out his notebook. Lucy grimaced and dabbed at the spots of blood on her face.

"Who's this then?" the policeman was saying to Ron.

"Roland Cumber. You know 'im don't you, Mr Perkins?"

Constable Marshall Perkins pulled at his chin.

"You mean 'im who drives the engines?"

"Yes, that's the one," Ron said.

"What happened to 'im then?" he asked unsympathetically.

"'E stepped in the drum and got 'is leg smashed; we cut it off to get 'im out."

Roland was groaning; his eyes opened and he raised a feeble hand towards Constable Perkins.

"What 'appened, my man?" the constable asked of Roland.

"It was that there girl, Lucy," Roland said in a shaky but determined voice, nodding towards Lucy who was standing at the pump watching, "she stuck me with the fork and I trod back in the drum, it was that girl."

Lucy stood rooted to the spot – her hands still lined with the blood of the man whose life she had just saved. Molly slipped her hand into Lucy's and gripped it tightly.

"Don't worry, Lucy, he won't get away with this – 'e's got what's coming to 'im and I'm gonna make sure 'e burns in hell for it."

Chapter Twenty-Six
The Investigation

"Are you all right, Lucy?" William asked his cousin.

The cart bearing Roland had just left and people were starting to disperse.

"Yes, but I'm going home," sighed Lucy.

"I'll come with you, you don't look very well."

"No, William," said Lucy firmly. "I'll be fine."

She turned and walked off down the track that would take her back to Cold Harbour.

Constable Marshall Perkins was crawling around the top of the drum – he beckoned to William.

"This is a rum thing, young William, a real rum thing," said the constable, stroking his chin.

"Why did he put his foot in it?" asked William. "He must have fed the drum thousands of times?"

"'E said it was 'cause young Lucy stuck 'im wiv the fork, and it made 'im jump back," sighed Marshall.

"You don't believe that, do you?" said William incredulously. "Lucy wouldn't do a thing like that."

"Well it could 'ave bin an accident I s'pose," muttered Marshall, looking around the drum.

"You can see the rest of 'is leg, such as it is, in the drum; 'ave you 'ad a look, William?"

"Yes I have. I s'pose someone has to get it out of there; what a mess."

"Start 'er up agin – it would go through now 'e ain't on the end of it."

William was silent – starting the machine again didn't seem the right thing to do in his opinion.

"What am I goin' to do now?" said Constable Perkins pulling his chin again and looking at William. "I'll 'ave to make a report you know, young William, and I'll 'ave to take some statements – that's what I'll 'ave to do. A report of the scene, a statement from Roland and I think a statement from Lucy Knighton."

He pulled a notebook and short pencil from his breast pocket; he licked the pencil twice, opened the notebook and was about to write when a look of confusion spread across his face. He put the pencil in his mouth, held his right fist in front of his face and slowly raised his fingers, mouthing numbers as he did so. He stared fixedly at his hand, shook his head and repeated the process twice more, before appearing to reach a conclusion. He turned to William.

"What's the date, William?"

"It's the twenty-eighth of April, Marshall," said William.

The constable nodded decisively, scribbled in his notebook and looked up.

"What I'm goin' to do, young William, is to go to Kimbolton and get a statement from Roland; you never know 'e might die and any road if I don't set off soon it will be dark by the time I get 'ome. Yes that's what I'll do. I can remember what I'm seen 'ere and I can find Lucy tomorrow; how about that?"

He turned to William for confirmation.

"Well, Marshall, it's up to you, after all, *you* are the policeman, not me."

Marshall straightened up, replaced his pocket book and made his way down from the drum to fetch his bike.

It was over half an hour before he arrived at the doctor's house, where Roland had already been carried in to the surgery. Constable Perkins knocked on the door and without waiting for an answer, strode importantly into the room. The doctor was leaning over Roland who was shaking his head vigorously from side to side; both looked up as they heard the constable come in.

"What are we going to do with this man, Perkins? Talk about a stubborn pig-headed fool," the doctor said crossly. "I don't know."

"What's up with him then?" said Marshall stupidly, pulling at his chin.

"His leg has been severed below the knee and is a real mess. The best way to proceed would be to send him to hospital to have it cut it off above the knee and make a good job of it – there's much less risk of infection that way; but he refuses. He wants me to patch it up."

"With due respect, doctor," Roland growled faintly, "it's my leg and I've knowed others with legs cut off and those with a knee get on better than those without – so please can you sew me up?"

He sighed heavily and collapsed back onto the bed.

"Where are you going to live then when I've done it?" asked the doctor severely. "You're not married and you will need someone to care for you, dress the stump and pull the ligatures out."

"I'll go to my sister's; she lives in Northampton. I'll stop in the van tonight and get someone to take me tomorra; the 'ospital is near 'er 'ouse so I can go there to get it seen to."

"But, my dear man, the risk of infection is severe unless you get it seen to *properly* – you know that, don't you?"

"You mean you won't do it or you can't do it?" said Roland testily.

"Yes I can do it but I couldn't honestly advise it as the best course of action," implored the doctor, his voice rising.

"Well do it then and it's my problem, ain't it," said Roland, shutting his eyes.

"Very well then," the doctor sighed, "At least there is plenty of skin to cover the stump."

"Yes she said she were to leave plenty of skin," Roland croaked.

"Who said?" asked the doctor.

"Lucy Knighton – she cut it off."

"Lucy Knighton? She cut you out the machine?"

"Yup."

"Well I never; she's a brave girl. I knew she wanted to be a nurse, but with work like this she should think about being a doctor."

"Doctor, can I ask a few questions?" interrupted Constable Perkins.

"Yes, but be quick, Perkins," said the doctor impatiently, "I'm going to give him some laudanum in a moment; he won't make any sense after that."

"Very good, doctor," said Marshall leaning close to Roland and peering into his face.

He cleared his throat, looked down at his empty notebook, hesitated a moment, then began.

"Roland, you said that Lucy stuck you with the pitchfork and that's why you trod in the drum, is that right?"

"Yea, that's right, in my other leg; you 'ave a look where she did it."

Marshall licked the lead of his pencil. The doctor looked up sharply.

"What did he say, Perkins? That Lucy stuck him with a pitchfork?"

"Yes, 'e's said it twice now, doctor – he says he has a wound on 'is other leg where she spiked him."

"Well I will have a look at that to confirm it," said the doctor firmly. "Now, Perkins, is there any more information you want or can I get on?"

"No, doctor, there ain't no time for me to get 'im to sign a statement, but I'm got it all down in me notebook so that'll be good enough."

He looked down once more at his notebook and closed it hurriedly.

"Very good, so will you leave us now please."

Marshall retreated through the low door, Ron was waiting on the other side.

"What you goin' to do with 'im?" said Marshall to Ron.

"No idea," Ron shrugged, "I s'pose I will 'ave to take 'im back to the van tonight; there ain't nowhere else. If he'd gone to the hospital like the doctor said 'e could 'ave stayed there."

"Ain't 'e got no wife?"

"'Im?" snorted Ron. "No one with any sense would marry that nasty bugger. 'Es a rum 'un as far as women are concerned, you mark me words, Constable Perkins, you mark my words."

"What about relations, then?" the constable asked.

"Well I don't rightly know; 'e 'as a sister in Northampton I think, but 'e never seems to see 'er, and I think he lives in lodgin's in the winter when 'e ain't on the engines, in the back of some pub somewhere, then 'e turns up when the work starts again."

"That ain't much of a life for a chap," said Marshall, his brow furrowing with concern. "Why don't 'e do sommut else? He must be a good engine man."

"You're right there; 'e's a good driver, there's no doubt on that. But 'e has to turn up every spring to get 'is overtime money."

The constable looked up, surprised.

"What overtime money?" he asked.

"The money we earn in overtime one year," explained Ron, "we're never paid until we set on the next year."

"You mean they keep it owin' to you all winter?"

"Yes, that's what happens," chuckled Ron. "And there's nothin' you can do about it."

"Well I never," said the constable, filing his notebook back into his pocket and ramming on his helmet. "Well I s'pose I better be orf else I won't be back afore it's dark the rate I cycle."

"What's goin' to 'appen then? About the accident I mean?" asked Ron urgently.

"Well I don't rightly know. I'll go and take a statement from Lucy Knighton tomorrow, but after that I don't expect anythin'. Mind you if 'e were dead that would be a different story – 'spect there would be an inquest then, we'll 'ave to wait and see."

And with a curt nod, he left. Ron continued to sit in the waiting room, the occasional groan reaching him through the surgery door. An hour later the doctor came out to see Ron.

"What are you going to do with him now, Ron? He's not in a fit state to do much and won't be for a long while; he'll be lucky if the wound doesn't get an infection in it."

"I were goin' to take 'im back to the van for the night," said Ron. "Then I don't know what after that." He shrugged hopelessly.

"He tells me he has a sister in Northampton and he's going there," said the doctor. "But he will need that stump dressing every day."

The doctor shook his head angrily.

"He should have had it cut off above the knee, but he wouldn't hear of it. Stupid man!"

"Well I s'pose we can get 'im to Northampton tomorra if the boss man don't mind. I can find a cart to take 'im in."

Ron sighed heavily; he did not want to have to go to Northampton, and he had no idea where he could get a cart from.

"When you take him Ron, go straight to the infirmary and get them to dress the wound before you take him to his sister; it will have to be done every day."

"Right you are, doctor, I'll sort 'im out; am I to take 'im now?"

"Yes, Ron, he's ready to go; we've got no crutch for him, but there's a broom there, that'll do for tonight. Get Flanders to make you a proper crutch tomorrow morning."

"Very good," nodded Ron, entering the surgery to help his charge back to the cart to take him home.

At the van, Bernard was frying belly pork for his dinner – smoke rose from chimney and wafted out the door, the smell of the coal fire pungent in the air.

"Where are we?" grunted Roland as the cart came to a standstill.

"Back at Harrowig, you get out, Roland and I'll put the 'orse away," instructed Ron.

"What's all that smoke then, Bernard?" Roland demanded of the cook-boy.

"Oh, I'm just cookin' some belly pork for me dinner; you goin' to 'ave some, Roland? I'm got a loaf of bread to go wiv it."

"No I ain't, or at least not at the minnit," snarled Roland, wiggling himself to the edge of the cart and prising himself off with the help of the broom. He put his weight on his good leg and stood up.

He groaned loudly, pursing his lips and looking about him; across the stack yard the engine and drum stood lifeless, the pulleys and belts stationary.

"Bastard thing," Roland cursed.

He swung his torso round to glare at Bernard, ready to take his foul temper out on the nearest innocent.

"Well, come on, you stupid bugger – get me a beer."

"We ain't got none, Roland," said Bernard, eyeing Roland beadily. "You drank it all last night."

"Well take the flagon and go and get a gallon won't you, you useless sod."

"But what about me dinner, Roland," said Bernard reasonably. "I'm got to 'ave me dinner."

"You just go and get the beer right, I couldn't care less about your dinner; you'll 'ave to 'ave it when you get back."

"'Ave you got any money then, Roland?" asked Bernard cunningly.

"No, I ain't! You know I ain't got any money; you just tell 'im it's for me and e'll put it on the slate. Make sure you go to the World's End; the beer's much better from there and get a packet of Capstan too."

"Yes, Roland," said Bernard, a faint smile playing around his mouth. The realisation that he was safe from the kicks and punches so frequently meted out to him had started to dawn on the huge man, and it was filling him with confidence.

"Does it 'urt much then, Roland?"

"What a bloody stupid question, does it look like it 'urts then?"

"S'pose it does," smiled Bernard, trotting off towards the pub, whistling as he went.

The next morning, Ron arrived with a trap he had borrowed from the butcher's shop to find Roland sitting on the steps of the van, his belongings in a long canvas bag beside him.

"That's a fine thing – going in a butcher's trap like a side of beef," growled Roland.

Ron sighed heavily.

"Well I ain't taking you all the way, Roland; William wants the trap back after dinner. I'm taking you as far as Wellingborough and you will 'ave to go on the train. William has lent you five shillings and 'e says that's enough for the train and a carrier to take you to the infirmary and to get to your sister's."

"S'pose I ain't got no choice, 'ave I," grumbled Roland, easing himself up to leave; the bandages on his stump were now crumpled, and blood had seeped through in places, drying a sickly brown colour. He looked across to the drum again, his jaw clenched.

"Ron?" he murmured.

"Yes, Roland."

"Is my leg still in the drum?"

"Yes, Roland, I ain't 'ad a chance to get things sorted out yet; but I'm put off all the others and told them not to come until I get it cleaned."

"Make sure you burn it, Ron."

He took a final look at the offending machine and hopped his way to the cart, his canvas bag dangling limply over his shoulder.

Constable Perkins was cycling to Cold Harbour to take a statement from Lucy. Although not far from Riseley, most of the journey was uphill and a southwesterly wind blew strongly in his face, hindering his progress. By the time he arrived he was quite worn out. In the scullery, he found Freda washing vegetables in the sink.

"Whoa up, Freda, 'ow are you today?"

"Well as can be expected," grumbled Freda, looking up. "In the circumstances that is."

"Well that sounds hopeful," replied Marshall cheerily.

"And what can we do for you then? You don't get up 'ere much."

"No, not often; I'm come to see Miss Lucy. Is she about?"

"She's out there gettin' in the eggs; do you want me to fetch 'er then?" Freda enquired.

"Well, if you don't mind, Freda, you will know where she is and in the meantime I can 'ave a sit down."

"Go in then," instructed Freda, pointing to the door of the kitchen. "Mrs Knighton's in there 'aving a sit down. That's all she does nowadays – sit down."

Marshall went into the kitchen, where Ann sat by the range.

"Mornin', Mrs Knighton, you look cold."

"Oh hello, Marshall, yes I do feel cold; I always feel cold these days," shrugged Ann, pulling a shawl tighter around her shoulders.

"What can we do for you then?"

"Well, it's Miss Lucy I'm come to see about the accident at Harrowig; you 'eard about it I 'spect."

"Yes we heard all the detail, nasty thing, losing his leg in the drum, Lucy said. It does happen, I've known plenty that have done it."

"Yes, 'e were a bit of a mess I must say," said Marshall, as Lucy hurried in through the door, followed by Freda.

"Do you want a cup of tea, constable?" Ann enquired.

"That would be very nice, Mrs Knighton, very nice."

"Freda, make a pot of tea will you; we will all have a cup, I expect."

Freda retreated as Lucy sat down at the table.

"Now Miss Lucy, I'm got to take a statement from you regardin' the accident that Roland 'ad in the drum at Harrowig yesterday an' I believe you were there and see everythin' that 'appened."

294

He pulled his notebook and pencil from his pocket with a flourish, his silver whistle tumbling out with them to dangle down the front of his jacket on its chain.

"Damn thing," he swore, thrusting it back.

"Oh I'm sorry, Mrs, shouldn't use them words, should I?" he said apologetically, licking his pencil and looking up at the clock on the mantelpiece. He looked back to Lucy.

"Now, Miss Lucy, you tell me what you saw and what happened; take your time now."

"Well I didn't see much; I was pitching the sheaves up so I didn't see it happen," she shrugged. "There was a big bang, the drum stopped and we couldn't see Roland on top anymore."

"Hold on, hold on – let me write that down, can you?"

Lucy paused, watching Marshall writing slowly and deliberately, his tongue poking from the corner of his mouth in concentration. He surveyed what he had written and looked up again.

"Roland said you stuck him in the leg with the fork; that's why he stepped in the throat of the drum. Did you stick him, Lucy?"

"No, I didn't," said Lucy sincerely. "I just threw the sheaves up; it was too far for me to stick him."

"'Old on, 'old on – let me write that down," insisted Marshall, his nose inches from his notebook.

"Why did 'e step in the drum do you think, Lucy?"

"He stepped in it because he was not looking at what he was doing," said Lucy simply.

"What were 'e looking at then?" Marshall asked.

Lucy did not reply.

"What were 'e looking at then?" Marshall repeated.

"He was looking at us women," said Lucy reluctantly. "'Specially Ruby – and I'm not saying any more."

"Very good, Lucy, let me just put that down."

His hand moved slowly across the page.

"Is there anything else you want to add, Lucy?" he asked eventually.

"No," she said firmly.

"They told me you cut 'im out the drum, Lucy, that were very brave of you. Not many girls would 'ave done that – I'm sure I couldn't 'ave."

"Well there was no one else," said Lucy defensively.

"Of course, and the doctor said you were wanting to be a nurse, although actually 'e said you should be a doctor not a nurse, so there – that's praise if there ever was any."

Lucy smiled slightly and looked down at her hands.

"What's going to happen now?" Ann enquired.

"Well I will send the report in and that's that. It would be different if 'e were dead as I said to old Ron, yes it would be very different then."

He looked down at his meticulous notes and frowned.

"S'pose you ought to sign this, Lucy. Yes! You read it and sign at the bottom and I will put the date again."

He handed his book to Lucy for her to read and passed her his stub of a pencil to sign the statement. "Who else saw what happened?" he asked.

"Just Ruby and Molly were there – that was all. The other men were round the other end of the drum and the two on the straw stack were too far away to see. Ron was on the engine so I don't know what he could see – but I don't suppose much."

"Well I s'pose I ought to go and ask them about it, 'adn't I?"

"They will tell you the same thing," said Lucy confidently. "But I s'pose it would be best if you asked them to confirm what I've said."

Freda had entered and was pouring out the tea.

"I don't like Roland Cumber," she said quietly.

Lucy looked up, surprised; Freda rarely participated in conversation.

"I don't like the way 'e looks at you," she continued. "I knowed it when 'e were up 'ere last year doing the ploughing; 'e ain't no good you know, no good at all."

There was silence – Freda was staring at the range, apparently lost in thought. Marshall coughed delicately.

"Well I can call and see Ruby on my way through Dean," he said. "And then I s'pose I could go along to Hardwick's to see if Molly were there."

He drained his tea and put on his helmet, thanked Ann for the tea and made his way back to his bicycle.

Twenty minutes later he arrived at the smithy. He could hear the banging of a hammer on the anvil ringing out down the road.

"Woo up, Art," he called, dismounting from his bicycle as Art looked up from his anvil.

"Woo up, Marshall, what are you up to today, then?"

The constable propped his bike against the wall of the forge and moved towards Art.

"It's like this," he explained, "you heard about Roland getting his leg in the drum, I 'spect."

"Yup, I got all the detail from Ruby – she were there, you know. What a mess it must 'ave bin."

"Well I'm goin' to make a report on it. I'm bin to see Lucy Knighton and I'm now come to see Ruby and then I'm goin' to see Molly to take statements, if you know what I mean. So that's why I'm 'ere, if you know what I mean," he finished uncertainly.

"You want me to find Ruby, then?" Art enquired.

"She about, then?"

"Yup."

"Well give 'er a shout then, it won't take a minute."

Art moved to the door of the house and hollered for Ruby, who came out with her hands covered in flour.

"What's up, then?" she demanded of Art, raising her hand to her eyes to fend off the brightness of the sun.

"It's the law come to see you, Ruby; to take a statement about old Roland getting 'imself in the drum," said Art, pointing to the constable.

"Oh it's you, Mr Perkins," said Ruby, squinting at the constable. "Well what do you want to know then? I ain't got all day, you know; I'm just doin' a bit of bakin'."

She wiped her hands on her apron, brushing the flour from her ample bosom.

"Now just a minute, let me get me book out," Marshall murmured, flicking open his notebook.

"Now I'm bin to see Lucy and she says that she didn't see 'im put his foot in; was that right?"

"Yes, course it was. We were nearly on the ground and 'e were up on the drum so you couldn't see 'im whatever."

"Right," said the constable uncertainly, "but Roland said that Lucy stuck 'im wiv the fork when she pitched the sheaves up to 'im. What do you reckon, Ruby?"

"No, she never, don't you believe any of that rubbish," snarled Ruby "

'E put 'is foot in that there drum because 'e weren't lookin' what 'e were doin' and that's all it were. Lucy never stuck 'im wiv the fork I'm sure on it. Lucy's a good girl; she would never do a thing like that, not even if it were by accident and don't you believe anyone who says anythin' else. And I'll swear to that, I will. You go and ask Molly and all she'll tell you the same, I know she will."

Ruby stopped – glaring angrily at the constable, who, with a small frown on his face, was scribbling furiously, muttering to himself. She turned questioningly to Art, who shrugged and shook his head despairingly. After three long minutes, Marshall looked up.

"Now, Ruby, if you read what I'm put and then you can sign it for me as the truth."

He offered her the notebook.

"Can't read," she said, refusing to take it.

"I'll read it to you then and you can sign it," said Marshall patiently.

"Can't write neither," said Ruby.

"Well I'll read it and you can put a cross, 'ow's that, Ruby?"

"No, let Art read it and then I'll put a cross. Then I know it's right, don't I?"

Marshall shrugged and handed the notebook to Art, who read it out very slowly. Satisfied, Ruby nodded and put a scruffy cross at the bottom of the page

"Well done, Ruby," said Marshall with a smile. "Is there anything else you want to add?"

"Only that Roland's no good and I don't like 'im. And what about what 'e did to Molly? What about that, then?"

She crossed her arms and directly met the constable's gaze.

"What did he do to Molly, then?" he asked curiously.

"I don't rightly know but she 'ad big bruises on 'er arms and none of the 'uvvers would 'ave done anything to 'er; they ain't got it in 'em to do it, I know all of 'em."

"Is that got anything to do with 'im gettin' in the drum then?" said the constable, looking at her closely.

"S'pose it ain't, but it ain't right. Whatever 'e did it ain't right."

"Well I better go and find Molly," said Marshall hurriedly.

"Yes, you better 'ad," said Ruby, turning back into the house.

As Constable Perkin's route to see Molly led him past Harrowig, he decided that it would do no harm to stop and take a few statements en route. The farmyard was abandoned, all the men had gone out into the field to work, with the exception of Bernard who was collecting kindling for the cooker.

"Woo up, Bernard," the constable greeted him.

Bernard started, dropping the kindling and looking about desperately for the source of speech. Eventually he focused on Constable Perkins.

"Woo up," he said touching his cap, and wondering belatedly whether his greeting had been quite suitable for an officer of the law.

"Mornin', constable," he stammered as an afterthought.

"Mornin', Bernard, and what are you up to today?"

Bernard, unsure of whether this was a chastisement for a lack of work on his part that morning, started to shuffle uncomfortably from foot to foot.

"I ain't done nothin', honest I ain't! I'm just bin 'ere mindin' me own business."

He looked apprehensively at the constable.

"No, Bernard. I mean what have you been doin'?"

"Oh yes, I see," nodded Bernard, relieved. "Well I ain't been doing nuffin', well not much any road," he admitted shyly. "I'm just bin gettin' the kindlin' and filling up the coal and water and all that."

"You ain't touched the drum?" the constable asked.

"No, no, I ain't touched that. Ron's gun to do that when 'e gets back from takin' Roland. His old leg's still in there, you know. I don't know 'ow 'e's goin' to get it out. Start it up, I 'spect and it'll come out wiv the straw I 'spect."

He faded out uncertainly, a frown puckering his forehead.

"Did you see the accident?" Marshall asked.

"No, I didn't see nuffin', not nuffin'," murmured Bernard. "I was in the van getting sorted out and gettin' the fire lit for our tea. No, I seen nuffin'."

He shifted the weight off his bad leg, leaning to one side and looking over at the drum.

"I've just thought," said Marshall suddenly, "did you see Roland wiv Molly yesterday at all?"

"Yes he was wiv 'er," growled Bernard, a frown on his face. "'E took 'er inter the van just afore we started yesterday arternoon; 'e kicked me out."

"You're sure of that, Bernard?"

"Course I'm sure," said Bernard confidently. "As sure as sure can be."

The constable looked at him steadily. Seemingly satisfied, he smiled and turned to make his way to Hardwick's.

"I'll see you later, Bernard."

"Right you are," nodded Bernard, looking after the constable, wondering if he had said the right thing.

From Harrowig to Hardwick's was about three quarters of a mile and the road was rutted so Marshall walked and pushed his bike alongside him. The farm yard was quiet, the odd sound of clucking chickens punctuating the quiet as they scratched in the straw looking for spilt grain or other morsels of food. An old boar had his front legs over the wall of his pen, watching Marshall's progress with beady black eyes. The gate to the cattle yards was open, the muck inside at least four feet deep and soon to be carted out into a heap in the fields. The dark brown puddles in the yard stank, filled to the brim with the oozing cow muck from the yards. All the stacks of sheaves had now been threshed, but the straw stacks remained and had been thatched to keep them dry for next winter's litter for the yards.

Constable Perkins picked his way across the yard, knocked on the door and entered the house through the scullery into the kitchen, where Molly sat on her own, watching the range. The kindling crackled as it caught light, and the coal above it shone as the flames licked around the black lumps. Molly looked sideways at the constable as he entered, but said nothing.

On the table, a bread board lay, half a loaf and a pot of jam standing on it. The room otherwise was quite bare – nothing covered the cold bricks of the floor save for a dirty rag carpet in front of the range. There were no pictures on the walls, just a dusty looking clock that ticked slowly away. Marshall read through the glass door to the pendulum case: "*Superior eight-day clock with extra brushed movement.*" Marshall had no idea what that meant. A cat sat on the table eyeing a jug of milk that stood next to the breadboard.

As Marshall moved into the room the cat took fright, charging past him out of the door into the farm yard. Molly continued to look into the fire; her shoulders sagged and her head hung sadly.

"Hello, Molly," said Marshall kindly. "Are you all on your own, then?"

"Yes," Molly replied, not taking her gaze off the fire.

"Where is everyone, then?" Marshall enquired.

"Father's down the butcher's shop; they're killin' today and Muvver will be back in a while. The boys are back at school."

Molly stood up, gave the fire a poke and lifted the kettle from the range. She filled it from a bucket before putting it back on the range to boil.

"Ain't you got no work to go to then, Molly?"

"No, we've bin put off. Can't go threshin' today 'cos of the accident."

"Yes, the accident," said Marshall. "That's what I've come to see you about."

"Me? Why me? I don't know nothin'," Molly snapped, staring hard at Marshall.

"Perhaps we better wait till your mother comes," said Marshall gently.

"She don't know nothin', she weren't there, was she?"

Marshall stared at the angry girl, unsure of what to say.

"When did you say your mother was coming back?"

"I don't know, do I? She said she wouldn't be long, but it takes a long while to walk down to Dean and back from 'ere – you try it."

She sat down again on the chair and stared angrily into the fire.

"I'll go and see if I can see 'er comin'," said the constable nervously. "You can see a long way down the track from the yard."

He hurried outside to find Ellen leaning against the wall, untying the laces of her boots.

"I'm goin' to take me boots off 'ere," she said. "I trod in some cow muck back there and it's all over 'em and I don't want to tread it in the 'ouse. Mind everyone else does so I don't know why I bother." She lifted her head, starting slightly when she caught sight of who it was.

"What are you doin' all the way up 'ere, constable?" she exclaimed. "We've never seen an officer of the law up 'ere, you know; what 'ave we done? 'Ave you come to arrest us then?"

She laughed throatily.

"I'm really come to see Molly; I want a statement about that accident at Harrowig. She were there, weren't she?"

"Yeah, she were there but we can't get much out of her about it, she seems a bit upset somehow. Mind you it can't 'ave bin nice to see it and Ray 'eard that she 'elped Lucy cut 'is leg out the drum; it don't bear thinkin' about, do it?"

"No, it don't sound very nice. Anyway I ought to take a statement about what she seen, just in case you know."

He followed Ellen back into the kitchen

"Molly Webb, are you only just lit the fire?" scolded Ellen. "Ain't that kettle boilin' yet?"

Molly looked up moodily and said nothing.

"We can't even 'ave a cuppa tea yet," sighed Ellen. "Sorry about that, constable."

"Oh don't worry, Mrs Webb; I can manage."

"Come on, Molly, out the way; let me get at that fire and sort it out."

She took the poker from against the range and gave the fire a poke.

"Now, Molly, Mr Perkins wants to ask you some questions about the accident yesterday," said Ellen. "Since you were there, 'e wants you to make a statement."

Marshall had sat at the table, his notebook in front of him. He licked his pencil expectantly.

"Are you listenin', Molly?" said Ellen loudly.

"Yes I'm listenin'," muttered Molly, her gaze still on the crackling fire.

"Right, Mr Perkins, you 'ave a go then; I don't know wever you'll get anything out of 'er," said Ellen with a shrug.

"Now, Molly, where were you when the accident 'appened?" Marshall said slowly.

"I were on the stack."

"And who was with you, Molly?"

"Lucy and Ruby."

"Look at the constable when 'e's speakin' to you, Molly," Ellen hissed.

Molly raised her eyes to meet Marshall's gaze.

"What did you see of the accident, Molly?" he asked gently.

"I didn't see nuffing."

"But you must have seen something, Molly," Marshall smiled.

"Well one minute 'e were there and then 'e were gone and the drum stopped. We were nearly on the ground and 'e were up on the drum; we couldn't see the throat where 'e stepped in."

"He said that Lucy stuck 'im with the fork that's why he stepped into the drum."

Molly looked up sharply.

"That ain't true, she never stuck 'im; she could 'ardly reach 'im any road. Lucy's a good person she wouldn't do that. Mind I would 'ave done if I could," she added bitterly.

"Molly, what are you sayin'?" said Ellen angrily.

"He's a rotten man, he deserved to get his leg in the drum, so there."

Marshall and Ellen looked at each other.

"Why do you think he stepped in the throat of the drum, Molly?" Marshall asked.

"'E weren't looking at what 'e were doin', was 'e?"

"Why not, Molly?"

"'E were lookin' at Ruby's tits, weren't 'e – that's why 'e stepped in the drum, the rotten sod."

"Molly, how dare you say such things," said Ellen furiously. "What would the parson say if he knew you used such words?"

"Well 'e was rotten," said Molly, her small frame shaking with rage. "Whatever words you use. You ask Lucy and Ruby, they will tell you."

"And Molly, you then helped Lucy get Roland out of the drum?" said the constable, trying to take control of the situation.

"Yes I did. I don't know why and I don't know why Lucy helped either; she should 'ave left 'im there. But Lucy's a good person."

Molly stopped; a tear came to her eye and she wiped it away hurriedly.

"How old are you, Molly?"

"Just sixteen," she replied.

He looked at her steadily and put down his pencil.

"Molly, Ruby said that you had got bruises on your arms; can I see them?"

Molly did nothing.

"Go on, Molly, roll your sleeves up," ordered her mother.

Molly sniffed, slowly rolling up her sleeves to reveal the imprint of four fingers and a thumb pressed angrily into her pale flesh. Ellen raised her hand to her mouth and gasped.

"Who did that, Molly?" her mother demanded. "Who in heaven did that? Look, Marshall, can you see?"

"Ruby said that Roland did it, Molly," asked Marshall. "Did Roland do it?"

"I ain't tellin' yer," mumbled Molly.

"Bernard said that Roland took you in the van, did he, Molly? Did Roland take you in the van?"

There was silence again.

"I ain't tellin' yer," Molly repeated more faintly.

"Molly, Molly, what happened?" her mother implored, wringing her hands. "Tell us what 'appened."

"I ain't tellin' and that's that," mumbled Molly, pulling her sleeve down quickly.

"What are we going to do, constable? What are we goin' to do?" begged Ellen, turning to Marshall.

"We ain't do nothin', Mrs Webb; she won't say, so there's nothin' we *can* do. Now, Molly, can you read?"

"Corse I can read," snapped Molly.

"Well when I'm finished this I want you to read it and put your name where I show," said Marshall steadily.

"I ain't put nothing except about the accident," insisted Molly, taking the notebook and reading slowly.

"Give us the pencil then," she said to Marshall, taking the pencil and scribbling her name.

"What's goin' to 'appen now?" she said.

"We'll 'ave to wait and see; probably nothing, I 'spect," said Marshall. "And about anythin' else – nothing will 'appen as you ain't made no complaint, Molly, so I can do no more. I will be on my way if that's all right with you."

He put on his helmet, said goodbye and left.

There was silence.

"Now, my girl," Ellen said, "are you going to tell me what 'appened? What did that brute do to you, Molly?"

Molly said nothing, the tears rolling down her face as she started to shake with sobs.

"Did 'e lift your skirt, Molly?" said Ellen quietly.

"What do you think?" sobbed Molly, turning angrily on her mother. "Why didn't you tell me; why didn' you tell me that that's what men do? Not that I could 'ave done anything, 'e just did what 'e wanted and I were completely 'elpless, just 'elpless. I were just like the old sow out there, couldn't do nothing. I wish I were dead, I wish I were dead and that's the truth." Ellen stood helplessly as Molly continued to shake. "And I wish 'e were dead as well. Why did Lucy 'elp 'im? I should 'ave stuck them scissors in 'im if I 'ad any sense."

She turned on her mother again

"And we ain't goin' to do nuffin' so don't think we will and we ain't goin' to tell no one, so there."

"But 'e can't just get away with it, just like that," Ellen begged. "'E can't just get away with it."

"Why not?" snapped Molly. "There's no proof, no one saw it 'appen,"

She wiped her eyes and sniffed.

"Bernard see it, the policeman said that Bernard see you get in the van."

"That ain't no good," laughed Molly bitterly. "Bernard's 'arf sharp! You know that, everyone knows that, no one would believe 'im anyway."

Ellen moved to her daughter and pulled her into her arms – Molly continued to sob into her mother's shoulder.

"What can I do for you, Molly?" Ellen said. "What can I do to 'elp? I don't know what to do."

She put her hand over her mouth as tears started to fall from her eyes, holding her daughter tightly.

"I know, Molly," she said decisively. "We'll give you a bath; that will make you feel better, that will take all the dirt away. The preacher says we should wash away our sin."

"Don't talk to me about washin' away sin," snarled Molly, pulling away from her mother. "I ain't sinned, 'ave I? I'm bin sinned against, ain't I? It's that Roland who's the sinner. That preacher don't know what 'e's talking about; 'e's got no idea."

Ellen went to reply and thought better of it.

"Let's give you a bath then, eh?" she said gently.

"I can't 'ave a barf now; not in the middle of the day. Anyway we ain't got any soap, so I ain't."

"Yes we 'ave; Dorcas gave me all the little bits that were nearly used up and I'm pressed them into one big bit; it really smells nice, it really does."

She smiled at her daughter.

"Go on, Molly, it'll make you feel better. No one's 'ere; your dad won't be back till tea time and the boys are at school."

Molly nodded dumbly. Ellen smiled and went to prepare – filling kettles and saucepans to empty into the zinc bath, which she brought into the kitchen. Twenty minutes later, the bath was ready.

"Come on then, Molly, get them clothes off and get in the lovely warm water; you'll feel better you see, I know you will and I'm got the soap 'ere–

you smell it! It's nice, ain't it?"

She held out the small patched bar to her daughter. Molly sniffed it reluctantly and shrugged.

She stood up, took off her dress and thick linen shirt, and climbed gingerly into the bath.

"Here's the soap, Molly, now wash yourself and I'll go and get a towel and a clean shirt and dress; I've filled the kettle for more hot water if you want it."

Molly sank into the warm water, the remnants of the tears still gleaming on her cheeks. She took hold of the soap and started to scrub – gently at first then harder and harder, trying desperately to scrub the memory of yesterday from her skin.

Chapter Twenty-Seven
Roland and Adelaide

At the infirmary in Northampton, Roland had to wait for two hours to be seen. He was irritable – the journey to Northampton had been uncomfortable and his leg throbbed agonisingly. Once he was eventually seen, the doctors showed similar concerns to that which Doctor Roberts had; they believed that Roland's leg should have been amputated above the knee. None of the doctors liked the look of the stump and although the amputation job had been competent, the risk of infection was high and Roland was ordered to stay in hospital for a couple of days. Roland objected vehemently to this, but the hospital doctors were a good deal more insistent than Doctor Roberts had been and took away his crutch to ensure he could not move. Roland named his sister – a Mrs Harding– as the person who would pay for his care; and the statement was never queried, the Hardings being well known in Northampton.

The rest of the Harding family remained blissfully unaware of Roland and his predicament. Rebecca Harding had returned home, having only completed half of her course at finishing school in Switzerland. She was desperate to have a career and as she spent much of her time with Mary – hearing tales of working life – she became increasingly determined that this was what she was wanted to do. Rebecca's father, however, would not hear of such a thing and persuaded Adelaide to redouble her efforts to marry Rebecca off, focusing her attention most heavily in the direction of Jimmy Brummitt.

In an attempt to cement the match, Adelaide would encourage Rebecca to go walking with Jimmy, and if Mary was staying, Rupert would accompany them, the four of them exploring the parks in Northampton, watching the football and cricket. That Sunday was a particularly balmy day and as the heat of the sun was relatively strong, the four of them took it upon themselves to walk all the way to Blisworth and back. Passing the infirmary, Mary noticed a man leaving the gates; he was swinging himself slowly along with crutches, having lost the lower half of one of his legs. Mary looked closely at the man

– she felt that she knew him but couldn't quite work out from where. He turned past them at the gates and made off in the opposite direction and Mary thought no more of it. At Dallington, neither of Rebecca's parents were in; Jimmy and Rupert said their goodbyes, leaving the two girls to play cards and discussing the merits of both of the men they had spent their day with. Halfway through a game of whist, the maid bustled in, her face flushed.

"Yes, Violet, what is it?" Rebecca enquired.

"Miss, there's a man come to the door and he won't go away, miss. He says he wants to see his sister Adelaide. I told him she wasn't here, miss, but he insisted and he won't go away. I've never seen him before, miss and I didn't know Mrs Harding had a brother, miss."

Violet stared desperately at Rebecca, wringing her hands.

"Very well, Violet, I'll come."

"And, miss?"

"Yes, Violet."

"He's only got one leg!"

Rebecca frowned at Mary.

"I had better go," sighed Rebecca, leaving with Violet.

A few minutes later, Rebecca returned. She hesitated in the doorway before turning to look at Mary.

"Mary, I don't know what to do with him," said Rebecca, chewing her lip. "He's in the kitchen now. He says he's Adelaide's brother and he does look a *bit* like her but—"

She broke off, frowning slightly.

"What is it, Rebecca, tell me? What is it?" Mary asked.

"Violet's right. He's only got one leg and he walks with crutches; he said he was in an accident with a threshing machine; he's all bandaged up. It can't be right, Mary; the smell is awful. Violet's going to make him a cup of tea, what do you think we should do?"

The face of the one-legged man slotted into place and suddenly Mary realised where she had seen the man by the infirmary before.

"It's Roland Cumber!" she said determinedly. "I know him – he's an awful man. He did have an accident about a week ago – Lucy was there, she cut him out of the machine."

"What are we to do then?" Rebecca said desperately.

"Shall I come and see him?" said Mary decisively.

"Oh would you? Thank you, Mary – especially if you already know him."

Mary stood up and followed Rebecca out of the room. In the kitchen the smell of putrefaction hit the girls as soon as they entered the room. Roland, his back to the door, was sitting on a chair; his stump, wrapped tight in dirty white bandages, resting on another. Violet was standing nervously at the range, waiting for the kettle to boil.

"Would you like anything to eat with your tea?" Rebecca asked, moving round the table to look at Roland.

"Not at the minute," Roland retorted rudely, looking up at the two girls. "But I could do with summut to take the pain away – if you know what I mean."

Rebecca, confused, looked to Mary.

"I think he means some rum or whisky, Rebecca," Mary advised her.

Roland looked searchingly at Mary.

"Don't I know you?" he said accusingly, a frown furrowing his brow. "Yeah, I know you, don't I? Well, well, fancy seein' you 'ere, Miss Knighton. It *is* Mary Knighton if I ain't mistaken, isn't it? Well, well, what a turn up for the books."

He chuckled to himself gleefully.

"Do you want some rum, then?" Rebecca said sharply.

"Whisky if you don't mind," leered Roland.

"Very well then," said Rebecca. "Mary come and help me find the key; Father locks all the drink up." She dragged Mary out of the room into the sitting room, turning desperately to her as soon as they were out of earshot.

"What am I to do with him?" she pleaded. "We can't turn him out on the street in that condition."

"You will have to wait until Adelaide comes back, Rebecca. Do you know when to expect them?" asked Mary.

"About half past nine I think. We will just have to wait and ply him with drink; he can't do us any harm in that state."

She scoured the room for the key to the drinks cabinet, finding it behind a visiting card on the mantelpiece, and delivered the bottle to Roland.

"'Ave you got another cup?" Roland demanded of Violet, looking scathingly at his half-full tea cup.

Violet scurried to the dresser, found a clean cup and placed it beside the man, stepping back quickly as if he might bite her.

Roland studied the whisky bottle, pulled out the cork with his teeth and poured a large measure into the fresh cup.

"Can't abide to put good drink into tea, it's a waste," he said, winking at Rebecca. "Much better on its own."

He took a long sup of the whisky, smacking his lips with satisfaction.

"That's better," he sighed. "Warms you up, that does."

He eased himself upright, wincing as his stump moved against the chair.

"Do you want anything to eat?" Rebecca asked.

"What you got, then?" Roland replied gracelessly.

"What have we got, Violet?" said Rebecca, turning to Violet who was standing as far away from Roland as possible, in the corner of the room.

"Well, miss, there's a pork pie and some bread and cheese; will that do?"

"I s'pose it'll 'ave to," interjected Roland. "Yeah, go on with yer – that'll do."

He turned curiously to look at Mary.

"And what's Miss Mary Knighton doin' in a posh 'ouse like this, then? Bit above your station, ain't it, Miss Knighton?"

Mary said nothing, but looked coolly back at him.

"Think yourselves better than you are, you Knightons, I knows that: I told you that afore, ain't I? As for that there sister of yours – she's the reason I'm in this mess."

"I'm quite sure she's not," Mary said coldly.

"Yes, she is," insisted Roland. "She stuck me with the fork – that's why I stepped back into the drum."

"You hold your tongue, Roland," snapped Mary. "We both know that isn't true, and if it weren't for Lucy cutting you out, you would still be in the drum! So just you stop saying such things!"

Mary's face was red – her eyes bored into Roland, her fists clenched. Roland grinned and poured himself some more whisky, shifting in his chair as he did so, then he winced.

"You should be in hospital, shouldn't you?" interrupted Rebecca. "That leg doesn't seem very good."

"I'm bin there and they kept me for a day or two, but I got meself out in the end. They ain't goin' to do me any good no more."

He took a long slug of whisky as Violet pushed a plate of food in front of him.

"Where are you staying?" enquired Rebecca, watching Roland tuck into his food.

"I don't rightly know," said Roland, through a mouthful. "I was hopin' that my dear sister might sort somethin' out – but you say she ain't 'ere."

"No, she's not, but we are expecting her shortly, aren't we, Violet?"

"Yes, miss," muttered Violet. "I think they will be back before long."

Roland shrugged and continued to eat. Rebecca grimaced in disgust.

"Come on, Mary," she said firmly. "We will go and wait in the drawing room, we will see them coming from there."

The two girls left the kitchen, Violet staring desperately after them.

"What are we going to do, Mary?" sighed Rebecca. "I do wish they would come home. Surely he can't be Adelaide's brother, can he?"

Rebecca sat, staring out the window before turning to Mary again.

"That leg of his smells terrible – it must be infected. We can't throw him out in that state, can we?" She looked at Mary, who was looking angrily down at her lap, twisting her dress in her fingers. Finally she looked up, blurting out,

"He's a dreadful man, Rebecca; no one likes him! He comes to our farm on the engines to do the ploughing and there's always trouble. And the awful things he said about Lucy! I'm sure it's not true; Lucy would never do a thing like that! I heard that she cut him out when he got his leg in the drum – she saved his life!"

She looked hard at her friend, just as the noise of car tyres on gravel met their ears. They hurried towards the front door.

Adelaide swept into the hallway, her gaze brushing superciliously over Rebecca and Mary.

"Oh it's you," she sneered. "What an unexpected pleasure to be greeted at the door by you two."

An expression of disgust crept over her face.

"What's that awful smell?"

"It's someone in the kitchen, Adelaide; he says he's your brother and he's injured."

"What's that, my dear?" Charles asked his daughter, pulling his coat off as he followed Adelaide into the hallway. "What's the problem?"

"It's Roland!" said Adelaide sharply. "Charles, you go in the drawing room, and get yourself a drink; let me deal with this one."

She turned to her husband urgently as he passed her.

"Charles, have you got any money on you?" she asked desperately.

"Yes, dear, how much?"

"Give me ten pounds – that will do," said Adelaide, holding out her hand for the two white five-pound notes that Charles pulled from his wallet.

"Now where is he?" she demanded.

"In the kitchen," said Rebecca, following Adelaide towards the source of the disruption, Mary right behind.

Roland was still eating as the women entered the kitchen.

"What do you think you are doing coming here, Roland Cumber?" demanded Adelaide of her brother, rounding the table furiously. "I thought I told you I never wanted to see you again."

"I'm come 'ere 'cos I'm injured– can't you see I am?" said Roland, indicating his stump and chewing slowly on a chunk of bread.

"Well, why ain't you in the hospital then, you stupid bugger?" hissed Adelaide. "You're no good, Roland Cumber, and you never were any good."

"I'm bin in the hospital," growled Roland, "but I got meself out; they won't take me back, I'm sure on it."

"Well you ain't stayin' here," snarled Adelaide. "Not another minute, and the stink of you! It's 'orrible."

"Where am I goin' to go then?" said Roland, a note of desperation creeping into his voice. "It's dark out there now."

"I don't care where you go – you should have thought of that before you came here," said Adelaide with a shrug. "And how did you find where we live anyway?"

"They told me in the hospital," said Roland shortly, adding slyly. "Everyone knows who you are, Adelaide; you've got a reputation, did you know that?"

"Shut up, Roland," snapped Adelaide angrily, shooting a sideways glance towards the two girls. "Just finish your food and shut your mouth."

There was silence – the siblings eyed each other suspiciously.

"You can't turn him out," said Rebecca quietly, "not in that state."

"Yes I can and I'm goin' to," said Adelaide triumphantly.

"Could we get Wilson to take him back to the hospital in the car?" Rebecca insisted.

"And let him stink the car out? No fear! He's goin' and that's that! He got himself here so he can get himself somewhere else."

She turned menacingly back to her brother. "I imagine that this injury is your fault anyway. You should be in jail by rights at any rate – it's only because that poor girl died that you got out of it the last time."

She glared contemptuously at her brother.

"You really are a rotten bastard, Roland – rotten to the core."

"She don't think so," said Roland nodding at Rebecca, "she's got a little bit of humanity in 'er, not like you or that other one."

He pointed accusingly at Mary.

"She knows what you're like, I guess," sneered Adelaide. "Now have you finished your food?"

"Yes," mumbled Roland.

"Well get your bag and get goin'," she snarled.

She threw the five-pound notes down in front of Roland.

"Here's ten pounds – and you're damn lucky to get that. Get yourself back to the hospital and get that leg sorted out, see."

Roland looked at the notes and back up at his sister, his face reddening.

"You're a hard old sod," he spat, glaring furiously at Adelaide.

He rounded on Violet.

"Get me me crutches then and me bag," he demanded.

He heaved himself up from the table, snatching the crutches from Violet and picking up the notes from the table. He took a glance at the whisky bottle, picked it up and stowed it in his jacket pocket. Hoisting the canvas bag onto his shoulder, he turned to look at his sister, his lip curling contemptuously.

"Well, my dear sister, I'll say goodbye but don't forget one thing! You ain't much better than me – we come out the same stable, didn't we?"

He tapped the side of his nose and grinned at Adelaide.

Adelaide gave a bellow like a wounded animal and moved angrily to the door

"Get out! Get out of my sight, you nasty bastard. And don't come back – not *never,* do you hear?"

Roland didn't answer – he took one last look at his sister and swung himself out of the door and into the night.

It wasn't until the next Thursday that Mary saw *The Northampton Echo* announcing the death of Roland Cumber, under the banner "*MAN FOUND DEAD IN PARK.*" The story read that the man – presumed homeless – had only had one leg and that his death was believed to be as a result of complications from his recent amputation. Roland Cumber was dead; Mary found it hard to find any pity for the man, but a sense of dread started to creep through her. If Roland was dead, what would happen to Lucy at the inquest?

Chapter Twenty-Eight
The Inquest

The date of the inquest into Roland Cumber's death was fixed for the last Thursday in May, and all those who had given statements were subpoenaed to attend the Coroner's Court in Northampton. Mary had asked for the day off to go and support her sister and Lucy, Ruby and Molly had come together by train to Northampton where Mary met them and took them to the court. The room was almost full when the four of them arrived. Rupert, having been sent to cover the case, sat at the back of the room and raised his hand to Mary as she moved into the room. Adelaide and Rebecca sat just behind him; since Adelaide had been the one to identify the body she had thought it best to attend, in case she was needed to testify. The coroner was perched behind a big desk at one end of the room, two clerks sitting either side of him. The jury of six men sat at a table in front of him, the members of public arranged on benches behind. The witnesses who had been subpoenaed sat in a row against the wall at the back.

The coroner was a man in his mid-forties with a long beard and very bushy eyebrows. He wore a black pinstriped suit, under a long frock jacket with velvet lapels. His moustache was stained yellow with nicotine and as he walked into the court room the smell of old cigar smoke wafted along behind him. His hair and beard were tinged with ginger, his cheeks a sharply contrasting red.

The court rose as he entered, crossed to his desk and sat to read the papers in front of him. The sound of footsteps interrupted the hush as Jimmy Brummitt crept into the room; his shoes squeaking as he tiptoed to a seat at the back of the room.

The coroner continued to read for a further three minutes; the shuffling and whispering growing more pronounced the longer he took. Finally, he glanced up, put the papers down and took a long look at his pocket watch.

"This court is now in session," he announced in a thick Scottish accent. "We will adjourn for lunch at half past twelve and if we have not finished by then we will reconvene at a quarter past two."

He turned to the clerk on his right.

"Have the jury been sworn in?" he enquired.

"Yes, sir."

"Very good," intoned the coroner, turning to address the assembled courtroom:

"We are here to determine the cause of death of a Mr Roland Cumber who was found dead in Abingdon Park on Wednesday the second of May 1902."

The coroner paused, shuffling impatiently through his papers before turning to the clerk.

"The body was found by a park cleaner, is that right?" he asked.

"That's correct, sir," agreed the clerk.

"Hmmm," mused the coroner, looking back to his notes, "well I don't think we need to see him. And the body was taken to the morgue and examined by Doctor Leach whose report is here."

He stopped, blinked and looked down at the paper in front of him, his brow furrowed in concentration.

"He tells us that Mr Cumber died of septicaemia caused by an infection in an amputated leg. Hmmmm. Don't have many of them, do we? Seems pretty straightforward."

He looked quizzically up at the court room and back at the clerk.

"So what are these people doing here?"

"To discuss the circumstances of the accident that caused his leg to be amputated, sir," said the clerk patiently. "That's what they are here for."

"Bless my soul, yes, I suppose it is; we must get on then," said the coroner with a sharp snort of laughter.

He looked round at the assembled company.

"Who identified the body?"

"Mrs Harding, sir," replied the clerk.

"Mrs Charles Harding?" said the coroner, surprised.

"Yes, sir."

"Well is she here?" he asked, scanning the courtroom. "Ah yes, I can see she is. Well I think we ought to hear from her. Please could you ask her to

317

come and take the stand?"

The clerk, recognising Adelaide, moved towards her and indicated that the coroner would like her to take the stand. Adelaide stood, smoothed down her dress and glided towards the stand, where she was sworn in before sitting down on the hard chair. She shifted uncomfortably.

"Mrs Harding, can I ask how you came to know the deceased?" asked the coroner.

"He's my brother," Adelaide said abruptly.

A small murmur of surprise rippled through the court room. The coroner raised a bushy eyebrow and continued.

"And when did you last see him?"

"On the Sunday before he died," she said, "he came to our house."

"Was he injured then?"

"Yes, he had lost the lower part of his leg in a threshing drum."

"And how did he say it happened?"

"He said that someone stuck him with a pitchfork which made him tread in the drum."

"And who had stuck him?"

"He said Lucy Knighton," said Adelaide simply.

Eyes swivelled towards Lucy, people craning their necks from their seats to catch a glimpse of her; the only person who seemed disengaged was Doctor Roberts, whose nose was buried deep in a book.

"And were you able to help your brother, Mrs Harding?" the coroner asked.

"Yes, I gave him ten pounds and sent him to the hospital."

"Very generous," the coroner remarked with a small nod.

"Now let me see," he said, "is there any mention of an injury from a pitchfork in the doctor's report?"

He picked up the report and read it quickly.

"Yes, sir," said the clerk. "He says that there was a deep graze on the right leg, sir."

"Ah ha," said the coroner, stroking his beard thoughtfully, "let's carry on then. Who have we got next?"

"Constable Perkins, sir, he attended the accident and took statements."

"Very good, call him then."

Constable Perkins was called, and trotted up to take his oath in the witness chair.

"Constable Perkins, did you see the accident?"

"No, sir, I arrived sometime after it 'ad 'appened," said Marshall carefully.

"And who was there when you arrived?"

"Well, sir, all the threshing gang and three women who were on the stack; oh and William Dunmore were there an' all."

"And you say here, constable, that Cumber spoke to you?"

"Yes he did, sir."

"And what did he say?"

"'E said that Lucy Knighton 'ad stuck him with a pitchfork, that's why he stepped in the drum."

"And what did you do then, constable?"

"Well, sir, I surveyed the scene of the accident and then follered 'im down to the doctor's in Kimbolton to speak to the doctor who was going to patch him up and examine 'im."

"Did the doctor know about the accusation that Lucy Knighton had stuck Mr Cumber with a pitchfork?"

"Yes, sir."

Marshall paused and fidgeted awkwardly.

"Carry on, constable; what happened then?"

"I went 'ome, sir, it were gittin' late by then, you see, sir—" he explained apologetically; the coroner nodded impatiently, gesturing for Marshall to continue.

"The very next day I went to see the three women – Lucy, Ruby and Molly."

"And what did they say, constable?"

"They all said that Lucy didn't stick 'im and that 'e stepped in the drum 'cos 'e weren't payin' attention to what 'e were doin'; it's all down there, sir."

Marshall pointed enthusiastically to his notebook, which lay on the coroner's desk. The coroner picked up the notebook and leafed slowly through Perkins's laborious notes.

"Well we had better hear from the three ladies," he said, putting the notebook down and looking to where the witnesses were sitting.

Lucy rose to take her seat first.

"You are Lucy Knighton?" the coroner asked.

"Yes, sir."

"And Lucy Knighton, you have heard the accusation made by the late Roland Cumber – that you stuck him with a pitchfork and that's why he got himself into the drum."

"Yes, sir."

"And what do you say to it, Lucy?"

"I didn't do it, sir, I'm sure I didn't stick him; I was just throwing the sheaves up and that was all. I didn't even see it happen. Anyway we were a long way down and I could hardly reach to throw them up, let alone to stick him in the leg."

"You're sure, Lucy?" asked the coroner, surveying Lucy sternly.

"Yes, sir."

"Let's have the next one then," sighed the coroner, gesturing towards Ruby, who rose to take Lucy's place.

"Did Lucy stick Mr Cumber?" he asked.

"No, sir, she never!" said Ruby forcefully. "Lucy is a good girl; she would never do anything like that, I'm sure she didn't. 'E got in the drum 'cos 'e weren't lookin' what 'e were doin' and that's all there is to it, I'm sure on it."

"Let's hear the last one then please," said the coroner with a glance towards his pocket watch, "then we will adjourn for lunch; we are not going to finish this one as quickly as I'd thought."

Molly walked to the witness stand, the tremor in her hand betraying the defiant tilt of her chin as she rose to swear her oath.

"Molly did you see Mr Cumber get himself in the drum?" asked the coroner.

"No, sir, you couldn't see from where we was; 'e were high up and we were nearly on the ground," replied Molly clearly.

"Did Lucy stick him with a pitchfork, Molly?"

"No she didn't, I'm sure on it. I never see that 'appen – she were just throwin' the sheaves up, that's all. 'E weren't looking what 'e were doin', that's why 'e got in the drum. Any road 'e would still be there in that drum if Lucy hadn't cut 'im out. I would 'ave left 'im if it were me – I'm glad 'e's dead."

"Now, now, Molly," chided the coroner with a quick look towards Adelaide in the crowd, "you should not say such things."

"Why not? It's true," Molly snapped back.

The coroner scratched his forehead and shuffled the papers on his desk.

"I think it is time we had lunch; I will ask everyone to return at a quarter past two."

He rose and left the courtroom. Everyone stood, before drifting out of the court room into the fresh air.

Ruby had brought a basket of food, and Molly and Lucy joined her to share the picnic. They were shortly joined by Mary and Rebecca who had been talking to Rupert and Jimmy.

"What's going to happen, Mary?" said Lucy nervously. "If he says it was my fault that Roland got in the drum, he'll say that I murdered him."

"Don't be so stupid, Lucy," said Mary sharply. "Of course he won't say that – you didn't do anything wrong, everyone says so."

"But they did say he had a graze on his leg, didn't they?" said Lucy miserably.

"I know," said Mary gently, "but there's no reason to think that you did it, is there? He could have done that anywhere."

"Don't you worry, Lucy," said Ruby, grasping Lucy's hand in hers. "I was there. I know you didn't do it – I told the man so, didn't I? You ain't goin' to get into trouble, I know you ain't."

She turned to Molly.

"That's right, ain't it, Molly? You was there."

"Yeah, I saw it too, Lucy – that rotten sod got all 'e deserved and I don't care who knows it. 'E only said you stuck 'im so 'e didn't look stupid for treadin' in the drum. If 'e ain't bin lookin' at Ruby's tits 'e would have never gone."

"Molly! Don't use words like that!" chastised Lucy.

"Well it's true!" said Molly indignantly. "We all know it and we ought to a' told that old judge what 'e were doin' – 'e should know that. Roland was a nasty man and we're all much better now 'e's dead."

"What did Jimmy say, Rebecca? He's a lawyer, isn't he?" Lucy asked.

"He says it will be an accidental death whatever happens and you're not going to be blamed for it, Lucy. I'm sure he's right."

Lucy sniffed, wiping a tear from her eye, before rising hastily and walking away across the park; Mary and Rebecca left to follow her.

Ruby and Molly started to pack away the food in the basket.

"Molly?" said Ruby.

"Yeah," Molly replied.

"You know the day that Roland got in the drum, somethink 'appened between you and 'im, didn't it? You'd got all them bruises, ain't you? I know what 'e's like, I do; 'e was a real rotter. Bernard said you was in the van wiv 'im."

Molly looked away across the park towards the figures of Rebecca and Mary comforting Lucy. Her face crumpled and tears started to course down her face, her shoulders shaking with the extremity of her emotion. Ruby put an arm round the girl's shoulder, pulling Molly in towards her.

"There, there, Molly; it's all right."

"I couldn't do nothing about it, Ruby," sobbed Molly. "He grabbed me, I couldn't get away – it were awful; I didn't know what 'e were doing. 'E were a big man; you ain't got a chance! It were just horrible." She sniffed and rubbed her eyes with the back of her hand. "I wish I were dead, Ruby, I really do! I'm just so ashamed – I really wish I were dead."

Ruby stroked Molly's hair gently.

"There, there, Molly. You don't think no more about it; 'e's dead now and 'e ain't goin' to trouble you again. When you feel bad you come down and see me at the smithy and we can 'ave a talk, can't we?"

"Thanks, Ruby," Molly sniffed, wiping her eyes and offering Ruby a watery smile.

Ruby smiled, and squeezed Molly's hand gently.

"Right, I'm got to go down the end before we go back in; I think there's one right over there – you comin', Molly?"

"No, I can last all day if I want to – you go, Ruby, I'll wait 'ere."

Ruby rose and made her way towards the buildings, leaving Molly gazing listlessly across the park. Two figures were making their way in her direction – the man's face reminded her of somebody. As they approached it became obvious they were heading straight for her – a man and a woman, both slightly rotund, smiles creasing both of their faces.

"Well hello, Molly, I bet you don't know who I am," said the man with a wink.

"I'm got no idea, sorry," said Molly cautiously.

"I'm Dorcas's brother Edwin – you know 'er, don't you?"

"Oh yes! My mum works down there along of 'er; she's a nice lady, ain't she?" said Molly eagerly.

"Yes," chuckled Edwin. "She is! I were born in Dean, a lovely place you know, a lovely place and where do you live, Molly?"

"Oh we live up at Hardwick's."

"That's a bit out in the wilds, ain't it?" tutted Edwin. "I bet it's a bit lonely up there."

"You're right about that," said Molly with a wry smile. "We don't see no one from one end of the week to the other and you're got to walk miles to get anywhere."

"What do you work at then, Molly? You must 'ave left school, ain't you?"

"Yeah, I'm bin left nearly a year now. I do a bit of this and a bit of that. I 'elp on the farm mostly and 'elp Mum sometimes; anyfink I can come across really."

Edwin looked sideways at Lizzie, who raised a wistful eyebrow to her husband and added,

"We would always give you a job, Molly; we're always on the lookout for young girls to 'elp in the pub, ain't we, Edwin?"

"Yes that's right," agreed Edwin. "We can never get enough 'elp, can we, Lizzie?"

"What is the job then?" Molly asked curiously.

"Oh cleaning, washing glasses, making the sandwiches, servin' at the bar; all that sort of thing, you know," said Edwin.

"Do you know where our pub is, Molly?" Lizzie asked.

"No I ain't never bin to Norfampton afore. I ain't ever bin on a train afore today either so I ain't travelled much."

"Well you know how to get hold of us if you do want a job, just go down and ask Dorcas, she'll tell you," said Edwin confidentially.

"I'll 'ave to ask Mum about it; but I know Mary works in Norfampton, don't she?"

"You mean Mary Knighton, don't you; I think she works at Tibbitts. We don't go in there," said Lizzie with a laugh. "It's a bit posh for the likes of us, ain't it, Edwin?"

They were interrupted by Ruby returning. She smiled weakly at Edwin and Lizzie, before addressing Molly.

"That's better," she said, "I wonder 'ow long we're gonner be this arternoon. I hope it don't go on too long or it will be dark afore I git 'ome and Art will be starvin'. Come on, Molly, they're about ready to start going back in now".

Molly stood and stroked down the front of her skirt. She smiled shyly at Edwin and Lizzie before following Ruby back to the front of the court, where people were standing chatting in the afternoon sun.

Jimmy and Rupert had returned from their offices and were talking to Mary and Rebecca.

"What will happen, Jimmy? If they say Lucy did stick him with the fork?" whispered Rebecca, out of earshot of Mary and Rupert.

"I don't know," shrugged Jimmy. "I don't see how she can be held responsible – but you never know. We will have to see what the doctor says."

A crunch of gravel announced the arrival of the coroner's carriage; the assembled crowd scurried into the court to take their seats, moments before the coroner trotted in, the smell of cigar hanging in the air around him. There was a scraping of chairs as everyone stood up and then sat down again.

"Now, where were we?" said the coroner, peering at the clerk.

"We have just heard Molly Webb, sir. I assume you have finished with her?"

The coroner stared down at his notes, reading back over what he had written.

"Hmm," he mused, "I see that the last two witnesses said that Mr Cumber was not paying attention and that's why he stepped in the drum but why wasn't he paying attention?"

He drummed his fingers on the desk thoughtfully.

"I think we are going to have to ask them why he was not paying attention. Call Molly Webb again."

"Molly Webb, will you come forward please?" called the clerk, indicating the witness chair.

Molly looked up, surprised, and made her way back to the front.

"Don't worry, my dear, you need not be sworn in again, just sit down I have a question for you." Molly sat on the chair, pushing her fist backwards and forwards across her nose and sniffing loudly.

"Molly Webb– you said that Mr Cumber was not looking at what he was doing. If that was the case – what was he looking at?"

Molly flushed, raising her eyes to look at Ruby and Lucy, who both lowered their heads and looked at the floor. Molly turned back to the coroner and shifted uncomfortably in her seat.

"Well, Molly," encouraged the coroner, "what was Mr Cumber looking at? Why wasn't he paying attention to what he was doing? Now speak up, will you!"

"Well, sir, he weren't looking at the drum," said Molly quietly.

"I know that, dear girl, but what was he looking at?"

"'E were looking at Ruby, sir."

"Who's Ruby?"

"Mrs Tuffnail, sir. You questioned her this morning, sir,"

"Oh, yes, yes, so I did! And why was he looking at Mrs Tuffnail, Molly?"

Molly looked desperately once again at Ruby, whose eyes were firmly downcast.

"Don't know, sir," mumbled Molly.

"Well if you don't know, Molly, we had better ask Mrs Tuffnail, hadn't we?"

"Yes, sir," said Molly.

"Thank you, Molly, that's all," sighed the coroner. "Can we have Mrs

Tuffnail again, please?"

Ruby's head snapped up – she put her hand to her mouth and shook her head gently – she could not bring herself to tell the assembled company what Roland was looking at.

The clerk beckoned her over and Ruby replaced Molly in the witness chair.

"Now, Mrs Tuffnail," said the coroner firmly, "in your evidence and in Molly's evidence you both say that Mr Cumber was not looking at what he was doing. Molly here says he was looking at you. Now tell us, Mrs Tuffnail, what was he looking at you for?"

Ruby sat up straight and looked towards the ceiling.

"Well, sir—"

She stopped.

"Yes, Mrs Tuffnail?" prompted the coroner.

"I don't rightly know that I want to say—" mumbled Ruby.

She blushed and looked down.

The coroner leant back in his chair, put his index finger to his lips and looked from Ruby, to Molly and then at Lucy.

"Hmm," he muttered, "I'm going to get to the bottom of this!"

He sighed again and shook his head.

"We must have Miss Knighton back to ask *her*. Clerk – if you would please."

Lucy came forward, a look of grim determination on her earnest face.

"Lucy Knighton," said the coroner firmly, "*why* was Mr Cumber looking at Mrs Tuffnail?"

Lucy swallowed nervously, and looked at her hands.

"Well, sir, Mrs Tuffnail was pitching the sheaves up and Mr Cumber was looking down the front of her dress in a lecherous manner, so she and I changed places, but he still kept on looking at her and we were all upset."

The coroner rolled his eyes, bending his head to write on the paper in front of him again, before looking down at Lucy.

"Thank you, Miss Knighton, I am *now* clear what happened; you may return to your seat. Is there anyone else to call?"

"Just the doctor, sir," advised the clerk.

"Very well then," nodded the coroner, as the clerk indicated to the doctor to take a seat.

"Doctor Roberts, can you tell us what happened when Mr Cumber attended your surgery?"

"Yes, sir," said Doctor Roberts, clearing his throat. "He came to me having lost the lower part of his leg in an accident. I advised him that he should go to the hospital and have his leg amputated above his knee. He refused and said I was to patch him up, which I did although I was reluctant to, as I felt he was at risk of infection."

"Were you aware of his accusation against Lucy Knighton?"

"Yes, sir, and I looked at the injury on his good leg."

The court fell completely silent; Lucy held her breath and looked to the ceiling.

"And your opinion, doctor?"

"The injury was not caused by a pitchfork as he said; the graze had been caused by a downward motion, not upward as the pitchfork would have been. It looked more like a kick from a boot and damage from the nails or some such object."

The coroner raised an eyebrow and continued to write.

"Very good, doctor, is there anything else you want to add?"

"Yes, sir, I would like to commend Lucy Knighton to you; she cut Cumber out of the drum. I think she was very brave and he would have had a lot to thank her for if he had lived."

The coroner nodded wisely and thanked the doctor for his evidence, before advising the jury that the only possible verdict here was accidental death. It did not take the jury long to come to the same conclusion and there was a collective sigh of relief from around the courtroom.

"Well I think that will do everybody," said the coroner, leaning back contentedly in his chair "and I think that I will second the commendation of the doctor, Miss Knighton – in a tricky situation you were very brave."

Lucy smiled weakly and sniffed.

Chapter Twenty-Nine
Life at Cold Harbour

The summer that year was a good one – long sunny days stretched into one another, making an easy time for the hay making and harvest. Lucy was preparing to go to Bedford in September, where she was to train to be a nurse. This made it inevitable that Mary would have to give up her job and return home to look after her declining parents. Henry and Martha were making plans to get married and move over to Church Farm in Brington, leaving John and his brother, Edgar, to run the farm at Cold Harbour. John's health now limited him to paying cheques – he could just about walk across the yard, but was unable to work on the farm. The Dunmore farm at Lower Dean continued to prosper. William, despite his youth, was a good farmer and businessman and was bringing the extra land into better shape. Thomas now did most of the work in the butcher's business, and left it largely to his son to develop the farm.

Life for the Webbs at Hardwick's, however, was still hard. There was not much work for Molly; she spent much of her time going to see Ruby, and she was always welcome at the smithy since Ruby had softened her initial, rather harsh, judgments of the girl. Ruby had noticed a change in Molly and on one of these visits she sat Molly down in the kitchen to tackle her on the point.

"Molly Webb, are you eatin' too much?" she said gently. "You're gettin' fat you know."

"No I ain't – or not much, I ain't, we don't get enough food to get fat," laughed Molly.

"Stand up, Molly, let's see," said Ruby, placing a hand on Molly's stomach.

"You know what, Molly?"

"What?"

"You're goin' to have a baby," said Ruby gently.

"I'm what?" gasped Molly, her eyes widening in disbelief. "No I ain't! I ain't goin' to 'ave no baby, so there! I don't believe you."

"Sit down, Molly," Ruby said calmly, "I'm tellin' you, you are; and if you don't believe me you'll 'ave to go to the doctor and ask 'im."

"I ain't goin' to no doctor! I ain't got no money for doctors," shrieked Molly, screwing her eyes tight shut and shaking her head.

"It were Roland, you see," said Ruby. "It were that rotten bastard that got you that way."

Molly said nothing.

"Just you feel it, Molly; you feel your belly – it's grown, ain't it and your tits are bigger, ain't they?"

"I'm just growin', that's what it is, I'm just growin'! I don't believe you – I'll go an' see Lucy, she reads all them books on medicine, don't she? She'll tell me I ain't having no baby."

"Yes, you go and see Lucy then," said Ruby kindly. "But she'll tell you the same, Molly. When you've seen 'er you come back 'ere and we'll sort you out."

Molly looked searchingly at Ruby, a look of dread on her young face.

"Right, I'm goin' there right now! I'll walk up to Cold Harbour and see 'er right now."

Ruby nodded, watching Molly stride out the door.

At the farm, Lucy was in the kitchen. Molly knocked at the door and entered to find her standing over the glowing range; she could smell the fragrant smell of warm buns wafting from a batch standing on the table. Lucy looked up.

"Hello, Molly, we don't often see you up here," she smiled. "I hope you haven't come for work as we don't have much on at the moment."

"No," said Molly curtly. "I don't want no work. I'm just bin down at Ruby's."

"Oh yeah, and how is Ruby?"

"She's all right," Molly replied, before falling silent.

"Well what have you come for then, Molly?" said Lucy dubiously.

Molly hesitated for a moment and then burst out:

"It's like this! Ruby say I'm goin' to 'ave a baby! That ain't right, is it Lucy? Say it ain't right – *you* know about these things, I know you do."

Tears rolled down Molly's face and she buried her head in her hands.

Lucy brushed her hands into the mixing bowl, wiped them on her apron, and sat down beside Molly. "Why did Ruby say that then, Molly?"

"She said my belly were gettin' fat."

"And is it, Molly?" Lucy asked.

"Well I s'pose! I don't know! You feel it, Lucy; you know about these things, you read it in books, I know you do."

Lucy put her hand on Molly's stomach, moving her hand up and down before sitting back.

"Ruby said if I were goin' to 'ave a baby my tits would get bigger," said Molly tearfully.

"And are they, Molly?"

"I s'pose a bit; but I'm still growin', ain't I?"

She looked pleadingly at Lucy.

"Well?" she said.

"Well what?" said Lucy.

"Am I goin' to 'ave a baby then?"

"Yes, Molly," said Lucy calmly. "I think you are."

Molly screwed up her eyes, slamming her fists into her legs.

"I wish I were dead you know that, Lucy," she wailed. "I wish I were dead; some people 'ave no luck, do they? It were that sod Roland you know that, don't you, Lucy? Course you know that; it were that day when 'e got in the drum. You were there! I bet Ruby said, didn't she?"

She glared accusingly at Lucy.

"What are you going to do then, Molly?" asked Lucy softly.

"What you mean, what am I goin' to do?" snarled Molly. "'Ow the 'ell do I know, 'ave the bloody thing I s'pose; you wait, Lucy, it could 'appen to you!"

The fight suddenly left her and Molly's shoulders sagged. Lucy put her arm round her, letting Molly cling to her like a child.

"You're a good friend, Lucy," whispered Molly. "And so's Ruby, she's a good friend, I know she is."

"I'll help, Molly, so will Ruby you see. And Mary, when she gets back."

"I'm got to go back to Dean," said Molly, disengaging herself from Lucy. "I'll go and see Ruby – she was right, wasn't she? Thank you, Lucy."

But before Lucy had time to reply, Molly had scuttled out the door and was gone.

Mary had certainly agreed to come back to Cold Harbour, but was putting off the day as long as she could. She had known for a year now that if Lucy wanted to train as a nurse she was the only one who could replace her. Her aunt, although sorry to see her niece go, agreed that it was now Mary's duty to return home to look after her parents.

So it was with a sense of dread that Mary went to tell Mr Tibbitt that she would be leaving the shop. She knocked timidly on his door.

"Enter," he shouted.

Mary let herself in to find Mrs Stevens sitting in the chair across from her boss.

"Mary, my dear, do come in; take a seat," smiled Peveril.

He looked at Mary quizzically for a moment – before turning distractedly to Mrs Stevens.

"I think something awful's happened! I feel it in my bones, yes I'm all come over."

He dabbed his brow theatrically with his handkerchief.

"You're going to tell us you have had your hand in the till and taken all the money," declared Peveril.

"No, sir."

"Well then you've had Mrs Harding in and you have been so rude to her, she will put it in the paper."

"No, sir," said Mary with a small smile.

"Well what then, Mary?"

Mary took a deep breath and said quietly:

"I'm afraid, sir, that I am going to give you notice that I am going to leave the shop."

"Oh the very worst!" cried Peveril. "The very worst that you could have said. Why, Mary, why? Aren't we paying you enough?"

"No, sir, it's not that; I am going to have to go home to look after my parents and the farm house. Lucy, my sister, wants to train as a nurse and I will have to go back when she leaves."

"Isn't there anyone else to do that, Mary? Surely there must be; don't you have any other sisters?"

"Yes, sir, but she is married and lives a long way away."

"Well what about your brother? I thought you said he was getting married; what about his wife? Why can't she do it?" pleaded Peveril.

"My brother's moving away, sir; he has taken a farm of his own. He fears that the mortgage on Cold Harbour is too much and the bank will take it in the end."

"What a calamity! What will we do without her, Mrs Stevens? What will we do?" wailed Peveril.

He wrung his hands desperately.

"I must have a drink to calm me down," muttered Peveril, standing and bellowing. "Frisby!"

Frisby scurried in obediently.

"Pour me a glass of port, there's a good lad; I have had such a shock."

He leant back and looked sadly at Mary.

"Mary, my dear, we will all miss you; but I can see that you have to do what is right and we will just have to put up with it, won't we, Mrs Stevens?"

"Yes, sir," said Mrs Stevens, turning to Mary. "But she's going to be a great loss; I don't know how we will replace her."

"I know, I know, but the show must go on as they say. When do you want to leave then, Mary?"

"The end of next week, sir."

Peveril sighed heavily.

"Very well then, if you must. I will get Frisby to do the necessary paperwork."

He leant forward confidentially.

"But if you ever want your job back, you only have to say, Mary, you know that, don't you?"

"Thank you, sir," said Mary quietly, before adding, "and can I thank you, I've been so happy here; it's the best job a girl could have – I'm sure it is."

Mary smiled and hurried from the room, afraid she would embarrass herself and disintegrate into tears, Peveril and Mrs Stevens staring sadly after her.

Mary arrived back at Cold Harbour two weeks before Henry left. He and Martha were married in Martha's local church in Derbyshire and then moved straight into the farm at Brington. Henry's place on the farm had been taken by John's brother, Edgar, who had been helping on the farm for some time and, having nowhere else to live, moved into the farmhouse with Mary and her parents. The daily grind of cooking and cleaning and washing drove Mary to distraction and the only solace she found was the freedom she gained from her bicycle – by which she could escape to go and see William or Verity, when she was home from school. She had letters from Rupert but he only visited very occasionally, as it was so far. Rebecca also wrote and called in when she was hunting in the direction of Dean, but Lucy was hardly ever home; she had very few weekends off and was completely absorbed with her career.

Mary's mother gradually got weaker and weaker; Doctor Roberts said her heart was not strong and he did not hold out hope for a long life for her. She now spent most of her time in bed; everything had to be carried upstairs to her and even with Freda to help, it was not easy. Uncle Edgar, Mary thought, was a very dour specimen, adding no colour at all to the household; he demanded his meals on time and a clean shirt every day; seeming to think Mary was more of a servant than a niece.

The winter grew colder and with it Mary's jobs more arduous – the pump in the yard was now frozen every morning, and needed a kettle of hot water poured on it before any water could be extracted from the well. It got increasingly difficult to nurse her mother upstairs; so Mary decided to move her. She wrote a postcard to Henry, demanding that he come and help move the heavy old bed downstairs into the front room – Henry agreed by return that he would ride over the next Saturday. He arrived at ten o'clock – the journey had taken him much longer due to the hard ground, but he had caught up with William in the pony and trap who was doing the butcher's round with George. Mary could see them all coming in the distance and put the kettle on for tea for when they arrived. Reuben was also at Cold Harbour; he had started coming up every Saturday to help collect the eggs and get the wood and coal in, or whatever small jobs Mary could think of for him to do.

"They're coming, they're coming," shouted Mary to Freda and Reuben. "Make the fire up Reuben, and, Freda, get the cups down and the cake out."

John, sitting in his rocking chair by the range, looked up but said nothing. Henry rode into the yard, dismounted and came over to embrace Mary as she came out.

"How are things then, lovely sister?" he said to Mary.

"They're awful, absolutely *awful* but don't mind me, come on in, *dear* brother – it's so good to see you."

She pecked her brother on the cheek, waving at William and George who were being enthusiastically greeted by Reuben.

"Do you want me to take the 'oss, 'Enry?" called Reuben, making his way towards Mary and Henry. "I'll put 'im in the stable for you."

"Well done, Reuben, you're a good lad," said Henry, pulling the reins over the horse's head and giving them to Reuben, who removed the horse's saddle and led it towards a stable.

"Does 'e need any hoats, 'Enry?" Reuben shouted.

"No, he's too fat! Just hay will do," called Henry, following Mary into the house tailed closely by William and George.

The kitchen, usually empty, suddenly seemed bright and joyful, full of people chattering away – John waved his hand frantically at Henry, struggling to be heard over the din.

"Henry, just go upstairs and see your mother, she wants to know what's happening. And William, you take a seat."

William pulled out a chair and put the butcher's basket on the table, as Freda placed a plate of warm buns next to the basket – George and Reuben eyed them beadily.

"Mary, just look in the basket and take what you want before we forget," said William, pulling a bun apart and shoving it hungrily into his mouth.

Mary moved to the basket and peered in.

"What is there, William? It all looks like beef."

"It is all beef on the top; but there's some sausages and nice pork chops nearer the bottom, and I think we've still got some liver in the trap, haven't we,

George?"

"Yes, William," George squeaked.

"Well I will take some sausages, ribs of beef and four chops; Freda come and put these away safe in the pantry," Mary instructed as Freda took the meat out of the kitchen.

"George, put the basket back on the trap out of the way," instructed William.

George leapt to his feet, grabbed the basket and moved towards the door; he turned in the doorway.

"'Ave you got anything for the pony, Mary?" he asked.

"Oh, take the crust of that loaf on the side, it will like that, George," she said, as Henry came thundering down the stairs and took a bun from the plate.

There was a shout from George at the door.

"William, William, come quick, the dog's bin in the trap and got a leg of mutton and I can't catch 'im."

Everyone rushed to the door and across the yard; in the straw the big collie was starting to gnaw at the joint of mutton. Seeing the approaching band of people, the dog picked up the joint and started to trot off, but the it was heavy, slowing him down and allowing William and Henry to move around and cut him off. William dived to get the dog, but despite being weighed down, it dodged him and William went down hard on his knee on the icy ground.

"I've got me catty," shouted Reuben. "I'll give 'im one, he'll drop it then."

He took the catapult from one pocket, a stone from the other and took aim.

"Don't hurt him, Reuben," Mary shouted, as Reuben pulled back the catty.

He released the elastic; the stone flew towards the dog and hit him hard on the flank. The dog yelped and dropped the meat, which William picked swiftly from the ground; he brushed the straw off it, examining the joint carefully.

"That will be all right," he said. "Good as new – we'll sell that, won't we, George?"

"No trouble, William."

"No, no, give it to me," Mary demanded. "We'll have mutton not beef this week; after all, it was our dog that had it."

She grabbed the cowering dog by the scruff of its neck and hauled him across to the kennel where she chained him up and returned with the others to the house.

"Mother don't look too good, Mary," said Henry softly as Mary re-entered the kitchen.

"No, but it will be much better to have her downstairs; you'll help, won't you, William? It won't take long but the bed's so heavy, I can't lift it. You lit the fire in the front room, didn't you, Reuben?"

"Yes, Mary."

"Right, we will move her when everyone's finished their tea."

"I've got some good news," said Henry suddenly to the assembled company, "Martha's going to have a baby!"

"Oh, Henry, that's splendid," said Mary delightedly. "Did you tell Mother? She will be pleased. That is good news, isn't it, William? I bet Martha's pleased, isn't she, Henry?"

"Yes, she is," beamed Henry, before adding thoughtfully. "I heard poor Molly's having a baby too, is that right?"

"Yes," said Mary. "I must go and see her, I promised Lucy I would. Is she all right, William?"

"Yes I saw her yesterday when I went up to Hardwick's. She seemed all right; she said that Verity had written to her and was going up to see her this weekend."

"Well I will make sure I go and see her this week," said Mary, draining the last of her tea and turning to the others. "Are we all ready, then?"

Everybody nodded.

"Go and stoke the fire up, Reuben. I'll go and get her out of bed; you come and get the sheets and blankets, Freda."

Mary trotted up the wooden stairs, helped her mother from the bed to a chair and started to strip the bed.

"George," she shouted down the stairs.

"Yes," he squeaked, rushing to the bottom of the stairs.

"Come and get the mattress, would you?" called Mary, rolling up the feather mattress as best she could as George came thundering up the stairs. Although the mattress was not heavy it was cumbersome, and George – who was still not very big – could hardly see over the top of it. He tottered off to the top of the stairs – but having no idea where the first stair was, he trod on the corner of the mattress, which started to spill out of his arms. In his effort to stop the mattress falling, he fell on top of it and surfed his way down the stairs riding atop.

"That's a quick way down the stairs," laughed Henry, as George rolled into the kitchen.

"George," shouted Mary, "are you all right?"

George picked himself gingerly off the floor and grinned at Henry.

"I'm fine, Mary, jus' a bit bruised," he said, brushing himself down.

"Henry," she shouted, "come with William and carry the frame now, can you please?"

Henry winked at George and made his way up the stairs followed by William. They carried down the frame and Freda started to make the bed up in the front room.

"Henry, I think you will have to carry Mother down; I don't think she can manage the stairs," said Mary quietly.

"We could take her down on the chair," he suggested.

"I think it would be best if you carried her," said Mary firmly.

"Come on then, Mother," said Henry, helping his mother to her feet and sweeping her up into his arms.

"Don't you bang me head, Henry Knighton, when we go downstairs," grumbled Ann.

"Don't worry, Mother, I won't bang your head," said Henry with a smile, carrying his mother down to the bed and helping her into it. Ann shifted in the bed, wheezing as she tried to make herself comfortable, before shooing Mary and Henry affectionately out of the room under the pretence that she was tired and wanted to sleep.

In the kitchen, William and George said their goodbyes to carry on with the butcher's round. Reuben hovered expectantly.

"Is there anything else you want me to do, Mary? I've got time," he said earnestly.

"No, Reuben, you've been a really good boy, thank you."

She ruffled his hair affectionately. Reuben vigorously flattened it down again, before smiling lopsidedly at Mary.

"I'll be off then, see you next week," he said, before scampering out of the door.

"You are going to stay to lunch, aren't you, Henry?" said Mary, turning to her brother.

"Yes, but I must be away soon after. I will have to go steady with the ground as hard as it is; don't want to damage the horse."

He looked furtively round the room to check that his father was asleep.

"What about Mother then?" he said quietly.

"She's not very good," said Mary. "I think that the doctor suspects she won't live very long."

"She's as light as a feather," said Henry. "There's no meat on her at all; I don't know how she stays alive."

"I know, but all we can do is take each day at a time. I wish Lucy were here, she would know what to do; she knows everything about medicine."

Mary sighed heavily.

"She must do her training, Mary," said Henry gently. "It's only fair; she has the chance and she must take it. I know you didn't want to leave Northampton, but we had no choice."

"Yes, I know, I know," said Mary defensively.

Henry fell quiet, the silence only disturbed by John's gentle snoring.

"You must come and see us again, Mary, when the weather gets better. Martha would love you to come; she gets a bit lonely at times."

Mary said nothing.

"Come on then, let's get some lunch together," said Henry, rising from the table.

Mary sighed and rose to help her brother, feeling more than ever like a caged animal.

Chapter Thirty
Reuben's Proposition

The winter remained cold – the ground was rock hard and there had been a light dusting of snow in early December. One of these mornings, Mary decided to make the visit to Hardwick's to see Molly; Molly's predicament was now general knowledge and whispers followed her whenever she went to the village, so much so that she now preferred to stay at home. Mary knocked on the door at Hardwick Lodge and made her way through the scullery into the kitchen. In the kitchen, Verity and Ellen were staring earnestly at Molly who was scowling; arms folded tightly across her chest. They greeted Mary warmly as she entered, Ellen jumped up to make a pot of tea and the frown lifted from Molly's face.

Ellen poured out four cups, passing one each to Mary, Verity and finally to Molly who turned away from the proffered cup angrily.

"Come on, Molly, 'ave some tea," said her mother.

"Don't want none," Molly replied grumpily.

Mary looked at Verity, who frowned before cheerfully sparking up conversation about Henry and Martha.

Suddenly Molly sat up straight.

"Mary?" she interrupted.

"Yes, Molly."

"You know that shop you worked at in Norfampton?" said Molly eagerly.

"Yes, Molly," said Mary with a look of disquiet.

"I fink I'm going to get a job there," said Molly decisively. "You got all sorts of nice clothes when you worked there, I knowed you did, I'm seen you in 'em. 'Ow do you go about gettin' a job there then, Mary?"

Mary looked at Verity and back at Molly, who was staring at her, an almost aggressive set to her jaw.

"Well it was through Verity really and a mutual friend of her father's – I met Mr Tibbitt through him."

"What 'appened then?"

"Well he said that if ever I wanted a job I had to write to him; so I did."

"Oh," said Molly, "well I ain't goin' to posh places with Verity like that, are I? So I guess that's that, ain't it?"

She sank lower in her chair, misery etched on her face.

"I could write on your behalf," said Verity a little uncertainly.

"I could write as well," said Mary, with a bit more confidence. "I know everyone at the shop."

"Could you, Mary?" said Molly gratefully. "I know I'm goin' to 'ave to learn to talk proper like what you do, but you learnt, Mary, didn't you?"

"What about the baby?" Ellen interjected.

"What about it, then?" Molly said defiantly.

"Well who's goin' to look after it then if you're goin' off to work?"

"I'll give it away," said Molly, tilting her chin up defensively.

"You can't do that, Molly," gasped Verity. "The poor little thing! It must have a mother to look after it; I'm sure when it comes you will love it, I know you will."

"No, I won't! I never will," Molly snapped determinedly. "I'll 'ave it 'cos I can't do any uvver fing, but I ain't keepin' it! Never, never, never! Not if it were anyfink to do with *him*, 'e were awful, 'e were an awful man."

She looked away angrily, slumping back into her chair. The others looked at each other in turn but said nothing.

"You wait, Molly," piped up Mary. "When you have had the baby and it's weaned, I'll write to the shop for you; I am sure they will give you a job, you trust me."

"Will you, Mary?" said Molly a note of hope creeping into her voice. "Will you really?"

She looked at Mary and almost smiled.

"I can't live 'ere no longer; not when I'm 'ad the baby anyway. They all look at me when I go down Dean and they're all whispering; I know they are. All except Ruby they are, Ruby's all right – she don't whisper."

"Now tell me, Molly, when's the baby due?" enquired Verity.

Molly did not answer; Ellen spoke for her.

"We think it'll be the middle of January, not long now," said Ellen quietly.

She looked down at her daughter who remained looking impassively into the distance.

"We must make sure you have everything, Ellen," said Verity officiously. "I will ask Mrs Tuffnail what you need and send up a parcel if I can't come myself. The baby will have to be christened as well, but we can sort that out later."

She rose to leave

"I must go; are you coming, Mary? It will be a cold walk back into the wind."

Mary nodded and picked up her coat – the pair said goodbye and left, walking along the track from Hardwick's until they met the bridleway where they were protected from the biting west wind. They chatted as they went, shivering in the cold air, their faces flushed by the chill. Verity was to go back to school the next day, so it was with an element of regret that Mary said goodbye to make her way back to Cold Harbour.

Arriving home, Mary found Reuben in the kitchen with Freda; he had been helping getting the wood and coal in.

"What are you doing, Reuben? You should be at school," chided Mary.

"I were," said Reuben indignantly, "but they sent us 'ome, so I come up to 'elp you, Mary."

"Why did they send you home then?"

"They couldn't light the fire 'cos the 'eap of coal 'ad got wet and then it froze and they couldn't get any on it; or not enough any road to light the fire – so they sent us 'ome. We are got to go agin tomorra when they've bashed it up a bit."

He grinned up at her.

"Well we could do with some help, couldn't we, Freda?" laughed Mary. "And you're just the man for the job."

She ruffled his hair.

"Are you going to chop some kindling for us then, Reuben?"

"Whatever you say, Mary."

"Go on then, boy, and you can have a bit of lunch when we have ours."

"Where's Father, Freda?" Mary asked.

"He's in with Mrs Knighton, Miss Mary; I don't think she's very good, he's sittin' by the fire in there."

"It's nice and warm in there, Mary; I'm made the fire up, ain't I, Freda?" said Reuben proudly.

"Go on, Reuben, don't just stand chatting," laughed Mary, shooing him out the door.

In the living room Ann was propped up in bed. Her face was drained of all colour and her hair hung lankly about her face – she had long since stopped putting it into curlers. Her breath rasped and rattled its way in and out through dry lips and any attempts to speak had become laboured. Mary sat down carefully on the bed, taking her mother's cold hand and telling her about her visit to Molly. Ann smiled wanly, her eyes slowly closing as Mary continued to chat to her. When she was asleep Mary returned to the kitchen, where Reuben was stacking the kindling he had collected by the range.

"They will dry if I leave 'em there, Mary. What do you want me to do next?" he asked.

"Just wait there," instructed Mary. "It won't be long before it's lunch and I'll find you another job after that."

Reuben sat on a chair at the table, tapping his fingers and humming quietly under his breath.

"Mary?"

"Yes, Reuben."

"When I grow up—"

"*When* you grow up?" interrupted Mary, laughing. "How old are you now then, Reuben?"

"I'm nearly eleven."

"Well you're nearly grown up, aren't you?"

"But, Mary, I mean when I'm *really* grown up."

"Yes, Reuben," Mary smiled, carrying on laying the table.

"Yes, well, when I'm really grown up will you marry me, Mary?"

Mary stopped, turned to look at Reuben's earnest face and burst out in peals of laughter.

"Did you say will I marry you?" asked Mary.

"Yes! I mean it, Mary!" insisted Reuben, looking crestfallen as Mary started to laugh again.

"You're a lovely boy, Reuben Heighton," she said, ruffling Reuben's hair gently. "What are we going to do with you?"

"Will you then?" said Reuben hopefully.

Mary placed her hands on Reuben's shoulders, stooping slightly to look him in the eye.

"Now, Reuben, when you are ready to marry there will be so many girls to choose from you'll not know which way to turn! They will all flock to you, Reuben; and I will be old and you won't look at me then – you will have to wait, Reuben, wait and see."

"Yes, Mary," said Reuben doubtfully, his face red, tears threatening in his eyes.

He sniffed and wiped his nose with his fist.

"Now, no more of that, Reuben!" scolded Mary. "You just get some more coal for the range and we will have lunch."

Reuben sniffed and scuttled off as Mary turned to go back to the living room to wake her parents for lunch.

Ann was still fast asleep; her mouth hung open and a little dribble crept down her cheek. As the door opened, she stirred, opening her eyes to register Mary. She inhaled, the air rattling into her fragile lungs, and dabbed at her cheek with a handkerchief. Mary approached the bed, straightening the sheet and tucking it in.

"Now, Mother, how are you feeling? Are you ready for some lunch?"

"Is it that time already?" said Ann softly. "It doesn't seem long since breakfast."

The door creaked open and Reuben's head poked round the door.

"Mary, are you there?"

"Yes, Reuben, what do you want?" said Mary a touch sharply.

"It's William – I can see 'im in the trap comin' up the drive."

"Very well, Reuben, tell him I'll be there in a minute. Now, Mother, is soup all right? It's on the range hotting up."

Ann's eyes focused faintly on Mary.

"What did you say?" she asked.

"Is soup all right?" Mary asked loudly.

Ann's eyes moved distractedly around the room – flitting from the fire, to John fast asleep in his chair, back to Mary again. Her voice rose slightly in panic.

"Where have you been, Mary? I know you've been out, where have you been?"

Mary sighed and gently took her mother's hand.

"I just went to see Molly Webb, that's all. Now – soup! I'll go and get it."

She returned to the kitchen, just as William and George were entering from the scullery. George heaved the large butcher's basket onto the table as William moved to the range, rubbing his hands vigorously in front of the fire to warm them.

"That's still freezing out there, I'm sure it is, the ice hasn't melted on the puddles yet," he grumbled, turning to warm his calves.

"How are we all at Cold Harbour?" he enquired jovially.

"Much the same, that's what I would say," Mary replied moodily, stirring the soup.

"And how's Aunt Ann?" William asked. "Can I see her? Mother will not be pleased if I don't pay a visit."

"Of course, William, she's in the front room with Father. I don't know if you will get much sense out of her, she's wandering a bit this morning."

Mary looked into the butcher's basket and chose the meat she wanted. Minutes later, William came back into the room.

"She's not making any progress, is she, Mary?" said William quietly. "I'd say she's going backwards if anything."

For a moment Mary didn't reply.

"I don't think she's got long," Mary said finally, staring into the soup.

"She wanted me to read to her from the Bible; I said I would come back on Sunday when I had more time. Sorry, Mary, I haven't brought the bread up today, the oven door broke this morning and old Frank couldn't start baking until Art had mended it; all the bread is late and he won't have time to come up here. I'm afraid I couldn't wait all that time for it to be ready."

344

"Blast!" said Mary. "We are more or less out. I will have to walk down and get it this afternoon."

She turned to her cousin.

"Now, William, are you going to have some lunch or a cup of something?"

"No, Mary, we must get on or we won't be home before it is dark. Come on, George, bring the basket – have you written down what Mary has had?"

George nodded and scurried out behind William, who raised his cap to Mary and left.

Mary left the soup on the range to prepare the trays for her parents; the squeak of the mangle could be heard from outside as Freda wrung out the washing. A sudden violent hissing came from the hob, as the soup boiled over onto the range.

"Damn and blast, damn and blast!" Mary shouted, rushing to pull the saucepan off the heat.

"You shouldn't swear Mary," Reuben said quietly, not really meaning her to hear.

"Don't tell me not to swear, Reuben!" she yelled. "Don't you dare tell me not to swear; if I want to I will."

Freda appeared in the doorway to check what the shouting was about. Mary glared angrily at her, and was about to snap at Freda to leave when there was a loud knock at the back door.

"Who the hell's that at this time?" Mary exploded again. "Freda, go and see who it is, come on, Reuben you take that tray to Father, and I will take the other one."

Mary seized the tray, rushed it to Ann's room and returned quickly to the kitchen.

"Who is it then, Freda?" she shouted.

"It's a gentleman, Miss Mary."

"What gentleman?" Mary said impatiently.

"He says his name's Rupert something and 'e's called to see you, miss."

"Rupert!" exclaimed Mary. "What's he doing here? Well show him in then, Freda, show him in – come on."

Freda scowled and made her way very slowly out of the room. Mary quickly took off her apron, combed her hair with her fingers and put her hands to her nose, pulling her fingers across her cheeks and blinking two or three times. Freda stomped in, followed by Rupert, who was wearing a heavy top coat and carrying a flat cap. His face was very red and he had grown a small moustache. He looked over the top of Freda's head towards Mary, smiling broadly.

"Rupert Nelson, what on earth are you doing here and on such an awful day in the middle of the winter?" exclaimed Mary.

"Well aren't you pleased to see me, then?" he laughed.

"Of course I'm pleased to see you!" laughed Mary. "I'm pleased to see anyone, living out in the wilds like this."

"Well I had hoped that I was not just anyone," said Rupert with a wink, moving forward to shake her hand.

"I didn't mean it like that, you silly thing!" laughed Mary, grasping his hand and then exclaiming. "But aren't your hands frozen! Come and get near the range and warm up."

Reuben came back into the room, quietly closing the door behind him. He looked curiously at Rupert, who still hadn't take his eyes off Mary, and pursed his lips. Moving to sit on the chair the other side of the dresser, he put his hands under his knees and began to swing his legs backwards and forwards, his boots scraping the stone floor as he did so. The noise caused Rupert to look over towards him; Mary looked too.

"Oh, that's Reuben," she explained. "He's been helping get the coal in. Say hello to Mr Nelson, Reuben."

Reuben scowled and muttered, "Hello, Mr Nelson."

"Now let's take your coat, Rupert, or you won't feel the benefit when you go out, and then we can have some lunch. Freda, take Mr Nelson's coat, can you and hang it in the hall?"

Freda rose and with as little enthusiasm she could muster, came across and took Rupert's coat and hat, bearing them away into the hall.

"Now, Rupert, tell me what are you doing here at Cold Harbour and how did you get here? It really is so good to see you; you will have some lunch, won't you?"

"Yes, that would be nice," Rupert replied, as Freda came back into the kitchen.

"Come on, Freda, we must get the table ready for lunch; Edgar will be in soon, get the bread out and the meat."

"We ain't got no bread," said Freda curtly.

"What do you mean we ain't got no bread?"

"I mean what I say! Don't you remember what William said – the bread's all late today and he ain't bringin' it 'cos the door of the oven broke and it got them all late."

"Yes, yes you're right, Freda, Mother had the last bit with her soup. What are we going to have?" Freda pushed out her bottom lip and shrugged her shoulders.

"S'pose we could 'ave some pickles and there's some cheese. There ain't no soup – your mother's 'ad all that – but there's some cold taters, you could fry them."

"Very well then, get it all out and lay the table, come on, Reuben – you help Freda set five places at the table. Rupert, sit down near the range to get warm; we can't go in the front room as Mother is in bed in there. Now tell me again what brings you here?"

"Well I had to go to Rushden to report on a fire in a boot factory, but as we were heading into Rushden, the train derailed and it's going to take them six hours to repair. So I reported on the fire, borrowed a bike from the landlord at the Victoria and it has taken me just over an hour to get here. I have been wanting to come for ages but I haven't had time."

Mary waved away his apology, asking,

"And Rebecca, how is she?"

"She's fine, she's been out hunting a lot; or at least she was until it started freezing. You know her – hunting always keeps her happy."

The back door opened and Uncle Edgar came into the scullery, his hobnail boots scratching on the stone floor. He hung his coat and cap on a peg on the back of the door and came into the kitchen. His boots and leather gaiters were splattered with cow muck and the smell started to seep through the room.

"Ain't lunch ready then?" he demanded.

"Very nearly," said Mary. "Come and sit down, Uncle Edgar; are you going to cut the joint or am I?"

"You do it, girl, my 'ands are all muck," he said, wiping his hands down his trousers and looking over at Rupert.

"Who we got 'ere then?" he said, sitting down in the chair at the end of the table.

"This is Rupert Nelson, Uncle Edgar; he's a reporter on the Northampton paper."

"What's 'e doin' 'ere then?" Edgar asked.

"He's paying a visit; he has been stuck in Rushden and the train has come off the rails."

"Oh," said Edgar lacking any interest.

"Come and sit up," she said to the others, starting to carve from a joint of beef. She passed the first slices to Edgar.

"Where's the bread then?" he demanded.

"There ain't no bread," said Freda with a hint of satisfaction.

"There ain't no bread, Mary Knighton?" exclaimed Edgar. "What are you up to?"

"It hasn't come, Uncle; the oven door broke at the bake house and it's all late. I expect I will have to cycle down and get some this afternoon; there's some fried potato and there's pickles."

"Well I don't know," he grumbled, "no bread! What's the world coming to?"

Mary said nothing and continued, with difficulty, to cut the joint.

"This knife is blunt," she complained.

"I know what to do, Mary," said Reuben eagerly. "Give it 'ere, I'll 'ave it sharp in a jiffy."

He grabbed the knife from her and ran to the back door where he rubbed each side of the knife as hard as he could on the doorstep, until he got an edge on it. He handed it proudly back to Mary, who wiped it on her apron and started to carve the meat again.

"Ah ha, that's much better, how did you learn that trick, Reuben?"

"My father all'as does it, he says the doorstep is the best sharpenin' stone there is."

He smiled smugly at Rupert, who smiled back at him nonplussed and took the proffered plate from Mary.

"Freda, be a dear and go and fetch the trays from Mother and Father. Reuben, you go and make the fire up when you've finished that," said Mary as Reuben stuffed the last of the meat into his mouth, leaving Rupert and Mary alone – Edgar being asleep in a chair by the range.

"Mary," sighed Rupert.

"Yes, Rupert," said Mary, a hint of a laugh in her voice.

"I've got something to tell you."

"Yes, Rupert," she repeated, curious now.

"Father's sending me to South America."

"He's doing what!" exclaimed Mary in dismay. "How long for?"

"A year or two he thinks; he says I should see more of the world and learn a foreign language."

"But why?"

"I don't know, but he thinks it will be good for my career and that I should not stay in Northampton all my life, so that's it."

"When are you going, Rupert, not before Christmas surely?"

"No, no, not until March but it will take two months to get there. I'm going to Buenos Aires in the Argentine, Father's got friends there who have a paper."

"But do you want to go, Rupert?" Mary asked, studying his face closely.

"Well I don't know! I suppose it will be good, but I will miss all my friends and I'll miss you, Mary! I'll miss you dreadfully."

"But you don't see me much now, Rupert!" said Mary carelessly "Or at least you haven't – not since I left Northampton."

"I know, but when I get a car I will! I'm sure I will."

"But you won't if you are in Buenos Aires!" Mary exclaimed, louder than she had intended.

"No, I suppose not," sighed Rupert. "But I will write; will you write to me, Mary?"

He looked imploringly at her.

"Of course I will, Rupert," she said softly, putting her hand over his and squeezing it. Rupert's cheeks immediately coloured.

Freda walked back into the kitchen, followed by Reuben with the coal bucket.

"Are they all right, Freda?" Mary asked.

"Yes, they ate it all and your father's smoking 'is pipe."

"And Mother?"

"She's alright; she says, who's talking in the kitchen – is it the King?"

"The King!" laughed Mary, nudging Rupert. "What did you say, Freda?"

"I said yes," snorted Freda, provoking more laughter from Mary and eventually from Rupert.

Edgar, woken by the noise, hoisted himself from his chair and without a word rose and made his way outside.

"Mary, I will have to go," said Rupert, standing up. "By the time I get back they will have mended the rail and I ought to get the report back to the office in Northampton this evening."

"Freda, fetch Mr Nelson's coat and hat, will you?" instructed Mary, moving towards Rupert.

Reuben stood by the scullery door watching the two of them.

"What do you want, Reuben?"

"'E's got a flat tyre on 'is bike, Mary."

"You mean Mr Nelson has, Reuben?"

"Yes 'im," Reuben said rudely. "Shall I pump it up, Mary?"

"Yes, yes, Reuben, go on then," said Mary, turning back to Rupert.

"Now, Rupert, you must send my love to Rebecca when you see her and tell her I will write and you must write and tell me when you are going and then I will come to Northampton and we can all meet to wish you goodbye, how would that be?"

"That would be lovely, Mary," smiled Rupert, taking his coat and hat from Freda and moving outside to where Reuben was holding up the bicycle.

"Has it got a puncture, Reuben?" asked Rupert

"No, mister, it was only the valve a bit loose, I tightened it up and pumped it; it's all right now."

"Well done," said Rupert, pressing sixpence into his hand.

Reuben looked down at the cold coin, his face splitting into a broad grin.

Rupert mounted the bike and waved as he rode off down the drive.

"I'm going to have to cycle down to Dean to get some bread," said Mary, watching him go, "or we won't have anything to eat for tomorrow. Now, Freda, while I'm away you make sure that Mother and Father are all right and help Mother to the commode if she wants to go. You can do the ironing in the meantime."

She looked round for Reuben.

"Reuben, have you made up all the fires and filled the buckets?"

"Yes, Mary."

"Well done, well I think that will be all; you can go home now."

"Very good, do you want me tomorra?"

"Can you come then?"

"I don't know," shrugged Reuben. "But I might be able to."

"Very good then; come only if you can."

"Can I have a ride, Mary?" he piped up.

"What do you mean a ride?"

"A ride on the carrier on the back of your bike," explained Reuben.

"You can't ride on that!" chided Mary.

"Yes I can, I do all the time on Mother's; we go a long way like that."

"What are you going to sit on as a cushion?"

"I'll use my cap and I can open the gates for you."

"All right then, we can give it a try," said Mary with a laugh.

She went to put on a coat and fetched her bag, returning to the yard to see Reuben ready with the bike; he had found a small hessian sack and rolled it up to make the seat on the carrier a bit more comfortable, tying it on with a piece of binder twine. Mary mounted the bike and rode through the gate which Reuben had opened; he quickly closed it and ran after her.

"Don't stop, Mary," he shouted, "just keep goin' slow and I can jump on."

He ran himself level with the bike, swung his leg over and nimbly installed himself on the carrier with a leg sticking out each side and his hands in his pockets. Despite the freezing weather, he was still wearing shorts; he did not seem to feel the cold even though his long woollen socks never stayed up. At each of the three gates down the drive he leapt off to open the gates for Mary to ride through, jumping deftly on again after he had closed the gate. At the end of the drive they turned right down the half-mile hill; the road was pock-marked with potholes, and towards the bottom of the hill, the holes became more pronounced. With several in a row, and avoiding all of them impossible, Mary realised she had no alternative but to choose the smallest and cycle through it – she selected the least offensive looking hole, aimed for it and stood on the pedals to take the impact of the bump through her knees. Reuben, taken unawares, was thrown six inches into the air, coming down again hard on the carrier. In agony, he immediately lost concentration and with it his balance, falling gently into the crisp frosted grass of the verge. It was another thirty yards before Mary realised she had lost her passenger. She stopped and looked round to see Reuben, doubled up in pain, his hands pressed into his crotch. She leapt off her bike, running back and putting her hand on his shoulder. Reuben's face was screwed up in pain – his eyes tightly closed and his lips clamped shut.

"Reuben, what happened? Where does it hurt? Let me have a look!"

"No, Mary," groaned Reuben, straightening up.

"Where does it hurt, Reuben? Show me."

"No, Mary, I can't show you," he croaked. "Not there! I'll be all right, you see, just winded a bit."

He turned his face away from her and grimaced.

"You sure, Reuben?"

"Yup, I'm sure," he puffed, straightening further.

"Come on then," she said, trying not to laugh. "Get back on again but this time hold onto me and don't fall off."

Reuben gingerly lowered himself onto the carrier and threaded his arms around Mary's waist, pressing his face into her back. He could smell the vague aroma of mothballs and just feel the flesh of her middle through the layers of coat and dress. Reuben thought that he'd never been happier.

They turned right at the bottom of the hill, which began to climb into Dean. The weight of Reuben on the back of the bike began to slow Mary up as she met the rise; Reuben jumped off and ran alongside, turning as he heard the sound of hooves on the road behind him. A man on a large bay hunter was trotting up behind them, leading two other horses from leading reins.

"Mary, you better stop and let 'im past," shouted Reuben. "Leadin' them two there ain't much room in the road."

Mary dismounted and pushed her bike to the side, waiting for the horseman to pass. When he got level Mary recognised the man as Noble Ladds. He looked very smart as usual and although the horse he was riding was clearly an expensive animal, the two he was leading were in need of grooming and looked underfed.

He pulled his horse up and dismounted by throwing his leg over the horse's neck and sliding nimbly to the ground.

He smiled at Mary and took off his cap; Mary could smell eau de cologne, and was reminded briefly of Peveril Tibbitt. Reuben bristled, taking an immediate dislike to the stranger and the familiarity with which he approached Mary.

"It's Miss Knighton, I believe," he said to her with a small bow.

"That's right," said Mary coquettishly. "But to whom do I have the pleasure of talking?"

"Ah my name is Noble Ladds, I farm next to your brother Henry and his wife; a splendid man, your brother."

"Well I'm glad you have made friends, but why have you stopped, Mr Ladds?" asked Mary, flashing an innocent smile at him.

Noble hesitated for a moment, before smiling indulgently at Mary.

"I think my horse may be going a bit lame! I must have a look. Come here, boy, and hold it for me."

He nodded at Reuben who reluctantly came forward and took the reins of the horses. Noble went round the horse one foot at a time, lifting each one and cleaning it out with a penknife to make sure there were no stones.

"There," he said, "all done! There was a stone in the front hoof, you see. I thought there was something."

He turned again to Mary.

"I must call and see your father, Miss Knighton; to see if we can do any horse business, but Henry tells me he's not in good health at the moment."

"No," said Mary. "He's not well and does not have much to do on the farm. Uncle Edgar does all that but I don't think he will be buying any horses at the moment."

"Aha, never mind," sighed Noble.

He winked at Mary.

"Perhaps I will call all the same. I'm going to call and see William Dunmore on my way home. You two are related, aren't you?"

"He's my cousin," Mary replied.

"He's a tough one, isn't he?" Noble Ladds whispered confidentially. "Not easy to get on with like your brother; yes I wish there were more like your Henry."

Mary said nothing.

"Well I must get going," said Noble cheerily, "or I will not get back to Bythorn before nightfall. Please send my regards to your parents, Miss Knighton and tell them I will call by soon to make myself known."

He snatched the reins back off Reuben, and vaulted onto the hunter, raising his cap once more to Mary.

"Good day to you, Miss Knighton, a pleasure to meet you."

He rode off.

"Who was 'e then?" said Reuben.

"'*E* Reuben was Mr Ladds and '*e,* Reuben, farms next to brother Henry, so there; why do you say it like that?"

"I don't like 'im," muttered Reuben sulkily.

Mary looked at the pouting boy and laughed.

"Well I don't remember asking your opinion, Reuben Heighton, so there."

Chapter Thirty-One
The Death of Ann Knighton

The next Sunday morning Lucy and Mary sat having breakfast at Cold Harbour. Mary had told Freda to have the day off as Lucy had the weekend at home and she was not expected back until Monday morning.

"What do you think about Mother, Lucy?" Mary asked. "You haven't seen her for a bit; she's no better, is she?"

Lucy hesitated, looking earnestly at her sister.

"No, Mary, I don't think she's got long. We should call the doctor really but it's Sunday and I don't think he can do much anyway."

Mary shook her head slowly and looked despairingly at her sister.

"What am I going to do, Lucy? When Mother dies? Stuck up here looking after Father who is in a poor way himself! And Uncle Edgar! It's going to drive me mad!"

"I know, Mary, but if things get really bad I can give up nursing and come back," Lucy said half-heartedly.

"Don't, don't! I know you can't do that, it's unfair I know," moaned Mary, sitting back in her chair and covering her face with her hands.

"I wish I had a cigarette to smoke."

"Mary! You know that Mother does not approve of women smoking and if Aunt Charlotte knew she would have a fit."

"I don't care what they think!" exclaimed Mary. "They're not stuck out here in the middle of nowhere looking after two old people and one old drudge! Never seeing anyone and never going anywhere! No wonder I want to smoke!"

She rubbed her hands over her face and fell quiet.

"I did see that Noble Ladds the other day," she said suddenly.

"Noble who?" said Lucy.

"Noble Ladds."

"You mean that horse dealer man who lives near Henry and Martha?" said Lucy disapprovingly.

"Yes – that's the one."

"I don't know about him, Mary," said Lucy. "William can't stand him, he's a bit of a jack-the-lad, don't you think?"

"Well I don't care what William thinks, he's not right all the time!" pouted Mary. "And if he is a jack-the-lad, so what? It's better than being like the rest of the dull specimens around here; not a bit of spark between any of them."

"I'm sorry, Mary," backtracked Lucy. "I didn't want to sound critical."

"Well, if you don't want to sound critical keep your mouth shut then, Lucy Knighton, do you hear me?" snapped Mary, leaning forward aggressively.

Lucy looked down and blushed.

"I'm sorry, Mary, I won't say any more about Mr Ladds," she said quietly. "We mustn't argue; especially with Mother so ill next door."

Mary rose from the chair and started to poke the fire vigorously.

"You're right, Lucy, we mustn't argue," she said, throwing down the poker and looking into the glowing range. She turned, smiled at her sister and laughed.

"I've got something to tell you, Lucy."

"Go on," said Lucy, "what's that?"

"I've had a proposal of marriage."

"You haven't, Mary, who was it?" said Lucy clapping her hands.

"You'll never guess," giggled Mary.

"No, I can't. Who was it?"

"Reuben Heighton," she grinned.

Lucy gave a hoot of laughter as Mary started to join in.

"Did he go down on one knee?" laughed Lucy. "Was it romantic?"

Both girls were creased over, and tears streamed from Lucy's eyes.

They were interrupted by a loud knock at the back door.

Before Lucy could make it to the door to see who it was, their visitor marched purposefully into the kitchen, took his bowler hat off, placed it on the table with his bag and started undoing his thick tweed coat.

"Well, Lucy, well, Mary," said Doctor Roberts, "I know you didn't call me; but I had to come past this morning on my way back from a patient in Melchbourne and thought I would call while I was in the area. And how is our patient?"

The sisters looked at each other.

"She's no better," said Mary.

"In fact I think she is quite a lot worse," said Lucy. "I don't think she's got long to go."

"Well let me see her then, and your father? Is he in with her?"

"Yes he is there, come this way, doctor," said Lucy, showing the doctor into the living room.

Ten minutes later he returned.

"I'm afraid it's not going to be long," he said solemnly. "I don't think she will last the day myself. I have told your father; not that he needed telling and he's not so good himself, poor man!"

The doctor put on his hat and coat and picked up his bag.

"Let me know when something happens and I will come and do the necessary paperwork."

The girls thanked him and he left.

There was silence – Mary and Lucy looked at each other sadly.

"Right," said Mary, "we must make plans. Lucy, you must stay here and look after Mother and Father; I will go down to the butcher's shop and tell Aunt Charlotte and Uncle Thomas and get William to ride over and tell Henry and Martha. We must write to Bessie; I know she can't come but she needs to know; give me one of those cards from the dresser, I can post it when I go down to Dean."

Lucy handed a card to Mary, who picked up a pen and ink pot from the drawer and started to write.

"Now, Lucy, where are we going to bury her, do you know?" said Mary, in a business-like manner.

"Don't say that, Mary," pleaded Lucy. "She's not dead yet."

"I know she's not," said Mary gently, "but you heard what the doctor said – she won't last the day. We can't just ignore that, and Father isn't going to be able to do anything to help – it's up to us. I will go to The Manse when I go to the village and tell Reverend Packham what is happening."

"I think she wants to go to Dean, don't you?" said Lucy slowly. "With all the others."

"Yes I'm sure she does; in the row in the churchyard."

"But what's the hurry, Mary?" insisted Lucy. "Can't we sort it all out when she's dead? Henry should be here surely."

"Don't worry, Henry will agree with what we say. We must hurry, Lucy – Christmas is in less than a week and we want her buried before then, don't we?"

"I suppose we do," said Lucy, sniffing.

"Don't sniff like that, Lucy!" scolded Mary. "I don't know how many times I have had to tell you."

Lucy scowled and looked away.

"Do you think we should go and tell Edgar, Mary, he's only just out in the cattle yard," she said finally.

"No! I don't like that man; I know he's our uncle but he drives me to distraction. He comes in here and demands his meals on the dot and a clean shirt every day as if he owns the place and he's really not much more than hired help. No, Lucy, you tell him when he comes in for his lunch and not before."

Mary stood up, moving to the range, where she pulled up the back of her skirt to warm the back of her legs.

"I wish you wouldn't do that, Mary," said Lucy, pained.

"What's wrong, no one can see, can they? Even you can't see, Lucy."

"I know, but Mother's dying next door and it doesn't seem right," said Lucy desperately, starting to cry.

Mary went over to sit down beside her, putting an arm around Lucy's shoulder.

"Lucy darling, Mother is coming to the end of a very good life. We have known she is going to die for months, the doctor told us so – isn't that right, eh?"

She shook her sister's shoulders gently.

"I suppose so," Lucy snivelled, wiping her nose with her hankie.

"And, Lucy, it's our job to make her going as peaceful as we can, isn't that right?"

"I suppose so," said Lucy softly.

She turned to her sister, despair in her eyes.

"But, Mary, I can't imagine it if she's dead, she's always been here," she stammered.

Lucy dissolved into tears again.

"Now, Lucy, you have got to be brave," said Mary impatiently. "I'm going to get going; Henry must know what is happening and so must all the people who need to in Dean. Now you must cheer up and think of all the good times we have had with Mother."

Mary stroked Lucy's hair gently and Lucy leant her head on Mary's shoulder.

"You're right, Mary; there is so much to do, especially if people come to visit. Is there anything to give them? Have we got any cake or any wine or sherry?"

Mary shrugged.

"I'm sure you might find some wine in the scullery."

Lucy stood decisively, determined to keep busy.

"What was the weather like, Lucy, when you went out to get the coal?" asked Mary, pulling on her coat.

"It's cold and grey and still freezing; the wind is coming along from Dean."

"Ooh, it doesn't sound very nice," shivered Mary. "I'm off; I will be about two hours I expect by the time I have seen everyone. I'll go to Aunt Charlotte's first and then on."

She smiled at Lucy, moved towards her and squeezed her hand gently, before leaving to collect her bike from the shed.

She arrived at the butcher's shop twenty-five minutes later, walking round the back of the house and in through the scullery, where Sarah was doing the washing up.

"Hello, Sarah, is Mrs Dunmore here?" she enquired.

"Yes they are all here even Master William – they're in the kitchen – go on in, Miss Mary."

Mary went in to find Thomas sitting at the range in a rocking chair reading yesterday's paper, William sitting at the table reading the *Farmer & Stockbreeder*, his mother next to him reading the Bible.

"Mary dear," said Charlotte looking up, "how lovely to see you! But what are you doing down here so early?"

She looked towards her husband, who hadn't looked up from the paper.

"Thomas! Say hello to Mary and stop reading the paper; you know I don't like that on a Sunday." Charlotte closed her Bible, marking her place carefully with a card, and turning to William.

"The same goes for you, William," she said sharply. "Now, Mary, what is it that brings you? I guess that it's news of your mother?"

"Yes," said Mary, "I'm afraid it is, she's no better and the doctor called this morning and he said he did not think she would last the day; it's awfully sad."

"There, there, my dear, if it is God's will, I am sure your mother will be looked after. We must be thankful for the good things in life and your mother has had a good life."

"Yes, Aunt Charlotte, that's just what I told Lucy," said Mary.

She put her hankie to her eyes, but no tears came.

"Now, Thomas, we must go up to Cold Harbour, is the trap clean?"

"Yes my dear, I'm sure it is; you cleaned it, William, when you finished last night?"

William nodded.

"Aunt Charlotte?"

"Yes, Mary?"

"I wondered if William could ride over to Brington and tell Henry to come home; it's a long way for me to go and I think I ought to be back with Lucy, she's very upset you know."

"William," said Charlotte, looking expectantly at her son.

"Yes, Mother, I can go. I'll cycle; it will be quicker than saddling up the horse. I can get the trap ready for you before I go and get George to come with you; he can open the gates and deal with the pony when you get to Cold Harbour."

"Thank you, William," said Mary appreciatively.

"And Mary?"

"Yes, Aunt Charlotte."

"We will call at The Manse and tell Reverend Packham that we won't be at chapel this evening. I will tell him how your mother is."

"Oh thank you, Aunt Charlotte. That will save me a job. I am going to the Rectory as we want her buried in the churchyard with the others. And I must see Harry Rawlins about the coffin, and doesn't Art Tuffnail dig the graves? I had better see him as well."

Mary passed a hand over her face, and shook her head.

"I can't remember; I don't know who else I have to see."

"Don't worry, my dear," said Charlotte quietly, laying her hand on her niece's arm, "I am sure you will manage; don't forget she's not passed away yet."

"I know, I know," cried Mary, "but it's all so difficult; it's so near to Christmas to get all these things done."

"Don't you worry, Mary, the good Lord will help you in your hour of need, I know He will and He will be soon looking after your Mother. Now, Thomas, you go and get changed; you can't go and see Ann looking like that and William, what about you?"

She surveyed William critically.

"Hmm, you don't look too bad. And, Mary, I nearly forgot! What about Bessie? Have you let her know?"

"I have a card for her in my pocket, I will put it in the box when I go past. Has Muskett already done the collection?"

"No, I'm sure he won't have done it yet."

"Good but I must go, do you mind, Aunt Charlotte?"

"No, my dear, you have a lot to do; you get along directly – your mother will want you back as soon as possible. We will do the rest and will be there directly."

Everyone sprang into action; William got the trap ready, running along the road to fetch George. Thomas changed and Charlotte put a cake in a tin to take with them. William pulled his bike out of the shed and cycled off to Brington. The journey took under an hour; the big hill between Dean and Brington made William puff and by the time he reached Henry's farm he was warm, despite the frosty weather. He went straight into the kitchen and found Henry and

Martha in their Sunday best, ready for church. Noble Ladds was sitting at the table with them.

"Who do we have here?" said Noble mockingly. "Your esteemed cousin, Henry – Mr William Dunmore, no less!"

He chuckled and grinned at William.

"William," exclaimed Martha, "what are you doing here so early?"

"It's your mother, Henry; Mary has sent me, she says you must come as soon as you can."

"Oh dear," said Noble, "I'm so sorry to hear that, Henry. I'll be getting on – you must have to go."

He stood up and put on his cap.

"Henry, if there's anything I can do let me know."

He tipped his cap to Martha and left, throwing a wink at William as he did. William looked at Henry but said nothing. Henry shrugged his shoulders and held up his hands.

"Now, William Dunmore, don't say it! I know you don't like him; but he's been a good neighbour to us that's all I can say. Now we must get ready."

He smiled at his wife and laid a hand on her shoulder.

"Martha, you just take it easy."

Martha looked up at William.

"I'm going to have a baby, William, did you know?"

"Yes," he replied. "What good news for such an otherwise sad day."

"What did Mary think, William? Has she got long – Mother, I mean?" Henry asked.

"Mary said that the doctor told her that your mother would not last the day."

"We must be quick then; we best go in the trap – I don't think that you should cycle all that way, Martha."

Henry threw his coat on and went out to catch the pony.

"What do you think I should take, William?" asked Martha, easing herself up from her chair, "I must take something; we haven't got much in the pantry, but there is our Christmas cake. I will take that – I haven't iced it yet, but no one will know what it is, will they."

"I'm sure you needn't, Martha," said William. "They won't be expecting anything, I'm sure."

"I know but I bet there will be a lot of people there," she said, bustling into the pantry to find a tin for the cake.

"Martha, tell Henry I'm going straight back to Cold Harbour, all right?"

"Yes, you get on, William; we will be there as soon as we can."

Back at Cold Harbour, Lucy had washed her mother and made her comfortable as best she could; she was just about to put a cake in the oven when there was a loud knock at the back door. She went to find Verity and Dorcas standing at the backdoor: a basket slung over Dorcas's arm.

"Lucy, my dear, we have come to see your mother, I know it's Sunday but I only just got back from school yesterday and couldn't come before. Dorcas wanted to come as well, she does so like your mother and saw her a lot at the chapel."

Verity smiled.

"Do come in, Verity; it's all a bit of a mess as we are having to live in the kitchen."

"Oh that doesn't matter, Lucy," said Verity, placing the basket on the table, "and how is your mother? I should have been before; I promised Mary I would."

"I'm afraid she is not very good," said Lucy shakily. "The doctor says he doesn't think she will last the day."

Lucy sniffed once and burst into noisy sobs, bringing her apron up to her eyes to stem the tears.

"Oh, Lucy, my dear, how sad," said Verity, rising and putting her arm round Lucy's shoulder. "You come and sit down dear. Dorcas, we must help; put the kettle on. Lucy must have a warm drink, tea or something."

Lucy sat down opposite Verity who held her hands and looked earnestly into her face which was blotchy with crying, her eyes very red.

"Where is your mother, Lucy?" asked Verity gently.

"She's in the bed in the front room," sniffed Lucy. "Father is in there with her."

"Well we must go and pay our respects and then we will be back to help. Dorcas – come – you must see her as well."

Verity and Dorcas made their way down the corridor, returning a couple of minutes later.

"Where is Mary, Lucy?" asked Verity softly.

"She's gone down to Dean to tell William and he's going to tell Henry."

Lucy's bottom lip quivered and Verity squeezed her hand again.

"Now, what can we do? Dorcas, you've got the tea on the go?"

"Yes, Miss Verity, we'll soon have you a nice cup of tea, Miss Lucy, you see, but your poor mother does look poorly, very poorly I would say."

Lucy sniffed and nodded silently, just as Thomas and Charlotte arrived.

"Lucy my dear," said Charlotte putting her arm round Lucy, who sniffed and buried her head in her aunt's shoulder.

"Now, Lucy," said Charlotte gently, "Thomas and I must go and see your parents; are they in the front room?"

"Yes, Aunt Charlotte, do go and see her, I don't know whether she will know you though. Father's in there by the fire."

"Very good, my dear, we will be back directly; come on, Thomas. Oh and Lucy – George is with us; I told him to put the pony in the stable and feed it so he should be in soon."

They took themselves down the corridor, as Dorcas started to pour out the tea.

"Now come and sit down, Miss Lucy; a cup of tea will do you good right now, it will build you up."

"That is kind of you, Dorcas, everyone is so kind." She looked up at Dorcas and smiled. "How did you get up here? You didn't walk surely?"

"Oh no – Walter brought us in the motor car," said Dorcas with the ghost of a grimace, "but we are going to walk back bein' as it's down'ill all the way."

"So it is," said Lucy vacantly as the door of the scullery opened to reveal Mary.

She threw her coat and scarf over the back of the chair.

"How's Mother, Lucy?" she said quickly, and before waiting for a reply she turned to Dorcas.

"Dorcas, how kind of you to come, you shouldn't have."

"Oh think nothin' of it, Miss Mary, I came up with Miss Verity, we did not know that your mother was so low."

"Yes, how is Mother, Lucy?" Mary asked again.

"Much the same; Uncle Thomas and Aunt Charlotte have gone in to see her and Verity's in there as well."

At that moment Verity came back into the kitchen.

"Oh, Mary," she said, "I'm so pleased to see you; but your poor mother, I'm mortified that she's so ill."

"Yes, so are we," said Mary quietly.

The scullery door clicked open again, George sidled in and smiled shyly, saying nothing. He sat down on a chair by the sideboard, surreptitiously moving to the biscuit barrel, where he lifted the lid and took a biscuit. Everybody else was too absorbed to notice or if they did notice, too absorbed to care. Edgar strode into the room, a bucket in his hand, stopping short as he saw the crowd in the kitchen.

"What are all these folks doin' 'ere? I ain't never seen anythink like it," he demanded of Mary.

"It's Mother, Edgar, she's taken a turn for the worse; the doctor says she may not last the day."

Edgar looked from Mary to Lucy, from Dorcas to Verity.

"Well then, no one lives forever, do they?" he grumbled. "Now 'ave you got some soap, Mary, and some 'ot water for me bucket; I'm got a calf I can't get out and I'm going to 'ave to put me 'and in."

He took a step forward, bringing with him the smell of cow muck, which was splashed over his boots and up his long woollen coat. Dorcas curled her lip in disapproval. He put the bucket down, straightening himself up and staring pointedly at Mary.

"What about it then, Mary, do you got any soap?"

"Yes, yes, Edgar, I'll get it from the scullery," said Mary, irritated.

"And 'ot water," he said, glaring.

"There's plenty in the kettle," said Dorcas, taking an oven glove and lifting the kettle from the range, pouring it into his bucket. Edgar turned, picked up the full bucket, and made to go out.

"I'll be in for me lunch on time," he ordered, leaving with as much grace as he had arrived.

Mary and Lucy sighed in unison. Mary looked over towards George, taking him in for the first time.

"George, be a good boy and go and get another bucket of water from the pump; the bucket's in the scullery."

George jumped up, almost knocking over Charlotte and Thomas as they came back into the room.

"Aunt Charlotte and Uncle Thomas, take a seat, we are going to have to sit in here but I don't expect it matters," said Mary.

"No, my dear, these occasions call for special measures, don't they?" replied Charlotte piously.

"Would you like a cup of tea, Aunt Charlotte?" said Mary. "Or would you rather a glass of sherry or wine? I think we even have sloe gin; Lucy, get the bottles and glasses out, I thought you were going to do that."

Mary looked intently at Lucy.

"Sorry, Mary," said Lucy quietly, moving to the sideboard, her lips quivering.

"Now you know, Mary, that I don't approve of drink, especially on a Sunday," started Charlotte. "We should all be thinking of other things on Sundays, you know. But –" she inclined her head slowly – "*but* this is one of those times, one of those occasions when special measures are called for and I will have a small glass of sloe gin."

"And you, Uncle Thomas?" Mary said, suppressing a smile.

"Thank you, my dear, I will have a glass of sherry, if I may."

Lucy nodded and poured them out.

"Mary?" came a small voice from the door.

"Yes, George," said Mary.

"The pumps froze, Miss Mary."

"Oh no!" Mary exclaimed putting her palm to her forehead.

"Don't worry, Mary, I can do it with a little 'ot water," assured George. "That'll do it in a jiffy."

"I'll bring it, George, there must be a little in the kettle," said Mary, picking up the kettle and following George to the pump. Outside, Reverend Packham was trotting into the yard – he greeted Mary with a rush of condolences.

"Do go in," she said when he had finished his address "Lucy is in there, she will take you to see Mother; I have just got to deal with the pump, just go straight in."

Reverend Packham bowed slightly, and made his way towards the house, tripping on a flagstone into the scullery as he did so. His glasses tumbled to the floor, rendering the Reverend momentarily sightless; he stooped and fumbled around on the cold stone floor, his fingers finally making contact with the frames of his spectacles. He pushed the glasses back onto his head and continued on to the kitchen. He opened the door to be greeted by Dorcas, who was passing the glasses of sloe gin and sherry to Charlotte and Thomas.

"Oh, Reverend Packham!" she said looking delightedly at Reverend Packham, who took off his bowler hat and held it for a moment before Dorcas grabbed it and hung it on the back of the door.

"I've come to see poor Mrs Knighton, I hear she hasn't got long to go," he said, addressing Lucy.

"Yes, Reverend Packham, she is this way, if you would like to see her?"

The Reverend nodded, following her blindly down the corridor, gripping the door posts as he went.

"I don't know whether you will be able to have much communication," advised Lucy. "She comes and goes a bit."

In the kitchen George, having unfrozen the pump, was filling the copper ready for the next day's washing; he looked up as Reuben entered.

"Look who's here," exclaimed Charlotte, "Reuben Heighton, what are you doing so far from home?"

"Reuben dear," interrupted Mary, with a smile. "What a blessing you are; now you know what I'm going to say, don't you?"

"Yes, Mary, you're going to say fill the coal buckets and make up the fires."

"How did you guess?" Mary laughed, pouring the full force of a radiant smile on Reuben.

"You've got him trained well, Mary," said Charlotte wryly, "and George as well!"

The Reverend Packham tottered unsteadily into the room, Lucy grabbed his arm as he came wobbling past her and sat him down at the table.

"Are you all right, Reverend Packham?" Charlotte enquired.

"Just fine," he said. "Just fine – it's my eyesight; it seems a little strange at the moment."

"Oh yes, and in what way is it strange, Reverend?"

"Well I don't seem to focus but I'm sure it will be all right soon."

He looked dubiously around the room.

"We are having a glass of something," said Charlotte loudly. "I really don't approve, you know, especially as it's Sunday and I know, Reverend, what you tell us about the demon drink; but there are occasions when one should make exceptions and I told Lucy this is one of them, don't you agree?"

She looked at him eagerly for guidance.

"Yes, I am sure you are right, Mrs Dunmore, quite right," murmured the Reverend.

"Would you like a glass of something, Reverend Packham?" enquired Mary.

"Well I ought not to but on the other hand I'm sure something would go to help my eyes to focus a bit better; is that wine Mrs Dunmore has?"

"No," said Lucy, "it's sloe gin; very good for the constitution, would you like some?"

Reverend Packham mulled this over for a while, before muttering,

"Well, I'm sure a small glass will do no harm."

Reuben came shuffling in, carrying two big buckets and sidling sideways towards the range to get past all the people.

"Look what I'm found in the scullery, Mary!" he exclaimed. "Looks like a bit of someone's glasses, what you fink?"

Out of his pocket, he pulled the lens that had fallen from Reverend Packham's glasses when he had stumbled.

"Oh!" exclaimed Lucy. "Reverend Packham, it must be from yours! I can see that one of them is missing; that's why you can't focus."

Reverend Packham pulled off his glasses, thrusting a finger through the hole of the frame.

"My goodness, you are right, Lucy, how clever you and how clever that boy was to find them. God guides the lowliest of His creatures."

He smiled benevolently down on Reuben, who stared back at him, slightly embarrassed. Reverend Packham hummed nervously and looked back at his glasses.

"But I don't know how I will get it back in," he admitted.

"I do," piped up George, who was sitting by the sideboard again. "I do it all the time for my mother, her lens is always falling out."

All eyes turned to George.

"It's only a little screw," he said quietly. "I'm got a screwdriver on my shut knife and I do it with that, give it 'ere – you see I can do it."

"Well, if you are sure," said the Reverend, handing the glasses to George, who got out his shut knife and stood at the table. He quickly unscrewed the screw where the arm of the glasses met the frame, took the lens from Lucy and slotted it in, before screwing the glasses up again and handing them back to Reverend Packham, who slid the glasses back onto his face.

"My goodness!" he exclaimed. "I can see again. I must say I did think I was coming down with something, and all it was was a lens missing! How wonderful! Thank you, my boy."

He patted George on the head awkwardly.

"George is going to Kimbolton Grammar School, Reverend Packham," said Charlotte. "What do you think of that then?"

"Very commendable, very commendable; I had not heard about that, my boy. You will learn a lot from Belpeel, he's a good man. When do you start, my boy?"

He peered down at George.

"Well I don't really know when I'm goin' but I'm got to sit the scholarship paper next term and then they will see."

"You will pass that George," said Thomas. "William did, so I'm sure you can."

"'Ope so," said George.

The door opened and William walked in; he was very red in the face having cycled for nearly eight miles, the last bit up the steep hill to Cold Harbour.

"Come on in, William," said Lucy. "I'm so pleased to see you, I feel better now you are here; is Henry on his way?"

"Yes, he's coming, he's not far behind in the pony and trap and Martha has come as well. I think he must have got out and walked up the hill to give the pony a bit of a blow. How's Aunt Ann?"

"No better, I'm afraid; you must come and see her, you said you would read the Bible to her, William, when you were here the other day. I'm sure she'd like that."

"So I did," remembered William. "Where's the Bible, then, Mary?"

"Oh, it's in there by the bed. She might be asleep when you go in but don't worry, I'm sure she will wake up when she hears you. Father is in there as well, he will like to hear you read, William."

"'Adn't we ought to go, Miss Verity?" said Dorcas quietly, as William and Mary left the room. "It's gettin' an awful crush in 'ere."

"No, Dorcas, we must stay to see if there is anything we can do; they might need help with Mrs Knighton. Anyway, I want to say hello to Henry and Martha."

"Very good, Miss Verity, whatever you say."

A face peered cautiously round the kitchen door, staring at the assembled company.

"Freda dear, you've come back early! That was kind of you," said Lucy. "We did not expect you until tomorrow."

"I know but I 'eard Mrs Knighton ain't got long, so I fort I better come on up to see if there's summut to do; 'spect there is, ain't there, there's always summut to do up 'ere, ain't there, Lucy?"

"Yes there always is, Freda," said Lucy with a sigh.

"And ain't you got to go back tomorrow?" said Freda.

"You can't go back!" declared Charlotte. "It's outrageous; and your mother on her death bed! You must write immediately to tell them, Lucy. You tell them that you can't come until—"

Charlotte stopped and shifted uncomfortably in her chair.

"Until the situation has *resolved.* Don't you agree, Reverend Packham?"

She turned swiftly to Reverend Packham.

"Yes you are quite right, Mrs Dunmore," said the Reverend hurriedly. "It is out of the question that you return tomorrow, Lucy. Would you like me to write? I'm sure I could explain the situation."

"Perhaps if I write and then you add a note of confirmation that would be sufficient but I don't like letting them down, you know," said Lucy, "especially at Christmas."

"Well what about letting your mother down?" said Charlotte fiercely, shaking her head. "I don't know!"

"Please don't make me feel guilty, Aunt Charlotte," begged Lucy. "I know Mother hasn't got very long but I want to do the right thing," and the tears started to trickle down her face.

"Now look what you have done," said Thomas crossly. "You have made poor Lucy cry and she was being so brave."

Charlotte blushed, and rose to put her arm round Lucy.

"My dear, I am so sorry. Thomas is right; I only meant that I'm sure they will understand if you write to the hospital. You can do it directly and we can post it on the way home and Reverend Packham can put in a note as well; I'm sure it will be all right."

Once again the scullery door clicked. Henry and Martha rushed in – they both embraced Lucy one at a time.

"Henry, Martha, I'm so pleased you are here," Lucy sniffed. "Come and see Mother first and then you can say hello to everyone else."

She led them down the corridor into the front room; William was sitting on the chair by the bed, Mary was standing by the fire near John, who was asleep in his chair, his head lolling back. Ann lay impassively in bed, showing little sign of knowing her son was in the room. William stopped reading and looked up.

"Go on, William," whispered Henry, "she knows what you are saying, I'm sure."

Henry moved to the bed, and squeezed his mother's hand – a faint smile spread over her face.

"She looks so peaceful, don't you think," said Martha gently.

"Come back into the kitchen, Martha and you too, Henry," Mary whispered. "We will get you a cup of tea and something to eat – you've had a long journey."

They left the room as William started to read again.

Back in the kitchen Henry and Martha greeted the assembled company, happily receiving everyone's congratulations on expecting the baby.

"I must see to the horse," said Henry, standing from the table.

"And get the things out the trap, Henry," said Martha.

"I'll do it," said Reuben.

"I'll help," said George, rushing to the door.

"Does it want feeding as well?" said Reuben.

"Just some hay, Reuben; don't give it any oats," instructed Henry.

"And, George," said Martha, "you get the things out the trap; there's a basket and a cake tin as well, bring them straight back."

"Very good, Miss Martha," said George, dashing out the door.

"Now, Martha, would you like a cup of tea or a glass of wine?" Mary asked.

"Oh, a cup of tea would be lovely, Mary."

"And what about you, Henry?"

"Oh, is everyone else having a glass of wine? I'll have some sloe gin if there is some."

Lucy poured out the last of the bottle for Henry.

"Is that all we have, Lucy?" said Mary, a little surprised.

"Oh no, there's one more bottle here and I think there is some more in the cellar."

"If that's the case, I think I will have a glass," said Mary.

"I don't approve, you know, and it being a Sunday as well," chipped in Charlotte.

"But you've got a glass, Aunt Charlotte," said Mary sharply, "and you've nearly finished it as well."

"Well I s'pose I have," sniffed Charlotte. "But it's the occasion, my dear, very special circumstances, isn't that right, Reverend Packham?"

"Quite right, Mrs Dunmore, quite right; there are occasions which make exceptions to the rule."

George came back in carrying the basket and the cake tin, which he placed on the table.

"Mary?" he said.

"Yes, George."

"There's someone comin' up the drive on a big 'orse."

"*Horse*, George Lowe, you will have to say 'horse' if you are going to the Grammar School," Charlotte scolded.

"Who is it, George?" interrupted Mary.

"I don't rightly know, but I think it might be the vicar – he's got a top 'at on, shall I go and open the gate?"

"Yes, George, run along."

A few minutes later there was a rap at the back door as the Vicar of Dean, Reverend Archibald Heaton announced his arrival by tapping the door with his riding crop. Mary went and greeted him, bringing him into the now very crowded kitchen. Mary took his top hat, putting it on the sideboard and hanging his coat over the back of a chair.

"Mary my dear, I thought that after your visit this morning I ought to pay a call on your mother and discuss the arrangements with you; it's getting very close to Christmas, you know, and I like to have everything organised."

"Mrs Knighton is still alive, Reverend Heaton and I don't think Mary and Lucy can make any arrangements at present," said Verity firmly. "I'm sure they would be pleased if you would go and visit their mother who is in the front room."

There was an awkward silence. The vicar blushed.

"Quite so, quite so, Miss Watson-Foster," intoned Reverend Heaton apologetically. "Please accept my apologies, Mary and Lucy, if I was a bit presumptuous. Now perhaps you would take me to see your mother."

Reverend Heaton was in the front room a matter of minutes before he returned to the kitchen.

"Now, Reverend Heaton, would you like a cup of tea or a glass of wine?" Mary asked.

"Oh, a glass of wine would be very hospitable of you; to keep the cold out on the way home, don't you think?" chuckled Reverend Heaton.

"It's sloe gin," said Lucy. "Is that all right?"

"Even better, Lucy, I am very partial to sloe gin particularly in the winter, you know."

The kitchen was now full to bursting, and the chatter grew louder and louder. The only people not drinking were Lucy, Martha and Verity who all had cups of tea and as the afternoon wore on, the noise in the house grew. No one heard the door when Edgar came in.

"Where's my dinner, then? I'm bin workin' all morning and I'm ready for my dinner," Edgar shouted loudly.

Mary put her hand to her mouth.

"Edgar! There is no lunch! I have completely forgotten!"

"What you mean, no lunch?" bellowed Edgar. "I need my lunch, I can't work on an empty stomach, you know! I need an 'ot dinner."

There was silence. Mary looked around the room, deciding how best to proceed.

"Sit at the end of the table, Edgar, we will get you something," she instructed. "Dorcas, do you mind moving – we must get Edgar some lunch and something for everyone else. Lucy, come and help see what there is in the pantry."

She clapped her hands.

"Now, everyone, find a seat and we will get the food on the table; Dorcas and Martha, you will help, won't you?"

They set to, finding plates, knives and forks. From the pantry came cheese, cold meat and pickles, which were all set out next to the biscuits that Dorcas had brought with her. Charlotte started slicing Martha's cake and Thomas was given the job of carving off the cold pork.

There was not room for everyone round the table and Reuben, George, Freda, Mary and Lucy had what they ate on their knees. Lucy took a small plate in for John but she was only able to get Ann to drink a little beef tea. Back in the kitchen Edgar continued to complain that he hadn't had a hot dinner; he flatly refused to talk to anyone and sat with his head lowered to his plate, grumbling under his breath. The sloe gin was having its effect, adding to the warmth that had built up in the room – red faces smiled at one another, as Mary refilled the glasses with sherry and sloe gin and Dorcas kept the teapot full. As they started to clear the plates into the scullery; a shuffle was heard in the corridor to the front room. The kitchen fell silent as John appeared supported by his two sticks; his gaunt figure framed in the doorway.

"I think we've lost her, Mary," said John helplessly. "I think we have. Lucy, you go and look at your mother, but I think we've lost her."

There was silence, as tears sprang to Lucy's eyes but she made no sound.

"Come on, Lucy," said Henry gently, "I'll come with you."

Taking her hand, Henry moved with Lucy towards the door, past John who remained motionless, staring into the distance.

"Are you going to come and sit down, Father?" said Mary quietly.

"No, my dear, I'm going down the end," said John gruffly, making his way across the kitchen.

"You can't go out there, Father, you'll catch your death," said Mary.

"Don't worry about me, dear, I've got a thick jacket on," he smiled weakly at his daughter, "and anyway, I want some fresh air."

He continued into the scullery and towards the back door.

"I'll come with you, Father," said Mary urgently. "We can't have you slipping on the cobbles, they're all ice, you know."

"Very well," sighed John. "Come if you must."

In the living room, Lucy felt her mother's pulse, putting her hand to her mother's forehead and her ear to Ann's mouth. She stood up and looked at Henry; her tears had gone now.

"She's dead, Henry."

"Are you sure, Lucy?"

"I'm sure, I've seen too many of them in the hospital."

Henry went up and squeezed his mother's hand, laying the lightest kiss on Ann's cold cheek.

The pair returned to the kitchen to relay the news to the others.

"We must tell the doctor," said Lucy. "He will have to come to confirm the death and issue the certificate, but it's getting late in the day – I'm sure he won't come today."

"I know," said Verity decisively. "What's the time, Dorcas?"

"It's five and twenty to two, Miss Verity," said Dorcas after checking her pocket watch.

Verity turned to Lucy.

"If we set off now we will be home just after two. I will get Walter to go and fetch the doctor in the motor car and he can bring him here and take him home after that, how about that, Lucy?"

Lucy smiled gratefully.

"That's awfully kind of you, Verity; are you sure you don't mind?"

"It's the least I can do," said Verity determinedly. "Come on, Dorcas, get your coat, we must get going."

"I will walk with you, Miss Watson-Foster, if you don't mind," said Reverend Packham, putting his hat and coat on.

Mary returned with John from the yard.

"Are you going to sit here, Father, by the range and keep warm?" Mary asked.

"No, my dear, I'm going to sit with your mother for a while; there is a fire in there."

He slowly made his way down the corridor. The Reverend Heaton rose and picked up his hat and coat.

"Can we talk about the funeral, Reverend Heaton? Can we have it before Christmas?" asked Mary.

"My dear, I can't see it happening before Christmas Eve. But if you don't mind having it then we could have the service before lunch – say eleven o'clock – assuming we can get all the other arrangements made."

"Yes that will do, don't you agree, Lucy? Henry, what do you think? Bessie should be able to get here by then."

Henry and Lucy nodded their assent.

"You can send a telegram," suggested William.

"Well that is all arranged then," said Mary, smiling sadly at Reverend Heaton. "Reuben, go and hold Reverend Heaton's horse for him and get him mounted."

Reverend Heaton lifted his hat to the women individually and was gone.

"Well, Mary," said Charlotte," I think we should go and then we will be able to get to chapel this evening; there's nothing else we can do here, is there."

"No, Aunt Charlotte," agreed Mary. "I'm afraid we will not make it this evening."

"No, my dear – you stay here in the warm and look after your father. William, are you coming?"

"I'll wait a bit, until Henry goes."

"All right then, we will see you in a little while. Come on, George, nip and get the harness on the pony and we will be on our way."

George scampered out of the room, Charlotte and Thomas trailing behind him.

Reuben stood up.

"Mary, should I get some coal for the front room?" he asked.

"Yes, Reuben, if Father is in there we must keep him warm."

"Aren't you going to see Mother, Mary?" asked Lucy.

"I suppose I must," sighed Mary, looking dejectedly round at the others.

"I'll come," said William. "I think I will feel better when I've seen her."

He led Mary down the corridor into the front room. They looked down at Ann's still form.

"She looks very peaceful; don't you think?" he said to Mary.

"I suppose she does," Mary said quietly, before adding, "shouldn't we pull the covers up over her face, William?"

William was silent for a moment.

"I don't know, perhaps your father wants to see her and you should wait until the doctor's been."

"Very well then, let's go back in the kitchen now; there are things to be done."

Henry and Martha were making ready to go when Mary and William returned.

"Are you going so soon, Henry?" said Mary. "Can't you stay a bit longer?"

"I want to get home in the light, Mary; it's dark soon after four on a cloudy day like this and I don't want Martha out in the cold longer than we can help."

"Yes I'm sure you are right," said Mary. "Martha, why don't you take the rest of the cake home with you – it looks like it is your Christmas cake."

She fetched the half-eaten cake and replaced it in its tin.

"She's all ready, 'Enry," said Reuben, who had rushed in from readying the trap for Martha and Henry.

"Very good, Reuben, you are a good lad. Do you want a lift home? It's downhill and flat so the pony can manage."

"Yup, if you don't mind and I can open the gates for you." He looked at Mary. "Is there anything else to do, Mary?"

"No, Reuben, you have been very helpful," smiled Mary, ruffling Reuben's hair.

Reuben beamed and followed Henry and Martha out to the trap.

William, Mary and Lucy sat silently round the table looking at each other. Freda was finishing the washing up in the scullery and the occasional mooing of cattle in the yards could be heard as Edgar moved through to feed them. Suddenly Lucy leapt to her feet.

"I just remembered I must write the letter to the Sister at the hospital!" she exclaimed. "Reverend Packham did not write a note to go with it either! What am I going to do?"

"Don't worry, Lucy," said William. "You write your letter and put it in the envelope but don't seal it and I will get Reverend Packham to do his note when I go to chapel this evening. I can put it in and post it. It won't go today, it's too late, but they will get it on Tuesday morning."

"You're right, William, I will do it now."

"I shall have to make a list," said Mary.

"What list?" said William.

"A list of all the things to do before the funeral; there's a lot to think about, William. I'm going to come and see your mother in the morning; she will tell me what to do. Father will not be much help."

Lucy wrote her letter and addressed it, giving it to her cousin as he left the house.

"It seems very quiet now," said Lucy, "now all the people have gone."

She sighed heavily, and looked at Mary who was staring into the coals of the range.

The evening passed slowly at Cold Harbour; they had their meal at half past five and John went up to bed. Lucy read the Bible, Mary wrote her list of things to do and Freda sat by the fire and darned some socks.

"I'm just going to see Mother," said Lucy, taking a candle and moving along the corridor.

Mary looked up when she came back.

"Is she all right?" Mary said, before gasping and putting her hand to her mouth. "I didn't mean it like that, Lucy, I meant—"

"I know what you meant," said Lucy gently. "Yes, she's all right. It's awfully cold in there now without a fire."

She sat down at the table again and opened the Bible; Mary continued to write.

"I'm goin' to bed now," said Freda, standing and removing a brick from the oven, which she wrapped in a cloth and clutched to her.

"Night," she said, leaving the room with a small nod of the head to the two girls.

"Time we went too, Lucy; light a candle and I will put the lamp out," sighed Mary.

Lucy sat staring into the distance. Without warning, she started to cry. Mary rushed to her sister and put an arm round her.

"Come on, Lucy, don't cry," pleaded Mary. "Mother had a good life and she was very sick."

"I know all that but –" Lucy stopped and took a deep breath, "let's go to bed."

In their room, the light from the moon was streaming in onto the floor. Lucy pulled the curtains to as they both got changed and got in bed; Mary blew the candle out. A minute or two passed.

"Are you asleep, Mary?" whispered Lucy.

"No," said Mary.

It was quiet for a while; Mary could faintly hear Lucy sobbing.

"Mary?" said Lucy a minute later. "Can I come in your bed with you?"

"Come on then," sighed Mary, making room for Lucy. Lucy hopped across the room and slid in next to Mary, who wrapped an arm around her younger sister.

"Mary?"

"What is it now?"

"We haven't said our prayers – we must do that."

"Lucy, you are exasperating! Lie down and we can say the Lord's Prayer together and then we can say God bless Mother – it's too cold to get out of bed now."

"But how can we say God bless Mother if she's dead?"

Mary sat up and turned to Lucy.

"I know Mother's dead but I'm sure she is in heaven; if we say God bless Mother, He will."

"Yes," said Lucy in a small voice, "I suppose you are right."

Chapter Thirty-Two
Laid to Rest
Christmas 1902

Mary went down to Dean the next morning to make the arrangements for the funeral. She went first to Reverend Heaton to confirm the time of the funeral on Christmas Eve and the position of her mother's grave alongside the other family members, before going to see Harry Rawlins who made the coffins.

"What do you want then, Miss Mary?" said Harry quietly, looking at her inquisitively.

"What do you mean, what do I want?" asked Mary, taken aback. "I want a coffin."

"I know that," he sighed, looking slightly exasperated, "but what *sort* of coffin; what sort of wood – oak or elm or pine?"

"What's the difference?" she asked.

"Well oak's more expensive," he said.

"We will have pine then," said Mary firmly.

"What about handles, do you want handles?"

"No, no handles," said Mary.

"Right you are," he nodded, "I'll come up first thing after dinner and you can 'ave the coffin tomorra. Do you want the hearse to bring her down to the church?"

"Is that expensive, Harry?"

"I don't rightly know, but I expect it will cost a fair bit."

"No then. I'll get Henry to bring her down; we can put the coffin in the church before the service, can't we? Then no one will see if we bring her down in the wagon. There's no money for extras, Harry – but I expect you know that."

Harry patted Mary on the arm and assured her that the coffin would be ready tomorrow. Mary thanked him and made her way to see Reverend Packham to organise refreshments after the service.

"There's no way we can get everyone back to Cold Harbour," Mary explained, "so I was wondering if we could give everyone sandwiches in the school room at the back of the chapel?"

Reverend Packham readily agreed – this was the usual custom for those who worshipped at the chapel – and he offered the services of his wife to make the tea, which Mary agreed to thankfully before heading back home via the butcher's shop.

Christmas Eve came; Henry and Martha arrived early and Henry fixed the horses to the wagon before enlisting the others to load on the coffin. He made his way to the church where Harry Rawlins and Art Tuffnail met him; the three men lifted the coffin into the church and placed it on the trestles. Henry then returned to Cold Harbour to collect Martha and John in the trap. Edgar had decided not to attend, claiming there was much too much work to do before Christmas and that the other men on the farm attending the funeral were leaving him short-staffed.

Lucy and Mary decided that they would walk; the ground was hard with frost and they would not get their boots muddy.

"I've never been to a funeral before," Lucy said to Mary. "Will they save us somewhere to sit? I can't remember what it's like in the church."

"Yes, you silly, we have to walk in behind the parson. Father and Henry will go first and then us and Martha and Bessie."

"But everyone will look at us!" groaned Lucy. "I don't like the idea of that, can't we just sit at the back?"

"No we can't, Lucy, we are the main mourners!" cried Mary incredulously. She turned to her sister gently.

"Don't worry, I will look after you."

They walked on in silence; the day was grey and overcast and a cold breeze blew sharply in their faces as they walked along the path across the top of the ridge. There were no cattle in the fields now and the cow muck lay frozen solid amongst the spindly trees, the trunks of which had been rubbed down by scratching cattle. The bark shone dully as they passed and the rooks rose noisily from the branches.

"I'm going to want to go down the end before I go into church," said Lucy. "I'll go behind the hedge before we get over the stile."

"No you won't," said Mary sharply. "Not dressed up like that! We can go round to Ruby's; she won't mind and she's right next to the church."

Ten minutes later they arrived – having called at Ruby's on the way – where the parson stood outside the church talking to Henry and John who stood supported by two sticks. William, Charlotte and Thomas were waiting to process in with the rest of the family and were standing with Bessie, who had just arrived from Kimbolton station. She rushed to greet Mary and Lucy as they arrived.

A single bell tolled mournfully from the bell tower and they could hear the organ playing inside the church. Reverend Heaton turned to the family, tossed his head back a little and in a loud whisper said,

"Ready, everyone?"

Henry and John nodded decisively, Bessie looked at Mary and smiled encouragingly; Mary looked at the ground. Lucy sniffed and held her hankie to her nose.

"Don't sniff like that, Lucy, I don't know how many times I have told you," Mary said sharply under her breath.

The little group moved slowly into the nave of the chapel, processing down the aisle. Some of the congregation turned round to look at their progress, others looked steadfastly forward. John Watson-Foster sat near the far side, where there was room for his wheelchair, Verity sitting next to him, and beyond her sat Rupert Nelson. The pews to the front were sparsely populated and on the right, four were left for the family. Mary noticed that in the very back pew, pressed in next to four other gentlemen, was Noble Ladds; in a very smart black coat with velvet collar.

For Mary the service passed in a blur – no sooner had they reached the pews than it seemed that they were being asked to leave them again, ushered out by Reverend Heaton who progressed to stand in front of the coffin ready to process out. It was a moment before Mary realised with horror that she had failed to select any pall bearers; she looked desperately around the church in embarrassment. Henry looked quizzically at her, before realising what had happened. He nodded to William, looking around him for other volunteers from the congregation. Art Tuffnail elbowed Harry Rawlins who was sitting next to him and rose to move towards the coffin. The four men lifted the box with ease and followed the parson into the churchyard round to where the grave had been dug. After some hesitation the ropes were passed under the coffin which was slowly lowered into the grave. The family stood around in silence as Reverend Heaton chimed out the last prayers, and only Lucy dabbed her eyes with her hankie, wiping away a tear. Mary and Bessie stood in silence looking sadly down at the coffin at the bottom of the deep grave, before moving to shake the hands of friends in the congregation. Mary, who noticed Molly in the crowd with her parents, went to talk to her.

"Molly," she smiled, grasping Molly's hand, "it was very good of you to come all this way, how are you keeping?"

"I'm fine, Mary," Molly replied. "But I was sorry to hear about your mother; she was always nice to me and give me biscuits when I went up to Cold 'arbour."

"Are you coming to the chapel school room? We've got some sandwiches and tea; you'll need them before you walk back."

"No, I ain't comin'," said Molly sharply, before adding apologetically, "Folks'll look at me, you know, Mary."

She blushed and looked down.

"No they won't," came a voice beside Molly's elbow. "You come with me."

Verity had come up behind them and had heard what was said.

"Don't you worry, Molly, Mary is right. You need all the energy you can get at the minute and the tea will warm you up."

She took Molly's hand and squeezed it, leading her off toward the school room.

A lot of people had come from Dean. The farmers from the area stood around in groups talking; amongst them Noble Ladds stood leaning on the lych-gate, smoking a small cigar and regaling two local farmers with the merits of a horse he had for sale. Rupert Nelson fought his way through the crowd to greet Mary.

"I'm so sorry about your mother, Mary," he said, gripping her hand and holding it tight. "I know she was ill; but what a difficult time for you just at

Christmas."

"I know," said Mary, "but God decides these things, not man – so we have to make do."

Mary blushed and looked down, wishing she had said something less banal. She shrugged and looked up again:

"But, Rupert, it's so good of you to come – how did you get here and how did you know about the funeral?"

"Oh, I cycled; it didn't take too long. I didn't want to rely on the trains today, and I heard from Dorcas's brother Edwin – he came round to the office with the news which was kind of him."

"I'm so pleased you came, Rupert," said Mary earnestly. "You must come and have some food before you go home. How is Rebecca? Have you seen her lately?"

"Yes I saw her yesterday; she said to apologise but she couldn't come – she has broken her leg. She fell when she was hunting about a month ago and it is still in plaster."

"Oh, poor Rebecca; I must write to her," said Mary.

"Well she wrote to *you,* Mary, and I have the letter somewhere."

He searched frantically through his pockets, coming up eventually with a sealed envelope which he passed to Mary. Their fingers brushed lightly as Mary took the envelope from him, Rupert blushed and smiled.

Gradually people moved to the school room at the back of the chapel; the fire was alight, the table full of sandwiches and Dorcas was pouring out cups of tea. John was assisted and placed in a chair near the door; with all the chatter in the room he could not hear what most of the people said to him, so he resorted to nodding and smiling at those offering their condolences. His hand shook as he held his cup of tea and slowly chewed a sandwich with the few teeth he had left. Noble Ladds continued to try and sell horses to anybody who cared to listen – be it draught horses, hunters or children's ponies. He stood out from the rest of the crowd, looking overdressed for a funeral in his high boots and checked waistcoat. Mary and Lucy tried to talk to everyone, but it was an impossible task and before they knew it, people started to leave to get ready for Christmas. Rupert came to say goodbye to Mary.

"Mary, I must see you again before I leave for the Argentine," Rupert begged. "It's just over two months before I go, can I come over?"

"No, Rupert," said Mary firmly, "I will come to Northampton and then I can see Rebecca; I expect I could stay with her for a night."

"That would be splendid, Mary; you could come to lunch!" declared Rupert.

"But your mother doesn't approve of me, Rupert," said Mary with a small laugh. "Didn't she call me a shop girl?"

"No, no, Mary, it'll be fine – you see if it won't be," said Rupert calmly, the lack of eye contact belying the truth in his words.

"I will write to Rebecca as soon as possible and then I will write to you, Rupert," smiled Mary, holding his hand and colouring a little as she did so.

"Oh, Mary, I nearly forgot – I've got you a small Christmas present," said Rupert, handing Mary a small square parcel in pretty paper. "I hope you like it, it's not much and I'm not much good at choosing, but there."

"Rupert, how kind – I had completely forgotten about Christmas with Mother and—"

She trailed off, and squeezed his hand, bidding farewell to him as he left to find his bicycle.

There was only a small group left now, they were all standing in a corner and Noble Ladds was surreptitiously handing round a hip flask; everyone in the group taking a quick sip from it before Noble slipped it away as he saw Mary moving towards them. He straightened up and addressed her.

"Miss Knighton, can I offer my sincere condolences on the death of your mother and could I add that you have given her a very good send off. The service was lovely and so many people turned out despite it being Christmas."

"Thank you, Mr Ladds," said Mary proudly, turning immediately to Henry. "Henry, I think you should take Father home, he's beginning to get cold by the door and it will take you a little while to get home."

Henry nodded and left to set up the trap. Noble Ladds shrugged his top coat on and followed Mary to the door to say goodbye.

"Miss Knighton —" he started.

"Do call me Mary," said Mary, "after all you are a good friend of my brother."

She smiled coyly.

"Mary, then," corrected Noble with a small bow, "I was going to say that I will call in to see your father when I come past, which I expect to be soon after Christmas – but I must say goodbye now."

He took her hand and grasped it firmly.

"Thank you, Mr Ladds," said Mary with a smile. "I am sure Father will be pleased to see you."

"And remember, *I* am Noble," he said with a wink.

"Yes," said Mary, "Noble, then."

She coloured a little and eyed Noble curiously.

"Goodbye then, *Noble*, thank you for coming."

Noble Ladds bowed deeply, kissed Mary's hand and swirled out of the room. Mary watched him leave until he was out of sight.

Chapter Thirty-Three
The Naming of Molly's Baby

Christmas had been noneventful – not a single present had been exchanged, no decorations had been put up, no cards delivered and the girls had not been able to summon the energy to make a Christmas cake or pudding. The only highlight for Mary had been the present she had received from Rupert – a brightly painted Swiss musical box – which stood in pride of place on her bedside table.

Her father's condition was declining; a few steps would make him breathless, and although he insisted on still sleeping upstairs, it took him five minutes to climb the twelve steps to his bedroom. It was becoming clear that before long the farm would have to be sold to pay the debts that John had accumulated over the years and Mary was not alone in secretly hoping he would die before this had to happen.

Life at Cold Harbour gradually folded itself into the pattern that Mary had dreaded it would. Lucy went back to her training and left Mary to look after her father, with only Edgar and Freda to talk to on a day-to-day basis. The frost had gone to be replaced by a cold, wet period – day upon day of rain blown in from the south-west. Mud seeped in everywhere and with Edgar refusing to take his boots off whilst walking through the house – except at night – the house got more and more difficult to keep clean. Mary was able to go on her bicycle down to Dean every so often to call and see Verity, but by the second week of January Verity had returned for her last two terms at school and another friendly face was lost to her. She wrote to Rebecca and quickly got a reply with an open invitation to stay with her in Northampton. Her broken leg was well on the mend, but it was unlikely that she would be able to hunt again this season, and she wrote to say that a visit from Mary would be a welcome distraction from having to cope with her stepmother.

On a cold morning in early January, Mary decided to go and see Molly. She knew that the walk would take her down muddy tracks, but anything to get her away from the day-to-day monotony of cooking and housework was welcome.

She left Freda to put on the lunch and with a basket of small gifts, set off at half past nine.

The first part of the journey along the grass fields on top of the ridge was good going; the path was not used that much and so not too muddy, but the bridleway was not as kind. They had been carting timber from the woodland near Kimbolton and the horses and carts had cut deep ruts into the soft earth, which now stood full of water. Mary picked her way along it, criss-crossing the road to avoid the worst of the ruts, her boots and the bottom of her thick coat getting more and more muddy. All the cattle had been taken from the fields, but there were still some sheep scattered around; they looked up curiously as Mary walked past before lowering their heads to forage again in the meagre pasture. All the leaves had fallen from the hedges, leaving crooked gaps through which Mary could see the mud of grey-brown fields; only the oak trees held tenuously to their browning leaves, which were just starting to flurry from the branches.

When Mary finally got to Hardwick's she called out and went straight into the kitchen. Molly was the only one at home, her mother having gone to work at the Hall, her father out in the yard with the cattle.

Contrary to Mary's expectations, Molly seemed quite bright – she had the range fire glowing and put the kettle on as soon as Mary came in.

"Cuppa tea then, Mary?" she asked cheerily.

She wore a thick dress with a jacket over it and had both shoes and socks on; her cheeks were rosy, her face clean and her hair was brushed.

"That would be nice, Molly," smiled Mary. "Don't you look smart this morning?"

"Yeah I s'pose," said Molly shyly. "But I ain't going nowhere."

"No," said Mary, "but that's a nice jacket you're wearing."

"Yeah, Miss Verity give to me; she said it don't fit 'er no more, nor the shoes neither; what you fink, Mary?"

"Very smart," said Mary.

"Yeah, I fort so; makes me feel better to 'ave somefink decent to put on."

She poured boiling water into the pot and they both sat down at the table while the tea brewed.

"And how are you keeping, Molly?" asked, pulling the packet of home-made biscuits out of the basket. "It can't be long now can it?"

"I s'pose it can't, but it'll come when it's ready, I 'spect."

"Yes I s'pose it will," Mary replied.

There was silence.

"I ain't keepin' it!" said Molly quietly. "You know that, don't you, Mary? I told Miss Verity that, I'm told everyone that and I mean it! I ain't keepin' any child of 'is and that's that."

She pressed her lips tightly together and reached for the teapot. Mary said nothing as Molly poured the tea.

"You know that shop you were at in Norfampton, Mary?" said Molly carefully.

"Yes – Tibbitts."

"I'm gonna work there!" said Molly determinedly. "You said you would write for me, din't you, Mary? You did!"

"Yes I did and I will when the time comes, but—"

Mary stopped and thought how to phrase her next sentence without causing Molly offence. Molly, however, seemed oblivious to Mary's discomfort; she looked at Mary slyly and said,

"'Ave you got a young man courting you then, Mary? I see'd one at the funeral; come on a bike, 'e did – I could see 'e liked you, Mary, 'e was goin' all red when 'e talked to you, I see'd 'im."

"I haven't got anyone! I don't know who you mean," said Mary sharply, colour rushing into her cheeks.

"I'm sure you do – look, you're goin' red, an' all. I knew I was right," laughed Molly. "'E weren't the only one even; there were a smart chap in ridin' boots and a check waistcoat, 'e couldn't keep 'is eyes off you, Mary!"

Molly paused and frowned slightly.

"I didn't like the look of 'im," she said quietly, with a small shake of her head. "I'm sure 'e's no good. I know I ain't very old, but I can tell a rotter when I see one."

Mary sipped her tea slowly, trying not to show she was irritated that Molly was making a joke at her expense. She thought of Rupert; she did like him a lot but they were not courting; she had never thought of it like that and it had never really crossed her mind that Rupert might be in love with her, she just liked the attention and thought he was nice. As far as Noble Ladds was concerned, she hadn't realised he had been looking at her, although she only had Molly's word for it that he was. The idea didn't displease her – it didn't displease her at all.

She finished her tea and turned to Molly.

"Molly, I must be off," she said offhandedly.

"So soon, Mary!" said Molly, surprised. "I thought you would stop and chat; I ain't said anything wrong, 'ave I?"

"No, no, Molly," said Mary quickly. "But I must get back to do the lunch, or Edgar will be cross."

"Very good then," said Molly disappointedly, watching Mary as she pulled her coat back on and left.

Three quarters of an hour later Mary arrived back at Cold Harbour to find a bay mare hunter tied to the yard gate. She went through the scullery into the kitchen where Freda stood next to the range waiting for the kettle to boil.

"We've got a visitor," she said without enthusiasm.

"Who is it, then?" asked Mary, hoping she knew the answer.

"Dun't know! Ain't seen 'im afore; looks a bit posh though – all dressed up, 'e is. Said 'is name were Noble summut. 'Rats' or summut like that?"

"Noble Ladds," said Mary. "Where is he then?"

"E's in wiv your dad now; but 'e's bin round the yard lookin' in all the stables at the 'orses. I'm gettin' 'im a cuppa tea."

"Very good, Freda. I'll go and have a word with him," said Mary, hanging up her hat and coat and smoothing down her dress. She cast a critical eye down at her clothes, sighed and moved back to the doormat in the scullery to wipe off the worst of the mud on her shoes, before moving down the corridor to the front room. The corridor was not well lit, but she stopped at the mirror, pushing her hair into place the best she could before putting her hands to her nose and pulling her fingers across her cheeks.

In the front room, Noble Ladds was in a chair with his back to her sitting opposite John on the other side of the fire. On hearing her come in, Noble leapt to his feet, and turned with a smile – he bowed slightly and offered his hand to be shaken.

"Miss Knighton! Ah, I'm sorry – Mary. It's a pleasure to meet you again; I have called in to see your father."

He smiled at her.

"Mr Ladds, Noble. It's a pleasure to see you again," said Mary with a small laugh. "I believe Freda has offered you a cup of tea; can I offer you something to eat? We will be having lunch soon; you are very welcome to stay, I am sure we have enough."

"No, no, I don't want to put you to any trouble," smiled Noble, with a wave of his hand, "and in any event I have an appointment at The Falcon at Bletsoe at one o'clock which I do not want to miss."

He flicked ash from his cigar onto the fire and turned questioningly to John.

"How long will it take me from here?"

"Under the hour if you have a good horse, well under the hour," John replied, before coughing and spitting into the fire.

Noble took a gold watch from the pocket of his waistcoat and flicked it open.

"Well I have time for tea – but that is all I'm afraid and then I must be off."

He turned to Mary.

"I've been talking to your father about horses; he tells me that the Cold Harbour team are a bit long in the tooth and I have a few good animals about me at present."

"I'm sure you do Mr L–, *Noble*," said Mary pointedly, "but I don't think we are in a position to buy until we sell some of the bullocks later in the year. Don't you agree, Father?"

John coughed again and looked into the fire.

"No, my dear, I suppose we are not able to at the moment," he murmured.

Freda entered with a tray – she placed the pot and three cups and saucers on the table and left without a word. Mary moved to the table to pour the tea out.

"That's a fine hunter you are on today, Noble," she said, passing him a cup and saucer.

"Yes, that's why I'm going to Bletsoe; I'm hoping to sell her to a Mr Harding. I believe you might know him, Mary?"

"You mean Mr Charles Harding from Northampton?" asked Mary.

"Yes – that's the one: a fine fellow, loves his hunting, I believe."

"Yes," smiled Mary, "as does his daughter."

John looked up towards Mary.

"Do you know them then?" he said, looking dubiously at his daughter.

"Oh yes, I've known them some time; Rebecca's a good friend and I saw a lot of her when I worked in Northampton."

"We must be talking about the same people then, mustn't we?" said Noble, raising an eyebrow.

"Oh yes, I am sure we are," said Mary, smiling again at Noble, who drained the last of his tea and rose to leave.

He said goodbye to John, who shook his hand and turned back to his newspaper. Mary followed Noble out into the yard, where he untied his hunter, mounting nimbly without the use of the block. Mary opened the gate and smiled up at him, admitting to herself that he looked a fine sight on the handsome mare. Noble raised his bowler.

"I will call again if you don't mind, Mary," he said.

"That would be nice," smiled Mary, blushing slightly, before adding, "it's a pleasure to see anyone up here, especially in the middle of winter."

Noble grinned, touched his bowler and rode off; Mary watched him trot down the drive, skilfully opening and closing the three gates in his way without getting off his horse. She sighed and moved back into the house, resolving that she would write to Rebecca that afternoon to fix a date to go and stay with her in Northampton.

She sat down at the kitchen table to write her letter, while Freda got the lunch ready. Edgar came in on the dot of one o'clock and shovelled down his food silently at the end of the table. Mary was growing more and more resentful of his demands, only speaking the bare minimum to him. With John incapacitated, Edgar had more and more power to run the farm the way he wanted to; although he worked hard, the other three men who worked for John did not like him. She looked up at her father, who sat limply at the end of the table eating very little; he no longer asked what was going on outside, seeming to have lost interest in what had once been his life's work.

After lunch Mary put her hat and coat on ready to go down to post her letter. She went to the shed to get her bicycle only to discover it had a flat tyre, so it was with a little reluctance that she decided she would have to walk. The day was mild, and the wind had dried the worst of the mud so the going was easier than it had been. As she walked into Dean along the road to the post-box, she caught sight of a motor car approaching and recognised it as John Watson-Foster's car, driven by Walter. Verity was sitting in the back, her trunk tied to the pannier at the boot of the car; Mary could hear her shouting at Walter to stop as he drew level with Mary.

"Verity, I thought you had gone back to school a week ago," Mary said.

"Yes I should have done but I have been in bed with flu and Father said I should not go back," shrugged Verity. "It's an awful nuisance; I don't want to get behind with my studies and fail the exam for Oxford; that would be a disaster."

"Verity, I'm sure you will pass no matter what," said Mary encouragingly. "You're so determined and I'm sure a bout of flu won't get in your way."

Verity smiled up at Mary, suddenly adding,

"Oh, Mary! I must tell you; Molly has had her baby. It's a boy and both of them are well and I have sent some things up for her with Mrs Tuffnail—"

Mary could sense that Verity was about to issue her with instructions and stood waiting expectantly, a small smile playing on her lips.

"Now, Mary, I don't suppose you would be so kind as to visit poor Molly on my behalf; I really couldn't face the walk all that way and I can't ride as you know. I really think she should have some visitors, it's awfully lonely up there."

"Yes," said Mary quietly, "it's just like living at Cold Harbour."

Verity looked up at Mary, taken aback – she fell silent for a moment.

"I s'pose it is," said Verity, before adding sharply, "but you haven't just had a baby, Mary."

Verity dropped her head and reddened, wishing she had stayed quiet.

"No, Verity, I haven't," said Mary with a small laugh. "Don't worry, I will go and see her and take something for the baby."

Verity smiled, grateful she had not offended her friend.

"And, Mary," she lowered her voice, "we must get the baby christened; I think it would be a good idea if I were the godmother. It would put me in a much better position to help, if you understand my meaning; I'm sure you will be able to suggest these things to Molly; she thinks a lot of you."

"Very well, Verity, I will see what I can do," said Mary taking Verity's hand and squeezing it.

"We must go now or Walter won't be home in the light," sighed Verity. "You will write to me, Mary and let me know all about Molly?"

"Yes, Verity, don't worry, I will write," promised Mary, as the car revved up and pulled off in the direction of Bedford.

With the news of Molly's baby, Mary decided she must visit Ruby to find out what was happening. After posting her letter, she made her way the short distance to blacksmith's forge. She greeted Art who was clanging away at a piece of red-hot iron on his anvil.

"Is Ruby in?" Mary shouted, trying to make her voice heard over the banging.

Art smiled and nodded towards the door to the house, bringing his hammer down hard on the glowing metal and sending sparks flying as he did so – Mary hurriedly brushed one from her coat to stop it burning a hole and moved into the house to find Ruby.

Ruby was in the kitchen on her knees in front of the oven, a dirty white oven glove on her right hand, looking critically at a tray of buns to assess whether they were cooked and muttering under her breath.

"They'll do," she said to herself, rising and pulling the tray of buns from the oven; she stood up, pushed the door of the oven shut with her foot and turning to put the buns on the table. As she did so she caught sight of Mary and leapt in the air with fright, nearly dropping all the buns.

"Gawd bless my soul, Mary Knighton, you did give me a frit standing there like that and not sayin' nuffing!" She put the hot tray on the table and pulled the oven glove off her hand. "I'm gone all goose pimples! You shouldn't creep up on an old lady like that, Mary, you really shouldn't."

"I didn't creep up, Ruby, you just didn't see me come in!" laughed Mary. "And you're hardly an old lady – I'd say you were in your prime."

"Be that as it may, Mary Knighton, to what do I owe the pleasure of your company or can I guess?"

"I expect you can guess, Ruby," said Mary. "I've come to ask about Molly – I saw Verity and she said she had had the baby and you've been to see her."

"That's right," said Ruby removing the buns from the tray. "She's 'ad it and I'm bin to see 'er but I don't know what to say."

"What do you mean?" Mary asked.

"Well she don't want it – says she's goin' to give it away and do I want it! Well I don't know," Ruby sighed.

"She still doesn't want it," Mary said with a shake of her head.

"She says she ain't goin' to 'ave anyfing to do wiv '*im* – I s'pose she means Roland – and any road she's goin' to work in Norfampton at that shop where you worked, Mary, you know the one, whatever it's called."

"Tibbitts," sighed Mary.

"Yes that's the one – she's got 'er 'eart set on workin' there and she says that you are goin' to write to them. She won't take no for an answer."

Ruby shook her head.

"Would you have the baby then, Ruby?" Mary asked.

"Well I didn't' say to 'er; but I would 'ave it like a shot," said Ruby gently. "I know we've got two but I all'as wanted more and we ain't 'ad no luck, not for three years now. I would give anyfink to 'ave another one."

She sat down and rubbed her eyes.

"'E's a lovely little thing, 'e really is, Mary – you must go and see 'im. She don't give 'im no love; they want love, do babies – you know that, don't you?" Tears rolled down Ruby's red cheeks, and she blew her nose on her apron, wiping her eyes. "I don't care where 'e come from, Mary and I don't care who 'is father was, all 'e needs is a bit of love and 'e will be a good boy, I know 'e will. It ain't right, you know, Mary, it ain't right! She ought to love 'im, but she don't and that's that."

"What are you going to do then, Ruby; you can't just take him, can you?" said Mary. "Does Molly know you would have him?"

"No, she don't," said Ruby sharply, "and don't you let 'er know I said so! She might come to like 'im, you never know. But I'm sure she ain't goin' to. I ain't goin' to 'ave 'im until he's weaned whatever and that's goin' to be six mumfs but 'e's a lovely boy; you go and see, Mary, 'e's a lovely boy. E's got blue eyes and fair 'air –what there is of it – although I know a lot of 'em are blue eyes to start off."

Ruby's eyes started to fill with tears again.

"Verity says it ought to be christened and she said that she would be godmother," said Mary hastily. "She told me that I had to sort things out."

"Quite right!" sniffed Ruby, her eyes brightening. "Miss Verity's got 'er 'ead screwed on for someone who's still at school. That baby won't want for nuffink if she's 'is godmother, I know that."

She looked up at Mary, pushing the hot buns towards her.

"'Ave a bun, Mary, you wouldn't get none fresher than that."

"Thank you, Ruby, I don't mind if I do," said Mary, grabbing a hot bun and pulling it apart. "Ruby, you could be another godmother, that would be very suitable. After all you're her best friend."

"S'pose so," sniffed Ruby. "But who's goin' to be the godfather, then?"

"I hadn't thought that far," said Mary slowly. "Who do you think should be, Ruby?"

"Don't know; can't think of no one for the minute. You want someone who's goin' to be of some use to the ol' boy, you know what I mean."

Ruby fell silent and picked up a bun.

"I know," she said suddenly, "I'm just fort of just the right man."

"Who then, Ruby?"

"You know 'im as well as I do, Mary Knighton; even better I s'pose."

"Who? Tell me," said Mary expectantly.

"Guess then," said Ruby with a sly look at Mary.

"Give me a clue then," said Mary impatiently, "I've got no idea who you mean."

"'E's your relation, Mary; there's a clue – now guess," said Ruby, enjoying the suspense.

Mary looked puzzled, mentally working through all her male relations. Finally she looked up and grinned.

"You don't mean William, do you, Ruby?"

"Yes, course I do! Ain't that just the best idea I 'ave 'ad today?"

"Brilliant, Ruby," said Mary happily. "What made you think of him? He's just the right person; but do you think he will do it?"

"'E will if you tell 'im, Mary and make sure you don't let 'im get out of it!"

"I'll go and see him now; I've just got time if I hurry," said Mary, pushing the rest of the bun into her mouth. "We can't have the christening until Verity is back, can we?"

"No, but don't worry, Mary, I can ask Dorcas if she knows when Verity's next home."

"And we'll have to have it in the church, won't we; there's no font at the chapel," said Mary excitedly, before adding, "what about Molly, Ruby? Hadn't we ought to ask her first and her mother and father?"

"Don't you bother, Mary; she'll agree to anyfing," said Ruby confidently. "Just get it sorted out and let me know."

Mary gave Ruby a hug and hurried to the butcher's shop where she thought she would find William.

When she arrived, she could see him through the window with George and his father Roy Lowe. Roy and William were cutting up a pig and George was turning the handle of the mincer, preparing the meat for the sausages. Mary pressed the latch and the door clicked open just as William brought the axe down with a thump to separate the chops. He looked up, surprised to see his cousin in the shop mid-week.

"Mary!" exclaimed William, wiping his hands on his smock and removing his cap. "What brings you here on a cold afternoon like this? We don't usually see you in the week."

"I've got a surprise for you, William! I bet you will never guess what it is."

"Well how could I have any idea; you haven't given me a clue," laughed

William.

"Is Aunt Charlotte in, William?" asked Mary.

"Yes, she's always in, Mary! You know that."

"Well, come in the kitchen and I will tell you the surprise."

She winked at George, taking William's hand and leading him through into the kitchen where Charlotte sat by the range in the rocking chair. She looked up as Mary entered.

"Mary dear, what a lovely surprise, we don't often see you down here in the week."

"No, Aunt Charlotte and I can't stop long as I want to be home before it's dark; but I've got a surprise for William."

"Oh yes, my dear and what's that, may I ask?"

She looked quizzically over her glasses at Mary.

"I bet you can't guess, Aunt Charlotte."

"Well how could I guess, you ninny, you haven't given me any clues! Have you any idea, William?" she asked, looking at her son.

"No, Mother, she won't give me a clue, will you, Mary?"

"Well I can't think of a good clue so I will have to tell you," said Mary, looking from one to the other.

"Go on then, silly, tell me!" said Charlotte impatiently.

"Well William's going to be a godfather!"

"A godfather?" said Charlotte.

"A godfather?" echoed William, surprised. "Who to then, Mary?"

"Molly Webb's son."

There was silence. Mary looked again from her cousin to her aunt; they both looked disapproving.

"She's had the baby, did you know?" said Mary, a bit uncertainly, desperate to fill the silence.

"Yes; I was up there this morning, I knew she had had it," said William quietly.

"Well," said Mary hurrying on, "I saw Verity on her way back to school and she said that the baby must be christened and that she would be godmother and left me to organise things with Molly. Anyway, I went to see Ruby and she said she would be another godmother and it was her idea that William should be the godfather so it's all decided."

Mary stopped expectantly, but still no one said anything. Charlotte eventually lifted her head and said,

"Well, William, if Verity is the godmother you must certainly be the godfather. Verity Watson-Foster is the most thoughtful person I know and that child will never want for anything if she is the godmother, wouldn't you say so, Mary?"

"Yes, Aunt Charlotte," said Mary with conviction. "William, you don't mind, do you?"

"I suppose not," shrugged William. "And if Mother says so, there's not a lot I can do! What are they going to call it?"

"I've no idea," said Mary.

"They can't call it after the father, can they?" said Charlotte under her breath.

"We had better ask Molly," said Mary.

"Oh!" harrumphed Charlotte. "She will have no idea, Mary, you must find a name from the Bible, dear, that's where to look! Molly will agree with what you suggest, I'm sure she will. Make sure it's easy to spell, Mary," she added cuttingly.

"Very well then – I must get along or I will be getting home in the dark," said Mary with a slight frown.

She said her goodbyes and left.

The next day Mary prepared herself to go and see Molly; she searched the house up and down to find something to take for the new baby, but could find nothing suitable. Edgar had been for his breakfast and her father had settled in the front room as usual. Mary paced up and down the kitchen.

"Freda," she shouted into the scullery where Freda was doing the washing up. She came into the kitchen at Mary's call, wiping her hands on her apron as she did.

"Yes?" she intoned, with as much insolence as she dared. "You shouted?"

"Yes, Freda," said Mary, "now you must help me. What am I going to take this new baby of Molly's? I can't go with nothing, it wouldn't be right. Rack your brains – we must have something here that would be suitable."

She strummed her fingers on the side of her mouth and looked eagerly at Freda.

"I dunno why you want to take anyfink; after all it's only a bastard child, ain't it?"

"Freda," Mary snapped angrily, "don't talk like that! It's a new baby, it's precious and we should be generous; you ought to read your Bible and learn some charity."

Freda lowered her eyes, hiding a scowl.

"Come on, Freda!" ordered Mary. "There must be *something*! I want to go now, so I can be back by lunch time."

Freda said nothing but walked over to the dresser, reaching up and taking down a small book.

"You could give 'im this," she said, handing Mary the small book.

"What's this, then?" she demanded.

"It's a prayer book."

"Whose prayer book? It's not new, is it?"

"It were giv' to your bruvver; the one that died. What were 'is name?"

"Edward, I think," said Mary quietly, turning the small book over in her hand. "I never knew him; he died before I was born."

"Well I fink it were 'is," shrugged Freda. "Your muvver used to get it down sometimes and look at it, that's how I know; don't it say 'is name in the front?"

Mary flicked open the book; there on the flyleaf written in copperplate writing it said,

"*Given to Edward Knighton by his parents on his Christening March 2ⁿᵈ 1879.*"

"I can't give him this, Freda," said Mary impatiently. "Not with that written in it."

"Yes, you can," insisted Freda. "It shows you care – to give 'im sumfing of your dead bruvver's."

Mary looked down at the book, deep in thought.

"I suppose I could tear it out," she mused, tracing the writing with her forefinger.

"No," she said decisively, "I won't. You're right, Freda; I will leave this and write more underneath, fetch me the pen and ink."

Mary sat down at the table and dipped the pen, drawing a line under the first inscription and laboriously writing,

"*To*"

She stopped.

"Ah bother, bother, bother," sighed Mary.

"What's up now?" said Freda resignedly.

"I can't write it."

"Why not?"

"I don't know what his name is, do I? We haven't chosen it yet."

"Don't Molly do that?" said Freda. "The choosing, I mean."

"In a manner of speaking, I suppose she does," Mary replied, blowing on the writing to dry the ink and closing the book. She rose abruptly, put on her hat and coat and marched out the room, Freda staring grumpily after her.

The day was clear and bright; there wasn't a cloud in the sky and Mary could feel the warmth of the sun on her face as it glanced across the fields from above the horizon. Rabbits darted into the hedgerows as she walked past and a hare stood on its hind legs, turning its ears this way and that, before loping off along the lane in front of her. In the distance she could hear the puffing of a steam engine, punctuated every so often by the shrill note of a saw blade as it cut through the trunk of a tree. Mary stepped around the deep pot holes in the bridleway; they were still deep and full of water but the tops of the ruts were dry and she stepped nimbly from one to the other up the lane towards Hardwick's.

When she arrived at the house, Ellen was stoking the fire of the range. Molly was sitting in the chair, doing up the buttons on her blouse which was open to her waist showing the very white skin of her chest. On the table was a drawer, which Mary could see had come from the sideboard. Mary tiptoed up and looked in. Swathed in a pile of blankets was the baby; he was only three days old and fast asleep. Ellen came over to Mary with a smile, putting her index finger to her mouth.

"Shhh," she said, "don't wake 'im; we're only just put 'im down."

She looked fondly into the makeshift cradle.

"'E's ever so good, you know, Mary; I ain't known a baby as good as 'im. Much better than she was," whispered Ellen, nodding towards Molly.

"Isn't he lovely," crooned Mary quietly, leaning over the drawer.

"Isn't he lovely, Molly?" Mary whispered to Molly, who looked up at her from her chair.

"S'pose he is, if you say so, Mary," grumbled Molly.

"Of course he is and is he good, Molly?"

"S'pose so, Muvver says 'e is, any road."

She turned her eyes from Mary and looked fiercely into the fire.

"I ain't keepin' 'im, you know, Mary," she said angrily. "I'm said that all along and I don't care what anyone says or anyone finks – I ain't keepin' 'im."

Ellen looked at Mary and back at Molly who was wiping a tear from her eye with her fist.

"Ruby'll 'ave it, I know she will."

"Did she tell you that?" Mary asked sharply.

"No she din't, but I know she will; she wants another one, I know she does."

Mary said nothing, looking at the small angry figure hunched by the fire.

"I've brought him a little present," she said gently, handing Molly the prayer book.

Molly took the book reluctantly, flicked it open and read the inscription on the flyleaf.

"This ain't 'is name," she said confusedly. "Whose name's that then, Mary? Edward Knighton? Don't know 'im."

Mary laughed.

"He was my brother, Molly, he died before I was born. I thought that you would like the book for your baby and I will write his name in it when he's got one. Have you thought of a name for him, Molly?"

"No 'e's just baby," mumbled Molly.

"I saw Verity yesterday and she said that he must be christened and I was to help in sorting things out for you," said Mary hesitantly.

Molly scowled and said nothing.

"Oh, that's kind of you, Mary and kind of Miss Verity to think of us," said Ellen quickly.

"Well he must have some godparents to be christened," said Mary, ploughing on through Molly's silent apathy. "Verity says she will be one and Ruby said she would like to be another. And I asked William if he would be godfather, if that's all right with you, Molly."

"William?" Molly said, surprised. "'*E* won't do it! You mean William Dunmore, Mary?"

"Yes, William," said Mary.

Molly gave a snort of laughter.

"Well, I don't mind if they want to do it – I don't see why we 'ave to!" shrugged Molly. "But if Miss Verity says so, maybe we had better."

She sighed and rose from the chair, stretching her arms upwards before bringing them down again and shaking out her limbs like a dog. She plucked a shawl from the back of a chair and wrapped herself in it.

"The other thing to do, Molly, is to choose a name for him," persisted Mary. "Aunt Charlotte said that we should look in the Bible for a name – what do you think? I've brought a Bible for you to look at." She pulled her worn Bible from the basket and offered it to Molly.

"I'm got one of 'em," Molly said, slightly indignantly. "Ain't I, Muvver?"

"Yes, you got it from the Sunday school at Melchbourne."

"So what about a name?" Mary said firmly.

"Don't worry, Mary, I'll choose the name and I will tell you when it's christened."

"Are you sure you don't want to do it now?" Mary asked.

"No," said Molly, throwing herself grumpily back in the chair.

"Well, I must go then and get lunch ready," said Mary quietly, aware that she had outstayed her welcome.

"Ain't you goin' to 'ave a cup of tea while you're 'ere?" Ellen asked.

"No, that will make me late," said Mary determinedly, before adding with a wink. "I would have to nip behind the hedge on the way home if I had any tea."

Ellen laughed, as Molly rose abruptly and moved towards Mary.

"Mary?" she said shyly.

"Yes, Molly."

"Thank you for comin' and for the book." She hesitated for a moment. "And, Mary?"

"Yes, Molly," Mary said.

"You ain't forgot that you said that you would write to that shop in Norfampton?"

"No, Molly," said Mary gently, putting her arm round Molly's shoulders and giving her a hug. Molly wiped her nose with her fist and smiled for the first time.

The day for the christening was fixed for Verity's half term and was to be at three o'clock on Sunday afternoon. The small group of people involved gathered at the church; Molly and her parents had walked down from Hardwick's, stopping at Ruby's house to feed the baby. Lucy had walked to the church with Mary, as she had Sunday off and William, Charlotte and Thomas all arrived with Verity and Dorcas. All the women stood in a crowd around Molly and the baby, cooing and admiring the little lad peeping up between the blankets. The Reverend Heaton arrived in a top hat and frock coat and made himself known to the congregation in loud, ringing tones.

"Just give me a few minutes and I will be ready," he said pompously, moving off into the church.

The congregation filed in – Verity and Dorcas sitting in their usual front pew, Molly and her family at the back.

The service started with prayers before Molly and the godparents were invited to the font to christen the baby. Reverend Heaton turned to Molly to ask the child's name.

"Goshen Hardwick Edward William," said Molly loudly.

Reverend Heaton started slightly and looked dubiously at Molly.

"You can't call him Goshen, Molly; that's the name of a place," he whispered urgently.

"I know it is," she replied aggressively. "It's in the Bible, ain't it? Mary said

I 'ad to choose a name from the Bible and I'm done it! I *can* read, you know."

She stared hard at Reverend Heaton, daring him to say any more.

"But Molly, do you really want to call him Goshen?" insisted Reverend Heaton.

"Yes I do," said Molly firmly. "I'm writ it down on this bit a paper; I can write too, you know."

She pulled a piece of paper from the pocket of her coat and thrust it towards the incredulous vicar.

"Goshen's a land of plenty, ain't it?"

"Yes, it is, my dear," agreed Reverend Heaton with a small shrug.

"But Goshen must 'ave been a bloke they named the land after, like 'Ardwick must 'ave been a bloke they named our farm after; ain't that right?"

"Well I suppose it might be," sighed Reverend Heaton – unable to argue with the logic being applied.

"I'm calling him Goshen after the land of plenty; Hardwick after where 'e were born, Edward after Mary's bruvver – 'e's got 'is prayer book you know – and William after Williyum and *that's* why!" said Molly crossly. Her bottom lip started to quiver and tears threatened as she turned and looked at William.

Verity grabbed her hand and held it tightly, before edging towards Reverend Heaton and whispering hurriedly in his ear.

"Of course," he said uncertainly, with a small flicker of the eyebrows. "Goshen it is then!"

Chapter Thirty-Four
The Manor

It did not take long for the excitement of the christening to wear off, but Mary still had her visit to Northampton to look forward to. She had arranged to spend two nights away, as Lucy's day off would coincide with her trip and it would be easier to leave the Cold Harbour household. She had written to Rupert telling him of her visit to Northampton and he had written straight back inviting Mary and Rebecca to lunch with his mother, which she had accepted.

After a quick breakfast, and having packed the night before, Mary left Cold Harbour at half past seven in the morning, leaving strict instructions with Freda as to her duties while she was away. It took her about an hour and a quarter to cycle to the station at Rushden and she arrived in plenty of time to catch the train to Wellingborough, from where she caught the connection to Northampton.

As the train drew into the station she could see Rupert on the platform waiting for her; she waved out of the window as the train came to a stop.

"How did you know I was coming on this train?" she said excitedly, skipping out of the carriage, putting her bag down and flinging her arms around Rupert's shoulders, an action which surprised Rupert and Mary alike.

"Oh, Mary, it's so good to see you again; it seems an age since I saw you last and that was such a sad occasion."

"Yes, but how did you know to meet the train?" she asked.

"I guessed!" laughed Rupert. "When I invited Rebecca to lunch tomorrow, she replied and told me the day you were coming, so I decided that this was the first train you could possibly be on! I decided to meet this one and all the others after that, how's that?"

He picked up her bag, slinging it over his shoulder and grabbing Mary's hand in his.

"How have you got the time off work then, Rupert? What will your father say?"

"Oh no need to worry; I'm supposed to be at the cattle market, but that's only just round the corner so I can soon be back, and I've got someone to note down the prices for me while I'm away."

They walked out into the station yard.

"Now, Mary, how are you going to get to Rebecca's home? A cab? Or there is a motor taxi if you would prefer?"

"No, no, Rupert, I'm going to walk."

"Are you sure, Mary, it's a long way and the last bit is uphill?" said Rupert, looking concerned.

"No it's not far," laughed Mary, squeezing his hand. "It can't be much more than half a mile and it will do me good to walk."

"But what about your bag?"

"I can carry that, can't I? I have done so far, didn't you notice?"

"Don't tease me, Mary or I may cry," said Rupert dolefully.

"Go on then, you silly," she laughed, putting her hand to the back of his head and tipping his bowler hat forward over his eyes, as she had seen her brother Henry do to William so many times. Rupert stopped in his tracks.

"I'm going to cry," he said determinedly.

"No, you're not!" giggled Mary, watching Rupert grin as he put his bowler back on again.

"No, I'm not," he agreed with a laugh. "Look here, Mary, I'll walk halfway with you and then I will have to run back, how about that?"

"That will be lovely," agreed Mary, squeezing Rupert's hand again.

"Now, you're coming to lunch tomorrow at half past twelve and Rebecca is coming as well," chattered Rupert happily.

"Yes, Rupert, but what about your mother? How does she feel about me coming?"

"Don't worry about Mother, Mary, I'm sure you can hold your own."

"I hope you're right, Rupert; I wouldn't want to blot my copy book, would I?" She laughed again.

"You won't do that, I can assure you, and Mother will be fine, you'll see."

"And what about your father? I haven't ever met him."

"Oh he never comes home for lunch; he's far too busy with the paper, we only ever see him at home on Sundays, he leaves most things at home for Mother to deal with."

The two walked on.

"Rupert, when are you off to the Argentine?" asked Mary suddenly.

"Two weeks," said Rupert gently. "Mother's bought me a trunk and she's packing it already! She does fuss so! I'm sure I could do it myself."

They walked a bit further in companionable silence.

"Now," said Rupert suddenly, "let's look at the time."

He stopped in his tracks and took his gold pocket watch from his waistcoat pocket.

"Blimey," he exclaimed, "I've got to go, Mary; they will be selling the best beef animals soon and I will have to get the details of those."

"I will see you tomorrow then, Rupert, at half past twelve," said Mary with a smile.

"I can't wait," he said, pecking her on the cheek and turning on his heel.

Mary waved as he ran off in the opposite direction.

It wasn't long before she was at Rebecca's house. Violet answered the door, but Rebecca wasn't far behind, limping up the hall with the aid of a stick. Mary thought how pretty she was, her long dark hair framing the sharp features of her handsome face. She had lost some weight since Mary had seen her last and a little of the colour in her face had gone, but she smiled broadly when she saw Mary and seemed to radiate pleasure.

"Mary, how lovely to see you – I've been longing for you to come!" Rebecca declared happily.

She dropped her stick with a clatter and flung both her arms round her friend, embracing her and pressing her cheek to Mary's. She leant back and let go of Mary's shoulders. This evidently was not a good idea – no sooner had Rebecca released her grip on Mary than she started to sink to the floor without the support of the stick; Violet lunged towards her, grabbing her firmly under her left arm, as Mary held onto her right arm. Violet handed her the stick as she regained her balance.

"You all right now, Miss Rebecca?" said Violet worriedly.

"Yes, I'm fine, Violet," said Rebecca sharply, drawing herself up to her full height. "Violet, can you take Mary's bag and bring us some coffee please; we will be in the drawing room. Come on, Mary, follow me."

She turned, and hobbled off down the hall into the drawing room. She put her hand on the back of a chair, pointing with her stick to where Mary had to sit and plonking herself down in an armchair opposite. She threw the stick disgustedly on the carpet.

"Bloody leg," she hissed, wincing with pain as she eased herself into the chair.

"Rebecca," said Mary with a cheeky smile, "you shouldn't swear you know."

"Mary, if I want to bloody well swear I will bloody well swear and I don't care a bugger," said Rebecca quietly.

She looked nervously round to make sure that Violet had not heard and they both giggled.

"Where did you learn all those words, Rebecca?" Mary asked.

"From my bloody stepmother, who else! Common woman! I will never know why Father married her, she is a complete nightmare."

She shook her head despairingly.

"But, Mary, tell me all your news; it's such a long time since I've seen you and I have been stuck here with a broken leg for months. I'm so sorry about your poor mother; how dreadful for you. And Rupert! Have you seen Rupert? He worships you, you know that, don't you, Mary? He really worships you."

The cascade of questions stopped sharply as Violet brought in the coffee, pulling up one table for Rebecca's cup and one for Mary's, before placing the cups down and leaving.

"No more swearing now," said Rebecca. "Can't let the servants think we use bad language!"

She winked at Mary, before listening as her friend related the story of her mother's death, Molly's baby and Rupert.

"Lunch!" announced Rebecca an hour and a half later. "What are we going to do for lunch? Let's go out, Mary – I haven't been out for ages and ages. Let's go to The County – it's the only place we will get in without booking."

"I'd like that," said Mary.

"How do we get there though?" sighed Rebecca. "That's the next thing; I can't walk all that way and the motor car is out taking Adelaide somewhere or other. I know – I'll get Violet to cycle down and get a cab from the station to pick us up."

Rebecca rang the bell and explained to Violet what she needed and minutes later – having seen a cab on the street moments earlier – Violet returned having successfully hailed the cab.

"Come on, Mary," said Rebecca, hopping along the corridor and making her way upstairs one at a time, "we've got to get ready – tell him to wait, Violet, we won't be two minutes."

Lunch at The County Hotel was much as it was when Mary had gone with Verity; like Verity, Rebecca took control, ordering all the food, wine and coffee, and putting the bill on her father's account.

"What would you like to do this afternoon, Mary?" Rebecca asked, as they sat in the lounge having their coffee.

"I would love to go to Tibbitts to see Mrs Stevens, if there's time," said Mary.

"Yes it would be nice to go there, and I'm sure I can get that far," said Rebecca, sipping her coffee. "Mary!" Rebecca's face lit up. "I've just remembered! Father met someone the other day who knew you; in fact Father bought a horse from him. Father doesn't like horse dealers but he said that the horse was so good that he had to buy it all the same. Do you know who I mean, Mary?"

Rebecca put down her coffee cup and looked questioningly at Mary; she laughed.

"Mary, you've gone red! You do know him, don't you? Father said that he was very smartly dressed and much younger than all the other horse dealers he had met. Come on, Mary, I want to know. Who is this man?"

"Well I don't know him well," said Mary, refusing to look Rebecca in the eye. "I only know him because he's got a farm next to my brother Henry and he knows him. He called in to see Father after Mother died, that's all."

Mary looked down, and swirled a spoon around her coffee cup vigorously.

"Come on then, Mary, what does he look like? Tell me more."

Mary shifted uncomfortably on her chair, unwilling to address the topic of

Noble Ladds.

"Well, he's well dressed and he's a horse dealer and farmer and that's about it," she said grudgingly.

"How old is he, then?"

"I don't know; he looks about twenty-five, but I really don't know."

"Well, well, well," said Rebecca with a small laugh, "you really are a dark horse, aren't you, Mary? Anyway, the horse is a splendid animal; Father's never had a better hunter, he's even entered it in the point-to-point and we're all going to see it race."

"Yes, I'm going to it as well I think, I had a card from Martha the other day," said Mary quietly.

"Splendid," said Rebecca. "Who are you going with?"

"My brother and his wife are taking me."

"Anyone else, Mary?" Rebecca asked slyly.

Mary sighed and reddened again.

"I think Noble Ladds is coming as well; they farm next to Henry you see, so they know him."

"So you can introduce me then, can't you, Mary?" giggled Rebecca.

"I suppose so," Mary agreed, with very little enthusiasm.

Rebecca sighed and shifted her leg to a more comfortable position.

"I wish I could ride in the point-to-point; don't you think that would be exciting, Mary? It's not fair that girls don't get any chances to have fun, we don't even have the vote."

"Yes, Verity says that women should have the vote," said Mary, glad of a change of topic.

"You must agree with that, Mary, surely you do?" said Rebecca pointedly.

"Yes, I suppose I do," shrugged Mary, who had given the subject very little thought.

"But it doesn't change the fact that I can't ride in the point-to-point," frowned Rebecca.

"So who will ride the horse? And what's it called?"

"It's called Speedy – but I don't know who will ride it. One of Father's friends, I expect, or he might get a real jockey, I suppose."

They finished their coffee, Rebecca signed the bill for their lunch and the pair made their way slowly towards Tibbitts, where they went straight to Ladies' Fashion. Mary recognised none of the girls behind the counter so she asked if she could see Mrs Stevens.

"Who shall I say, miss?"

"Just say Mary Knighton," said Mary, as the girl went towards the office. No sooner had she gone than she was back again, followed by Mrs Stevens.

"Mary my dear, how good it is to see you!" exclaimed Mrs Stevens, beaming. "You look so well and Miss Harding – this is a great pleasure! What can I do for you ladies?"

"Oh I only came to see how you were, Mrs Stevens," said Mary, "as I was in Northampton."

"You don't want your old job back, do you, Mary?" said Mrs Stevens hopefully. "You can have it right now – I'm sure Mr Peveril would agree."

"I'm so sorry, Mrs Stevens, I would love to come back, but I'm afraid my mother died at Christmas and I still have my father to look after at the moment."

"Oh I'm so sorry to hear that, Mary," said Mrs Stevens kindly. "What about your sister? I can't remember her name."

"Lucy, yes. She's training to be a nurse now; she stayed at home all last year so it's my turn now," shrugged Mary. "How is Mr Peveril?"

"He's very well, thank you, but I expect he's having forty winks at the moment and I wouldn't want to disturb him."

"No, no, don't do that," agreed Mary with a smile.

"Well is there anything I can interest you in, Mary, or perhaps you, Miss Harding?" said Mrs Stevens, smiling the smile of a good saleswoman.

"What about a winter coat, then?" said Rebecca. "I know it's nearly the end of the winter but I bet they are cheaper now; Father would be pleased if I could knock the price down."

"Just give me a moment, Miss Harding, and I'm sure we can show you something," beamed Mrs Stevens.

She turned and shouted at a small blonde shop girl to go and fetch a selection of coats.

"We know your size don't we, Miss Harding?"

"I hope so," said Rebecca, "I spend enough money here."

At that moment Frisby entered the room.

"Just the man," Mrs Stevens said. "Frisby – look who's here."

"You don't say!" squeaked Frisby, bobbing up and down excitedly. "It's Mary Knighton, it is! How splendid, absolutely capital and how are you, Mary?"

"Very well, Frisby and you?" said Mary shaking Frisby's outstretched hand.

"Oh I'm all behind as usual but you know how it is."

He suddenly noticed Rebecca.

"Oh beg my pardon, Miss Harding, I didn't notice you there! I hope you are well and Mrs Stevens is looking after you."

"Yes, I am well and yes, she is," said Rebecca, amused.

"Mrs Stevens," said Frisby determinedly, "I will go and see if Mr Peveril is awake; he will not want to miss Mary, I know he won't."

He scuttled out, to return moments later.

"Sound asleep like the proverbial log he is; but you will be a little while – we will see if he is still asleep then. Shall I send for some tea, Mrs Stevens?"

"Yes do that, Frisby; Miss Harding, can we offer you some tea?"

"That would be nice," Rebecca replied, easing herself into a chair to rest her leg. Frisby went off to order the tea and Rosy came back laden with coats, only to be sent immediately back for the right size. Frisby returned and leant on the counter, examining his fingernails before rubbing them on the sleeve of his jacket.

"You know what I'm going to do, Mrs Stevens?" Frisby said, staring up at the ceiling.

"No, what are you going to do, Frisby?" asked Mrs Stevens, with a good deal of apprehension.

"What I'm going to do is to have a look at Mr Peveril and if he's still asleep I'm going somehow to wake him! He will be so cross, Mary, if we let you go without him knowing."

He tottered off again down the corridor, wiggling his hips as he went.

"Mary Knighton!" came a roar from the corridor, followed by the owner of the voice, almost skipping down into the department.

"Mary, is that really you?" exclaimed Peveril, rushing towards Mary and grasping both her hands, before pressing his cheek to hers.

"My dear girl, it is so good to see you! Can I immediately offer you your old job back! When can you start? Tomorrow I hope, I will increase your pay and what else do you want, eh?"

He gazed hopefully at Mary, who blushed and looked down.

"Oh, I am so sorry," said Peveril, turning to Rebecca, "how rude of me, Miss Harding! I did not see you there." He grabbed Rebecca's hand and kissed it. "It is always a pleasure to see you in our shop especially with Miss Knighton."

"And without my stepmother," Rebecca added with a smile.

"I didn't say that, did I, Miss Harding?" said Peveril, with a wolfish grin.

"Now, my dears, step this way! Please come into my office for some refreshment."

"I have ordered tea, Mr Peveril," interjected Mrs Stevens.

"Ah so kind, Mrs Stevens, we will have it in my office and you come as well and Frisby – Frisby! Where are you, man?"

"I'm here, Mr Peveril," said a voice at Peveril's elbow.

"Come and sort out chairs and pour the tea and things," instructed Peveril.

Frisby dashed ahead of the entourage to the office, arranging three chairs in front of Peveril's desk and a table for the teacups.

"Can't tempt you to anything a little stronger, can I?" said Peveril hopefully, looking over his glasses at them; they all shook their heads.

"I'll have one, Frisby, if you please," boomed Peveril, adding with a wink, "– for medicinal purposes, you understand."

He turned with a smile to Mary.

"Now, Mary, what have you been up to since you left us, busy I hope?"

"Yes, sir, but I'm afraid my mother died before Christmas, which we have had to deal with."

"Yes, yes, yes, I did hear that. Can I offer my sincere condolences, my dear; what a blow to lose one's mother, I know just how it feels."

He sipped delicately from his glass of port.

"And of course, Miss Harding, you have been through the same loss at a much earlier age; it must have been awful for you."

"Yes," agreed Rebecca wryly, "it would be better not to lose one's mother, but often there is no choice in these matters."

"Quite so, quite so, my dear," mused Peveril, absently running his index finger around the top of his glass until it hummed.

"Mary Knighton," he addressed Mary again, "I am assuming that you are not going to take up my offer of your job back?"

"No, sir," said Mary, "I'm afraid as much as I would like to, I have to continue to look after my father who is also in poor health."

"I quite understand, my dear, but is there anything else I can do in the meantime?"

Mary sat forward in her chair and placed her teacup down.

"There is one thing, sir," she said.

"Go on then."

"There is a young girl in our village who has set her heart on working here and I said I would ask if there were any positions available."

"Oh," said Peveril, glancing at Mrs Stevens.

"Is she like you, Mary?"

"No, sir," admitted Mary quietly.

"Is she assistant material? Does she say Northampton with an 'F' or a 'TH', Mary?"

"With an 'F', sir," said Mary, trying not to laugh.

"Can she spell, then?"

"Yes, sir," said Mary eagerly. "She reads and writes and can do sums, I know she can; I know she would have to work her way up."

"Mary, there's more to this girl than you are telling me," said Peveril suspiciously. "She wants to get out of Dean for a reason; something has happened; I can see that. There is more, Mary, isn't there?"

"Yes, sir," admitted Mary reluctantly.

"Come on then," said Peveril impatiently.

"She had a baby recently out of wedlock; but she will have it adopted and then wants to move on to somewhere new."

"Ah, I thought as much," said Peveril, nodding his head sadly. "Well, Mary, I don't hold out much hope, but we may have something in six months or so; certainly not now. And we always need girls to hire as cleaners or for the sewing room. You must ask again in six months."

They chatted for a little longer and Rebecca tried on several coats, but as she could not find anything she liked, they sent for a cab and went home.

For the lunch party the next day, the two girls were to be taken in the motor car. The Nelson's house, the Manor, was even bigger than the Hardings'; it had a huge garden peppered with enormous trees and the lawns ran down to a small lake on the edge of the town. They rang the doorbell and a maid answered the door, ushering the two girls into the drawing room where Rupert and his mother Christiana were talking heatedly. Rupert rose and shook Rebecca and Mary's hand before offering them a glass of sherry and asking them to sit down. It became instantly apparent that lunch was going to start with a thorough interrogation from Christiana; she already knew Rebecca well, addressing her by her Christian name and enquiring after the health of her father.

"He's very well," Rebecca replied, "but it's coming to the end of the hunting season and I don't know how he will occupy himself after that."

"And his wife?" Christiana enquired absently, as if she had forgotten Adelaide's name.

"She's well; but we don't see a lot of her – she has lots of friends, you know."

"Yes," Christiana replied condescendingly, "I suppose she has."

She smiled frostily, and turned to Mary – her cheeks noticeably straining under the effort of forced civility.

"Miss Knighton, Rupert tells me that your mother is recently deceased; can I offer my sincere condolences to you and your family. And is your father still with us, Miss Knighton?"

"Her name is Mary, Mother," interrupted Rupert, a little nervously. "We all call her Mary."

Christiana looked round at him over her glasses.

"Thank you, Rupert," she said icily.

"My father *is* still with us, Mrs Nelson," replied Mary hastily, "but he is in poor health."

"And he is a farmer, I believe, Miss Knighton?"

"Yes he is, but he does not do much now, due to his infirmity."

"And you have brothers and sisters, Miss Knighton?" Christiana asked.

"Yes – I have one married sister and one married brother, and my younger sister is training to be a nurse," replied Mary, determined to stick to the barest bones of information.

Rebecca yawned obviously, twisting her glass of sherry between her fingers and looking out of the bay window distractedly.

"And where were you educated, Miss Knighton?" fired Christiana, as Rupert started to shift agitatedly in his chair.

He looked desperately towards Rebecca, but Rebecca put her finger to her lips and looked back out into the garden.

"I went to the school in the village, Mrs Nelson."

"Hmm," sniffed Christiana, tapping the table impatiently, "you have no French, then?"

"Yes, I have learnt a little French from my cousin William and my friend Verity."

"Verity who?" demanded Christiana.

"Verity Watson-Foster," Mary replied.

"You mean John Watson-Foster's daughter?" said Christiana, visibly sitting higher in her chair.

"Yes, Mrs Nelson, she goes up to Oxford in the autumn and she's a good friend."

"Yes, we had heard that she was going to Oxford; a great achievement *and* without the help of a mother, like you, poor dear," she sighed, looking pityingly at Rebecca.

"Rebecca, did your parents host Miss Knighton when she worked at that shop?"

"Oh no," said Rebecca languidly. "Mary *has* stayed with us quite a lot, but when she was at Tibbitts she stayed with her uncle in Rushden."

"And who is your uncle, my dear?" Christiana addressed Mary again.

"George Henry Chambers, Mrs Nelson," replied Mary.

Christiana sat up again, rocking from side to side a little in excitement.

"George Henry Chambers is your uncle?"

"Yes, Mrs Nelson."

"Well I never, who would have thought it," muttered Christiana, shaking her head a little.

The gong sounded in the hall and Christiana rose imperiously.

"Rebecca, Mary, lunch is served if you would like to follow me into the dining room. Rupert, you will have to carve."

After lunch the girls and Rupert walked in the garden, Rupert promising he would write every week to Mary while he was in the Argentine. The car arrived to collect them and they thanked Mrs Nelson and said goodbye to Rupert. As soon as the car moved off Rebecca turned to Mary.

"Well, Mary Knighton," she said with a wink, "he's yours for the taking if you want to wait, but I rather suspect you know that, don't you?"

Mary smiled and looked out the window as the huge house passed out of sight.

Chapter Thirty-Five
The Point-to-Point

The last Saturday of March brought with it the day of the point-to-point. The point-to-point was the first time Mary had been out since her trip to Northampton and she made every effort to look as smart as she could, putting on a small amount of cosmetics left over from her time at Tibbitts before going down to collect her things from the kitchen, where Freda stood in front of the range.

"Oh, Miss Mary, you do look lovely," exclaimed Freda, taking Mary by surprise, "I didn't know you had cosmetics, Miss Mary; it does look smart."

Mary smiled and fussed with her coat.

"Freda, help me a moment; are all my buttons done up and is my hair straight at the back?" she said urgently, spinning round to show Freda her hair.

"They're all done up, miss and your 'air is straight," assured Freda, as Mary put on her straw hat, pushing the pin through and straightening the hat as best she could.

"Come over, let me do that," said Freda, standing on tiptoe to level Mary's hat and helping her on with her coat. She stood back as Mary did up the buttons of her coat.

"You do look a picture, Miss Mary; you are going to turn all the heads today, you really will," she said, gripping Mary's arm and giving her a peck on the cheek. "Now I'll give you an 'and to get all this on your bike; are you sure that they can't come to pick you up? You're goin' to get all dirty gettin' down the 'ill."

"Don't worry, Freda, I'll be careful; just you look after Father, won't you."

"Don't worry about 'im, miss, 'e'll be fine," assured Freda, following Mary out to her bike and helping her load it with food for the picnic. The day was cloudy but not cold, although it looked like there might be a chance of a shower, so Mary tied an umbrella to the panier of her bike next to the food. Freda opened the gate for her to ride down the track and with a wave she was off.

At the bottom of the hill, she parked her bike against the hedge, unloaded her picnic and waited by the gates that led to Melchbourne Park – Henry and Martha were to pick her up from here. She could see a long way along the road back to Dean; there was no sign of the racing party, but she could see a bicycle approaching from the top of the small hill. It was William; he waved as he approached, drawing up and stopping next to his cousin, his face scarlet with the effort from bicycling.

"Are you going to the point-to-point, William?" Mary asked, surveying her cousin's red face.

"Yes, I'm trying to beat Henry there, but he's soon going to catch up, I'm sure," panted William.

"How far back are they? I'm supposed to be being picked up by them," moaned Mary.

"Don't worry, they're on their way," puffed William. "They stopped at the butcher's shop to water the horses and give them a rest, but I think Mother has been talking to Martha and that has held them up."

He spun his pedals backwards and sat back on his bike.

"Noble Ladds is with them," he said disapprovingly.

Mary rolled her eyes.

"I know you don't like him, William Dunmore, but he's been a good friend to Henry so just keep your opinions to yourself," ordered Mary.

William spun his pedals again and looked at the ground.

"Anything you say, Mary," he muttered, pushing the pedals round the right way and starting off up the hill, standing up to put all his weight on the pedals.

"I'll see you when you arrive," he shouted back over his shoulder. "I think I can see Henry coming now."

Mary looked back down the road to see a carriage moving quickly down the hill, pulled by two bay horses. As it approached, she could see Noble Ladds sitting up at the top driving, with Henry and Martha side by side in the carriage, admiring the countryside as they travelled along.

"Whoa," Noble shouted to the horses, pulling the reins as the carriage came to a halt. He lifted his bowler to Mary and jumped down as Henry got out the back.

"You made it then," she said with a hint of impatience, before hurriedly adding, "what a splendid carriage, where did you get it?"

"Oh, I borrowed it from a friend," said Noble casually, "but it's seen better days I'm afraid; I don't know whether the roof would go up without falling to bits, so let's hope it doesn't rain."

"And the horsehair's all coming out of the seats," called down Martha. "It's awfully prickly to sit on." Henry took the two baskets from Mary's hands and passed them to Martha, before sharply slipping behind Mary and tickling her waist. Her right arm flailed round in a flash and Henry jumped back to avoid being hit.

"Don't do that, Henry; you don't get any better, do you?" she shrieked, leaping back to avoid a repeat.

"You tell him, Mary!" said Martha. "He's always doing that to me and I'm having a baby in four months."

Noble Ladds pulled the step down to get Mary into the carriage, the bracket breaking off as he did so, leaving the step hanging limply in his hand.

"Oh no," he groaned, "there won't be much left of this old girl before long." He looked teasingly at Mary.

"Now how are you going to get in, Mary?"

"The one the other side's all right," said Martha, but Mary had already pulled her skirt up and put her foot on the niche by the door, ready to haul herself in. Noble put one arm under her knees and one behind her back and lifted her daintily up into the carriage. Mary could smell his cologne, mixed with the smell of the small cigars he smoked. She turned round and looked down on Noble.

"Thank you, kind sir," she said, reddening a little, and sitting down next to Martha.

"Isn't this grand?" Martha said. "It beats our trap any day. I know it's seen better days, but we can't have everything, can we?"

"Let's be off then," said Noble as Henry jumped in beside Martha and pulled the small door shut. It was a three-mile trip to the point-to-point and the last bit of the journey was up a steep hill; at the bottom of the hill Noble pulled up.

"Everyone out," he shouted. "Except for Martha, that is."

He jumped down from the driver's seat and opened the door of the carriage for Mary. Mary stood up and went to open the door with the unbroken steps – it was stuck fast. She turned to see that Noble was standing by the other door, both arms outstretched. She moved towards him and he gripped her round the waist, pulling her towards the little door.

"Come on," he said, "jump!"

Mary launched herself to cover the thirty inches to the ground. As she fell, Noble pulled her close to him, lowering her gently; she felt the front of her coat brush his jacket. He squeezed her waist briefly before releasing his grip.

"I'll lead them," shouted Henry, who had grabbed the reins of the horse and started up the hill.

"Are you sure you don't want me to walk?" insisted Martha. "I know I could; it makes me feel like an invalid to sit up here."

"You sit there, Martha; they will manage with only you," said Noble, walking beside the carriage with Mary.

The nearer they got to the course the more people they met; many were walking, but some rode and some were in a variety of wagons, carts, traps and carriages. There were also several motor cars, belching out smoke and frightening the horses as they went past. At the top of the hill they could see the course entrance, where William was stood waiting for them.

"There's William," shouted Henry. "Give him a whistle, Mary – that'll wake him up."

Mary put two fingers in her mouth and blew a piercing whistle; everyone around looked up including William. Mary tried to hide her face, giggling at the reaction of the rest of her party.

"I didn't know girls could whistle like that," said Noble admiringly.

"I can't do it," admitted Henry. "I've tried and tried but I can't make a sound, can you, Noble?"

"No, I'm hopeless; do it again, Mary."

"No," laughed Mary. "Everyone's looking now; come on, let's get going."

She hoisted her skirt and leapt into the carriage before Noble had a chance to lift her up again. He took a sidelong glance at her and jumped into the driver's seat.

Towards the bottom of the field where the start and finish line lay, there were already a lot of people milling around; a band was playing and the bookmakers were chalking their boards ready for the first race. In a small marquee, race organisers sat writing down the entries as each entrant came up to pay the small fee for racing their horse; all the horses had to have hunted with the Oakley that season or they would not be eligible to race. Another smaller tent housed the bar and another served food; pigs and sheep were being spit-roasted over log fires and the smell wafted tantalisingly round on the wind. Horses of all shapes and sizes roamed around the fields – some being ridden, others led and some tethered to rails or stakes in the ground, nonchalantly grazing, their ears flicking intermittently back and forward. Henry led the carriage to a spot against the hedge, taking the horses from their harnesses and tethering them on a long rein to the carriage. The first race was at half past one, so they decided to have a look round before coming back to eat the picnic and watch the racing.

"Have you brought any food, William?" Mary asked her cousin, who had joined them. "We've got plenty if you haven't."

"Mother made a few sandwiches."

"Where are they, then?"

"In my pocket," he said, tapping his jacket pocket.

"There can't be very many," laughed Mary. "You had better come and have some of ours. Come with us, we're going to have a look round before we eat."

After their picnic, Noble and Henry made for the beer tent, Martha, Mary and William following slowly behind them. In the distance Mary could see a girl walking with a stick; she immediately excused herself from the party to run across to the limping figure.

"Rebecca," she shouted, waving frantically, deciding against whistling.

Rebecca was in deep conversation with her father; they were admiring the mare that he had recently bought from Noble Ladds, and she looked up as Mary approached.

"Mary, how lovely to see you. I'm so pleased you could come! Father, look who is here, it's Mary." Mr Harding took his cap off and shook Mary's hand.

"Have you ever seen such a splendid animal, Mary? This is the best hunter I've had," he said proudly.

"I have seen it actually, Mr Harding, I saw it the day you bought it from Noble Ladds."

"Ah you know him, then."

"Yes, he farms next to my brother and brought us all here today in his carriage."

"Well it's the first time I've seen the animal," said Rebecca. "And I'm so jealous; I wish I could ride it – I would show them a thing or two. Isn't it a splendid animal, Mary, don't you think so?"

"Yes, it really is and it looks in really good condition," Mary agreed.

"I keep it at old Allibone's; he looks after horses better than anyone I know," said Mr Harding wisely. "Mary, you must introduce me to Mr Ladds, come on where is he?" demanded Rebecca.

"He's over there with my brother Henry and his wife Martha."

"Come on then, let's go," said Rebecca, hobbling towards Henry. "Father, I am going to be introduced to Mr Ladds, are you coming?"

"I'll come over in a jiffy," replied Mr Harding, having caught sight of one of his old hunting friends, "you go on, I'll catch up."

Rebecca nodded and walked on with her stick – progress was very slow.

"Isn't your leg better yet then, Rebecca?" Mary asked.

"No it bloody well isn't! It's so frustrating; I can't ride for another three to four months, that's what the doctor says."

She shook her head angrily and hobbled on.

"That's your cousin William, Mary, isn't it?" Rebecca asked.

"Yes that's him," said Mary with a smile.

"I feel so embarrassed every time I see him after falling off on the hunt in front of them. I'm sure I was awfully rude, did he say anything to you, Mary?"

"No, he just said you were very pretty," said Mary with a grin.

"No, he didn't," cried Rebecca, reddening.

"Yes he did, so there!" laughed Mary, sticking her tongue out at Rebecca.

Henry and Noble Ladds both had pints of beer in their hands when Mary and

Rebecca approached; on noticing them, both men raised their caps and Mary introduced Rebecca to them and then to Martha and William.

"Can I get you a drink, Miss Harding and Mary, what would you like?"

"I don't drink beer," said Rebecca, "but what's that Martha and William are drinking?"

"It's golden lemonade – it's good," said Martha.

"I'll have that then," she said.

"So will I," said Mary, "I really don't like beer."

"Don't you like beer, William?" Rebecca asked.

"His mother does not approve, does she, William?" Henry said laughingly. "Ain't allowed to have beer – it's sinful."

William looked at the ground but said nothing.

"Don't you take no notice of him, William," said Martha angrily. "He has too much of it on a regular basis, I know he does."

"Mr Ladds," Rebecca said loudly, turning to Noble in a bid to change the subject, "I believe that you sold my father 'Speedy'. Where did you get such a splendid animal? I have never seen one as good as that out with this hunt."

"I bought her in a sale, Miss Harding," said Noble with a smile, "and rode her myself for a while; but that's my business – horse dealing."

"And you look very much the part, may I say," said Rebecca.

"Should I take that as a compliment, Miss Harding, or otherwise?" said Noble, with a rakish grin.

"I said it as a compliment, Mr Ladds; you can take it how you wish," Rebecca retorted simply.

"Now, now," interjected Mary, who had been watching this interaction with interest, "we must keep an eye on the time or won't be able to have our picnic before the first race. William, what's the time?"

"It's about midday, Mary, give or take a little."

"Very good; then everyone back to the carriage for food. Are you coming, Rebecca? We have plenty."

"I had better go back," said Rebecca. "Father will be wanting me to meet some of his friends, no doubt; but where are you, Mary? I will come over if I can."

"Just over there by the hedge," said Mary, pointing to where the horses were tied to the rather decrepit carriage.

Rebecca eyed the carriage but said nothing, waved a farewell and limped back towards her father. The others made their way back to the promised picnic, only to be intercepted by Reuben and George moving across the field.

"How did you two get here?" William asked.

"Walked," George said shortly.

"That's a long way," laughed Mary, "for little legs."

"It ain't far across the fields; and any road we ain't got little legs," said Reuben defensively.

Mary ruffled his hair and laughed – Reuben managed a small grin.

"I know," said Henry, "you're just the two people I need; do you want to earn a penny or two?"

Reuben and George's faces lit up and they nodded furiously.

"Doin' what?" said George.

"Take them two horses down to the brook at the bottom of the field to water them; it'll be a lot quicker than trying to find a bucket."

"'Ow much then?" said Reuben, squinting up at Henry dubiously.

Henry turned to Noble, trying not to laugh.

"How much is it worth, Noble?"

"Tuppence a horse, I would say," said Noble.

"Thruppence," said Reuben firmly.

"Done," said Henry, with a wink towards Noble.

Reuben and George trotted up to fetch the horses and led them down to the brook, chattering excitedly.

It was decided it was too damp to put the rug on the grass for the picnic, so everyone sat in the carriage and Mary handed round the sandwiches. William sat in the driver's seat and ate the slightly flabby sandwiches that his mother had packed him.

"I can see some horses in the ring," he said through a mouthful.

"Come on then," said Henry, swallowing down the last of a piece of fruit cake, "we don't want to miss anything; there won't be time to put a bet on if we're not there soon."

Mary and Martha started to pack away, just as Rebecca made her laborious way towards them.

"Oh dear, we were just packing up," said Mary. "Have you had food, Rebecca? I can get out the sandwiches again."

"Yes, I'm fine; we had masses and I'm full."

"Are there a lot of your father's friends with you, Rebecca?" asked Mary.

"Yes, but he's got a disaster on his hands, there's no one to ride Speedy."

"What happened?"

"I don't know exactly. He hired a jockey called Tim Tricket, but Tim has now booked to ride another horse and can't ride Speedy; so it's all a disaster."

"I know that Tricket," said Noble who had overheard all this. "He's an unreliable character if ever there ever was one; I'm not surprised he's let your father down. Tell your father, Miss Harding, that if he wants someone to ride it, I will; after all I know the horse."

"Do you mean that, Mr Ladds?" said Rebecca, a smile lighting her face.

"Yes, I mean it all right," said Noble with a snort of laughter. "That horse is one of the best I've ever sat on."

"I'll go and tell him," said Rebecca gleefully, rushing off as fast as her damaged leg could take her.

The racecourse was roughly a mile and a half long and the horses had to go round twice to complete the race, which was marked by stakes in the ground. There were ten hedges to jump – which had been cut down, trimmed and marked with posts – and a brook which had to be ridden through twice. Each end of the course was out of view of the crowd, but there was a good view of the racing across the meadow on the other side of the brook from the spinney to the farm buildings before they turned back to the finish. Before each race, all the horses were paraded in the ring to be viewed by the crowd; who could then put bets on the one they fancied. There were six races and Speedy had been entered in the last at half past four.

"Which one have you chosen, Mary?" Noble asked, as they watched the horses for the first race prancing round the paddock. "You must have a favourite."

"I hadn't thought," said Mary absently. "They all look good, don't they? Anyway, I'm not going to bet; I'm sure I would lose my money."

"That's right, Mary," said Martha wisely, "it's money down the drain, that's what I say."

"Oh, don't be a spoilsport, woman," laughed Henry. "It's only a bit of fun and you only have to put a shilling on. I'm going to have a bet, aren't you, Noble?"

"Yes I will," agreed Noble, before turning with a smirk to William. "And what about Mr Dunmore?"

"I can't pick a winner out of this lot," shrugged William. "I won't put any money on this race."

Noble said nothing, but raised his eyebrows and turned back to the paddock.

George and Reuben, having spotted an opportunity for some easy money, were now dragging their third lot of horses down to the brook.

"Come on, George," urged Reuben, "we're goin' to miss the first race if we don't get these back quick, let's turn round now – they won't know."

"No, silly," said George. "We'll see the race as they go through the brook right near where we're takin' 'em to water. We'll see just as much of the race from there."

They led the horses down to the water, a little way downstream from the crossing for the racehorses and waited for the race to start. A loud cheer echoed around the fields as the starter gave his flag a quick wave and crashed it to the ground. There was a field of twenty horses in this race; each rider had a number pinned to the front of their shirt and another on their back. Some wore coloured shirts, but most riders wore what they had arrived in, with broad braces holding up their trousers. The first two fences were not very challenging, everyone cleared them with ease before turning the corner to head down towards the stream where Reuben and George waited for them.

"Here they are, George," Reuben shouted above the pounding of hooves on the ground.

The field burst into view, jostling one another as they rounded the corner and pelted down the hill. The crossing of the brook here was shallow and as the competitors galloped through, great fountains of water streamed into the air, falling thickly down on Reuben and George and the animals they were holding; the drinking animals skittered and whinnied, eager to join the field.

"Hold 'im, George," Reuben shouted as George's charge reared up and tried to make off after the others. George was pulled over as the horse plunged and bucked, but he did not let go of the leading rein, the horse dragging him a little way through the river before he regained control. Reuben, being a bit bigger than George, was able to keep his animal in control.

"Are you all right, George?" he shouted as George rose from the brook with a scowl.

"Yeah, just wet," moaned George, water dripping from his sodden clothes.

They watched the field climb the hill before turning left along the edge of the spinney. The field disappeared, all except the last horse of the group, who instead of following the others had slowed up and ridden into the line of trees of the spinney.

"What's 'e doin'?" said George.

"Don't know," said Reuben. "Why ain't he going after the others? I'm goin' to 'ave a look. 'Ere, George, just 'old this 'un for a mo."

Reuben darted up to the edge of the spinney and disappeared from sight; a few minutes later, he was back.

"I dun know what 'e's doin'; 'e's just standing there waitin'," said Reuben, taking back his horse from George.

"Can't we get back somewhere?" shivered George. "I'm gettin' froze stood 'ere in these wet things."

"Just wait a mo, George, until they come round again. I want to see what that bloke does."

Five minutes later the field were round again; a bit more strung out this time and without the full complement that had started the race.

"'Ere they come, George," said Reuben as the sound of the hooves increased.

George gripped his leading rein tightly and watched the horses pound down the hill; they were slower this time, the horses straining with the effort of the two miles they had already galloped. Through the brook and up the slope they galloped; Reuben and George watched apprehensively as the rider in the spinney burst from the trees to join the back of the field as they passed.

"Look, George, look what that old sod's done, 'e's come out again and started racin'," Reuben shouted.

"'E's missed a whole round," said George. "I bet 'e wins! Number firteen, ain't 'e, Reuben?"

"Come on, George," shouted Reuben, dragging his horse back in the direction of the assembled crowds, "we 'ave to see who won the race."

The two boys ran back with the horses, collected their threepence each and trotted over to see who had won the race; as expected it was number thirteen.

"How did he do that?" marvelled Henry, who was standing with the others at the edge of the paddock. "He should never have won on that old nag."

"That was Tim Tricket," said Noble. "I bet he's been up to something."

"Well he won, didn't he?" interjected Mary.

"Not fairly I bet," muttered Noble, tearing up his bookie's slip and throwing it on the ground.

"What's up with George?" said Martha who had been watching Reuben and George's progress towards them.

"I don't know," said Mary looking round. "Where is he?"

"He's over there with Reuben; but he looks wet through."

She waved towards the two boys, who trotted towards them.

"George, look at you! How did you get so wet?" Mary asked.

"I fell in the brook, Miss Mary; I were tryin' to 'old that 'orse."

"We can't leave him like that, he'll catch his death," said Martha. "But we haven't any dry clothes. What clothes are in the carriage, Henry?"

She turned to her husband.

"Nothing, only my big coat and that won't fit him."

"But look at him! His teeth are chattering like anything and he's shivering. Reuben, run across to the carriage and get Henry's coat, there's a dear," said Martha. "Come on, Mary, we can dry him out by that fire over there where they're cooking the pig."

She took George's hand and marched him towards the tent, Mary following in their wake. The fire was very hot, stoked by a great heap of logs; and the pig on the spit smelt wonderful.

"Come here, Reuben, give me that," said Mary as Reuben emerged carrying Henry's huge coat, "Now, George, take off your jacket."

George peeled off his sodden jacket and stood shivering by the fire.

"Now your shirt," Mary ordered.

"No I can't, miss, everyone will see," hissed George.

"Well, we'll put the coat round you to cover you up; give me a hand, Martha."

The women put the coat around George, buttoning it up at the neck and down beyond his feet, where it spread out over the ground like a bridal train.

"Now give me your shirt, George," instructed Mary.

George wiggled under the coat, finally pushing his shirt out to Mary from between the buttons; she laid it to dry on the heap of logs by the fire.

"Now your trousers, George."

George blushed and looked at the ground.

"I can't, Miss Mary, it ain't right to take 'em off," he stammered.

"Do what I say, George," Mary demanded. "You can't walk about in soaking trousers, can you?"

"No, miss."

"Well take them off then."

George sighed, looked furtively round him and quickly unbuttoned his trousers, before pushing them out from under his coat.

"Just a minute, Miss Mary, there's my money in the pocket," he said, as Mary picked up his sodden trousers. She retrieved the pennies and dropped them into George's outstretched hand.

"Now have you got anything else on, George?"

"No, miss."

"Very good then; well you will just have to stand there while they dry, it won't take long with that heat."

She turned to Reuben.

"Now, Reuben; you make sure they don't scorch."

"Don't you dare leave me, Reuben," hissed George.

"Don't worry so, George," said Reuben with a sly smile.

George scowled.

"We're going now, but I'll come back in about twenty minutes," said Mary. "You look after him, Reuben."

"Yes, Mary," Reuben replied, turning the clothes over by the fire and looking adoringly after Mary's retreating figure.

"Reuben?"

"Yes, George."

"'Ow much money 'ave we got?"

"I dun't know," shrugged Reuben. "You were counting."

"I think we've got two shillin's and I think we should 'ave a bet; William'll do it for us if we can find 'im."

"Good idea," agreed Reuben. "But we've got to get your clothes dry first."

"Well I don't think we 'ave to look far," said George nodding in the direction of the paddock. "William's coming over 'ere now."

William, having decided he could no longer put up with the delicious aroma of pig without eating some, was making his way towards the fire. It was all he could do not to laugh when he caught sight of George trussed up like a snowman by the fire, Reuben meticulously turning his clothes every couple of minutes.

"Do you know someone cheated in the last race, William?" said George eagerly.

"How do you know that?" said William sharply.

"That there number firteen, 'e 'id in the spinney and only went round once, we see 'im, din't we, Reuben?"

"Yes that's right," said Reuben.

"Well that's no surprise," said William, chewing thoughtfully on his pork and passing the boys a piece of crackling each, "the jockey's a well-known cheat."

The boys were still crunching on crackling when Mary and Martha returned; Mary moved to George's clothes and felt them.

"They're not quite dry but they're a lot better than they were; come on,

George, put them on again." The clothes were passed under the coat until George was dressed again and could safely remove Henry's coat.

"Now run Henry's coat back to the carriage, George," Mary said.

"Very good, Miss Mary," smiled George, starting off towards the carriage. He stopped suddenly, and turned.

"Reuben, ask William about – you know."

And off he trotted.

One by one the races were completed; in the middle of the afternoon there was a parade of the hounds and then the racing resumed. The band had long since stopped; most of the musicians had made their way to the beer tent, their jackets undone and their caps on the back of their heads. The pork had been eaten almost entirely down to the bones. Everyone was waiting for the last race and Noble and Henry had gone to inspect Speedy. Reuben and George had managed to persuade William to place their money on Speedy and were waiting in a state of anticipation for the race.

"George? What if that bloke hides in the spinney agin; 'e's goin' to win, ain't 'e?" said Reuben worriedly.

"S'pose 'e is," said George with a frown.

"'Ave you got your catty wiv you, George?"

"Yes, it's in my jacket."

"Just the job; we'll go back down near where we were – we can sort that chap out this time, you see."

The horses for the last race were being led into the ring, some by their riders, others – like Speedy – by a groom. Charles and Rebecca stood in the middle of the ring with Noble who was smoking one of his small cigars, watching the horses stalk around the ring

"Which is Tricket?" asked Rebecca.

"He's number thirteen," said Noble. "He's already mounted. Come to that, I had better get ready."

He tossed his cigar to the ground and moved to the rails where Mary, Martha and Henry were standing. He took off his jacket and handed it to Mary.

434

"I don't suppose I can prevail on you to hold this for me, Mary?" he asked with a smile.

"It would be a pleasure, Mr Ladds," said Mary with a laugh.

Noble bowed, and peeled off his waistcoat and tie, handing them to Mary as well, before rooting through his pockets to empty them of anything that might be lost in the course of the race.

"All my worldly possessions, Mary; don't lose them, will you?" he said with a wink.

"Have you got a whip, Noble?" said Henry loudly.

"Blast, no," cursed Noble.

"Don't worry; here's a crop I found in the carriage, that will do. I took the lash off it for you."

"Good! Now wish me luck, folks."

He turned on his heel and strode off to mount, turning his cap round so the peak pointed down his neck and brushing the dust from his riding boots. Despite Speedy's seventeen hands of height Noble had no trouble mounting from the ground, leaping deftly onto the horse's back. Speedy shifted edgily as Noble threaded his feet into the stirrups and followed the rest of the field out to the starting line. Tim Tricket looked much more like a jockey than the rest – he had a proper riding hat, a silk shirt and a racing whip. He had also shortened his stirrup leathers so that his knees rested near the horse's withers. His horse, Nightjar, was a black gelding somewhat shorter and more compact than the other fifteen horses in the field.

The starter raised his flag, the competitors fighting for position, their mounts impatient to be off. The flag fell and the horses burst forward in a surge of power.

William had walked down to the stream with George and Reuben to where the two boys had stood last time. Reuben had taken George's catapult and moved on from the brook, positioning himself just into the spinney so he could not be seen. The field thundered through the water as before, close together, the horses fresh and full of running. Noble was tight in the middle of the pack, but Tricket was at the back and fell back as the field galloped away from the stream, guiding his horse into the spinney as before.

"Bless my soul," gasped William, "you were right; he's going in there to wait for the next round."

George nodded and looked up to where Reuben was stood waiting. Tricket manoeuvred his mount behind a tree, stopping ten yards in front of where Reuben was standing with his loaded catapult; he drew it back to its full extent and released. The stone scythed through the air, hitting the animal in the middle of its rump. The horse started and reared – almost throwing Tricket off as it did so – before taking off at full pelt through the trees and back onto the course after the other horses. Reuben swaggered out of the spinney, grinning all over his face and handed the catapult back to George with a wink.

The next time the field passed them, the order had changed; Noble was narrowly in the lead, with Nightjar tucked in close behind him in third. Along the back of the course, Tricket drew level with Noble – they leapt the next fence together, bumping into each other as they landed. Noble took a sidewise look at his competitor; Tricket smiled, drew his horse closer once again and with a powerful sweep of his arm, knocked Noble's foot from his stirrup. Noble – a very competent horseman – did not fall, but realising there was no way he could get his foot back in his stirrup, rode on without, fully aware that Tricket would try to win by any means necessary. With Tricket riding on such a short stirrup, Noble could see one chance to get his own back whilst the eyes of the crowd would not pick up what was going on. He manoeuvred Speedy almost level with Tricket's mount, closer and closer until he could reach the saddle. With one swift movement, he flipped up the saddle flap and seized the leather strap securing the girth, pulling sharply upwards. Nothing seemed to have happened and Noble returned both hands to the rein to negotiate the next fence. The two horses leapt together, landing at the same moment; as they did so Tricket gave a shout. Noble looked over to see Tricket's saddle slipping slowly to the side as he tried desperately to cling to the galloping animal and slow it down at the same time. Two seconds later, Tricket was deposited on the ground, shaking his fist angrily at the retreating field.

With no competitors near enough to trouble him up to the finish, Noble won by twenty lengths. He trotted Speedy back to the paddock where Charles and Rebecca were standing with the groom and Mary, Martha and Henry.

"Well done, my man, what a splendid ride you had!" cheered Charles, as Noble swung his foot over the horse's neck and slithered down to the ground. The groom slid the saddle from the horse's back and rubbed it down with straw, before throwing a rug over it and walking it around, steam rising in great clouds from its sweaty back. Noble shook Charles's hand and Rebecca's and went to retrieve his clothes from Mary, who gave him the slightest peck on the cheek.

"Well done, Noble, you're a hero," she said with a small laugh.

Noble winked.

There was a cup for Charles as owner of the horse, and a rosette for Noble, and ten shillings in winnings to be collected for Reuben and George, who grabbed their loot and set off delightedly across the fields to home. As Noble had had such a strenuous ride, Henry hitched up the horses and volunteered to drive home, which Noble readily agreed to, sitting himself down next to Mary and opposite Martha, who fell asleep within ten minutes of leaving the racecourse. Noble put his hand gently on Mary's knee and squeezed it, turning to smile at her – Mary smiled back, but lifted his hand off lest anyone should see. It was not long before they arrived back at the Park Gates where Mary had left her bike; Noble hopped out and lifted her down again, helping her to load the baskets onto her bike. They stood in silence for a moment, looking at one another; finally, Mary blushed and looked down.

"I will call and see your father again shortly," he promised, grasping her hand and kissing it, before leaping back into the carriage. Mary pushed her bike off in front of her, her cheeks flushed and a knowing smile on her face.

Chapter Thirty-Six
Courtship

As winter ended and spring arrived, Mary saw more and more of Noble Ladds. He would regularly call with the excuse that he had come to see John, but this only thinly disguised his actual intentions. Similarly, Mary made more and more frequent visits to Martha and Henry, playing the dutiful sister-in-law particularly since Martha lost her first baby. She was soon pregnant again and Mary took it upon herself to be ready to attend to Martha's needs when the baby was born as Henry would be managing the farm. There was only one incident regarding Noble that sat uneasily with her. She kept in regular contact with Rebecca, and it was through Rebecca's correspondence that she heard the story. Rebecca's father had ridden into town on Speedy and had been accosted by a man who had recognised the horse. Upon her father stating that the beast had been bought honestly from the horse dealer Noble Ladds, the man had insisted that it had not been Noble Ladds's to sell. That had been all the information that Rebecca had given her – and it appeared that Charles's meeting had had no further consequence. Mary was confident that there was a rational explanation, but she determined to pluck up the courage to ask him should the opportunity arise.

Noble had taken to coming over to Cold Harbour every Sunday. As the days got longer he would visit Mary's father for an hour before walking along the ridge and down into Upper Dean to meet Mary on her way back from chapel, where they would walk together back to the farm. At first he would hold Mary's hand as they walked along, but as the weeks went by he would put his arm around her shoulder or waist. He would usually smoke a small cigar and occasionally would take a sip from a flask he carried in his jacket pocket.

"What's in that?" Mary enquired one day.

"Just brandy, do you want to try some? Have a sniff."

Mary took the flask and held it to her nose, inhaling deeply. She coughed, pulling the flask from her nose and waving her hand in front of her face.

"How do you drink that stuff?" she spluttered, closing the top and handing it back.

Noble laughed and led her on through the field. At the next stile Mary stepped onto the first step; Noble still holding her hand, pulled her round to face him; she stood a little taller than him now and looked down into his face. He threaded his other arm round her and pulled her towards him, kissing her hard on the lips. She tried to push him away, but there his grip was strong and after a while she did not resist. Finally, Noble stood back, her hand still tightly clasped in his.

"Come on, we must get home," said Mary quietly. "Father will want to know where we are."

She scrambled over the stile, pulling her hand from his. They walked along in silence for a while, before Mary piped up.

"Noble?"

"Yes, Mary."

"You know that horse that you sold to Charles Harding."

"Yes, Mary."

"Who did it belong to before you owned it?" asked Mary quietly.

"It belonged to a farmer in the fens at Ramsey back where I was born," said Noble. "Why do you ask?"

"I heard that you didn't own it and you should not have sold it," said Mary nervously.

"And who told you that then; you must have big ears?" said Noble sharply, pinching her ear and pulling it down hard.

"Don't do that, you horrid man," Mary snapped, whirling around and twisting herself free of his grip.

"Who told you then?"

"A little bird told me," said Mary sharply.

She looked at him squarely, hands on hips.

"*Did* you own it, Noble?" she demanded.

"At the time I did own it; I had simply not paid for it, which I have done now. So tell your little bird to mind its own business."

The frown dropped from his face, he grinned, gave her a playful pat on the bottom and looped both arms around her; she could feel his fingers tickling her ribs. She squirmed backwards, turning herself around in his arms and beating her fists on his chest until he stopped tickling her. Her arms pinned between them, Noble kissed her again. This time she took longer to pull away; she smiled and tossed back her hair, scampering on towards home with Noble trailing after her.

The following week Noble came up to Cold Harbour on the Saturday instead to have lunch; he had been early to Bedford Market, selling one horse and buying another.

"What are you doing this afternoon?" he asked Mary. "Perhaps I will stay a little while to give the old nag a bit more rest."

"I was going down to see Aunt Charlotte to get a sewing pattern, but that was all."

"Will your dear cousin William be there?" said Noble with a wolfish grin.

"Oh no, he's on the round on Saturdays, he usually doesn't get home until at least six o'clock."

"Then I will walk with you!" declared Noble. "That is, if you are not going to be too long."

When lunch was cleared and her father settled, the pair set off on the hour long walk to Lower Dean, where they found Thomas working in the shop and Charlotte in the kitchen reading the Bible. Sarah was using the other end of the table to cut a loaf of bread for sandwiches of cheese and finely chopped onion, the smell of which wound round the kitchen as Mary and Noble entered from the shop.

"Mary dear, and Mr Ladds!" exclaimed Charlotte. "How nice to see you; come and sit down – we must have a cup of tea. Sarah dear, put the kettle on will you and get out the china."

Charlotte patted the chair next to her, signalling to Mary to sit down as Sarah retrieved the kettle and on finding it empty, moved past Noble to the scullery to fill it up. As she brushed past him and out of view of Mary and Charlotte, Noble put his hand down, gently squeezing her bottom. Sarah jumped forward, spinning to face Noble with a scowl – Noble stared at her, daring her to retaliate. She frowned and continued into the scullery, filled the kettle and returned around the other side of the table to put the it on the range.

"I think I will have a chat with Mr Dunmore while the kettle boils," said Noble, making his way into the shop with an indulgent smile towards Charlotte.

"You've been seeing him a bit then, Mary Knighton," said Charlotte, nodding towards the door of the shop.

"Now and then, Aunt Charlotte," said Mary noncommittally.

"A bit more than now and then from what I've heard," retorted Charlotte in a disapproving tone.

"William doesn't get on with him," she continued, leaning forward in her chair. "But we can't see much wrong with him; Thomas likes him, anyway."

She rose and moved to the sideboard, opening the cupboard and taking out a cake tin, which she placed on the table, before turning to the sideboard to retrieve a big envelope from the top of her sewing basket.

"Is this what you want, Mary?" she asked, sliding the pattern from the envelope.

"Yes; that is just what I need! It gives me something to do now the evenings are so long and Father is in bed."

"And how is dear brother John?" asked Charlotte gently. "I haven't seen him since the funeral, you know, my dear, isn't that terrible of me?"

She shook her head.

"He's not so good, Aunt Charlotte," sighed Mary. "He can only just manage to get out to the yard and that's it."

"I don't like to say it, Mary, but he's going to follow your mother before long," said Charlotte knowingly.

"Don't say that, Aunt Charlotte!" said Mary sharply.

"There, there, my dear, don't take on. I'm sorry to upset you, but you know what I mean."

She patted Mary kindly on the arm as Sarah filled the teapot, placing the cups and saucers on the table.

"Go and tell Mr Ladds tea's ready, Sarah, and Mr Dunmore will come as well I'm sure."

Noble re-entered the room, placing his cap down on the sideboard.

"I do admire your lovely boots, Mr Ladds," cooed Charlotte. "I do like to see well-polished boots; it sets a man off, don't you think, Mary?"

Mary smiled at Noble, who looked down at his boots.

"Thank you, Mrs Dunmore, I spend a lot of time keeping them like that," he admitted.

"You mean you polish them yourself? Don't you have someone to do them for you?"

"Oh no, I don't have anyone in the house and there are only two chaps on the farm."

"My word!" exclaimed Charlotte. "So who cooks and cleans for you and does your washing, you must have someone?"

"Oh yes, Miss Gaunt comes in and cleans and does the washing. The cooking I mostly do myself if Miss Gaunt has remembered to light the range."

"Well I never, a man doing the cooking, what will the world come to?" said Charlotte admiringly. "I could not do without dear Sarah here, could I, Sarah?"

"You all'as say that, Mrs Dunmore," said Sarah blushing.

"Martha's baby, Mary, tell me about that! When is it due?" asked Charlotte.

But before Mary could reply Noble had spoken up.

"Mrs Dunmore, thank goodness you said that! I have a letter from Martha for you, Mary."

He took an envelope from his pocket and handed it to Mary, who opened it and started to read.

"It says she's keeping very well and the baby's due in about two weeks. She wants me to go and stay for a day or two when she has it, she says she will send someone over as soon as she starts, to fetch me I suppose she means."

She folded the letter back into the envelope and shoved it in her pocket.

"You must go, Mary, it's your duty," said Charlotte firmly.

"But, Aunt Charlotte, I don't know anything about babies! I wouldn't know what to do."

"Stuff and nonsense, Mary, it's easy. Anyway, you've got to learn sometime – you must go. Don't you worry about your father and that nasty man Edgar;

Freda is quite capable of looking after them. I'll get William to drive me up to check on him. So you go back and write a reply and Mr Ladds can take it with him."

She took a sip of tea.

"Isn't that right, Thomas?"

"Yes, dear," Thomas replied.

Mary and Noble finished their tea and started off up the hill back to Cold Harbour. The sun was high in the clear blue sky, beating down on them as they walked. Noble removed his jacket and rolled up his sleeves and Mary had removed her shawl and stuffed it into her basket. The wheat and barley was above knee height now and the hay was nearly ready to cut. The pair held hands as they wandered along, Mary's brown arms and face contrasting sharply against her pale pink dress. A cock blackbird sang determinedly from the top of an elm tree and a magpie chattered, hopping from branch to branch along the top of the hedgerow looking for plunder from the nests of small birds.

"I must write to Martha as soon as I get home, Noble," said Mary. "If you will take the letter for me?"

"Anything for you, Mary," laughed Noble, pulling Mary to a stop and turning her to face him "You know that? Anything!"

He pulled her a little closer.

"Do I get a kiss for taking a letter?"

"You haven't done it yet," smiled Mary.

"I know but I will! Come on – one kiss."

Mary laughed and leant in towards him, just as Noble leant back, tilting his head to the side and looking up.

"Noble, what are you doing?"

"Listen! What's that noise?"

"I can't hear anything," giggled Mary.

"Shut up and listen!"

Mary frowned and tried to hear beyond the clamour of the birds.

"Yes I can," she whispered. "What is it?"

"It's a swarm of bees! But where, can you see it, Mary?"

He scanned the trees for sight of the swarm.

"No, Noble, I'm frightened – where is it? Can't you do something?"

"Just shut up, Mary, and look," Noble hissed impatiently.

Mary looked around the hayfield in which they were standing; oak trees were dotted about the field to the line of the hedge, where a stile crossed into the next wheat field. Behind was another pasture with cattle grazing and to the left was a spinney of elm and ash trees.

"I can see it," Mary screamed suddenly, pulling her hand from Noble's to point. "Down there, look! Coming up the hill."

Noble turned to where Mary was pointing, picking out a moving black mass – almost thirty yards long and five yards wide, a low loud buzz emanating from it.

"Can't we run?" begged Mary.

"No," said Noble. "There's no telling which way it's going. At any rate, it travels faster than you can run. Just wait and watch it to see which way it's going."

They stood still, Mary trembling in fear.

"Noble? Noble!" she whimpered. "What are we going to do?"

"Get down on the ground, Mary; they're coming towards us, but they are quite low."

He grasped her hand and looked at her earnestly.

"Don't worry, they never sting when they're swarming unless you upset them."

Noble pulled Mary into a crouch as the swarm approached, the buzzing louder than Mary thought she could bear. As they approached Mary flung herself flat to the ground, wrapping her hands desperately over her head as Noble put his arm round her and watched the progress of the bees as they flew a few feet overhead. The buzzing, which had reached a deafening crescendo, suddenly subsided as the swarm settled on an old gnarled oak twenty feet behind them.

"Have they gone?" Mary whispered, opening her eyes and raising herself up on her hands to check for the swarm.

"Yes they're over there; look on that oak tree."

He pointed to the large black mass milling around the trunk of the tree.

"Thank the Lord, Noble! I thought we were done for," laughed Mary. "I'll give you a kiss for that."

She wound her hand round the back of his head, pulling him towards her and kissing him with as much passion as she could muster. Slowly she sank back to the ground, Noble's hands twined in her hair. As they lay locked in their embrace, Mary felt one of Noble's hands wander from her face, down over her throat, lingering briefly on her bosom and travelling down over her stomach to her legs. She lifted his hand, bringing it back up to her shoulder, but no sooner had she done this than she felt the hand wandering again. The weight of his body pressed down against her right shoulder, and although she was enjoying the experience, she knew that she had to stop it. She slid her free hand under his waistcoat, up to his ribs, dug her fingers in and tickled. Noble jumped back immediately, squirming away from her on the ground. Mary leapt to her feet and brushed the grass from her dress, picking up her hat as she did so.

"What did you do that for?" Noble complained.

"Time to go," said Mary with a small laugh, offering her hand to him to help him up.

They started back across the hayfield, Mary five yards in front. At the next stile she turned and waited for him

"Come on, Noble Ladds," she laughed, "don't sulk like that, it's not becoming."

"Hmm," mumbled Noble with a scowl, scuffing his heels like a schoolboy and refusing to walk next to her all the way back to Cold Harbour.

At the farm, Lucy had arrived home for the weekend. Noble greeted her moodily and left with Mary's hastily scribbled letter to Martha – a scowl still etched to his face.

Next day was much the same as most Sundays, but it was a welcome change for Mary to have Lucy at home. After lunch they decided to go down to the butcher's shop to see if they could find William before they had to go to chapel.

The Dunmores were all sitting in their Sunday best, ready for chapel in the kitchen at the farm: Charlotte was reading the Bible, Thomas *The Farmer & Stockbreeder* and William was reading the paper.

"Bless my soul," Charlotte cried. "We don't see you in weeks, Mary Knighton, and here you are twice in two days."

Mary laughed and beckoned Lucy into the kitchen.

"Lucy is back from training Aunt Charlotte; she wanted to see William and it's awfully boring sitting up at Cold Harbour, there's no one there only Edgar and Father."

Lucy smiled but said nothing.

"My word, Lucy, I'm sure you've grown since Christmas!"

She cast a critical eye over her niece.

"Yes, you have grown I'm sure – but you haven't filled out much yet. I suppose there is time for that." Lucy looked down at her flat chest and sniffed.

"Yes, Aunt Charlotte," she said, sitting herself on a chair next to William.

"Don't you think she's grown, Thomas?" insisted Charlotte.

"Yes dear, I'm sure she has. She's certainly grown prettier."

He winked at Lucy, who showed little reaction.

"I don't know about that Thomas," Charlotte muttered.

"Mary dear, it's Sarah's day off, so we've got to manage. Be a dear and put the kettle on for a cup of tea – you want one, I expect."

Mary nodded and went to put the kettle onto the range.

"William, what's in the paper, then?" whispered Lucy, sidling up to her cousin and reading over his shoulder.

"I'm reading about stocks and shares and all that," William replied, concentrating hard on the paper in front of him.

"What are stocks and shares then, William?" Lucy asked.

William dragged his eyes from the paper, and tried to explain the system to Lucy.

"What are you two whispering about?" demanded Charlotte.

"Stocks and shares, Mother."

"Oh," said Charlotte, a puzzled frown knitting her brow.

"Have you made any friends in Bedford, Lucy?!" asked Charlotte.

"Reverend Packham said that when he went to preach at your chapel, a young man walked you home."

The room fell silent. Mary turned from the range, Thomas lowered *The Farmer & Stockbreeder* and William shut the paper.

"Who's that then, Lucy?" demanded Mary. "You didn't tell me and I'm your sister!"

She turned accusingly to William.

"Did you know, William?"

William shook his head.

"She must tell us, mustn't she, Aunt Charlotte!" insisted Mary.

"No, dear, she will tell you when she's ready and that's time enough," smiled Charlotte. "Don't you bully her, Mary. Lucy my dear, you wouldn't mind coming into the other room in a moment and having a look at my bunions, I could do with a medical opinion."

She closed her Bible decisively and moved into the adjoining room to prepare for her examination.

"Who is he?" William whispered, as his mother left the room.

"His name's Roderick."

"Is that all?"

"That's all I'm going to tell you, William," laughed Lucy.

"Come on, Lucy, you bring your tea and I'll bring mine and we will go next door," called Charlotte from the door. Lucy rose and followed her aunt out of the room.

Mary handed out the tea and sat down by William.

"What did she tell you then, William?"

"About what?" William said vacantly.

"About her young man, you silly, you know what I mean," hissed Mary, gripping William's arm and pinching it sharply.

"She said his name was Roderick and that was all," complained William, wrenching his arm from Mary's grasp.

"No more?" hissed Mary.

"No, nothing."

"I'll get it out of her later, you see if I don't."

She drummed her fingers on the table and turned to her cousin with an angry sigh.

"William, how are we going to deal with Father and Cold Harbour? You've had a chance to look at the situation?"

"Yes, Mary, and I'm afraid it's not good; there's no money, the payments on the mortgage are too big for what the farm brings in, and Edgar isn't much good at managing it. Henry was much better but even he couldn't make enough to meet the payments."

"What are we going to do then, William?" said Mary desperately.

She had known things were bad but had tried her hardest to put it to the back of her mind and forget about it.

"In the end, Mary, the farm will have to be sold. In a way the sooner the better; then there will be money left to support your father."

"But if we sell the farm where will we live?" cried Mary, wringing her hands.

"Just take things slowly, Mary," soothed William. "There's no immediate rush; the bank isn't worried yet. Best to decide after harvest and don't worry about where you will live, Father has several cottages down the street in Lower Dean – they come up all the time."

"Are you sure, William?"

"Yes, I'm sure," said William firmly.

"And if Edgar goes," said Mary tentatively, "would you run the farm until we can sell it?"

"Yes, of course I would."

Mary smiled gratefully and squeezed her cousin's hand.

"William, I don't know what I would do without you; you've got your head screwed on, which I haven't all the time. Lucy's like you, she's careful and thinks things out, but I don't always do that do I?"

"No, Mary, not always," laughed William, laying his hand on Mary's.

"Time for chapel," announced Charlotte, rushing back into the room. "William – you go and get the trap ready, we will ride and you girls will have to walk. You did bring hats, I hope? Mary? Lucy?"

"Yes, Aunt Charlotte," chimed the two girls.

"And you better go down the end before you go, you two."

"Yes, Aunt Charlotte," they answered again, Mary looking down to avoid giggling at her aunt.

Chapel was, as ever, tedious. Mary sat in a state of half awareness; the background drone of Reverend Packham drowned by her thoughts of Noble Ladds. She thought about lying in the grass with him, the bees swarming over them, his hands over her body. She shut her eyes and clenched her fists, trying to bring her thoughts back to the sermon. This dragged on and there were still two more hymns to sing, and the collection to take. She looked at Lucy who seemed to be concentrating, but Mary wondered whether she was thinking about Roderick. William sat with his parents; Mary could tell he wasn't listening, he was probably thinking about stocks and shares and the farm.

She looked down at her hands; they had lost all the daintiness that they had had when she was at Tibbitts and were red; her palms were hard and rough and most of her nails were broken. She ran her thumbnail under her fingernails and flicked the pieces of dirt onto the floor. Lucy looked sideways at her and frowned – Mary turned her nose up at her sister, sticking out her tongue. Lucy sniffed and looked away.

The service ended, they bid goodbye to their relations and set off up the hill back to Cold Harbour. The two girls chatted as they walked.

"Who's Roderick then, Lucy?" asked Mary, unable to keep it to herself any longer.

"Who told you about him then?" Lucy snapped.

"William said his name was Roderick, that's all I know," placated Mary.

There was silence.

"Well?" said Mary.

"Well what?"

"Who is he?"

There was a longer silence, but Mary knew she was winning; she could tell Lucy wanted to tell her about him and it would soon all come out.

"He's a boy I see at chapel," said Lucy finally, breaking off into silence again.

"And?" said Mary.

"And – he walks home the same way as I do; so we walk together."

"*And?*" insisted Mary.

Lucy sighed.

"He works at the hospital. He's a porter, he does all the heavy work pushing the beds and wheelchairs about. He's a bit younger than me and he lives in a small house with his mother; his father died years ago."

"And what does he look like, Lucy?" asked Mary curiously.

"Just ordinary," shrugged Lucy. "He's not handsome but I—"

She broke up, looking down at her skirt.

"Well he's not like Noble Ladds or anyone like that," finished Lucy shyly.

They made their way into a field filled with cattle; cattle that came prancing up to them as they walked along, trying to lick the hems of their dresses as they swung from side to side. Mary turned round and clapped her hands as she felt one nudge her.

"Goo on, get away, you buggers," she shouted, waving her arms at the cows, who ran off only to turn round and follow them again at a distance.

"I wish you wouldn't swear, Mary, it's a sin," Lucy reprimanded. "Didn't you hear what Reverend Packham said about it in the sermon?"

"Everything's a sin if you listen to him," snorted Mary.

They reached the stile into the next field; the hayfield where Mary and Noble had encountered the bees.

"Lucy?"

"Yes, Mary."

"Did Mother tell you anything?"

"About what?"

"About having babies and that sort of thing."

"No," said Lucy, turning to her sister curiously. "Did she tell you?"

"No," said Mary wistfully.

She could not think how to continue the conversation.

"You're a nurse, Lucy, they must tell you about that sort of thing."

Mary stopped in her tracks and looked at her sister.

"Martha. She's having a baby, isn't she? So what happened? I mean what do men *do*? What happens? Nobody ever told us, Lucy, *you* must know, Lucy, you *must!*"

Mary twisted her hands in agitation. A tear sprang to her eye and she wiped it away.

"Mary, they don't tell us that bit," insisted Lucy. "I know about babies in the womb and how they are born but we're not told anything else; I think they expect you to know."

She stopped to think for a moment.

"It must be like pigs, or bulls and cows – it must be."

"I know it must be something like that, but it can't be exactly the same, can it? Anyway we weren't supposed to see the animals doing that; Mother always took us inside when it happened."

"Why do you want to know, Mary?" Lucy asked innocently.

"Because I do!" cried Mary. "We should know! You should know, we should all know before it happens."

"But it won't happen until you're married, Mary, will it?" said Lucy, a note of warning in her voice. Mary sighed heavily.

"No, you're right, Lucy; there's nothing to worry about and there is no one to ask now Mother's dead, is there?"

"You could ask Martha, she must know," suggested Lucy.

"But that would be embarrassing, wouldn't it?" asked Mary. "She's our sister-in-law! But you're right, she must know."

"Mary," Lucy said firmly, "if you find out you must tell me – promise me you will; you're right, we should all know."

They continued to walk on, past a spot where the grass had been flattened by Mary and Noble lying there yesterday. Mary shivered and told Lucy about the bees.

"Now, Lucy, you must tell me about having babies because I have to go down and help Martha when we get home. You must tell me what to do and I will write it all down so I know."

"I'm not a midwife, Mary!" laughed Lucy. "But I'll tell you what I know. Aren't they having a midwife? Most people do."

"Most people do if they can afford it, Lucy; I think that's the problem," sighed Mary.

Chapter Thirty-Seven
Martha's Baby Born

Early on Wednesday morning, Mary was woken by Noble Ladds shouting up at her window that the baby was on the way.

"What time is it?" Mary yelled back.

"Half past five."

"Give me ten minutes and I will be ready," shouted Mary, running to wake Freda, before dressing and dashing down to open the door for Noble.

"I'm coming on my bike, Noble, is there going to be time?"

"Yes, I'm sure there will be," assured Noble. "First babies are often a long time coming – you know that, Mary."

"I suppose I do," she said doubtfully.

"Let me take your bag with me and I'll go back along the fields and tell them you are coming."

"Good idea," Mary said, handing him the bag that she had packed on Monday in readiness.

Freda stumbled down the stairs, trying unsuccessfully to stifle a yawn.

"Freda, I'm going!" said Mary. "You know what to do, don't you?"

"Yes, Miss Mary," yawned Freda, before adding "off where, Miss Mary?"

"The baby's coming, you ninny, I just told you."

"So you did," Freda replied, opening and shutting her eyes.

It took Mary just over an hour to get to Martha, having stopped at the butcher's shop on the way past to tell them the news. Henry was with Martha, who was upstairs in a bed in an enormous room which had very little furniture and no carpet on the floor. She looked hot and sweaty and Henry sat with her.

"Ah, Mary," he said, rising, "it's good you're here; I can go and get on with the hay now."

He kissed Martha lightly on the forehead and left the room.

"How are things then, Martha, what can I do? I must get the notes that Lucy gave me."

"Don't worry, Mary," smiled Martha through short puffs. "I know what to do; I helped my mother with four or five of my brothers and sisters; just sit down for a minute and let's have a chat."

Martha's calmness put Mary's mind at rest and she left moments later to make them both a cup of tea. Returning to the bedroom, she found Martha red in the face, her eyes tight shut, her lips white and pressed tightly together; she was clearly holding her breath. She suddenly exhaled, before breathing in again deeply. Mary stroked her hair.

"Poor Martha, does it hurt? What do you want me to do?"

"Nothing, Mary, sit down and have your tea, it ain't comin' yet, I'm sure of it, and it don't hurt too bad, not yet anyway."

"I don't know why you're so calm, Martha," wondered Mary. "I would be going to pieces, I'm sure I would."

"Now, Mary, just sit down like I said and give me my tea," laughed Martha. "I'll tell you what is going to happen and what you have got to do; but you must just keep calm, it's all going to be all right. I helped my mother so many times I am almost an expert, although I do say it myself."

"And is the doctor coming?" asked Mary.

"No, or at least he ain't comin' yet. Henry has seen him and he says he will call in later to make sure everything's going all right."

Mary sat nervously at the bedside, whilst Martha told her what was going to happen and what she was to do; the main priority being to get dinner ready for Henry.

"Don't look so worried, Mary," laughed Martha. "It's all going to be fine, you'll see."

Mary squeezed Martha's hand and went to start carrying out Martha's instructions. She went up and down the stairs time and time again; she went out to the well to get water, she emptied the potty, filled the kettle, ironed more bed sheets, and so it went on, until in the middle of the afternoon she heard Martha shout.

"It's comin', Mary! Come and give an 'and, can you!"

Mary clattered up the stairs as fast as she could. Martha had folded the bed clothes back and pulled up her nightdress, her hands holding tight to the brass rails of the bedstead as she puffed and puffed.

"Can you see anything?" said Martha between gasps.

"See what?" said Mary looking desperately into Martha's face.

"The baby, you silly! Go on, look down there!"

She nodded to between her outstretched legs and Mary paled. She took a few nervous steps towards the foot of the bed and glanced to where she had been instructed to, before looking hurriedly away. Martha gasped again and laid her head back.

"Well," said Martha, "can you see its head?"

Mary took a deep breath and looked again, before looking back at Martha.

"I'm not sure," said Mary.

Martha panted and shut her eyes, screwing her face up and straining with all her might.

"What now?" she groaned. "Look, Mary!"

Mary did as instructed, before beaming up at Martha.

"Yes, Martha, yes I'm sure it is the head and it's nearly out!"

Martha panted.

"Can you see its face or the back of its head?"

"The back," said Mary. "What shall I do, Martha?"

"Nothing at—" Martha stopped, screwing up her eyes again, her face reddening.

Mary looked desperately at her sister-in-law and back down to where a baby had appeared in its entirety. She gasped, and picked it up, laying it in the sheet she had ready.

"Careful, Mary, is the cord still attached?" panted Martha.

"Yes, yes, it is," Mary said.

"Now, do what I said, Mary: you remember! Get the string and tie it in two places and cut between it."

The baby mewled angrily.

"It's crying, Martha!"

"Good, it's alive then," Martha laughed, lying back and breathing heavily.

Mary did as she had been instructed, as the baby continued to cry.

"Will it hurt it where I cut the cord, Martha?"

"You silly thing, Mary Knighton," exclaimed Martha, "just cut it like I said."

Mary cut the cord and folded the sheet round the baby, handing it proudly to Martha.

"Come here, you lovely thing," crooned Martha, clutching the baby tight to her chest and rocking it gently until it stopped crying.

"What is it, Mary?" she asked, looking hopefully up at Mary.

"What do you mean what is it, Mary?" Mary asked bemusedly.

"Is it a boy or a girl? Didn't you look?"

"No," Mary gasped, looking embarrassed. "I was just too busy worrying about the cord!"

Martha pulled back the sheet from around the baby, looked it over and pulled its legs apart.

"It's a boy, Mary, look! It's a boy."

And she flicked with her index finger; Mary reddened and looked at the floor. Martha burst out laughing.

"Mary Knighton! Ain't you seen one of them before? It ain't goin' to bite you, or at least this one won't."

Mary lifted her head and looked at Martha, who reached out for Mary's shoulder and pulled her forward, kissing her cheek.

"Now you go and make me a cup of tea, there's a dear, while I get myself sorted out; you've got the range goin', ain't you?"

"Yes, but can't I do anything?"

"No, no, you go and make the tea," insisted Martha.

Mary reluctantly left, not knowing what she should do otherwise, Martha shouted after her,

"Bring a jug of 'ot water as well, Mary."

Mary made the tea, pouring out a cup and carrying it upstairs in one hand, a jug of hot water in the other. She pushed the door to the bedroom open with her foot – Martha was suckling the baby, who was wrapped up in a pale blue woollen shawl, the top of his tiny head peeping above the blanket.

"Put the cup on the floor, Mary; there ain't nowhere else," instructed Martha.

Mary tiptoed round the bed; a small newspaper parcel lay folded on the floor, bloody finger marks streaking its outside.

"Put that in the fire when you go down," said Martha nodding to the parcel. "Now put the water on the stand and come 'ere and 'old the baby for me."

Mary did as she was told and Martha handed her the sleeping child.

"What are you going to do, Martha?" Mary said as she folded down the blanket. "You can't get out of bed so soon."

"Course I can!" laughed Martha. "Only your la-di-da friends think that. I'm goin' to 'ave a wash then I'm goin' to change the sheet and get back in the bed for an hour or two."

She eased herself from the bed, peeling her nightshirt off over her head; Mary looked away and carried the baby over to the window, rocking it gently in her arms.

"Bring 'im 'ere then, Mary," instructed Martha a few moments later, having washed and changed her nightshirt.

"What are you going to do with him?" Mary asked in a worried voice.

"Put 'im in 'ere," said Martha nodding at a drawer she had pulled from the chest of drawers in the corner. She took the baby, laying him gently on a pillow she had lined the drawer with and covering him with a small blanket.

"Don't you have a crib, Martha?" Mary asked.

"We ain't got no money for 'fings like that," snorted Martha. "We've got enough bills to pay as it is; you know what farming's like, Mary. Now 'elp me change the sheet and I can get back in bed. If you fetch a couple of chairs from downstairs we can put the drawer on them, so 'e ain't on the floor." Mary's shoes thumped along the stairs as she lugged up the heavy wooden chairs, setting them opposite each other to the side of the bed next to Martha and carefully lifting the drawer onto them. For the first time she looked into the drawer, pulling the blanket back with her index finger to look at the sleeping child.

"He's a lovely baby, Martha," she sighed. "What are you going to call him?"

"'Enry, I s'pose; but we ain't really thought of names."

Martha leaned over from the bed and stroked the child's cheek before looking up at Mary.

"You don't know much about all this sort of thing, do you?" she said with a smile.

Mary bowed her head and looked at her hands, wrapping them round one another nervously.

"No I don't," she admitted.

Martha grabbed her hand.

"Don't you worry, Mary; I know everyfing about 'avin' babies – I will soon learn you."

She squeezed Mary's hand encouragingly.

"Now what about 'Enry's dinner? 'E'll be in within the hour. There's some taters to boil down there somewhere and some cold meat in the safe in the pantry. 'E'll 'ave a raw onion with it if you peel it for 'im, and you can bring me up a bit when 'e's 'ad 'is."

The next day Martha was out of bed and down in the kitchen before Mary, the baby in its drawer on the kitchen table. Henry had gone out to feed the cattle and milk the few cows he had. The range was alight but not yet hot enough to boil the kettle.

"Martha, you shouldn't be doing that," insisted Mary. "That's my job! I'm sure you should be resting in bed after having the baby yesterday."

"Blow that," said Martha, "I can't lay in bed when there's things to do; my muvver never did, so I ain't goin' to! Although you could go and get a bucket of water from the pump, I don't think I want to lift one of them yet."

Mary tied a shawl round her shoulders and went out to the pump with the bucket. It was cold outside; there was a little ice on the ground from a late frost and a thin sheet of ice glistened on the surface of the puddles. She was the first one to use the pump that day so had to work the handle up and down for some time before the water started to rise up into the throat of the machine and out into the bucket. She tipped a little out so as not to spill it down her skirt and made her way back across the yard to the back door. The sound of hooves on the cobbles startled her into turning round, just as the figure of Noble Ladds on a splendid black hunter emerged from around the corner of the house. He wore a bowler hat as usual and a long dark green trench coat, his highly polished brown riding boots contrasting with the shiny black coat of the hunter. He dismounted and raised his bowler to Mary.

"Good morning, Mary, what a pretty sight on such a cold morning! Come here, let me take that."

He grabbed the handle of the bucket and handed Mary the reins of the horse.

"Just hang onto him for a moment, Mary, while I take this into the kitchen."

He was soon back to take the horse, tying it to the gate and loosening the girth before returning to Mary.

"I've come to offer my congratulations to the new parents," announced Noble.

"At this time of the morning?" laughed Mary. "It's a little early, isn't it?"

"Well I suppose it is," agreed Noble. "But I'm on my way to sell this horse and won't be back for a couple of days; so I thought I had better call in before I go."

"Come on in then," said Mary, leading the way into the kitchen, where Martha sat by the range feeding the baby.

Martha looked up as the pair entered and smiled politely. She did not like Noble Ladds; he led Henry into the wrong company and kept taking him to the pub drinking.

"Don't let me interrupt," said Noble, "I can come another day when it is more convenient."

"No, no, come in," said Martha, turning away and doing up the buttons of her blouse. "Here, Mary, you have the baby for a while, I'll make some tea; the fire's hot enough now. Would you like some tea, Mr Ladds?"

"You must call me Noble, my dear," said Noble smoothly, "we have been neighbours for over a year now and yes I would like a cup of tea!"

He put his bowler hat on the table and threw himself into a chair.

"Shall I put him down, Martha?" asked Mary, looking down at the child in her arms.

"No just rock him for a bit – let his breakfast go down."

"But he might cry," said Mary worriedly.

"No he won't, you silly; he's a good baby."

Noble moved over to Mary, taking a cursory glance at the child before returning to his seat.

"I came to congratulate you and Henry, Martha, on your firstborn," announced Noble. "What are you going to call him?"

Martha turned from the range, where she was holding the handle of the kettle – willing it to boil so she could make the tea and get rid of Noble before Henry came back. Her face was red and she looked flustered by the unexpected visitor.

"I expect we will call it 'Enry," she said shortly.

"Quite right, after his father and I have a present for young Henry."

He worked his index finger round his waistcoat pocket, pulling out a shiny sovereign and spinning it onto the table.

"There we are – gold for luck, and mind you keep it safe, Martha."

"That is very kind of you, Mr Ladds, very generous I'm sure and course I will keep it safe."

The kettle boiled and she poured it into the waiting pot.

"Just let it brew a minute, Mary, I will take him now," said Martha, taking the sleeping baby and tucking him up in the drawer. Mary poured out the tea and went to join Martha and Noble at the table.

"You're all dressed up today, Mr Ladds – I mean Noble – goin' somewhere important, then?" asked Martha.

"I'm goin' to London to sell that animal out there," said Noble, nodding towards the door.

"You ain't goin' to ride it all the way are you? It'll be legless by the time you get it there," said Martha.

"No, no, I think I can put it on the train at Huntingdon and if I sell it, I will stay the night and come back tomorrow."

"I've never been to London, have you, Martha?" Mary asked.

"No, I ain't and I don't want to, if all's true that I 'ear about it."

"I would go," said Mary. "Mr Peveril used to talk about it all the time; it sounds wonderful! Is it, Noble?"

"Oh yes, you should go, Mary," nodded Noble. "I could show you round; the fast train is only just over the hour from Huntingdon."

Mary watched him as he lit a small cigar and puffed the smoke towards the ceiling. He was not like the other men Mary knew; his clothes were clean and fashionable, his hair was smoothed down and his moustache was trimmed exactly to the line of his top lip. His hands were clean, there was no dirt in his fingernails and he wore a gold signet ring on the little finger of his left hand. He finished his tea and stood up, flicking ash from his cigar into the hearth and taking a gold repeater from his waistcoat pocket. He flicked open the cover.

"I must go, I don't want to miss the train and it will take me over an hour to get to the station."

"Very good," said Martha, barely disguising the note of relief in her voice. "Thank you so much for young Henry's present; now show Mr Ladds out, Mary."

Noble picked up his bowler hat and with a small bow to Martha, followed Mary out the door.

"Let me hold the horse for you," said Mary as Noble tightened up the girth and untied the horse from the fence.

"He's a lovely animal, isn't he?" she said, stroking the gleaming coat of the gelding in front of her.

"Yes," agreed Noble. "One of the best I've had for some years; let's hope I get a good price for him."

He deftly mounted the house as Mary held its bridle. The horse shook its head impatiently and snorted, as Mary loosened her grip on the reins. Noble lifted his bowler and winked at Mary.

"Goodbye, Miss Knighton. I'll bring you a little something from London if I make a good sale."

With the slightest touch of his heels to the animal's flank, he urged the horse forwards across the cobbles and into the road. Mary watched him leave wistfully, clutching her shawl round her shoulders to stave off the cold. Back in the kitchen, Martha sat by the range, cooing at the baby.

"I don't like that man, Mary," said Martha as Mary entered the kitchen. "I can see you do though."

The colour rose in Mary's cheeks; Martha laughed.

"There you go; you're goin' red, Mary, I can tell."

"No, I'm not," gasped Mary, bringing her hands up to her cheeks.

"Yes you are; I'd tell you to look in the mirror, 'cept we ain't got one."

Martha finished her tea and eyed Mary.

"Any road I don't like 'im; did you smell 'im, Mary? He got scent on, I'm sure 'e had; men that put scent on can't be no good that's what I say."

"That wasn't scent, it was cologne! Mr Peveril used to put it on," Mary said defensively.

"Well I don't know what it is, but it don't sit with me right," said Martha rising from her chair. "I'm just goin' down the end; so just keep an eye on young 'Enry for me, Mary."

"Put a shawl on, Martha, it's cold out there; you don't want to get a chill."

"Oh don't fuss, Mary, I'm as strong as an ox, you know that."

She smiled at her sister-in-law and walked out into the door. As she did so the dogs in the yard started barking.

"Who's that then?" said Martha. "It's a bit early for most folk."

She opened the door from the scullery into the yard.

"It's William! Mary, put the kettle on! I'll be back in a mo."

Martha hitched her skirt and rushed across the yard, waving and shouting at William as she did so.

Mary went to the door as William approached the house put her arm through his and led him into the kitchen.

"William Dunmore! What a lovely surprise to see my dear cousin," exclaimed Mary, pecking William on the cheek.

William blushed and looked away.

"And aren't you pleased to see me?" teased Mary, turning him to face her.

"Yes of course I am!" said William. "But Mother sent me with things for Martha and the baby."

"Yes dear Aunt Charlotte, she's got you where she wants you, eh William?" laughed Mary, as Martha walked back into the room.

"William dear, how lovely to see you!" exclaimed Martha, kissing William on the cheek and making him blush again.

"What's that smell?" said William, sniffing the air with a look of disdain.

"You mean my house smells?" exclaimed Martha in mock horror. "Did you hear what he said, Mary, he thinks my house smells! What a thing to say to a lady, don't you think?"

"Dreadful," said Mary, as the two girls giggled at William's further embarrassment.

"The smell, William," announced Martha grandly, "is Mr Noble Ladds, who has just bin in 'ere and 'e wears scent, or what did you call it, Mary?"

"Cologne."

"Yes, cologne, that's what it is, do you know any men who put cologne on, William?"

"No, I don't think I do."

"Well you do *now*," said Martha with a snort of derision. "What is the world coming to? Men putting on scent, I really don't know."

William said nothing, and rummaged in the basket he had brought.

"Martha, Mother sent this for the new baby and she says not to lose it."

He handed Martha an envelope.

"And she sent another present – I think it's something she knitted – and some sausages and a bit of salt bacon."

"William, that is kind of her, I will write a note for you to take back."

"She says she wants to know all about the baby!" said William looking around the room. "Where is it? Don't babies cry?"

"Not this one," said Mary with a smile. "Look – he's over there."

She pointed at the drawer on the table. William went to look at sleeping child, and Martha cooed at it over his shoulder.

"I'll give him a feed and then we can put 'im upstairs, Mary," said Martha, starting to undo the buttons of her blouse. William turned, aghast and hurried towards the door – calling back to the girls over his shoulder as he pelted from the room.

"I'll go and find Henry, he's probably feeding the cattle!"

Mary turned to look at Martha; before both girls burst out laughing at William's expense. Mary began to unpack the basket that William had brought with him. She put the sausages in the safe and hung the piece of bacon from a beam across the kitchen ceiling; there was also tin of biscuits and a knitted jacket for young Henry. Under all this, right at the bottom of the basket was an envelope addressed to her with a stamp she did not recognise. She looked closely at it and read "Argentina". She looked up sharply to check that Martha wasn't looking at her, and stowed the letter hurriedly in the pocket of her dress.

Chapter Thirty-Eight
Noble Ladds

Mary sent a note back with William to her father and Lucy to say that all was well and she would return as soon as Martha was able to cope on her own. In truth, Martha was coping very well and although a little weak for the first day or two she recovered remarkably quickly. Noble Ladds returned from London having sold his horse and as promised he brought Mary a present; a small lacquered, painted jewellery box which Mary had hidden from Martha so as not to be teased. She had read the letter from Rupert several times; he was much better at expressing himself in a letter, and although enjoying his time in Buenos Aires, he was clearly somewhat homesick and missing Mary. He had asked for a photograph of her to keep with him; she only had one, of her and Lucy, which had been taken ten years ago. She decided that she would go to Rushden and get a portrait done when she next got a chance.

Noble Ladds called most days, much to Martha's annoyance.

"What does that man keep comin' 'ere for?" she would grumble. "It's 'cos of you, Mary, 'e's coming to see you, I know 'e is."

Mary said nothing; but it was true and she knew it. She was unapologetic about Noble's presence – she liked his company.

As the chapel in Brington had recently closed down, Mary walked the two miles to Bythorn for the evening service. The congregation was pitifully small and the closure of this one was imminent. Although Noble lived in Bythorn he did not go to chapel, preferring to spend Sunday afternoon sitting in the sun outside the front door of his farm house, sleeping off the beer he had drunk at lunchtime. Mary's journey home took her past his farm and that Sunday as she returned past his house, she had caught sight of him asleep against the trunk of a tall pear tree. He had no jacket on in the warm spring sunshine, but his smart check waistcoat was cut tight to his body, showing a fine athletic figure and no sign of a paunch. Mary smiled at the sleeping figure and walked on.

A cry echoed up behind her, a couple of hundred yards further up the track: "Mary, wait a moment! Let me walk you home, you don't know who you might meet along the road."

She turned to see Noble grab his jacket from the ground beside him, before trotting down the path to meet her.

"You don't go to chapel then, Noble?" asked Mary curiously.

"No, I'm a church man myself," he said lightly.

"So you went this morning then?"

"Well not exactly," he laughed. "I was busy and didn't make it today."

"You really don't have to walk me back; I can manage on my own you know," Mary said, turning to smile at him coyly from under the brim of her boater.

"No, Mary, it's my pleasure; it is really. Besides, what else do I have to do on a Sunday afternoon?"

"Very well then," Mary said. "But aren't you going to shut your front door?"

They looked back to where the front door yawned open.

"No there's no need," said Noble with a dismissive wave of his hand. "Spot is in there; he keeps guard."

"Who's Spot?"

"He's my terrier, best dog I've ever had. He won't let anyone in."

Mary raised an eyebrow, and turned along turnpike road to Brington. It wasn't the quickest way, but in her best coat and Sunday shoes it was the least muddy path.

"Bless my soul, Mary, slow up a little, you walk faster than I can keep up with," Noble complained, looping his arm through hers to slow her pace and pull her closer. Mary did not resist but did not slow down.

"I have to get home to get the tea you know; it's only a few days since Martha had the baby and she is hardly fit yet."

"Be blowed for a tale, Mary Knighton," laughed Noble. "Martha is as strong as an ox, there's nothing that will slow her up. And any road, Henry will help."

"Don't you believe it, Noble!" said Mary. "Henry won't even hold the baby; he says that's woman's work."

She sighed and shook her head.

465

"How long are you staying, Mary?" asked Noble.

"Just a few more days, then I have to go back to Cold Harbour," sighed Mary. "I dread it."

"It's a lovely spot up there on the hill," insisted Noble earnestly. "Why don't you like it?"

"Stuck up there all day with no one to talk to!" sighed Mary. "No one ever comes to visit, and with only Father and Edgar in the house it would drive anyone mad. I don't know what I would give to get away."

Noble looked at her, surprised, and for a moment was silent.

"I'm going to look at another horse tomorrow," he said after a while. "I'll bring him round for you to have a look at if you like?"

He pulled her a little closer as they walked along.

"Will you, Noble? I could have a ride then."

"You can't ride him anyway, I don't have a side-saddle," said Noble with a laugh.

"Yes I can! I always rode Henry's horse; I don't need a side-saddle – I can sit astride."

"That ain't very ladylike, Miss Knighton," scolded Noble. "Not very ladylike at all."

"I don't care whether it's ladylike or not! You bring it round; I'll show you I can ride."

Noble pulled out his silver cigar case as they continued along the path, lighting one as they chatted.

"That's a nice smell," she said.

"Do you want one, then?" Noble asked.

"No," said Mary, wrinkling up her nose. "You don't have any cigarettes, do you? I'll have one of those."

"In my jacket pocket," he said with a smile.

Mary pulled her arm from his, putting her hand in his pocket and pulling out a packet. She opened it, pulled out a cigarette and tapped the end on her thumb before bringing it to her lips.

"Light, please," she said imperiously to Noble, who lit a match, cupped his hands around its flickering flame and brought it to meet the end of the cigarette. Mary inhaled deeply, blowing a thin stream of smoke out of the corner of her mouth and smiling flirtatiously up at Noble.

"I didn't know you smoked, Mary Knighton; that's a turn up for the books!"

The road bent sharply to the left, and although the setting sun warmed their backs, the wind was cold and blew full in their faces, stinging their cheeks mercilessly. Mary lowered her head and pulled her shawl tighter around her shoulders; she shivered and walked a little faster.

"Come on, Mary, let's go and shelter in Old Miles' barn for a while to get out of the wind," Noble said, indicating a stone barn set slightly back from the road, not too far removed from a dilapidated farm. He smiled at Mary, waiting for a reply.

"I'm not going to walk through all that mud and cow muck in my best boots!" huffed Mary "What do you think I am?"

"I can carry you over that bit – it's not very far," said Noble with a laugh, looked imploringly at Mary.

"What do you want to go in there for? We will soon be home – look, I can see their place now, it's only going to take another five minutes!"

She pursed her lips and looked up the road towards Henry and Martha's farmhouse.

"Mary, just for five minutes," Noble begged, taking hold of her arm.

"No, Noble!" Mary snapped, pulling her arm away.

She softened and smiled at him gently.

"Come on, you can have a cup of tea when we get there – I must get back to help Martha; they will be expecting me, don't you see."

"Hmm," Noble grunted, evidently displeased.

Mary turned, looped her arm through his and smiled.

"Come on, Noble Ladds, cheer up and take that miserable look off your face."

She dug her fingers into his ribs to tickle him; Noble squirmed and jumped back. He scowled, looked away and then rushed forward to grab her; but Mary was too fast and danced away from him with a delighted laugh.

"Look," she said, pointing, "I can see Henry over there bringing the cows in!"

She put her index fingers in her mouth and blew a shrill whistle, making Noble jump. In the distance they could see Henry waving his arms; they waved back.

"Want some of this?" asked Noble, pulling his flask from the inside pocket of his jacket.

"What's that?" asked Mary suspiciously.

"Whisky."

"I've never had that," said Mary with a small frown.

"Try some. It's lovely," he said, taking a good swig, "it warms you up on a day like this when the evenings are getting cold."

"If you say so, Mr Ladds," laughed Mary, grabbing his arm. "Come on, I would much rather have a cup of tea."

Martha returned to full strength very quickly and it was clear that Mary would not be needed much longer. That Tuesday, Thomas and Charlotte came to visit on their way back from Thrapston market. Charlotte rarely went away from Dean but she could not resist the opportunity to see her new great-nephew. When they arrived Henry took Thomas off to look at the cattle in the yard and the three women admired the baby in the warm kitchen. Mary picked him up deftly and gave him to Charlotte to hold.

"Look at you, Mary Knighton; I didn't know that you were so adept with babies; it doesn't seem like you."

"Aunt Charlotte, I've hardly had a chance until now, have I?" protested Mary.

"No, dear, but you will get married one day and have some of your own."

"There's not much chance of that, living at Cold Harbour, is there Aunt Charlotte," muttered Mary.

"Why can't you have babies at Cold Harbour, dear? It's a lovely place and such a view!"

"I mean getting married, Aunt Charlotte; no one ever goes up there and I don't meet anyone except Father and Edgar. It might as well be a prison."

There was an uneasy silence.

"Noble Ladds comes to see you up there," said Martha with a sly smirk.

"Hmm," murmured Charlotte, disapprovingly, rocking the baby with renewed vigour.

"Your father asked when you were coming home," she said, tearing her eyes away from young Henry to look at Mary. "He passed the message to William on Saturday."

Mary put her hand to her forehead and shut her eyes.

"I can manage now, Mary, I'm sure I can," said Martha gently.

Mary sighed heavily and smiled at Henry waving his little feet in the air.

"Tell William to tell him I'll be back by the weekend," said Mary quietly. "But I'm going to miss the baby. Aunt Charlotte, isn't he a lovely boy?"

"Yes, Mary, he really is," she cooed, handing him reluctantly back to Mary who tucked him up in the drawer.

"It's a pity he has to start life in a drawer though, Martha," she said with a sniff, staring hard at Martha.

"Well, yes I suppose it is," said Martha lightly, "but he's doing awfully well, isn't he?"

"Yes, my dear, you must be very proud, and so must Henry."

She looked distractedly out the window.

"Where are Henry and Thomas? We can't stay much longer! I get so cold sitting in the trap these days and it will take us over an hour to get home."

"I will go and give them a call," said Mary, making for the door. "You sit here with Martha and the baby."

Mary went out to the yard to Thomas and Henry, who were putting the horse back in the shafts of the trap after a feed. Charlotte was summoned from the house and she bustled out, climbing into the trap and wrapping herself in a blanket for their trip home. They gave a cheery wave, Thomas shook the reins at the horse and they were gone.

Mary and Martha went back in the kitchen, while Henry went back to attend to the cattle.

"Martha," said Mary, "why don't you have a crib for young Henry? Aunt's Charlotte right, a drawer is a bit humble, isn't it?"

Martha looked down at Henry, who was feeding greedily, and chewed her lip.

"He's not in a crib, Mary, 'cos we don't have any money for fings like that. Uncle Thomas lent Henry a lot of money to start 'ere and we 'ave to pay 'im back in the end. William helps Henry with the figures but he says we are not making any profit yet and what money we do have goes, it just goes!"

She sniffed and drew her sleeve across her nose, her lip quivering.

"And then Henry goes down the pub with that Noble Ladds and more goes! I suppose he's got to 'ave some fun, he works 'ard enough – but it don't help. So that's why he ain't got a crib."

Martha sniffed again and fell silent.

"Martha, I'm so sorry," said Mary, "I didn't realise that things were that bad, I really am sorry, Martha."

Martha wiped her eyes on her sleeve and smiled.

"Don't worry about me, Mary, it will be all right, you see. I was brought up like that, my mum and dad never 'ad any money and all my bruvvers and sisters were started in a drawer and it did them no 'arm."

On the Thursday before Mary was due to go home, Noble arrived in the afternoon as usual; bringing with him a new horse that he had bought at the market. Mary, Martha and Henry stood and admired his new purchase; a bay gelding of fifteen and a half hands. Henry found half an apple left over from the store in the barn, which he fed to the beast, who chomped happily on the apple, his bit clattering in his mouth.

"Now, Noble, you said I could have a ride," Mary said firmly. "Tell him, Henry; he doesn't believe that I can ride a horse."

"She can ride all right, Noble," chuckled Henry. "She always rode my horse at Cold Harbour – even bareback at times."

"But you don't have a side-saddle," said Martha.

"She won't worry about that, if she can get on the thing," laughed Henry, holding the bridle with both hands and nodding to Mary.

"Hold this for me then, Martha," said Mary excitedly, taking her shawl from around her shoulders and handing it to her.

"Noble," she said pleadingly.

"Yes, Mary?"

"Can you shorten the stirrups?"

"I didn't say you could ride him, did I?"

"Didn't you?" she said, looking wistfully at him.

"Very well then," shrugged Noble, lifting the flap of the saddle and raising the stirrups up three notches.

Mary took the reins and with both hands held onto the saddle. She tried to reach the stirrup with her left foot, but was not tall enough. She looked around at the incredulous trio.

"Come on, someone; give me a lift," she laughed.

She bent her left knee, sticking her foot out behind her and looking indignantly at Noble.

"Noble, come on, give me a lift!" she ordered.

Noble smiled and hoisted Mary into the air. As she rose level with the saddle she threw her right leg over, her skirt and petticoat flying in all directions. There was an ominous ripping sound.

"What was that?" screamed Martha, laughing.

"Just a bit of my petticoat tearing," Mary said unworriedly, landing lightly on the saddle, the leather cold against her skin.

"As long as that's all," giggled Martha.

The skirt of Mary's dress fell down the flanks of the horse and flowed out along its back. She wriggled her feet wriggled from under the material, trying to find the stirrups.

"Noble," she demanded, "stirrups!"

"Yes, Miss Knighton," Noble said, touching his cap quickly.

He grabbed Mary's left foot and slid it into the stirrup before moving to the other side to do the same, quickly squeezing Mary's calf as he moved back to join Henry and Martha.

"You look a real picture sat up there, Mary; all you need is a smart 'at and you would be real la-di-da," wondered Martha.

"Quite so, my dear, quite so," said Henry, in his best upper class accent.

Henry let go of the bridle and the horse stepped gently forward, before shifting on the spot uneasily, ears flicking backwards and forwards. Mary pulled the horse to a standstill, and patted its neck. She looked in complete command of the animal.

"Have you got a leading rein, Henry?" enquired Noble.

"I don't want that, Noble!" snorted Mary. "I want to give him a gallop."

Noble ignored her and grabbed the reins.

"I'll lead him just out the yard and then we can go up the top meadow," insisted Noble. "It's dried up in this sun and the cattle have not been out yet, that's all right with you, Henry?"

"That's fine," said Henry as Noble led the horse across the cobbles, its hooves clacking as it danced a little in anticipation of the ride.

"Come on, Noble, let the reins go – I can manage!" grumbled Mary.

"Just wait till we are past the cattle yard and the stables and then you can go."

"I feel like a child," said Mary grumpily.

Up past the gate of the yard, on the track, Noble released the reins.

"You be careful, Mary, and mind the rabbit holes," warned Noble. "I don't want any damage to him; I paid a lot of money for that horse."

"Don't worry, Noble Ladds, I told you I could ride," laughed Mary, squeezing her legs into the side of the animal; with a slight jab of her heels the beast responded immediately. "I'll see you up there," she shouted back over her shoulder.

"Very good, miladyship," Noble called back with a decadent wave of his hand, as she cantered off.

He could see that she was right; she was an extremely good horsewoman in complete command of the horse, which responded to her every instruction. The ground underfoot was dry and the sun beat powerfully down, the grass waving gently in the breeze. Rabbits scurried into the undergrowth as Mary urged the horse on, only pulling up at the entrance to the meadow where she waited for Noble.

"What's his name?" she called to Noble, who was swaggering up the hill with an admiring smile. "He's a fine bit of horseflesh, isn't he?"

"Yes, but he's not as good as Speedy," said Noble. "He hasn't got a name."

"Oh, he must have one!" insisted Mary. "I will think of one now, can I have a gallop?"

"Yes, yes, go on then, just twice round and I'll meet you up by that oak tree at the top."

Off Mary went, standing in the stirrups and crouching over the animal's neck as she took him flying round the field, her hair flowing in a stream behind her, her cheeks flushed with exertion. She arrived at the tree before Noble; dismounting away from him to ensure her torn drawers did not show.

"That was wonderful, Noble; I love horse riding, we don't have one any more at Cold Harbour."

She patted the horse's velvety nose as Noble attached the leading rein to the bridle, tying it the hedge; the horse put its nose down and started to graze.

"I think you should call it Tinker, Noble; that would be a good name."

"Well I suppose it would," Noble said, moving slowly towards Mary, a smile playing on his lips. "If you want to call it Tinker, that's what its name shall be."

He gripped both her forearms, pulling her forwards to kiss her on the lips; Mary turned her head slightly and took the kiss on her cheek.

"You're hot, Mary," he whispered.

"I'm out of puff from riding, it takes a lot out of you, doesn't it!" laughed Mary.

Noble looked at her and smiled.

"Let's sit down for a while; the ground's dry and you can get your wind back."

"No, it's not!" said Mary with a laugh. "The grass is wet."

"Very well then; I'll put my jacket down for you to sit on," said Noble, taking off his jacket and spreading it out on the grass.

"A seat for my lady," he said with a low bow.

Mary laughed, curtseying at Noble before sitting down on the makeshift rug. The sun was still high in the sky, warming their upturned faces. Mary lay back, her arms above her head, and looked up at the branches of the oak tree. Noble leant over her and she remembered the day with the swarm of bees and sat up sharply to avoid his advance. She pulled her knees to her chest, locking her arms around them, before realising with a stab of embarrassment that she had torn her drawers getting on Tinker. Hurriedly, she stretched her legs out in front of her.

"Noble, I'm sitting on something hard here," she complained, shifting on the grass.

"Oh, Mary, be careful that's my flask," said Noble, putting one hand on her thigh and leaning over to pluck the flask from the pocket of his jacket.

He sat up and unscrewed the top of the flask, as Mary removed his hand from her thigh.

He took a small swig and offered it to her.

"Want a drop?" he said.

"The smell is awful," she said. "I couldn't."

"Yes, you could," laughed Noble. "Go on; it will do you good. I didn't like it the first time but I do now."

Mary sighed and reached for the flask.

"Go on then let me have it," she relented, sniffing the contents of the flask.

"Euergh," she spluttered, "I can't drink that."

"Yes, you can," insisted Noble. "Go on, just tip it up."

Mary shut her eyes, tipped her head back and took a huge swig from the flask. She swallowed hard, her eyes widening as the liquid burnt its way down her throat. Her hand rose to her mouth, her eyes tightly shut as she turned her head away from the flask which she offered back to Noble. She opened her eyes and took several deep breaths.

"You didn't tell me it was going to be hot like that!" she croaked. "It burns your throat – like eating fire."

"Did you like it, then?" Noble enquired.

"No I didn't," gasped Mary.

She paused, before adding,

"At least, I don't think I did."

He smiled at Mary, who smiled back.

"I don't know how you can do it, Noble; I don't know anyone who drinks whisky. We hardly have any drink at Cold Harbour. Reverend Packham always reminds us about the demon drink and the sins of the flesh."

"If you say so, Mary," said Noble unconvinced.

"Yes I do say so," insisted Mary. "And that reminds me; I'm going back to Cold Harbour tomorrow, back to looking after Father and Edgar." Mary shuddered. "I hate Edgar more and more; why Father puts up with him I don't know! I wish Henry were back running the farm."

She turned to Noble.

"Noble," she said quietly, "you will call, won't you? It's so awful living up there; it's like going back to prison. William says we are making no money and we will have to sell up in the end because we owe the bank so much, what is the point? What is the point?"

She sighed and lay back on his jacket again, looking up at the branches of the tree. Once again Noble leant over her and once again Mary sat up as his lips lightly swept her cheek. Suddenly, she clasped her hands together, banging them down hard on the ground between her legs angrily. She paused and banged them down again and again. A tear trickled from each eye, as she leant her body forward over her legs – her forehead almost touching her knees.

Without warning, she sat up and with her left arm she grabbed Noble's shoulder, pulling him towards her and kissing him quickly on the mouth. She rested her cheek against his and wrapped her arms tightly around him. Moments passed before she released her hold, pushing him away from her. Her face was red; her cheeks damp with tears.

"You will come, won't you, Noble? Promise you will, I will go mad I'm sure I will if I stay up there much longer. I'm over twenty, Noble, I'll soon be an old maid. Please say you will come!"

"Of course I will come, Mary," promised Noble. "Now dry your eyes and don't upset yourself so; it won't do you any good. Have another tot of the whisky – that will make you feel better."

Mary examined him closely, her eyes boring into his. Noble shifted uncomfortably and reached again for his flask. He undid the top, took a swig and once again offered it to her. Mary eyed the outstretched flask and looked back at him. She wiped her eyes on the sleeve of her blouse, sniffed and took the flask, holding it in both hands; her arms resting on her knees, her body leaning slightly forward. She looked down accusingly at the flask before blurting out,

"Yes, I bloody well will! I don't care what bloody Reverend Packham says, I need another tot of the sins of the flesh if I've got to live at Cold Harbour."

She raised the flask to her lips, tipped her head back and took a big swig, shaking her head as if to rid her mouth of the taste as she let the flask fall from her mouth.

"That's better," she said firmly. "I feel better for that."

She handed the flask back to Noble with a bleary smile.

"You're right, Noble, the whisky does make you feel better. I didn't realise that it had that effect. I feel quite light-headed, like I've just lit a cigarette." She stopped and considered. "I've got the rest of your packet from the other day! It's in my pocket! That is if they're not squashed." She rummaged about the folds of her skirt to find the pocket, finally pulling a crumpled packet from within. "There we are and they are not crushed at all," cried Mary triumphantly.

She hiccupped loudly.

"Noble?" she wheedled.

"Yes, Mary."

"Have you got a light, my dear?"

She pulled a cigarette from the packet, tapping the end impatiently on her thumbnail.

"Yes, my lady, I'll be with you directly," said Noble mockingly, pulling the matches from his waistcoat pocket and lighting the match.

Mary raised the cigarette to her lips, moving towards the flame, and putting her hand on his thigh to steady herself. Noble looked sharply down at her hand and watched as she lit the cigarette and took a deep draw. Mary felt dizzy and shut her eyes to steady herself. She took another pull on the cigarette and looked out towards the farm. She could just see the tops of the chimneys – the setting sun glinting across the pots. Rooks floated on the breeze, swinging over the fields on their way back to roost and on the far hill Mary could see smoke drifting up to the horizon from a hedge cutter's fire. As she stared out towards the fire – the smoke started to lose focus – the horizon seemed to tip to the side – pulsing furiously in the distance. The colour drained from her cheeks and she raised her hands to her face, feeling dizzy and slightly sick, the effect of the tobacco making her lose control; she turned and looked at Noble, who she could see was talking to her.

"Do you feel all right, Mary?" asked Noble. "You look a bit funny."

She could see his lips moving, but couldn't work out what he was saying – the sound echoed around her head, muddying in her skull. She tried desperately to focus on the horizon again – but it wouldn't stay upright.

"I'm fine," she mouthed, but the words wouldn't seem to come out.

She looked at the cigarette between her fingers, knowing she must get rid of it. She rolled it between her index finger and thumb, flicking it away.

"No, I don't feel well," she said, blinking rapidly. "It's the cigarette – I know it is and—"

Speech petered out and Mary fell backwards – her head lolling onto the collar of Noble's jacket. She could see the branches of the tree still, but they weren't in focus – it was as if they were moving towards her, threatening to fall. Mary could see Noble leaning over her – he seemed to be undoing the buttons of his waistcoat, she wondered vaguely what he was doing that for? She could feel the cold breeze on her legs – the warmth from the sun had gone. And then she felt his weight on top of her – and still the branches moved towards her – she wondered vaguely if they would collapse on her entirely.

Gradually, she felt herself regaining control; the dizziness was receding and the branches returning to their rightful place. She pushed herself up on her arms and felt the cold on her legs. She looked down to see that her skirt had been pulled up round her waist. She looked confusedly up at Noble who stood over her, pulling his braces over his shoulders and doing up the buttons of his trousers. He bent down and pulled her skirt down from her waist as she sat up and looked around. Tinker was still tied to the hedge, absently chewing some of the smaller branches. She pulled her legs under herself and knelt on her heels for a moment, trying desperately to retrieve the last few moments in her mind. Noble offered her his hand; she took it and stood up.

"Are you all right?" he asked, bending down to pick up his jacket.

"I'm fine," she said without looking at him. She felt uncomfortable but couldn't work out why.

Noble thrust his arms into his jacket, turning his collar down and brushing the grass from the arms. He picked up his flask and put it in his inside pocket.

"I'm going," she said quietly.

"Do you want to ride back?" Noble asked.

Mary shook her head.

"Do you want me to come with you?"

"No."

"I'll go back across the fields then," Noble said.

"Suit yourself," mumbled Mary.

She brushed down her skirt, pulled the sleeves of her blouse down and started back across the field. She felt unsteady and uncomfortable as she walked past the big horse grazing; she looked into his eyes – big and brown and deep. The horse looked back and then looked away without expression – seeing all but knowing nothing.

Chapter Thirty-Nine
Suddenly All Alone

Mary walked slowly back to the farm house. The sun was in her eyes and the breeze had dropped, the smoke rising straight up from the chimney; Martha must have just made up the range because Mary could smell the coal. The two dogs barked and rushed out of the gate to meet her, licking her hands and rubbing up against her skirt as she walked. She stumbled to the wall that circled the yard, leaning heavily against it before turning and being violently sick. She could hear the cattle moving about in the yard and the clank of a bucket handle as Henry was doing the feeding.

She waited until he went into one of the loose boxes and made her way to the back door, through the scullery and into the kitchen where Martha was preparing the evening meal, standing by the range, stirring a large saucepan.

"Is that you, Mary?" she shouted without turning round. "I'll be there in a minute, just got to stir this a bit more."

The room was warm and cosy but seemed dark to Mary– she had been outside in the sun for so long – and it took a while for her eyes to get accustomed to the gloom. The warmth of the room made her feel sweaty again, and the urge to run outside again and be sick rose up in her; she took several deep breaths and the sensation started to dissipate.

"There we are," said Martha, putting the lid on the saucepan and pulling it to the side of the hob, "that will go along slowly now."

She turned round and looked at Mary.

"Mary, Mary!" she exclaimed. "What's wrong? You're white as a sheet and your hair! Come and sit down."

She pulled a chair out from the table and Mary sat down.

"Now tell me what's wrong?" said Martha, looking hard into Mary's white face.

"It's nothing, I just came over a bit sickly," said Mary weakly, looking at Martha and forcing the faintest of smiles.

"What's that smell, Mary, you smell of something? It's smoke! You've been smoking, Mary, that's it! That's made you feel upset I bet that's it."

"Yes, that's probably it," said Mary looking down.

"You smell just like Henry does when 'e's bin in the pub, but I s'pose you would if you've bin smokin'."

She pulled up a chair for herself and sat in front of Mary, holding her hands and peering into Mary's face.

"Why don't you go and 'ave a lie down, Mary? That will make you feel better, you see if it don't."

"Yes, you're right, Martha," nodded Mary weakly. "I'll just go down the end first."

"You do that, Mary, and I'll make you a cup of tea to take to your room."

When Mary came back, Martha had the tea ready. She was still unsteady on her feet and had to hold onto the chair to stop herself falling.

"Come on, Mary, you go up and I'll bring the tea and then you can 'ave a lie down."

The latch of the door clicked as Martha opened it to let Mary up the stairs, the soles of their shoes banging on the stairs as they climbed.

"Where's Noble Ladds then, Mary? Why didn't he bring you back if you didn't feel well?"

"Oh, he took the horse back over the fields to Bythorn," said Mary absently.

"Well I don't know!" scolded Martha. "He could have come this way! That's men for you, Mary, they don't think, do they?"

They walked down the landing into Mary's room at the end of the corridor; the room faced west and the last of the sun was streaming through the sash window. In the room stood a bed and one chair with a split cane seat which was falling through, but no other furniture. Mary's bag lay against the wall, packed with all her clothes, her coat hanging from a nail on the back of the door.

"Shall I close the window, Mary?"

"No, Martha, leave it open please, I feel a bit hot," said Mary faintly.

Martha moved the chair next to the bed, balancing the cup and saucer on the corner.

"Come on then, Mary, you lie down; you'll feel fine in a little while, I'm

480

sure you will."

Mary sat on the bed and swallowed, beads of sweat standing on her forehead. Martha eyed her worriedly.

"I'm goin' down now to feed the baby and give Henry 'is tea, you come down when you are ready," she advised.

She squeezed Mary's hand and moved out of the room, closing the door after her.

Mary took a small sip of tea but could not drink it. She lay back on the bed, a dead weight sitting in the pit of her stomach. In the last two hours, the whole course of her life seemed to have changed fundamentally yet she could not work out why. She felt cold and alone and miserable beyond belief. The sunlight from the window moved across the back wall of the room and little by little disappeared. The darkness crept across the room, lengthening shadows and heightening noise in the house. She could hear the baby crying intermittently – stopping when she supposed Martha must have been feeding it. She could hear the click of the scullery door as Henry came in from feeding the cattle, the sound of his boots ringing out on the stone slabs. Her thoughts flicked from Noble to Cold Harbour to Tinker to the baby and back to the oak tree in the top meadow. She rose from her bed, kneeling by it and clasping her hands together to pray; but when it came to it she didn't know what to say. She went to retrieve her Bible from her bag, but it was too dark to read and she had no candle. She crawled back into bed, pulling the blankets up to her chin and staring desperately at the ceiling. What was going to happen? What had happened? She pored over the haze of the afternoon, trying desperately to remember. Nothing.

The back door clicked again, squeaking open, followed by the sound of footsteps on the cobbles – it was Martha; she could hear the nails in the heel of her shoes scratching the stones as she crossed the cobbles and a clank as the handle of a bucket dropped. The pump handle squeaked as Martha worked it up and down; the splosh of the water falling into the bucket sounding out against the faint whooshing effort of the pump.

Endlessly, she pored over the events of the afternoon, searching for answers as to what had happened. She shivered and drew the blankets closer around her. She didn't know; only Noble knew. Noble and the horse; the horse with its dark, dark eyes. She sobbed once, desperate to dispel the fug of whisky. If only she could remember!

There was a clatter as plates were laid on the table – the scraping of the legs of Henry's chair, and the quiet murmur of conversation drifting up to Mary. It was now dark; Mary could see stars through the little window, shards of light pierced the darkness of the room, and Mary could hear the hooves of a horse as it trotted up the road – the farm dogs barking at the noise until it retreated into the distance. What was she going to do? What could she do? Who could she talk to? She was in complete disgrace; of that she was sure. Lucy! She should talk to Lucy; Lucy was level-headed and had good judgement. But Mary knew she couldn't talk to Lucy, knew she couldn't talk to anyone. She shivered and went to find her nightdress, taking off her clothes and throwing them on the floor. She felt her way round the room to the door, took her thick coat off the nail, put it on and got back in bed.

Henry and Martha had finished their meal; she could hear Martha washing up and cooing as she dealt with the baby. There was a clink and rattle as the top was taken off the range and more coal poured in from a bucket. Then it all went quiet; she knew Henry would be asleep in the chair by the fire and Martha would be sitting at the table, mending or knitting. She heard a squeak from above her head and a scrabbling noise as rats scurried around in the ceiling. An owl hooted outside, another one answering a little way off; they hooted backward and forwards for some time and then there was silence. A little more light had started to seep through the window. Mary knew there must be a moon, but all she could see outside was the faint silvery outline of the hay barn on the other side of the yard.

Time passed, and Mary had no idea how much, having no watch. There was a click at the door at the bottom of the stairs, footsteps coming up the stairs. It was Henry, Mary could tell by the thump of his feet on the treads of the stairs. She could see a faint light flickering under the door as he moved to his room, where she could hear him rummaging around. He went back to the top of the stairs and shouted,

"Where's the money, Martha?"

There was a brief pause as Martha moved to the bottom of the stairs and hissed,

"Just keep your voice down, Henry Knighton, you'll wake the baby and Mary; she's not well, I told you that, and any road what do you want money for this time of day?"

"Oh, sorry," he whispered loudly, "I'm going up the pub."

"No, you're not!"

"Yes, I am! I'm going to see Noble, so where's the money?"

Mary's heart sank when she heard Noble's name; she shivered again and pulled the blankets closer around her neck.

"I'm got the money safe so there," Martha hissed up the stairs.

"Just tell me where it is."

"You can 'ave two shillin's I'm got it 'ere; that'll be plenty for one night."

Henry grunted and moved along the landing and down the stairs. A few more words were exchanged and Henry left the house; Mary could hear his boots crunching across the cobbles and out into the road.

Not long after her brother had left, Mary heard a gentle tap on her door.

"Mary dear, how are you? Are you awake?"

Martha came into the room holding a candle which lit her face from below; Mary thought how pretty she was.

"Yes I'm on the mend, thank you, Martha," said Mary with a faint smile

"Can I get you anything? You didn't drink your tea and look at all your clothes on the floor! Come, I'll fold them up for you."

She put the candle on the floor and moved the cup from the chair, picking up Mary's clothes and folding them one at a time, hanging some on the back of the chair and others on the broken seat.

Last of all she picked up Mary's drawers.

"Look 'ere, Mary, I can see what ripped when you got on that 'orse this afternoon," laughed Martha, putting her hand through the gaping hole and wiggling her fingers.

Mary managed a small smile.

"I'll take 'em down and sew them up for you."

"No, no, Martha, I'll do that; I'll come down, Henry is out, isn't he?"

"Yes, he's gone for the night, won't see him till ten o'clock."

"What time is it, Martha?"

"About quarter to seven I guess," Martha said.

"Is that all?" sighed Mary, getting out of bed and following Martha out.

In the kitchen, the oil lamp cast a dim light around the room; the coals glowed in the range, and a cat sat in Henry's vacated armchair, warming itself by the fire.

"Come on then, Mary; push that cat out the way and sit near the fire and warm yourself up. You look half starved, you really do, are you goin' to 'ave anything to eat or a cup of tea?"

Martha stroked Mary's hair as she sat down.

"Perhaps a cup of tea then, but I'm sure I couldn't eat anything," said Mary quietly.

She looked around the room as a stranger might, seeing details of the kitchen as if for the first time; her eyes came to rest on the drawer where young Henry lay.

"Martha, I must have a look at him," said Mary, rising and hurrying to the table, pulling the blanket back a little. Henry gurgled up at her, his mouth wide in astonishment as she smiled and mouthed words to him.

"Isn't he wonderful?" sighed Mary, pulling the blanket back up and sitting down again.

Martha smiled and poured out the tea, bringing it to Mary and sitting opposite her in the dim light.

"Martha," said Mary tentatively, "when's Henry coming back?"

"Oh, no telling, when he gets in the pub with Noble. But I know it will be at least 'arf past ten, I know that."

Mary took a sip of her tea and was quiet again.

"Martha?"

"Yes, Mary?"

"You know Mother died a bit back?"

"Yes, Mary, I was there," said Martha, at a slight loss as to how to respond.

"Well, she didn't tell me anything."

"What you mean she didn't tell me anything?"

"Well you know what mothers tell daughters," persisted Mary. "She died before she could."

Tears sprang to her eyes; Martha rose, putting her arm around Mary's shoulder and pushing her cheek against Mary's.

"Come on, Mary, you mustn't cry, it's not like you to do that. You are usually so strong."

Mary wiped her eyes on her sleeve, sniffed and looked at Martha through watery eyes.

"She didn't tell me what men and women do to have a baby," whispered Mary.

"Oh," said Martha with a small frown, sitting back, "well you've come to the right person to ask then, Mary; I'm an expert, ain't I?"

She laughed and nodded at the baby, Mary was looking at her expectantly. Martha smiled and without embarrassment explained everything to Mary, who listened in complete silence. She shuddered slightly as it gradually dawned on her what had happened that afternoon.

"So that's that," said Martha when she had finished.

There was silence, Mary looked up.

"And how often?" she asked quietly.

"Every night; sometimes twice."

"Oh Martha, that must be awful," Mary said sympathetically.

"No, I like it," laughed Martha.

Mary eyed her dubiously and sat back in her chair as Martha continued to chatter on. What Martha had told her made things infinitely worse. She looked up suddenly, aware that Martha had asked her a question.

"Mary, you ain't listenin'?" asked Martha, leaning forward and looking intently at Mary.

"No, what did you say, Martha?"

"What made you ask, Mary? Was there somethin' else to tell me?"

"Oh no, it was just that Lucy and I were talking about it," said Mary weakly. "We agreed to find out."

"Oh," said Martha doubtfully.

She rose to change the baby's nappy, before handing the little bundle to Mary.

"Here you are; he'll cheer you up, Mary, even if I can't."

She handed the baby to Mary, who took Henry gratefully and rocked him slowly to sleep.

"Now where are those drawers? I'll sew up that seam and they'll be as right as rain."

"No, Martha, I'll do it," said Mary urgently, grabbing the drawers from where Martha had laid them on the table. Martha frowned slightly and nodded, sitting back in her chair and finally dozing off as Mary sat gazing at the baby she held in her arms.

Chapter Forty
The Refuge of Cold Harbour

The next day Mary packed her bag, tied it to the pannier of her bicycle and set off for Cold Harbour. She had to pass the butcher's shop on the way and normally looked forward to visiting but today she did not want to go in. She felt changed, she felt dirty and she felt sure that Aunt Charlotte would know somehow. However, she knew there was no avoiding it; if she rode straight past someone would see her and in the end that would make things worse.

She leant her bike up against the wall and went into the shop where Roy Lowe was cutting up joints.

"Is Mrs Dunmore in, Roy?" she asked.

"She's always in, Miss Mary, 'cept when she goes to chapel," laughed Roy, "so being Friday, she is here."

Mary smiled and went through into the kitchen where Charlotte sat at one end of the table; Sarah was rolling out pastry at the other.

"Mary dear, do come in, come in," exclaimed Charlotte. "I want to hear all about this new nephew of yours! Come and sit down, and Sarah, put the kettle on, there's a dear. I'm sure Mary would like a cup of tea."

Charlotte pulled a chair out for Mary and patted it invitingly, Mary sat down with a small smile.

"My word, Mary, you've lost all your colour," clucked Charlotte. "You do look peaky, are you feeling all right?"

"I'm fine, Aunt Charlotte, I just had a little upset yesterday," explained Mary carefully. "But I'm much better now; I just haven't eaten much."

"Well you make sure you look after yourself, my dear, it's not like you to be under the weather. Now tell me about this boy."

Mary recounted as much detail as possible about Henry until Charlotte appeared satisfied.

"Now, Mary dear, fetch me my Bible– it's on top of the chest of drawers– and a pen and ink and I will write his name in."

Mary did as instructed and Charlotte opened the Bible at the front where she noted all family events.

"Here we are, Mary, here's you! Look, 1883! My goodness, you will soon be twenty-one."

"Yes. An old maid, Aunt Charlotte," sighed Mary.

"Fiddlesticks, Mary, you're no old maid," scolded Charlotte. "You're the prettiest girl for miles. You'll see – you will find a husband and be married soon, you see if I'm not right."

Mary's heart sank a little more, the terror of uncertainty unfurling in her stomach.

"Mary, you're daydreaming, did you hear what I said?"

"Yes, Aunt Charlotte, you said—"

Mary trailed off, watching Charlotte laboriously scribing the details of the new arrival in the Bible. She looked up sharply.

"Is he just Henry, Mary; did they give him any other names?"

"Just Henry, Aunt Charlotte."

"Your brother hasn't got a lot of imagination, has he, Mary, not much at all," muttered Charlotte, blowing vigorously on what she had just written.

She laid down her pen and looked up at Mary.

"As I was saying, you're not an old maid, dear, and you will soon be married and have children of your own; as long as it's not with Noble Ladds you will be fine."

Mary was silent. She wanted to leave, she could not face talking to her aunt anymore.

"Is William here, Aunt Charlotte?"

"I don't know, dear; Sarah, have you seen Master William?"

"No, Mrs Dunmore, I think he's gone farming," replied Sarah.

"He's always farming these days," sighed Charlotte.

Mary poured her tea into the saucer, drinking it from that to cool it more quickly.

"Don't do that, Mary; that's just what a man would do," scolded Charlotte. "You have to be more ladylike – just remember that."

"Yes, Aunt Charlotte," said Mary, gulping down the scalding tea.

"We will see you in chapel on Sunday, no doubt," Charlotte said as Mary rose to leave.

Mary nodded, kissed her aunt on the cheek and set off back home on her bicycle.

She had been dreading going back to Cold Harbour yesterday, but as she cycled nearer she realised that everything was different; Cold Harbour's isolation was now an advantage. Even the prospect of dealing with Edgar seemed a minor issue compared with the events of the last twenty-four hours, and she was looking forward to seeing her father again. She pushed her bike up the hill, turning left down the drive to Cold Harbour. She mounted her bike again, riding in and out of the pot holes and deftly avoiding the first lambs that had been turned out to grass. The dogs barked as she rode into the yard where Freda was at the washing-line, banging a rug with a paddle, clouds of dust rising into the air. She looked up, catching sight of Mary and dropping her paddle.

"Thank God you're back, Miss Mary," she cried. "I couldn't have stuck it much longer, I can tell yer, I'm 'havin' a day of it right now. 'Ow anyone can put up with that there Edgar I don't know, 'e's a dreadful man, truly dreadful. If it weren't for lookin' after your farver, Mary, I would 'ave gorn long ago."

She rushed to pick up the paddle, bustling after Mary into the kitchen.

"Where's Father, Freda?"

"'E's in the front room. I'm got the fire lit for 'im and 'e's readin' the paper or somethin'; I think William brought it."

Mary went through to greet her father and give him the news of the baby before returning to the kitchen, where Freda was boiling the kettle for tea.

"Now, if you are back, Miss Mary, I fink I ought to 'ave my day off if that's all right wiv you. You can give that horrible man 'is dinner."

Freda scowled.

"Very well, Freda," nodded Mary. "You certainly deserve it."

"Cuppa tea, Miss Mary?"

"Very good, Freda."

"Now before I go, Miss Mary, tell me all about the baby. I ain't got one of my own, ain't likely to never. Not wiv no man around. But I've allus liked babies. Don't you like babies, Miss Mary? I bet you're going to have some one day."

Freda broke off from her stream of narrative, put the cups and saucers on the table and looked up at Mary.

"Are you all right, Miss Mary?" she asked, examining Mary's face. "You look a bit peaky, you know."

"Yes, I'm fine," said Mary, casting her eyes down.

"What's 'is name, then?" asked Freda eagerly.

"Henry," said Mary, before elaborating on the details of the little boy.

As they chatted, Mary started to pull her clothes out of her bag, ready for washing on Monday. A letter tumbled to the floor and Freda quickly bent down and picked it up.

"'Ere we are, Miss Mary," she said, looking at the envelope, "don't know where this come from, some foreign place by the look of it."

Mary looked numbly at the letter and said nothing.

"I'll take your farver a cup of tea, then I'll go," said Freda softly. "It's funny, Miss Mary, now you're 'ere I don't really want to go for my day off; you've calmed me down no end, you 'ave. Oh, and Miss Mary, I think Miss Lucy is comin' 'ome for the weekend, there's a card up there; I 'ad to read it out for your farver 'cos he 'ad lost his glasses."

She bustled off down the corridor with the tea.

Mary looked at the letter and thought of Rupert; he seemed to have left such a long time ago.

"I'm off then," declared Freda, re-entering the room. "The dinner's in the bottom oven; 'e won't be long, it's half twelve now."

The door banged as she left. Mary stood stock still in the middle of the kitchen, still looking at the letter. She swallowed hard and started to prepare dinner for her father and Edgar.

"Oh you're back," grumbled Edgar as he barged into the kitchen, leaving a trail of mud across the floor. He shovelled down his lunch without speaking before going to sleep for half an hour in the chair by the fire and stomping out again.

Mary helped John back to the front room and made up the fire. She wandered back into the kitchen, Rupert's letter still lying on the table, inviting her to reread it. She sat on the chair by the fire and opened the crumpled letter.

"Dear Mary,

It seems so long since I left home and saw you last that I don't know what to tell you first. However I must tell you how much I am missing you; it seems so long before I will see you again."

Tears rolled down Mary's cheeks, landing messily on the letter, the ink spreading out tendrils of black across the creamy paper. She dabbed at the paper, but the writing was already smudged.

"I got here last week and am staying with a family in a grand house in the middle of Buenos Aires; it is a truly amazing place, I wish you could see it..."

The letter went on for five pages, finishing:

"Do write to me soon Mary, I can't wait for a letter from you.
Much love and best wishes,
Rupert."

Mary looked down at the letter, folded it back into the envelope and put it back into her pocket; she would deal with the reply another day.

The next day was Saturday and Mary knew that William would call with the meat. Her father was sitting in the kitchen as she had not yet lit the fire in the front room. Edgar had already been in for his breakfast and Mary had cleared the table. The dogs barked to announce the arrival of William and the butcher's trap; he was accompanied by Reuben and George. William walked straight into the kitchen and put the basket onto the table, pulling a paper out of the pocket of his brown smock coat and handing it to John, who winked at him and grabbed his hand and shook it.

"You're a good boy, William; have you read it all, can I keep it?"

"Yes, Uncle John, we've all read it at the butcher's shop except Mother, who refuses to read anything except the Bible."

"Well, I don't know about that," said John, "but your mother was always keen on the Bible and all that sort of thing."

"Tea, William?" interjected Mary.

"Thank you, Mary," smiled William.

He looked hard at his cousin.

"Mary, Mother asked specifically to ask how you were; she thought you looked very down yesterday. You know she fusses."

"Tell her that I am much better, just a little tired, I expect," assured Mary, pouring the tea out.

"George? Reuben?" said Mary to the two boys, who had just scurried into the kitchen.

"Yes, Mary?" they answered in unison.

"Biscuit?"

"Yes please, Mary."

"You know where they are then – just one mind – I know what you boys are like."

The boys rushed to the sideboard and opened the barrel. George stood on tiptoe and thrust his hand in.

"There ain't none, Mary."

"What do you mean there ain't none?" asked Mary, moving to have a look in the barrel, which as George had said, was empty.

"Well that's it, then!" sighed Mary. "Edgar's had them all and I haven't baked any cake yet! Lucy is coming home as well, oh I don't know; I'll have to get a move on this morning."

"Mary?" said George. "Do you know what?"

"Do I know what *what*, George?" said Mary with a hint of impatience.

"Reuben's got new lacky in his catty."

"No, I didn't know that, George, how interesting," replied Mary, struggling to keep the sarcasm from her voice.

"Yes, it is. Anyway we're going to get some rats, ain't we, Reuben?"

"You mean *I* am," said Reuben a touch smugly.

"Well yes, but we've still got mine."

"Well go on then," said William, picking up on his cousin's frustration and ushering the boys to the door, "you see if you can get one while I drink my tea."

The two boys dashed out of the door, past John who looked up briefly and returned to his paper.

"I saw Henry yesterday, Mary," said William. "He said how good you had been with the new baby and how well you got on with Martha."

"Yes I did, William!" agreed Mary. "I didn't think I would like babies; but he was lovely, he was so good and Martha knew all about it and it was easy."

"He asked me to be a godfather," smiled William proudly. "That will be the second time I've done that in a year."

"You must be a godly person to be asked to so often, William," laughed Mary.

"I suppose," said William dubiously. "He said that he wanted to ask Noble Ladds as well, but Martha didn't like the idea. He was sure that they would ask you."

William looked closely at Mary, who said nothing.

"Are you all right, Mary?" William enquired. "You've gone a bit white; Mother said you weren't up to much when you called in yesterday."

"I'm fine, William, just a little lack of sleep," insisted Mary, busying herself by rattling the poker pointlessly in the fire.

"I'll get some fresh air in a while; I will have to go down and get some bread if Lucy's coming back, she is always hungry."

Mary lifted the filler plate from the range and moved to get the bucket of coal.

"I'll do that," said William, lifting the bucket and pouring it into the top of the range.

The fire crackled, yellow-grey smoke puffing briefly out into the room, before threading its way back up the chimney again. Mary inhaled deeply.

"I always like that smell, don't you, William? It's full of memories, that smell."

She smiled at her cousin, then frowned slightly into the fire.

"William, have you had a chance to look at the figures from the farm? I mean the bank and all that sort of thing."

"Yes, Mary," said William quietly. "I looked with your father while you were away."

"Well, what do you think?"

"You want the truth then, Mary?"

"Yes."

"There is not enough coming in to pay off the mortgage. To get out of debt the best thing would be to sell the farm after this harvest."

"You really mean that, William?"

"Yes, I can see no way round it. You could go on for another year, but with prices as they are, you would be worse off after that and there would be nothing left over to live on."

Mary wrung her hands and frowned.

"I blame Henry, you know, William," she blurted out angrily. "If he had stayed at home, we wouldn't be in this situation. If I had been here and known what was going on; I would never have let him go, I'm right, aren't I, William?"

"I don't think so, Mary" said William gently. "The mortgage was always too big and if he had stayed there would have been more mouths to feed and no money to buy anything."

"But we have to feed Edgar," Mary cried, stamping her foot. "I was born here, William, you know that?"

"Yes, but I thought you didn't want to come back," said William reasonably. "You've always said you didn't like living here because it was so isolated."

"But that's not the point!" snarled Mary. "I might change my mind! I might like to live on my own!"

She threw herself into one of the chairs, banged her elbows down on the table and held her face in her hands. She sighed, rubbed her hands over her eyes and looked up.

"Things aren't going right, are they, William? At least not for me."

William said nothing.

"You are sure you are right, William?" she asked desperately. "We've got to sell up, you're sure?"

She looked hard at him. William spread his hands desperately.

"Mary, I can't see any other way to get out of the debt! At some point or other the bank will have to have its money back and you can't do that by farming this farm; the only way is to sell it."

"Does Father realise?" Mary asked.

"Yes I'm sure he does, but he just ignores it. He's waiting for someone else to make a move."

"It makes me mad to think of Henry over there at Brington," complained Mary. "Why isn't he here to sort this mess out?"

"It would make no difference, Mary," assured William. "He would have to sell just the same as you will, he knew that before he went."

William sighed.

"But he's got no money *now*, has he?" fired Mary.

"No he hasn't," said William carefully, "and what he has, he borrowed from my father. He will struggle to make a go of things, we all know that."

"Well why are you doing so well, William?" said Mary accusingly. "It looks like you're making a lot of money."

She glared at him.

"We have the butcher's shop, Mary, which helps," said William calmly. "We can sell through the shop some of what we produce."

"You're a better farmer, William, even I can see that," sighed Mary, leaning back in the chair.

She chewed her lip and looked at her cousin.

"Where are we going to live if we sell up, have you thought of that?" asked Mary desperately.

William didn't reply, but sat looking into the flames in the fire. He cast a look towards John, who still had his head in the paper.

"Your father's not going to live for ever, is he," he said in a low voice. "And I expect you will get married some time, Mary."

Mary's head flooded with images of Noble Ladds and of Rupert, so far away in Argentina. Her temper flared.

"You're going to marry me off then, are you, William? Like a prize heifer

495

at the market! Marry me off and then all will be all right?"

She was shouting now, her face red with anger. John looked round the side of his paper, and said nothing. Mary sat back in the chair, chewing her nails; tears welled up in her eyes but she did not cry.

"I didn't mean it like that, Mary; I don't want to upset you but you know what I mean," said William pleadingly.

"Yes, yes I know," said Mary angrily. "But you don't have to remind me, William Dunmore. It's all right for you – there's only one of you and there were four of us!

William said nothing, but downed his tea and rose from his chair.

The latch on the back door clicked and the two boys came back in, Reuben holding a large rat by the tail.

"Look, look, Mary, William! I got one! I told you I would," exclaimed Reuben gleefully.

The boys grinned happily, moving into the kitchen to give Mary a better look.

"Stand still, you two!" shouted Mary. "Look at your boots! You're just like Edgar! Freda's not here today and I've got to clear that up!"

She pointed angrily at the rat.

"And take that damn thing out!"

The smiles slid off the boys' faces.

"He didn't really kill it, you know," said George quietly. "He knocked it off the stack and the dog 'ad it."

The boys turned and tiptoed out.

"I must be going," said William, taking the cloth from the basket to let Mary choose the meat she wanted and hurrying out after the two boys.

Mary stood looking after her cousin, anger boiling in her veins. She stomped towards the coal bucket and slammed out into the yard to fill it. Reuben was outside, scraping and brushing his shoes.

"What are you still doing here, Reuben?" Mary demanded. "Aren't you going on the round with the others?"

"No, I'm stopped 'ere to 'elp you, Mary," said Reuben, staring up defiantly at Mary. "Now give me that bucket, I'll get the coal."

He took the bucket and opened the door to the coal hole.

"Are you sure, Reuben?" asked Mary quietly.

But Reuben either did not fancy answering or didn't hear, leaving Mary to make her way back inside. In a few minutes he was back – holding the brimful bucket of coal with two hands.

"Do you want me to light the fire in the front room, Mary, so your dad can sit in there?" he grunted. "I'm took me boots off so I don't make no muck on the floor."

Mary smiled at the young boy puffing in front of her.

"Reuben, you are a darling," she laughed. "Go on then, that would be very helpful."

She ruffled his hair as he went past with the coal, grasping his shoulder briefly.

"I'll come back for the kindling," he said.

Mary busied herself tidying, whilst Reuben lit the fire.

"What next?" he asked eagerly, as he walked back into the room.

"Are you going to stay a while, Reuben? Are you sure? After all it's Saturday, you know."

"Yes, I ain't got anyfing else to do so I can 'elp you, Mary; that's what I come up for."

"Reuben," sighed Mary gratefully, "I don't know what I would do without you. I want to go down to the baker's and get some things so if you could do a few small things while I'm gone."

She thought hard, reeling off a list of jobs: fetching the water, chopping the logs, sweeping the back yard; the list went on. Reuben listened carefully to the instructions and scurried off to start.

It would take Mary half an hour to walk to Dean, longer than it would take on her bicycle, but she preferred walking through the fields as it was now getting drier after the winter. At the crossroads in the bridleway between Kimbolton Woods and Dean, Mary could see someone walking in her direction; it was Molly, who waved and started to run to catch her up.

"Mary, Mary, wait for me," she shouted, "don't walk so fast; I can't catch you up."

She trotted up beside Mary, a little out of breath.

"Mary I writ to that shop in Norfampton; you know the one where you worked," she said a little breathlessly.

"And?" said Mary.

"They writ back."

"And?" repeated Mary.

"They said that they ain't got no jobs at the present; but I was to write again in six mumfs and they might have somefink then."

Molly smiled delightedly.

"That ain't so bad is it, Mary, and do you know what?"

"No, Molly, what?"

"I'm got a job in Norfampton."

"Well done, Molly, what's that?"

"I'm goin' to work for Dorcas' brother in 'is pub, cleanin' and that to start wiv, and servin' when I get used to it. Then I can go down the shop if they 'ave a job in six mumfs! Ain't that good! I'm goin' next week – away from 'ere! Ain't that good, don't you fink, Mary?"

"Molly dear, you've done very well," agreed Mary, "but what about the baby?"

The smile slid from Molly's face and she bowed her head a little.

"What do you want to know about 'im for?"

"He is a lovely little boy, isn't he?"

"Hmm," said Molly chewing her lip nervously, "Ruby's got 'im; she wanted 'im, so she can 'ave 'im."

She walked a little way in silence.

"Anyway, he'll be better wiv Ruby; she likes babies and I ain't got nuffing to give a boy like that."

Molly shuddered.

"What if 'e grows up like 'is farver, eh Mary, what if he did?"

She fell silent for a bit.

"There's only one good thing about all that 'appened," she said firmly, after a minute.

"What's that, Molly?"

"I didn't 'ave to marry 'im; can you imagine it, Mary?"

Mary said nothing. Molly looked concernedly into her face.

"Are you all right, Mary?" she asked, concerned. "You ain't sayin' nuffin' and you look a bit white. You ain't cryin', are you, Mary?"

"No, Molly, I'm not crying," sniffed Mary, wiping her sleeve across her eyes.

"You sure?" said Molly.

"Yes, I'm sure," said Mary peevishly.

"Well I didn't 'ave to marry 'im –" continued Molly, "and any road 'e's dead now and the baby's got a good 'ome and I'm got a job and it's all lookin' a bit better, don't you fink, Mary?"

Molly looked at her again.

"Yes, it's all a lot better for you, Molly," she agreed, sniffing.

"Mary?"

"Yes, Molly?"

"You look so sad, Mary," whispered Molly, grabbing Mary's hand as they walked along.

"Don't look sad, Mary, you're not a sad person, are you?"

She squeezed Mary's hand.

"I'll try not to be," Mary replied, forcing a smile and squeezing Molly's hand in return.

Mary and Molly continued on into Dean, splitting up at the baker's, where Mary made her way on past the smithy. In the garden she could see an old pram sitting – she assumed Goshen must be tucked up inside and she thought again of Molly's words. She could see a car moving up the street – as the only car in the village belonged to the Watson-Fosters, she backed down the lane a little, so as not to be seen. As the car passed she could see Verity sitting in the back; she ducked further back into the lane, but Verity was chatting enthusiastically to Walter.

Reuben was still chopping the logs and Edgar was out with the cattle so the kitchen was empty when Mary returned home. She placed the shopping on the table and hung her coat and hat on the back of the door. Lucy, who had been in the front room with their father, was still in her uniform when she came into the kitchen. Mary, who had forgotten that her sister was coming home, was suddenly overcome at the sight of her. She rushed towards her, wrapping her arms around Lucy's back in a tight embrace, sobbing slightly.

"Mary, what is it?" asked Lucy, gently pushing Mary back and looking her full in the face.

Mary lowered her head, tears dripping down her nose to the floor; Lucy pulled her sister back in towards her, hugging her tightly.

"Mary, what is it?" begged Lucy, stroking her sister's hair. "You must tell me; you never cry like this, what is wrong?"

Reuben entered with a big basket of logs; unnoticed by either of the girls, he put the basket down and took a step backwards into the scullery.

Mary fumbled in the pockets of her skirt until she found a handkerchief, which she pulled out, wiping her eyes and blowing her nose.

"Now tell me, Mary, what's wrong?" said Lucy firmly, holding Mary's arms and looking at her closely.

"Don't be upset, Mary; you are always so strong. I've not know you cry like this for years."

Mary turned her head to one side to avoid Lucy's gaze and sniffed twice, swallowing hard before sniffing again.

"I wish you wouldn't sniff like that," Lucy said teasingly, nudging Mary gently.

A smile crept across Mary's face and she laughed softly, before wrapping her arms around Lucy again. Reuben edged a bit farther back into the shadows of the scullery, as Lucy and Mary sat down at the table and Lucy took both Mary's hands in hers.

"Now, you have to tell me what it is, Mary," urged Lucy.

Mary bowed her head.

"Did you speak to Father?" she asked.

"Yes," said Lucy.

"Did he tell you anything?" said Mary, sniffing again.

"Tell me what?" asked Lucy.

"Tell you that we've got to sell Cold Harbour."

"No, why have we got to sell?" asked Lucy, taken aback.

"There is no money left; the mortgage is too big and we can't make enough to pay it," shrugged Mary.

"How do you know all this, Mary?" Lucy demanded.

"William says so."

"What does William Dunmore know about our affairs?" said Lucy indignantly. "What's he interfering for? It's not his place to say these things; it's for Henry to decide and he should be back here helping."

She shook her head angrily and looked desperately at her sister.

"We can't sell, Mary!" she exclaimed. "We were born here, weren't we?"

Mary sighed and looked at her sister.

"William knows because I asked him to look at the bank accounts and the earnings and he says there is no money," said Mary gently. "Henry went because he could see there was no chance of paying back the bank, he knew we would have to sell in the end. You and I have known for years that things are bad and are getting worse so it's not really a surprise, is it?"

"I suppose not," agreed Lucy grudgingly, "but where are we going to live if we sell up?"

The two girls sat in silence for a while, looking at each other.

"You will have to get married, Mary," said Lucy decisively. "That's all there is to it and I will live in the nurses' home; I've got a room there."

Mary frowned – everyone's advice one way or another seemed to lead her back to Noble Ladds.

There was a cough from the scullery; Reuben picked up the log basket and carried it through to the front room.

"Hello, Reuben," said Lucy, with a hint of surprise.

"Hello, Lucy," he replied.

"You're a good boy," said Mary, ruffling Reuben's hair as he went past. "I don't know what I would do without him."

Reuben grinned and disappeared outside.

"William says Father knows about the farm," said Mary sadly, "but he just ignores it."

"He hasn't got long, that's why," said Lucy. "I can tell he's gone downhill every time I come back. There's plenty like him in our hospital."

There was a shout from the yard:

"Mary, Mary, there's a motor comin' down the drive, I can see it from the front room winder."

"I'll look," said Lucy, rushing down the corridor to the front door and looking through one of the small panes in it.

"Yes, it's Mr Watson-Foster's car."

"Go on then, Reuben," said Mary, "go and open the gates for him."

Reuben dashed off at full speed only to return a few moments with a card in his hand, which he handed to Mary.

"I'm goin' to 'ave a ride back down the drive with 'im to open the gates," said Reuben, hopping from foot to foot in an effort to control his excitement. He dashed off to join Walter.

"It's from Verity," said Mary reading the note. "She has had to go back to school, but says she would like to call in three weeks when she is on her Easter holiday."

"I will be back then, Mary," said Lucy, "that will be nice; I've got to go back first thing tomorrow but next time I can stay for at least two nights, maybe three."

Mary continued to read the calling card.

"Verity says she wants to hear all about the new baby."

"Oh, the new baby," gasped Lucy, "you haven't told me, Mary! I had forgotten clean about him; I must hear, come on then!"

The latch on the back door lifted and Freda poked her head into the kitchen.

"You're back early!" said Mary with surprise.

"Yes, I want to 'ear more about this baby before I start – oh hello, Miss Lucy; I didn't' see you there – 'ave you 'ad all the detail?"

"Not yet, Freda, but I'm just about to," said Lucy with a smile, motioning for Freda to sit at the table.

"I think it's so wonderful," uttered Lucy with utmost sincerity. "A new life come in the world. We should thank God for him, shouldn't we?"

No one answered. Mary looked at Freda who was looking pointedly at the ceiling.

"Don't you think so, Mary?"

"Think what?"

"We should give thanks to God for the birth of the new baby."

"Yes, I'm sure," agreed Mary somewhat uncertainly.

"We will when he's christened, won't we?" said Lucy.

Mary was saved from having to answer by the entrance of Reuben.

"What's this young ruffian doing 'ere?" said Freda.

"Oh don't call him that, Freda," said Mary. "He's been very helpful while you were away; he lit the fire, filled the coal and chopped logs, didn't you, Reuben?"

"Yup," he answered, beaming at Mary.

"And what was the ride in the car like then?"

"Wonderful," he said with a lopsided grin, "we went twenty mile an hour; I've never bin so fast in my life."

"Do you want to stop for some dinner, Reuben?"

"Yes please," he said.

"Right," said Mary, setting about organising the lunch, filling in Lucy and Freda about Henry's progress as she went.

Lucy looked hard at her sister and thought she seemed much like her normal self.

That evening the two girls sat in the kitchen discussing what they would do when the farm was sold. After debating the subject for several hours and reaching no definite conclusion, they decided to go to bed. They could hear Edgar snoring as they walked down the landing, Lucy carrying the candle to light the way.

"Don't worry about waking him," said Mary loudly. "Nothing would wake up that old sod."

"Mary, don't say such things," said Lucy crossly.

"Why not? It's true; he is an old sod and I don't mind saying it, so there."

"But what if he heard?" whispered Lucy.

"He won't," said Mary, opening the door to their room.

Lucy moved to the chest of drawers, putting the candle down next to a pencil and piece of paper lying on the top of the polished oak. The paper had a few recent dates written on it and a series of pencil marks and crosses, which Lucy could extract no logic from. She picked up the piece of paper and studied it.

"What's this, Mary?"

"Oh nothing," shrugged Mary, taking the paper off her and placing it on the chair by her bed. They changed into their night clothes.

"Can we say prayers together, Mary, like we used to?" asked Lucy.

"If you're not too long, Lucy; it's still very cold," said Mary, kneeling by her bed.

Lucy said the prayers and Mary joined in with the amens. When they had finished the pair climbed into bed, Lucy blowing out the candle before they did so.

"Are you awake, Mary?" Lucy whispered.

"Yes, what now?"

"You know the other day; what we were talking about?"

"What do you mean? We talked about a lot of things."

"No! You know what we were talking about! What we didn't know about what Mother never told us… about babies and how they come."

"Yes," said Mary apprehensively.

"Well I found out – the sister on the ward told me. I said we didn't have a mother and I had a sister and we really wanted to know so she told me or at least most of it."

There was silence, before Mary replied.

"I know as well."

"Who told you, Mary?"

"Martha."

"Oh."

There was silence.

"Doesn't it sound awful, absolutely awful, I couldn't imagine it."

There was silence.

"She said she liked it though, Mary," said Lucy incredulously. "How could she? I don't want to talk about it I really don't, but she said she would tell me about how you know when you're going to have a baby next time we are on nights together."

Mary did not answer.

"Are you asleep, Mary?" Lucy whispered again.

"Yes," said Mary.

Chapter Forty-One
Mary and Lucy Make Plans
Spring 1903

Lucy left early the next morning to walk the six miles to Sharnbrook station for the train to Bedford, leaving Mary to decide whether or not to go to chapel on her own. She desperately didn't want to see anyone, but knew that if she did not go, they would all think she was ill, or imagine that she had met a sticky end on the road and someone would be sent up to find out where she was. Reluctantly she realised that she had very little alternative. She prepared the Sunday lunch for her father and Edgar and when they had eaten, and Freda had cleared away; she started to get herself ready for chapel.

As Mary put her smart dress on, she could feel an edge of something scraping on her leg from the pocket – it was Rupert's letter. She sank to the bed and started to read it again, words that she had almost memorised. She sighed heavily – he was a good man, with lots of prospects but as the days drew on she knew that she would never marry him. Rising from her bed, she brushed her hair and pinned it up ready to put her straw boater on, moving to the mirror to ensure she put it on straight. The person staring back at her from the small mirror was pale and drawn – cheeks pinched, bags blue under her eyes. She wondered if she dared put any cosmetics on; people wouldn't approve at chapel if they knew, but if she applied a little bit she would look healthier. She sat and rubbed some rouge into her cheeks – not daring to use lipstick which she knew people would notice. She carried the mirror to the window, turning her face from side to side, confident that she looked better than she had done before. In the kitchen, Freda was sitting at the table frowning deeply at Edgar, who was by the fire, snoring loudly – he never worked on Sunday afternoons. Mary put her hat on and turned to Freda.

"Is that on straight, Freda?" she asked.

Freda shut one eye, cocking her head to the side and squinting myopically at the angle of Mary's boater.

"Yup," she confirmed. "You goin' to chapel, Miss Mary?"

"Yes, are you coming?"

"Yes, I'll come, I ain't sittin' 'ere wiv 'im," said Freda, rising briskly and nodding at Edgar, "drives me mad, 'e does, I'll get me coat and 'at."

Mary laughed as Freda clattered up two flights of stairs to her room – Mary had never known her go to chapel in all the time she had worked at Cold Harbour. Freda re-emerged and threw her things on the table.

"Can you 'ang on a bit, Mary, while I go down the end? There ain't nowhere to go down the chapel 'cept behind a bush."

She turned on her heel before Mary could answer, her shoes clattering across the stone slabs in the scullery.

"That's better," she said, returning and throwing on her coat.

She looked at Mary curiously.

"You look better this afternoon, Miss Mary; you've got some colour in your cheeks for a change." Mary smiled and led the way out towards chapel. There was little conversation on the journey – Freda was not one for small talk – and Mary was happy to walk on in companionable silence to Dean. As they were passing the smithy a voice echoed from the doorway.

"Mary, Mary!" came the voice. "Mary, you must come and see what I'm got 'ere, I ain't coming to chapel 'cos 'e's asleep, but you call in on your way back."

Ruby emerged onto the street, beaming and pointing happily into the house.

"Very good, Ruby, I will call on the way back," Mary shouted, walking on towards the chapel.

"Hmm, what she wants to show that one off for I don't know; I'd be ashamed of it, I would" murmured Freda.

"Freda!" said Mary sharply.

"I'm only saying what people think and you know it, Miss Mary," said Freda determinedly.

"Have you got any collection, Freda?" Mary asked sharply, desperate for a change in conversation.

"No, but I can pretend –no one'll know," sniffed Freda.

"No you can't," reprimanded Mary, handing Freda twopence from her handbag.

"I ain't goin' to sit wiv you, Miss Mary, you sit with William and them, I sit at the back," said Freda, scuttling off before Mary had a chance to try and change her mind.

Mary moved into the chapel, hoping that she would not have to talk to her aunt. A couple of moments later, William eased himself into the pew next to her, his parents following suit.

"You look much better, Mary; you've got some colour in your cheeks again," whispered Charlotte, leaning forward to address her niece down the row of the pew.

Mary smiled and sat back against the cold wood of the pew as the formal tones of Reverend Packham from the back of the chapel announced the start of the service with a hymn, *Onward Christian Soldiers*. Miss Poynter flexed her fingers and began to play the organ with gusto – George was pumping today and every so often Mary could see his head poking out from behind the organ, listening to Miss Poynter's whispered instructions.

As usual, few people seemed to listen to the sermon; William spent the time scribbling on a little scrap of paper, his pencil moving up and down columns of numbers. Mary sidled closer along the pew and snatched at the paper, gently prising the pencil from William's other hand; she turned over the paper and drew two vertical lines, crossing through them with two horizontal ones. In the bottom left-hand corner of the grid, she drew a small cross. William looked at his cousin and back at the paper, his expression blank; he looked to his left at his father who was gently nodding off. If he leant forward he could just see his mother – an expression of adoration etched on her face as Reverend Packham continued to sermonise. William winked, grabbed the pencil and drew a nought in the middle of the grid, the game continuing into the opening bars of the next hymn, when William hurriedly shoved the paper back into his pocket and rose to sing.

On the way home from chapel, Mary stopped at the smithy, knocking lightly on the door of the cottage.

"I ain't stoppin'," said Freda, who had joined Mary for the walk home. "I'm goin' on, I don't want to see 'im."

508

She tossed her head and set off at a trot, as Ruby's door opened.

"Mary dear, come on in, I'm just givin' 'im his tea; come and see 'ow 'e's getting on."

Mary followed Ruby into the kitchen – Ruby stopped at the table and beamed at the child.

"Look at him, Mary, just look at 'im, ain't 'e a grand lad?"

In a highchair sucking a biscuit sat Goshen; very blond, almost white hair, framing a chubby face with blue eyes and rosy cheeks. Mary moved to the high chair and tickled him under the chin.

"Ain't 'e lovely, Mary? How Molly come to give 'im up I don't know. You've got to forget all about 'ow 'e was conceived; 'e's an 'uman bein', ain't 'e, like all of us, and 'e should have just the same chances."

"I'm sure you're right, Ruby," agreed Mary, who wasn't really listening. "Can I hold him?"

"Course you can," grinned Ruby.

Mary lifted Goshen out of the chair and bounced him on her knee, smiling at the little blond boy staring up at her in fascination.

"I didn't know you liked babies, Mary," Ruby said, watching Mary pulling faces at Goshen as he gurgled with delight.

"Nor did I, Ruby," smiled Mary. "Until I had to deal with Martha's new one."

"Oh, of course," said Ruby. "Did you get on all right then?"

"In the end I did," laughed Mary.

She looked at Goshen and then up at Ruby.

"Are you going to adopt him properly, Ruby?"

"Not on your nelly," snorted Ruby. "Molly's never goin' to want 'im back, so what's the point? My other two don't mind so that's fine by me."

"And are you going to call him Goshen then?" Mary asked.

"I s'pose so but 'e'll get a nickname of some sort soon, I 'spect."

She smiled down at the baby.

"As long as 'e don't turn out like 'is father I don't mind," she frowned. "You wait, Mary, you will 'ave a family one day; everything changes then. You see if it don't; you ain't the centre of things then, you've got others to think on. I love children – you know I wish we 'ad 'ad more."

Mary swallowed and rose hurriedly, handing the baby back to Ruby.

"I must go," she said, "or it will be dark before I get home and Edgar will be shouting for his tea."

Ruby took the child back, a look of surprise etched on her face and watched as Mary scurried out the door, bidding a hasty goodbye as she went.

Lucy next came home on Good Friday; Roderick was coming to see Lucy on Sunday so they spent the day cleaning out the dining room, where the bags of seed corn had been stored for the winter to keep it safe from the rats. The next morning Lucy was up early and dressed quickly.

"Come on, Mary, it's time to get up," she ordered.

"I'll be there in a minute, you go," croaked Mary from the bed as Lucy left the room to go down stairs.

Lucy hadn't reached the top of the stairs before she heard Mary being violently sick in the bedroom. She rushed back along the landing and opened the door.

"Are you all right, Mary?" she asked gingerly.

"Yes I'm fine," Mary snapped. "Just go and help Freda; I'll be there in a few minutes."

Downstairs, Freda had lit the range, but it would be a little while before it would boil a kettle. Lucy readied the table for breakfast and went to see if John was ready to get up. Edgar had gone out some time ago and would be back in soon. The back door clicked revealing Reuben, who remained standing awkwardly in the doorway from the scullery.

"Reuben, what are you doing here so early?" Lucy asked.

"You're 'avin' visitors tomorra, aren't you?"

"Yes, but how did you know?"

"I were 'ere when the card came and I fort you might need an 'and with the fires."

"How thoughtful," said Lucy, "you are a dear boy."

Reuben smiled bashfully and rushed out to get coal and sticks, as Mary came slowly downstairs, carrying her potty.

"I'm just going down the end," she said quietly.

She looked white, her face very drawn and tired.

"What's up wiv 'er?" said Freda, as Mary left the room.

"She's a little under the weather this morning, that's all," shrugged Lucy.

Freda raised an eyebrow and said nothing.

When Mary came back, some of the colour had returned to her face.

"Sorry if I snapped, Lucy, I'm just having a bit of an off day, that's all." She smiled at her sister.

"Now did I see Reuben? Isn't he a good boy?"

No sooner had she said it than Reuben staggered into the room under the weight of the coal bucket.

"Reuben, I don't know what we would do without you," exclaimed Mary, coming up to him and giving him a peck on the cheek. Reuben blushed deeply and Mary laughed.

"I'm sorry, Reuben, I shouldn't embarrass you," said Mary, ruffling his hair. "Now, Reuben, can you light the fire in the dining room first?"

"But you can't get in there, Mary," protested Reuben. "It's full of seed corn."

"Not any more, it isn't, the seed was all drilled this week."

"Right then," said Reuben, hoisting his bucket and tottering off down the corridor.

He was back moments later.

"You can't light that fire; there's a jackdaw's nest up the chimney. It won't be safe unless I can get it down."

"Well can you do it, Reuben?" asked Mary.

"I can if you've got some rods and a brush."

Mary turned to her sister.

"Have we, Lucy?"

"I don't know."

"Have we, Freda?"

"I don't know," grumbled Freda, throwing some bacon in the frying pan.

"Go and ask Father, Reuben; he's in bed but he's awake, he'll know," said Mary, as Reuben dashed off upstairs.

"No, 'e said that William borrered them," said Reuben on his return.

"So we can't have a fire. Damn, damn, damn!" exclaimed Mary.

"Don't swear, Mary," said Lucy, with a sniff.

"Don't sniff, Lucy," retorted Mary, sticking her tongue out at her sister. "What are we going to do?"

"I know," said Reuben.

"Go on then," said Mary impatiently.

"We can shoot it down."

"What do you mean, shoot it down?"

"That twelve bore in the corner there; fire it up the chimney, that'll fetch it down; Uncle Len always fires the gun up to sweep the chimney, I'm seen 'im do it."

"You're pulling my leg, Reuben," laughed Mary.

"No I ain't, it's true, I'm seen it done," insisted Reuben.

He looked hopefully at Mary, who looked at Lucy, then at Freda and back to Reuben again.

"You go and ask your dad," Reuben urged. "He'll tell you."

Mary raised an eyebrow and went to consult her father, returning moments later with a somewhat incredulous smile.

"He says it's worth a try, but to be very careful and put the butt of the gun on a sack, whatever that means."

"Don't worry, Mary, I know," insisted Reuben, taking the shotgun from the corner of the room.

"Where are the cartridges, Mary?" asked Reuben, brushing the dust off the gun.

"I don't know. Lucy, go and ask Father where they are."

Lucy sighed and trudged up the stairs, as Mary turned to look sceptically at Reuben.

"I really don't like this, Reuben, I hope you know what you are doing."

Reuben grinned at Mary, as Lucy came back, reaching for a mug above the shelf on the range.

"Father says there are a few in here," she said, bringing down the mug and shaking three cartridges into Reuben's outstretched hand.

"Can someone go outside, Mary, and look to see what comes out?" Reuben asked.

"You go, Lucy," ordered Mary.

"But the front door won't open! It's stuck with the damp."

"Well go round and push from the outside; we'll pull from here. Come on, Freda, let's unbolt it first," Lucy ran off out of the scullery, knocking on the front door to alert the others that she had made it round.

"Push, Lucy, push," shouted Mary, who was tugging the door towards her by the door handle.

She stopped for breath.

"It won't budge," yelled Mary.

"Get out the way, I'll give it a good kick," shouted Lucy, before kicking hard at the door with her boot. The door creaked and Mary pulled it open wide, and went to check on Reuben who was lying on his back, looking up the chimney.

"Can't see much but it looks like it goes straight; can I 'ave that cushion to rest the butt of the gun on, Mary?"

Mary handed him a cushion from the sofa, as Reuben loaded the gun, pointing the barrel up the chimney and resting the butt on the cushion. He looked round at Mary and Freda excitedly.

"Ready?" he asked.

Mary nodded and waved out towards Lucy who was looking up at the chimney just outside the open window. She stuffed her fingers in her ears and squeezed her eyes closed. Reuben pulled the trigger; the gun clicked. He pulled the gun down, opened the breech and looked critically at the cartridge.

"Dud," he muttered, looking at where the firing pin had hit the casing and tossing it to the side. He took another and reloaded.

"Ready?"

Mary and Freda nodded, re-covering their ears.

There was a loud bang, and sticks clattered down the chimney, soot billowing behind in their wake. Reuben smiled.

"There you are, Mary, it works! Did anything come out the top?" he shouted towards Lucy.

"Nothing except one jackdaw," she shouted back.

"I'll give it another," said Reuben, clearing the smoking cartridge and reloading. He fired again, releasing a sea of sticks, which cascaded down and nearly filled the whole fireplace.

"That shifted it," he said with a smile.

"Did anything come out, Lucy?" yelled Mary.

"Yes, a few sticks," called back Lucy.

"One more," said Reuben, whose foot was now black, caked with dust and soot.

A cloud of dust drifted across the room and began to settle on the furniture and floor.

"Look at this mess," moaned Freda. "I s'pect you want me to clear this lot up."

Reuben fired again; twigs, soot and dust shot from the chimney in a column and clattered onto the roof, the pellets of lead hailing onto the tiles.

"'Ave you got a match?" Reuben asked. "We can light all this lot and you see, I bet it draws."

"Don't you dare, Reuben, till you've got the cushion out," ordered Mary, as Reuben pulled the blackened cushion from under the twigs.

He pulled a scrunched piece of paper from his pocket, surveyed it, crumpled it up and lit it, before holding it out to the twigs. The fire roared into life – Reuben beamed delightedly.

"Look, it worked," he grinned; his white teeth glowing from his blackened face.

"But look at the mess, Reuben!" exclaimed Mary.

"Don't worry, Mary, I can help you; see it won't take long when me and Freda get at it and the fire's burning well – it'll be fine for tomorra."

The next morning was Easter Sunday; Mary was once again sick in the morning, but had managed this time to avoid Lucy's notice as Lucy was far too excited by Roderick's impending visit. He was to get the train to Sharnbrook and then walk the six miles to Cold Harbour. Lucy rushed down the drive an hour before he was due to come, waiting impatiently for him where the drive met the road. It was a cold morning and she tucked her chin into her thick coat, the wind blowing in her face, reddening her cheeks to a rosy hue. Within the hour Roderick came into view, appearing up the hill from Riseley; he waved at Lucy. He was wearing his Sunday clothes, all of which seemed too small for him. His trousers were a little short, revealing the top of his boots, and the sleeves of his jacket finished three inches from his wrist, his cuff poking out. His collar looked tight and uncomfortable and was circled by a thin, worn tie which tucked into his waistcoat; the only part of his apparel which seemed to fit. He raised his flat cap to Lucy, exposing a mop of mousy wiry hair, which clung to his scalp in great uncontrollable billows. The two shook hands, chattering and exchanging pleasantries about Roderick's journey and the weather.

They walked up the drive, Lucy taking Roderick's hand to guide him round the ruts and puddles, dropping it gently as soon as she got within sight of the house. Mary and Freda watched the pair's progress from behind the curtains of the front room. The fire had been lit for some time but the room was still cold.

"They're 'olding 'ands, Miss Mary, look!" exclaimed Freda.

"So they are, so they are," smiled Mary as Lucy guided Roderick towards the front door.

"'E ain't much to look at, is 'e," Freda commented loudly. "Looks like 'e could do with a new sooot." She took a rapid step back from the curtains as Lucy looked towards the house.

"Freda, come on," whispered Mary, "they're coming to the front door – we need to open it."

Mary drew back the bolt at the top of the door, but the bottom one would not budge.

"Push the door in, Freda and I'll kick the bolt," instructed Mary.

Freda leant on the door as Mary kicked the bolt, the heel of her boot catching the ankle of her other foot as she swung it back.

"Damn, that hurt," she snarled, bending down to rub her ankle.

"Right, you pull that coat hook and I'll pull the handle. When she gets to the door; she should remember to shove and it might come open with any luck."

Mary squatted down and put her eye to the large keyhole so as not to be seen.

"Ready?" she whispered to Freda.

"Yes."

"Pull now!" hissed Mary.

They both tugged and the door flew open with very little persuasion. Lucy had hold of the handle outside and had been preparing to discreetly shove the door with her shoulder, when it had flung itself open. Taken by surprise, she tumbled inelegantly onto the hallway floor at Freda's feet; Freda turned away and put her hand to her mouth to stop herself laughing, while Mary helped Lucy picked herself up off the floor. She pursed her lips and frowned furiously at Mary.

"We couldn't help it," insisted Mary. "We just went to open the door – we thought it would be stuck again."

Lucy sniffed and then started to grin.

"Come on then, Lucy, you must introduce me," laughed Mary.

"Oh yes, Roderick, this is my sister Mary," said Lucy, standing aside to let Mary and Roderick see one another.

"Pleased to meet you," said Roderick, pushing his hand towards Mary, who shook it and ushered Roderick into the front room. She sat him on one side of the fire and called Freda in to order the tea. Lucy said nothing as Mary skilfully extracted from Roderick all the basic details of his life and work.

"Lucy dear," Mary said, "you must take Roderick and introduce him to Father; he won't come in here, but he's up now, you can go while Freda gets the tea."

Lucy escorted Roderick to the room the other side of the hallway where John sat reading an old paper. After the introductions had been made, the couple returned to Mary to drink their tea.

"And your father?" enquired Mary. "What did he do for a living?"

"Oh he was in the army, Miss Knighton; he was killed in Africa before I was born, so I never knew him, God rest his soul. Mother and I pray for him every day."

Roderick looked down at the carpet.

"Oh how sad for your mother to lose her husband so young," said Mary sympathetically.

"He wasn't her husband," said Roderick calmly.

Mary and Lucy looked at each other in horror.

"No, they weren't married," said Roderick with a quiet chuckle. "He went before they could get married."

He spread his hands apologetically.

"Mother says that I have to tell people, because they always find out in the end and it's best to tell the truth –that's what it says in the Bible. There's just Mother and me, Miss Knighton; we have no other relations and I look after her now. She never worked except as a cleaner briefly at the vicarage. She said that no one else would give her a job as she had a child out of wedlock. So she just looked after me and did the cleaning, and now I look after her."

The colour drained from Mary's cheeks as she forced a smile onto her face, her knuckles white from gripping one hand tightly in the other. Roderick's words seemed to swell in her brain – she forced herself to concentrate on what he was saying.

"Mother says that if we trust in God we will all be forgiven. She says we should all be thankful for what we have and pray to God for forgiveness."

"Quite so," said Mary quietly. "I must go and make sure Freda has the lunch on."

She rose, leaving Lucy and Roderick both sitting looking at the carpet. After a moment Lucy stood and went to sit by Roderick on the sofa.

"You didn't have to tell us, Roderick, you hadn't told me before," she said gently, putting her hand on his.

Roderick looked at her and smiled.

"Mother said that I should tell you and then you can decide if you want to see me again. She said if I didn't tell you, it would make things worse in the end and I agree with her."

They both looked at the carpet again. Lucy sniffed.

"It makes no difference to me, Roderick," said Lucy quietly, taking his hand and squeezing it gently.

Roderick smiled.

In the kitchen Mary and Freda were preparing the lunch.

"What's 'e like then, Mary; 'e looks a bit steady to me," said Freda confidentially.

Mary said nothing, but carried on lifting the lids off the saucepans and checking their contents.

"Ain't you saying nuffing then?" Freda said. "About 'im in there."

She glared at Mary indignantly.

"'E could do with a new sooot, I can tell you that for nuffing," she scoffed.

"He's a very nice young man, he's very polite and he's honest," Mary said loudly, whipping round to face Freda.

"All right then, I only asked," Freda said defensively, banging down the cutlery on the table.

"Lucy," Mary shouted down the corridor.

"Coming," Lucy shouted back, clattering down the flagstones in the kitchen.

"Lucy dear, can you go and get Father in," asked Mary.

"Mary, what if he wants to go down the end?" whispered Lucy urgently.

"He went this morning," said Mary with a frown. "Anyway, he's got a potty."

"No, no, not Father: Roderick!" giggled Lucy.

"Well ask him."

"I can't do that!" hissed Lucy.

"Yes, you can."

"I can't, it's too embarrassing!" she insisted.

"I'll do it," barked Freda from the scullery, carrying an extra chair into the kitchen and eying Lucy steadily.

"You ain't very brave, are you?" she teased. "What 'is name then, Miss Lucy?"

"Roderick."

"Roderick what?" said Freda impatiently.

"Roderick Coyle."

"What?" said Freda, before attempting to repeat Roderick's surname.

She sighed.

"Don't worry – I'll call 'im sir."

She stomped off down the corridor into the hallway and from the door the girls could hear her announcing snootily:

"Lunch is served, sir, and if you want the facilities please be kind enough to follow me."

Lucy snorted with laughter and turned to hide her face, as Freda marched back up the hall, through the kitchen and out through the scullery, Roderick scurrying in her wake.

By the time Roderick had returned, Edgar had come in for lunch and was sitting moodily at the table. John slowly made his way to his seat and sat down. Roderick and Lucy both stood behind their chairs; Mary moved to sit down, stopping to stare at Lucy and Roderick.

"What are you waiting for?" she asked.

"We haven't said grace," said Lucy.

"So we haven't," said Mary with a small tut, her chair scraping the flags as she stood up again.

"You do it then, Lucy."

Lucy blushed, said a short grace and they all sat to eat.

After lunch, Lucy and Roderick went to look at the cattle, before setting off to Lower Dean to see Aunt Charlotte and Thomas, arranging to meet Mary at the chapel at six o'clock. Charlotte was very impressed with Roderick; he told her he read the Bible every day and he knew the names of the books of the Old Testament off by heart – she had checked. At chapel they all sat in one pew; Mary and William at the end, Roderick between Lucy and Charlotte. After the service Roderick had left promptly in order to catch the last train. Lucy walked with him to the park gates where he went up the hill and on to Sharnbrook station, leaving Lucy with a smile and a touch of his lips to her hand.

Back at Cold Harbour, Edgar and John had taken themselves to bed and Freda had left as she had the Bank Holiday Monday off.

"Mary, let's sit in the front room," said Lucy. "We could make the fire up and take the lamp in there; I haven't got to go back until tomorrow evening. It would be just like when Mother was alive and Henry and Bessie were still at home."

Mary smiled and went to make up the fire – Lucy took her Bible to read and they sat in the front room and talked. They talked about Verity and Roderick; they talked about Martha and the new baby. Eventually Lucy brought up the subject that Mary had been dreading that she would.

"Mary, did you see Noble Ladds while you were over with Martha?"

There was silence. Despite the heat of the fire, the colour leached from Mary's face and tears started to well up in her eyes. She sniffed and covered her face with her hands.

"Mary, what is it?" gasped Lucy, rushing to her sister and putting an arm around her shoulders. "You never cry! What is it?"

Mary shuddered, sniffed again and wiped her eyes with her handkerchief.

"You're right, Lucy, I never cry and I'm not going to now," said Mary determinedly. "That's the only way to cope with this."

"Cope with what?" asked Lucy desperately.

Mary was quiet for a moment; when she spoke, her voice was calm.

"You know this morning when Roderick came and told us about his father. How he said that his mother and father were not married?"

"Yes."

"Well he was very brave, wasn't he? To tell us? But he said it was the best thing to do and everyone would be forgiven in the end."

"Yes," said Lucy, worried about what might be coming next.

"Well, I've got to tell you something, Lucy."

"Yes, Mary, what?"

There was a pause while Mary collected herself.

"I think I'm having a baby," said Mary quietly.

Lucy gasped and covered her face as Mary had done, shaking her head incredulously. She looked back at her sister.

"Did you say that you are having a baby, Mary?" she whispered. "You didn't, did you?"

"Yes," said Mary. "Yes, Lucy, I think I am having a baby."

Lucy's hands flew back to her face; she began to cry, her body shaking as she sobbed into her hands. Mary grabbed her arms and pulled Lucy round to look at her.

"Now, Lucy, you mustn't cry," ordered Mary. "You've got to help me, you are the only one I can talk to. Please, you must help."

She grabbed her sister and shook her gently.

"Please, stop crying; that's not going to help," said Mary desperately.

Lucy sniffed and wiped her nose with her fist.

"But how?" she said to Mary incredulously.

"Don't let's worry about how at the moment, I want to make sure I am having one. What did the sister tell you about the signs?"

Lucy sniffed again and asked Mary to go over what symptoms she was having.

"What do you think then, Lucy, you're a nurse?"

Lucy looked at Mary and sighed heavily.

"If you've missed again at the end of next week you must be, Mary," she said gently.

"Yes, Lucy, that's what I think."

She squeezed her sister's hand.

"I've got to be strong and you have to help me, Lucy, I've got no one else," she said pleadingly.

"Of course I'll help, Mary," said Lucy, before adding quietly, "but who is the father?"

Lucy looked into Mary's eyes, turning away again almost immediately. Mary looked down and said quietly,

"Noble Ladds."

"How dreadful," gasped Lucy, adding quickly. "I didn't mean it like that, Mary."

She threw her arms round her sister and hugged her, before sitting back and looking hard at her again.

"But what are you going to do, Mary, what on earth are you going to do?"

"I'll have to marry him," said Mary firmly. "That is the only answer. If I do and do it quickly, what will it matter? The child will have a father – that's the main thing."

"But do you love him, Mary?" Lucy asked gently.

"Not anymore, but that's not the point now, is it?" said Mary with an angry shake of her head. "I was such a fool, Lucy."

She sighed, forbidding tears to overcome her again.

"I have to marry him, don't you agree?"

"Yes, you must," Lucy nodded. "But he hasn't asked you has he? Does he know about the baby?"

"No he doesn't, I haven't seen him since that day."

Mary shuddered.

"If I tell him – what do you think he would do?" asked Mary quietly.

Lucy looked thoughtful.

"I don't know; but he ought to ask you to marry him – surely he ought, don't you think?"

"He ought to," said Mary doubtfully. "But would he? I don't know, he's very sharp, you know; he could take all his horses and leave – sell up and go. He hasn't much to hold him here, all his family went to Canada a long time ago."

"It's a risk," said Lucy honestly.

"That's what I thought," said Mary.

"You'll just have to get him to ask you somehow. You were always good with boys, Mary; you can get them to do anything for you, it comes naturally."

Mary laughed bitterly.

"Yes, it does," she said with a wry smile. "But will it work with him? I don't know."

"Well you've got to try."

There was silence.

"What I've got to do is to seduce him."

"To what?" said Lucy bewildered.

"To *seduce* him."

"What's that mean?"

"It means I've got to get him to do it again."

Lucy sat up straight and looked at Mary, horrified.

"Mary, you couldn't, how could you; it is all so horrible!"

There was silence; a log rolled lazily out of the fire, smouldering on the carpet, Mary rose and kicked the log back into the fire, stoking it with the poker and adding another log.

"So if you did it again, would he ask you to marry him?" said Lucy dubiously.

"He might," shrugged Mary. "But it's got to be quickly – before the baby shows."

She chewed her lip and thought hard.

"He will need a push," she muttered, pulling Rupert's letter from her pocket and thrusting it at Lucy. "Here, Lucy, look at this."

Lucy took the letter from the envelope. She started to read, mouthing the words as she read. When she had finished, she looked up at Mary.

"Well, have you replied, Mary?"

"No, but I've got to soon – I've had it about a month or more."

"But he doesn't actually ask you to marry him, does he?" said Lucy.

"No, but—" Mary paused and chewed her lip again.

"But he implies that," said Lucy. "And he's asking you to wait for him. I read that as him intending to ask you as soon as he gets back."

"That's how I read it," agreed Mary.

"So what are you going to do?" asked Lucy. "Would you rather marry Rupert or Noble Ladds?"

Mary thought for a while, then shook her head.

"I have to marry Noble Ladds – what I would prefer is irrelevant."

"So?" said Lucy impatiently.

"So—" said Mary, "I am going to tell Noble Ladds what Rupert wrote in his letter – tell him that I am about to reply to him to give him my answer. That should be enough of a prompt for him to ask me." Mary was silent.

"That could work, Mary," said Lucy, "But—"

"But what? It's the only idea that has a chance of working without him smelling a rat," Mary said.

"But it's so sinful to seduce someone and then trick him into marrying you – it doesn't sound right."

Mary looked incredulously at her sister.

"He was the sinner, Lucy!" she hissed angrily. "Don't talk to me about sin; I'm the victim of that. Anyway, what did Roderick say this morning: 'All sins can be forgiven?' What's the point of going to chapel if not to get our sins forgiven?"

"I know, I know," said Lucy hurriedly. "Don't shout so, Mary, it frightens me. But Roderick's mother didn't get married!"

Mary rose and stood with her back to the fire.

"That was different," she said quietly "Roderick's father was killed in battle. Lucy, I am not having a baby without a husband and if it has to be Noble Ladds so be it. If I have to trick him to marry me so be it; it's the best way out of this dreadful situation."

There was silence again.

"It's the only way," conceded Lucy. "You don't want to be like poor Molly; that would be awful."

"Good, you agree then."

"Yes," said Lucy quietly, standing up to give her sister a hug.

Mary lifted the back of her skirt, holding it round her front and warming the length of her legs.

"I wish you wouldn't do that, Mary, it's so common," sighed Lucy.

"No, it's not, Lucy – it's good sense," laughed Mary. "You try it – go on."

"I couldn't," gasped Lucy, horrified.

"Yes, you could," said Mary firmly.

She beckoned to her sister.

"Come on – just stand here like me; no one's looking, the curtains are shut."

Lucy looked around surreptitiously and rose with a small smile, lifting her skirt gingerly to warm her legs.

"You're right, Mary, that is nice," agreed Lucy.

"It's funny, Lucy, now I have told you and we've got a plan, I don't feel worried anymore."

She sighed heavily.

"Lucy, he's not much good and I don't expect much of him as a husband;

he goes to the pub and keeps bad company, but at times he is good fun and exciting."

She dropped her skirt and sat in the chair by the fire.

"Now here's the plan. Sit down, Lucy."

Lucy let her skirt fall and fell into the chair opposite as Mary continued.

"I will write to Noble Ladds asking him to come to lunch two weeks today; I will know then if I have missed again. Will you be home that weekend?"

"Yes, on the Sunday I think I will be."

"Can Roderick come?"

"I don't know."

"Well bring him if you can. After lunch we will all walk as usual down to Lower Dean and then go to chapel on the way back. After chapel you go home with Roderick to sort out Father, but keep him awake till I get back with Noble."

"When will that be?" said Lucy.

"About half an hour later, fingers crossed."

She held Lucy's hands and squeezed them.

"What do you think?" she asked Lucy quietly.

Lucy looked at her calmly.

"You're my sister and I would do anything for you, you know that. I just hope that it works."

Chapter Forty-Two
A Rat in a Trap

The appointed Sunday arrived. Mary had invited Noble Ladds, who was more than surprised at the invitation, but wrote back by return accepting. Lucy and Roderick arrived at half past eleven and Noble rode up at twelve o'clock. The two men contrasted vastly in their dress; Noble was as usual immaculately turned out, making Roderick look shabby in his ill-fitting suit.

After lunch Noble and Roderick sat in the front room chattering for a while before Noble drifted off to sleep, leaving Roderick to leaf through an old newspaper. Lucy and Mary went up to their room to get ready to go out to tea; Mary took her boots off and pulled a pair of long drawers out of the chest.

"You can't wear those, Mary, the seams all torn," said Lucy, holding them up.

"Don't ask questions, Lucy, just give them here," snapped Mary, pulling on the drawers.

Lucy slumped onto the bed, tears welling up in her eyes.

"Don't cry, Lucy, don't cry, we don't want any of that," begged Mary.

"No, Mary, I won't cry. I will say a prayer for you," sniffed Lucy, taking her sister's hand and following her downstairs.

At half past three the party set off for Lower Dean to the butcher's shop, where Charlotte was waiting impatiently for Roderick's arrival. She had decided to take him under her wing as a fellow devout Christian. Thomas chatted happily to Noble as William and Mary handed round the tea.

When they had finished, they all walked up to chapel.

"I know you don't usually go, Noble," said Mary apologetically, "but once in a while won't matter, will it?"

She smiled coyly and looped her arm through his as they walked the mile to Upper Dean.

"No, I don't mind, Mary; if that's what you want, I'm happy to come along."

He smiled at her and entered the chapel.

After the service Mary and Noble followed Roderick and Lucy back to

Cold Harbour. They walked arm in arm at a leisurely pace along the high street of Upper Dean, up along the bridleway until they met the path to Cold Harbour. Noble could not disguise his surprise at how accommodating Mary was, having not seen her for so long. He decided that she had obviously come to terms with what had happened and thus he could resume the relationship as though nothing had happened.

The clouds loomed on the horizon, threatening rain, and it was clear that there would be a shower before long. They ambled on, past the spot where the swarm of bees had trapped them and on over the last stile, seeing Cold Harbour in the distance. As they approached the farm, spots of rain started to fall.

"Come on, Noble, we must run or we are going to get wet," said Mary, grabbing his hand and dragging him the last two hundred yards up to the wall of the farmstead.

"Come on," she said, pulling him into a stable, "let's go in here."

To one end of the stable, three carthorses stood grazing from the manger and tethered halfway down the barn, chomping on hay from a mound in front of him, stood Tinker. Mary moved up to him, stroking his nose and running her hand down his flank.

"Isn't he a lovely animal, Noble?" sighed Mary, looking round at Noble.

Noble moved towards her and wrapped his arms around her – she turned towards him and let him kiss her. She ran her hands down his waistcoat, feeling the flask in his pocket and breaking away to look at him.

"Is that your flask, Noble?" she asked, tapping his jacket.

"Yes, do you want some?" said Noble, pulling out his flask and unscrewing the top.

She grinned and accepted the proffered flask, putting it to her mouth and taking the smallest of sips. She handed the flask back to Noble, who took a deep swig. Mary eyed him carefully.

"Noble," said Mary, "I've got something to tell you."

"Go on then, Mary, what is it?"

"I've had a letter from Rupert Nelson; do you remember him? You met him at the point-to-point."

"Yes," said Noble with a small snort of derision. "Well, what about him?"

"His father sent him to the Argentine; he's been there about four months now. We were good friends when I worked in Northampton and he has been over a bit since then. Well, you see he's written me this letter and—"

She stopped, feigning reluctance.

"What did he say, then?" Noble asked impatiently.

"Well, he said that he was very much in love with me," said Mary coyly. "He told me if I waited until he got back he would ask me to marry him."

There was silence. Noble took another long swig from the flask and offered it to Mary; she took it and once again had only the smallest sip.

"Oh," Noble said, walking up the stable and back, patting Tinker on his way past.

"Why are you telling me this, Mary?" he said finally.

"Well, Noble, I want your advice," said Mary innocently. "No one has ever asked me to marry them before and I don't know what to do."

She looked at Noble, who took another swig from his flask and paced the length of the stable again. He breathed in deeply and came to stand in front of Mary.

"I don't think you should marry him, Mary," he said decisively.

"Why not, Noble?" said Mary curiously.

Noble looked hard at her again and offered her the flask; she shook her head.

"Because he's a long way away and you've got to wait all that time."

"I know that," said Mary. "But he's a good man and he will keep his word – I know he will."

Noble seized Mary by the waist and pulled her to him.

"You shouldn't marry him, Mary," he murmured, kissing her gently on the lips.

"Why, Noble?" Mary asked again.

"Because you should marry me, Mary."

Mary froze in his grip.

"What did you say, Noble?"

"Will you marry me?" Noble whispered, kissing her again – his hands moving up and down her body, undoing the buttons of her coat.

She pushed him gently away from her and looked at him carefully.

"You mean that, Noble?"

"Yes."

"You mean right away? I wouldn't have to wait like I would for Rupert?"

"Yes, right away!" said Noble. "As soon as it can be arranged, next week if you like."

"And you will go and see Father now, yes?" said Mary with a laugh.

He nodded and they kissed again, Mary responding to his embrace as they gradually sank into the pile of hay that was aside ready to be fed to the horses. She pushed herself up on her elbows and smiled at him.

"Yes I'll marry you, Noble, as soon as possible."

"Let's drink to that then," he said with a smile, taking another large swig from the flask.

Fifteen minutes later they rushed into the house where Lucy and Roderick were in the kitchen; Mary shook her coat in the scullery and came into the kitchen, Noble following, looking very flushed – his hair not quite as smooth as usual.

"Hello, you two, is Father still up?" said Mary hurriedly.

"No," said Lucy. "But he's still awake – I just took him some tea."

"Noble, did you want to pay your respects before you go?" said Mary pointedly. "You know where Father is."

"Very good, Mary," said Noble, making his way to John's room.

"Roderick, you sit still," Lucy ordered, leaping from the table and tiptoeing with Mary to John's door, where they pressed their ears to the door.

As John was a bit deaf, Noble was forced to speak loudly – so the girls heard every word of Noble asking for Mary's hand in marriage. Lucy smiled at Mary, who giggled and grabbed Lucy's hand, the two girls rushing back to the kitchen and sitting down. Roderick looked up in surprise, but appeared to be none the wiser. After a while Noble returned and sat down.

"Well," said Mary. "What did he say?"

"He said yes," said Noble simply.

Mary smiled.

"Tell Lucy and Roderick then, Noble."

Noble moved round the table, gave Mary a peck on the cheek and said,

"I'm pleased to announce that Miss Mary Knighton and Mr Noble Ladds are engaged to be married," he declared.

Lucy and Roderick clapped loudly.

"On...?" said Mary.

"I don't know," said Noble. "Who's got a diary?"

"Get that calendar down, Lucy," Mary instructed.

They pored over the calendar.

"Four weeks yesterday, which makes it the fifth of June."

"Let's drink to that," said Noble, pulling out his flask and offering it to the table.

Everyone declined.

"Oh well, suit yourself," he said, taking a swig.

"We will have to go, Lucy," said Roderick, rising. "I think we will have missed the train by now, so we'll have to walk all the way."

"I'm not coming, Roderick," said Lucy apologetically. "I have to talk to Mary. Can I give you two notes – one for the nurses' home, you pass that so that you can drop it in – and one for the sister in case I am late in the morning."

She grabbed a pen and paper from the sideboard, quickly scribbled the notes and handed them to Roderick.

"Now get your coat, Roderick, and I will walk down the drive with you," she said, rising from the table.

"I must go as well, I am off to London tomorrow and I want to call and see Henry and Martha to tell them the news," said Noble, grabbing his coat and leaving to saddle Tinker, giving Mary a peck on the way past.

When they had all left, Mary and Lucy sat down in the kitchen.

"It worked then, Mary, he's going to marry you then," said Lucy dolefully.

"Yes, so far so good! Now we have to get things organised; there's the parson to see, the banns to organise, the wedding to fix. It's not ideal I know that, but it's the best I can do in the circumstances."

Lucy sniffed.

"I know you've done the best you can, Mary, but what happens when he finds out? He will be able to work out that you were already pregnant."

Lucy wrung her hands.

"I will cross that bridge when I get to it; as long as he doesn't find out until after the wedding I am safe."

She took Lucy's hands.

"Now listen, Lucy, I realise he is not an ideal husband, but I had no choice. There is no way I was going to have a baby without a husband. What would everyone say? Aunt Charlotte, Aunt Sarah and Verity and all my friends in Northampton? Think about the child, Lucy, it will be legitimate."

"But Roderick isn't," protested Lucy, "and it doesn't matter."

"I know he isn't and he's done very well; but I'm going to do it my way."

Mary stood up and took the poker to the range; Lucy looked sadly after her.

The four weeks passed quickly. The service was to be at twelve o'clock at Melchbourne church and the congregation would then be invited to Cold Harbour. William was to give Mary away, as John was too infirm to come.

Edgar had been particularly unaccommodating about the plans that were being made and before long Mary could no longer stand it. A week before the wedding, having grumbled the whole way through breakfast, Edgar sat at the table for lunch to find it was not quite ready. He continued to complain bitterly until the food was served. Mary, already flustered, placed a plate in front of him; Edgar peered at it dubiously, took up his fork and raised a mouthful to his mouth; he grimaced, ate the mouthful, chewed it several times and pushed his plate away, protesting that it was inedible. Mary turned furiously to face him.

"What exactly could I do to improve it?" she asked icily.

Edgar scowled at her.

"I am doubtful you could do anything at all," he snarled. "Most of the food I get served in this 'ouse is just as filthy."

Mary glared at him angrily, moved calmly towards him, picked up the plate and tipped the contents into Edgar's lap. Edgar roared and leapt up from the table, grimacing at Mary in expectation of an apology, but he wasn't going to get one. He turned and stormed up the stairs, returning later with a packed bag, which he hoisted on his shoulder and with one last furious glare at Mary, left the house.

Despite being initially concerned at the difficulties this might cause on the farm, Mary and Freda found it difficult not to celebrate Edgar's disappearance. William was already in control of the farm's finances and some of the workmen were only too happy to take on some extra responsibility, so Edgar's absence was not a particular disaster. However, the one area that the lack of finance did impact on was the wedding, and Mary was forced to economise where she could. She was just about able to afford a new dress, which she went to Northampton to buy; but Lucy, who was the bridesmaid, had to make do with what she had. They could not afford for the bells to be rung and there was no photographer. The number of invited guests stretched to only as many as they could accommodate at Cold Harbour after the ceremony; Noble's family had all moved to Canada so there were no relations from his side. Mary had to make all the arrangements herself, including getting the banns read at Melchbourne and Bythorn, which she dragged Noble along to hear, much to his annoyance. There was no honeymoon planned; instead they were to go to Noble's home, Elgin Farm at Bythorn, for the first night of their married life. Mary knew where the farm was, having passed it a couple of times, but had never been inside. Her father was to stay at Cold Harbour until the summer, when Mary planned to move him over to live with them when the farm was sold.

On the weekend of the wedding, Lucy arrived home on the Friday to help Mary get the wedding breakfast ready. Bessie was coming up by train from Surrey on the day of the wedding with her husband and two children. Noble had borrowed the same tattered carriage that he had taken to the point-to-point and had promised that he would send it to Cold Harbour to fetch the bride and her small entourage.

Freda was in the kitchen when Martha arrived on the morning of the wedding, Mary and Lucy were still upstairs getting ready.

"Cuppa tea, Martha?" Freda asked.

"No, it will make me want to go in the church if I drink too much, thank you," said Martha.

"Well it will soon be over any road," said Freda. "And best of luck to 'er, that's what I say."

She shook her head despairingly.

"What a lovely girl like that is marrying that good-for-nothing for, I don't know."

"Freda, you shouldn't say such things," said Martha, but her voice held little conviction.

"Why not? It's true and you know it, Martha, if no one else does."

Martha sighed and shook her head.

"You're right, Freda," agreed Martha, lowering her voice. "He is a good for nothing man and I wish Henry would see that."

"Master William knows," grumbled Freda

"Yes, I know he does," agreed Martha. "Where is he by the way?"

"'E's in with the master; talkin' farmin' no doubt."

Mary and Lucy clattered down the stairs and burst into the kitchen; Mary in a long cream coloured dress, holding a small posy and her veil, which she had not put on. Lucy was wearing her best floral dress with a white rose pinned to it.

"Martha dear, don't you look nice," said Mary distractedly. "Now what have I forgotten, Lucy? Look at me, what have I forgotten?"

"Nothing, Mary, nothing, just keep calm," said Lucy quietly, picking a loose thread from Mary's dress. "Now I'm just going down the end so just keep calm."

Lucy dashed out the door, Mary looking desperately after her.

"That's what I have forgotten!" cried Mary. "I must go down the end!"

"Now wait a minute till Lucy comes back, Mary," said Martha. "And make sure you lift that skirt up so as not to get it in the mud."

Lucy came back into the kitchen moments later, Reuben right behind her.

"Reuben, where have you been?" cried Mary delighted. "I haven't seen you for two weeks at least."

"I'm 'ad scarlet fever, I'm bin in bed," mumbled Reuben.

"Oh, that's nasty."

"Is it right you're getting married, Mary?" asked Reuben quietly.

"Yes, today!"

"To that Ladds?"

"Yes, Noble Ladds."

Reuben scuffed the floor with his boot.

"'E ain't no good, Mary," he burst out. "Everyone says it – I know 'e ain't."

He thrust his hands into his pockets and looked at the ground.

"What a thing to say, Reuben! And to a lady when she's just about to get married," Mary said with a small laugh. "You're just jealous."

She ruffled his hair and looked up as William walked into the kitchen.

"What time is the carriage due, Mary?" he asked.

"Quarter to twelve," said Mary nervously.

William looked at his watch.

"It's nearly that now."

"Go to the front room, Lucy," said Mary, "and see if it's coming."

"He's not coming up the drive," said Lucy, having been to look.

"Well we will have to wait," said Mary.

She sat down, fidgeting with her bouquet of flowers distractedly. Five minutes passed.

"Go and look again, Lucy," demanded Mary.

Once more Lucy went to the window in the front room and came back.

"No sign of it," said Lucy apologetically.

William looked at his watch.

"We're going to be late now; it's nearly five to and it'll take five minutes to get up the drive."

"Where can it be?" said Mary again. "Reuben run out into the field! You can see all the way to the The Grape Vine, you will see where he is then; go on run!"

Reuben did as he was told, scampering out the door and returning moments later.

"Well?" said Mary.

"'E ain't comin'," said Reuben quietly.

"What do you mean he isn't coming?" said Mary incredulously.

"'E ain't! I can see the carriage outside the pub and it ain't movin'."

"Damn and blast the man," cried Mary at the top of her voice. "What are we going to do now?" William looked to Mary for instruction, unable to keep a blank expression on his face.

"Don't look at me like that, William Dunmore," hissed Mary angrily. "I know he's no good before you say it; but I am going to marry him for better or for worse, do you understand?"

There was silence. William sighed and looked down.

"We will have to cycle and quickly," he said quietly.

"But we've only got three bikes," said Lucy.

"Well you ride on William's crossbar, Lucy," instructed Mary. "Martha, you have Lucy's bike and I will go on mine. Reuben – run and open the gates for us."

"I'll get them out the pub, Mary," said Martha angrily. "I'll box Henry's ears for him, you see if I don't, I've never 'eard of such goings on."

They rushed out the door to collect the bicycles.

"Hold your skirt up, Mary, don't let it get in the chain," said Martha, as Mary hoisted herself onto her bike.

Lucy backed up to William's crossbar, hitched herself on sideways and held the handlebars as William started to pedal as steadily as possible, standing up to see past Lucy's small form. Reuben scampered off ahead to open the gates.

Sure enough, as they passed the pub they saw the carriage stood outside.

"You go on, I'll catch you up," said Martha, braking and laying her bicycle against the wall of the pub. Her furious shouts reached them as they cycled on towards the church.

At the church, the vicar was waiting impatiently – William moved towards him to explain their transport problems. The vicar was easily placated and led Mary and Lucy round the back of the church to wait for Henry and Noble. William peered in through one of the lower windows – he could see the few guests in the church shuffling impatiently in their seats.

It wasn't long before Martha appeared on her bike, with Reuben sitting on the pannier, followed by Henry and Noble in the carriage. They pulled up next to the lynch gate and jumped down.

"Boy, take the horses will you and turn them round," ordered Noble, spinning Reuben a threepence piece and making his way up the path with Henry.

Mary's thoughts strayed to Rupert; she had written to him but hadn't posted the letter. What would he say when he got the letter, what would he do? It didn't matter really, she thought – Rupert was a long way away and she had never promised him anything. She sighed and tried to think of the upcoming ceremony with a sense of positivity.

The vicar poked his head round the side of the church and beckoned to the three of them. Lucy squeezed Mary's hand and smiled – Mary found it hard to smile back. She sighed heavily and followed the vicar into the church.

The service passed in a blur, Mary didn't think that she would be able to remember a single detail of it, only that she managed to get through it with a smile of sorts plastered to her lips. After the service most of the small congregation made their way up to Cold Harbour, Mary and Noble being driven in the carriage by Henry. At Cold Harbour, sandwiches and cakes were laid out in the front room and Freda, who had rushed back on her bike, had put the kettle on for cups of tea. Noble had brought two bottles of whisky in the carriage, unbeknown to Martha, which he laid out on the sideboard. After a while he took the bottle round, offering everyone a tot; everyone except Henry and Art Tuffnail refused.

Charlotte took Martha to the side, eyeing Henry critically.

"You must take Henry in hand, my dear," she said. "I notice he's drinking whisky; it's a sin you know, Martha, you've got to deal with it."

"I know, Aunt Charlotte," agreed Martha. "But it's not easy at a wedding – and when he's with Noble Ladds I can do nothing with him, nothing at all!"

She turned and watched her husband guffawing loudly at one of Noble's jokes; both men became increasingly boisterous as they drank more whisky from their tea cups. Charlotte furiously beckoned William over.

"William," she said in a loud whisper, "when do you think we can go?"

"Not quite yet, Mother, someone will have to make a speech first; then we can go."

"Who's going to do that, then? It should be dear John, but he's not fit enough."

She looked over at John, who was sitting, smiling benignly at the proceedings. Lucy was offering him a small plate of sandwiches; Charlotte beckoned to her as she left John's side.

"Who's going to do a speech, Lucy dear?" she whispered.

"I don't know, Aunt Charlotte," shrugged Lucy.

"Well get someone to do it and then we can go."

"Very well, Aunt Charlotte," sighed Lucy, leaving to find Mary.

Mary was in the kitchen, arranging the next batch of sandwiches.

"Mary, Aunt Charlotte wants to know who's going to make a speech because she wants to go" said Lucy sighing.

"She is an old spoil sport," frowned Mary, "and at my wedding as well."

"But who's going to do it?" insisted Lucy.

"I've no idea! Father can't, that's for sure, what about Henry?"

"No, no, no," said Martha urgently, "I know him, he's had too much to drink – you never know what he will say."

"William will have to do it," said Mary with a sigh. "Go and ask him, Lucy and tell him to get on with it."

Lucy left the kitchen to find William, passing Verity in the doorway, who was talking to Aunt Sarah and Uncle George, the trio slightly removed from the other guests.

"What a very nice service," said Verity with little sincerity.

"Yes," said Sarah, "but a pity she had to marry such a dreadful man, don't you think, my dear?"

She looked disapprovingly over at Noble.

"Just look at him with his jacket off, drinking spirits out of a tea cup; how common can you get?"

"Well she must have had her reasons for marrying him," said Verity with a shrug.

"We had such great hopes for her, didn't we, George?" Sarah said to her husband.

"Yes dear," he said, winking at Verity.

"Such a lovely girl, lived with us you know for some years," continued Sarah. "Yes, we had great hopes for her."

She sipped her tea.

"Of course I blame that useless brother of hers; he's nearly as bad as Noble Ladds. Why he could not stay at home and run the farm, I do not know, it's disgraceful, that's what I say. Young people these days have no sense of responsibility: none at all, aren't I right, George?"

"Yes, dear," said George, grinning at Verity again.

"Present company excepted, my dear," corrected Sarah, clutching at Verity's arm and forcing a smile.

"What about William?" said George.

"What did you say?" Sarah said turning to George directly.

"What about William, dear?" repeated George. "You can't accuse him of shirking his responsibility."

"William, yes – well, yes," spluttered Sarah. "He's an exception too; doing very well by all accounts *and* he's younger than Henry, running Cold Harbour as well, I hear. Of course he's got a little more class, don't you think?"

She lowered her voice and looked around surreptitiously.

"Went to a good school as well, Miss Watson-Foster; don't you agree, makes all the difference, that's what I say."

"I'm sure you are right, Mrs Chambers," said Verity deferentially.

Sarah sniffed and cast her eyes snootily around the room.

"Who's that drip?" she said, her eyes lighting on Roderick.

She pointed in his direction.

"Oh, that's Roderick!" exclaimed Verity. "He's Lucy's young man, he is sweet; got a heart of gold."

"He could do with a new suit, don't you think?" sneered Sarah.

"You mustn't be rude, dear," George reprimanded.

"No," Sarah said, without the merest hint of an apology.

The sound of a spoon being banged on the sideboard announced the start of the speeches.

"We are about to have a toast," William said, "Freda is bringing the glasses round, so please help yourself."

"Thank goodness for that," Sarah whispered. "Then we can go, eh, George?"

"Yes, dear," muttered George.

"The only thing you can say about Noble Ladds, Miss Watson-Foster," said Sarah in a hushed whisper, arms folded tightly across her chest, "is that he's a fine figure of a man; you can see that with his jacket off."

She grabbed a glass from Freda's tray and waited for Lucy to come and fill it up.

William banged on the sideboard again, and shortly proposed the health of the bride and groom. Mary smiling winningly as Noble made a brief reply.

"They look a handsome couple, don't they, Freda?" Martha whispered, from the back of room.

"'E's a fine lookin' man I'll give you that, Martha, whatever you say about him you 'ave to give 'im that. 'E don't carry no weight, can't if 'e's all'as ridin' 'orses."

She sipped her wine delicately.

"Mind, Mary is a bit heavier than usual, don't you think, Martha; not like 'er, is it?"

"I 'adn't noticed to tell you the truth," admitted Martha, with a frown.

"Well I'd say she's carryin' a bit of extra weight," said Freda again. "Strange really, women usually lose weight before their weddin' day, wouldn't you think?"

Martha shrugged noncommittally and said nothing.

After the speeches, people started to leave, either by foot or on bicycles. Walter brought the car up for Verity, who got in and prepared to ride back to The Hall. Reuben was standing by the gate, having opened it for Sarah and George's motorcar which had left moments later; as they passed him, Verity instructed Walter to stop the car.

"Would you like a lift, Reuben?" Verity enquired, knowing riding in the car was one of Reuben's favourite things.

"Yes please, miss," Reuben answered, but without his usual enthusiasm. "Shall I get in the front, miss?"

"If you like, Reuben."

Five minutes later they were at The Hall.

"Thank you, miss," Reuben said, climbing out the car and walking up the drive towards the road, his head hung low. Verity watched him go; it took her a moment to realise he was crying.

"Reuben, Reuben, are you all right? What's the matter?" she called, rushing after him.

Reuben stopped and leant against the big oak tree at the end of the drive, his forearm pressed against the bark of the tree, his head pressed to his arm. He kicked the tree hard with his boot.

"My dear, what is it?" insisted Verity. "You must tell me."

Reuben gave a small sob but said nothing – Verity put her arm around him and prised him off the tree, seeing the tears rolling down his face.

"Come, come, Reuben, it can't be that bad. Come on back and we will get Dorcas to get you some tea."

Reuben sniffed and let Verity guide him back into the kitchen at The Hall.

"Dorcas, look what we have here," said Verity, leading Reuben into the kitchen. "Come on, Reuben, sit down at the table. What's wrong with him, Dorcas?"

Reuben sniffed, the tears had stopped but his face was wet.

"I don't understand it," said Verity helplessly.

Dorcas came round the table, sitting opposite Reuben and looking at him long and hard.

"I know what's wrong with 'im."

"What then, Dorcas, tell me?"

"A broken 'eart, that's what 'e's got; a broken 'eart, ain't you, Reuben?" said Dorcas knowingly.

Reuben looked up at Dorcas with surprise.

"Yes," he sniffed, crossing his arms in front of him on the table and laying his head on them. He sobbed again.

"What is it, Dorcas? I don't understand," said Verity, nonplussed.

"E's got a broken 'eart, Miss Verity, because Mary Knighton got married; Reuben carried a torch for her, see."

"Yes," said Verity, trying not to show the incredulity she felt, "I suppose I do; but Reuben's so young."

"That don't matter, Miss Verity, 'e were smitten and that were that; I knowed all about it, I'm seen 'im go up to Cold Harbour, yes I knowed."

"Yes, well what do we do?" said Verity impatiently.

"Nothing, 'e'll get over it, you see, or rather 'e will get used to it."

Dorcas ruffled Reuben's hair gently.

"'E's a lovely boy mind, ain't 'e, Miss Verity?" she said with a smile. "One of the best and 'e will be a good looker, you can see it now."

"I suppose he will," said Verity.

"Reuben?" said Dorcas.

Reuben looked blearily up at her, his eyes bloodshot, his face wet with tears.

"How old are you, Reuben?" Dorcas asked.

"Twelve," he answered.

"How old's Mary?"

"I don't know."

"Well, I do know," replied Dorcas. "She's twenty-one."

"Twenty-one?" said Reuben in disbelief. "She ain't."

"She is, you ask Miss Verity," Dorcas said.

"Yes she is," said Verity gently.

"She's too la-di-da for the likes of you, Reuben, with all 'er posh friends an all, and she's educated, Reuben."

"I know she is," sniffed Reuben.

"Do you read and write, Reuben?"

"I do, well I do a bit," insisted Reuben.

"They tell me George Lowe does all your school work for you," said Dorcas, with a small smile.

Reuben sat up and looked from Dorcas to Verity.

"'E does a bit on it," said Reuben defensively. "But I look after 'im, see, they pick on 'im else."

"I know," said Dorcas.

Reuben looked at her and bowed his head.

"I know I ain't much good at that sort of thing, but I could learn, I just don't bovver."

He sighed heavily.

"But why did she marry 'im? 'E ain't no good, Dorcas, I know 'e ain't; you know that, Dorcas."

"I know that, Reuben and you know that and Mary 'ad 'er reasons for marrying 'im and that's good enough, don't you agree, Miss Verity?"

Dorcas looked pointedly at Verity.

"Yes, you are right, Dorcas," agreed Verity weakly. "She had her reasons."

"Mind he's a fine figure of a man," mused Dorcas. "Don't carry no weight, do 'e and 'e smells nice when you get near 'im."

She blushed.

"Not that I 'ave of course," she added quickly, "but that's what they tell me."

"Yes, he's always very smart," Verity agreed.

"Now, Miss Verity I would like some fresh air if you don't mind and I thought I might walk along the road to Lower Dean with Reuben."

"Please do, Dorcas," said Verity.

"Come on, boy, gimme your 'and, I'll walk you 'ome."

Reuben sniffed once more, offered Dorcas his hand, and allowed himself to be led from the kitchen.

Chapter Forty-Three
Goodbye Cold Harbour

The wedding was over and all the guests had left Cold Harbour. Mary, Martha and Lucy were clearing the plates, glasses and teacups into the scullery where Freda was washing them and William was in the front room with John discussing the sale of the farm.

Noble Ladds and Henry sat in the kitchen finishing off the bottle of whisky.

"The first night of married life approaches then, sister dear," laughed Henry as Mary brought another tray through to the scullery. He punched Noble Ladds playfully on the forearm.

"Eh, Mr Ladds?" he laughed again.

"You keep your mouth shut, Henry Knighton, I heard that and it wasn't called for," shouted Martha from the scullery.

"Sorry, Martha," said Henry with a giggle.

"Don't come that tone with me," Martha shouted from the door of the scullery. "I'll box your ears for you if I have any more of that. You can go and make sure the 'orses is bin fed and you are ready to go, Henry – you can go with 'im, Noble Ladds, you need some fresh air, I'm sure; we want to get 'ome afore it's dark."

Henry and Noble left without a word passing Roderick in the doorway, who was preparing to leave.

"Wait a minute, Roderick, I'll get my coat and come with you down the drive," said Lucy, pulling on her coat and following him outside.

They walked down the drive hand in hand, walking in silence.

"Lucy, is Mary having a baby?" said Roderick suddenly.

Lucy stopped and looked at him hard.

"Why do you say that, Roderick?"

"Mother said it," Roderick shrugged. "She says you can always tell when a wedding comes so quickly."

Lucy said nothing.

"Is she, Lucy?" said Roderick gently.

"Yes she is," blurted out Lucy. "But, Roderick, you must promise not to tell anyone, you must promise."

"Of course I promise," laughed Roderick. "And who do I have to tell anyway, only Mother!"

Lucy smiled wanly and said goodbye, making her way slowly back up the drive to where Mary was putting her bag into the carriage. Noble helped her into the seat next to Martha and leapt into the driver's seat next to Henry.

"All ready?" shouted Noble.

"Yes," said Martha. "But don't forget to stop and pick up young Henry from Ruby's."

Lucy said goodbye and waved as the carriage made its way down the drive. Mary looked back at her sister standing in front of the old house, misery welling up in her, threatening to drown her.

She could hear Noble and Henry chattering in the front.

"You look sad, Mary, and on your wedding day," said Martha gently.

"That's where I was born, Martha," said Mary gently, desperate not to let the tears overwhelm her. "And I'm leaving for good, that's why I'm sad."

"Course you are, Mary," said Martha quietly, falling silent.

At Brington, Noble dropped off Henry, Martha and young Henry, who they had picked up on the way past. The air was cool as they rode on and even though it was May, Mary shivered in her coat and moved closer to Noble. There were no lights on at Noble's house, which stood starkly against the starry night sky. The moon was half grown but provided enough light for them to see and added to the ghostly aspect of the forbidding house. Noble pulled the horses to a stop, the bridles rattling as the horses chomped on their bits and shook their heads. Noble carried Mary's bag to the threshold and opened the door.

"I'm supposed to carry you across the threshold, isn't that what they say?" he said with a wink, taking Mary's hand.

"That's what they say," repeated Mary wistfully.

Noble swept Mary up and carried her into the hall, kissing her as he put her down.

"Stay there, Mary, I'll just go and light the lamp," he murmured, making his way down the hall to where Mary presumed the kitchen was. Mary could see the light gradually appear as Noble brought the lamp back down the hall, illuminating the dark corridor with the flickering flame; shadows danced across the bare walls, speeding into the distance behind him as he walked towards her. The only furniture in the hall was a coat stand – a light fitting hung limply from the ceiling bereft of a lamp. Mary managed a weak smile.

"There's light," declared Noble, handing her the lamp. "You have a look round while I see to the horses – I won't be long."

The front door slammed as he made his way out into the yard, the bang echoing around the empty house. Mary stood dejectedly in the hallway – she could see doors to either side of her, very much like they were at Cold Harbour and she moved to each room in turn to examine them. Neither of the rooms held any furniture; no tables or chairs, carpets or curtains – each was completely empty and her footsteps sounded hollowly around as she walked across the boards of each room, dust shifting lazily as she walked. At the end of the hall there were two more doors, one to the kitchen and one to another smaller room which, like the others, was empty. Mary went into the kitchen; it was neat and tidy, but with nothing to suggest that it was a loved home. The range was large and black, the tops showing rust as though they had not been used for a long time, and the back was piled with dusty pots and saucepans. A spindly oak table stood in the middle of the room, surrounded by four chairs, and a rocking chair sat next to the range. Mary pulled open a drawer in the dresser, but it was empty – most of the drawers were, save one that housed a few mismatched items of cutlery. A cupboard to the left of the range revealed a few sad looking plates, cups and saucers, but none of them matched.

The pantry was also empty except for a meat safe, and a few shelves with large glass jars of pickled onions standing side by side. In the safe Mary found a jug of milk and a piece of cheese on a plate. Out in the scullery a stone sink stood to the left facing a copper that had not been used for years and was full of potatoes, which had all started to sprout.

Mary moved out of the kitchen to see what was upstairs. The metal on the heels of her boots banged on the boards of the treads as she climbed each creaking step, making her way up to a wide landing where a window at the end overlooked the church. Four doors led to four identically proportioned rooms, three of them void of any furniture. The room at the back was furnished with a double bed, flanked on either side by a small table, and a chest of drawers stood in the corner next to a washstand. A fireplace stood opposite the window, a bucket of coal and sticks next to it, ready to light the fire. Two imposing cupboards stood either side of the fireplace – Mary opened the door to one to find half a dozen jackets and three suits hanging from the rack, all immaculately pressed and smelling faintly of moth balls; on the floor of the cupboard was a row of shoes. The other cupboard housed smart riding coats and jodhpurs, with various caps and hats hanging off hooks on the side. A line of riding boots stood along the bottom of the cupboard. Mary pulled open the drawers of the chest to find socks, shirts, underwear, handkerchiefs, gloves and woollen jackets all folded and laid out very precisely.

She moved back down the stairs again to find Noble washing his hands in a bowl in the sink by the light of a candle.

"What do you think?" he said without turning round as he heard her enter. "It's a big house, isn't it? Could get a family in here."

"Yes, Noble," said Mary hesitantly. "But there's no furniture, no curtains, no nothing – it's empty."

"What do I need furniture for?" he scoffed. "It's only been me since all the rest of them left; they took all that with them."

"But there's no food, Noble," said Mary quietly. "What are we going to eat?"

"I don't eat here," said Noble, turning to face Mary. "I go up to Miss Gaunt's for my breakfast and I'm mostly out after that, and if I'm here she cooks me something, or I go to the pub."

"But what am I to eat then, Noble? I'm not going to Miss Gaunt's," said Mary.

"No, I didn't think of that," he said thoughtfully. "Well we don't want anything now; let's go up to bed, eh?"

"Can't we have a cup of tea?" Mary said, turning to look at the cold range before adding, "I suppose not."

"Let's go to bed then," said Noble again.

"I want to go down the end," said Mary shyly.

"Out the back door, turn right and across the yard, you can't miss it," said Noble cheerfully. "It's light enough out there with the moon."

Mary went out the back door into the cold night air to the closet – it was a two-seater which she had never seen before. She pulled the door to behind her, but it immediately swung open again. She pulled it shut again, fumbling up and down the door for a hook, but there wasn't one. She sighed and let the door hang open – there was nobody around anyway.

Back in the scullery she washed her hands, took a candle from the kitchen and made her way by its light into the hall to collect her bag. She padded slowly up the stairs, the light from the moon slanting in through the window at the end of the landing to lie coldly on the boards of the floor. In the bedroom Noble was in bed, smoking a cigar. Mary put her bag on the floor and began to unpack her belongings onto the floorboards, laying her long flannel nightgown on the bed. Noble watched her amusedly – he had no shirt on and for the first time Mary saw his slim, athletic body. She blushed and turned away.

"Blow the light out, Noble," she instructed.

"Why?" he laughed.

"I'm going to get changed," Mary replied.

"So?"

"So, there aren't any curtains and I want to get changed in the dark, thank you very much," she retorted sharply.

Noble sighed and blew out the lamp, the glow of his cigar illuminating the bottom half of his face as he inhaled every now and then. Mary fumbled her way to the bed, pulled her nightgown over her head and started to pull her dress off from under the gown. She carefully folded her clothes, put them neatly on the floor next to the unpacked ones and knelt by the bed; she began to whisper her prayers.

"What are you doing?" said Noble sitting up a little, peering through the gloom towards Mary.

"I'm saying my prayers."

"You're what?" he said with a snort of laughter.

"I'm saying my prayers," said Mary firmly, whispering a hurried Lord's Prayer and climbing into the bed.

Noble took another draw from his cigar, rose from the bed and moved to the window, which he slid open before throwing the end of the cigar out. Mary peeped out at him from behind the bedclothes – she could see that he was naked – she shut her eyes tightly, hearing him pad back towards the bed. Mary lay on her back with her hands by her sides, she could feel Noble's breath on her face as he lay on his side facing her. His right hand reached across to her, moving over her neck, her chest and down across her stomach. Mary tensed up completely as he touched her, willing him not to notice; his hand came to a rest on the slight swell of her belly, then moved up and then back over the lump again. He sat up quickly.

"Mary?"

"Yes, Noble."

"Are you having a baby?"

There was silence.

"Mary, answer me, are you having a baby?" said Noble icily.

Mary shivered.

"Mary," he said once more.

"Yes."

"You didn't tell me, Mary, why didn't you tell me? You must have known when I asked you to marry me."

His voice was rising.

"I wasn't sure, I didn't know then, not for sure," stammered Mary.

"And all that about Rupert, was that true?"

"Yes it was," Mary snapped back, pulling the covers from her face to look at him. "It was true and I wrote back and said I was getting married."

"You took advantage of me, Mary," Noble said, rage etched in his voice.

Mary sat up, her hair tumbling down each side of her face.

"Took advantage? Took advantage? Don't you dare say that to me, Noble Ladds," shouted Mary angrily. "You took advantage of me, you know you did, and I'm with child; it's not me to blame – it's you. You filled me with drink and did as you pleased, although you knew I didn't know what was happening.

And you say I took advantage."

She stopped, breathing heavily and looked away. When she looked back, her face was contorted with contempt.

"There's a word for what you did to me, Noble Ladds, did you know that? Yes there is; it's rape – that's what the word is."

She glared at him angrily.

"We're married now, Noble," she hissed. "For better for worse, you said that, Noble – and we have a baby coming and it's your baby whatever the circumstances of its conception, but when it's born it will have a mother and a father and we will bring it up to be a good and God-fearing child, you and I."

She could feel Noble losing confidence in himself, she could feel the power that she had over him in that instance and realised that she was more in control of the situation than she could have dreamed she would be. Noble was silent.

"Noble, are you listening to me?" said Mary threateningly.

"Yes," said Noble quietly.

"Then don't you ever say again that I took advantage of you, do you hear me?"

There was silence.

"Do you hear?" Mary roared.

Noble lay back on the bed, closing his eyes resignedly.

"Yes, Mary," he said.

Chapter Forty-Four
One Leaves the World and Another Arrives

Bythorn life was very different to that of Dean; the village was much smaller and Mary tried to establish some sort of routine as soon as possible. Noble's family had always been church people, but since they had left for Canada, Noble had not set foot in the church. However, on the first Sunday after the wedding Mary insisted that they should attend the evening service, much to the surprise of the rest of the congregation. Mary enjoyed the more relaxed attitudes of the church, preferring the bumbling sermon of the portly vicar to Reverend Packham's zealous ravings on sin and damnation. She had quickly come to terms with Noble and his waywardness; she was much more confident than she had expected and was able to guide their lives in the way in which she wanted them to run, particularly in the home. At the insistence of the bank, the sale of Cold Harbour was postponed for a year and she decided that she would have to move her father over to Bythorn to live with them. William agreed to run the farm for the last year of their ownership and they could close the house up and bring the furniture over to Bythorn. Freda, on account of her virulent dislike of Noble Ladds, refused to move too, telling Mary she would have to find someone else to help in the house.

Although they lived on a farm Noble Ladds did not do much farming, spending his time instead dealing horses, which involved him spending a lot of time at sales and visiting clients. The farm itself was all pasture and as well as the horses, they had a few cattle and sheep. Noble employed two brothers from the villages, Cyril and Dennis Baxter, to handle the workings of the farm for him. Cyril was a good man and kept the place going in Noble's absence but Dennis was slow and really not up to much. Horses came and went – except for two shires which were used permanently on the farm and Tinker, who was kept as Noble's riding horse.

In early July, Lucy came home to Cold Harbour for the weekend to find John's condition very much worse; she immediately summoned Mary, who rushed home as soon as she could. She arrived in the kitchen to find Freda and Lucy sitting at the table, both looking very glum.

"What is it, Lucy, is he worse?" asked Mary.

"Yes, Mary, I don't think he's got very long – you go and see him."

Mary hurried down the corridor and into John's room. He was still in bed and his eyes were shut, his skin looked papery and almost transparent. She whispered to him,

"Father, it's me – Mary."

There was no reaction. She tried again, laying a hand on his cold hand and calling to him softly.

John's eyes fluttered open – he focused his watery eyes on his daughter and tried to speak but no words came. He moved his head slowly from side to side, little bubbles of froth lining the edge of his mouth as he tried again to form words. Slowly his eyes closed and his breathing slowed again. Lucy appeared at the door with a flannel; she moved to her father and gently wiped his face.

"He's not got very long, Mary," said Lucy quietly. "I've seen it too many times. You can tell when someone is about to die."

"How long then, Lucy?"

"A day or two," shrugged Lucy. "Maybe a week, or maybe tonight."

"We must tell Aunt Charlotte."

"Yes," said Lucy, "But we need someone to be here tonight, Freda can't do it all and I've got to go back I can't be late again, can you stay, Mary?"

"No not tonight, I can come back tomorrow and stay but I've got no things, and I've got Noble to see to; he's going to be away all week."

"Who can we get?"

"I know," said Mary, "I'll go down and see Aunt Charlotte then I'll go to see Ruby; she might do one night."

At the butcher's shop Mary found Aunt Charlotte and Thomas both asleep in their chairs in the kitchen; William was sitting at the table reading the paper.

On seeing Mary, William put his finger to his lips and pointed to the front room; they tiptoed next door where the fire was roaring in the grate and the two sat and discussed John's deterioration. To William the news was no surprise, he had seen John the day before.

"William, who have you got in there?" Charlotte shouted from the kitchen.

"Only Mary, Mother, she's come about Uncle John."

"Just a minute, I'm coming," Charlotte shouted again. "Thomas, wake up, wake up, it's Mary come about John."

Charlotte and Thomas appeared at the door.

"Aunt Charlotte, Lucy says Father hasn't got long to go – maybe a week but probably not even that."

Mary blew her nose loudly.

"There, there, dear, don't take on, he's had a good life," soothed Charlotte before adding, "but he's no age, is he? Fifty-three, if I'm not mistaken?"

"Fifty-four we think, Aunt Charlotte."

"It's no age, is it?" mused Charlotte. "Worn out by hard work, you know, Mary: trying to pay off that wretched mortgage. Never borrow money, Mary, it ruins people."

A tear came to her eye, and she wiped it away delicately.

"Only me and Sarah left now," she continued, "oh, except Edgar of course but we don't count him really."

She sat down heavily in her armchair, resting her face on her hand.

"All those years we lived in Raunds, it doesn't seem possible he's dead," she continued.

"He's not dead, Aunt Charlotte," said Mary with a frown.

"I know dear, I know, but you know what I mean."

Charlotte looked at Thomas.

"We had better go up and see him, don't you think, Thomas?"

"Yes, dear," he replied.

"William, you must drive us up after chapel," instructed Charlotte.

"Yes, Mother."

"Will you be there, Mary?"

"No, Aunt Charlotte, but I'll be back tomorrow. I've got to go and sort Noble out and get some things from home; but I'm going to see Ruby to see if she can go up tonight because Lucy can't stay either."

"She might, dear, but try Mrs Lowe if Ruby can't do it."

Mary nodded and rose to go.

"Mary dear," said Charlotte, catching her niece's arm as she passed, "have you got something to tell us?"

Mary blushed.

"Aunt Charlotte?"

"Are you expecting a baby?" whispered Charlotte.

"I think so," said Mary, nodding.

"You look so, Mary. How wonderful, don't you think, Thomas?"

"Yes, dear, it's great news," said Thomas dutifully.

"And when's it due, dear?"

"In the New Year I think, Aunt Charlotte but I'm not quite sure."

"Let's hope it doesn't come early, Mary," said Charlotte confidentially, "a lot of first ones seem to these days."

Mary smiled ruefully and left, cycling along the road towards the Tuffnail house. At the doors of the chapel, a great throng of children were waiting to go in; Mary spied Ruby's two daughters pushing a pram with Goshen in. Mary waved and moved to the pram, pulling back the cover to reveal Goshen fast asleep.

"We're taking 'im to Sunday school – 'e's ever so good, never wakes up," they told Mary.

"Is your mother at home?" asked Mary.

"Yes, she's at home somewhere," they said.

Mary walked to the smithy – the door was shut and the curtains on the upstairs of the house were shut. Mary knocked on the door and waited. The dog barked at the back of the house, Mary knocked again, standing back to look up at the windows of the house. The curtain twitched in the bedroom and the window slid open, revealing Ruby, very red in the face; she looked as though she was wearing her nightgown. She poked her head out of the window.

"What do you want, Mary?" she said peevishly. "I were just 'avin' a rest while the kids were at Sunday school."

"I'll go then," said Mary apologetically.

"No don't, Mary, what is it?"

"It's Father," Mary said, lowering her voice and explaining her predicament.

Ruby listened in silence.

"Did you 'ear that, Art?" she called back into the room, when Mary had finished.

Mary could hear a grunt from the bedroom.

"Yes, I'll do it for you, Mary," said Ruby, closing the curtains quickly.

With a smile Mary turned away and turned her bicycle back towards Bythorn.

When Mary returned to Cold Harbour the next morning; Freda was struggling to cope. There were sheets to wash, clothes to wash, the cow to milk, the eggs to collect, the breakfast to get and many other jobs; Freda was sitting at the table with her head in her hands, with no clue as to where to start.

"How's Father, Freda?" asked Mary as she rushed in.

"E's very low, Mary – very low. 'E ain't ate nothing only just 'ad a little tea and that's all and we're got to wash and change him – but I ain't lit the copper yet, you'll 'ave to give me a 'and, Mary."

"You light the copper then, Freda and I will go and see how he is."

She hurried to her father's room. John was fast asleep, but covered in flies.

"Oh, how dreadful," she screamed, taking a towel and desperately fanning the flies away.

"What is it, Mary?" shouted Freda, rushing into the room. "Is 'e dead?"

"No, it's the flies," gasped Mary, hitting out in every direction with the towel.

"Oh, I opened the winder for fresh air," said Freda in horror, "but the flies come in from the yard; shut it, Mary, it's the only thing."

"Look at him, Freda, he will get fly-blown just like the sheep," said Mary in horror. "Eurgh, how horrible and the smell!"

"I know, I told you we've got to wash him," said Freda indignantly. "I'll just get the copper going and then you put the kettle on for some 'ot water and we'll do it."

Freda went to fetch bowls, soap, hot water, towels and clean pyjamas and after twenty minutes John was clean again and in fresh clothes. Mary looked at him sadly.

"Look at him, Freda; he needs a shave – I've never done it, have you?"

"No, Miss Mary, but Miss Lucy did 'im on Saturday; 'e don't look too bad, do 'e?"

"I am going to shave him, Freda," said Mary decisively. "I will just have to learn how. If Lucy can, then so can I."

She looked critically at the razor and brush on the table, unsure of how to start.

"Master William is across the yard, Mary – you go and see 'im while I make some tea, I'm sure he could do with a cup."

William was directing the men who were clearing the muck from the cattle yards. Mary could see that the farm had already changed dramatically under William's management; the yard had been cleared, all the equipment had been put away, the stables were clean, the horses groomed, the sheep had been shorn and everything seemed to be running smoothly. Mary walked up to her cousin, and looped her arm through his.

"Come on, William, come and have some tea," she said, guiding him back into the kitchen.

William allowed Mary to lead him back into the house. In the kitchen, Mary turned to her cousin.

"Father's dying, William, it's not going to be long," she said quietly.

"I know," he replied sadly.

She turned to him suddenly.

"William, I want you to show me how to sharpen the razor."

She scurried off to John's room to retrieve the razor and strop.

William flicked open the razor, hooked one end of the leather strop to the door latch and wedged his foot against the door, pulling the strop tight. He ran the razor rapidly up and down the strop, turning the razor over and over as he ran it against the leather.

"That can't sharpen it," said Mary, incredulously.

"It does," said William, using the edge of the razor to shave some hair from his forearm. "Be careful when you use it, Mary."

He closed the razor and put it on the table, picking up the cup of tea.

"Well—" he started, pouring his tea into the saucer to cool it.

"William, do you have to do that?" reprimanded Mary.

"That ain't very posh, William," scolded Freda.

"No, I know but I'm in a hurry, got to get back to Hardwick's by lunchtime," said William with a shrug.

"You're a real farmer now, William, not a butcher anymore," chided Mary with a grin.

"And you're a farmer's wife," William shot back. "Bully your own farmer."

"She ought not 'ave bin," chipped in Freda.

"I beg your pardon, Freda?" said Mary.

"You ought not be a farmer's wife; you should 'ave married one of them posh friends of yours from Norfampton and that's the troof."

Freda's accusation hung uncomfortably in the air. William coughed, excused himself and left. Freda stood by the range unapologetically, daring Mary to contradict her.

"Come on then, Freda," said Mary quietly. "You will have to give me some help with this."

She rose and headed to John's room. After laying the implements on the bedside table, she started to lather his face with soap and warm water; when his face was covered she gingerly picked up the razor.

"Hold his head for me, Freda," she said, pushing the skin up on one side of John's face with her thumb and tentatively scraping the blade across the skin.

"This is easy, Freda, it cuts well now William has sharpened it," she said, carefully shaving down one side of John's face and then the other.

"Mary?" said Freda quietly.

"Yes, Freda?"

"I'm sorry what I said; I didn't mean any offence."

"I know, Freda, don't worry about it. Pull his head back a little, so I can do under his chin."

The razor scraped up again.

"Bugger," said Mary suddenly, "I've cut him; give me that flannel, Freda."

She dabbed the small wound.

"Let's 'ave a look," said Freda, as Mary held the flannel away.

"That's nuffing, don't you worry," said Freda, tearing a small corner off an old newspaper and pressing it on the cut.

"There we go, that'll stop it."

They laid John back on the pillows and pulled the blankets up over his chest, which rose and fell very slowly.

"He looks all right now, doesn't he, Freda?" said Mary, smiling gently at her father.

"Very smart, Mary, very smart," agreed Freda.

She paused and then added,

"Mary?"

"Yes, Freda?"

"Are you 'avin' a baby?"

There was silence.

"Yes, Freda."

"Oh lovely, Mary, that's lovely when's it doo?"

"In the New Year."

"Let's 'ope it's not early then," said Freda wryly, picking up the bowl and moving back into the kitchen.

After lunch, Mary went to sleep in the chair by the range, only to be woken ten minutes later by Freda.

"Mary, Mary, wake up it's the doctor come," hustled Freda, shaking Mary's shoulder.

"What is it, Freda? I was dreaming."

"It's the doctor, 'e's come to see your father."

Mary rose from her chair and rushed into her father's room, to see Doctor Roberts listening to John's faltering breathing.

"We didn't expect to see you, doctor," she said.

"And I did not expect to see you, Mary; but I was passing and they told me down in Dean how your father was."

"That was very kind of you, doctor. But—"

"Don't worry, Mary," said Doctor Roberts quietly. "I won't bill this one."

He stood back from the bed.

"He's not got long, you know that," he said gently.

"Yes, we realise," sighed Mary. "Lucy has been back and she said it would be a matter of days."

"Ah, Lucy Knighton. That girl should be a doctor, Mary, not a nurse; there's precious few women in our profession and there should be more, although not everyone thinks that."

He shrugged.

"But she's right; I'd would say it's hours now, not days, I'm sorry to tell you."

"Thank you, doctor," said Mary calmly.

"What about you then, Mary, having a baby?"

"Yes, Doctor Roberts," said Mary slowly.

Doctor Roberts grabbed her hand, pulled out his watch and took her pulse.

"Fine," he said. "Open wide!"

He looked in her mouth.

"Say aaah."

"Aaah," said Mary.

He turned Mary round, put his hand on her back and tapped it with the other one.

"Good," he said. "Any sickness, Mary?"

"Not any more, doctor."

"Good."

"Ankles swollen?"

"No."

"Putting on weight?"

"Just a bit."

"You will do," he said walking out the door. "Fit as a fiddle! How old are you, Mary?"

"Twenty-one," said Mary, following him out through the kitchen.

Doctor Roberts smiled approvingly.

"Let me know when he's gone, Mary," he said, nodding back to the house and mounting his horse.

Mary watched him trot off down the drive.

The next morning Mary woke, dressed and went immediately to her father's room. John lay where she had left him the night before, his mouth slightly open, hands lying delicately on the blanket. Even from looking at him from the doorway she knew that he had gone. She moved towards him, laying a hand over his and planting a kiss on his forehead.

She was sitting at the kitchen table by the time Freda came into the kitchen.

"He's gone," she said quietly.

Freda moved to Mary and wrapped her in her arms.

"There, Mary, 'e's gone to a better place, I'm sure 'e 'as. I'll make you a cuppa tea, you need it I'm sure. You know, Mary, when my mum and dad died, me mum died first but it weren't till me dad died that I felt really sad. It's the second one goin', Mary that gets you."

She sniffed and wiped her eyes.

"You're all on your own when they're gone; they brought you into the world and now they're gone." She sniffed again and hugged Mary a bit tighter.

Having arranged her mother's not long ago, Mary was familiar with what preparations needed to be arranged for the funeral. Nobody came to pay their respects this time, except for William and there was no wake after the service; just a cup of tea and biscuits at the butcher's shop to save everyone the trek back to Cold Harbour. Noble and Henry had brought wagons to take the furniture from the house and Freda had already collected her belongings and taken them to The Hall, where she had secured herself a job helping Dorcas. When the house was finally empty; Mary walked out through the scullery, turned the key in the lock and walked away. She had already said her goodbyes to the house when she had left with Noble, and she didn't look back as she made her way to the butcher's shop to give the key to William, who was to take charge of the farm for a year before it was put up for sale.

After John's death, summer went quickly for Mary; she gradually got the new house in order, filling the rooms with furniture and making it into a home where she felt comfortable. At Bythorn she saw little of the family except Henry and Martha; Lucy only came to see her twice that summer, although it wasn't that much more difficult for her to get there than Cold Harbour. Mary put down her absence to how hard she was working but she knew that Lucy disapproved of her brother-in-law.

Noble's business appeared to make money; he continued to buy and sell at all the local markets and went often to London to see clients, leaving for days at a time, meaning Mary had to organise the farming with the help of Cyril. The birth of Mary's child was expected around Christmas; Martha was to come and act as midwife, despite the fact that she too was pregnant again. On Christmas Eve, Mary started to go into labour. As Noble was away Mary had to get Cyril to go and fetch Martha. Martha, having had plenty of practice in delivering her mother's children, was a consummate professional, and kept Mary calm throughout the labour. Jack was finally born on Christmas Day 1903 – his early arrival wasn't commented on; the fact that he was born on Christmas Day seeming to distract any unkind comments. Six weeks later he was christened in the church at Bythorn, with Lucy, Verity and William as the godparents.

In the middle of September the next year, Mary received a letter from Rebecca Harding who had only just heard that Mary was married and had had a baby; she wanted to come and visit when she came cub hunting. Mary wrote back by return inviting her to stay and offering stabling for her horse, but as it turned out Rebecca didn't currently have a horse, so Mary and Noble agreed that she could ride Tinker at the hunt. The hunt was due to meet on the village green on Wednesday the seventeenth October and Rebecca would come on the train the day before.

As Noble did not have a pony and trap, Mary had to borrow one from Michael Smith who farmed at the other end of the village to pick up Rebecca from Raunds station, and Cyril drove, Mary and Jack riding behind him. When they arrived at the station, Mary made her way up to the bridge so that Jack could watch the train as it struggled up the hill from Thrapston. Jack stared in awe at the plumes of steam huffing into the cold autumn air, grabbing Mary's hair with his tiny plump fingers and gurgling happily. As the train ground to a halt, Mary rushed down to meet her friend. Rebecca was the only one to get off, sweeping out of the carriage and turning to retrieve her bags from somebody still on the train. She took them with a smile, placed the bags on the platform edge and looked around for Mary. Mary had forgotten quite how elegant she was – her long dark coat edged with maroon cuffs and epaulets clinging to her slim figure, and a heavily feathered hat framing her handsome face. She was taller than Mary remembered her, but it had been a while since the pair had seen each other.

Mary ran down the platform to greet her friend, embracing as best they could around Jack, who was staring in wonderment at Rebecca's hat, trying to grab at the feathers.

"Mary, this is wonderful, I have been so looking forward to coming," gushed Rebecca. "And let me look at this young chap."

She smiled down at Jack who stared goggle-eyed up at Rebecca – mouth open in wonder – as they made their way back to the trap, the station master collecting Rebecca's bags and carrying them out for her. Cyril raised his cap to Rebecca and the station master, who placed the bags in the trap and accepted the tip that Rebecca had just finished rummaging in her purse for. Rebecca and Mary chatted the whole way home; heads turned as the two passed through Bythorn, people wondering how Mary Ladds was friends with such a finely dressed lady.

At the farm Mary showed Rebecca her room and around the house, before putting Jack to sleep and returning to the kitchen, where the coals were glowing warmly in the range.

"Now, Rebecca, stay here a moment – I'm just going to light the fire in the front room and then we can go in there," instructed Mary, moving hurriedly out of the kitchen.

"Don't you have anyone to do that for you, Mary?" Rebecca asked, as Mary returned.

"Not at the moment," shrugged Mary. "Noble says he doesn't like other people in the house, although I expect he just doesn't want to pay for them. Now shall I make the tea?"

"Can I see the horse first?" pleaded Rebecca. "I have been so looking forward to riding him tomorrow – I'd love to see him in the flesh."

Mary laughed and led her friend out into the yard, where Cyril found a halter and walked Tinker out into the yard.

Rebecca approached him approvingly, patting his neck and running her hands along his back and down his legs.

"He'll do," she said, straightening up. "Your Noble knows a good horse when he sees one."

Mary smiled.

"We've got a side-saddle for you, Rebecca," she said. "Do you want to have a look?"

"Don't worry about that, Mary, I'll ride astride – I've had a new skirt made, I'll show you later."

Mary raised an eyebrow and led her friend back into the house, moving into the front room for their tea.

"Is Noble here then, Mary?" asked Rebecca, looking around as if Noble might be hidden behind a curtain.

"No, he's away on business," said Mary. "He's away a lot, buying and selling."

"You will have to keep an eye on him, Mary," said Rebecca with a wink. "A good-looking man like that."

"I don't know what you mean, Rebecca," Mary said defensively.

Rebecca laughed and took another sip of her tea.

"I'm just saying that your husband is a good-looking man," said Rebecca.

"And what about Jimmy?" Mary enquired.

Rebecca sighed heavily.

"Jimmy is fine. I suppose I will have to marry him if no one else turns up to carry me off."

She laughed again, and this time Mary joined in.

"Don't say it like that, Rebecca," scolded Mary. "That wouldn't be right."

"Yes it would – it would be wonderful," said Rebecca with a smile, "otherwise I will be forced to marry Jimmy out of sheer desperation. How depressing."

Mary bit her lip and said nothing just as a howl reached their ears from upstairs. Mary leapt gratefully to her feet, excused herself and dashed from the room.

The next morning was bright and frosty. The sun glinted across the yard – Cyril and Dennis, who had been up since five, had groomed Tinker until his coat gleamed; they wanted him to be the best turned out horse that morning.

Rebecca came down to find Mary in the kitchen with breakfast ready for her. She looked splendid in a dark green skirt, velvet bodice and black jacket. Her white stock was fixed into place with a large jewelled gold pin and in her hand she carried her hat, which she threw onto the table.

"Breakfast, Rebecca?" Mary asked.

"Oh yes, got to keep my strength up, you know."

"Tea?" Mary asked.

"Only half a cup, Mary, must not drink too much, if I have to get off him I'll never get on again and I'll have to walk home."

The dogs barked as the door latch clicked and Martha and Henry entered, followed by young Henry who could now walk.

"Morning, Mrs Ladds," said Henry, coming up behind Mary and pulling the cord of her apron, undoing the bow.

"Don't do that, Henry Knighton," scolded Mary. "I've never met anyone as annoying as you; now just you behave when I've got guests here."

Mary turned to Rebecca, who was watching this sibling display with an amount of curiosity.

"Do you know my brother Henry and his wife Martha?" she asked.

"Yes of course, we met at the point-to-point," said Rebecca graciously. "But I didn't meet this little chap."

She bent down to say hello to young Henry, who frowned and buried his head in Martha's skirt, hiding his face from Rebecca's view.

"Where's the baby, Martha?" asked Mary.

"'E's tucked up in his cot in the trap, sleeps like a log, don't 'e, 'Enry?"

"Yes, never makes a sound, 'cept fer when he's hungry," agreed Henry, looking around the kitchen hopefully. "Anything to eat then, Mary?"

"No," Mary snapped.

"Don't you give 'im anything, Mary, he's just 'ad a great plateful at 'ome," said Martha, smacking Henry's hand which was snaking towards the pan full of bacon.

"Goin' 'untin'?" Martha asked Rebecca, who was putting her hat on.

"Yes, I must go or I will miss the meet; they get very sniffy if you're late," said Rebecca.

"We've come to watch," said Martha, hoisting her son onto her hip. "Young 'Enry ain't see it before."

Rebecca smiled indulgently at Henry, pulled her veil down, and turned to Mary.

"Is it straight?" she asked.

"Yes, perfect," said Mary.

"Let me 'ave a look at you, Rebecca," said Martha, turning Rebecca gently round so that she could look at her.

She step back and sighed.

"What a picture don't you think, Mary? I wish I could look like that, don't you? There will be no one out there to compare with you, Rebecca, not a soul."

"Well," said Rebecca, blushing slightly at the compliment, "it must be time to go."

She led the way into the yard, where Cyril was walking Tinker round on the cobbles. The sun had risen high in the sky, melting the frost of the grass, the rime of which covered the leaves. Tinker snorted a blast of steam from his nostrils and shook his head impatiently.

"Have we got a mounting block?" Rebecca enquired. "I can't get on him from the ground without."

"Yes, you can," said Henry. "I'll lift, you grab 'old of the 'orse and put your foot up."

Cyril brought the horse round, holding him still as Rebecca grabbed the reins and the saddle, sticking her foot out for Henry to grab.

"Just my foot, Henry," she warned as Henry approached and took hold of her outstretched leg.

"Don't worry, Rebecca, I'm watchin' 'im," said Martha.

"Lift then, damn you," said Rebecca.

Henry lifted her skywards as Rebecca swung her right foot over Tinker's back and lowered herself into the saddle, arranging her skirt around her. Tinker's ears pricked up as the call of the hounds reached them on the breeze. Rebecca shook her reins and nudged the animal forwards, giving a little wave as she trotted towards the gate.

"Are you comin', Mary?" asked Martha.

"Yes of course, just let me put something on the baby and I will be there," said Mary, rushing upstairs.

When they arrived at the meet, the hounds were already out of their pen, trotting here and there nosing people's pockets in the hope of titbits, and Rebecca was talking earnestly to a portly whipper-in, who was responding heartily to her questioning. The huntsman raised his horn to his lips and blew steadily, booting his mount towards the gate of the field – the hounds trotted gamely after him, followed by the whips and the rest of the field.

"Isn't it a lovely sight," sighed Mary, "and look at Rebecca; doesn't she look lovely – you would hardly notice she wasn't riding side-saddle."

"She's very pretty, isn't she, Mary?" said Martha wistfully. "I wish I could look like 'er."

The two women admiringly watched Rebecca ride off until she was out of sight.

"Are you coming back for another cup of tea, then?" Mary asked, turning to Martha and Henry.

"I'm going up the hill to follow for a bit; you go on, Martha," said Henry, "I'll be back in half an hour or so. I'll check they ain't broken all your fences down, Mary, like what they usually do. Spend half the time mendin' 'em again."

"I suppose they catch the foxes though," said Mary. "That must be good; the foxes won't eat our chickens then."

"If they catch them at all," said Henry dubiously. "It's only twice a year they come here and they can't get them all."

"But it's lovely to see 'em, 'Enry," said Martha.

"It's all right for them who can afford it, Martha," said Henry sharply, "but not all of us can. Sittin' up there on an 'orse looking down on the rest of us."

He shook his head crossly and stomped off after the field.

Chapter Forty-Five
The County and the Griffin

With the coming of the better weather and longer days, Mary decided that she would take Rebecca up on her invitation to visit her in Northampton. She was expecting her second child later that year and wanted to go before it became too difficult. She had written to Rebecca arranging a date, and Martha had offered to look after Jack. Noble was away; but he was away a lot of the time, and Mary had taken over the day to day running of the farm, whilst her husband travelled and traded horses. The sale of Cold Harbour had gone through the previous autumn and after a profitable harvest the farm was sold. There was a little money left over after paying off the loans, which had been split between the Knighton children. Mary had been careful not to tell Noble exactly how much she had inherited; taking her cheque to the bank in Thrapston and opening an account in her own name.

The evening before she was due in Northampton, she took Jack over to Martha and Henry's house; Martha always seemed happy to look after Jack despite now having three of her own.

"I wish I were comin' wiv you, Mary," sighed Martha, as young Henry tore round the kitchen after his younger brother. "I could really do wiv gettin' away from this place sometimes and away from the kids for a bit, you know what I mean?"

"Well, Martha, you will have to leave all yours with me one day and go yourself," said Mary firmly.

"But you've got someone to go wiv and I ain't," reasoned Martha. "'Enry wouldn't go for love nor money, but then I don't s'pose Noble would either, would 'e."

"Well he's away a lot," said Mary quietly.

"I know 'e is, Mary; you want to watch out what 'e's up to, you never know these days."

She gave Mary a mischievous smile.

"He's doing his buying and selling," said Mary firmly.

"That's what 'e tells you, Mary, but a good-looking man like that! You ought to keep 'im closer to 'ome, Mary, so you know what 'e's up to."

Mary smiled politely, but did not answer. She kissed her son goodbye, waved to Martha and left to pack for her trip the next morning.

The next day she was up early to walk to Raunds station to catch the nine o'clock train. It was a bright day, but chilly and she was glad that she had worn her warmest coat for the walk to the station. At Raunds, she could see the smoke of the engine in the distance as the train left Kimbolton and she rushed to buy a ticket. She had to change twice, once at Kettering and once at Wellingborough, which would make the whole journey nearly one and half hours.

When she arrived at Wellingborough, she had to wait ten minutes for the Northampton train to arrive. The wind had built up and she paced up and down to keep warm. Standing halfway down the platform she noticed a man that she thought she recognised – he wore a bowler hat and a dark suit which was a little too small for him.

As she walked past him the second time, he raised his bowler exposing his bald shiny head.

"Good morning, Miss Knighton," he said.

Mary turned and smiled at the man, desperately trying to place him.

"It's Edwin, Miss Knighton; you know, Dorcas's brother."

"Ah," said Mary, her face lighting up, "I knew I recognised you! Pleased to meet you."

"Yes, Miss Knighton, I remember you," said Edwin. "I were born in Dean if you remember; I recall you when you were just a dot but I left soon after that."

"Well, Edwin, what a surprise and how is Dorcas? I haven't seen her for a long time."

"She's well, Miss Knighton, very well; I've just bin to see 'er and on my way back to Northampton."

"I'm Mrs Ladds now, Edwin," said Mary with a small smile, "but perhaps you didn't know."

"Yes, yes, course you are!" exclaimed Edwin, clapping his hand to his forehead. "I just forgot. Yes, I know Mr Ladds; fine gentleman 'e is, fine gentlemen. Are you goin' to Northampton, Mrs Ladds?"

"Yes," said Mary.

"Well we 'ave got another Dean lady with us at the Griffin," continued Edwin.

"Yes, of course you have," said Mary curiously. "How is dear Molly? I haven't seen her for ages."

"She's fine, just fine," said Edwin. "Course she gets fed up with the cleaning and all. She wants to go and work at Tibbitts, I know that, but still she does us proud; yes, does us proud I must say."

"Is she there today then, Edwin?" Mary asked.

"She should be! I 'ope she is or Lizzie will have been a bit short 'anded," he chuckled.

"Well," said Mary, "if I get time I might pop in and see her. Where is the Griffin, Edwin?"

"Wellingborough Road, Mrs Ladds, you can't miss it but we ain't used to well-dressed ladies like you in there, Mrs Ladds."

"Don't worry about me, Edwin," laughed Mary. "I'll be able to cope."

"Very good, Mrs Ladds, I'll be seeing you then. 'Ere comes the train."

He lifted his bowler again and made his way towards third class.

When she arrived at Northampton Mary walked up the hill into the town, making her way straight to Tibbitts, where she went to the Ladies' Fashion Department to find Mrs Stevens.

"Mary, my dear, how lovely to see you. It's been such a long time and you're married now I understand," said Mrs Stevens, ushering Mary into her office.

"It seems so long since I was here," sighed Mary. "But now I'm here, it only seems like yesterday."

She sighed.

"I was so happy here, Mrs Stevens, you don't realise," said Mary wistfully.

"Well, Mary, so were we; it's not been the same since you left – Mr Peveril always says that – he's not here today, gone out for lunch I think and then to London this afternoon. Now did I hear you had had a baby, Mary?"

"Yes," laughed Mary. "Jack, and the next one is coming in the autumn."

"How wonderful," said Mrs Stevens, "and are you shopping today, Mary?"

"Oh yes, I need clothes for myself, Jack and the new baby but I have to meet Miss Harding here at twelve o'clock before we go out for lunch."

"That gives us plenty of time then, Mary," smiled Mrs Stevens.

She hesitated for a moment and then added,

"By the way, Mary, that young lady you recommended was here the other day."

"You mean Molly?" said Mary.

"Yes that's her; we haven't got anything for her at the moment."

She lowered her voice confidentially.

"She's well, not quite what I was expecting, but she's had a difficult time, I understand."

"To say the least," said Mary with a shake of her head.

Mrs Stevens nodded sympathetically and led Mary back into the shop to choose her clothes; she was done by the time Rebecca arrived at twelve o'clock and was waiting with Mrs Stevens.

"I'm sorry, Mary, but we've got to go to The County for lunch," said Rebecca with a frown. "It's really the only place that two old maids like us can go unescorted; it really is *such* a bore."

"Don't worry, Rebecca; I know we've been there before when your leg was broken and I also went there once with Verity – it's not that bad."

"Verity," muttered Rebecca, "I remember her I think – Rawson-Foster or something like that?"

"Watson-Foster," corrected Mary.

"Yes, hmm," said Rebecca, raising an eyebrow.

"She's going to Oxford University in the autumn, you know."

"Yes," said Rebecca again. "A nice girl, but she's anti-hunting as far as I remember and that won't do, will it, Mary?"

"No, Rebecca," said Mary with a small smile, "but she's all for votes for the women."

"Well we are all for that, aren't we?" laughed Rebecca, raising her voice. "And no more side-saddles!"

Mrs Stevens, who had been serving another customer at the till, looked up in surprise – Rebecca grinned at Mary, who gave Mrs Stevens a small wave and hurried from the shop giggling.

The County Hotel was much fuller than it had been all those years ago when Mary had been with Verity, but Rebecca had booked a table so they went straight into the dining room. Mary scanned the large room, catching sight of Peveril Tibbitt having his lunch with Mortimer Allibone by the window; unwilling to get sucked into conversation with him, Mary and Rebecca took a table at the far end of the dining room. They started with soup – watery and tasteless – which was gracelessly cleared away by a waiter just as apathetic as Mary had remembered the first time she'd been to the hotel with Verity. From where they sat, Mary had a clear view through the wide double doors into the lounge of the hotel, which housed a selection of low chairs and tables where guests would take tea and coffee. Mary looked up, glancing into the lounge where a tall dark man wearing a smart coat with a velvet collar stood with his back to them. There was something about his carriage which Mary recognised. She looked harder towards the lounge then to Rebecca, who frowned and swivelled in her chair to follow Mary's gaze. The man appeared to be looking for someone and as he turned his head they both could see that it was Noble. Mary's face lit up and she lifted her hand to wave to him as a woman in a long fur coat and fur hat sashayed up to him. Mary's mouth fell open in amazement and Rebecca put her hand to her mouth – her eyes widening. It was Adelaide.

The pair faced each other, talking quickly – Noble pulled out his pocket watch as Adelaide twisted her wrist to look at her wristwatch – the pair spoke a few more words and made to part. Noble made a slight bow to Adelaide, who winked, made a little wave with her gloved hand and swept out of the room. Noble went back to the market where there was a horse sale. Rebecca and Mary stared at each other speechlessly as the waiter entered and laid their main course in front of them. Mary looked down at her plate of food and said nothing.

"Mary, was that who I thought it was?" whispered Rebecca.

Mary looked up at Rebecca and frowned.

"Yes," she said quietly, tapping the table with her fingernails.

"I don't know what to say," said Rebecca. "That awful woman and your husband; that was who it was, Mary, tell me I'm right?"

"Yes, you're right, it was Noble and Adelaide," said Mary quietly.

"What were they doing?" Rebecca hissed.

"Just talking. They didn't leave together, unless they were making plans to meet later." Mary looked back down at her food and gnawed at her lip.

"It's so awful, Mary, what was she doing with your husband? I really don't believe it."

Mary grimaced and picked up her fork.

"Come to think of it, what was my husband doing with your stepmother?" she said angrily. "Are you going to tell your father, Rebecca?"

"No way," said Rebecca firmly, "I could never do that to my poor father."

She slammed her hand down angrily on the table.

"Why he married her I will never know! She is awful, Mary, awful!"

An old couple at the next table looked worriedly over at Mary and Rebecca – Rebecca smiled graciously and looked back at Mary.

"Are you going to ask him, Mary?"

"No – never," said Mary with a frown. "There's no point; I know what he's like and I've guessed what he might get up to."

She sighed and pushed her food around her plate.

"If it wasn't her it might have been someone worse," she shrugged. "Come on, Rebecca, eat your lunch; there's nothing we can do about it."

"Mary, how can you be so calm?" said Rebecca urgently. "That was your husband!"

"Rebecca, what did we see?" demanded Mary. "They spoke for less than a minute, looked at their watches and went; what does that mean? I'm sure they know each other so maybe it's all very innocent. Come on, eat your lunch."

Rebecca looked at her friend dumbfounded; she shook her head incredulously.

"Mary, I don't know how you can be so calm, I really don't."

"You already said that, Rebecca," frowned Mary.

"I'm sorry, you're right, let's eat," agreed Rebecca, although neither woman really had the appetite any more.

When they had finished lunch, Rebecca put the bill on her father's account and they parted; Mary didn't think she could have borne the look of pity of Rebecca's face any longer. She said a hasty goodbye to her friend and headed to the Griffin.

At the Griffin, the lunchtime rush was over; Edwin was sitting at a table with Lizzie, having a sandwich and Molly was sitting desolately on a stool at the other end of the bar, her elbows leaning on the chipped wood, cupping her face in her hands and studying a paper in front of her.

"Molly!" Edwin shouted from the other end of the room.

Molly looked up reluctantly, but did not move.

"Molly," Edwin said again, "come on over 'ere, me duck."

Molly stared down the bar, slick with beer stains, the smoke hanging in the air between them.

"What is it now?" said Molly defiantly, pushing herself away from the bar and sauntering over to Edwin

"I ain't going upstairs again; I'm bin twice today already, so there."

"No, no, Molly," hushed Edwin, "it ain't that; come 'ere I've got somethin' to tell yer."

Molly took a suspicious step closer.

"Come on then, gal, sit down," said Edwin impatiently.

Molly sat and looked sulkily at Lizzie and Edwin.

"I were goin' to tell you, Molly, that I see an old friend of yours from 'ome and she said that she might call and see you this afternoon."

Molly looked at Edwin and then at Lizzie, the expression of dissatisfaction not lifting from her face.

"Hoo were that then?" she asked, folding her arms and leaning back in her chair.

"'Ave a guess," said Edwin, smiling at her.

"'Ow can I guess, it could be anyone, couldn't it? I dun't know, do I?"

shrugged Molly nonchalantly.

"Go on then," Edwin said again, "'ave a guess."

"No, I ain't gonna! I'm goin' if you ain't goin' to tell me."

She pursed her lips and glared at Edwin angrily. He groaned and rolled his eyes.

"It were Mary then," he said.

"Mary hoo?"

"Mary Knighton, I mean Mary Ladds I suppose," said Edwin.

Molly's face broadened into a grin, her eyes lighting up in genuine pleasure.

"You're kidding, Edwin, where did you see 'er then?"

"She was on the train from Wellingborough, she's come to see 'er friend, what's 'er name."

He tapped his head impatiently.

"Rebecca, that's it! Rebecca 'Arding – got that big 'ouse on the 'ill in Dallington, lots of money there."

He tapped the side of her nose and Molly ignored him, desperate for news of her friend.

"But she ain't comin' 'ere, is she, not 'ere I mean?" Molly questioned.

"Yes why?" said Edwin indignantly.

"This ain't the sort of place that Mary goes to, I'm sure it ain't."

"What's wrong with it?" demanded Lizzie.

"Well, if you don't know I ain't goin' to tell you," Molly snapped.

"Molly," Edwin said sternly, "that's enough of that, thank you, come on, you get on clearing up if Mary's coming; we can give her a cup of tea – that'll be more in her line."

Molly leapt up, brushing down her apron with her hands, before trying to push her hair into some semblance of tidiness. The door opened– Molly turned to it expectantly, only to see Adelaide Harding swooping into the room. She was shrouded in black and immediately began to undo the buttons of her coat as she walked to the bar. She scanned the room snootily before turning to examine Edwin.

"You still alive then, Edwin?"

"Grimly hanging on," Edwin replied with a smile. "And what can we do for you, Adelaide, it's not often that we see you here?"

"That's my good fortune, ain't it, Edwin," she laughed, taking a packet of cigarettes from her handbag. "You forget, Edwin, I were brought up 'ere all them years ago; I were glad to get out of 'ere, I can tell you, yes, leaving here never came soon enough for me."

She tapped the cigarette packet on the bar and placed one between her teeth.

"Got a light, Edwin?" she asked.

Edwin took a box of matches from his grimy pocket, struck one and cupped the flame in his palms for Adelaide to light from. Adelaide straightened up, blowing the smoke firstly towards Edwin and then upwards above his head. She tossed her head haughtily and looked down her nose at Edwin.

"Gin, Edwin," she demanded.

"Coming up," said Edwin, scuttling behind the bar and lifting down a gin bottle.

"Anything in it, Adelaide?" he asked.

"Splash of water," she said distractedly, her eyes slowly scanning the room.

"What brings you here, then?" Edwin asked.

"Business," she replied, seizing the proffered glass and tipping it back in one swift movement. "'Nother one, Edwin," she said, taking a puff on the cigarette.

Edwin filled the glass again.

"Has Noble Ladds bin in?" Adelaide asked casually.

Molly stopped brushing and looked up curiously, Lizzie also stopped wiping to look at Edwin, who looked blankly at Adelaide.

"You know who 'e is, don't you, Edwin?" laughed Adelaide.

"Yes, yes, course I do but 'e ain't bin in, well not for a while any road."

Molly looked down and started to sweep again as the door swung open to reveal Noble Ladds. Before he could catch sight of her, Molly dodged through the door at the end of the pub – leaving it slightly ajar so she could listen to what was happening.

"Glass of whisky, barman," he sneered, striding to the bar to greet Adelaide.

They shook hands and Noble slid himself onto the stool next to her.

"About time, Noble Ladds," she complained. "I've been here hours, haven't I, Edwin?"

"I had some business to attend to," Noble said impatiently.

"So have we, young man," said Adelaide, tapping the ash from her cigarette onto the floor.

"So we have," said Noble with a wink, leaning over the bar towards Edwin and adding in a low voice: "Edwin – got a room upstairs?"

"Yes," said Edwin blankly.

"Is it warm?"

"The fire's laid" said Edwin, "only needs a match."

"How much?" said Noble.

"Depends how long," Edwin replied cannily.

Noble did not answer, instead turning to smile at Adelaide.

"Shall I lead the way?" Edwin asked.

"No need," said Adelaide, "I could find it with my eyes shut."

And with a swish of her coat, she had gone, leading Noble through the bar and out into the corridor behind her.

Molly opened the door to the yard and scurried back into the pub.

"What if Mary comes, Edwin, that's 'er 'usband up there," she hissed to Edwin.

"Well we will just have to see," said Edwin with a shrug. "Any road she didn't say she would definitely come, only just she might. Goo on, get on sweepin', Molly, and get this place clear."

Five minutes later the door to the Griffin swung open again, announcing Mary's arrival. The smoke trails had gone from the room, the fire had crackled to life and Molly was just finishing cleaning the bar when she saw Mary arrive.

"Molly, how are you? I saw Edwin and he told me you were here today," exclaimed Mary, moving to the bar and embracing Molly enthusiastically. Molly accepted the hug awkwardly, arms pinned to her side. She stood back, a look of embarrassment creeping over her face, and smiled at Mary nervously.

"It's lovely to see you, Mary," she said gratefully, "but I don't know why you come here, it's not a very nice place, is it? Not for someone like you."

"I came to see you, Molly," laughed Mary, "And it doesn't look too bad, there's a nice fire and—"

She looked round the room at the grubby furniture and tobacco-stained ceiling, the smell of stale beer and smoke thick in her nostrils.

"Well it must keep you busy, Molly," she finished feebly.

"Yeah, it does," nodded Molly, "and it ain't too bad now when there's no one 'ere; but when the factories close they all come in and it's awful – you can't imagine how awful it is, Mary."

She shuddered.

"Now would you like a cup of tea?" Molly said hopefully. "I put the kettle on, it won't take a moment."

"That would be nice, Molly but I can't stay long. I've got to go back and pick up my shopping before I catch the train; it will take forever to get back to Raunds."

She sat at a small table by the bar as Molly rushed off to collect the tea tray.

"'Ave you bin to Tibbitts, Mary?" said Molly hopefully, pouring Mary a cup of tea. "I went a little while ago but they ain't got no jobs; I wish they 'ad then I could move from 'ere."

"Poor Molly," said Mary, "they said you had been; they really haven't got any vacancies – I asked them."

"I know," shrugged Molly. "I'm got to go back in six mumfs – that's what they said, so I s'pose I'm got to stay 'ere."

She put down the kettle and looked scornfully around the room of the pub. "I wish—"

She stopped, shaking her head and passing Mary a cup of tea.

"Well," she lowered her voice, "it just ain't nice 'ere."

Mary looked at her kindly – Molly looked tired; dark rings circled her eyes and she looked older than her years.

"You could come and work for me, Molly," she said suddenly. "I couldn't pay you much – but I really need some help; I've got another one on the way and the farm to look after while Noble is away."

Molly's eyes lit up; she grabbed Mary's hand and held it tight.

"You mean that, Mary?" she asked earnestly.

"Well, I've got to ask Noble first so don't count on it," said Mary earnestly "he wouldn't agree before, but I'm sure I can persuade him."

"Mary, where do you live now then?"

"Bythorn."

"I ain't never bin there," said Molly quietly. "What am I got to do if I come?"

"Housework, cleaning, cooking, looking after children, feeding chickens, calves, you know all about that sort of thing, Molly," said Mary with a shrug.

She smiled at Molly.

"Come on, what do you say, Molly?"

Molly smiled joyfully.

"I'll come, Mary – of course I'll come, if 'e agrees that is, it can't be no worse than 'ere, can it be?"

"Don't say it like that, Molly," laughed Mary.

"Oh sorry, Mary, I didn't mean it like that, I really didn't," insisted Molly.

"I'll take your word for it," said Mary, rising from the table. "Now, Molly, as soon as I have seen Noble I will write, then you tell Edwin and let me know when you are coming. Now, I must get on or I will never get home."

Molly rose, hugged her friend and walked her to the door of the pub; she watched Mary leave, her thoughts straying to the man in the room upstairs and how little he deserved his kind wife. She moved to collect her duster and Brasso, starting to polish the brass handles and fingerplates on the front door.

Moments later, the door was barged open from the inside and Adelaide pushed her way out. She looked contemptuously down at Molly and the can of Brasso that she had knocked over. She sniffed, threw her head back and walked off in the direction of the town centre. It wasn't long before she heard footsteps from the inside of the pub; she grabbed the can of Brasso and stepped away from the door; Noble Ladds swept out the door, eyes brushing Molly as he did so. He walked two paces, stopped, turned and came back towards her.

"Don't I know you, girl?" he asked, eyeing Molly curiously. "Yes I do, you come from Dean, don't you? Yes, I've seen you there, your father works for William Dunmore, doesn't he?"

"Yes," said Molly sulkily.

Noble tutted and looked up the road where Adelaide had disappeared into the distance.

"Did you see me come in here? What's your name?"

"Molly," said Molly.

"Yes, that's it, Molly Webb," mused Noble. "Had a baby a bit back, I remember."

He looked her up and down warily.

"Did you then, Molly?"

"Did I what?"

"See me come in here?"

"Yes," said Molly incredulously.

"Did you see who I was with?"

"Yes, you weren't 'idin', were you," sneered Molly.

Noble did not reply, pulling at his chin with his hand.

"Come on in a minute, Molly," he said with a small frown.

He gripped her arm forcefully and pushed her into the bar.

"Edwin!" Noble shouted.

Edwin, who was polishing glasses at the bar, looked up.

"Edwin, can this one keep her mouth shut?" he said nodding at Molly.

"I s'pose so if she 'ad to, Noble, why?" said Edwin.

"Why, you oaf, why?" yelled Noble, moving angrily towards Edwin.

He spun on his heel, rounding on Molly and grabbing a handful of her hair, twisting it in his hand and bringing his face close to hers.

"Are you going to tell my wife about this, Molly? Are you? Do you know who my wife is, Molly?"

"Mary Knighton," Molly said through clenched teeth.

"Well, are you going to tell her?" Noble hissed menacingly.

"Well I ain't done yet."

"What do you mean, you ain't done yet?" roared Noble.

"She were 'ere this afternoon while you were upstairs and I didn't tell 'er, so there," Molly spat angrily.

Noble released her hair, surprised, and turned to Edwin.

"Mary, here?" he asked.

"Yes," shrugged Edwin, "I met 'er on the train this mornin' and she wanted to come see 'ow Molly was gettin' on."

"She offered me a job an' all," said Molly, delighting in Noble's predicament.

"A job?" he sneered contemptuously. "What job? What as?"

"'Ouse maid."

"Over my dead body," Noble snorted.

He paced the room angrily, sat at the table and looked from Molly to Edwin, furiously reviewing his options. A thin smile spread across his face.

"On second thoughts," he said, rising and lunging for Molly again, wrapping his hand in her hair and looking her in the eye.

"Are you going to tell, Molly Webb?" he hissed.

Molly gritted her teeth and stared back at him.

"Not if I'm got a job I want, stands to reason, don't it," she said grudgingly.

Noble loosened her hair and smiled wolfishly down at her.

"I don't think she will tell, do you, Edwin?"

He gripped Molly's chin and lowered his face to hers.

"Don't 'spect she will," said Edwin slowly, "but we won't 'ave a cleaner then."

"Don't worry about that, Edwin, you'll soon find another and I can make it worth your while to lose her. You can get another young soul from somewhere I'm sure."

He released Molly and moved towards the bar.

"If you say so, Noble," said Edwin sceptically.

"I do say so, Edwin," said Noble, taking a five-pound note from his pocket and putting it on the bar, his hand covering it.

"Molly, what did my wife say she was going to do about hiring you?" he demanded.

"She said she would ask you and then she would write and then I could leave 'ere and come over to your 'ouse."

"Now did you hear that, Edwin?" chuckled Noble.

"Yes, Noble," said Edwin.

"Well here's five pounds for your trouble and you make sure she leaves when Mary writes – no monkey business, all right?"

"If you say so, Noble," said Edwin, easing the five-pound note from Noble's grasp.

"I do say so, Edwin," said Noble menacingly.

He let go of the note and walked round Molly, slowly looking her up and down.

"What are you lookin' at?" Molly demanded.

"Never you mind, my dear, never you mind."

He took one last look at her and swept from the pub.

Chapter Forty-Six
Molly and Reuben come to Elgin Farm

The trip to Northampton had been very successful for Mary; she had been able to get herself some new clothes with the money she had inherited, replacing the shabby old ones that had been wearing thin. Enlisting Molly had pleased her, she was desperately in need of help in the house and on the farm, and she had been pleasantly surprised at how readily Noble had accepted the idea of Molly coming to work for them. She wrote to Molly straight away and arranged that she would arrive the next weekend.

Verity was immersed in her studies at Oxford and had proved to be a model student. She spent most of her time away and saw Mary very little, using her vacations from university to tend to the poor of the parish of Dean, which she looked on as her responsibility. When she heard that Molly had started to work for Mary, Verity decided that she should pay a visit and check how Molly was getting on. She wrote a card to Mary who replied by return inviting Verity to come over for tea the following Saturday.

With the furniture Mary had obtained from Cold Harbour, the room at Elgin's was now quite respectable, with the exception that there was no carpet – only a rug in front of the fireplace. All the carpets from Cold Harbour had fallen apart when they were taken up and Mary had burnt them. For Verity's arrival, Mary had put a new dress on and Jack, who was now walking, had been dressed in a sailor's suit which she had bought from Tibbitts. Molly wore an old dress of Mary's – which between them they had altered to fit her – over which she had a pretty floral apron. It was now mid-summer and Verity had just returned from a holiday with her father in the South of France. The wheat had all been cut and the stooks stood upright in the fields, topped with crows, who stood pecking at the corn. At three o' clock the motor car drew up outside the farmhouse; Walter parked in the middle of the road, hopped out and moved round to open Verity's door.

"This is the place, Miss Verity," he announced. "I'll just go and turn the motor round so we are pointing the right way for goin' 'ome."

"Very good, Walter."

Mary had walked down the path to meet the car, Jack holding tightly to his mother's hand and Molly standing at the door.

"Mary, how good it is to see you!" exclaimed Verity. "It's been so long – too long in fact, and look at this young man."

She peered down at Jack with a strained look of pleasure, making no attempt to make any contact with him.

"Mary, you do look well," she said, turning back to her friend, "and another one on the way I can see."

She held out her hand to shake Mary's; Mary brushed it aside and pressed her cheeks to Verity's, who looked taken aback.

"It's wonderful," agreed Mary, standing back to look at her friend. "And you've grown, Verity, I know I shouldn't say that but you have."

She bent down and scooped Jack up in her arms, ushering Verity towards the house where Molly was standing at the front door.

"And here is dear Molly," said Verity with pleasure. "Doesn't she look well and what a pretty dress."

"Fank you, Miss Verity," said Molly with a little curtsey.

"Now I am so silly," said Verity, "I brought everyone a present and now I have left them in the motor car. Molly, be a dear, will you, and run out to Walter to fetch them; they are in a basket on the seat."

Molly performed her odd little curtsey again and rushed towards the car as Mary showed Verity into the front room and offered her a seat.

"Now, Verity, you must tell me all about Dean," said Mary. "It's ages since I've been back and I only see William when he comes over and he knows none of the gossip."

Molly entered with the basket, handing it to Verity with a shy smile.

"Molly, take Jack, will you, and put him to bed – he's ready for a sleep now, and when that's done we can have the tea," said Mary, handing over her son and turning back to Verity.

Verity filled Mary in on life in Dean and her work in the parish, while

Molly, having put Jack to bed, brought in the tea; sandwiches and cakes sitting daintily on a tray with a teapot, milk jug, water jug and sugar bowl that all matched – Mary's pride and joy. Mary rose and poured the tea, which she handed to Verity.

"Now, Molly, I must hear all about you and how you are getting on," ordered Verity.

"Go and get yourself a cup, Molly, and have your tea with us," Mary suggested.

Molly nodded, leaving to return moments later; she poured her tea and sat herself in an upright chair at the table, while Verity quizzed her.

"I'm so glad you are happy here, Molly," said Verity, a touch pompously.

"And she's so good with Jack, aren't you, Molly?" smiled Mary.

"If you say so, Mary," said Molly dubiously.

"I'm sure she is," said Verity. "And where did your dress come from, Molly?"

"Oh, it's only Mary's old one, she got a noo one see, so I 'ad 'er old one; we made it fit, didn't we, Mary?"

"Yes, Molly," smiled Mary.

"Mary always looked smart, not like me, Molly; I have no idea how to dress myself – just like a sack of potatoes, someone said to me at university the other day. Do you remember, Mary, I had to take you to choose my clothes that time?" laughed Verity. "We went to Northampton!"

She suddenly looked at Mary quizzically.

"We met that boy on the train; what was his name – Rupert or something. Yes Rupert Nelson! What a day that was and Dorcas came as well, poor old Dorcas."

"I see 'im the uvver day," piped up Molly.

"You saw who the other day?" asked Verity.

"That Rupert Nelson; not the uvver day, but afore I left Norfampton."

Mary looked up sharply, her cheeks colouring.

"Oh," said Verity, looking at Mary.

"Yes," continued Molly, "'e were goin' into the noospaper office; I knowed it were 'im 'cos I seed 'im wiv Mary when 'e come over to Dean."

There was silence; Mary fidgeted on her chair uncomfortably.

"You should 'ave married 'im, Mary, 'e were a much better man than the one you got," blurted out Molly.

"What a thing to say!" Verity snapped, turning angrily to Molly. "Now say you're sorry to Mary."

Molly lowered her head and wrung her hands in her lap.

"Sorry, Mary," she sniffed, looking at Mary earnestly, "sorry, Mary; I dint fink what I were saying! I dint mean it, you know that, don't you."

"Let's forget about it, Molly, can we?" said Mary quietly. "Just clear the tea things please."

"I must be going now, Mary," said Verity, draining her tea and rising.

She collected her coat and followed Mary out of the front door to where Walter was waiting in the motor car. She turned to Mary, embracing her and holding her at arm's length.

"Molly was right, Mary – about Rupert Nelson, I mean; he came back from South America in the spring. Father met his father, that's how I heard."

She shrugged a little and smiled at Mary, squeezed her hands and climbed into the car. Mary stood desolately in the driveway, staring after the departing car.

The days began to get shorter; the sheaves were carted from the fields and the blackberries started to ripen on the hedges. Noble had decided that they should plough up some of their pasture and plant wheat for next year and he had hired a steam ploughing contractor to come and do the work after they had completed the ploughing on Henry's farm. The morning they arrived, Noble was away, leaving Mary to organise the team with Cyril. Jack, who had never seen a ploughing gang, stood at the garden gate waiting for the team with Molly.

They could hear the engines from some way off, and when they finally came into view Molly recognised the driver as Ron Seamarks – she waved enthusiastically. Jack took one look at the vast engine belching out smoke, squealed and ran back towards the house, hiding himself behind a holly bush by the front door.

The first engine drew the plough behind it, the mould boards glinting in the morning sun. Behind them the second engine chugged onwards – Molly read its nameplate, making out the word "Dread" and another word she could not decipher.

"What's that one's name, Mary?" she called to Mary, who was standing by the entrance to the farm.

"Dreadnought," Mary shouted back over the hissing and puffing of the engine.

"What's that mean?" Molly asked.

"It's the name of a warship," Mary shouted, "and so's Victory; they are both named after ships."

"Well I never," said Molly with a shake of her head.

The second engine passed the garden gate, pulling the green painted living wagon behind it. Molly momentarily froze to the spot – staring at the peeling paint on the wagon as it passed – she shuddered and rushed back to the house to find Jack, who had crept out of his hiding place and was looking curiously at the engines. Behind the living-wagon plodded an old horse pulling the water barrel, and perched on a board in front of the tank was Reuben. As soon as he caught sight of Mary he leapt off, tying the horse to the gate and rushing over to greet her.

"Mary, I knew it were goin' to be your farm," he exclaimed delightedly. "I knew it were! They said it weren't, but I knew it were."

He took his cap off, threw it on the ground and grinned broadly.

"Reuben!" laughed Mary, placing her hands on his shoulders and turning him towards her.

"Look at you, boy, haven't you grown? You will soon be as tall as me! But shouldn't you be at school?"

"Not no more," he said happily, "I'm left and good riddance to it! I'm goin' to be an engine driver."

"Are you sure, Reuben?" Mary asked.

"Yes I am absolutely sure and I always 'ave bin."

He looked up as Molly walked towards them, holding a very cautious looking Jack by the hand.

"Look, Jack! Look at the engine," urged Molly, pointing towards the machinery, which had come to a halt in the farm yard.

Jack whimpered and hid his head in Molly's skirts.

Ron waved and leapt down from the engine, moving towards Mary and raising his cap.

"Well, Mrs Ladds, it's a long time, ain't it?"

"Yes, Ron – I wasn't very old when you came up to Cold Harbour," agreed Mary with a wistful smile.

"Now, Mary, coal you have to provide, where is it?" he asked.

"Cyril has organised it," said Mary, pointing to Cyril who nodded furiously.

"Yes, Mrs Ladds, there's a heap at the back of the barn over there, do you want us to cart it?" said Cyril.

Mary nodded.

"And water," said Ron, "where is the water? We want to fill up before we go."

"We've got two wells in the yard and there's the pond just out the gate there. Do you want us to cart that as well?"

"No, Reuben can do that as long as it's not too far," said Ron. "Which field are we working?"

"Cyril, you show Ron where it is," instructed Mary. "It's our biggest one, it's just over twenty acres."

"Very good, Mary," nodded Ron, "and you tell 'im not to sow wheat in it, or at least not in the first year; that's the best thing, you tell 'im."

"Why's that, Ron?" Mary asked curiously.

"Wheat is always ate by the wireworm in the first year, you see if I'm not right."

He lifted his cap to her.

"We will be off if you will show us where to go."

Cyril walked off in front of the engines, indicating that Ron should follow. The two engines made their way slowly to the field, leaving the living-van in the yard. Reuben led the horse and tanker to the well in the cattleyard, lifted one of three planks covering it and dropped his pipe down into the well, moving to work the pump at the back of the tanker.

Molly led Jack up to watch.

"'Ow long's that goin' to take you then, Reuben?" Molly asked.

"Nearly 'arf an 'our, I guess; the water's a bit down in the well."

"Look, Jack – the man's filling the tank," said Molly bending down to Jack's level.

Jack quivered, listening to the splosh of the water as Reuben moved the handle of the pump backwards and forwards, his eyes widening with curiosity.

"What's George doin' now, Reuben?" Molly asked.

"Oh, 'e ain't left school yet; 'e's a year younger 'an me and he's good at sums and writin' and that, so 'e's got another year to go."

"I'm good at writin', ain't I, Mary?" Molly said, as Mary came to join them.

"Yes, Molly, you are very good – but not so good at sums, are you?" she said with a smile.

"Don't 'spec so," said Molly.

"Reuben, do you want a cup of tea?" Mary asked.

"That would be very nice as long as the others don't see," Reuben grinned. "They won't like it if I get one and they don't."

"Don't worry, they can't see," she said as both the engines started to make their way up to the field.

"I better light the fire in the living-van after this," he said to Mary, "or it won't be 'ot enough to cook the lunch."

"You mean you are going to do the cooking, Reuben? I thought Bernard was the cook boy?" said Mary surprised.

"No, not now! Bernard's on the plough with Jeff; he fills up with coal if the plough's going all right so I do the cooking and fetch the water."

He looked at Molly and Mary's doubtful expressions and laughed.

"And I've got to go and get some fags for them and some bread; where do I go for them, Mary? Is there a pub 'ere?"

"Well, there's a pub but there isn't a bakery. But you're in luck, Ulick comes today delivering from his bakery in Catworth, so you can get some from him."

She moved away from the well, returning to the front of the house just as Noble trotted into the yard, leading two shire horses. Mary waved and moved to help him, holding one of the huge creatures as Noble dismounted from Tinker and tied the other to a fence post.

"What do you think, Mary? Aren't they splendid; just wait till they're groomed and shod properly."

He stood back and admired his purchases.

"They look very good, Noble, but where did you get them? I thought there was no market today," Mary asked.

"A farm sale at Ramsey; an absolutely bargain, there was no one there! He should have withdrawn them but he wasn't very bright," sneered Noble. "They're all like that out there."

"That's not true, Noble," said Mary with a frown. "So what are you going to do with them?"

"I'm going to take them up to old Gun now and get them shod properly; then I'm going to feed them, groom them and take them to Thrapston Market tomorrow and sell them."

"Couldn't *we* do with them, now we've got some ploughed land?" Mary asked.

"No, I'm going to make a good profit," Noble insisted.

He untethered the largest of the horses and led it the hundred yards to the smithy. Mary shrugged and returned to the house.

Reuben, having filled the water cart and lit the fire, rushed to the pub to get the supply of cigarettes before the others stopped for lunch. Noble Ladds was sitting in the tap room when he entered, perched next to the unlit fire reading a paper, a pint on the table in front of him, his usual cigar hanging from his fingers. He looked up as Reuben strode in, sneered slightly and turned back to his paper. Reuben peered round the dingy room and into the scullery where the beer was kept.

"He ain't here," said Noble without looking up.

Reuben shuffled awkwardly on the spot, unsure of what to say.

"He's helping to shoe my horse," said Noble. "You'll find him out the back if you want a drink."

Reuben still said nothing. Noble looked up at him again, recognition dawning on his face. He laughed.

"No," said Noble, "you don't want a drink, do you, Reuben? I didn't recognise you, boy, you're all black."

"It's the coal, Mr Ladds, I all'as ends up black, whatever I do."

"What are you doing here then?" Noble asked.

"I'm cook boy for the ploughing gang and they've sent me for some fags."

"Left school already? You don't look old enough."

"Well I am," said Reuben. "I'm workin' now."

"Well, you will have to go and fetch him," said Noble, nodding at the door and turning back to his paper.

Suddenly, he threw down his paper and leapt up.

"No, on second thoughts I'll give you them. I don't want him to stop with the horses, I've got another one to do yet. How many do you want?"

"They said forty but they ain't got no money; they'll come in tonight to sort things out," said Reuben as Noble moved to a drawer in the sideboard, took out two packets of cigarettes and handed them to him. Reuben doffed his cap and left Noble to get back to his paper.

Back at the farm Reuben put the beef on to boil; there was no other way to cook it, the stove in the living wagon had no oven. ′

"What's the time, Molly?" he shouted across the yard to Molly, who she was hanging out the washing.

"No idea," she yelled back. "I ain't got no watch, I'll just go and ask Mary."

She bustled into the house with her empty basket, re-emerging at the door to shout:

"'Arf past eleven."

She disappeared into the house again.

Before long the boiled beef in the living-van began to give off a delicious aroma; Reuben was boiling it with onions, something he had seen his mother do. He found a bucket, pumped a little water into it, half-filled it with potatoes and sat down on the steps of the van to peel them.

"What smells so good, Reuben?" came a voice beside him; Mary had come up to see what he was cooking.

"Just old boiled beef," he said, "and taters if I get them done in time."

He kept peeling with his shut-knife.

"You don't all live in there do you, Reuben? There doesn't look like much room," Mary asked, peering up the steps.

"No, Jeff and Ron go 'ome most nights, so it's only me and Joe and Bernard; but there ain't much room all the same. All the spares are in there as well, you know."

He continued to peel his potatoes at breakneck speed. Mary smiled.

"Have you seen Noble, Reuben?" Mary asked.

"'E were in the pub when I went to get the fags, but they must 'ave done one 'orse and 'e's took the other one up I should think."

"He's in the pub *again*," sighed Mary. "Don't you start drinking, Reuben, it doesn't do you any good; I'm sure of that."

"I ain't never 'ad a drop of it, my muvver don't approve of it."

Mary laughed and returned to the house.

At three o'clock Noble returned, leading the second horse into the stables to join the other one. He made his way into the house.

"Come on, you two," he hollered at Mary and Molly, "we've got to get these animals ready for tomorrow and I could do with a hand."

There was no immediate response from the house.

"Come on then, look sharp about it, Molly, you can brush them and, Mary, bring the scissors; we can trim the manes and tail, that always makes them look good, and I will oil their hooves. Mary! Molly!"

Mary and Molly emerged somewhat reluctantly, following Noble out to the stables. Noble threw the hand brush to Molly which she caught rather clumsily.

"There's a curry comb over there if you need it," he said, taking off his jacket. "Come on then, get on with it, girl!"

Molly started to brush the huge horse with limited enthusiasm; but the more she brushed, the more the coat seemed to gleam and she began to warm to her task. Noble was on his knees with a rag and a can of linseed oil, vigorously oiling the hooves and Mary – having combed the mane of one horse –was clipping at it ineffectually with her sewing scissors.

"I'll have to go and get the other pair of my mother's," she said to Noble, "these ones aren't man enough."

She left the stable and made her way back to the house. Molly continued to brush the horse, humming slightly under her breath and reaching up to brush the creature's neck. She jumped as a hand snaked around her waist, moving up past her ribs and squeezing her breast. Molly spun round, smacking Noble's knuckles hard with the back of her brush. The brush connected with his hand with a snap; Noble grimaced and blew on his knuckles.

"You little bitch," he hissed, gritting his teeth.

"Don't you dare do that to me or I'll tell 'er about what you get up to, Mr Noble Ladds," snarled Molly.

She had backed up against the wall of the stable and looked frightened; her lower lip quivered and tears threatened.

"Don't you dare touch me," she warned, holding the brush out in front of her as a weapon.

"But you won't tell, will you, Molly, I know you won't," Noble said quietly, his voice laced with menace.

"Why won't I tell?" she said indignantly, dashing the tears away with her fist.

Noble leant towards her, bringing his lips close to her ear.

"You won't tell, my little precious, because you want a job. You like it here; you don't want to go back to the Griffin, do you? Don't want to go back to trotting up and down them stairs two or three times at lunchtime and the same in the evenings, do you?"

He drew back and looked Molly in the eye.

"Do you?" he hissed.

Molly looked down at the straw on the floor of the stable. The horse snorted, stamped his foot twice and began pawing at the straw.

"Do you, Molly?" Noble repeated.

"No," Molly said, hurriedly turning back to the horse as she heard Mary making her way back to the stable.

The ploughing was completed by the end of the next day, the gang moving their engines on to the next farm.

"See you next year," Reuben shouted, as he led the horse with the water cart out of the yard. "Mary, the top of that well's all rotten, you must get it replaced – you don't want young Jack getting down it."

Mary shouted thanks and watched him leave, Jack holding her hand tightly next to her, gazing in awe at the retreating engines.

It was the autumn of 1905 and in November Mary's new baby arrived; they named her Ethil and she was christened in Bythorn, with Rebecca, Martha and Henry as her godparents. Rebecca had arranged to go hunting on the Saturday before the christening and came to stay at Elgin Farm that night.

"You know Rupert is back, Mary?" said Rebecca.

The pair were sitting by the range in the kitchen, Noble having gone to the pub with Henry.

"Yes. Molly said she saw him just before she left Northampton. I wouldn't expect Molly to recognise him, but she must have been right."

Mary rose to poke the fire in the range distractedly. She gave a small laugh.

"She said I should have married him and not Noble. Poor Molly, she doesn't know when to keep her mouth shut, does she?"

"She was right, wasn't she," said Rebecca bluntly.

She looked closely at her friend.

"But then you couldn't have done anything else, could you, Mary?" she said gently.

Mary said nothing, but continued to stir the coals in the range.

"You don't mind sitting in the kitchen, do you, Rebecca?" she asked with forced cheeriness "But we've cleaned the front room ready for tomorrow and I've got a carpet now, you will be pleased to know. I had a little money when William sold Cold Harbour and Noble has been doing well with his horse dealing."

"And the farm's doing well," added Rebecca, "and you're the farmer, Mary, I can see that; Noble's never here so you have to do it, don't you?"

She smiled at her friend.

"But Mary Ladds can do anything she sets her mind to, can't she?" she added. "I don't know anyone as capable as you, Mary; ever since I've known you I've been jealous of you."

Mary looked up, surprised; Rebecca laughed.

"Not like that," Rebecca explained. "I know I've got a lot of money, or rather Father has, but I always wished I had some of your skills. And so pretty with it, Mary; you could make anyone do what you wanted."

Mary blushed and waved a hand at Rebecca.

"Rebecca, stop it – it's not true and you know it. Now tell me about Jimmy."

"What about him?"

"Are you going to marry him?"

"That's what everyone thinks, that's what Adelaide wants and Father I suppose."

She sighed.

"But I just don't know about Jimmy. I think he feels the same as me; he's pushed towards me by his mother and I'm pushed towards him by Adelaide and so it goes on. We are really quite good friends in an odd sort of way."

She gave a small laugh.

"We have similar enemies and that makes us think the same. I suppose I will marry him in the end."

She picked at her dress and sighed again.

"And what about Noble, Mary?" she asked. "Did you ask him about Adelaide; you can't ignore it – they were both there, you know that we both saw them."

Mary thought for a while.

"I know what Noble's like, Rebecca and I know we saw them together," she said slowly, "but I've decided that I will never find out about what he gets up to whilst he is away, so why worry? As long as he behaves at home and around here I don't mind. If he steps out of line here, I would have to deal with him and I know that I would be able to."

She chuckled wryly.

"He wouldn't stand a chance."

"Oh ho," giggled Rebecca, "poor chap, he'd get his marching orders if he blotted his copy book then, eh, Mary?"

"Yes," said Mary firmly.

"And William, Mary; isn't he going to marry?"

"No sign yet," shrugged Mary. "He doesn't go out with girls. His mother keeps him on a very short rein, she lives by the Bible and makes William do the same."

"Pity," said Rebecca, "but he's a bit young for me."

"He's good with money, Rebecca," said Mary. "He has invested mine for me; he reads all the papers, you know, and he helps me with the farm and Henry with his as well."

She laughed.

"Henry's not very bright, but you can see that, can't you? William does the business for him and Martha keeps him in order. He's coming tomorrow so you will be able to meet him."

"And Rupert, Mary," probed Rebecca. "Are you going to arrange to meet *him*?"

"What would I say?" said Mary helplessly. "It wouldn't be right."

"Well," said Rebecca with a shake of her head, "at least you know that he's back; if you ever did want to see him."

Mary sighed and said nothing.

Chapter Forty-Seven
A Departure

Over a year had passed since the birth of Ethil and she could already walk. Mary was now able to manage the day-to-day running of the farm with ease; hay time was some time away, but the cattle had all been turned out to pasture so they no longer needed feeding. At present there were no horses on the farm; they had all been sold with the exception of the two farm carthorses and Tinker. Against the advice of Ron, Noble had sown the newly ploughed field with wheat the first year, and it had duly been destroyed by wireworm and had had to be sown with beans in the spring. Mary had obtained more chickens and the old sow had had an early litter of piglets, which were now ready to be butchered.

One morning that spring, Mary took the two children to Brington to visit Martha and their cousins, leaving Molly at home to clean the rooms. The afternoon was bright, and high clouds scudded across the sky in the early summer breeze. Most of the hedges were in leaf, the blackthorn blossom was just over and the hawthorn beginning to shoot. Mary meandered along, accompanied by the chirping of birds busy looking after the young of their early broods, and Jack toddled curiously from hedge to hedge, asking for names of flowers and picking up empty bird egg shells. Not far from the trio, Noble was making his way back from Thrapston. He rode a big bay hunter and led two draught ponies behind him, whistling as he went and occasionally raising his bowler to passing acquaintances. At the top of the hill at Obelisk Farm, eight bullocks were being driven into a small field next to the road. Ray Clarke, who worked for William, was in charge of the driving, and was being assisted by George Lowe; it didn't take the pair long to herd the last of the bullocks into the field.

Ray raised his cap.

"Thank you for waitin', Mr Ladds," he groaned. "They're bin a cantankerous lot; it's taken us all day to get 'em 'ere, ain't it, George?"

"Yes, Ray," said George obligingly.

"Shouldn't you be at school, George?" asked Noble. "They tell me you're a good scholar."

"They let me have a day off to drive these cattle. William's going to write a note to the teacher," explained George, wiping a dirty hand across his nose.

"Aha, William Dunmore's word is law in Dean, I expect," said Noble with an almost imperceptible curl of his lip.

George squinted up at Noble bemusedly.

"I suppose it is," he shrugged.

"But William went to the Grammar School, didn't he, George? So he's much grander than all you, isn't he?"

"I suppose so," said George a touch uncertainly. "I were going to go to the Grammar School."

"You mean, 'I was going to go to the grammar school'," said Noble with a snort. "You'd never get in if you don't know your 'was' from your 'weres', George. Why didn't you go to the Grammar School?"

"I passed all the exams and that but Father wouldn't let me go," said George with a shrug.

"And why was that?"

"He said that he never took charity and he wouldn't take it to send me to school. Neal's Charity people said they would pay, but Father would have none of it. He's very strong chapel, you see, and that won't let him do a lot of things," he added by way of explanation.

"Shame," said Noble wryly.

"That's what I said," interjected Ray. "The boy had a chance and they wouldn't let 'im go; I think that's criminal waste, real criminal waste."

"Maybe you're right, Ray," said Noble, giving his hunter a kick and turning it back towards home. "'Ow's Molly getting on?" Ray called after him.

Noble turned in his saddle,

"Very well, yes, very well; Mary is very pleased," he said, urging his mount into a trot.

Noble arrived back in Bythorn at two o'clock, stopped at The Stags Head, tied the horses up and went in for a beer. There was no one behind the bar, so he helped himself, sat down and started to read one of the old papers from the pile on the sideboard. He pulled a cigar from a packet in his jacket pocket, patting his trouser pocket for his matches. On finding none he stood and ran his hand along the high shelf above the inglenook fireplace until he came upon a box. He could hear the sound of wheels outside on the cobbles and looked out the window to see Ulick, the baker, pulling up in his pony and trap. Noble watched him tie the pony to the railings, heave his basket of bread from the cart and make his way up the steps into the pub.

"Morning, Ulick," said Noble. "There's no one here."

"I bet there is," Ulick said, plonking his basket on the bar, "but she ain't 'eard you; you wait, I'll fetch 'er out."

He moved to the door into the kitchen and shouted at the top of his voice,

"Dora, Dora, come out, you old hag!"

He chuckled and turned back to Noble.

"You'll see, she'll come now."

Sure enough, they could hear the scraping of a chair against the flagstones.

"That's a fine way to address a lady – 'old hag', isn't it, Ulick?" reprimanded Noble.

"She ain't no lady, and you know it, Noble Ladds, she's an old hag just like I said," laughed Ulick.

Dora shuffled into the bar; she was short, largely due to her stooped posture and had to angle up her head awkwardly to look at them. Her grey-black hair hung uncombed round her shoulders, as if she had just got out of bed. Her face was weatherbeaten and wrinkled and one eye did not open as much as the other; her mouth was small and sunken and when she opened it, the seven remaining teeth in her mouth looked like miniature weathered tombstones leaning in all directions. She wore a dark brown woollen dress, covered by a cotton wraparound floral pinny with a pocket in the front.

"What did you say?" she hooted at Ulick, cupping a grubby hand over her ear.

"Do you want any bread?" Ulick shouted back.

Dora squinted up at him, stretching her neck towards him.

"Four loaves," she said gruffly.

"I'm only got three and then I'm out."

"You what?" she said, putting her hand to her ear again.

"I'm only got three and that's all I'm got and I'll 'ave a pint when you're ready, an all," Ulick said loudly.

"You've only got three, you said?" snorted Dora. "What sort of a baker do you think you are, then? Only got three, well I never; that's a rum un, ain't it?"

She looked round at Noble, her chest rattling a little as she breathed in deeply. Her mouth gaped open, grey spittle on her bottom lip joining with that on the top in a thin thread which expanded and contracted like an elastic band.

"What you doin' 'ere?" she demanded.

"I'm having a pint of your beer which I poured myself as there was no one here," said Noble pointedly. "And very poor beer it is too, must be weeks old."

"That's good beer, don't you tell me any other," grumbled Dora, with a wave of her hand.

"Pour me one, Dora, and I'll tell you what it's like," said Ulick with a wink.

Dora laboriously pushed herself upright, stuck her chin forward and shuffled into the scullery for the beer.

"See, Noble, what did I tell you? She's a stupid old hag," said Ulick.

"Well," said Noble, "there's nowhere else to go so you will have to put up with it."

Dora shuffled back with the pint, her grubby thumb gripping the rim, beer slopping onto the floor and over her slippers. She steadied herself against the wall with her other hand and extended the beer towards Ulick, who took it and sat on the bench by the wall. He held the beer critically up to the light creeping in through the small window, took a large swig and screwed his eyes up in disgust.

"Well," he said, "well, I do declare."

"Declare what?" asked Noble.

"I do declare," said Ulick again, "I do declare it tastes like weak woman's water, yes weak woman's water or in other words piss."

He grimaced and took another gulp.

"But it always does taste like that 'ere, don't you agree, Noble Ladds?"

Noble didn't look up from his paper.

"Don't you agree, Noble?" Ulick said again.

Noble looked up, took his watch from his waistcoat and flicked it open.

"If you say so, Ulick," he said absently. "I'll have another pint as well, Dora, and do you have anything to eat?"

Dora looked up from the bar where she had been picking at a scab on her neck.

"I've got some cheese and there's some bread 'ere now 'e's bin," she grunted.

"Right I'll have some of that," said Noble, "and I'll go and get the beer."

He pushed his way past Dora out into the scullery.

"I'll 'ave some as well, Dora, if you're gettin' it for Noble and I'll 'ave another pint an all. 'Ave you got an onion to go with the cheese?" Ulick asked.

"'Spect so," said Dora, shuffling to the sideboard and retrieving a bread knife and two plates, which she proceeded to clean on the sleeve of her dress. She sniffed and went out to find the cheese, returning five minutes later with an old looking piece of cheese and two onions in her hand; she divided the food between the two plates and leant back against the bar, wheezing.

"Is that all?" she gasped, looking up at Ulick.

"Is that all, woman?" scoffed Ulick. "There ain't nothin' else is there, so of course that's all, ain't it?"

He fumbled in his pocket for his shut knife, taking it out and bending down to cut up the cheese.

"Ooh, you don't 'arf pong, Dora, ooh," he groaned, sniffing and looking round at Noble who had returned with the beers.

"Don't she pong, Noble? You tell 'er."

Noble said nothing, but moved to the bar and cut two slabs of bread, tossing one towards Ulick's plate and standing by the bar to eat. Dora shuffled back out to the kitchen muttering under her breath.

"You haven't run out of bread, Ulick, there's some more in here," Noble said through mouthfuls, pointing towards where he could see some objects beneath a cloth in Ulick's basket. He lifted the cloth to reveal two more loaves of bread.

"No, no; don't tell 'er that; I want them for one of me specials a bit later on," he whispered, tapping the side of his nose. "You know, Noble?" Ulick winked, grinning at Noble lopsidedly.

"Know what?" said Noble,

"Her up Black Lodge."

"Who up Black Lodge?" Noble asked.

"Frances," said Ulick. "Yes, she ain't got a lot between 'er ears, but that don't matter."

He took a mouthful of food and chewed it thoughtfully.

"But it's a long old way up that drive and she don't get back till after dinner," he mused, tapping his foot on the floor; the sound echoing across the empty room.

Ulick took another gulp of beer and looked at Noble.

"I see your missus just before I come in 'ere," he said. "She were off along the road with your two young uns. She's a fine lookin' lady, your wife, Noble Ladds; one of the best, yes one of the best. Too good for you, me boy, you bein' away all the time. You want to watch out; I wouldn't leave one like 'er alone for long, no I never would."

Noble chewed some cheese slowly and said nothing. Ulick, uncomfortable in the silence, started tapping the floor with his foot before continuing.

"Mind, Noble, you should be all right, your missus away and that young Molly at home. She's all right for a trick or two from what I 'eard about 'er in Norfampton."

Noble looked up sharply.

"Don't you ever shut up, Ulick?" he snapped, downing the rest of his beer and slamming the glass back down on the bar.

Ulick opened his mouth to answer, just as the door swung open and Gun, the blacksmith, sauntered in. He was a huge man with closely cut hair, a big leather apron slung on over his shirt and trousers. He looked slowly at the two men.

"Ulick, Noble," he growled.

"Gun," said Ulick.

"Gun," said Noble, pushing past him to take his equine purchases home.

Noble led his charges down towards the farm, turning out the two ponies in the orchard and leading his horse back to the stable to unsaddle him. He removed the saddle, threw the bridle over the door and wandered into the house. There was nobody in the kitchen and the fire in the range was nearly out; Noble opened the biscuit barrel on the sideboard, selected a biscuit and nibbled at it. He removed his jacket, hanging it over the back of one of the chairs, which he sat on to pull off his boots. He could hear noises from upstairs and smiled; that would be Molly cleaning the bedroom. He strummed his fingers on the table, thinking hard. He looked about the room, rose from his chair and left the kitchen, mounting the stairs quietly. In the main bedroom, Molly was brushing the rug, leaning on the doorpost to do so. She didn't hear Noble come in and it wasn't until she turned around that she noticed him.

"Argghh!" she shouted, bringing her hand to her chest. "You gimme a fright stood there like that." She bent down, picking up the brush and pan.

"I'll get out of your way then," she said, making to leave the room.

Noble moved to block her way.

"Let me past, then," she demanded.

Noble smiled.

"Where's Mary?" Noble asked, knowing full well where his wife was.

"She's taken the children over to Martha's for the afternoon," said Molly.

"When's she coming back?" Noble asked.

"I don't know, but she's generally gone a fair while when she goes there," said Molly indifferently.

Noble leant back on the door post and surveyed Molly slowly.

"Well, then?" said Molly.

"Well, then?" repeated Noble, moving towards Molly until they were standing close enough that Molly could feel his breath on her face.

Molly glowered at him, and stood her ground. Noble smiled and wound his hand round the back of her head, pulling her towards him. He kissed her cheek slowly, grabbing hold of her shoulders and asking:

"Are you ready, then?"

"Ready for what?" Molly demanded, shrinking away from him. "I know your sort, you're all the same! I'm seen too many of 'em at the Griffin."

She stared at him angrily, breathing heavily.

"Well, are you going to be nice to me or do I have to—?"

He broke off, standing back and eyeing Molly carefully.

"What's in it for me, then?" demanded Molly.

Noble looked at her, surprised.

"You've got a job, haven't you?" he laughed. "Isn't that enough?"

"No," snarled Molly, "it ain't. I'm bin finking about it. I knowed this were goin' to happen, see. I could tell a year ago."

She wagged a finger warningly at Noble.

"I know what you're like, Noble Ladds, you see. So I'm reckoning if it's goin' to 'appen then there'd best be somat in it fer me."

She raised an eyebrow at Noble and smirked.

Noble stood up straight, put his hand deep into his trouser pocket and pulled out a gold sovereign. He held it up to the light and let Molly inspect it.

"'Nother one," she demanded.

Noble stared her in the eye:

"You drive a hard bargain, Molly Webb," he said with a small chuckle, putting his hand into his pocket and pulling out another coin.

Molly walked closer, holding her hand out for Noble to drop the two coins into it. She smiled, turned the coins over in her hand and placed them carefully on top of the chest of drawers. She moved back to the bed, removed her pinny and started undoing the buttons of her dress.

Mary was walking back along the road to Bythorn; she had left Martha's early as she wanted to see Cyril before he went home to organise the cutting of the hay. The road was bumpy and the pram hard to push through the pot holes, but it wasn't long before she arrived home. She went to find Cyril, made plans with him for the morning and made her way into the house. She knew Noble was home as the horse was in the stable, and his jacket slung over the chair. She cut two slices of bread from the loaf that Ulick had left on the table, buttered them, gave them to the children and sent them outside, before picking up her hat and coat and making her way up the stairs to put them away.

It took her a while to fully comprehend the scene in the bedroom that

603

confronted her, and even when she realised what she was seeing she was not sure whether she could honestly believe it. Her hat dropped from her hand, rolling a little across the wooden boards of the room and coming to rest against a leg of the bed. Noble jumped and raised himself up enough to turn and look for the source of the noise. Mary could see Molly's terrified face and bare chest beneath her husband's broad shoulders. Noble shut his eyes, turning his head away from his wife and mouthing a silent curse. Mary stepped back, clinging to the doorpost to steady herself, unable to form any coherent thought or to tear her eyes from the bed. Finally she turned to walk away, still leaning heavily on the doorframe. She shuddered, stopped and started to shake with rage.

"I don't believe it," she hissed, moving back into the room, her anger boiling in waves towards Noble.

"I don't believe it," she repeated, her voice shaking. "In my own house, in my own bed!"

She turned her head away, fists clenched, her body taut with fury.

"Noble!" she screamed.

For a moment Noble did not reply.

"Yes," he said finally.

"Come downstairs immediately," ordered Mary, her voice trembling with rage.

She spun on her heel, walking to the top of the stairs before turning again and adding,

"Molly, go to your room and stay there until I say."

The heels of her boots clattered on the bare treads of the stairs as she descended.

In the kitchen Mary sat down at the table and covered her face with her hands. Her face was red and there were tears in her eyes; she sniffed and rubbed her nose with her sleeve, before standing up. She looked out of the scullery towards where the children were scampering around outside on the grass, blissfully unaware. She shuddered, moved to the shelf over the range, took down a pewter teapot and opened the lid. She pulled out two white five-pound notes and tucked them through the buttons of her dress before emptying

604

the coins into her hand and putting them into her pocket. From the top drawer of the sideboard she lifted up two strategically placed books and removed another crisp white five-pound note, stuffing it into her dress with the others.

Noble sloped into the kitchen, the cuffs on his shirt hanging open, his collar only attached by a stud at the back. He sat himself on one of the chairs by the table, slowly pulling his boots on before turning to her.

"Well?" he said truculently.

Mary stood by the door, her arms lightly folded, looking out through the scullery at Jack who was instructing Ethil in the making of a mud cake. Noble tapped the table impatiently – his wife scowled and turned to look at him.

"How could you?" she snarled. "And in my own home? How could you?"

Noble said nothing, tapping the table. Mary did not move.

"How could you deceive me?" she hissed.

"No more than you deceived me," snapped Noble, but there was little fight in his voice.

"I deceived you?" Mary screamed. "I deceived you? And when, pray, did I do that?"

"When I asked you to marry me, don't you remember?" Noble sneered.

The look of fury on Mary's face grew, her lip curled.

"You do remember that you had just got me pregnant, don't you?" she retorted. "What was I expected to do? When you had forced yourself on me, Noble Ladds, you rotter?"

There was silence. Noble looked moodily at the ground, before leaping to his feet and moving to the pewter teapot.

"I'm not staying here and listening to all this from you," he hissed, reaching up to pull the teapot from the shelf.

"Good," she snapped, "I'm glad! Go, get out of here, go! I never want to see you again."

Noble pulled the teapot down, opened it and thrust his hand in; he glared angrily at Mary and moved to the drawer in the sideboard, once again returning empty handed. He looked at Mary.

"Where's the money then?" he said threateningly.

Mary said nothing.

"Where's the money?" he shouted.

Mary took a step back to the range, grabbing the poker as she did so.

"I've got it and you're not having it," she snarled.

"Just give it to me!" growled Noble, holding out his hand.

"No," said Mary, gripping the poker with both hands.

"Just give it to me!" Noble yelled, taking a step towards her.

"Don't you dare touch me," Mary screamed, lifting the poker to shoulder height and taking a step towards Noble. Noble stepped back, but said nothing; the poker was long and heavy and his wife was strong and as tall as Noble was himself.

"I'm going then," Noble said quietly, searching his wife's face for some clue that she would back down.

"Good," she said quickly. "Go, pack your bags and leave."

Noble took a step towards her; Mary raised the poker again.

"All right then, I will!" shrugged Noble. "I should have done it years ago. This damn farm will never make any money; I should never have married you – I should have gone to Canada with the others, but you fooled me, didn't you, Mary Knighton. Well, you can look after yourself from now on!"

He turned, slammed the door and stormed upstairs.

Twenty minutes later he returned with two large suitcases; Mary was sitting at the table, the two children standing by her. Noble was dressed smartly again – he took his jacket from the back of the chair, put it on, pulled out his wallet and counted the money. He carried the cases to the scullery, before running out the back door to hail Ulick who was passing in his trap. Ulick – a little startled by the shouts – pulled his pony up.

"Noble Ladds, what can I do for you? I ain't got no bread, you know that, don't you," he said with a shake of his head.

"I want you to take some cases up to Raunds station for me," said Noble hurriedly.

"Can't do that," said Ulick, "I ain't goin' that way."

"Oh no," groaned Noble, "I can't carry them all that way."

"I can take 'em to Kimbolton," offered Ulick, "but that won't make much difference."

"Ah, that will do," said Noble, dashing back to the scullery to pick up his cases.

Mary stood in the doorway to the kitchen and said nothing. Noble took a cursory look at his wife and children and left without a backwards glance.

Mary sank down on a chair at the table and looked at the children.

"Where's Daddy gone?" said Jack.

"I don't know, dear," said Mary quietly, ruffling her son's hair.

She rose, cut both of the children another slice of bread and ushered them outside again to play. She took a deep breath, walked to the bottom of the stairs and called up for Molly.

Molly came slowly into the kitchen, her face blotchy with tears and stood in front of Mary, her head slung low.

"You will have to go, Molly," said Mary calmly. "Go and get your things."

Molly started to cry, tears rolling down her face.

"It weren't my fault, Mary, it really weren't; 'e made me," she sobbed. "I'm bin 'appy 'ere, Mary, you know that; I don't want no wages, but please don't turn me out – I ain't got nowhere to go."

"You heard what I said, Molly," Mary said firmly, her voice rising slightly.

"But he made me, Mary, you know what he's like!" begged Molly.

"How do I know he made you?" Mary snapped. "It didn't look like it."

"'E said I couldn't 'ave a job if I didn't; that's what 'e said," Molly snivelled. "You know what 'e's like."

Molly sank to her knees, howling with despair.

"Mary!" Molly pleaded, desperation and anger in her voice. "I bet 'e made you the first time, I bet 'e did! I can count, you know, Mary, and I've 'ad it done to me, don't you remember. I bet 'e made you, din't 'e, Mary? Jack was inside you when you went up the aisle, I know 'e was."

Mary grimaced and said nothing.

"You can't do nuffing about it when it 'appens, can you?" said Molly desperately. "I couldn't; it just happened, it's rape, ain't it, Mary? That's what they call it. Did 'e rape you, Mary, is that what 'appened?"

Molly grabbed Mary's hand, holding it to her tear-stained face.

"Don't throw me out, Mary, I can't go back to Norfampton and that horrible place; you can't imagine what I 'ad to do there – it's 'orrible."

Tears coursed down Molly's cheeks, falling onto Mary's hands.

"Look, Mary, look, you 'ave this," begged Molly, thrusting the two sovereigns into Mary's hand.

"'E gimme them; you 'ave 'em! You 'ave 'em, I don't want 'em, not now any road."

Mary looked at the coins and then back at Molly kneeling in front of her.

"Mary, Mary, tell me it weren't my fault!" Molly begged. "I could do nuffing about it, Mary; don't frow me out, Mary, don't frow me out. I can't go back to Dean, never! Not wiv the boy at Ruby's, it wouldn't be right."

Molly let go of Mary's hands and sat back on her heels. The tears had stopped now but her face was red and blotchy; she sniffed and wiped her hands on her sleeves, looking desperately up at Mary. Mary's eyes were not focused on Molly. She sighed heavily several times, trying to stop herself from breaking down. She could feel Molly's hands winding her fingers around her own as Molly continued to stare up at her. Finally, Molly slowly got to her feet.

"I better go and get my fings," she said dolefully, making her way to the door.

"Molly," Mary said gently, "don't go."

"I'm only goin' upstairs to get my stuff."

"No, I mean don't go," said Mary quietly.

She paused.

"I mean – you can stay."

"You mean it, Mary?" said Molly, her face beaming.

"Yes," said Mary firmly.

Molly sobbed, throwing her arms around Mary's neck and hugging her tightly. Mary raised her arms and hugged Molly back; as she did so the two gold sovereigns fell from her hand and rolled across the stone flags. She pushed Molly back and held her at arm's length.

"I believe you, Molly," she said. "Just sit down for a minute."

Molly ran her fingers through her hair and sat down.

"Now, Molly, Noble has gone; do you understand?"

"Yes, thank God," said Molly.

"If anyone asks you where he has gone you say he's gone to Canada to see his parents and to look for a new life for the family, you understand?" said Mary sternly.

Molly nodded.

"And, Molly, you say nothing to anyone about what went on this afternoon and we never speak about it again, you understand?"

"Yes, Mary, but –" Molly stopped, "but 'e ain't took the 'orses, Mary; I seen from my window."

"Yes, Molly, I saw that; I expect he will come back for them, but we can't worry about that now." She held Molly by the shoulders and looked into her eyes.

"You understand what I've told you, Molly?"

"Yes, Mary, don't worry about me – I'll never let you down, not never, you're bin good to me when no one else 'as."

She stood on tiptoe and kissed Mary lightly on the cheek. Mary smiled weakly.

"Now go and get the children, Molly," she instructed, "and we will tell them the same thing."

Ulick cracked his whip and the pony trotted off up the road towards Catworth.

"What you got in them bags then, Noble?" Ulick asked as they trotted along.

Noble said nothing.

"Where you off to then, Noble?" Ulick said, undeterred.

"I haven't decided yet," said Noble, "but probably Canada."

"You got family over there, ain't you, Noble?" said Ulick, pulling the pony round to the right and stopping at the gate of a long drive.

"What we stopping here for?" demanded Noble.

"I told you," said Ulick. "This is Black Lodge."

"I know that it's Black Lodge," said Noble scornfully.

"I told you, I always make a special delivery," said Ulick with a wink.

"We haven't got to go all the way up there, have we?" groaned Noble.

"It won't take long, 'specially if you do the gates, you see."

"Why didn't you go on the way?" said Noble.

"She ain't 'ome until this time; she works at the Rectory and she don't get away till after dinner," chuckled Ulick.

Noble sighed.

"Come on then," he said, jumping out to open the gate.

Some way up the drive, they reached an old pair of cottages at Black Lodge. Ulick leapt out and scurried across the yard, passing a dog who rushed out of the kennel, only prevented from biting Ulick by the chain around its neck, which tightened suddenly as it reached the end of its length. Noble lit a cigar and waited. Fifteen minutes later, Ulick appeared with his empty basket, the tail of his shirt just visible over the belt of his trousers.

"Very good, Noble, we will be off then," said Ulick contentedly, picking up the reins of the cart and urging his pony on. As they approached Catworth, Ulick's chin dropped to his chest, the reins slipping from his fingers as he fell into a gentle doze. Not one to look a gift horse in the mouth, Noble picked up the reins and drove the trap the extra mile to the station at Kimbolton. As the trap ground to a halt, Ulick woke with a start.

"Where are we?" he said looking from one side to the other confusedly.

"Where do you think we are?" sneered Noble. "Now, Ulick, you wait for me this time."

He leapt from the trap and carried his two bags into the ticket office where he got his bags labelled and dispatched to the Griffin in Northampton. He returned to the trap and set off back to Catworth.

Mary sat in the kitchen of Elgin Farm, silently looking out across the farm. Molly entered, carefully closing the door to the hall so not to wake the children who had just been put to bed.

"As 'e come for the 'orses yet, Mary?" Molly asked.

"Not that I've seen," Mary sighed.

"I'll go to the other room at the top," said Molly. "I'll tiptoe – I won't wake 'em up but I can see all the way down the road."

Molly went back into the hall and up the two flights of stairs to the attic room; moments later she rushed back into the kitchen.

"I can see 'im comin' or someone like 'im," said Molly.

Mary stood up.

"We had better lock the doors, Molly," Mary said.

"There ain't no keys, Mary; there ain't never bin."

"There's bolts though, Molly; you go to the front door, I'll do the back."

The two women secured the doors and stood by the small window in the scullery looking out across the yard to the stables. The barn door squeaked as Noble led Tinker out onto the cobbles and tied him up. He tacked up the horse, before taking a small bucket with some food in it to catch the two ponies that were in the orchard. He looked scathingly around, mounted his horse, dug his heels into its sides and rode off, dragging the two ponies behind him.

Chapter Forty-Eight
Reuben is Injured

Mary decided that despite Noble leaving, her only course of action was to continue running the farm; she had no other source of income and her savings from the sale of Cold Harbour were small. She explained to the rest of the family that Noble had gone to Canada to see his family and to decide if they should all emigrate. Whether they all believed this story she did not know; certainly Aunt Charlotte had reacted to this news with suspicion, but William appeared to take what she had told them at face value and did not ask any awkward questions. Lucy had also responded to the news without querying it, but Mary was certain she had guessed that there was something more to it. Noble had left a lot of debt; the rent had not been paid for the last six months and Mary was forced to go the landlord to ask if she could have sole tenancy and for time to pay. With her natural charm, she had no trouble in getting him to agree to both these requests. There were also outstanding bills at all the local merchants. Mary dealt with these one at a time and was gradually able to get some stability into their farming business, selling the eggs from her chickens and the pigs from the litter earlier in the year.

In early November, Mary was walking back from Thrapston where she had been to the bank to pay in the money from the sales; the frost lay thick on the ground and the day was sharp and clear. She could hear the ploughing engines following her – they were going a bit faster than she could walk and at Obelisk Farm she stopped to let them pass. They did not have a plough with them as they had been pulling out old apple trees from an orchard in Woodford, the last job before they would be laid up for the winter. As the engines passed, a familiar figure leapt down from the water cart to walk along with her, grabbing the reins of the cart horse as he did.

"Reuben, look at you!" exclaimed Mary. "Every time I see you, you've grown! You're much taller than me now; I can remember when you were just a little lad in short trousers."

She leant towards him and ruffled his hair like she always used to; Reuben smiled and smoothed his hair down with his grimy hands.

"Where are you going now?" she asked him.

"Back to the yard for the winter and then we're all laid off," he said.

"Oh, that's hard, Reuben, what will you do?" said Mary.

"I'm got to find a job as best I can. Mother says that she can't afford to feed us wiv nuffin' comin' in; so I'm got to find a job."

"Do you want to work for me?" blurted out Mary. "I can't pay much but it's a job."

Reuben's eyes lit up.

"Oh, I don't worry about the pay as long as I'm got my board and lodge so Muvver don't have to feed me," said Reuben with a wave of his hand.

"When can you start?" asked Mary.

"Soon as you like, I can come over tomorra I fink," said Reuben. "I know 'e's goin' to set us all off when we get the engines back to the yard; I'll come over tomorra like I said and we can get things fixed up."

He grinned at her, threw his cap in the air and caught it.

"I better catch 'em up," he added, watching the engines move further away; he gave the horse a tap on its rump and made off after the engines.

The next day Reuben turned up at nine o'clock and immediately set to work as he had always done; getting the coal, lighting fires, feeding the cattle with Cyril and Dennis and the numerous other jobs that needed doing. They agreed that he would be fed at breakfast and midday and would have a small wage at the end of each week, which he took home to his mother. Initially he walked every day from Dean; a journey which took about an hour and a half each way, but as the nights drew in he decided to lodge overnight in the tack room. As there were no longer many horses, most of the tack was moved into a redundant stable to make room for him. With Molly in the house and more help outside, Mary was able to get away from the farm more often to do some shopping or visit relations and one cold morning she took the opportunity to cycle over to Dean to see Aunt Charlotte.

"Have you heard from Noble lately?" Charlotte demanded, before Mary had even had time to sit down.

"Not for some weeks now," said Mary quietly – her standard reply.

"And where has he gone? You did tell me but I have forgotten," Charlotte said curiously.

"Canada, Aunt Charlotte," Mary replied.

"Yes," said Charlotte, raising an eyebrow, "your brother Henry always talked about Canada, but the poor boy is easily led, you know, my dear."

"Aunt Charlotte," Mary said indignantly, "you mustn't say things like that."

"Like what?" said Charlotte.

"That Henry is easily led," said Mary, frowning at her aunt.

"But it's true, Mary, isn't it?" said Charlotte bluntly.

"I suppose he is a bit," said Mary. "Not like William. How is William? Has he got any lady friends? He will be twenty-three soon, Aunt Charlotte; Henry was married and had children by that age."

"Lady friends!" said Charlotte with a laugh. "He's got no time for them, with all the work he has on. Anyway, I don't know any around here that would suit him; or at least none that your uncle and I think would suit him."

"I know someone, Aunt Charlotte," said Mary suddenly.

"Do you now, Mary, and who might that be?" said Charlotte with little enthusiasm. "I hope she goes to chapel, Mary."

"No, Aunt Charlotte, she goes to the same church that I do," said Mary pointedly. "There isn't a chapel in Bythorn, you know that, and the children can't walk all the way to Catworth."

Charlotte frowned.

"And what is the name of this *someone,* Mary?" said Charlotte disapprovingly.

"Grace. Grace Brawn," said Mary.

"And where does *Grace Brawn* come from? I've heard the name Brawn, I'm sure I have."

"She comes from Woodford," said Mary, warming to her subject. "Her father's a big farmer there; got a big herd of cows and Grace has lots of brothers and sisters, there must be eight or ten of them. She's nineteen, Aunt Charlotte, she is a very good singer and artist, and she's very pretty."

Charlotte looked up at Mary with a little more interest.

"I've heard of the Brawns," she said slowly. "Thomas knows a John Brawn, it must be the same lot. Are they a good family, Mary? You say they go to church?"

"Yes, Aunt, they live right next to the church in a very big farmhouse; I think they own the house and the farm. They farm some of the Bagshot Estate and her father's on the Board of Guardians; I think she said he was the chairman."

Charlotte sat up and put down her sewing.

"How do you know this Grace then, Mary?" she asked, hardly able to contain her excitement.

"I meet her in church, she comes with her uncle and aunt – the Flaxsteads, you know them, Aunt Charlotte?"

"Yes, I know them," mused Charlotte. "And how old do you say she is?"

"Nineteen."

"Hmm," said Charlotte, sitting back in her chair and smoothing down her white hair; she pulled a pin out of her bun and pushed it in again.

"William is coming over to yours next week," she said pointedly. "He has been invited to shoot on the estate: rabbits and hares and one cock pheasant each."

"Yes, I heard," said Mary. "They want Cyril and Dennis to beat and Reuben, I suppose."

"I heard you've got Reuben, Mary," said Charlotte, "a good boy, a very good boy."

She turned sharply to her niece.

"You don't have him in the house though, Mary?" she said suddenly. "I hope not, it wouldn't be right, you know."

"No, he's not in the house, Aunt Charlotte," laughed Mary. "Well, he comes in for meals."

"Well that's enough, Mary, you don't want to encourage them, you know that," said Charlotte firmly.

"Yes, Aunt Charlotte," said Mary, lowering her head to hide her smile.

"I don't expect this Grace will be in Bythorn next week, will she, Mary?" asked Charlotte nonchalantly.

"I wouldn't think so, she normally comes home on the weekend," said Mary, turning with a smile to her aunt: "Do you want me to let you know?"

"No, not yet, dear, but I will make some enquiries and then I will send you a card," said Charlotte importantly, turning back to her sewing.

The shoot day was always highly anticipated as it meant a day off from farming. Cyril, Dennis and Reuben had been up two hours earlier than normal to get round all the milking, feeding and littering before they went off shooting. William had cycled over, his shotgun tied to his crossbar, and had called in at Elgin Farm for some breakfast and to polish his boots, which had become dirty on the journey over. Cyril, Dennis and Reuben were standing in the kitchen watching Mary furiously brushing down William's jacket to make him look smart. The door opened and Henry wandered in.

"Hello, Henry Knighton, what are you doing here?" asked Mary.

"I'm beating," announced Henry, picking up William's cap from the table and putting it on.

"But look at this – Squire Dunmore, eh? We didn't get an invitation to shoot, did we, Cyril? We've got to beat! And how did Squire Dunmore get an invitation to shoot, then?"

He picked up William's cartridge bag and tipped it upside down, the cartridges flooding over the table, rolling off every which way onto the floor. William looked embarrassed.

"Don't look like that, cousin dear," laughed Henry. "I'm only joking. But how *did* you get to shoot?" he added with a wink.

"I met the agent at market," shrugged William. "We got talking and he invited me."

"You mean Wilson or the other one?"

"Wilson," said William.

"He's all right," said Henry. "And who else is shooting?"

William listed the names he knew as Molly and Jack collected the cartridges, putting them back into the bag.

"You should be going," chided Mary, inspecting William for any missed dirt.

William picked up his gun and followed Henry and the others out of the kitchen to join the rest of the guns and beaters.

The shooting day covered a large area of land, and they mainly shot hares. There was a break for lunch, which was taken at the pub at Clopton, before they blanked the area back to Bythorn. The day had gone smoothly, with plenty of shooting for the ten guns, until they returned to within half a mile of the village. The guns, lining several hedges, had their backs to the village and the hares were being driven towards them, many coming through the gate directly in front of them. Lord Vilossa, standing poised halfway up the hedge, aimed his gun towards a hare which had come dashing along the side of the hedge. With the hare in his sights he squeezed the trigger and fired. A howl rose from behind the hedge as the hare pelted away in the direction it had appeared from. On the other side of the hedge Reuben lay flat on his stomach groaning; finally he crawled to his hands and knees and winced. William, who had been standing next to Lord Vilossa and could see his prone figure beneath the hedge line, rushed to his aid.

"That don't arf sting, William," gasped Reuben, staggering to his feet.

"Let's have a look, Reuben," said William, turning him round and pulling up his shirt a little.

"You're just peppered, Reuben; go down to Mary, she'll get them out," advised William. "There's very little blood – you're going to be fine."

Lord Vilossa tottered up, a look of embarrassment on his face.

"I'm so sorry, me boy, don't know how it happened – I was sure there weren't to be beaters behind the hedge, thought I had a clear shot at the bugger. Are you going to be all right?"

"Yes, sir, I'm fine," said Reuben, touching his cap. "I'm going down to Mrs Ladds, she'll get them out."

"Very good, very good," said Lord Vilossa pompously. "I will come and see how you are when we've finished."

He turned to William.

"Come on, Dunmore, we must get in position for the next drive."

Reuben walked gingerly down to the farmhouse, entering through the scullery; he knocked at the kitchen door and went in. There was no one there, but he could see Mary crossing the yard through the door, having just shut up the chickens.

"Reuben, what are you doing back?" she asked him.

"I'm bin shot," said Reuben moodily.

"You've been shot, Reuben? You don't look very shot," said Mary with a laugh. "Where have you been shot?"

"In me back."

"Well just sit down and I'll come and have a look."

Reuben held onto the table and lowered himself into the chair, jumping back up again immediately with a yelp.

"Reuben!" gasped Mary from the scullery. "Does it hurt that much?"

Reuben screwed his eyes tight shut, opening them slowly to reveal a tear in the corner of one eye.

"You're crying, Reuben," said Molly accusingly, having returned from cleaning the front room.

"No I ain't," Reuben hissed, looking worriedly to the door where Mary was returning from drying her hands.

Molly smirked.

"Take your jacket off," Mary ordered.

Reuben slowly removed his jacket, hanging it on the back of a chair.

"Molly, give the fire a poke and put the kettle on," instructed Mary. "We will need hot water. Now, Reuben, turn round and let me have a look. Come to the light by the window."

She led him over to the window, turned him round and pulled his shirt out of his trousers. Reuben yelped again.

"Molly!" shouted Mary. "Come here and hold his shirt up."

Molly rushed over, holding Reuben's shirt to his shoulders and staring at his peppered back.

"Ten, eleven, twelve," counted Mary. "There's a lot, Reuben; some have broken the skin and some haven't. Go and get the tweezers, Molly, from the sewing basket."

Mary looked down towards Reuben's trousers.

"How far down does it hurt, Reuben?" Mary asked.

"I think there's some in the top of me legs," mumbled Reuben.

"Well take your trousers down and we can see," said Mary firmly.

"No, I can't do that," said Reuben in dismay.

"Why not?" said Mary.

"Cos you're 'ere," said Reuben reddening. "I'm bin private all me life and I'm goin' to stay that way." Mary and Molly looked at one another; both simultaneously raising their hands to their mouths to stop their giggling reaching Reuben, who was standing with his head lowered, shaking it gently back and forth.

"Right, take your boots off," ordered Mary.

Reuben bent down, letting out a small moan of pain as he started to undo his boots.

"Now take your braces off, undo your belt and the buttons on your trousers and lie on the table."

"I can't do that," Reuben protested, but with less confidence than before.

"Yes you can," said Mary gently. "You can't get the pellets out yourself, can you, Reuben?"

"No," he said quietly.

"Well do what I say then, Reuben, and quickly. Now get on the table and undo your trousers."

Reuben turned and stared at her, furiously assessing his options; Mary looked back at him, no flicker of embarrassment on her face. He sighed, slipped his braces off, undid the buttons of his trousers and giving another heavy sigh, climbed a chair and manoeuvred himself onto the table, stretching himself out on his front.

"Let's have a look at you," said Mary, pulling his shirt up to reveal a dozen or so pock marks where the pellets had entered.

"Give the fire a poke, Molly – got to keep Reuben warm," said Mary as Molly thrust the poker into the fire of the range.

Mary examined the pellets.

"Now gently pull his trousers down, Molly," instructed Mary.

Reuben's hands flew to his waistband, holding as tight as he could.

"Reuben, take your hands away and let Molly pull them down," Mary ordered sharply.

Slowly, Reuben's hands released their grip – Molly tugged at his trousers.

"I'm never pulled a chap's trousers down afore," giggled Molly.

"Molly!" said Mary sternly.

Molly looked down, biting her lip furiously to stop herself laughing. Mary examined the twenty or so pellet marks running down to the top of Reuben's legs.

"Now we want some hot water, some Dettol and cotton wool and iodine; we've got all those, I think. Oh, and I want a pin. Come on, Molly, look sharp."

The two women sourced the implements necessary and returned to Reuben, who was shivering despite the heat of the fire. Mary, with tweezers in one hand and a pin in the other, started to ease the first pellet from halfway up Reuben's back; Reuben winced and let out a whimper.

"Go and hold his hand, Molly," instructed Mary.

Molly moved to the end of the table, pulled up a chair and took Reuben's outstretched hand, stroking his hair as she did so.

"There, there, Reuben," she soothed, "it's goin' to be all right; Mary won't be long."

A tear rolled down Reuben's cheek onto the table.

"Get me a saucer, Molly, to put the shot in," said Mary holding out the first pellet in her tweezers.

Molly fetched a saucer and extended it towards Mary, the pellets tinkling benignly onto the china. As each pellet was extracted Mary dabbed iodine onto the wound – the iodine fizzed as it met the exposed flesh.

"Nearly all done now," said Mary fifteen minutes later. "Are you all right, Reuben?"

"Mmm," groaned Reuben between clenched teeth.

"Last one," said Mary, dropping the last pellet into the saucer.

Reuben hurriedly started to push himself up.

"No, no, Reuben," Mary said, "you just lie there for a bit while we clean these up."

Mary wiped each wound with the Dettol, dried off the excess with a towel and examined her handiwork. She smacked Reuben playfully on the side of his bottom; Reuben yelped and Molly dissolved into laughter.

"Put your trousers on now, Reuben," Mary said.

Reuben rolled himself onto his side and smiled. Suddenly, the realisation that he was naked hit him. He clumsily hefted himself off the table, pulling his shirt down with one hand and his trousers up with the other. There was a knock on the scullery door.

"See who that is, Molly," Mary shouted.

Molly hurried to the door to reveal Lord Vilossa standing in the doorway; Molly had only seen him at a distance, but immediately realised who he was.

"Is Mrs Ladds in?" Lord Vilossa asked, taking off his cap.

"I'll just go and see, milord, I won't be a minute."

She pushed the door to, rushing back to Mary.

"Mary," Molly hissed in a loud whisper, "it's Lord Vilossa."

"My goodness," Mary gasped, patting her hair and brushing her pinny down.

She looked desperately around the room.

"Look at us," Mary said in exasperation. "He can't come in with the place like this."

She looked worriedly at Molly.

"What shall I do?" Molly asked.

"Oh show him in, Molly, show him in; he's no better than us after all."

Molly trotted back to the door.

"Mrs Ladds says would you like to step this way, milord?" Molly said grandly, leading Lord Vilossa into the kitchen.

"Lord Vilossa – Mrs Ladds," announced Molly.

"Lord Vilossa, how nice to see you," said Mary. "May I apologise for the mess; we have been dealing with some of your wounded game."

She nodded towards Reuben. Lord Vilossa laughed heartily.

"Quite so, my dear, quite so; so good of you. All my fault, you know, what! Yes, all my fault and how are you, me boy? So sorry and all that."

Reuben pulled himself to attention, which seemed to him to be the best thing to do.

"I'm very well, sir," he barked, avoiding eye contact.

"Is he really all right?" Lord Vilossa said dubiously, turning to Mary.

"Yes, sir, he will be fine we took –" she turned to Molly, "how many pellets out of him, Molly?"

"Thirty-seven I counted, Mrs Ladds," Molly said precisely.

"Well I never, well I never; I didn't know they put so many pellets in every cartridge, what!" he guffawed.

Molly looked at him confusedly.

"And what's your name, me boy?" he said, turning back to Reuben.

"Reuben Heighton, sir," Reuben said, stiffening up again and looking ahead.

Lord Vilossa pulled out a smart leather wallet and started to flick his way through the notes inside.

"Now, Reuben Heighton, I am sure you are a good boy if you are working for Mrs Ladds and I have a little something here for you to... um—"

He paused and looked up with an expression of puzzlement.

"To, erm to help with your savings, my boy."

He smiled and handed Reuben a crisp white note. Reuben smiled, and made eye contact for the first time, taking the note.

"Thank you, sir," he said, standing back to attention.

Lord Vilossa turned back to Mary.

"My dear, I can't thank you enough for being so kind and patching this young man up; I won't forget what you have done. And now I must be off."

He nodded and picked his cap up from the table.

"Thank you, my lord," said Mary with a smile. "Molly, please show Lord Vilossa out."

"If you would like to step this way, my lord," said Molly grandly, leading Lord Vilossa out towards the scullery.

At the back door, Lord Vilossa turned, took Molly's hand, placed a coin in her palm and with a wink he left.

"Look, Mary, look what 'e giv me!" exclaimed Molly, rushing back into the kitchen, the shilling outstretched before her.

"Look!" she wondered. "A shillin', a shillin'! What's that for, Mary?"

"Don't you worry what it's for, Molly; you did very well, I'm proud of you," smiled Mary.

Molly grinned and looked over towards Reuben.

"What 'e give you then, Reuben?" she asked curiously.

Reuben held up the note.

"I don't know what it is," he said with a frown, handing the note to Mary.

"It's a five-pound note," she said.

"It's what?" gasped Reuben.

"A five-pound note, Reuben," Mary said again.

"Gor," marvelled Reuben, "I'm never seen one of 'em afore."

He took back the note and examined it carefully.

"You mean that's five whole pounds, Mary?" he whispered.

"Yes, Reuben," laughed Mary.

Reuben stared at the note in his hand, his eyes gleaming in awe.

"Five pounds, eh?" he sighed happily. "I'd get shot again for that."

Chapter Forty-Nine
Horses get Stuck in the Pond

The weeks and months went by and still Mary heard nothing from Noble. She knew that he had gone from the farm to Northampton and stayed at the Griffin, but after that she had no idea. There were no letters or other communications and no one came forward with information of his whereabouts. She assumed that he may have gone to Canada, but she had no address to write to or any other way of contacting him. Since he had often been away on business, at first no one commented, but as the months passed she had difficulty making excuses. Aunt Charlotte had already guessed that he had left for good and told Mary so; Martha and Henry had also put two and two together, but did not talk about Noble openly.

William came to visit Mary regularly, often on his way back from market on Tuesdays. He did not talk about Noble either, not knowing quite what to say. He did, however, help Mary with the farm, advising her on how to manage the livestock and what to buy, although even with his help there was very little profit. Lucy visited on some of her weekends and would either stay with Mary or at the butcher's shop with Aunt Charlotte. She had one more year left of training and then she would have to decide where to go, and although she was still seeing Roderick there was no sign of them getting married.

The early spring of 1908 at Elgin Farm was bitterly cold and the first job every morning was to unfreeze the pumps on the wells and break the ice on the water troughs in the cattle yards. One morning in early February, Reuben went to fetch the two carthorses from the field above the farm to find that they were both stuck in the pond. They had walked in for a drink and had fallen through the ice, managing to freeze themselves to the spot. The frost that night had been hard and throughout the course of the night the ice had thickened around the horses' legs. Cyril and Dennis brought axes and sledge hammers to start breaking the ice around the legs of the animals and Mary and Reuben waded in to help pick up the great horses' hooves, but no sooner had they cleared one and moved to another leg, than the pond froze over again. Both horses were exhausted and cold; the effort of trying to pull their legs from the deep mud at the bottom of the pond had taken its toll on them and their eyes glowed with pain. Mary, exhausted and soaking in the freezing water, instructed Reuben to fetch Henry to help – the four of them would not be sufficient as each leg had to be pulled out one at a time and the big horses were by now incapable of helping themselves.

Henry arrived, bringing men from the village and eventually they managed to get the horses free from the pond. However, the ice was thick everywhere and the great creatures slid to their knees once free of the sucking mud. Mary turned to Cyril, Dennis and the rest of the helpers, who were all shivering violently in the cold, and sent them home to change their clothes and get warm.

"We must give them something to pick them up," said Henry, looking worriedly at the shaking beasts. "What have you got in the house, Mary?"

"Like what?" Mary asked.

"Any whisky or anything like that?" said Henry urgently.

"There's some brandy somewhere," said Mary, turning to Molly who had come out with cups of tea to warm the workers.

"Molly, go and fetch it," ordered Mary. "It's in the sideboard in the front room."

Molly scurried off and Henry turned to Reuben.

"Reuben, go and get some rolled oats and put a little each in a couple of buckets," he instructed.

Molly returned moments later with the half-full bottle of brandy and Reuben with the oats; Henry poured half of the bottle of brandy into each bucket, mixed it with the oats and placed a bucket in front of each horse, who both started to pick uninterestedly at the food.

"We've got to get them up," said Henry, tugging at the closest horse's halter.

The horse refused to move. Henry turned to the other and tried again, but could induce neither creature to move from the ground.

"Go and get a whip, Reuben," he instructed, yanking on the horse's halter again.

"Now, Reuben, grab the halter of that one," instructed Henry, when Reuben returned. "What do you call it?"

"Sharper," said Reuben.

"Right, Sharper," said Henry, moving to pat the great horse's neck, "you've got to get up! Take his head, Reuben."

Reuben pulled at the halter as Henry cracked the whip across the animal's back. It struggled up onto its front feet.

"Go on with you, giddy-up," shouted Henry, cracking the whip again until the horse was finally up on all four legs.

"Molly, lead it in the stable while we get the other one up," ordered Henry. He turned to the other horse.

"What you call this one, Mary?" he asked.

"Caddy," said Mary.

"Caddy," said Henry scornfully. "What a stupid name; now let's have you, Caddy."

He cracked the whip as Reuben and Mary pulled at the halter; Caddy needed less encouragement, having watched her friend being led away, and was soon up on her feet.

"Now get her in the stable, Reuben, and we'll all go and rub them down," said Henry, following Reuben towards the stables.

In the stable the four of them took great handfuls of straw from the floor and rubbed the horses vigorously. Bit by bit, the tremor of cold seemed to leave them; they snorted and turned with more interest to their brandy-infused oats. Mary leant back on the stable door, puffing and surveyed the two animals.

"I think you will manage now," said Henry with a smile. "I need to get home."

"Thank you, Henry," said Mary gratefully. "We couldn't have done it without you."

Henry laughed, doffed his cap and left the stable.

"Come on, Reuben, you must have some dry trousers," said Mary, looking down at Reuben's soaking legs.

"I ain't got none, Mary; Mother washes my other pair each week and they're at Dean."

"Haven't you got anything else to wear then?" Mary asked.

"No," Reuben replied.

"Well I think there is still a pair of Noble's upstairs; let's go inside and Molly can go and look in the chest in our room."

They hurried back into the house out of the cold, Molly appearing minutes later with a very smart pair of jodhpurs with leather inside legs.

"Is this what you mean, Mary?" said Molly sceptically.

"Is that all there is?"

"Yes, there's no more trousers."

"Well they will have to do," nodded Mary. "Here you are, Reuben – go and put those on and if you bring yours back we will wash them. And take that pair of boots in the scullery – no one else is going to use them."

Reuben went off to his room. Moments later Mary could hear hoots of laughter from Dennis and Cyril as Reuben hurried across the yard, his wet clothes bundled in his arms.

"Do I have to wear 'em, Mary?" sighed Reuben, walking into the kitchen.

"Yes, you do, Reuben," laughed Mary. "Yours are sopping – you will just have to put up with it."

The frost and snow stayed well into February, giving way eventually to a balmy summer. William had organised a threshing gang to come to handle the two stacks that Mary had in the yard from the one field of wheat that she had grown that year. Cyril and Dennis stood expectantly awaiting the arrival of the engines, Jack wedged between them, all terror of the engines long forgotten. The engines were arriving from Henry's farm, and everyone could hear the whistle of the engines as they left Brington to make their way to Bythorn.

Molly was cleaning the floor of the kitchen when Mary rushed in to announce the arrival of the gang.

"Aren't you coming out to watch?" she said. "I love the smell of the engines, Molly, don't you? The smoke and the oil; it's so unforgettable."

"I know it is," said Molly grimly, eyes fixed firmly on the mop.

"I'll finish that, Molly; you go and see them," insisted Mary, moving towards her to take the mop.

"No, I ain't goin'," said Molly moodily. "Too many bad memories."

"Of what?" Mary said blithely.

She raised a hand to her mouth and gasped, ashamed at her own stupidity. Molly continued to mop the floor.

"You know; what happened to me when we were threshing that time up on that 'ill at Dean," said Molly sarcastically, "it might've bin a long time ago but it seems like yesterday to me."

She stopped mopping and looked pointedly at Mary.

"I were only fourteen," she cried, "That rotten bastard. But then, you know what it's like, don't you, Mary?"

Mary said nothing.

"There's no turning the clock back when it's done, is there, Mary?" she added quietly.

Molly stared into the fire, her eyes pricking with tears.

"You're right, Molly," said Mary gently. "We can't turn the clock back; what's done is done and we have to get on with it."

"Hmm," said Molly, wiping her eyes, "it were all right for you, Mary, you got married; I didn't, although I wouldn't 'ave been if 'e weren't killed," she added with a grimace.

Molly straightened up, a look of angry determination on her face.

"'E were a rotten bastard and I were glad when 'e got 'is leg in the drum," she continued. "I hope it 'urt 'im and I was glad he died, so there. I know Lucy tried to save 'im, an all, but she's like that; she's a good person – she ain't got no 'ate like what I 'ave."

She gripped the mop tightly, turning back to Mary.

"You know what 'appened, Mary, don't you? Lucy must a told you," she said quietly.

"Yes, I know," said Mary.

There was a knock at the kitchen door; Reuben appeared, grinning from ear to ear.

"'Ave you seen the engine?" he asked.

"Yes, Reuben, you saw me out there, didn't you?" laughed Mary.

"Yes, I suppose I did," he shrugged. "They say can they 'ave a kettle of 'ot water as they ain't lit the fire in the livin'-wagon and they want a cup of tea."

"Very well, Reuben. Just push the kettle off the heat, Molly, it's nearly boiling," said Mary.

"Mornin', Missus Ladds," came a shout from the door.

Ulick barged his way past Reuben into the kitchen, bread piled high in his basket.

"You'll be wantin' more bread today by the look of all what's goin' on 'ere this mornin'," he said loudly.

"Yes, Ulick, we will," agreed Mary. "Reuben, you nip out and ask them how many loaves they want and the kettle will keep till you get back."

Reuben spun on his heel and clattered out of the scullery.

"S'pose you want a cuppa tea, Ulick?" said Molly, watching Ulick make himself at home at the table.

"If there's one going, my dear," he said, taking the loaves from his basket.

"Six," he counted. "Is that going to be enough? I've got more if you want."

"Just wait till Reuben comes back, Ulick," said Mary, pulling out a wooden spoon to make a start on a cake, which she had forgotten in her excitement at seeing the engines.

Molly placed a cup and saucer in front of Ulick, added milk and started to pour out a cup of tea. Ulick's hand dropped from his side and made its way towards Molly's backside. Mary hissed and whacked him hard across the knuckles with the wooden spoon. Ulick yelped and grabbed his hand to his chest.

"That 'urt, Missus Ladds," he whined.

"I meant it to," snapped Mary. "And that's not all that will hurt if you don't learn how to behave yourself in my house."

Molly look round in surprise, unsure of what had happened.

"Do you understand, Ulick?" shouted Mary.

Ulick cowered under her furious gaze.

"Yes, Missus Ladds," he said, subdued.

Reuben came back to the kitchen door.

"They want four loaves, they say, Ulick; big 'uns if they can 'ave 'em," he called.

"And I'll have three, Ulick," Mary added.

"I'll go and get another one from the trap when I've 'ad my tea," said Ulick quietly.

"Is the kettle ready?" asked Reuben from the door. "Are you comin' to 'ave a look, Molly? I'll show you 'ow it works; it's a compound engine, you know, nearly new it is, only free years old, 'e says."

Molly hesitated and looked at Mary, who smiled at her encouragingly.

"Go on with you, Reuben," said Molly with a small frown. "I'll come then, an' you show me 'ow it works."

She lifted the kettle from the range and followed Reuben out.

Ulick sat back in his chair and looked at his boots, as Mary pulled out the scales and started measuring ingredients for the cake.

"Heard from Mr Ladds lately?" Ulick said carefully.

"Not at all," said Mary, cracking eggs into the bowl.

"Gone far, 'as 'e?" said Ulick with feigned disinterest.

"Canada," replied Mary.

"His family live out there, I seem to remember," Ulick said.

"Yes," Mary replied.

"He'll be back soon, then?" Ulick asked.

Mary pursed her lips and beat the eggs vigorously.

"You going up to Black Lodge today?" she said glibly.

Ulick sat up, discomfort etched on his brow and wilting under Mary's innocent smile.

"I s'pect they will need some bread," he mumbled. "They usually do."

He pulled at his collar and straightened his tie.

"They tell me it takes you a long time to drop two loaves up there, Ulick," continued Mary. "Does it then?"

Ulick said nothing, but started to drink his tea in great scalding gulps.

"I'm seeing Mrs Handly tomorrow, Ulick – I've got to go to Catworth, I always say hello to her in the bakery," said Mary sharply.

Ulick stood up hurriedly from the table and picked up his basket.

"I'll just go and get the other loaf and get out your way, missus," he said loudly, scuttling out the door.

"What's got into Ulick?" Molly asked, walking into the kitchen with the kettle in one hand and an extra loaf of bread in the other.

Mary said nothing, pounding the ingredients for her cake angrily together in the bowl.

Half way through the afternoon, Mary had another visitor – Percy Blinkhorn, who owned the engines being used for the threshing.

"Go and see who that is, Molly," said Mary, hearing the sharp rap at the back door.

Molly opened the door, not recognising the man but recognising the expensiveness of his apparel she gave an awkward little deferential bob.

Percy swept off his bowler hat off and enquired,

"Is Mrs Ladds in, my dear?"

"I'll see, sir," said Molly. "Who shall I say is calling?"

"Percy Blinkhorn," he said.

Molly performed her bob again and rushed into the kitchen.

"Mary, it's Mr Blinkhorn – the man with the engines."

"Ask him to come in then, Molly," said Mary, patting her hair and removing her flour-stained apron.

"Mrs Ladds says would you like to step this way, sir?" Molly said, returning to the door and imitating Mary's voice as best she could.

Mr Blinkhorn followed Molly into the house.

"Gooday, Mrs Ladds," said Mr Blinkhorn, bowing slightly to Mary as he entered the kitchen.

"Mr Blinkhorn, how nice to see you!" said Mary. "I would invite you into the drawing room, but we have not lit the fire and it will be very chilly in there; if you don't mind the kitchen I think we would be more comfortable."

Percy Blinkhorn nodded, the crown of his head gently brushing the low beams in the kitchen. He spread his hands with a smile.

"Please, Mrs Ladds, I am most happy to be in here; it is as we would be at my own home, I can assure you."

He sat down in the chair that Molly had pulled out for him, crumpling his huge frame into what seemed an impossibly neat and small posture. His hair was wavy and dark brown in colour, parted down one side and rising up on the other to a ridge, giving the impression of waves about to break. His face was broad and plain and bore the effects of a life working outside.

"Can I offer you some refreshment, Mr Blinkhorn?" asked Mary. "Some tea or maybe a piece of cake – it's freshly made."

"That is kind of you, Mrs Ladds; can I say yes to both?" said Percy with a smile.

"Molly?" Mary said, sitting down across the table from Percy.

"Yes, Mrs Ladds," said Molly, bobbing again and turning to busy herself with kettles, teapots and plates. She placed the cake in front of Mary, handed her a large knife and set the pot of steaming tea next to her.

"Is that all, Mrs Ladds?" she said in her carefully accented new voice.

"Thank you, Molly," said Mary, as Molly bobbed twice for good measure and made her way into the scullery.

"Mr Ladds is away, I understand," said Percy.

"Yes," said Mary, "he's visiting his family in Canada and has been away some time now."

She smiled winningly.

"I expect you have come about your outstanding account, Mr Blinkhorn," continued Mary, "but I do hope to clear it as soon as we have been paid for the wheat. I think that I have sent you two cheques since Noble left, so I hope to have cleared the rest before long."

She broke off, aware that a pleading tone had entered her voice.

"Oh no, Mrs Ladds, it's not that," said Percy with a wave of his hand, "although can I thank you for the cheque and I am sure you will settle, as you say, when the wheat is gone. No, it was about the boy Reuben."

"What about him?" said Mary surprised.

"Well I am a little short of labour for these threshing gangs," said Percy slowly, "and I know I put him off in the autumn, but I would like to take him back on again, right away, if it does not inconvenience you. He's a good boy and I'm sure he will make a driver after the summer; he's got the talent, you know. But I did not want to say anything to him before I spoke to you; I know he likes it here and I don't know how much you rely on him."

Percy sipped his tea, eyeing Mary curiously over the rim of his cup.

"Well I don't know what to say, Mr Blinkhorn," said Mary quietly. "You are right; he is a good boy, honest as the day is long and a hard worker. He's very helpful to us but I can't afford to pay him much, he gets his keep but not a lot else from here; so if you can pay him he ought to go. I know there are lots of mouths to feed back at home in Dean and any extra cash he can take home to his mother would be welcome. We know he loves the engines; he talks of nothing else."

She nodded decisively.

"So I think he must go if you want him, and if he wants to go of course."

"Well, Mrs Ladds, I'll see what he has to say," said Percy with a smile, draining his cup and moving out into the yard to find Reuben.

"Did he say 'e wants Reuben?" said Molly, having shown Percy out.

"Yes he did, Molly," said Mary with a frown, "but you shouldn't have been listening!"

"I wasn't listening – you was talking so loud I couldn't 'elp 'earin'," said Molly indignantly.

Mary waved her hand impatiently to stop Molly's protestations.

"Well you heard what I said, Molly," sighed Mary. "I can't afford to pay him much and he needs the money."

"You don't pay me very much, Mary, but I don't want to go," Molly replied snootily.

"I know I don't, Molly, but I haven't got much and you know you could go if you wanted."

She turned to Molly with a smile.

"And, Molly Webb, where did you learn all this 'yes, sir, no, sir'?" teased Mary. "You talked like a real lady's maid to Mr Blinkhorn and come to think of it to the old lord the other day! Quite gone up in this world, have we?"

"You didn't fink I could do it, did you, Mary?" said Molly with a grin. "It's easy; I just copy you, I can act la-di-da wiv the best of 'em."

"That's good then, Molly," laughed Mary.

"But it ain't good that Reuben's goin'," said Molly with a frown. "'E's lovely, 'e is."

She sniffed and looked at the ground.

"Come on, Molly," Mary soothed, putting her arm round Molly, "he's not going far and I bet he will come over at the weekends."

Mary pulled her close.

"I s'pose I will see 'im then," Molly snivelled.

"Well there's not much of him you haven't seen, is there, Molly?" laughed Mary, tickling her ribs. Molly yelped away from Mary's embrace and giggled, giving Mary a playful smack on her forearm. Mary laughed and moved out into the yard to find the children.

It wasn't until later that evening when the children were in bed that Reuben plucked up courage to come and talk to Mary. He entered the kitchen and stood awkwardly, twisting his cap in his hands.

"Mary?" he said slowly. "Did Mr Blinkhorn speak to you today about givin' me a job for the rest of the winter?"

"Yes, Reuben."

"Well, what do you fink, Mary?" he asked earnestly. "I don't want to go, mind, 'cos I don't want to let you down. I said I would stay till the ploughin' starts and I'll do that if that's what you want; or I'll tell 'im I 'ave to stop 'ere, 'e won't mind."

Mary looked calmly at Reuben.

"But, Reuben, I can't pay you any more than I do already and Mr Blinkhorn can," said Mary kindly. "You love the engines and he says you will be a driver soon. Think of your poor mother, Reuben; just imagine if you could send her some money to help feed and clothe all those brothers and sisters of yours. No, Reuben, if you want to go, you must and we will manage."

"I could come back at the weekends, Mary, and 'elp then?" said Reuben hopefully.

Mary smiled.

"I know you could, Reuben," she said gently. "You are welcome whenever you want. So when does he want you to start?"

"'E said as soon as I like, but we've got to finish the threshing 'ere, so I told 'im I could come next Monday if that's all right wiv you, Mary."

Molly, who was sitting at the table finishing a jigsaw puzzle, sniffed and blew her nose; her eyes looked very red in the light of the lamp hanging from the beam.

"We don't want you to go, Reuben," said Mary quietly. "*I* don't want you to go and Molly doesn't want you to go; but you have to and that's that."

A tear trickled down Reuben's cheek; he brushed it crossly away with his fist.

Mary got up and put her hand on his shoulder.

"Come on, Reuben," said Mary softly, "time you went to bed."

Chapter Fifty
Grace Brawn

It was now over a year since Noble had left and Mary had not heard a word from him. Jack was nearly five now and would go to the school in the village that autumn. In the first week of July, Mary had a letter from Aunt Charlotte; she had written regarding Grace Brawn, deciding she wanted to meet her. Mary wrote back assuring Charlotte that she would cycle over to Dean at the earliest opportunity to discuss how a meeting could be arranged. Finding herself able to do so the following week, she dropped the children with Martha early that morning, and set off for Dean. The hill up into Catworth seemed steeper than ever and Mary got off to push her bike the last quarter of a mile. The sun was high in the sky, but the hill was shaded by the large elm trees which lined the road. As she walked, the rooks took off one by one from the trees, cawing loudly as they rose into the sky on the warm summer breeze. At the crest of the hill she met Ulick setting off on his bread round.

"Good day, Missus Ladds," he said, lifting his cap, "out for the day, are we?"

"Yes, I'm off to see Aunt Charlotte," Mary replied.

"Ah and Thomas my landlord, no doubt?" said Ulick with a deferential nod.

"I didn't know Thomas owned your place, Ulick," Mary said, surprised.

"Yes, 'e has done ever since he were left it by his father, who were left it by his father, who he got from 'is wife who were a Catworth lady."

"So," said Mary with a small laugh, "you learn something new every day."

"Shall I leave any bread, Missus Ladds?" Ulick enquired.

"Three, Ulick, just put them on the kitchen table," instructed Mary.

"Young Molly there, then?" he said.

"No, she isn't," Mary snapped. "You remember what I said, Ulick."

Ulick recoiled hastily and snapped his whip at the pony, making a hasty retreat. Mary shook her head angrily and remounted her bicycle; the rest of the way was flat, so she was soon in Dean.

In the shop, Aunt Charlotte sat at the desk, writing in a ledger from a small notebook: adding up the columns of figures at the side of each page.

"Mary, I'm so glad you have come," she said gladly, throwing down the pen in disgust. "I am fed up with doing this; William's writing is so bad it's very difficult to read what he has put, I have to guess half the time."

She rose from the stool.

"Come on, dear, let's have some tea."

She closed the ledger and led Mary into the kitchen.

"Sabine," she called, "put the kettle on!"

She turned confidentially to Mary.

"We've got a new girl, you know; Sarah left to go back home and get married – this one is a real dolt." She lowered her voice: "Nothing between her ears except bone, that's what Thomas says."

Sabine bustled in, tripping up the step from the scullery as she did so, but managing not to drop the kettle. She was short and plump and can't have been much over fourteen Mary thought. She had a pleasant face, with rosy cheeks but her most noticeable feature was that she was cross-eyed.

"Hello, Sabine," said Mary.

There was no answer; Sabine was concentrating hard on lifting the kettle onto the range, which was a little high for her and the kettle was very full.

"Say hello to Mrs Ladds, Sabine," said Charlotte, as Sabine managed to push the kettle onto the hot-plate.

"'Ello, Mrs," said Sabine distractedly, turning and fixing one eye briefly on Mary.

"Mrs Ladds," corrected Charlotte.

"Mrs Ladds," parroted Sabine, shuffling back out of the kitchen.

Charlotte shook her head despairingly.

"I don't know what we are going to do with her, I really don't; you can't get anyone good these days, you know, Mary."

She sighed heavily.

"Of course you have Molly, don't you; she's all right, isn't she?"

"Yes, Aunt Charlotte, she's very good," said Mary. "And I don't have to pay her too much, thank goodness."

Aunt Charlotte nodded approvingly.

"Now sit down, dear, have you heard anything?" Charlotte's question was very direct and Mary assumed it referred to Noble.

"No, Aunt," said Mary.

"I didn't think you would have," said Charlotte, raising an eyebrow. "Now, dear, what about Grace? I have done some investigations and all reports are good, so I must meet her and I must meet her soon in case there is other competition; you never know who might be looking for a wife."

"Exactly, Aunt," agreed Mary, suppressing a smile. "Why don't I invite her for tea and you can come over as well. She is often over at the weekend and I have got to know her quite well now; she's a lovely girl, she really is. There's a big family of them; she's got four sisters and four brothers I think, but one of the brothers was born blind."

"Yes, Mary, your information is the same as mine," nodded Charlotte wisely.

She leant forward and whispered.

"I got Thomas to ask when he was at the market."

"Does William know about her, Aunt Charlotte?" Mary asked.

"Oh no, my dear, I don't worry him about such things. He spends all his spare time playing cricket in the summer and shooting in the winter, so he has no time for girls."

"But what will he say if he finds out that you are arranging things for him?" asked Mary incredulously.

"Don't worry, dear, he won't know – as long as you don't tell him," added Charlotte with a severe frown.

"Aunt Charlotte," Mary said indignantly, "as if I would! I don't know how you could think such a thing."

"Very well, my dear," said Charlotte contentedly, "you make the arrangement, Mary, and let us know the date; but it *must* be a Saturday – we are too busy the rest of the week, and it would not be suitable to meet on a Sunday what with chapel to go to."

Aware that her visiting time was over, Mary bid her aunt goodbye and made her way to The Hall. She cycled to the back door and entered the kitchen, where Dorcas was making pastry. On seeing Mary, Dorcas clapped her hands over the mixing bowl to rid herself of the flour, wiped them on her apron and rushed forward to embrace Mary.

"Miss Mary, how lovely to see you – it really is! Miss Verity has been so looking forward to your visit."

She frowned slightly.

"But you should have come to the front door – not in this way," she scolded.

"Do you remember the first time I came, Dorcas?" laughed Mary.

Dorcas blushed and squeezed Mary's hands gently as Verity came rushing into the kitchen. She smiled delightedly, offering her hand out, before thinking better of it and raising her arms to give Mary a very quick hug.

"Mary, it's so lovely to see you," she exclaimed. "Come on, let's sit in the garden – you can stay for some lunch, I hope?"

"Yes, the children are at Martha's so I've got time," replied Mary.

"Dorcas, we will be on the veranda – can you serve lunch out there?" instructed Verity. "Oh and, Dorcas, we will have some wine, white, I think – get Walter to open a bottle."

Verity and Mary walked round the garden for a while, chatting and throwing a ball for the dog before sitting down in the shade under the veranda.

"Mary," said Verity earnestly, "have you heard from Noble?" She waited momentarily for an answer before hurrying on: "Forgive me for asking – you might not want to talk about it."

Mary composed herself.

"No," she said quietly, "I've heard nothing since he left."

"Dorcas tells me that Noble stayed with her brother Edwin for a while before he left. Apparently he sold the three horses he had with him and told Edwin that he was going to Canada."

"Yes I know that," said Mary. "His family are in Canada."

"So do you expect him back?" asked Verity.

Mary thought for a while.

"At first I thought he might, but as time goes by I think it's not so likely."

"So what will you do, Mary?"

Mary shrugged, turning the wedding ring distractedly round on her finger.

She looked back at Verity.

"I don't know," she sighed. "I do know I won't keep the farm if he doesn't come back within the year. I'll sell up; I'm not going to be a farmer all my life."

She gave a small laugh.

"It's not very ladylike, is it?"

Verity was quick to answer.

"I think it should be possible for women to do what they want; no matter if they want to be farmers, or judges or doctors. Men do all the best things and it should be possible for women to do them too."

She was silent for a moment, before adding with a small smile,

"But I agree, Mary, being a farmer is not very ladylike; I know what you mean – it's more for the clodhoppers of this world."

Mary raised an eyebrow.

"William's not a clodhopper and he's a farmer."

"You're right, Mary," said Verity, changing her mind again, "that theory doesn't really hold water when you take him into account."

She sighed happily.

"Thank goodness for William, he keeps me afloat. He's a tenant of ours now – but who knows for how much longer," she explained, "he always pays the rent on time, which is more than most of them do."

"But the prices are so bad, Verity," protested Mary. "It's difficult for people."

"I'm sure," said Verity with a shrug. "But now, Mary, to other things – a glass of wine, how about that?" She rang a small bell that was on the table.

"I didn't think you approved of drink, Verity; what's made you change?" laughed Mary.

"I still don't really approve, Mary, you're right," said Verity slowly. "But at Oxford we drank; well at least, all the men did—"

Mary lowered her head and suppressed a smile as Dorcas wandered over with a silver tray which bore two glasses and a bottle. She placed down the glasses and poured the golden liquid into each of their glasses.

"Mary, you smoke, don't you?" said Verity sharply.

"I do sometimes."

"Dorcas," shouted Verity at the servant's retreating figure, "bring Father's cigarettes, can you, there's a dear, and the lighter?"

Dorcas was back moments later bearing a silver cigarette box and matching silver lighter, which she put on the table.

"Now, Mary, if you would like a cigarette, you have one. I think that it's a disgrace that people frown on women smoking; why shouldn't we smoke if we want to? That's what I say, don't you agree, Mary?"

"Yes, Verity," said Mary.

"Well have one then, you *must* have one – just for me."

"Don't you want one then, Verity?"

"No, I'm sorry, Mary," said Verity with an embarrassed smile. "I did try, but they make me sick; it was *most* embarrassing and I was trying to be so elegant," she added a little sadly.

Mary opened the case and took out a cigarette which she tapped on the box and lit from the lighter. She took a deep breath, puffing the smoke up into the midday air. Verity watched intently.

"Mary, that was wonderful," she sighed. "You look so sophisticated when you do that; I am hopeless and always was hopeless, you know that."

Mary took another puff at the cigarette; she found the smoke and wine were making her feel slightly faint and the sensation was provoking memories that made her uncomfortable.

"Are you all right?" asked Verity. "You look a little vacant, Mary."

"I'm fine," smiled Mary, the feeling subsiding.

She picked up a book from a small pile lying on the table.

"Now, what are you reading, Verity?" she asked.

She scanned the title.

"*The RSPCA, a Short History*," she read out, looking up at her friend. "You are a keen supporter of this, aren't you, Verity?"

Mary flicked open the first page and a photograph fluttered out from between the pages. Verity leant violently forwards as Mary picked the photo up, snatching it from Mary's hand, but not before Mary had seen the picture of a handsome young man in military uniform.

"Verity," gasped Mary, "Verity, who's that?"

"Oh, it's no one important," insisted Verity, tucking the photograph into the next book in the pile.

"Verity, you're not telling me everything! Who is he and where did you meet him?" demanded Mary, grabbing Verity's hand. "Come on, tell me!"

"Aha," boomed a voice from the door of the house, "the lovely Mrs Ladds! My dear, what a pleasure it is to see you."

Mary turned to see John at the French windows; he indicated for Walter to wheel him up to the two girls, where he grabbed Mary's hand and kissed it enthusiastically.

"Walter says he opened a bottle of wine so I've come to help you finish it, what, eh?"

He looked up at Walter.

"Glass," he said to Walter, who stomped off to fetch one.

"I don't know if I approve of ladies drinking on their own and look," he said pointing to Mary, "smoking as well! What is the world coming to?"

He winked at Mary out of sight of Verity.

"Father, how could you?" Verity exploded. "Mary is our guest; of course I offer her a drink and a cigarette in the same way that you would when you entertain your friends. You know my views, Father."

"Yes, dear," said John with another wink at Mary.

"I asked Mary to smoke to make my point clear," continued Verity.

"Yes, dear."

"And we are just having a drink before lunch and why shouldn't we?" rebuked Verity. "I don't know why you are always so old fashioned, Father; it really is trying."

"Yes, dear," John sniggered, before shouting: "Where's my glass then, Walter?"

"Comin'," said Walter, returning with the glass.

"Pour me a glass then," John instructed, winding his finger round and round in a circular motion until Walter had filled the glass to the brim.

"Your good health, my dear," he said, raising his glass to Mary.

She lifted her glass in return as John looked down at the books on the table.

He reached forward and plucked one from the table top.

"*Women's Social and Political Union*, hmm," he murmured, opening the book.

"Pankhurst," he declared, putting the book down and turning to Mary.

"Do you belong to this union, Mary? I bet you don't, you're too busy keeping the wolf from the door, I bet eh?"

"No, I don't," said Mary, "but I do agree with the *principle* of votes for women; I read about it in the papers."

"Quite right too," agreed Verity.

John raised an eyebrow.

"Now I'm not stopping," he murmured, drinking his glass of wine down in one large gulp.

"Don't let us drive you away, Father," said Verity with little conviction.

"No, dear," said John, "you're not; I'm going out to lunch with old Allibone if the motor will start, eh, Walter?"

He turned and raised an eyebrow at Walter.

"It will start, sir," Walter assured him. "Don't you worry!"

"Right, let's go and see then," said John, raising his cap as Walter pushed him away.

Dorcas arrived to lay the table, as Verity left to put the dog in her kennel while they ate. Dorcas banged a bottle of yellow-green liquid onto the table.

"Holive hoil, Miss Mary!" she said incredulously. "'Ave you ever 'eard of such stuff? You're 'avin' salad, you know – not a proper meal – not to my thinkin', any road."

She lowered her voice.

"Got all these ideas when she were in France, you know," she whispered, shaking her head slightly.

Verity made her way back to the table, stopping to survey the layout critically.

"Vinegar, Dorcas," she tutted, "there's no vinegar."

"Very good, Miss Verity," said Dorcas, with a pointed look at Mary as she made her way slowly back to the kitchen.

"Who's the man in the photograph, Verity, you still haven't told me? Where did you meet him?" prompted Mary, keen to find out the identity of the man.

Verity looked down at her food.

"His name's Maurice and I've never met him," said Verity quickly.

"What do you mean you've never met him?" laughed Mary. "How did you get his photograph?"

Verity raised her eyes slowly to Mary, took a surreptitious look around the garden and lowered her voice.

"Promise you won't tell anyone if I tell you?" she whispered.

"Of course not," said Mary. "Anyway who would I tell? I don't mix in the same circles as you do, Verity."

"Oh don't say it like that, Mary, it's unfair," said Verity, stung. "I'm not a snob and I think of you as a real friend, not like all the people I am forced to meet."

"I'm sorry, Verity, I didn't mean any offence," soothed Mary, before adding, "but it's true, we're not from the same background, are we?"

"No," conceded Verity, "we aren't; but I must tell you about Maurice, Mary, I am desperate to tell someone and a lot of my friends don't approve of men – well, you know what I mean—"

Her voice trailed off.

"Go on then," urged Mary.

Verity took a deep breath.

"Maurice is the brother of a friend who I was at Oxford with and he is in the army. He's in India and she asked me if I would write to him because he gets very lonely and there are no English girls out there. I've been writing for over a year now; I write every month and he writes back. He sent me this photograph and I sent one of me."

Suddenly, without warning Verity started to cry; the tears rolled down her cheeks as she looked at Mary miserably.

"Verity, don't cry," pleaded Mary, jumping up and putting an arm around her friend. "Verity! Why are you crying?"

Verity sniffed and blew her nose.

"Sorry, Mary, I never cry; I shouldn't, should I?" she said tremulously.

"So why are you so upset?" asked Mary.

"Because, Mary, Maurice last wrote that he was moving north," Verity sniffed. "That's where they are fighting and he will be in the thick of it. They've been doing training with machine guns – just imagine! Machine guns! Doesn't it sound awful?"

Verity sighed, sat back in her chair and threw her head back to look at the sky. For a moment she was still, then she slowly sat up again.

"I do hope he's not hurt, Mary; just tell me he won't be hurt, I've never met him but I feel know him so well, he writes lovely letters."

She took Mary's hand.

"Mary, I think I'm in love with someone I have never met, isn't that silly?"

"No," said Mary firmly. "Verity, it's not silly and I'm sure he won't get hurt; it's not a real war, is it? William told me, he said that he had read about it – he told me it's only skirmishes."

Verity sighed and smiled weakly at Mary.

"I'm sure you're right, Mary, and he comes home on leave in October, so maybe I will meet him."

She released Mary's hand as Dorcas made her way slowly back towards them, banging a jug down on the table.

"What's that?" asked Verity with a sniff.

"Vinegar," said Dorcas with a frown. "You said you wanted vinegar, din't you?"

Verity picked up the jug and sniffed it.

"That doesn't smell like the vinegar in France. What did it say on the label, Dorcas?"

"It didn't say nothin'."

"What do you mean it didn't say nothing?"

"I mean what I said!" growled Dorcas. "It said nothing. We ain't got no vinegar – so I poured that out of a bottle of pickled onions and that ain't got no label on it 'cos I put 'em in it; I can see there's onions in vinegar so that's vinegar, ain't it?"

Verity shrugged wearily.

"Yes, Dorcas, thank you."

That evening, having returned home in the afternoon, Mary sat at the kitchen table with writing paper, a pen and a bottle of ink, trying to work out what to write to Grace.

"What are you finking about, Mary?" asked Molly, looking up from her jigsaw puzzle.

"I'm thinking what to put in my letter," said Mary, sucking the end of the pen.

"Who you writin' to then?" Molly asked. "I shouldn't ask that, should I? It's bein' nosy, ain't it?"

"Oh I don't mind, Molly," sighed Mary. "I'm writing to Grace, you know the girl that comes to stay at Dingy Farm."

"Yes I know 'er, she's always in church when we go, ain't she? Comes from Woodford or somewhere like that."

Mary nodded.

"I'm going to invite her to tea when Aunt Charlotte and Uncle Thomas come over."

"We ain't see them for a long time, 'ave we, Mary?" admitted Molly.

"No, they haven't been over this year, that I can remember," agreed Mary.

She looked back down at the paper, absently writing her address in the right-hand margin.

"Mary?" said Molly, still looking for pieces of the jigsaw.

"Yes, Molly?"

"Is Williyum coming?"

"Not this time, Molly."

Molly stared intently at the jigsaw, her tongue poking a little way out the side of her mouth, furiously concentrating on the picture in front of her. She frowned and looked up at Mary.

"Mary?" she said again.

"Yes, Molly."

"I've worked it out."

"Worked what out?"

"Why your Aunt Charlotte and Uncle Thomas are coming over."

"Why's that then, Molly?"

"They're looking for a wife for William, aren't they, and they're comin' to see if Grace's suitable; ain't I right, Mary? I bet I am."

"Hmm," said Mary, focusing on the letter more determinedly than before.

"She would have to be all right for your Aunt Charlotte, Mary," continued Molly. "She's very particular, ain't she? She would make sure this Grace said her prayers every day and she would 'ave to go to church every Sunday at least once, or even better, chapel."

Molly shook her head and bowled on.

"But Grace don't go to chapel, Mary, she goes to church – that will be a black mark."

She put two more pieces in the puzzle and smiled contentedly. Mary looked up from the letter.

"What do you think of Grace then, Molly?" she asked.

"She's lovely," smiled Molly. "Do anythin' for anyone she would, a bit scatterbrained at times but that's all right and she's quite pretty, ain't she?"

"And who do you think would make a good wife for William, Molly?" Mary asked interestedly.

Molly didn't hesitate.

"Me of course," she declared, standing regally and posing as if she were a bride.

Mary laughed.

"I'm the right age and I am quite pretty, aren't I, Mary? I can read and write and I can speak all posh now I'm copied you, Mary, but—"

Molly paused, a mocking smile playing on her lips.

"But I ain't a maiden, am I, Mary? That wouldn't' do for William Dunmore Esquire, would it?"

Mary did not answer, but folded her finished letter and slid it into an envelope, before addressing it and thumbing through her writing box to find a stamp.

"You know who I'm goin' to marry, don't you, Mary?" said Molly, looking up from the puzzle again.

"No, Molly, who?"

"I'm goin' to marry Reuben; but 'e don't know it yet. He's lovely. Don't you fink he's lovely, Mary?"

"Yes he is but he's not old enough – he's only sixteen and you've got to get him to ask you, Molly," said Mary with a small laugh.

Molly put the last piece into the jigsaw and sat back.

"That won't be difficult," Molly said. "I know what men like; any road, you got Noble to ask you."

"Molly," snapped Mary, "that's none of your business."

"Sorry, Mary," cried Molly, aghast, "I didn't mean it; it just come out, I din't mean it, 'onest."

Mary frowned and left Molly sitting dejectedly at the puzzle.

The day of the tea party was set for the next Saturday; Grace had written back saying she would be pleased to come and asked if she could bring her brother who was going to be over as well that weekend. The front room was spick and span; sandwiches had been cut and cakes made and the two children were dressed in their Sunday clothes. Charlotte and Thomas had arrived early to avoid any chance of arriving after Grace.

"What's the name of this bruvver of Grace's, Mary?" asked Molly curiously.

"Carvell, she says in the letter."

"Wonder what 'e's like, then?" said Molly with a grin.

"Molly, stop it, all you think about is boys," scolded Mary.

Molly looked down but continued to smile.

"Here they come," Mary exclaimed suddenly, watching Grace and Carvell driving up in a trap.

"Molly, get Dennis to come and deal with the pony for them and then lead them through the kitchen into the front room."

Molly scurried out to shout at Dennis before rushing back to open the door for the visitors.

There was a knock at the front door.

"Molly!" Mary shouted.

"Coming, Mrs Ladds," said Molly, haring down the corridor to open the front door.

"What's come over her, Mary?" whispered Charlotte. "She's lost all her accent, she really has come on."

Mary laughed.

"She's not like that all the time, Aunt Charlotte, but she *has* come on, yes; she says that she copies me."

"Quite right, my dear, I'm sure you are a very good example to follow," said Charlotte wisely.

Charlotte hesitated, before adding in a pointed whisper,

"Have you heard from Noble, Mary?"

"No, Aunt," Mary replied impatiently, making her way out of the kitchen to the front door.

Molly opened the front door to reveal Grace and Carvell standing on the doorstep. Grace was wearing a plain coloured dress with a rose pinned just below the collar and a straw boater with a striped ribbon round it. Carvell, who had his hand resting lightly on Grace's forearm, wore a suit with a collar and tie, plus-fours with woollen socks and highly polished brown shoes. He took his cap off to reveal blond hair and a strong, good looking face, but where Grace's eyes were bright and engaging, Carvell's were opaque and grey; there was no pupil or iris to be seen. He blinked rapidly, holding his head back just a little, looking upwards and slightly to the side as if he were listening.

"Miss Brawn, Mr Brawn, would you step this way?" said Molly grandly. "Mrs Ladds is expecting you."

She led them into the front room, Grace guiding Carvell and whispering, "Step," as they crossed the threshold of the door.

Molly stood to one side and announced,

"Mr and Miss Brawn; Mrs Ladds."

Mary came forward and shook Grace's hand and then Carvell's. Thomas rose and shook hands with both guests, but Charlotte determinedly stayed put, her large black hat casting a forbidding shadow over her face. Grace moved forward to her, shook her hand and guided Carvell in her direction so that he might do the same. Charlotte continued to eye Grace critically as the six of them drank their tea, but Grace's assured recitation of all the books of the Bible soon thawed Charlotte's icy countenance and by the end of tea the fact that her family went to church rather than chapel was a minor consideration.

Grace stayed for an hour, before asking if she might take Carvell for a walk round the village, asking if perhaps the two children might like to come with her. Ethil and Jack seemed delighted by the opportunity to leave the stuffy atmosphere of the front room and skipped happily out of the house, Ethil holding tight to Grace's hand, and Jack to Carvell's.

"Well, Aunt Charlotte, what do you think?" asked Mary bluntly, as they watched the small procession walk down the drive.

"What a splendid girl, Mary, really splendid," uttered Charlotte with a degree of fervour. "Now all we have to do is to get William to think the same; that's right, Thomas, isn't it?"

"Yes, my dear, she would make a perfect daughter-in-law, but will her father approve of William, we must think of that, you know."

"Why would he not approve of William?" cried Charlotte indignantly. "I've never heard such rubbish! William is a fine young man, a good catch for a girl, don't you agree, Mary?"

"Oh yes, Aunt Charlotte, I am sure you are right," said Mary with a smile.

"Very well then, let's hear no more of this approval business and get them introduced."

"Leave that to me, Aunt Charlotte," said Mary.

Chapter Fifty-One
Bath Time

It was now over eighteen months since Noble had left and it was becoming increasingly difficult to explain his absence. Mary decided that the only person who might know what had happened to him would be Adelaide Harding after seeing them together at the County Hotel; so she wrote to Rebecca asking if she could visit. If she were to give up the farm, which she had been struggling to make money from, she did not want Noble returning and causing trouble after the decision had been taken. She also decided to tackle Molly to see if she knew any more; many of his work trips had taken him to Northampton and she knew that Noble had been on friendly terms with Edwin and Lizzie.

The day before she was due to go Northampton, she sat Molly down in the kitchen to question her. Molly was nervous, unsure why she had been summoned; she looked up apprehensively as Mary sat down opposite her.

"Now, Molly, you know I'm going to Northampton in a couple of days," Mary started, "I'm going to see if I can find out where Noble has gone."

Molly said nothing, but started to fiddle with a loose thread on her apron.

"I'm going to see Adelaide Harding because I think she was friendly with Noble," continued Mary. "Do you know who I mean, Molly?"

Molly continued to fiddle with her apron.

"Yes, I know her," she said slowly.

"How did you know her, Molly?" asked Mary, surprised.

"She used to come in the pub, din't she; she used to say she were born there."

"And was Noble ever there as well?" Mary prompted.

"Sometimes 'e was," she shrugged. "I s'pose 'e was quite a lot and—"

She broke off and stared helplessly at Mary.

"And what?" said Mary.

Molly squirmed in her seat and said nothing.

"*What*, Molly?" Mary said severely.

Molly swallowed hard, fighting to find the right words.

"He used to 'ire a room off of Edwin and go upstairs," she said quietly. "They were up there when you come to see me that time."

"Oh my God!" exclaimed Mary. "Why didn't you tell me before?"

Molly shifted uncomfortably and spread her hands.

"You din't ask me afore," she said. "And any road, 'e said 'e would do sommat dreadful if I ever told you."

She looked desperately at Mary.

"'E frightened me, Mary; 'e really did and when 'e went I just 'oped 'e would never come back and – and ..."

Molly started to whimper, wringing her hands.

"I din't know what to do, Mary," she finished feebly.

Mary sighed heavily, and put a hand over Molly's.

"I know, I know," she said quietly. "What did Edwin say about it?"

"'E din't say nuffing – just took the money; 'e knowed 'im quite well though, you could tell that."

"And what about Adelaide?"

"She were all dressed up like a dog's dinner – acted like she come out the top drawer; but she din't, I know that much."

Molly shook her head angrily and looked away.

"Molly, you know you mustn't tell anyone about this; no one, or—"

Molly held up a hand and looked squarely at Mary.

"I know, Mary, you've bin good to me," she interrupted. "I shan't tell no one, you can be sure of that."

"Good," said Mary quietly.

"But, Mary, what if you do find where 'e is? What you goin' to do then? I fink you're goin' to get rid of the farm, ain't yer?"

"I don't know, Molly," sighed Mary. "I want to make sure where he is, so I'm prepared if he comes back."

"What will I do if you give up the farm, Mary?" cried Molly. "I ain't got nowhere to go; you know that."

"Molly, don't worry about that yet," said Mary with a laugh. "I haven't given up the farm yet."

She looked at Molly earnestly.

"But I don't want to be a farmer all my life!" she said gently. "You can understand that, can't you?"

Molly chewed her lip pensively and nodded.

That night was a bath night. Molly had fetched in the tin bath and heated the copper and the kettles on the range; the curtains were drawn against the black of the frosty night and all the doors to the kitchen were shut. After the children had been bathed and dressed in their nightclothes, they were put to bed and Molly, having topped up the bath with hot water, hung her towel by the fire, undressed and slid into the bath. Mary was sitting by the stove reading the Bible; she raised her gaze and marked her page, turning to Molly.

"Molly, I've been thinking," she said, looking down at the Bible in her hands.

"Yes, Mary," said Molly, swishing the water over her white skin.

"When you were in the pub in Northampton—"

She broke off, turning over in her mind what she wanted to say.

"What about when I were in the pub?" said Molly levelly, turning her head to look at Mary.

Mary put the Bible on her lap and wound her thumbs round one other, first one way and then the other, watching them intently.

"When you were in the pub, Molly, did you go upstairs with people?" Mary asked. "Men, I mean?"

Molly stopped swishing the water and turned away from Mary, looking down into the murky water. She shut her eyes tightly, sobbed once very quietly and rubbed her nose with her fist.

"Yes, I did," she admitted quietly. "But it's not like what you fink."

She sniffed again.

"I din't want to do it – there were no choice; they made me, I 'ad to, it were 'ow it was. I din't get nuffin', they all'as paid Edwin."

Molly stopped and rippled the water again, furiously chewing her bottom lip.

"And I know what you're goin' to ask, Mary; did I go upstairs wiv Noble and no I din't, so there."

She looked down angrily.

"It's all right, Molly dear," said Mary, leaning forward and placing her hand on Molly's shoulder. Molly shrugged it off.

"I know you couldn't help it," Mary continued gently. "I just want to know about Noble, that's all; I know you're not to blame for anything."

Molly raised herself from the bath and grabbed the towel off the chair. She wrapped it round herself and Mary helped her dry her back.

"I didn't mean to upset you, Molly; it's just that I want to know about Noble, that's all," Mary persisted. "You must see that."

Molly looked at her.

"S'pose so," she said grudgingly, "but I din't go wiv him; mind, I fink Lizzie did from what she said."

Mary retrieved her towel and hung it on the chair where Molly's had been, putting the kettle on to boil again.

"Mary," Molly said shyly, standing by the fire wrapped in her towel.

"Yes, Molly?" Mary replied, poking the fire through the bars to get it to burn up and boil the kettle.

"You know in your room you got some powder on the top by where you got your 'airbrush and fings? Don't s'pose I could 'ave a little to put on me? I never 'ad powder afore and it smells nice, I know it does and you could 'ave some too – I can go and fetch it?"

Mary smiled and looked at Molly.

"No, no, I'll go," she insisted. "You'll catch your death up there with nothing on."

"Fanks, Mary," said Molly, as Mary hurried away to fetch the powder. She came back and put the pot on the table.

"Sure you don't mind?" said Molly, reaching for the tub.

"No, go on, Molly; not too much mind, that's all I've got."

Molly shook a small amount of powder over herself and patted her skin; little clouds of white powder puffed into the air before slowly floating to the ragged rug in front of the fire, leaving a dusting of white on the dark mat.

"Come on, Molly, get dressed; your clean clothes are there, then you can put the water from the kettle in when it's boiled."

Mary peeled off her dress and stepped into the bath, pulling her knees up to her chin as Molly poured the hot water from the kettle in at the other end.

"Is that enough?" Molly asked.

"It's lovely," sighed Mary, lying back in the water.

"I'll put some more on just in case," said Molly, filling the kettle from the tall enamel jug and placing it back on the hob. She sat down in the chair by the fire, picking up the tin of powder from the table and sniffing it.

"I like that smell, Mary; what is it?" she asked.

"Lavender, I think," said Mary absently, swirling the water round the bath with one hand. "Are the children asleep, Molly?"

Molly went to the door to the stairs, opened it and listened.

"Can't 'ear 'em," she said.

"Shut that door!" cried Mary. "The draught is enough to freeze me!"

"Sorry," said Molly, quickly pulling the door to. "Can't 'ear them; they must be asleep."

She sat down again and stared into the fire; Mary shut her eyes and relaxed in the warm water.

Suddenly the dog barked; Mary's eyes flicked open and she scanned the room quizzically. Molly sat up straight and went to speak but Mary lifted a finger to her lips. The pair both listened; the dog barked again twice and then was silent.

"Is that someone?" whispered Mary.

"Don't know," said Molly.

Mary pulled herself up in the bath and listened again. There was a knock at the scullery and the latch clicked.

"Bugger," cursed Mary. "Give me that towel, Molly, quickly, come on."

She grabbed the towel from Molly as the footsteps steadily advanced across the flagstones of the scullery. There was a tap at the kitchen door and the latch clicked; Molly jumped in front of Mary, her arms outstretched, as the door opened. The light from the kitchen fell on a dark figure filling the doorway; it was Reuben. At eighteen he was now over six feet tall, with a broad strong body and jet black hair; his face was always tanned and he had red shiny cheeks. He gave Molly a broad smile as he moved into the light of

655

the kitchen.

"Hello, Molly, it's me, Reuben," he said, staring at Molly confusedly. "Don't look so at me, I ain't done nuffing."

"You can't come in, Reuben!" hissed Molly, her voice rising.

"What you mean, I can't come in?" laughed Reuben, taking a step forward and standing up to his full height as he moved from under the low doorway. All of a sudden he caught sight of Mary over Molly's shoulder; clutching the towel to her front, her bare white shoulders glistening in the gloom of the lamplight. Reuben's smile slid from his face in a flash, to be replaced by a look of terror; his eyes widened momentarily and he clapped his hand to his face, closing his eyes tightly shut.

"Oh, I'm so sorry," he cried. "So sorry, Mary – I didn't mean—"

He turned abruptly to retreat, his hand still covering his eyes, hitting his forehead on the half open door from the scullery as he did so.

"Ouch," he shouted, fumbling for the door, which had shut when he had banged into it. Molly turned to Mary, giggling; Mary, with a wicked grin on her face, pulled the towel away from her body with a seductive pout, as Reuben, eyes still tightly shut, continued to fumble towards the door. Both Mary and Molly were now in hysterics, tears streaming from their eyes as Reuben finally found the door, opened it and scurried out.

"Go and fetch him, Molly," Mary gasped. "Don't let the poor boy go; I'll get dressed. Tell him to wait and we will give him a shout."

Molly rushed out.

"Reuben!" she shouted, trotting to the scullery door where Reuben was making his exit, "Reuben, come 'ere! Don't go, you silly thing."

She grabbed his hand and pulled him back.

"Wait 'ere till we give you a shout; Mary says so, see."

Reuben said nothing, his cheeks still flushed crimson. Molly laughed and went back to Mary, who was half dressed.

"I stopped 'im," she said, grinning at Mary. "You ain't put any powder on, Mary," she added, handing Mary the tin.

"Bother," said Mary, taking the tin and pulling her bodice forward.

She shook some powder on her bosom, pulled her bloomers forward and shook some more powder down them, handing the tin back to Molly with a quick laugh as she patted herself.

Mary finished dressing, brushed her hair and helped Molly to empty the bath.

"Where's Reuben, Molly?" she asked finally.

"Standin' in the road, I fink," said Molly with a snort of laughter.

"Go and fetch him then, girl, before he runs off."

Mary put the kettle on once more and gave the fire another poke.

Molly returned, Reuben following shamefacedly behind. As he entered the kitchen he took off his cap, holding it tightly across his chest with both hands. His eyes darted every which way, focusing anywhere except on Mary.

"I'm found 'im," said Molly triumphantly.

"So I can see," said Mary. "And it's very nice to see him; but why do we have the honour of your company on a Thursday night, Reuben?"

Reuben reddened again but said nothing.

"Well?" she asked, looking at him.

"I din't mean to come in like that, Mary, I really din't," blurted out Reuben. "I'm ever so sorry; I really am, I din't know you was—"

He stopped to reform the words.

"I din't know you was –" he stopped again, "you know."

"I know, Reuben," laughed Mary. "But next time don't make it such a surprise."

"Yes, Mary," mumbled Reuben, looking at his cap as he folded and unfolded the peak in his hands. Molly grinned at Mary, who smiled back.

"Come on now," said Mary, "that's enough of that; now, Reuben, sit down and have a cup of tea and tell us why you have come."

Molly looked up at Reuben, took his hand and patted it. Reuben sat, but still said nothing. Molly made the tea when the kettle had boiled, putting the cups on the table with the sugar and a jug of milk. Mary sat at the other end.

"Now, Reuben, tell us why you are here," she instructed.

Reuben looked up at Mary; his eyes were watery and his face was still red.

"'E's set me off for a bit and I'm come to see if you want any 'elp," Reuben mumbled.

"Reuben, you are a dear, we always need help, don't we, Molly, but for how long? When can you start?"

Reuben finally looked at Mary.

"'E says there ain't no more work till we start ploughing the fallow and that won't be till after Easter but 'e says 'e's goin' to make me a driver when I go back."

He smiled proudly.

"A driver?" said Molly. "You ain't eighteen yet, 'ow can you be a driver?"

"Well I am gonna be any road," shrugged Reuben. "I'm nearly eighteen and 'e says I will be the best one he 'as afore long."

Reuben tapped the table once with his knuckles.

"Well done, Reuben; that is good news, you always wanted to be a driver," smiled Mary. "So when can you start back here?"

"Tomorra," Reuben said quickly. "I'm got to go home to see Muvver for tonight, but I can be back in the mornin'."

"I can't pay much, Reuben, but you can have your board and lodging as usual."

"That don't matter," he said. "Mother can't afford to feed me with no money comin' in, so that will be fine."

Molly smiled and clapped her hands delightedly.

"Least we'll 'ave a man about the 'ouse," she said.

She gasped and put a hand to her mouth, horrified by what she had said. Mary pursed her lips and said nothing.

"Sorry, Mary," Molly whispered.

"How are you going to get home, Reuben?" asked Mary.

"Walk," he said. "I'm walked here already, it won't take long."

"Take my bicycle, Reuben; but you must be back by eight in the morning as I have to catch the train."

"I'll be back, don't worry," assured Reuben, jamming his cap on his head and leaving with a grin.

"He's a lovely boy –*man* I mean, ain't 'e?" sighed Molly, as they heard the bicycle rattling out of the yard.

"Yes," agreed Mary with a wry smile. "He's a good man."

Chapter Fifty-Two
Mary questions Adelaide

Reuben was back by half past six the next morning. The children were up, Molly had given them their breakfast and Jack was getting ready for school. Mary was dressed in her Sunday clothes ready for her trip to Northampton; the bicycle had had its tyres pumped up in preparation and was parked by the back door ready for her departure.

"Molly, you know what to do?" asked Mary, fussing with her hat.

"Yes, yes, Mary, you can trust me; I know what to do."

"Reuben, have you seen Cyril?"

"Yes, Mary, don't worry, I've got plenty to do."

"Molly, is my hat straight?" she demanded, whirling to face Molly.

"Let me look," said Molly, "yes, it's fine – now come here, Mrs Ladds, while I brush your coat."

Mary stood obediently as Molly swept stray hairs and specks of dirt from her thick winter coat.

"You be good, you children, do what Molly tells you and I should be back before you go to bed," instructed Mary, turning to leave.

"Yes, Mother," they chimed.

"Reuben, where's the bike?" she asked, doing up the buttons on her coat.

"Outside, Mary, all ready for you."

"What's the time, Molly?"

"It says a few minutes after eight by the clock on the sideboard, but that's a little fast, I think."

"Right, I must go – train's at just before nine and that gives me time to get a ticket."

She rummaged through her bag, took out her purse out purposefully, shook her head and put it straight back again.

"Right I'm off then, bye everyone!"

She smiled in a harried sort of way and rushed out of the door.

It only took an hour and a half for Mary to make the journey to

Wellingborough, where she waited for the train to Northampton. The clouds had cleared to reveal the pale yellow sun, which beat down through the cold and warmed her cheeks in the late winter air. It was ten years since she had stood at that very spot waiting for the train with Verity and Dorcas; how much had changed in that time, she thought. What possibilities had lain before her that day!

"Good morning, Mary," a voice at her elbow shattered her reverie.

It was a man's voice, and one that she instantly recognised, although she had not heard it for some years. She did not turn immediately, instead composing herself and manufacturing a smile to mask her initially alarmed reaction.

"Rupert," she said, turning to look at the speaker, "what a pleasant surprise; I did not expect to see you waiting for the train."

"No, neither did I," smiled Rupert. "I usually go everywhere by motor car now, but it so happens that ours, alas, has broken down."

There was silence, Mary was unsure of what to say, unsure of how to proceed in the situation; she shifted uncomfortably and smiled.

"Are you going shopping, then?" said Rupert. "You were that first time I met you, do you remember all those years ago? You were with that girl from Dean, what was her name?"

"Verity," said Mary, "Verity Watson-Foster."

"Yes, that was it," said Rupert with a small laugh. "Must be ten years ago or so now."

"I suppose it must be," replied Mary with a small frown.

She turned to look at him.

"No, I'm not shopping today," she explained. "I'm going to see Rebecca Harding; you remember her, don't you?"

"Oh yes," said Rupert, "I saw her the other day at the races; she was with Jimmy."

The whistle of the train drew their eyes back to the train track.

"Shall we share a carriage, Mary?" said Rupert.

"I've only got a second class ticket," said Mary, embarrassed.

"That's all I have," smiled Rupert.

"Very well then," said Mary with a forced smile.

She was at a total loss; the last time she had had contact with Rupert was when she had written to tell him she was getting married, and she had never heard from him since. The train slowed up into the station – Rupert opened the carriage door for her and followed her into the compartment. There was already a passenger sitting by the window who looked and smelt like a farmer, cow muck plastering his black hobnail boots and leather gaiters. He lifted his cap to Mary.

"Mornin', missus," he grinned, pulling a cigarette from a yellow packet in his pocket and lighting it. Mary smiled and sat down, gazing out of the window as the train moved off, trying desperately to think what she should say.

"How was South America?" she blurted out finally.

"It was fine," said Rupert with a shrug. "Although a long time ago now, I've been back for nearly two years."

"You're running the paper now, then?" she asked, determined to keep the subject off her.

"Oh no, nothing like that, in fact it's much the same as it was; Father does not want to give up the reins, you know."

There was a pause.

"And your mother?" said Mary desperately.

"She's well, yes very well," Rupert replied.

There was another awkward silence; the farmer took the cigarette from his mouth and tapped the ash onto the floor of the carriage, eyeing Mary and Rupert amusedly.

"You've got a family, Rebecca tells me," said Rupert.

"Yes, I've got two children: a boy and a girl," said Mary in an honest manner.

She looked out of the window, dreading the question she knew was coming.

"And Noble, how is he? Such a good rider as I remember," said Rupert politely.

Mary cleared her throat and started to reply, but the words somehow would not come. She swallowed once and then began again.

"He's – he's well; he's in Canada," she stammered.

"Oh," said Rupert.

Mary looked out the window again, holding her breath, waiting for him to ask what Noble was doing out there, just as many had asked before him. Rupert said nothing; he was evidently having as much trouble as Mary keeping the conversation going. She glanced at him, their eyes meeting briefly before they both averted their eyes in embarrassment. Rupert was now in his early thirties, and still very good looking; he had lost the boyishness that she remembered and a little hair at the front of his head, but it was still fair. She could faintly smell his cologne, a similar fragrance to that which Noble had used to wear. The train slowed to a stop at Wilby, pulling away again with a jerk. Mary concentrated hard out of the window, seeing nothing.

"I've got a friend in Canada," Rupert said quietly, breaking the silence.

"Oh yes."

"He has a paper in Toronto."

"Oh yes," said Mary again, dreading where this conversation might lead.

"He says there are great opportunities out there."

"So I understand."

"Twelve mining railways and all sorts, he says."

"I'm sure," said Mary, twisting her hands agitatedly in her lap.

"Mary?" said Rupert.

"Yes," she replied.

"When I was talking to Rebecca she said—"

He broke off briefly.

"Look, look!" cried Mary, pointing out the window, "See there, some lambs, they would be the first I've seen this year."

She smiled at Rupert, a smile born of genuine relief that he had not revealed that he knew that her marriage was over; she had averted the question and made it obvious that she would not reply to any questions if they were to be asked.

At Northampton the pair shook hands as they went to go their separate ways out of the station.

"Would it be all right if I call to see you?" asked Rupert earnestly. "I am sometimes in Thrapston which is not far away."

Mary looked at him straight, unsure how to respond.

"Well that would be nice," she said after the briefest of pauses, "but you must let me know when you are coming, so I can make sure it is convenient."

Rupert doffed his bowler hat, smiled and walked purposefully away.

At the Harding residence, Violet answered the door, although Mary could see Rebecca behind her, limping towards them up the corridor.

"It's Mrs Ladds, Miss Rebecca," announced Violet, calling over her shoulder to Rebecca.

"Yes, I can see it is," exclaimed Rebecca, barging past Violet and embracing Mary in a tight hug.

"Oh, Mary, it's so good to see you after all this time. You don't know how much I miss you; you look well, how are the children? Violet, bring us some coffee in the drawing room, will you?"

"Yes, Miss Rebecca," said Violet, bobbing.

"And, Violet, take Mrs Ladds's coat."

"And my hat please, Violet," said Mary, handing over her hat. "I hate wearing hats, don't you, Rebecca?"

Rebecca seized Mary's hand and led her into the drawing room.

"Now sit down, Mary, I think I'm going to open the French windows; I know it's only March but it's such a lovely day. We will have to shut them when the old hag comes back but that won't be for a while."

She swung round to walk to the windows, her skirt arcing after her; as she walked, she limped slightly, her skirt giving a small flip as she did so.

"You're limping, Rebecca," said Mary, concerned, "I thought your leg was better."

"So did I; too much horse riding, the doctor said, but I don't take any notice."

She moved back to sit opposite Mary as Violet came in, setting down a tray of coffee on the low table between them.

"Is that all, Miss Rebecca? I must get on with the lunch; there's only me here today, you know."

"Yes, yes, Violet, that will be all," said Rebecca with a wave of her hand.

"Now, Mary, tell me all the news," demanded Rebecca, pouring out the coffee. "Have you heard from Noble?"

She looked at Mary in anticipation.

"You know I haven't, that's why I am here," tutted Mary. "You did read my letter, didn't you?"

"Yes I know, I did read it," said Rebecca, clapping a hand to her forehead as if to wake herself up. "And you want to see the awful Adelaide to see if she knows where he is. Do you think there was something between them?"

Rebecca looked at Mary and waited.

"Yes," said Mary after a while, "I'm sure there was."

"So will you have him back if you find him, Mary?"

"I hadn't thought that far," said Mary with a small shake of her head. "I just want to know where he is and what he's doing."

"You could have another lover, Mary, wouldn't that be exciting?" whispered Rebecca with a wink.

"Rebecca, how could you?" said Mary in horror. "I'm still married and I took vows in church!"

"I know, Mary," said Rebecca disinterestedly, with a wave of her hand, "but I've been reading Mr Engels; he says marriage is a trap for women and that there should be sexual equality. I'm quite sure Noble wouldn't wait for you, why should you wait for him?"

Mary sat stunned, but unable to argue with the logic of her friend. Rebecca barrelled on.

"I joined the Labour Party," she continued lowering her voice slightly, "but don't let Father or Adelaide know, will you, Mary; life is so boring here I had to do something."

She stopped, handed Mary a cup coffee and continued determinedly.

"And I've joined the Suffragettes; you must agree with votes for women, Mary, surely you agree with that?"

"Yes," said Mary, "I agree with that, but I have no time for meetings; I've got a farm to run and children to feed and money to earn, it's not as easy for me, Rebecca."

"Mary, dear, you don't have to say it; I know it isn't. And I've got plenty of money and nothing to do; but that's why I do all these things and I believe in them – votes for women, being a socialist. After all life's not fair for poor people, is it?"

Mary smiled wryly.

"You sound like Verity; she says that."

"Verity, yes I remember her; how is she?" said Rebecca with interest. "She went to Oxford University, didn't she? I wish I could have gone there but I haven't got the brains."

Rebecca sighed heavily and sat back in her chair, staring up at the ceiling.

"Verity is well," said Mary, "or she was the last time I saw her, but I don't think her father's estate is making any money; she says they will have to sell some of it."

Rebecca sat up again.

"I know," she declared, "we will have a cigarette; you smoke, Mary, and I do."

She jumped up and took the silver box from the mantelpiece, offering one to Mary, before taking one herself and lighting them both from a small matchbox. Rebecca drew the smoke into her lungs, puffing out the smoke in pillows of white towards the ceiling.

"I'm going to have to sit down," said Rebecca. "The first puff always makes me feel dizzy; does that happen to you, Mary?"

"It does sometimes," Mary replied quietly.

"Now, Mary," said Rebecca seriously," what will you do if you find Noble?"

"If I can be fairly sure he's not coming back, I'm going to give up the farm and train as a nurse," said Mary firmly.

"Mary, how wonderful," Rebecca exclaimed. "How absolutely wonderful! You will have your own career, not dependent on any man! I think that is splendid, let's hope you don't find him then, eh?" She looked Mary in the eye.

"So what about Adelaide, Mary? What are you going to say to her?"

"I'm going to ask her if she knows where he is," shrugged Mary.

"Are you sure you want to ask her about Noble?" asked Rebecca, taking

Mary's hand. "You never know what lies she will come up with."

"Yes, I must," said Mary firmly. "I must do everything I can to find out what has happened."

"We will wait for the Dragon to return then; I don't think she will be much longer now. Come on, let's walk out into the garden."

Both women extinguished their cigarettes and walked through the French doors into the warm sunshine.

"You will never guess who I met this morning on the train," Mary said, turning to Rebecca

"No," laughed Rebecca, "I'm sure I will never guess, so tell me! Was it a man?"

"Yes, it was Rupert Nelson," exclaimed Mary.

"Mary, you didn't!" said Rebecca with surprise, before turning confidentially to her friend and adding, "You know he's still in love with you, don't you? He always asks after you when I see him and he knows about Noble being away; Adelaide told him, I heard her when we were at the races."

"Yes, I gathered that," Mary replied slowly.

"Well then?" said Rebecca.

"Well what?" said Mary.

"Did you arrange to meet him, he must have asked you to lunch or something?" Rebecca questioned.

"No," Mary said, "nothing like that, he just said he would call at the farm when he comes to Thrapston."

"Well that's better than nothing," said Rebecca. "And did you he tell you, Mary, he's got friends in Canada?"

"Yes, he did," Mary replied. "He said they are in the newspaper business."

"There we are then," said Rebecca. "You must put an advertisement in their paper to find Noble."

At that moment the noise of wheels on the gravel of the drive reached them. Adelaide had evidently returned. Moments later, the front door banged as Adelaide stormed into the hall.

"Violet? Violet? Where are you? Come and take my things at once, and what's that draught? I bet that dratted girl has opened the French windows!

Violet?"

Adelaide marched into the drawing room, flinging her coat, hat and bag into an armchair and striding over to the French windows to bang them shut and bolt them, looking over to Rebecca and Mary walking in the garden as she did so.

"Violet!" Adelaide shouted again.

"Yes, Mrs Harding?" Violet said sheepishly, entering the room slowly.

"Where have you been, girl, didn't you hear me call?"

"Yes, Mrs Harding, I came as soon as I could."

"Well hang my things up," ordered Adelaide.

"Yes, Mrs Harding," said Violet, not looking at Adelaide.

"And who's that with Rebecca? Not that Ladds woman, she's the last person I want to see."

"Yes, Mrs Harding, Miss Rebecca asked her to stay for lunch," said Violet.

"That's all I need," Adelaide scowled, glaring out the window. "I suppose she wants to know what happened to her husband; she shouldn't have driven him off, should she? Some women don't know when they're well off."

"No, Mrs Harding," Violet said under her breath, taking Adelaide's belongings out the door, "they don't."

As the French windows had now been shut, Mary and Rebecca made their way round to the front door and into the house.

"Come on," said Rebecca, "let's go and see what the old Dragon has got to say for herself."

Adelaide was in the drawing room, standing next to the fire, cigarette poised to be lit in her hand.

"Oh it's you, Rebecca," she drawled. "And who do we have here? It's Mrs Ladds, Mary Knighton that was; the shop girl from Tibbitts if I remember correctly."

She moved smoothly across the room and flung herself into one of the large armchairs.

"Violet!" she shouted. "Violet!"

Violet rushed in, bobbing once in front of Adelaide.

"Mrs Harding?" she said.

"Get me a glass of gin," Adelaide snapped. "And be quick about it; no water, mind, just gin."

She drew deeply on the cigarette, blowing the smoke in an angry blue stream across the room.

"And what about our guest, Mrs Ladds? Are you going to join me?"

She forced a wolfish smile as she looked at Mary.

"Not at the moment, thank you, Mrs Harding," said Mary levelly, staring right back at Adelaide.

"Rebecca?" she asked, looking at her stepdaughter, before adding with a sneer, "No, I know you won't; so I will have one on my own."

Violet handed Adelaide the glass on a silver tray – Adelaide snatched it up and shot a look over to Mary.

"And what brings you here, Mrs Ladds? I haven't seen you in Northampton for a long time. But I did hear a little whisper, yes a little whisper."

She sniggered and rose to throw the end of her cigarette into the fire, as Mary and Rebecca sat themselves down opposite her.

"Yes, I did hear a whisper that you had misplaced your husband; careless thing that, to misplace your husband, eh, Rebecca? You know about it, don't you? Know that Mrs Ladds has misplaced her husband?"

She sniggered again.

"Adelaide, don't talk like that, you're embarrassing Mary," Rebecca said quickly.

"Why shouldn't I?" Adelaide sneered contemptuously. "It's true, isn't it, and don't call me Adelaide, young woman; I'm your mother – you should show me some respect."

There was silence; Rebecca scowled furiously at Adelaide. After a moment Mary spoke.

"You are right, Mrs Harding," she said slowly. "My husband Noble has been out of touch for some time and I wondered if you had heard from him, after all you were – friends."

Adelaide turned to the fire, took another cigarette from the box on the mantelpiece, lit it and took a long slurp from the glass of gin. She pursed her lips, drawing air in through her teeth as the spirit spilled down her throat and turned to Mary.

"No, I ain't heard from your husband, Mrs Ladds," she drawled, her refined accent slipping. "I don't expect to 'ear from him and I don't want to 'ear from 'im."

She paused and stared contemptuously at Mary.

"That sort don't bother; he uses people and then chucks them aside and he don't care a toss. He ain't comin' back; no he won't, not never, or at least not back to you. The sooner you realise that the better."

She flicked her ash into the fire and turned to Rebecca.

"And don't you tell me I'm speaking out of turn, Rebecca 'arding. You think I'm common, I know that; but I've got my head screwed on when it comes to men and don't you forget that."

Rebecca did not reply, Mary looked at her hands.

"Must be lunchtime soon," Adelaide said.

"We are going out," Rebecca said quickly.

"Suit yourself," said Adelaide. "Well if you're going I'll wish you good day, Mrs Ladds."

She turned and stomped out of the room, downing the last of the glass of her gin as she went.

"Isn't she absolutely awful?" Rebecca said quietly. "And to say such things like that; she was trying to upset you the best she could."

"Don't worry, Rebecca," Mary smiled. "I got the answer I wanted, she hadn't heard from him, that's the main thing."

"Come on then, Mary, I can't stand it here, let's go to The County Hotel for lunch; we can put it on Father's account."

Chapter Fifty-Three
Engagements

Mary was now more determined than ever that she wanted to give up the farm. Adelaide had provided no new information but her comments had confirmed what Mary had feared; she would never see Noble Ladds again. Her last hope was to advertise in Rupert's friend's newspaper in the hope that Noble might see it and reply; so it was with a sense of dread that Mary wrote to Rupert and asked that he put in an advertisement, citing her reasons that she had not now heard from Noble for quite some time. Rupert readily agreed and whatever his thoughts on Mary's request, he never let on. After four months there still hadn't been a reply to the advertisement in the paper in Canada. It was clear that Noble would not now return so Mary decided that she would sell the farm and write to the London Hospital for an application for the nursing course. Reuben had left in early May to go back to the engines – this time as a driver – but once the cattle were out in the fields, Cyril and Dennis could manage the rest of the work on their own.

Mary had written to Lucy to ask for her help with the application form for the London Hospital and Lucy and Roderick turned up on their bicycles the next Sunday to help. Mary had prepared lunch early and the afternoon was spent filling in the application form – pencil first, ready for Mary to ink it in later.

"Why do you want to go to London to train, Mary?" Lucy asked. "It's so far away; there are plenty of places nearer."

"I want to get right away from here," shrugged Mary. "I don't want people asking where Noble is all the time; can't you understand that, Lucy?"

"I suppose so," said Lucy. "Who's going to be your reference? It says here you need a character reference."

Lucy ran her finger along the writing of the page, checking the criteria for a referee.

"I know," she said decisively.

"Who?" said Mary.

"Mr Watson-Foster; he is just the man, I'm sure he would do it."

She hesitated.

"But he will ask me about Noble; I wouldn't like that," said Mary, wringing her hands.

"I'm sorry, Mary," said Lucy gently. "You will have to tell him if he doesn't know already; I think most people have guessed what has happened."

"I suppose so," sighed Mary. "And I could see Verity at the same time and I have to go to Dean anyway to see Aunt Charlotte to ask about Jack."

"What about Jack?" said Lucy.

"Martha says she will have one of the children, but not both; so Ethil will have to go to her and I want to ask Aunt Charlotte if she will have Jack."

"Oh," said Lucy, "what do you think she will say? It could be a long time, you know; the training takes three years and you don't get much time off."

"I know, I know, but I think William is going to get married soon."

"Who's he going to marry?" asked Lucy, surprised.

"Me of course," Molly said from the other end of the table, her arms crossed, her chin resting on her hands as she looked up at the two sisters. Lucy laughed.

"I didn't notice you there," Lucy said.

"No one does," Molly grumbled.

Mary laughed and leapt to her feet, rounding the table to give Molly a quick hug.

"You're going to marry Reuben, Molly, that's what you said," laughed Mary.

Molly looked up at Mary and said quietly,

"Reuben wants to marry you, Mary, you know that."

The three women looked one to the other and said nothing.

"Where's Roderick?" Mary said to break the silence.

"He's out with the children collecting the eggs round the yard, I think," said Lucy.

"When you goin' to marry 'im, then?" Molly asked Lucy.

"Molly, what a question!" Lucy said indignantly, standing up distractedly. "Can't we have some tea, Mary?"

"Yes, put the kettle on, Molly," said Mary with a small smile to Molly.

The next day Mary decided that she must go to Dean to see Aunt Charlotte and John Watson-Foster. She knew that Charlotte would be at home and she would have to hope that John Watson-Foster was as well. She gave Molly instructions to deal with the children and set off on her bicycle.

On arriving at the butcher's shop she found Aunt Charlotte in the kitchen sitting in the rocking chair by the range reading the Bible, while Sabine made pastry at the table.

"Mary my dear, come in, come in; how lovely to see you, come and tell me all the news! Sabine, fill the kettle, can you; we will have a cup of tea."

Sabine looked up, wiping her hands on her apron.

"You want me to stop doin' this then?" she said, nodding at the ball of pastry.

"Yes, dear, stop doing that and fill the kettle, we want a cup of tea."

"But there 'ent no water."

"Well go to the pump and get some then," said Charlotte calmly.

Sabine stomped out; Charlotte tutted.

"I just don't know what we are going to do with that girl; she's like a light gone out, she really is."

Mary sat down.

"So, Mary, let's not beat around the bush, you don't come to Dean that often; you must have finally decided to come and tell me something about Noble – so what is it? You must tell me everything."

Mary sighed and explained.

"Well, my dear," Charlotte said finally, "I am not entirely surprised at what you are telling me. That man was no good at all and will never get any better. And although you haven't asked yet, I expect you want me to have the children; there is no one else to ask, is there."

Mary smiled gratefully.

"Well, Aunt Charlotte, Martha says she will have Ethil; but it's Jack I was wondering if you could have, after all—"

Mary broke off.

"After all, what?" said Charlotte. "After all William won't be here much

672

longer, that was what you were going to say?"

"Well," said Mary with a shrug.

"I hope so too, my dear; I do hope that he gets married to Grace – she's wonderful, wouldn't you agree?"

"Yes she is, Aunt Charlotte," agreed Mary. "Does that mean you would have Jack?"

Mary looked imploringly at her aunt.

"Yes, of course I would; he's a good boy, we would love to have him."

Mary thanked her aunt repeatedly and finished her tea.

"Do you think I can call at The Hall without warning, Aunt Charlotte?" she asked.

"Yes, I'm sure you can, dear; I know Verity is at home, I saw her go past in the motor car yesterday."

Mary rose from the table, said goodbye and made her way towards The Hall.

She went to the back door and knocked; Betty came to the door.

"Miss Mary, what a surprise! I mean Mrs Ladds," exclaimed Betty.

"Who is it, Betty?" a voice came from inside.

"It's Mary," Betty called back into the house.

"Well, bless my soul," Dorcas said, rushing to the door. "Bless my soul, we haven't seen you for ages; come in, my dear, come in."

She ushered Mary delightedly into the kitchen.

"Miss Verity is here somewhere, Betty, you go and find her and tell her Mary is here."

Betty hurried off; Dorcas surveyed Mary with a beaming smile.

"And the children, Mary, how are they?" she asked.

"They're well, thank you."

"Their father not turned up yet, I s'pose?"

"No, he's still away," murmured Mary.

"Hmm," said Dorcas, as Verity came running into the kitchen.

"Mary dear, how lovely to see you; what a surprise!" she cried, giving Mary a hug.

"Mary, you will stay to lunch; Dorcas, bring us some coffee in the drawing

673

room, will you? I've got so much to tell you, Mary."

Verity led the way out of the kitchen down the long hall into the drawing room. Mary sat on the long settee and Verity sat beside her, positively brimming with excitement. Able to contain herself no longer she turned to Mary with a squeal and held out her left hand to Mary; a large engagement ring glittered on her fourth finger.

"Look, Mary, look! I am going to get married! I'm so happy, really I am."

Mary laughed delightedly and hugged her friend.

"I assume you are marrying Maurice, Verity?" she asked with a laugh.

"Yes, of course I am, who else would I marry? I really can't believe it."

She spread her fingers and admired the ring.

"Some of my friends say that marriage is a trap and women rush into it; they don't approve of men. I used to think that, but then this all happened when he was back on leave."

"So when are you getting married, Verity?"

"Oh, not yet; he's gone away again and it will be at least a year before he is back, but I can't wait! Even Father was pleased; Maurice's from a good family, you know, and his prospects in the army are good, I just pray that he doesn't get hurt. And then there's the wedding to plan and all the people to invite. You will come, won't you, Mary? I don't know how Father is going to pay for it but we will cross that bridge when we come to it. I'm so excited, Mary, I really am."

She pulled up short, frowning slightly.

"Oh, Mary, I'm so sorry; there's me going on about getting married and you –" she stopped for a moment to summon the right words, "you having all your difficulties. How are things, Mary? Have you heard from Noble?"

Mary gazed at her hands, turning her wedding ring round and round on her finger.

"No, I've heard nothing," she sighed. "I'm going to sell up and train as a nurse."

"Oh, Mary, I'm so sorry that things have not worked out for you."

Verity squeezed her hand.

"The reason I have come, Verity, is to ask your father to write a reference for me in my application for training; do you think he would do that?"

"Yes, I'm sure he would, we can probably find him; he is about somewhere."

She dragged Mary from her seat and scurried round the house looking for her father. Once they had found him in his study, it didn't take John much persuading to agree to write a reference. Once it was done Mary and Verity had lunch and Mary prepared to leave.

"Everything is changing, Mary," sighed Verity, clasping her friend's hand at the front door. "I do hope we don't lose touch now you are going to London."

"If I'm accepted, Verity," laughed Mary.

"You will be, Mary, I know you will."

She hesitated and looked earnestly at Mary.

"We have been good friends, Mary; you have been my best friend really. I hope so much that it all goes well for you, I really do."

"It will, Verity," smiled Mary, "you'll see; I will be fine."

She pecked Verity on the cheek, pushed her bike out in front of her and left The Hall.

On Wednesday of the next week Rebecca came to visit – she had sent Mary a letter insisting she must come as she had much good news to impart. She arrived in the middle of the morning, driven by the chauffeur, and sprang from the car up to the front door. She bustled straight past Molly, who had opened the door in her clean dress and apron intent on practising her manners once more and hared towards the front room, Molly rushing after her.

"Miss Harding to see you, Mrs Ladds," she called over Rebecca's shoulder as Rebecca spun into the room.

"Mary dear, I really couldn't wait to get here to tell you all the news; it's so dramatic. But first could Jupp – he's the chauffeur – have a cup of tea or something?"

"Of course," said Mary. "Molly, invite Mr Jupp in and give him a cup of tea when you have brought ours in. Do you mind having tea, Rebecca? I'm afraid we do not run to coffee in Bythorn."

"Tea will be fine, Mary," said Rebecca distractedly.

Molly smiled, bobbed and left them.

"What is the news, Rebecca? It must be important for you to come all this way."

Rebecca sat and shook her head.

"Well, you will never guess so I will have to tell you."

She looked at Mary dramatically.

"Adelaide has left! Yes, she has gone, I was so pleased! She just packed all her things one day, called a taxi and left for the station and we haven't seen her since. She didn't even tell Father, just left him a note which said she was going abroad and he was not to try and find her. She took all her jewellery that Father had given her and emptied the bank account that Father had allowed her and that was that."

"But what made her go?" Mary asked.

"Well, Violet said that about a week before she left, she had a letter from Canada and Violet also seemed to remember there had been another letter about two weeks before. It makes you wonder, doesn't it?"

"It could be Noble, couldn't it, Rebecca?" said Mary quietly.

"Yes it could be and if so, good riddance to the bloody pair of them. But it won't make any difference, will it, Mary?"

"No, I have made up my mind," said Mary firmly. "There was no reply to my advertisement and if he came back now I would carry on with my plans either way."

"I'm so glad, Mary," said Rebecca. "I'm sure you are doing the right thing. Noble was a rotter and so is Adelaide and if she has gone to him they deserve each other, don't you agree?"

"Yes."

"But there's more news to tell you, Mary, and you won't guess that either, so I will have to tell you; I'm going to be married! I can't believe it, but it's true I'm going to be married."

She pulled her glove off, revealing her diamond engagement ring.

"But, Rebecca, you didn't tell me about any man the last time I saw you."

"I know I didn't, but I hadn't met him then," laughed Rebecca.

"But who is he, then?"

"His name is Aubrey Hurrell and he's a painter."

"He's a what?" said Mary.

"He is a portrait painter, he's from a good family but has no money; his father died and he lives in London."

"How on earth did you meet him?" asked Mary.

"It was Father; he wanted me to have my portrait painted and he organised it and sent me to see this painter at his studio in London and that was it."

"Love at first sight, as they say," said Mary.

"Yes," smiled Rebecca, beaming down at her diamond ring.

"But what did your father say? Does he approve?"

"Well, I wouldn't say he exactly approves, but Father has to do what I say and he likes Aubrey; that's the main thing – even though he doesn't earn much, but I've got plenty of money so that doesn't matter."

"But where will you live?"

"At home in Northampton I think; it's a whacking great house and now Adelaide's gone we are free and Aubrey can keep his studio in London and have one at home."

"And when's the wedding, Rebecca?"

"Next year, you must come, Mary; you have to come!"

Rebecca sat back in her chair and smiled happily at Mary.

"Well, what do you think to that news then?"

"I'm so pleased, Rebecca; so pleased you are so happy, it's splendid," smiled Mary.

She stood and gave her friend a kiss.

"Now tell me your news, Mary; you have heard nothing from Noble, then."

"No, nothing," grimaced Mary. "I have decided to give up the farm and I'm going to train to be a nurse like I told you."

"It's so sad, Mary," sighed Rebecca. "Here's me all excited about getting married and your marriage is breaking up; it's not fair, is it?"

"Don't worry about me, Rebecca; all my arrangements are made and I'm looking forward to having a career. The only person I haven't dealt with yet is Molly; but I'm sure I can find her a position with someone I can trust before long."

"Well *we* will need someone soon," said Rebecca. "Violet is going to leave to get married in the autumn so I would have her. What's she like, Mary, is she clean?"

"I have got on very well with her," said Mary thoughtfully. "But I have known her since she was a child and she has been through some very difficult times; I would recommend her, her heart's in the right place."

No sooner had she finished speaking than Molly entered.

"Will you be having lunch in here, Mrs Ladds?" she said grandly.

Mary stifled a giggle.

"Yes, Molly, we will have our lunch in here; you can lay the table by the window and give Mr Jupp his lunch in the kitchen when Reuben comes in."

"Yes, Mrs Ladds. Will you be having wine with your lunch?"

Mary looked incredulously at Molly; as far as Mary could remember they had no wine in the house. "Shall I fetch one from the cellar?" said Molly sincerely.

Mary had not been down the cellar for years, she could not say whether there was wine down there or not. She continued to stare at Molly.

"Very well then, Molly," she managed, "but hurry up, time is getting on, you know."

Molly bobbed, left and returned to lay the table, placing a bottle of red wine in the centre as she did so.

"I got Mr Jupp to open it, Mrs Ladds, was that right?" she announced.

"Yes, that's fine," said Mary with a slight frown as Molly went out. "I don't know where the wine came from, Rebecca, but we might as well drink it."

As it turned out the wine was not bad at all and Molly had surpassed herself with the lunch preparations. When the dishes had been cleared, she called Molly back into the sitting room.

"Molly dear, you know that I am going to leave the farm in the autumn, and you will have to find another job?"

"Yes, Mrs Ladds, but I try not to think about it," said Molly candidly.

"Well, Miss Harding will have a vacancy in the autumn for a housemaid; would you like to go and work for her?"

"You mean in Norfampton?" asked Molly, her eyes brightening.

"Yes."

"With Mr Jupp?"

"Yes, he works for Mr Harding," said Rebecca.

Molly looked at Rebecca and then at Mary.

"Well, I would 'ave to fink, I mean *think* it over," said Molly thoughtfully.

"Very well," said Rebecca, raising an eyebrow. "But when will you let me know?"

Molly looked a little confused, pursed her lips and put her finger to her mouth.

"Well I'm thought about it and I will say yes, I would like the job," declared Molly, turning to Rebecca and bobbing heartily.

"Thank you, Miss 'Arding... I mean Miss *Harding*," she beamed. "I'll just go and see if Mr Jupp wants any tea after his dinner."

She had been gone only a few minutes when she suddenly rushed back into the room.

"Mary, Mary, you've got to come quick; all the cattle are got out and they're all up the village and everywhere and Reuben says could 'e 'ave a 'and."

"I'm coming, sorry, Rebecca, this shouldn't take too long," said Mary, hurrying out of the room after Molly.

"I'll wait until you get back," Rebecca shouted after her.

In the back yard there was no sign of any cattle.

"Where are they, Molly? And where are Reuben and the others?" Mary shouted at Molly.

"They're all gone out of the gate and up into the village and Reuben's gone to get Cyril and Dennis – them are up the field cuttin' the hedge."

"Well you run off and fetch them; I'll go up the street and see if I can bring the cows back."

Cattle escaping was common and at times every farmer lost his animals, so when Mary ran up into the village, she wasn't surprised to find two of her neighbours had already held the animals up on the piece of green land in front of the church, where they were all quietly grazing the new grass. It wasn't long before Reuben and Molly appeared; both out of breath from running, pursued at some distance by Cyril and Dennis.

"Are you all right, Mary?" Reuben said, taking great gasps of air.

"We're fine now. Wait until the others get here and we will soon have them back; have you got a stick?"

Reuben shook his head and trotted to the hedge – he pulled two branches out, quickly cutting them to length with his penknife. He handed one to Molly and they began to turn the cattle home in the direction of the farm. Cyril and Dennis led the way, ready to turn the cattle in when they got to the yard gate. The beasts were mainly bullocks, which were being fattened, but there was one cow and calf and another two dry cows, making twenty animals in all, which would all be sold in the autumn to provide Mary with the finance to get her through the training.

The cattle moved calmly down the road, Mary, Molly and Reuben following slowly behind them and Cyril and Dennis in front. Once they were through the gate they could be driven straight into the meadow. Rebecca and Jupp stood in the front garden watching as the cattle trotted through the yard.

"That wasn't too bad," said Mary to Rebecca. "Give me a few moments to get them in the field and I'll come and say goodbye."

"Don't worry, Mary, take your time," Rebecca replied, quietly fascinated by the workings of the farm.

Dennis opened the gate to the meadow, walking slowly round to help the others drive the beasts into the field. They tapped the ground with their sticks, as the animals milled around in a circle refusing to go into the pasture. Suddenly one of the larger bullocks dashed between Molly and Mary, tanking about behind them, head high in the air, searching for a way out of the yard.

"Just hold on, Mary, I'll go round the back of it," instructed Reuben, moving slowly round the bullock. It trotted down towards the loose boxes, along the wall of the yard and stood by the pump attached to the well. Snorting, it stopped and turned to look at Reuben; its back to the wall. Reuben looked at Cyril in horror.

"'E's on that—"

But before Reuben could finish the sentence, there was a loud bang as the wood under the bullock split, the hind quarters of the animal sinking out of view. It started to struggle, trying feverishly to get its back legs out of the well, but the well was wide and as much as it pawed the ground it could not get a grip. With nothing to support its back end the bullock started to slide slowly into the well, bellowing loud and long.

"Reuben, do something," screamed Mary. "Do something for God's sake!"

Reuben dashed off to get a rope; by the time he returned the animal had slipped to the ribs, struggling desperately. For a moment it was motionless and lay panting – its front legs jutting out uselessly in front of it; Reuben slid slowly forwards, managing to secure a rope around one front leg as the animal started to struggle again, slipping further and further into the well. Everyone rushed to grab the rope, heaving the animal up out of the well, but the creature was heavy and before Reuben managed to secure the rope to the barn, the animal threw its head up and bellowed, moving its centre of gravity backwards. With a terrified cry the bullock disappeared down the well.

"Let go! Let go!" screamed Reuben.

Everyone released the rope, which snaked across the yard and followed the creature down the well. There was a great splosh, silence and then the animal began to bellow again, its cry echoing up from the depths of the well.

"Do something, Reuben," begged Mary. "Do something, I can't bear it."

She clamped her hands over her ears as Reuben crawled to the edge of the well, looking down into the pit as the animal bellowed again.

"There's no hope, Mary, we can't get him out; he's too heavy and anyway the rope's gone."

"Can't you shoot him, Reuben?" Mary screamed. "It's awful."

She looked at him imploringly.

"We've only got a shotgun; that won't kill him," said Reuben quietly.

Everyone stood helplessly looking at one another as unnoticed, the other animals made their way back into the field. Rebecca put her hand on Mary's shoulder.

"There's nothing you can do, Mary," she said gently as the animal continued to cry.

Reuben peered into the murk of the well – he could see just the bullock's head, its big eyes staring up at him through the gloom. It tried to bellow again, but as its mouth opened, it took in a lungful of water and sank lower into the well.

"It's goin' to drown, Mary," Reuben said, still on his knees and looking down into the well.

Mary stood with her hands over her ears, her eyes shut tight as tears rolled down her cheeks. Molly put her arms round her, hugging her tightly. One more strangled gurgle echoed from the well, then all fell quiet.

"Is it over, Reuben?" asked Mary, opening her eyes and taking her hands from her ears.

"I think so," said Reuben, still looking down, as bubbles rose to the surface of the water, breaking sadly on the surface.

"That was awful," said Rebecca, holding Mary's hand. "Come on into the kitchen, Mary; Molly, will make you some tea."

Chapter Fifty-Four
The Interview

The incident of the bullock falling down the well cast a long shadow over proceedings at Elgin Farm. Not only was there a sizeable financial loss, but Mary couldn't help but blame herself for the way in which the creature had died. The only way to get the body of the animal out in the end was to get Blinkhorn to come with one of his ploughing engines and haul it out. William arrived to help and supervise the construction of a tripod over the well; ropes, blocks and tackles were attached to the rope of the ploughing engine. Reuben was sent down the well to loop a chain round the front legs of the animal and then, very slowly, it was hauled out. It lay sadly in the yard until the knacker men came, winched the carcass into his trailer and after giving Mary a cheque for a fraction of its value, took the animal away.

William came into the house for a cup of tea while Reuben talked endlessly to the engine driver.

"Molly dear, go and see if any of those men want any tea," Mary said, indicating the men outside.

Molly scurried into the yard as Mary turned to William.

"Now, William," she sighed, "I'm not sure that with that beast dying, the sale of the farm will raise enough money."

She turned desperately to her cousin.

"I'm really worried, William; I don't want to ask your father for help but I don't know what else to do?"

"How many bullocks are left?" William asked, picking up a pencil to do some calculations.

"And how many acres of wheat have you got?"

He looked up at Mary, who was thinking hard, a frown puckering her brow.

"You still have the carthorses, don't you?"

"Yes," agreed Mary. "And I suppose there are the two wagons that Henry has borrowed – the chickens and the furniture in here."

William scribbled furiously, adding up the columns he had made in the back of his diary.

"Well according to these calculations you should be all right; you will easily cover your bank debt and expenses and have some to spare. No, I'm sure you need not worry, Mary."

"That's a relief then," said Mary quietly. "I just wonder what will happen next."

"So when will you go to London?" William asked.

"I don't know, but I have to go for an interview in three weeks. I've never been to London, William, but you have."

"Only twice, Mary."

"Well, Lucy says she will come with me," said Mary.

She turned and eyed her cousin critically.

"So, William, what news do you have?" she asked.

"Well," William said, trying unsuccessfully to hide the smirk on his face, "I'm going to get married."

"Oh, William, that's wonderful news but who to, or need I ask?"

Before William could answer a voice from the door said,

"To me of course."

Molly was standing in the doorway.

"Molly, how could you listen to our conversation!" Mary remonstrated.

"I weren't listenin'," huffed Molly. "But if you're talking loud and I've got to come in to get the tea I can't 'elp 'earing, can I?"

"Don't worry, Mary, leave the girl, it doesn't matter," William chuckled.

"I know who you're goin' to marry any road," continued Molly. "You're goin' to marry Grace, ain't you, William, and I'm going to be the first to congratulate you."

She skipped up to William and gave him a peck on the cheek.

"There we are!" she declared. "That's the one and only time I'll do that."

She stood back and grinned at William, who reddened but grinned right back.

"Thank you, Molly," he said, turning to her cousin. "She's right, Mary, as you guessed – I am to marry Grace."

"Well done, William!" said Mary, rising to give him a kiss.

"There din't I tell you, Mary – Mrs Ladds, I mean," Molly corrected herself.

"You wretched girl, you drive me to distraction at times; just you go and make the tea and keep your opinions to yourself," Mary cried in false anger.

"And there's something else, Mary," William continued, "we're buying a farm at Covington– about two hundred acres. We have been renting land for so long it's about time we had some of our own."

"That is good news, William," smiled Mary. "You have done well, haven't you – not like Henry and me, we just struggle along."

William accepted his tea from Molly and said nothing.

The day of Mary's interview was not far away and Mary was becoming apprehensive. It was 1909 and twelve years since she had been at school, and she wondered if she could concentrate on study again. Although she was not yet twenty-seven, she had lost the bloom of youth and her complexion was weatherbeaten from working on the farm.

She had laid her clothes out ready for the day and had been to Thrapston to draw some money from the bank for the expenses of the trip. Her interview was at two o'clock and to get to the London Hospital would take her some time. She had arranged with Lucy to be on the train that arrived at Bedford at half past ten and so was up at six on the day to have her breakfast; Molly having been up earlier to light the range.

"Now, Molly, you're in charge; send the children to school and make sure they stay around when they come back, don't let them go roaming. I will be back late so put them to bed. And, Molly, when Ulick comes, don't let him in the door, we just want four loaves as usual."

"Yes, Mary," said Molly with a smile.

"Don't say it like that, my girl, you know what he's like," scolded Mary.

She made a face at Molly and went upstairs to put her best clothes on, returning five minutes later.

"How hot is it, Molly? Do I need a coat?" demanded Mary. "How do I look? Is my hat straight?"

"I don't think you need a coat, you will be too hot; the jacket will be fine," said Molly calmly.

Mary buttoned up her jacket, looking at herself in the mirror.

"How do I look, Molly?" she asked again.

"You look very smart, Mary; you always look smart when you dress up, smarter than anyone I know."

"Thank you, Molly, that's very kind; now have I got everything, gloves, map, letter, money?"

"Hankie," said Molly.

"Hankie," Mary repeated. "What else, Molly?"

"Nuffing, I don't fink," said Molly, frowning hard. "What about somefing for Miss Lucy," she said suddenly. "She's been good coming wiv you."

"What a time to say that, Molly!" shrieked Mary. "What have we got to give her?"

Molly looked round the kitchen.

"What about a jar of 'unny?"

"Good idea, Molly, go and fetch one," ordered Mary.

Molly dashed into the pantry.

"The bike, Molly?" Mary called to her.

"I'm got it out; Reuben looked at it and pumped up the tyres," Molly reassured her, passing Mary a jar of honey.

"Very good then – time to go," said Mary, taking a deep breath and glancing once more at her reflection in the mirror.

It was just before seven when Mary set off on the bike for Raunds, where she caught the eight o'clock train for Kettering. At Kettering station, she waited for an hour for the train that would take her to Bedford and on to London. Just before half past ten the train pulled up at Bedford station. Mary looked out the window for Lucy who she could see dressed in a dark suit and a black boater, carrying a small black bag. Mary waved out of the window and Lucy climbed into the train and joined Mary in her compartment.

"Did you get the right ticket?" Mary asked.

"Of course I did," said Lucy with a sniff.

"I wish you wouldn't sniff like that, Lucy," hissed Mary.

Lucy said nothing, took a hankie from her sleeve and wiped her nose.

At St Pancras they caught a bus to Whitechapel and the London Hospital;

they arrived at the address given for the interview an hour early.

"I'm hot," said Lucy, as the sun beat down on them.

"There's nowhere to sit," moaned Mary. "My legs are killing me."

"Are you sure this is the right place?" Lucy asked.

Mary got the letter out and read out the address again.

"That's right, isn't it?" she asked, looking up at the imposing building front and showing Lucy the letter.

Lucy nodded.

"Have you got anything to drink?" Lucy said.

"No, one cup of tea at the station is enough, I will want to go down the end in the middle of the interview."

"Look," said Lucy, "there's a church up there; let's go and sit in that – we can pretend we are praying if anyone comes."

They made their way up the street and into the church. Inside it was dark, the stained glass cutting out most of the power of the sun. The pair sat on a bench at the back, leaning on the pew in front, as if in prayer. After a few moments Mary sat back, undid the buttons on her jacket and leant down to untie the laces on her shoes.

"Let me have your hankie, Lucy; I want to clean up my shoes," she whispered.

"You can't do it with my hankie. What am I supposed to use?" Lucy protested.

"I can't do it with mine, can I? I can't go in there with a dirty hankie, can I? Come on, give it here."

She held out her hand expectantly, Lucy sighed and passed Mary her handkerchief.

"You haven't got cosmetics on, have you, Mary?" Lucy said, looking Mary straight in the face. "They won't like it you have; we are never allowed cosmetics."

"No, I haven't," said Mary.

"Well, you've got a smut on your cheek," Lucy said.

"Where, where?" asked Mary, her hands flying to her face.

"Come here, give me the hankie, I'll get it off," said Lucy.

She took the hankie, pulled it over her index finger and spat on it, holding Mary's cheek and turning her head to wipe off the offending smut.

"There we go, all done," she smiled.

"You didn't do it with the hankie I've just cleaned my shoes with, did you?" Mary demanded.

"Just a clean corner, don't you worry."

Mary rubbed her cheek.

"What's the time, Lucy?"

"I don't know."

"Well have a look then!"

Lucy opened her small bag and took out her nurses' watch.

"Twenty past one; you needn't go yet, it will only take five minutes to get there."

Mary sighed.

"I wish it were over," she said. "I've only had one interview before."

"I've never had one," said Lucy.

"How did you get in then?" Mary asked.

"They took anyone who applied to be a nurse when I went, they were short of people and it was only Bedford, not a posh place like this."

"It doesn't look very posh to me," Mary complained.

"Don't say that, Mary, it's very famous, you mustn't let them think you don't approve."

Mary leant down and retied the laces of her shoes, before sitting back and doing up the buttons of her jacket.

"Is my hat straight, Lucy?" she asked, removing her hat pin, readjusting her hat and turning to Lucy.

"Not quite," said Lucy, reaching up to adjust the hat.

"Let me put the pin in, I will get it straight then," Lucy said, taking the long pin.

"Be careful then," said Mary, wincing as Lucy pressed the pin through the hat and set it straight.

Mary stood up, walked out of the pew and brushed down the front of her skirt, picking off specks and hairs.

"Brush me down the back, will you, Lucy?" she demanded, turning round.

Lucy brushed from the collar down, picking off the odd long hair.

"You're fine," she said.

"Well, we will go but walk slowly," said Mary nervously as they left the church. "What are you going to do while I'm in there?"

"I'm coming in with you," Lucy said.

"No, you're not! I will look such a fool dragging my sister along," exclaimed Mary.

"There will be a waiting room and I'm not standing out here in the street. What do you think I am?"

Mary pursed her lips and frowned.

"You really embarrass me, you do," she muttered.

Lucy whirled angrily round on her sister, her eyes sparkling with fury.

"Well you asked me to come, didn't you!" she hissed. "And I've spent *all* day and all that money on the train, and you – you—"

Lucy broke off, shaking her head and marching ahead of Mary.

"I'm sorry, Lucy, I'm sorry," Mary called after her, catching up with her sister and threading an arm round her shoulder. "I'm just a bit nervous; you know how it is."

Lucy said nothing, maintaining her icy glare as they arrived at the hospital entrance.

"Here we go then," said Mary.

She took a deep breath and walked up the steps and through the large oak panelled doors. Inside, a smart looking woman sat at a desk to the right of the large entrance hall. Mary went up to her and introduced herself.

"I have come for an interview; my name is Mrs Ladds," she said quietly, her voice echoing around the huge antechamber.

"Very good, Mrs Ladds, let me see."

The lady opened a large diary, running her finger down the list of appointments.

"Mrs Mary Ladds, is that?" she asked, peering up at Mary.

"Yes," Mary replied.

"Yes, two o'clock, Dr Barclay's panel. If you would like to go to the waiting

room down on the left I will call you when you are required. There is a ladies'
room further down if you require it."

"Thank you," said Mary. "Is it all right if my sister waits with me?"

Mary nodded to Lucy who stood a little behind her; the lady looked up as
Lucy took a step forwards.

"Of course it is," she said, smiling up at Lucy, recognition spread over her
face.

"Don't I know you from somewhere? Are you a nurse?" she asked.

"Yes," Lucy said. "But not here, I am a nurse in Bedford."

Lucy looked at the woman, but could not make any connection.

"I'll think of it in a minute, where I've seen you before," smiled the woman.
"But take a seat with your sister, please."

Mary and Lucy went to sit on the hard wooden chairs opposite the door;
the smell of carbolic thick in their nostrils. Chairs lined the walls and a table
stood in the middle of the waiting room, littered with copies of the *Illustrated
London News*. Two long windows opposite them looked out onto a small quad.
There were three other people in the room. A woman and teenage girl, who
looked like mother and daughter, sat on one side of the room, and a man in a
poorly fitting suit on the other. Everybody eyed each other as surreptitiously
as possible, snatching quick glances before looking away. The girl put her
hands under her legs, swinging them backwards and forwards under the chair;
her mother sighed and looked at her. The man, who smelt of cigarettes –even
from where Lucy and Mary were sitting – shut his eyes, his chin gradually
falling to rest on his chest.

The mother sighed again as she eyed her daughter. She scanned the room,
her eyes alighting on Mary.

"What time's her appointment, then?" the woman said, nodding at Lucy.
"We've been waiting ages."

Mary looked up, disconcerted.

"Half past one, they said we'd be in, but it's gone that ages ago," the woman
continued, looking at the girl who was still swinging her legs.

"We're two o'clock," said Mary.

"She's your daughter, then?" the woman asked, nodding again at Lucy.

"She looks just like you."

"No, she's my sister," Mary said indignantly.

Lucy suppressed a snort of laughter as the door opened.

"Miss Moon?" said the lady from the desk.

"That's us," said the woman, rising and ushering her daughter to the door. "I'll come too if that's all right."

Another twenty minutes passed before Mary was finally called in.

"Good luck," whispered Lucy as Mary followed the lady across the hall, through some double doors and into a huge room. The walls were hung with large pictures; two long tables ran down the length of the room and at the top of the hall a panel of four people sat behind another table, an empty chair standing ominously opposite them. The four were deep in conversation – suddenly one looked up and addressed Mary across the room.

"Come, come, take a seat," he boomed, waving his hand and pointing to the empty chair.

"Who do we have here, then?" he said, looking down at his papers, but not at Mary.

"Mrs Ladds, Dr Barclay," said the reception lady, who had followed Mary in.

"Very good," he said. "Sit down please, Mrs Ladds."

Dr Barclay was old; he had white hair, long side whiskers and a white moustache, his tight winged collar cut into his neck and looked to be very uncomfortable. Mary could see that he was reading her application as she sat down. He looked up and pierced her with ice blue eyes. He smiled.

"Let me introduce the panel," he said, clearing his throat, "I am Dr Barclay, this is Dr Knox, on my left is Sister Goodbody and Reverend Philpott represents the Trustees of the Hospital."

He looked down again at the application form.

"Mrs Ladds, you are somewhat older than most of our applicants," he stated simply.

Mary, thinking of no suitable answer said,

"Yes, sir."

"And you are married, Mrs Ladds, not a widow?"

He looked at her sharply.

"Yes, sir, but my husband has been abroad for some years."

Mary shifted uncomfortably on her chair.

"Ah ha, now I see; you have a family, Mrs Ladds?"

"Yes, sir: a boy and a girl."

"And their upbringing is taken care of, Mrs Ladds?"

"Yes, sir."

"Very good," he murmured, running his index finger each way along the underside of his moustache.

"Why do you want to be a nurse, Mrs Ladds?" he asked, pushing himself back in his chair and pinning Mary with an icy stare – palms of his hands flat on the table and fingers spread out. Mary composed herself; should she tell them the truth or should she go and parrot the required line of wanting to help others? She decided to tell some of the truth, and leave out the awkward detail.

"With my husband abroad," she said slowly, "and our income under some pressure I have decided to have a career. I have a sister who is a nurse; she enjoys her work and finds it rewarding so I chose nursing. It also gives one a chance to help others in times of stress."

She pulled up short, looking along the members of the panel; she could see the Reverend Philpott was nodding off to sleep.

"What does your husband do, Mrs Ladds?"

"He is in business, sir, but I have no detail."

"Very good," he said wiping his moustache again.

"Now your education, Mrs Ladds; are you a scholar?" Dr Barclay asked, leaning forward on the table.

"I was educated until I was fifteen at our local school and was considered good in reading, writing and arithmetic. We also learnt history, geography and Bible study and I am able to speak a little French."

"Sounds good, Mrs Ladds, and this fellow who gave you a reference, who is he? He sounds a gentleman."

"Yes, sir, he is a local landowner and businessman."

"Now, sister, do you have any questions of Mrs Ladds?" said Dr Barclay, turning to Sister Goodbody.

Sister Goodbody sat up straight in her chair; clearly she had not been expecting to have to say anything. There was a moment's pause while she composed a question.

"Are you in good health, Mrs Ladds?" she intoned in a deep voice, which took Mary by surprise.

"Yes, I enjoy very good health," Mary replied with a smile.

There was another pause.

"And do you have all your own teeth, Mrs Ladds?" the deep voice drawled, drawing out the sentence slowly. Dr Barclay sighed and looked at the ceiling.

Mary nodded.

"Do you have any infectious diseases, Mrs Ladds?" the sister continued, eyeing Mary from under her starched cap.

"No," Mary answered simply.

There was another pause, which Dr Barclay leapt into.

"Do you have any more questions, sister?" he asked a touch impatiently.

"No, Dr Barclay," she replied.

"And, Dr Knox, do you have anything to ask?"

Doctor Knox sat up in his chair and smiled. He was much younger than Dr Barclay, clean shaven and wearing a very smart suit.

"Mrs Ladds, are you able to cope with the sight of blood?" he smiled at her.

"I have no problem with it, sir; I have always lived on a farm so I am able to deal with that sort of thing."

"And, Mrs Ladds, do you know what the normal bodily temperature is for a human?"

"Ninety-eight point four Fahrenheit," Mary answered quickly.

"And normal blood pressure, Mrs Ladds?"

"One hundred and twenty over seventy, sir," Mary said confidently, silently thanking her sister for her knowledge.

"Very good," he said, with an impressed nod, "I have no more questions, Dr Barclay."

"Reverend Philpott?" Dr Barclay said loudly, leaning forward and looking along the line at the sleeping cleric.

"Reverend Philpott!" he said again. "Do you have any questions of Mrs Ladds?"

Revered Philpott opened his eyes and spoke as if he had never been asleep.

"Yes," he said, clearing his throat, "do you go to church, Mrs Ladds?"

"Yes, sir, every Sunday."

"You're not a Catholic, are you?" he whispered.

"No, sir; I have been brought up as a Methodist, but I now go to a Church of England church."

"That's what I like to hear! No more questions, Dr Barclay," he smiled at Mary.

"Well, Mrs Ladds, I think that concludes the interview," said Dr Barclay, standing up to shake Mary's hand. "If you would like to wait for a while we will call you back when we have discussed your case."

Mary thanked him and made her way back to the waiting room, where Lucy was in discussion with the receptionist.

"Mrs Ladds, you have finished," smiled the woman. "We have worked out where I have seen your sister – at Bedford hospital, isn't that a coincidence, she nursed my mother. Now I must go or Dr Barclay will be out looking for me."

She scurried out of the room.

"Well how did it go?" said Lucy.

"Well I don't know; all right I think, but they will give me an answer this afternoon so we have to wait a while."

Half an hour later Mary was called back in front of the panel.

"Well, Mrs Ladds, I'm pleased to say that we would like to accept your application and would like to offer you a place in our training scheme. However, we would like you to specialise in midwifery after your initial training as we have so many vacancies in that field. Would you accept this condition?" Mary thought for no more than a second, her heart racing.

"Yes, sir. I'd be delighted to," she smiled.

694

Chapter Fifty-Five
Reuben

For Mary, the rest of the summer flew by. The sale of the house took place in mid-September; everyone from all around came and Mary dressed in her best clothes, encouraging people to buy either the stock or the implements. She did not want to sell the furniture, but it all had to go; she needed the money and there was nowhere to store it. She wasn't sad to see the back of the house, she had never been happy there – it had never really been her house and even with Noble gone his presence loomed around every corner.

Once her course had started, Mary had very little time off; only making it back to Dean about every six weeks, but as she was so busy, time passed very quickly and it wasn't long before she had finished the three years of training and was ready to start work on her own. Verity, Rebecca and William were all now married, but due to her heavy schedule she had not attended any of the weddings. William had moved from the butcher's shop so there was more room for her to stay with Charlotte and Thomas and Jack. She decided she would use her skills as a midwife to go to the mother-to-be's home a week or so before their confinement and stay until the she was able to cope with the new baby. Not only would this pay more, but it would also give her more time to come back to see the children between each client.

Her first customer was the wife of a mine owner near Doncaster and on her departure, having successfully brought the first son of the family into the world, she was paid far in excess of the fee she had been told to charge. She returned from Doncaster in early February 1914 and with a week to spare before her next assignment, she went back to the butcher's shop to see Jack, and the rest of the family. She visited Martha and Henry and Ethil at Brington, and William and Grace who lived in the big farmhouse at Dean Way Post. Verity was not in Dean having travelled with Maurice on a posting.

The weather was cold and frosty. There was a dusting of snow on the ground, but despite this, the ground was hard so walking was easy. Mary decided that she would walk to Cold Harbour to have a look at her old home, so set off after breakfast, having wrapped up warmly first. She walked out of the back of the shop and headed across the frozen fields. At the top of the hill she heard a shout.

"Mary, Mary, wait a minute!"

She turned to see Reuben standing on the other side of the hedge in a small paddock above his parents' home. He ran along the hedge until he reached a gap where rails had been put in, climbed over and ran over to Mary. Reuben had grown into a handsome man, with jet black hair, a pure dark complexion and fine white teeth. Mary held out her hand to greet him and he lifted his cap.

"Reuben Heighton, how are you?" said Mary, beaming at him. "I haven't seen you for ages, you do look well."

She held his hand for a moment and smiled.

"But why are you at home? I thought you were on the engines."

"I am, but 'e's laid us off for a few weeks; all the winter ploughing's finished and there ain't no work till March, when we're goin' down to Kent to pull up some orchards."

"You're still a driver then, Reuben?" Mary asked.

"Yes, but 'e's made me foreman and I'm in charge of the jobs now."

He smiled shyly.

"Well done, Reuben, I knew you would make good," Mary laughed, releasing his hand.

"And you, Mary, are you well?" Reuben asked.

"Yes," she said, "I've finished my training and completed my first job, and I have a few days before I start the next one, so I came back to see Jack and Ethil."

"Where are you goin' then?" he asked.

"I was going to walk up to Cold Harbour; I haven't been there since we left all those years ago."

"Can I come along wiv you?" asked Reuben tentatively. "I ain't bin up there for years either – well only to do ploughing, that's all."

"That would be nice," Mary smiled, leading the way up the hill.

It was cloudy and cold; Mary pulled her coat tightly around her as they reached the top of the hill, the wind biting at her cheeks. She looked up at the old house and smiled

"You know there's no one at Cold Harbour, Mary?" said Reuben thoughtfully.

"No, Reuben, I didn't know; since when?"

"Don't know quite," he shrugged. "But the last folk left about three months ago when the bank shut them down, and I ain't 'eard that anyone else has gone in."

As they reached the farm Mary could see that Reuben was right; the place was deserted and the house locked. The cattle yards were empty and just two lonely stacks of straw lined the wall – no dogs barked, no chickens clucked, and a solitary jackdaw called throatily from the chimney stack.

"How sad," sighed Mary, "it's so quiet, so unloved. I will have to ask William what's happening, he will know."

Reuben looked at Mary thoughtfully.

"I saw William the other day," he said. "He says he thinks there's going to be a war."

"Going to be a war?" Mary repeated incredulously. "With who?"

"William says with Germany."

"I've never heard such nonsense," Mary snorted, turning to retrace her steps back to Lower Dean. "I wouldn't believe everything that William Dunmore says."

Reuben laughed and followed Mary back down the hill.

Now that Mary was working, her financial situation had dramatically improved and she was no longer eating into her meagre savings. She still had to rely on Thomas and Charlotte to look after Jack and Martha to look after Ethil, but she decided that if she did well as a midwife she might have enough money to send Ethil to boarding school. Jack, on the other hand, had already set his heart on joining the navy. She found herself home at the butcher shop and decided to follow Charlotte, Thomas and Jack to chapel. As she left the shop, she caught sight of George walking along dressed in his Sunday best, obviously heading to the same place.

"Hello, George, are you going to chapel?" called Mary.

George turned and seeing Mary, smiled broadly.

"Yes, Mrs Ladds," he replied, lifting his cap to Mary.

"I know why you're going to chapel," Mary said as she walked along beside him.

"Oh yes?" said George.

"Yes, you're going to see all the girls, you can't fool me, George," she laughed. "Who is your favourite, George? Go on you can tell me."

She smiled at him lopsidedly; George blushed and looked at the ground.

"Who then, George?" Mary persisted.

"Well," said George, "I haven't really got a favourite, or I have – but she's spoken for."

"Oh dear, George, so are you anyone's favourite? A smart young chap like you must turn a few heads."

George's blush deepened.

"Perhaps there might be one," he said looking up slyly at Mary. "But most of them all fall for Reuben; they all fall for Reuben."

"Where is Reuben?" Mary asked. "He normally goes to chapel."

"He's off ploughing somewhere and ain't come home this weekend; now he's foreman he's more important."

"And who's *his* favourite, George?" Mary teased.

George looked at Mary with a slight frown.

"Well," said George, "it's none of the girls; I thought you would know that, Mary – I mean Mrs Ladds."

Mary blushed and walked a little faster, unwilling to engage any further in the conversation.

Some weeks later, Mary was cycling back from Rushden. She always left her bicycle with her Aunt Sarah before taking the train to an appointment and had arrived back and collected her bicycle to ride back to Dean. She had balanced one bag on the front of the bike and was in the process of balancing her second bag on the back when the unmistakable smell of a traction engine reached her. She pushed her bike to the top of the hill, from where she could see the living-van attached to the chugging engine a hundred yards or so down the road. Little whispers of smoke drifted from the chimney and Mary could make out a figure sitting on the steps of the living-van; it was Reuben. She smiled, propped the bike against a gate post and walked over to him. Reuben sat with a small notebook in his hand and Mary could see a list of names and figures in the book; she touched him gently on the shoulder. With a sharp intake of breath, Reuben swung round, leaping to his feet, his fist clenched, a look of thunder on his face. Realisation dawned as to who it was and his expression softened.

"Mary, you shouldn't do that!" Reuben exclaimed. "I din't 'ear you comin'; you really frit me, you really did."

His face split into a grin, his fist unclenched.

"I'm sorry," said Mary, "I didn't mean to make you jump but you were so taken up with your notebook."

"I know I were," said Reuben. "I'm bin tryin' to add up the acres we ploughed and I keep comin' to a different number; I'll 'ave to get George to do it for me, 'e's good at that."

He closed the notebook and smiled again at Mary.

"And where 'ave you sprung from, Mary, out 'ere in the wilds?"

"I've been at a meeting in Northampton," explained Mary. "Why aren't you working, Reuben?"

"We're run out of coal and I've sent the others off to get some, the farmer should bring it really but this ol' sod says we've got to fetch it from 'is yard which is two mile away."

"Oh dear," said Mary with a smile.

"Do you want a cup of tea, Mary? It won't take long for the kettle to boil."

"That would be nice, Reuben," she replied.

Reuben climbed up the steps into the van, opened the bottom of the little stove and put the kettle on the hob.

"You can sit here, Mary," he said, pointing to the steps and brushing them clean with a muddy hand. Mary sat down gingerly on the cleared area as Reuben placed two enamel mugs on the top steps ready for the tea.

"You don't drink out of those do you, Reuben?" Mary said, examining the filth-stained mugs.

"I s'pose they ain't very clean, are they," sniffed Reuben, "I'll swill 'em out with some 'ot water first."

"Well," said Mary hesitantly, "I'm not sure."

"Ah, I just fort," Reuben said, "there's one china mug up 'ere; you can 'ave that – it's clean as a whistle."

He plucked the mug down from a high shelf, wiped it on his sleeve and handed it to Mary, pouring some milk into the mug as Mary peered into the van.

"I don't know how you all fit in here," Mary said, looking about in the gloom.

"It's a bit cosy," said Reuben. "But I don't stop 'ere at the moment; I'm near enough to get 'ome every night and any road it's Sunday tomorra and we don't work Sundays."

He warmed the pot with the boiled water and brewed the tea, placing a packet of sugar – with a spoon sticking out the top – on the top step next to the mugs.

Mary walked across to the engine, looking up at its gleaming metal. The engine was silent except for the occasional hiss of steam. She read the name on the brass plate on the side of the boiler.

William.

"Reuben, that name," she said, walking back as Reuben poured out the tea, "William."

"What about it?" Reuben said.

"Didn't Roland Cumber used to drive it?"

"Yes," said Reuben.

"And the living-van? Is it the same one?"

"Yes," said Reuben.

They sipped their tea tentatively. It was scalding hot and Mary put hers down.

"He's been dead quite a while now," Mary said thoughtfully.

"No one will miss 'im, Mary; 'e were no good and that sums it up."

"You're right, Reuben," she said quietly.

"Mary?" Reuben said, looking down into his tin mug.

"Yes, Reuben?"

"Are you goin' walkin' tomorra?"

Mary thought for a while.

"I might be, I don't know yet, why?"

Reuben pulled at his chin with his large hand.

"I was wonderin'—"

He broke off and looked down at his tea again.

"You were wondering what, Reuben?"

"Well I was wonderin' if you were goin' walkin', could I come too?"

Mary said nothing but sipped again at her tea.

"Well I don't know whether I will or not," she said evasively, "it depends on the weather and chapel and all sorts of things."

She looked away across the field.

"Well if you do go, can I come along?" asked Reuben gently.

Mary did not reply but brushed at her skirt to clear imaginary dust. She looked at Reuben.

"I don't see why not, I can't stop you really," she said nonchalantly.

Reuben smiled and stood up, stretching out his back as he did so.

"How will I know when you're goin'?" said Reuben curiously.

"I'll whistle; that will be the sign," said Mary simply.

"Very good," he said.

They sat in companionable silence for a while, before Mary handed Reuben back the mug, thanked him for the tea and left.

The next day, Mary decided that she would go to chapel once, in the evening. Thomas and Charlotte attended in the morning as well and Mary announced that while they were out she would get some fresh air and walk to the top of the hill. She walked from the back of the butcher's shop across the paddock, turning through the gateway up the hill. From here she was only fifty yards from the Heightons' house. She put her two index fingers in her mouth and gave a sharp whistle and walked on. As she hadn't slowed her pace, she was across the next pasture field before Reuben caught her up.

"Hang on, Mary," he shouted, running to catch her up," you're walking so fast."

Mary smiled at him and pressed on.

"You din't go to chapel then, Mary?"

"Not this morning, we are going this evening."

"Our lot 'ave gone as well," Reuben said, opening the next gate for Mary to walk through.

"How many of you at home now then, Reuben?" Mary asked, always amazed that such a big family could fit in such a small house.

"Only me now," he said, "all the rest – Robert and all the others – are gone and married, except Amy and she's in service so she don't live at 'ome anymore."

"So why aren't *you* married, Reuben; they say all the girls chase after you," Mary joked.

"Well—" said Reuben, breaking off and chewing at his lip.

"Well what?" Mary pushed him further.

He thought for a moment and then replied,

"Well I just ain't married –so what."

He shrugged as they walked on, finally reaching the top of the hill from where they admired the view. Reuben inhaled once deeply and gently took Mary's hand, squeezing it tightly.

"Reuben!" Mary said sternly, snatching her hand away.

"I din't mean no 'arm, Mary," said Reuben forlornly.

She sighed as Reuben looked at the ground.

"Reuben, look at me," said Mary gently, grabbing both his hands and pulling him to face her.

"How old do you think I am, Reuben?"

Reuben shrugged his shoulders.

"I'm not sure," he said.

"I'm thirty-one, Reuben; I must be nine years older than you."

"So what?" Reuben challenged.

"So I have two children and I am still married, Reuben, that's what," said Mary, her voice rising.

702

"'E ain't never comin' back, Mary," countered Reuben sharply. "You know that, 'e were never any good – you ain't 'eard anything from 'im fer years, I bet."

"No, I haven't but until I know what's happened, I can't—"

She stopped herself and looked down at the ground.

"Well I can't anyway," she said quietly.

Reuben hung his head dejectedly. Mary raised her hand, stroking his cheek with the back of her fingers.

"Come on, Reuben," she soothed, "don't look like that; you'll find someone and fall in love and get married, you'll see."

"No, I won't," Reuben snapped. "I ain't goin' to marry no one else, so there."

Tears formed in his eyes and his fingers bunched into fists as he looked away angrily.

"Come on," she said, putting her arm through his, "time to get back."

She shook him and laughed.

"Cheer up, Reuben, you're such a lovely looking boy, I can't bear to see you miserable."

Reuben sniffed and wiped his nose on the sleeve of his jacket.

"Go on, smile," she said with a laugh, peering up at his determinedly downturned mouth.

He shook his head again, unable to stop the smile creeping across his face. Mary laughed delightedly.

"There you go, Reuben, that wasn't that difficult, was it?" she teased.

Reuben laughed and grabbed up Mary's hand, looping her arm through his. Mary smiled up at him, and didn't pull away.

Chapter Fifty-Six
Nurse Ladds delivers Arthur

William's prediction about the war proved to be correct and on the 28th of July 1914, England declared war on Germany. William was one of the first in the area to volunteer for military service but was turned down as he was a farmer. George and Reuben decided that they would join the army if the war was to go on much longer, but the general feeling was that it would be over very quickly. Verity returned home to await Maurice's return in the autumn as he had been recalled for service in France.

Mary completed an assignment in London and returned to Dean in late August to find a letter from Rebecca. She was expecting her first child and wanted Mary to attend as her midwife. The baby was due in late November so Mary made the necessary arrangements with her agent and arranged the dates in her diary. Rebecca also had news of Molly who she hoped was going to marry Jupp, their chauffeur.

The three months to November passed quickly and it was with a sense of excitement that Mary packed her bags to leave; she was looking forward to renewing her friendship with Rebecca and also to seeing Molly again. At the station, Jupp was there to meet her in the car.

"Did I hear that you have some good news Jupp?" Mary asked as they drove up the hill.

"Yes, Mrs Ladds, you mean me and Molly are goin' to be married?" smiled Jupp. "Yes, we are."

"And when will the happy day be?" Mary enquired.

"Well, Mrs Ladds, we don't rightly know. I'm goin' to volunteer, you know, and we think we will marry when the war's finished."

Mary smiled and looked out of the window.

When they arrived at the house, Molly excitedly pulled open the door as soon as she heard the car on the drive; Rebecca rushed past her to greet Mary first.

"Mary my dear," she gushed, "how wonderful to see you and don't you look smart in your uniform! I didn't expect you to come dressed like this. Molly, come on, take Mary's cloak."

The uniform was indeed very smart; a black cloak over a grey striped blouse with a white skirt and apron. On her head she wore a small black cap tied with a white ribbon under her chin; a thick belt with a smart silver buckle circled her waist. The whole outfit looked very smart and could not disguise what a youthful figure Mary still retained. Molly took the cloak, folded it over her arm and waited while Mary and Rebecca embraced. Rebecca turned to Jupp who was standing at the door with Mary's two bags.

"Vincent, run those up to Mrs Ladds's room, will you," she instructed, before turning back to Mary. "I am so pleased to see you; I've got lots of plans to discuss, but first, Molly, show Mrs Ladds to her room, will you and then we will have some tea in the drawing room."

Molly nodded and slowly led the way upstairs to Mary's bedroom – a large room with huge gabled windows overlooking the vegetable garden and beyond, with views into the large park over the road. Molly put the cloak on the back of the chair and turned to Mary, who took off her cap and smiled back at Molly. Finally, unable to contain herself any longer, Molly rushed forward, flinging her arms round Mary, tears springing to her eyes as Mary held her closely.

"Don't cry, Molly, please don't, you'll make me cry as well," Mary said, holding Molly's shoulders and looking at her earnestly. Molly wiped her nose on her sleeve and smiled at Mary, using her knuckles to push the tears from her eyes.

"You look so well, Molly, and you're going to get married, I hear."

"Yes, it's good here, Mary. It's really good and Vincent's a good man," Molly smiled, adding with a small laugh, "it were no good me waitin' for Reuben, was it?"

"I s'pose not," said Mary quietly.

"And how are Jack and Ethil, Mary? I mean Mrs Ladds."

"Molly, call me Mary in here," smiled Mary. "Jack and Ethil are well; they send their love."

"And Miss Lucy and Martha and Henry, and Mr and Mrs Dunmore?"

"Yes, yes, everyone is well," laughed Mary.

"And what about poor Reuben, Mary? Is he still the same? 'E would die for you, Mary, you know that."

"Molly, don't say such things," said Mary helplessly. "He's busy ploughing and I haven't seen him for months. Now come on, I must go downstairs."

When she returned to the drawing room, Rebecca's husband Aubrey had returned.

"Aubrey darling," Rebecca said, standing up and smiling at Mary, "can I introduce Mary Ladds our midwife; Mary this is my husband Aubrey Hurrell."

Aubrey walked forward, bowed very slightly and shook Mary's hand.

"My dear, I've heard so much about you," he smiled. "What a pleasure to finally meet you."

Mary looked carefully at the man in front of her; Aubrey was not what she had expected, he was very much more conventional looking and in no way bohemian.

"The pleasure's mine, Mr Hurrell," she smiled, offering no more comment than that.

"You're well qualified, Mrs Ladds, in the art of midwifery, I hope?" he said.

"Yes, Mr Hurrell."

"Aubrey, you shouldn't be so rude; of course Mary is well qualified," Rebecca interrupted with a frown.

"Yes, sir," Mary said. "I trained for three and a half years at the London Hospital and this will be my eleventh delivery since then."

"Thank you, Mrs Ladds, just thought I would ask, you know," he nodded. "Got to go, my dear, a client is waiting; see you at dinner, Mrs Ladds."

With a small bow, he left.

The next day Jupp drove them into Northampton. The baby was due in nine days and the doctor was coming the day after tomorrow for his last visit so Rebecca had planned that they would go shopping for the last time before the baby arrived, stopping for lunch at The County Hotel, as they had used to.

Rebecca insisted that Mary not wear her uniform, saying it made it look like Rebecca was an invalid. They went into Tibbitts to get things for the baby, but in the years since Mary had left, all had changed and Mary could see very few people she knew. Peveril had long since retired due to ill health and Mrs Stevens had left. The only person she recognised was Frisby scurrying around the corners of the shop as he always had done, and he made no attempt to be friendly.

At the County Hotel they were shown to their seats by a waitress.

"Did you notice that, Mary: waitresses in here!" Rebecca whispered. "Never been seen before; it's the war, you know, all the men are going to the war."

She smiled and accepted a menu from another waitress, before turning with a worried look to Mary.

"Aubrey says he will volunteer in the New Year if the war goes on and Jupp has been to get his papers; it's awful, I think, just awful."

"I know," sighed Mary. "William already tried to volunteer and they turned him down, but Reuben says he will sign up in the New Year."

"Who's Reuben, Mary, do I know him?" asked Rebecca.

"He's just a boy lives next to the butcher's shop; I don't think you know him," said Mary distractedly, concentrating hard on the menu.

Rebecca leaned back in her chair and fanned her face with the menu.

"Are you all right, Rebecca, nothing is happening, is it?" Mary said, concern etched across her face.

"No, no, don't worry; just had a bit of a flush – you know how it is."

She fanned her face more vigorously, and looked around the room.

"Oh, look who we have here, Mary!" cried Rebecca with a small wink at Mary. "You will know who this is."

Mary turned, to see a man in uniform talking to the waitress at the door; it was Rupert Nelson.

"That's the trouble with coming to this place," whispered Rebecca, "you always bump into someone you know. Do you want to say hello to him, Mary? I'm sure he'd like to see you, he always carried a torch for you, and he does look good in uniform, don't you think."

Before Mary could say anything Rebecca had waved over towards Rupert, who looked up and smiled. Mary, with her back to Rupert, didn't turn round. Rebecca beckoned more vigorously and Rupert started to walk somewhat self-consciously across the dining room.

"Now, what have we got here?" said Rebecca with a laugh. "General Lord Nelson? You look quite the part, Rupert; doesn't he look smart, Mary?"

Mary turned round and smiled at Rupert.

"Very smart," she said quietly.

"Mary... Mrs Ladds, how are you?" stammered Rupert, blushing and bowing slightly, first to Rebecca and then Mary.

"I'm well," Mary said.

There was an awkward silence. Rebecca surveyed the pair of them with a flicker of amusement.

"Well go on – say something," Rebecca challenged.

"Well, it's such a surprise," Rupert said desperately, flushing scarlet.

"I can see that," Rebecca sniggered. "You look a bit red; it must be the thick uniform, don't you think, Mary?"

"Rebecca," Mary reprimanded.

"Well I'm hot as well," cried Rebecca indignantly. "But it's my condition, you know."

She winked mischievously at Mary. Rupert looked puzzled.

"I'm sorry to hear that," he said uncertainly.

"Rupert, I'm having a baby in a week or so, didn't you notice?"

Rebecca raised an eyebrow at Mary; Rupert blushed again and looked away from Rebecca who laughed heartily. Rupert swayed a little, moving his weight from one foot to the other, searching desperately for something else to say.

"Congratulations, Rebecca, when is the baby due?" he said finally.

"In just over a week; that is why Mary is here, she's a top-class midwife now."

She fanned herself again and looked pointedly at Mary. Mary looked down at her menu distractedly.

"Well, Rupert, what are you doing in uniform? Come on, sit down and tell us all about it," Rebecca ordered.

"Well I'm supposed to be meeting Mother," he said, looking hopefully at his watch, "but I suppose it will be five minutes before she arrives."

He stood dithering, looking towards the door.

"Well tell us all, Rupert, spill the beans," said Rebecca, pointing to the spare chair at their table.

"Well there's not much to tell," shrugged Rupert, "I have volunteered for the war, you know."

"And?" Rebecca prompted.

"And I was accepted," said Rupert with a small laugh. "But I'm a bit old so I'm going to be a war correspondent for the *Daily Mail*. I've been made Acting Second Lieutenant and I've got to do basic training but then I go off to report the war."

"How exciting and you shouldn't get shot doing that," exclaimed Rebecca eagerly.

"I suppose not," Rupert answered uncertainly as Rebecca suddenly pushed her chair backward, stood up and bent over to whisper in Mary's ear:

"I'm going 'down the end' as you would say, I will leave you two to coo at each other."

She winked at Rupert and waddled slowly across the dining room.

Rupert looked at Mary and smiled, cleared his throat to speak, then hesitated. Mary cast her eyes down to her gloved hands and said nothing.

"Did you have any reply to that advertisement, Mary?" he asked quietly.

Mary looked up.

"Oh dear," she said with a small frown, "that was a long time ago. No, I've heard nothing."

The pair looked away from each other; this time Mary took the initiative.

"Your uniform looks very smart, Rupert," she said simply.

"Do you think so?" he said with a smile. "It's not army issue, you know; Mother said the issue ones would not fit well enough, so I got it made in London."

"Very nice," said Mary.

"But the boots are from Northampton," he chipped in quickly. "Northampton is doing well out of supplying army boots; you ask Mr Harding, I think he will make a fortune."

"I suppose he will," said Mary.

Rupert nodded calmly and then leant forward earnestly.

"Could I call and see you while you are with Rebecca, Mary?" he said.

His cheeks coloured again. Mary fingered her napkin and considered his proposal.

"Well, Rupert, I really don't know," said Mary. "Rebecca will have the baby soon and we will be very busy and have so much to think about."

She looked up to see Rupert's mother standing behind his chair looking critically down at her.

"Ah ha," she coughed, tilting her chin up and looking at Rupert questioningly, "Rupert darling, you must introduce me."

She sniffed, looking over her glasses at Mary again.

"Mother, I'm sorry I didn't see you," said Rupert with a start. "Can I introduce Mary Knighton—?"

He stopped and shook his head.

"I'm sorry, Mary, I mean Mary Ladds. Mrs Mary Ladds; Mother, you must remember Mary!"

Mary stood up and offered her hand to Christiana, who took it limply and gave Mary a frosty smile.

"I remember," she said. "You were behind the counter at Tibbitts, weren't you; yes, Peveril always spoke very highly of you. And I nearly forgot your uncle is George Henry Chambers; I remember you telling me when you came to lunch"

Rebecca had now returned and stood waiting to take her place again.

"Rebecca darling," cooed Christiana, whirling round with a delighted smile, "look at you – the size of a house! When's it due?"

She pecked Rebecca's cheek and stood back.

"Mother," Rupert said warningly; but Christiana paid no attention.

"You look a picture of health, Rebecca; come, when's it due?"

"In just over a week; that's why Mary is here, she's my midwife."

"Ah, Mary, now I understand," said Christiana, giving Mary something approaching a genuine smile.

She turned to her son.

"Now come on, Rupert; these two want to talk about things that are not for your ears."

She linked her arm through Rupert's and turned to Rebecca again.

"Rebecca dear, we will call as soon as the baby has arrived and you are recovered."

She smiled, nodded to Mary and dragged Rupert off to the other side of the dining room.

"Well then, Mary," Rebecca said, sitting down again. "How did you get on? Didn't you think I was clever to leave you alone!"

Mary frowned, as Rebecca laughed delightedly and lowered her voice confidentially.

"What did he say? He must have said something. I'm sure he is in love with you, Mary; I know he is," Rebecca looked at Mary in hopeful anticipation; Mary shrugged.

"He didn't say much, but he asked if he could visit."

"What did you say?" Rebecca demanded.

"I said we would be too busy with the baby about to arrive."

She cut off Rebecca's denial with a wave of her hand.

"I'm right, Rebecca," she insisted. "This is your first one and we will be busy."

"I suppose so," said Rebecca grudgingly.

"And don't forget, Rebecca, I'm still married, I can't—"

She stopped and looked down.

"I got married in a church and I believe –" persisted Mary, before stopping again, "well if you make promises you should keep them, that's all I mean."

Mary pursed her lips and looked straight at Rebecca who raised an eyebrow and stared right back at Mary.

"I know!" Rebecca said suddenly, her face lighting up. "That's what it must be! There must be someone else, someone else in your life and who could it be? Let's think."

She put her hand in front of her mouth and rolled her eyes theatrically. She grinned at Mary.

"I know – it's that chap you mentioned last night, the one who had volunteered."

"I don't know who you're talking about," Mary answered defensively.

"Yes, you do," Rebecca said, "I'll get his name in a moment."

She paused for a moment, enjoying Mary's discomfort.

"Reuben! That's his name."

She leant forward.

"Who's Reuben?"

Rebecca grinned at Mary, who for a moment bowed her head and chewed her lip before looking up again, avoiding Rebecca's gaze.

"Don't be silly, Rebecca," she said quietly. "Reuben is just a farm boy who lives near the butcher's shop."

"Mary, you're going red!" exclaimed Rebecca.

"No, I'm not."

"Yes, you are," laughed Rebecca. "Just a farm boy where?"

"He's not a farm boy."

"Well, what is he then?"

"He drives the engines, ploughing engines I mean; well he's foreman now, helps to organise the business."

Mary sniffed, took out her hankie and blew her nose.

"Rebecca, don't go on," she begged. "All these people are going to the war and William is sure it won't be finished for ages. Some of them will be killed or injured. Your Aubrey says he's going, Jupp is going, Rupert is and Reuben and thousands more; they won't all come back, Rebecca."

She sniffed again and looked down at her food.

"Please can we change the subject?" she said quietly.

Rebecca frowned slightly and nodded.

The next day the doctor came to visit. They waited for him in the drawing room, Mary now wearing her uniform and looking very much the part.

"When's he coming?" Mary asked.

"When he's done his surgery, you can never tell; sometimes it's ten o'clock, sometimes it's midday before he gets here."

The bell rang and moments later Molly showed in the doctor.

"Doctor Pingstone, Mrs Hurrell," she announced.

"Thank you, Molly; would you like some refreshment, doctor?" Rebecca asked. "Coffee, tea, a glass of something?"

"Coffee sounds very nice but let's do the examination first," said the doctor with a smile.

"Very well; coffee, Molly, in about fifteen minutes," Rebecca demanded.

Molly bobbed and disappeared.

"Can I introduce Nurse Ladds, doctor; she is my midwife."

Mary stood up and shook the doctor's hand.

"Pleased to meet you, Nurse Ladds," he smiled. "Now, Mrs Hurrell, if you would like to go and get prepared for examination and I can have a word with the nurse."

Rebecca smiled.

"Give me two minutes," she said and left the room.

"Now, Nurse Ladds," said Doctor Pingstone sharply, looking at her severely, "where did you train?"

"The London Hospital."

"For how long?"

"Three and a half years."

"How many confinements have you attended?"

"This will be number eleven, doctor."

"Are you confident you know what you are doing?"

"Yes, doctor," said Mary firmly.

The doctor walked over to the window, looking interestedly into the garden.

"Lovely garden this house has, doesn't it, Nurse Ladds?" he said softly.

"Yes, doctor," agreed Mary, as he turned back to her.

"Nurse Ladds, the reason I ask all these questions is because I have seen too many disasters in childbirth caused by incompetent midwives who don't know what they are doing; especially when the mothers are older. However, you seem to be well qualified; I was at the London Hospital myself, not a better place to train. Did you meet Dr Barclay?"

"Yes, doctor."

"He's still alive then?"

"Yes, doctor," said Mary.

Molly entered.

"Mrs Hurrell says she's ready for you, doctor."

"Very good," nodded the doctor, "come, Nurse Ladds."

He left the drawing room, taking the stairs three at a time and marching down the corridor. Mary scurried after him, indicating the room in which Rebecca was.

As the doctor examined Rebecca he questioned Mary, assessing her depth of knowledge and pointing out and suggesting things. He completed his examination and picked up his bag.

"All seems well, Mrs Hurrell, and I think you are in good hands with Nurse Ladds. If I can wash my hands, I will see you downstairs. Nurse Ladds, would you come with me."

The doctor was shown the bathroom, as Mary moved back to the drawing room to wait for him. She heard him galloping downstairs moments before he entered the room, sitting himself down opposite her.

"Nurse Ladds, all seems fine but when the confinement comes you are to contact me if there are any complications or you are in any doubt. Do you understand?"

"Yes, doctor."

"Very good," he nodded, as Rebecca returned and started to pour out the coffee.

Eight days later, Mary was writing letters in her room, enjoying the afternoon sunshine creeping through the window when Molly banged on the door and entered, all of a fluster.

"Mary, come quick, she says she's started."

"Very good, Molly, I'm coming; where is Mr Hurrell?"

"In the studio I think, shall I go and fetch 'im?"

"No, not yet," Mary said calmly. "Let's make sure things are happening first."

She rushed downstairs to find Rebecca on the settee.

"Rebecca, are you sure? Have your contractions started?" Mary asked.

"Yes, I'm sure, Mary; that's the fourth," gasped Rebecca, wincing.

"Very good, upstairs with you and Molly, you go and tell Mr Hurrell."

She looked at the clock – it was four in the afternoon and just getting dark. Upstairs everything was prepared for the delivery in the spare room and Mary was confident that she was well organised. Molly had been briefed on her role; to keep Mary supplied with tea, sandwiches, towels and sheets, and Jupp was instructed not to go home in case he was needed to fetch the doctor.

Evening disappeared into night and no one except Aubrey had gone to bed. Jupp was sound asleep in a chair in the kitchen, Molly napping quietly beside him. It was daylight before Molly crept upstairs, meeting Mary on the landing.

"Is everything all right, Mary?" she whispered. "It's bin a long time."

"I think we are fine," said Mary. "I've known many longer."

Molly frowned and chewed her lip.

"Should I tell Vincent to fetch the doctor?"

"No," Mary said firmly. "I can manage; you give Mr Hurrell his breakfast and bring us something to eat and some coffee, Molly."

Molly nodded and went down to fetch some food and prepare the coffee. She returned a short while later, tapping on the door and entering with the tray.

"Everything all right, Mary?" said Molly, looking over at Rebecca, who was pale, a sheen of sweat glistening on her brow.

"Yes, I think so," Mary replied – but the note of certainty had disappeared.

"You don't want me to send for the doctor?" asked Molly.

"No, we should be fine," Mary replied.

Molly hesitated a moment, opened her mouth to speak, thought better of it and disappeared back downstairs.

An hour later, she tiptoed into the delivery room again. There was still no baby and Rebecca looked very uncomfortable; her breathing was shallow and a small tremor shook her from time to time.

"Mary?" Molly whispered.

Mary looked up distractedly.

"Is she all right?" asked Molly.

Mary did not answer. Molly looked again at Rebecca.

"She ain't right, Mary, I'm seed plenty of babies bein' born but she ain't doin' too well; let me send Vincent."

Mary said nothing; she just sat staring at Rebecca, wringing her hands.

"Mary, say something!" begged Molly.

She moved to Mary and shook her shoulders gently – Mary shuddered.

"I'm goin' to send Vincent to get 'im whatever," said Molly, rushing to the door.

"Very good then, Molly," Mary said, suddenly alert, as if all she had ever needed was somebody else to make the decision for her.

"Tell him to hurry."

Fifteen minutes later, Jupp returned with the doctor who bounded up the stairs into the delivery room, took one look at Rebecca and moved quickly to her side. An hour later the baby was born, a boy who appeared healthy. Rebecca was handed her son, wrapped tightly in a blanket. Her face was lined with exhaustion as she looked down at the little bundle in her arms and smiled. Doctor Pingstone gestured for Mary to follow him out of the room.

"Well done, Nurse Ladds; that wasn't the easiest of deliveries," he said quietly.

Mary nodded. Doctor Pingstone eyed her earnestly.

"You should have called me earlier; you left her too long. You know that, don't you? You should have called me,"

"Yes, doctor," Mary said quietly, "perhaps I should have."

Chapter Fifty-Seven
The War

It wasn't long before Rebecca was out of bed proudly showing off her son – Arthur George – and Mary left three weeks later. She had only a day in Dean before she had to leave again for her next job in London. From London she moved to Yorkshire, from Yorkshire to Devon and it was early March before she was able to return to Dean again. She arrived at the butcher's shop at ten o'clock on Friday morning, leant her bike against the wall and went into the shop. George was cutting up joints ready for the round in the afternoon as Mary took off her hat and undid her coat.

"Mrs Ladds," he said quietly, nodding to Mary.

"George, you look well!" exclaimed Mary. "It seems like yesterday that William was bringing you for your first day at school and now here you are running the shop."

George smiled.

"Not for much longer," he said.

"No, George, why's that?" Mary asked.

"I've joined up!" he said proudly. "Reuben and me went last week to Bedford and we go for a medical on Monday; if we pass we go to war."

"Oh George, are you sure you want to?" said Mary worriedly.

"Yes, Mrs Ladds!" insisted George. "It's all right, they say we can go together, Reuben and me. There's lots more going you know, some are in already and lots more say they will sign up. I don't want to miss it, do I? Got to fight for the country, haven't we?"

"If you say so, George," said Mary dubiously. "Now who is about?"

"Well Mr Dunmore has gone to market, Mrs Dunmore is in the kitchen, William is at Covington but will be back and I think I heard that Miss Lucy was coming to see Mrs Dunmore."

George picked up a steel and started to clash a knife up and down it furiously.

"Don't let me stop you," laughed Mary. "I'll go and find Mrs Dunmore."

In the kitchen, Charlotte sat by the range in her rocking chair, her Bible on her lap and a shawl around her shoulders. At the table stirring a mixing bowl was a young girl in a black dress and flowery apron. Charlotte looked across the room at Mary.

"My dear, how lovely to see you, it's been so long!" Charlotte cried. "Come and give me a kiss; you look well, Mary, you do look well. You've put on some weight, dear, if I'm not mistaken and it suits you! A woman of your age shouldn't be skin and bones. Ivy, put that to one side and get the kettle on. Oh—" She turned to Mary.

"This is Ivy, Mary; say hello to Mrs Ladds, Ivy."

"Hello, Mrs Ladds," Ivy said hesitantly.

"You will need some more water, dear; you will have to go to the pump."

Ivy went out with the kettle. Charlotte turned to Mary conspiratorially and said,

"We had to let Sabine go, she was useless; like a light gone out, Thomas said. This one's much better; I'll knock her into shape quite quickly, you'll see. Now tell me your news, Mary; sit down, my dear, sit down. *And* – I nearly forgot to tell you, guess who's coming today?"

Charlotte excitedly clasped her hands together and grinned at Mary.

Mary shook her head.

"Lucy!" Charlotte exclaimed.

"Well I never, what a lovely surprise," Mary said, with a small smile.

Ten minutes later William arrived, followed moments later by Lucy.

"Ivy dear, get some more cups and some plates and get the cake out," instructed Charlotte "Everyone sit down at the table; come on, Lucy, take your coat off."

"Have you walked all the way from Sharnbrook, Lucy?" William asked.

Lucy sniffed and rubbed her nose.

"It's only about seven miles," she said with a shrug. "Now tell us about young Thomas then, William." Thomas had been born to William and Grace just before Christmas – William's eyes lit up as he started to relate stories of his young son. A knock at the door interrupted his tales – the latch clicked and George's head appeared around the door.

718

"Mrs Dene is in the shop, Mrs Dunmore," announced George.

"Hang on, George, I'll be there directly," nodded Charlotte, who was always alerted when important people came into the shop.

Charlotte scooted out the door and the others could hear her saying,

"Mrs Dene, how lovely to see you, is George attending to you?"

"Yes thank you," replied Verity. "Mrs Dunmore, is that Mary's voice I can hear?"

"Yes my dear, would you like to see her? Do come in; Lucy is here as well and William."

"Oh, Mrs Dunmore, do you mind? It's such a long time since I have seen them," replied Verity, following Charlotte into the kitchen, calling back over her shoulder,

"Dorcas, you stay here and talk to George."

"No, no, Mrs Dene, bring Dorcas in, she knows everyone," insisted Charlotte, chivvying Dorcas into the kitchen. "Ivy, bring up the chair, can you for Mrs Dene? More cups and saucers, plates!"

"Come on," said Dorcas, "I'll give you an 'and, Ivy."

Verity beaming at everyone.

"Mary, Lucy and William," she exclaimed, "how wonderful to see you all together."

Verity kissed Mary and Lucy and shook hands with William.

"William, I was just on my way to see Grace and the new baby," Verity said.

"Yes, she is expecting you."

"I mustn't be too long then."

"Don't worry, Verity, Grace's never early; there will be plenty of time," laughed William.

"I should have been before but what with getting Maurice ready to go to France," said Verity hesitantly, trying to keep the smile on her face, "I have had no time."

"This wretched war," said Charlotte vehemently, "I wish it were over all; those poor chaps getting killed and George is going now, I don't know who's going to run the shop."

"George is going?" said Verity.

"Yes," said William, "and Reuben."

"Roderick has already gone," Lucy said quietly.

"Yes dear, but he's not fighting," Charlotte soothed her.

"Aunt Charlotte, Roderick is a stretcher bearer; he is right in the middle of the battles!" said Lucy angrily.

Charlotte blushed and said nothing.

"It's much worse than it says in the papers," said William, adding: "they try to make it sound like it's glorious and that we're doing so well but in reality—"

"I'm going," said Lucy quietly.

There was silence.

"You're doing what, Lucy?" Charlotte said sharply.

"I have volunteered to nurse in the hospitals behind the lines," Lucy sniffed, wiping her nose.

"You can't do that, Lucy – not with all those men, it's not right," said Charlotte indignantly.

"If Roderick is out there, I am going as well," said Lucy firmly.

"Lucy my dear, how brave you are," interrupted Verity. "William is right –Maurice says the same – it *is* much worse than it says in the papers. I think you are so brave, Lucy, you really are; I wish I could go, but I'm not trained or as brave as you are, and I could never leave Father."

Verity put her arm round Lucy and hugged her.

"That's what I came to tell you, Aunt Charlotte," said Lucy, sniffing again.

Charlotte turned to Mary, glaring at her fiercely.

"Don't you dare tell me you are going too, Mary Knighton, I won't have it; you can't leave two children, tell me you are not going."

She turned with a degree of panic to Verity.

"I'm sorry to speak to her like this, Mrs Dene, but she has no mother and someone has to tell her."

"I have no mother either, Mrs Dunmore," said Verity quietly.

Charlotte reddened and looked down, before recovering her composure.

"I realise that, Mrs Dene," she said slowly, "but it's not quite the same.

Now tell me, Mary, that you aren't going."

"I'm not going, Aunt Charlotte; I'm a midwife not a nurse," soothed Mary.

"But you're very headstrong, Mary; you always were, and people don't change," continued Charlotte, reaching for her Bible and laying it on her lap for comfort.

Lucy, Verity, William and Mary exchanged glances, hiding their smiles.

"Shall I pour the tea, Mrs Dunmore?" said Dorcas.

"If you please, Dorcas," said Charlotte. "Ivy, you cut the cake."

When they had finished their tea, Verity rose to leave.

"We must go, Mrs Dunmore; it was so kind of you to entertain us and so lovely to see Mary and Lucy."

She looked earnestly at Charlotte.

"You mustn't worry; Lucy is doing a wonderful thing going out to nurse the troops. I think it is absolutely splendid."

She gave Lucy a kiss and then Mary and turned to Dorcas.

"Now, Dorcas, are you coming with me or going back to cook the lunch?"

"I'll come with you, Miss Verity, if you don't mind; I'd love to see the new baby and lunch is cold so it will be all right."

"Very well," said Verity, following William out into the butcher's shop.

"When have you got to go back, Lucy?" Charlotte asked as they left. "Why don't you stay the night?"

"Well I thought I would go back after lunch and I haven't got anything with me," Lucy protested, "and there's no room is there?"

"You can borrow some of my things," Mary said, "and there are two mattresses on my bed; we could put one of them on the floor."

She turned pleadingly to her sister.

"Do stay, Lucy, if you are going away, we might not see you for a long time! Say you will."

"Very well then," Lucy smiled.

"And we can go for a walk to Cold Harbour, it's nice and dry – is there time before lunch, Aunt Charlotte?"

"Lunch is cold," said Charlotte, "so it doesn't matter if you were to be a little late."

"That would be lovely," Lucy said. "I haven't been up there since we left; I'll just go down the end then I will be ready."

The two sisters made their way towards their old home, wrapped up tightly against the cold. Halfway up the hill towards the bridleway, they could see a figure on their knees by the hedge.

"What's he doing?" Lucy asked. "Who is it?"

"I don't know, let's go and have a look," Mary said.

As they got closer they recognised Reuben; he leapt to his feet and pulled off his cap as he saw them approaching.

"Reuben Heighton, what are you doing? Saying your prayers?" teased Mary.

"No, I'm ferreting," said Reuben with a smile. "William said he don't mind; he wants me to get rid of the rabbits. And Mother says she can't afford to feed me if I don't bring no money so I'm gettin' our dinner."

"Poor rabbit," said Lucy.

"George tells me you've joined up, Reuben," Mary said.

"Yes, we are goin' for the medical on Monday; we start soon if they pass us fit."

"You will pass, Reuben, you look fit," Mary said, before looking down and blushing.

"Did you know that Lucy is going out as well? She's going to nurse in the field hospitals," she added hurriedly.

"We might see you then, Miss Lucy," Reuben said.

"I hope not, Reuben," said Mary sharply.

"Oh yes, I suppose I wouldn't want to be seeing you, would I?" said Reuben worriedly. "But I ain't going to get 'urt, you see, nor will George. I hope it lasts till we get there, it might be all over soon, some folks say."

"Where's your ferret, Reuben?" Mary asked, unwilling to carry on this vein of conversation.

"In this 'ere box," he said, pointing to a small oblong box which lay on the grass next to four dead rabbits.

"Do you want to see 'im then?" grinned Reuben, bending down and opening the box to pull out the ferret. The animal was completely white and tumbled through his hands, wriggling furiously to be let back into the hedge.

"Do you want to 'old 'im?" Reuben asked Mary. "'E won't bite you."

"No, I don't," said Mary firmly. "You keep him away from me, he smells awful."

"I'll put 'im down the 'ole," Reuben said, bending down and slipping the ferret into a hole which was covered with a tightly woven net.

"Quiet!" he whispered. "I'm got all the other 'oles netted."

He put his finger to his lips and they waited in silence looking from hole to hole. Suddenly there was a scuffle; a rabbit had bolted into one of the nets. Reuben threw himself over it, grabbing the rabbit and with one quick blow with the side of his hand, killing it. He disentangled the limp body from the net and threw it down with the others. Lucy winced.

"Come on, Lucy," Mary said. "We must get on; goodbye, Reuben."

Reuben lifted his cap as they left.

"I'll be in uniform next time we meet I dare say," he called out.

"I'd like to see that," Mary called back with a smile.

Lucy frowned.

"Mary," whispered Lucy that night, after they had gone to bed.

"Yes," Mary replied, shifting in her bed to face her sister.

"You know all these men going to the war?"

"Yes, what about them?"

"Some of them are going to get killed; I know they are."

She sniffed. Mary said nothing.

"When you think of them all; Roderick, George, Reuben and all the others, they're not all going to come back, you know that?"

Mary rolled onto her back looking at the ceiling where the dim light of the moon slanted in from a chink in the curtains.

"Yes, I know," she said quietly.

Lucy was silent, as the tears rolled down her cheeks. She sniffed and rubbed her eyes with her hands.

"It's worse for some of them; if they're injured I mean. I've seen some of them in the hospital, Mary, it's horrific. They're not really people anymore, just bits of people."

Lucy sobbed twice. Mary left her bed, moved to her sister and sat down on the edge of her mattress. She wiped the tears from her sister's eyes, kissed her cheek and climbed back into bed, unable to offer any consolation that she herself could really believe in.

Chapter Fifty-Eight
Enlisting

Six weeks later Roderick was shot dead by a sniper while recovering wounded men from the battlefield. Mary had returned to Dean on a Friday to find a letter from Lucy who was now in France. Her letter was matter of fact – it read like a report, not a letter to her sister. Mary shuddered and dropped the letter to the table.

"What should I do, Aunt Charlotte, what can I do?" she asked Charlotte desperately. "I can't go and see her, can I? I must write, but it's so difficult."

"There is nothing you can do except write to dear Lucy," shrugged Charlotte. "But you must pray, dear, yes you must do that; pray for his soul now it is in heaven."

She clutched her Bible to her, something she was doing more and more frequently these days.

"Pray! Pray?" Mary shouted angrily. "That won't bring him back, will it?"

"No, my dear, it won't," said Charlotte quietly, folding her hands over the Bible and shutting her eyes.

"I'm going to see William," Mary announced, putting on her hat and marching out the door.

William and Grace were still living at Way Post Farm for the moment until the farmhouse at Covington was made ready for occupation, which they had been told would be quite soon. It only took ten minutes to walk to Way Post Farm where William was rolling up newly shorn fleeces and putting them in large sacks. He knew immediately from Mary's expression that something was wrong, leaping to his feet and clasping his cousin's hand as tears rolled down her cheeks.

William ushered her into the house and sat her at the table with Grace.

"What can I do, William?" Mary asked. "She's out there all on her own, how will she cope?"

"There, there, Mary," said Grace soothingly. "She will have friends with her."

"I know, I know, but I'm her sister, I ought to be there!"

725

She banged the table with her fist, shaking her head angrily.

"When was he killed, Mary? We have all the papers here, let's look to see if it gives us a clue as to where they are."

Grace picked up a pile of *Daily Mails* from the chair, hefting them onto the table and pushing them towards William. William opened a recent edition to the list of deaths.

"What was his name, Mary? Roderick what?" William asked.

"I don't know," cried Mary, her hand flying to her mouth in horror. "I don't know if she ever said, how stupid I am; why did I never listen to her?"

She put her head in her hands and leant her elbows on the table.

"I'm pretty sure it's Dalby," said Grace quietly. "I'm sure she told me he was Roderick Dalby."

"Here it is," William said, "it must be him. Roderick Dalby: killed in action."

He dropped the paper, and looked sadly at Grace.

"What can we do?" Mary cried. "Poor Lucy, how can we help? We don't know anyone who could see her, we only know soldiers, she needs us and we can't go."

"William said that you know a reporter on the *Daily Mail* who comes from Northampton?" suggested Grace. "He might be able to see her, he would have more chance of finding her than any of the soldiers; does she know him, Mary?"

"Yes, yes, you're right, Grace," gasped Mary. "Rupert Nelson! Yes, she does know him, she's met him more than once, I'm sure. I will write to him; he would try and see her, I know he would if he could and I've got an address which will find him; but I must write to Lucy first."

"Yes, I will write as well. Have we got anything to send her, Grace?" William asked.

"I'll think of something," said Grace. "You go and get on writing, Mary; we should catch the second post."

Mary rose decisively, folding herself into her coat. She stopped suddenly, sighing heavily.

"Roderick, dead, I can't believe it!" she whispered. "Such a gentle chap; he was a good man – a bit strange – but he had a good heart."

"He's not going to be the last, Mary, you know that," warned William. "This war won't end yet and it will get worse before it gets better."

"Don't say that, William," begged Mary. "It sounds so depressing."

"William's right, Mary," Grace agreed sadly. "We have to come to terms with the fact that there will be many more men who won't come home."

Mary stood lost in thought, a sad frown creasing her forehead.

In the middle of Saturday afternoon the bell on the shop door announced the arrival of a customer.

"I'll go," said Mary, to her aunt and uncle. "You sit still while I find out what they want."

She opened the door into the shop to reveal George and Reuben standing to attention in their new uniforms. They had both taken off their caps and held them under their arms. The brass buttons on their shirts and the buckles on their belts sparkled and the toecaps of their boots shone brightly. Both of them wore broad grins masking a small amount of self-consciousness.

"My, my," smiled Mary, before calling into the kitchen, "Aunt Charlotte, Uncle Thomas, look who we have here, come you must see these two!"

The pair rushed to the door to see Reuben and George; Thomas nodded delightedly, moving to shake both boys by the hand as Charlotte clapped.

"Come into the kitchen and sit down, you boys," she demanded, leading the way and pulling out a chair for each of them. She placed the biscuit barrel on the table, opening it and turning to George and Reuben with a wink.

"Mother," chided Thomas, "they're not children anymore, you can't give them biscuits! Mary, there's a bottle of sherry on the sideboard in the front room, bring the glasses –we will drink a toast."

"I don't approve of drink, you know that, Thomas," said Charlotte with a reproving tut.

"I know you don't, my dear, but this is a special occasion. Mary, run along then."

Mary went to fetch the sherry as Charlotte turned to the boys.

"We've got some bad news," said Charlotte. "Roderick was killed, you know Lucy's – erm – friend."

"Yes, we know," said George." There's more getting killed now. We heard about him two days ago. Reuben said he met him up at Cold Harbour."

"You know Lucy is out there, don't you?" said Mary, returning with the sherry and pouring out four glasses. "It's so awful."

She looked pointedly at her aunt.

"Are you going to drink their health?" she asked.

"Hmm," said Charlotte, "just a small one then."

Mary smiled and handed her aunt a glass.

"Good luck and good health, George and Reuben," toasted Thomas, looking proudly at the boys.

Reuben and George looked at each other, their cheeks colouring.

"When are you going?" Thomas asked.

"Well we've finished our training and we have to go back on Tuesday but they haven't said exactly when we go, just that it will be within the next month."

"I'm in London for nearly a month," said Mary. "If you let me know when you go, I will come and see you off. Can you do that, George?"

"Yes, Mrs Ladds," he said. "I can send a card if you give me an address."

The atmosphere in chapel the next afternoon was very sombre; the names of those who had been killed in the area were read out, and Charlotte had ensured that Roderick's name was among them. Quite a few of the congregation wore uniform, including George and Reuben and after the service people did not stop to talk as usual, the triviality of chit-chat seeming to be beyond them. Mary walked back to Dean with Dorcas.

"That were a bad thing about Miss Lucy's young man," she said sadly. "I never met 'im, but she will be upset, poor thing, and out in France as well with no family."

She dabbed her eyes with her hankie and blew her nose; Mary's mouth quivered and she looked ready to burst into tears again, Dorcas put her hand on her arm.

"Don't cry, Mary," said Dorcas quietly. "She will manage, you'll see;

there's nothing else to do, but get on with it."

She squeezed Mary's arm and walked away towards The Hall. Mary walked back on her own; the sun was going down and the rooks scattered in the sky, making their way back to the roosts near the butcher's shop. Her thoughts miles away, she did not notice that Reuben had caught her up and was walking beside her. She looked round startled, as she heard his footsteps.

"Sorry, Reuben," she said, "I was miles away and didn't notice you."

She eyed him approvingly – he looked handsome dressed in his uniform, his shiny boots lightly coated in dust from the road.

"Do you mind if I walk with you, Mary?" he asked.

"No not at all," she smiled.

They walked for a while in companionable silence.

"I'm ever so sorry about Miss Lucy's young man, Mary," said Reuben suddenly. "'E were a nice bloke, weren't 'e, a bit odd like, but a nice bloke."

Reuben stopped uncertainly.

"Yes, Reuben, thank you, he was very nice," agreed Mary.

They walked on in silence. At the short cutting, banks lined with trees flanked the road; Mary turned suddenly to Reuben. She seized his hand and looked desperately into his innocent face – Reuben blushed and looked away.

"Reuben, you won't get hurt, will you, when you go to the war?" she said despairingly. "I really wouldn't like that; tell me you won't get hurt!"

She squeezed his hand and held on tight, her eyes never leaving his face.

"No, you need not worry, Mary; I won't get 'urt," he said firmly. "Any road, I've got George to look after me, that's what 'e says."

He looked at her and smiled.

"Yes, I suppose George will look after you, Reuben," she laughed.

They walked on, Mary still holding Reuben's hand. As they approached the butcher's shop, she pulled her hand from his, bid him goodnight and went into the house without a backwards glance.

Three weeks later, true to his word, Mary received a postcard from George with a picture of the Embankment on the front – informing her that he and Reuben were leaving for France in three days' time. They were due to arrive from Bedford at St Pancras and catch a train on from Victoria to Dover, but George did not know the exact times. As Mary was due to leave London later that day, she made her way to St Pancras early that morning.

The station and streets were full of soldiers, all of them in full kit with webbing packs on their front and back, rifles slung over their shoulders. A portion of them were very unkempt, their uniforms were covered in mud, and Mary supposed they must be coming home from the trenches. Inside the station were thousands more uniformed men. Mary looked around her desperately, unsure how she would be able to find George and Reuben in the sea of identically dressed men. She chewed her lip impatiently, looking from face to face. Suddenly she had an idea – she put her index fingers in her mouth and whistled as loudly as she could manage – a few people looked round in surprise, but she didn't care. She was just about to try again when two smartly dressed soldiers materialised in front of her, both grinning from ear to ear.

"Look at you both!" she exclaimed. "With all that kit and a gun as well."

"Rifle," George corrected her.

"Rifle then," she laughed.

"George has got to go soon," said Reuben. "He's in the advance party, takin' some of the kit."

"So what are you doing, Reuben?"

"They told us to make ourselves scarce for two hours but we've got to be back 'ere at half past twelve; we're goin' to march through London to Victoria they said, that's right, George, ain't it?"

"Yes," confirmed George. "But I must go now; I will bid you goodbye, Mrs Ladds."

He smiled and went to shake Mary's hand. Mary laughed and pulled him towards her, pressing her cheek to his. George stood back, lost for words. Slowly, a smile spread across his face, he touched his cheek, waved and disappeared into the crowd.

"Now, Reuben, let's find somewhere to sit; that kit looks awfully heavy," said Mary, grasping Reuben's arm and leading him towards Tavistock Square.

When they reached the square, Mary found them a seat as Reuben undid the webbing belts which held the packs on his front and back. He put them on

730

the seat between them and leant the rifle against the packs.

"What's that thing?" asked Mary, pointing to an object hanging from his belt.

"That's the bayonet, goes on the end of the rifle," Reuben explained.

"You mean it's that long? How dreadful," she exclaimed, "you mean—"

She stopped and looked down, her hands shaking a little.

"I just don't want to think of it," she whispered, looking across at him – she reached across his pack and took his hand.

"Now, Reuben, you're going off to war and it's a very dangerous place," she continued, looking earnestly at Reuben. "I've known you since you were a little boy and all those times at Cold Harbour when you came to help me; I couldn't bear you getting hurt."

"Don't upset yourself, Mary, I won't get 'urt, you'll see; we will both be together to 'elp each other, George and me, I told you that!"

He smiled and squeezed her hand. Mary wiped her eyes.

"You're right, Reuben, I mustn't get like this; it's not fair, you're the one who's going to war, not me!" she sighed.

"I'm sure I'm doin' the right thing," said Reuben quietly. "Everyone else is goin'; I couldn't sit at 'ome while everyone else went off fightin'. Any road, I am proud and the uniform looks good, doesn't' it?"

He turned to her with a wink.

"Yes, you look very handsome in it, Reuben."

"And it's right to fight for your country when it's in danger, ain't it, Mary?"

"Of course it is, Reuben."

"And I ain't never bin abroad before; in fact, I ain't never bin to London till today," he laughed.

"Perhaps you will learn to speak French, Reuben," said Mary with a grin.

"I ain't much good at English let alone learnin' French," he chuckled. "George can speak a bit mind and I know William can, but then 'e ain't goin', is 'e?"

Mary was silent.

"What's the time, Mary?" asked Reuben.

Mary looked at her watch.

"Just gone half past eleven, you've got to be back," she said.

"I don't want to be late, Mary, 'ow long did it take us to get 'ere?"

"About ten minutes or a little more, we'll leave in about quarter of an hour; that will give you plenty of time."

"Very good," said Reuben.

"What shall we talk about?" Mary said with forced cheeriness. "Not the war – something nice."

"Cold Harbour," said Reuben.

Mary smiled.

"Cold Harbour was lovely," she sighed. "Me, Lucy, Henry and Bessie; it was a lovely home. You used to come up and help, do you remember, Reuben? You helped on the farm and in the house, got in the coal and the wood and the water."

"I liked that," said Reuben.

He smiled suddenly, remembering.

"I got a lift once in Miss Verity's motor! First time I ever bin in a motor that was."

"I remember," said Mary.

"I asked you to marry me, Mary, when I was up there once, do you remember?"

"Yes, I remember," she said quietly.

She turned and looked at him.

"I'm still married, you know that, Reuben?"

"I know, Mary, I know," he sighed.

With his free hand he picked up his rifle and put it across his knees.

"Mary," he said, unable to hide the tremor in his voice. "I think I ought to go, I don't want to be late."

"Of course, Reuben, you best get your kit on," said Mary, helping him buckle up the webbing harness that held the packs. Reuben put his arm through the sling of his rifle and hauled it onto his shoulder. Mary inspected him, brushing specks from his uniform. She looked up at him, smiled and threw her arms around him, hugging him tightly. Her face close to his chest, she could feel him trembling.

732

"Oh, Reuben," she cried, pushing herself away.

"You know I love you, Mary?" he exclaimed violently.

"Yes, Reuben," she said quietly. "Come on then."

She took his shaking hand and walked him back to St Pancras. As they neared the station, the noise of hundreds of soldiers reached them – the pavements and side streets were crammed with men enjoying their last drink before they had to leave for Victoria station and military police strutted about, eager to ward off trouble. A strident voice was suddenly heard loud and clear above the hubbub.

"A Company, come on let's be 'aving you, and then B and C."

"That's me," said Reuben. "Look, there's Harry and all the others."

He released Mary's hand and turned to her.

"I've got to go now, Mary."

He looked at her, leant down and pressed his cheek against hers. He gave her a strained smile and disappeared into the throng of soldiers.

"Come on, chaps!" shouted the sergeant major. "Come on, let's 'ave you; three ranks form up on 'im. Rawlins, stand still, will you!"

The men continued to chatter and shift slowly into place, the scrape of their hobnail boots on the tarmac deafening.

"Quiet now!" he shouted. "No more talking!"

Lines started to form and talking subsided as the companies shuffled into the desired order. The sergeant major walked up and down shouting and pointing until he was happy with the parade. As the station clock struck half past twelve, the colonel mounted his horse.

"Very good, sergeant major; time to get going," he instructed, spurring his horse on to the front of the column.

One at a time each company moved off, turning right and marching off up the Euston Road. Mary watched and waved as Reuben's company started to follow A Company out onto the road – but she had lost sight of Reuben, all the men looked the same. All eight companies were now marching; people were waving, some ran along the pavements as the troops marched off. Suddenly– without any warning – the men began to sing; one voice was joined by another, and ten joined them, before the voices of almost a thousand men filled the streets, a joyous deep sound that echoed round the tall buildings. Half of the column was now out of sight and the sound of the singing started to fade as the men continued on towards Victoria station. Mary watched as they disappeared – making out the last few lines of the song:

"*Mademoiselle from Armentieres*
Never been kissed for forty years
Hinky pinky parlay voo."

She shuddered as the tail end of the procession disappeared from sight, the emotion of the scene overcoming her as tears rolled down her cheeks.

Chapter Fifty-Nine
A Wounded Soldier

On her return to Dean that afternoon, Mary found two letters waiting for her; one from Lucy and the other from Rupert. Lucy wrote that she had seen Rupert and that she had had a letter from William. There was no more detail than that – the letter was cold and impersonal and gave Mary no real comfort. Rupert's letter, on the other hand, was more specific. He said that he had managed to see Lucy and had done the best he could to comfort her.

"Your sister Lucy is not an easy person to get close to," he wrote. *"But I saw nothing to think that she will not cope through this difficult time. Her deep Christian beliefs are certainly providing her with a good deal of comfort."*

He also wrote that he would visit her again as and when he was in the area and that he was due leave in eight weeks' time.

A couple of months later, on a job in London, she received a letter from Rupert to say that he had called at the butcher's shop in the hope of seeing her, and that William had given him her address. He was due to go back to France the following Monday, but would be in London that day to see his editor; he asked if they could meet at a time convenient to her. Mary sent a telegram back arranging to meet at Nelson's Column at midday.

Monday came cold and wet; Mary arrived at Trafalgar Square in good time to find Rupert was already waiting, dressed in his army uniform. He had booked a table in the Lyons Corner House at the end of the Strand and they hurried there to get out of the rain.

"Now, Rupert," said Mary, sitting and taking off her long cloak, "I want to hear all about Lucy, it was so kind of you to go and see her; I had no one else to ask, I hope you don't mind."

"Not at all, Mary, I was only too happy to oblige, and I was based quite near her."

He turned and signalled to a waitress.

"Tell me, how was she?" asked Mary. "Was she upset? Was she depressed? Did she look ill?"

She looked intensely at Rupert across the table.

"Just a minute, Mary, one question at a time," Rupert laughed, breaking off to order wine from the waitress. He turned back to Mary.

"She didn't look ill; she did not seem depressed; she seemed very calm," he answered slowly. "It was actually a bit unnerving. She said that they had discussed the possibility of him being killed and that they had decided that if he was, then God would have ordained it and that she was to accept it. Her faith is really very strong, Mary. She said she prayed for him every night and looked forward to the day when she would meet him in heaven. She thanked me for coming and asked me to see you and assure you she was fine and that she sent her love."

Mary sat back in her chair, clasping her hands together and collecting her thoughts.

"I suppose if I had thought about it, I would have realised that's how she would see it. She's a very strong character," Mary said.

"So are you, Mary," said Rupert gently. "Very strong; to cope with all you have had to over the last few years."

Mary blushed a little under his steady gaze.

"Well I don't know about that," she said with a small laugh. "Now, Rupert, tell me about France; is it as bad as William says? He says that it is much worse than it says in the papers."

She gasped and raised her hand to her mouth.

"I suppose you write what's in the papers, don't you, Rupert?" she said quietly.

"Yes I do," he said slowly. "But we are very carefully monitored."

He sighed heavily.

"William's right, the reality of it is terrible," he said with a shrug. "It's the awful mud and the horrific injuries; you just really could not write about them – if people really knew how horrific—"

He paused and looked out of the window.

"And do you fight or will you have to fight?" asked Mary gently.

"I don't think so, I feel guilty, but I'm well over thirty now and they need someone to report what happens."

"Well at least you won't get killed or injured like poor Roderick," said Mary.

"I hope not," Rupert said.

Mary swallowed hard and changed the subject. They chatted about Jack and Ethil and Rebecca over lunch – the topic not straying back again to the war – and an hour later Mary rose to leave.

"Mary, do you mind if I write to you? It would mean a lot to me and after all, we have been friends for a long time," he added quickly.

Mary looked away for a moment and then back to Rupert.

"You know I am a married woman, don't you, Rupert? And your mother doesn't really like me, does she?" she said simply.

"I'm sure she means to like you, Mary, but I'm all she has got and well, you know how it is," he finished feebly.

"I know you're still married," he pressed on. "But you are not in contact with him are you?"

"No," admitted Mary.

"Well then, Mary, do you mind if I write?" he implored.

Mary chewed her lip thoughtfully.

"If you write, Rupert, address the letters care of William – don't send them to the butcher's shop or Aunt Charlotte will never stop," she said. "I don't know where I will be, so that is the most likely way that I will get the letter."

Rupert smiled broadly, stood to shake Mary's hand and watched her leave.

The autumn turned to winter and the cold weather set in. In February Mary was due to go back to Yorkshire to help deliver the second child for a woman she had worked for before. William drove her to Sharnbrook in the pony and trap to catch the train to Bedford. She had to wait half an hour for a train and paced up and down the platform to keep warm. A slow train arrived from London, the passengers piling out and rushing towards the ticket barrier. A door halfway down the train swung open to let the last passenger out, and a kit bag was thrown onto the platform followed by the passenger himself – a man in uniform who hopped out of the carriage on crutches, holding up a heavily bandaged foot. His uniform was plastered in mud and he was having difficulty finding his ticket in his greatcoat. Eventually he pulled the crumpled ticket from his pocket, placed it in his mouth and hopped over to the kit bag; he moved both crutches to one hand, bent down and picked up the end of the bag to try and swing it up onto his shoulder. Mary, seeing that the manoeuvre was going to be difficult, rushed up to help.

"Wait, wait," she said quickly. "Let me give you a hand."

The man turned to look at her, a look of desperation on his young face – and with a start of surprise Mary realised she was staring at Reuben. She looked carefully at his face; it was the face of somebody she hardly knew. His rosy complexion had faded and he looked grey and drawn. His eyes did not sparkle and two days' stubble grew where before he had always been clean shaven. His hands were ingrained with dirt and he smelt strongly of carbolic from the dressing on his foot, although the metallic tang could not mask the musty stench of sweat and unwashed body. He said something that Mary could not hear and she leant towards him as the train let off a billow of steam that enveloped the two of them. Mary reached up and put her arms round him, hugging him tightly; but his body did not respond, held against her like a stiff board. He dropped the two crutches, which clattered to the ground as Reuben tried desperately to balance himself so as not to fall into Mary. He placed his bandaged foot momentarily to the ground, wincing as he did so and inhaling sharply – his eyes tightly shut. He hopped a couple of times on his good leg to regain his balance as Mary bent down and picked up the crutches, handing them to him as he opened his watery eyes.

"Ooh, that's better," he said, leaning once more on the crutches as the kitbag fell to the ground.

He smiled at Mary.

"Mary, what are you doin' here, you ain't come to meet me, have you?" he asked hopefully.

"No, I'm catching a train for Sheffield in about fifteen minutes, I'm going to deliver another baby."

"Oh," said Reuben, "you haven't come specially then."

"Well no," said Mary quietly.

She looked critically at Reuben's foot.

"What's happened to you, Reuben? Your foot, what happened, were you shot?"

"No, no nuffing like that," sniffed Reuben. "I trod on a six-inch nail sticking out a duckboard in the bottom of the trench and it went through me boot, right into my foot, very painful it was. Anyway it got infected and swelled up and I can't get me boot on and they send me home to recover."

"Oh, Reuben, poor you, how awful," exclaimed Mary. "Come on, sit over here, I have a few minutes to spare."

She grabbed the long round kit bag and dragged it across the platform to a seat.

"So where are you going? Home, Reuben?" Mary asked as Reuben lowered himself to the seat.

"No, I'm got to report to the barracks but I expect they will send me home to recover when I'm seen the M.O. or when they think it's on the mend."

His eyes fell on a travel warrant lying on the platform in front of them where he had dropped it. He nodded to it.

"Mary, I don't suppose?"

"Yes, of course," she said, rising and retrieving the form.

"But, Reuben, how are you going to get to the barracks? They must be a mile away and with that big kit bag as well."

"Oh don't worry, Mary; I got here, didn't I? If I balance the kit bag right and 'old the drawstring I can do it easy."

"But your poor foot, does it hurt?"

"It does if I put it to the ground," he said cheerfully.

He smiled at Mary – a little colour had returned to his cheeks.

"You look very smart in your uniform, Mary, like all the nurses in the field 'ospital; they were good to me. I looked out for Miss Lucy – someone said she were out there, but I din't see her."

"No, I'm not sure where she is now," Mary replied.

She took one of Reuben's hands and squeezed it; it felt hard and rough to the touch.

"It's lovely to see you, Reuben, even though you are hurt; at least you were not shot," she smiled at him.

"No, but I wish I had been," he said gruffly. "Treading on a nail don't get you much sympathy from your mates, I'm tell you; it's more embarrassing than anything. A lot of them said I did it on purpose but I din't, George knowed that, he told them. Any road, I have been shot; one went through me tunic but it only grazed me arm, it weren't much, and one nicked my tin hat!"

He put his hand instinctively to his head to find the tin hat and on finding his cap there instead, he immediately pulled it off and put it on his knees.

"Sorry, Mary, I din't think to take it off," he said shyly.

He sniffed, put his hand inside his tunic, scratched and pulled his hand out again. Mary looked at him inquisitively.

"Yes?" she said.

"I'm got visitors," Reuben said.

"Visitors?" Mary echoed, with a small laugh.

"Lice, we're all got them; can't help it, they just come, get everywhere – you better not sit too close, Mary."

"Ugh," she said, "how horrid."

She edged back a little and looked up at the clock.

"I must go," she said, "I've got to cross the bridge and my train will be here in a few minutes."

"Very good," said Reuben, standing and placing his crutches under his arms. She helped him to sling the kit bag over his shoulder and collected her suitcase.

"I will be back in Dean in about four weeks," she said, turning to him hopefully.

"Well I may still be here," Reuben said with a shrug.

Mary moved forward, thought better of it and held out her hand – Reuben took it and shook it gently.

"That's right," he said with a wink, "don't get too close – they jump, you know."

It was in the end five weeks before Mary returned to Dean in late March. There was no one in the shop when she arrived, so she went straight into the kitchen where Ivy was laying the table and Charlotte was sitting by the range, knitting.

"Mary my dear, how wonderful to see you," smiled Charlotte, laying down her knitting and holding out her arms. "Come here and give me a kiss!"

"In a mo," Mary said. "I'm dying to go down the end, I didn't think I would make it."

She sped out the door – no sooner had she returned to the kitchen than Charlotte started to fuss.

"Now dear, we have long since had dinner and we won't have supper for a good while yet so what would you like to eat? Come and sit down, dear, and tell us all the news. Ivy can make you a sandwich and a cup of tea."

Mary sat and filled Charlotte in on her recent job, before remembering Reuben.

"When I was on my way up north I met Reuben Heighton at the station; he had been wounded and they sent him home to recover, is he still here?"

"Yes," answered Charlotte, surprised. "He has recovered very well; he has given up the crutches and has a stick now. Every week he reports to the barracks where they dress the foot and in between he goes to the doctor in Kimbolton."

"That's good," sighed Mary. "He was in a lot of pain when I saw him."

"Did you notice the way he speaks now?" said Charlotte, raising an eyebrow.

"No, not really, Aunt Charlotte; I only saw him briefly."

"Well, dear, he is much more refined now, doesn't drop his 'h's' anymore and he says his 'th's" and doesn't turn them into 'f's'; something has happened in the six months he's been away."

She gave a knowing wink, turned to Ivy and said,

"Ivy, can you leave for a while, I have something to say to Miss Mary."

"Very good, Mrs Dunmore; I'll go and clean up in the shop, shall I?"

Charlotte nodded, watching Ivy's progress out the door. She turned to Mary and lowered her voice.

"Now, Mary, I must tell you something that I'm sure you don't know; it's a little delicate and it concerns young Reuben."

She stopped and looked hard at Mary, who averted her gaze.

"Yes, Aunt Charlotte, and what about young Reuben?" she said innocently.

"Well, my dear, it is clear to me that Reuben shows more than a passing interest in you," said Charlotte confidentially. "I think the term would be infatuation. Now, my dear, I am sure you are not interested in Reuben – him being so much younger than yourself and in any event you are married, but the problem is how you handle it and what I want to say is—"

She stopped and shifted in her chair, looking at the ceiling as if it might provide her with the right words.

"This is very difficult, Mary," she said plainly, "but poor Reuben will soon be going back to France and things are so awful out there and he may not come back or he might get wounded again. So, dear, what I am trying to say is that you should try not to hurt his feelings if you can help it. Don't encourage him but neither must you make him feel unwanted. So if you could see him once or twice before you go off again he would appreciate it."

Mary looked at Charlotte, trying to mask her incredulity. She laughed slightly and turned to her aunt with a smile.

"Don't worry, Aunt, I will try and see him and I will try to be kind."

Charlotte nodded and returned to her knitting.

The next day Reuben came to the butcher's shop.

"Mother said I was to call for her order, Mrs Dunmore, if that's alright; she says she will come along on Saturday and pay," he said.

Charlotte peered down at Reuben from the height of a tall wooden stool, where she was working slowly through a stock take.

"My word, Reuben, you do look smart; I do like to see someone in uniform," Charlotte smiled, turning and stepping off the stool to fetch his order. She scanned the various piles of meat and sausages until she found the name of Heighton.

"Here we are, Reuben," she said, picking it up and putting it on the block in front of him. She eyed him with a casual smile.

"By the way, Mary's back and she was asking after you," she said, trying to keep the enthusiasm from her voice, "I'll give her a call."

She opened the door into the kitchen.

"Ivy, just go and tell Miss Mary that Reuben's here," she said.

A few minutes later Mary rushed into the shop, pushing her hair up and making sure her bun was straight.

"Reuben, don't you look smart!" she smiled. "Much better than the last time I saw you; how's that poor foot?"

"Much better thank you, Mrs Ladds," Reuben said formally, conscious of Charlotte's presence.

"Look how his buttons and buckles shine, Aunt Charlotte, and his boots and look at those creases! Quite the young soldier."

"Thank you, Mrs Ladds," Reuben said proudly, grinning at Mary.

"Come on," said Charlotte, "let's have a cup of tea; do you want one, Reuben?"

"Well I wouldn't mind if you're sure you have time, Mrs Dunmore," replied Reuben gratefully.

"Of course we do, don't we, Mary?" said Charlotte pointedly.

"Yes, Aunt Charlotte," smiled Mary, leading the way into the kitchen.

Reuben stood to attention in the middle of the kitchen, his head to one side of the low slung beam.

"Sit down then, Reuben," said Charlotte. "You're not on the parade ground now."

Reuben put his cap on the table and his stick on the floor.

"Now, Reuben, I want you to tell us something," Charlotte quizzed.

"Yes, Mrs Dunmore," replied Reuben, a touch nervously.

"What we can't understand, Reuben, is that you talk differently," said Charlotte. "You don't drop your 'h's' and you don't pronounce 'th' as 'f' anymore and we wondered why, didn't we, Mary?"

She turned to Mary.

"Well it's a long story," Reuben said, "our company commander, Major Barnett, had a man – a batman they call them – that looked after him. Well this batman got killed and there was no one to do the job, so he selected me."

Reuben looked up at Mary and shrugged.

"Well it turned out that this Major Barnett had been a teacher at one of the posh schools – Heeton, I mean Eton," Reuben smiled, correcting himself. "He said that I would never get anywhere if I spoke like a country bumpkin and

743

every time I dropped an 'h' or the like he pulled me up. So after a while I got to know what I was doing wrong and I guess I started talking better."

He ran his fingers round the brim of his upturned cap and shrugged again.

"Well isn't that splendid, Mary? What a lovely story," said Charlotte.

"He also made me write home. I never did before; George always wrote for me, but he said I had to write for myself. I can write but I've never been very confident, I'm not sure about the spelling and all that so I never did it if I could get out of it. Anyway when there was no one about in the dugout he would make me sit down and write and would correct it, so I'm much better now."

Reuben looked up past Charlotte and Mary, his eyes focusing behind them.

"He was really good to me, he really was," he said more vehemently. "And he didn't let on to anyone what he was doing, not even the other officers."

"He sounds like he a lovely man," said Mary with a smile.

"He was," said Reuben. "He was."

Reuben lowered his head.

"Was?" said Mary gently.

"Yes. He was killed," said Reuben quietly, his face crumpling as if he was about to cry.

"He was just—"

Reuben pulled up short, he sniffed.

"Well, he was just checking the men around the trenches and a mortar—"

Reuben sniffed again.

"Well, at least he wouldn't have known much about it – it were quick."

A tear came to Reuben's eye and he fumbled in his pocket to find a handkerchief. Mary started to rise to comfort him, but Charlotte waved at her to remain seated. Reuben found the handkerchief, wiped his eyes and sniffed as calm gradually returned to his contorted face. Ivy stood behind Charlotte's chair, transfixed by what Reuben was saying, tears rolling down her cheeks. There was silence for a moment, even Charlotte could think of nothing to say.

"Ivy, pass me my Bible and prayer book," she said finally.

Ivy went to the table by the rocking chair and retrieved the books, placing them on the table in front of Charlotte.

"Reuben, we will say a prayer for Major Barnett, and I will read a little from the Bible; you sit down, Ivy, and shut your eyes."

They all bowed their heads and waited while Charlotte composed a prayer. When she had finished they all sat in silence, unable to think of anything adequate to say. The sharp whistle of the kettle broke the quiet of the room – Charlotte nodded at Ivy who rose and went to make the tea.

"How's that foot getting on?" Mary asked.

"Nearly better thank you, Mrs Ladds," said Reuben, looking straight down the table. "I have to go the doctor tomorrow, but it has healed and Mother took the dressing off the other day; I hardly need the stick now."

"Then what?" said Charlotte.

"Well, he will tell me when to go back and then I have to report to the barracks. So I'm going to get my hair cut while I'm in Kimbolton, much better than the barber at the barracks."

"You have got to look smart to go back to France," Charlotte agreed, smiling at Reuben, who blinked several times and clasped one hand over the other.

She watched him pick up his cup and raise it to his lips, but his hand shook as he did so; slopping tea down over his hand and into the saucer. He quickly placed the cup down again with a clatter, nudging the spoon onto the table as he did so, where it lay rocking gently on the table top. A couple of moments later he tried again, but the shaking of his hand was still violent and once more he failed to raise the cup to his mouth. Mary clenched her fists and wished fervently that the shaking would stop, deeply pained by Reuben's struggle.

"What time have you got to be at the doctor, Reuben?" Mary asked as cheerily as she could.

Reuben did not answer, he was concentrating fiercely on the tea cup.

"I'm sorry, Mrs Ladds, what did you say?" Reuben asked suddenly, looking up.

"I said, what time do you have to be at the doctor in the morning?"

"Oh I all'as get there at 'arf past –"

He stopped and shook his head gently.

"I mean half past eight, Mrs Ladds."

Mary smiled at him and he grinned.

"And then you are going to have your hair cut?"

"Yes," said Reuben.

"Well I will look out for you, Reuben, and we can walk back together," said Mary gently.

"That would be nice," added Charlotte deliberately.

Reuben smiled again and picked up his cup. His hand did not shake.

The next day Mary found Reuben sitting in the covered arch leading into the churchyard; he rose as she approached and took off his cap, revealing his smart short haircut.

"All done then, Reuben?" she asked.

"Yes, Mrs Ladds, I'm all done," he grinned.

"Well I have just got one or two more things to get and I will be ready," she said, hurrying off towards the grocery shop.

Half an hour later they made their way home.

"Let's go back along the bridleway, Reuben; it's a bit nearer and the ground is bone dry now, it would be nice not to walk on the road."

They set off up Span Oak Lane, turning right at the top of the path to curve back towards Dean. Reuben pulled his finger round the collar of his tunic and shifted uncomfortably.

"What are you doing, Reuben?" Mary asked. "Have you got lice again?"

"No, I haven't," he replied indignantly. "Mother got rid of them. No, it itches from having my hair cut all around my collar."

"Come here then," Mary said, turning him round to face her, "take your tunic off and I will brush the hairs off the inside."

Reuben did as he was told, undoing the shiny buttons and handing the tunic to Mary. She shook it vigorously and swept as much hair as she could from the collar; Reuben continued to itch at his neck.

"Is it on your shirt as well?" Mary asked.

"Yes, that's the worst bit," grumbled Reuben.

"Well take your shirt off then," she demanded.

"I can't do that," he protested. "It ain't right."

"Come on, you stupid boy," laughed Mary, "get on with it, you've got something underneath, haven't you?"

"Yes, my vest," he replied stiffly.

"Come on then," she demanded, holding out her hand for the shirt.

Reuben gingerly slipped his braces off his shoulders, took his tie off and then his shirt. He held the tunic coyly in front of him whilst she dealt with the shirt, which she shook out and handed back to him. Reuben hurriedly pulled the shirt back on, rebuttoned it and slipped on his tunic; buttoning the buttons into the wrong holes in his haste.

Mary laughed and reached out to help him.

"Come here, silly," she said, unbuttoning his tunic and starting again.

Reuben watched her as she carefully realigned the tunic, working slowly from bottom upwards, her hands moving methodically. As she reached the top button, he held his head back so that she could fasten it. She looked up at him and smiled – Reuben smiled gently, looped his arms around her waist and kissed her hard on the lips. Mary didn't resist; she wound her arms around his shoulders, pressing her body to his with all her might. Finally, she pulled back from him, hands still linked loosely around his neck. She was red in the face and her hat was a little to one side.

"Reuben Heighton, where did you learn to kiss like that?" she asked with a small laugh. "You must have been taught by some of those French girls – I bet you have, Reuben, you wouldn't have done that before you went to France, would you?"

Reuben grinned in embarrassment and turned his head away.

"Reuben, look at me," she laughed.

Reuben looked to the sky and said nothing. Mary snaked her hands to his waist, dug her fingers into his body just under his ribs and tickled him.

"Tell me, Reuben, what are the French girls like?" she giggled.

Reuben squirmed, but could not get away. Seeing his only defence was to tickle her back, he laughed and dug his fingers into her ribs. She writhed away from him – the pair laughed and fell to the thick grass locked together. Mary rose quickly, laughing as she did so and gave Reuben her hand, pulling him up and towards her and kissing him gently.

"Now, Heighton, about turn," she said formally, standing to attention. "Let's look at that uniform; can't have any dirt on it, you know."

Reuben laughed and allowed her to turn him round and brush the grass off his uniform. She picked up her basket, grabbed his hand and they walked on hand in hand to the ridge from where they could look down to Dean.

"Reuben, you didn't tell me what the doctor said," said Mary suddenly.

"No, I didn't," Reuben replied.

Mary felt the grip of his hand tighten.

"Well then?" she said gently.

She turned to look at him; his face was pale.

"He said I was better and that he would sign that I was to return to the barracks next Monday."

Mary could feel his hand shaking now and she pulled him a little closer.

"What then?" she said quietly.

"I see the M.O. there and if I'm passed fit I will go back to France."

Mary looked down; the trembling of Reuben's hand told her what she would find written on his face. Finally, she looked up at him. Tears rolled down his cheeks and his face was twisted in anguish.

"I don't want to go back, Mary, I really don't," he sobbed. "I just can't describe how horrible it is; it must be worse than hell is in the Bible, truly worse."

Mary shuddered and wrapped her arms around him, hugging him tight.

"Reuben, what can I do? How can I help?" she whispered, gripping him tightly.

Reuben sniffed and composed himself, his expression hardening.

"You can do nothing, Mary; I have to go or I will be shot," he said baldly. "I'm not a coward and I am going to go back, but I am frightened."

He stopped and looked down.

"I don't think I'm going to come back," he whispered. "I just don't think I will."

"Don't say that, Reuben," Mary cried angrily.

"Well I just don't think I will," he said simply, looking away from her.

Mary gripped his hand, turning him back to her – he could see tears in her

748

eyes now.

"Don't be upset, Mary, please don't be upset; I don't want to make you unhappy, really I don't," he insisted, drawing her back towards him.

She wiped her eyes with her sleeve and stifled a sob.

"I know, Reuben," she said quietly, "and after all George is out there and you always said he looks after you."

"You're right, Mary," said Reuben with a small smile, "I hadn't thought about George; it will be good to see him again."

Mary looked at him, remembering the small boy from all those years ago, imagining him in that horrible place. She shuddered.

"Let's say goodbye now, Reuben; you go along the path and I will go onto the road and back. I am away first thing tomorrow and you're gone on Monday."

She untangled herself from his arms and looked back down towards the village.

"Yes, Mary," said Reuben firmly. "That's the best idea; can I write to you though?"

"Yes of course you can, Reuben," laughed Mary. "Send them to William; he will know where I am."

"Goodbye then, Reuben," she said with a smile, reaching up to ruffle his hair.

"Goodbye, Mary," said Reuben with a grin, his hands rising instinctively to smooth down his short hair.

She turned and walked back towards the road.

"Mary?" he called after her.

Mary turned.

"You know I love you, don't you?"

"Yes, Reuben," said Mary quietly, "I know."

Chapter Sixty
Molly

Five months later, on the 21st July, Reuben was killed in the battle of the Somme. He was hit by a shell blast and neither his body nor any of his uniform or effects were ever recovered. His parents were notified by the War Office and outstanding pay was returned to them; other than that, they were able to do nothing – there was no body so there was no funeral in France and no funeral in Dean and in the end the only reference to Reuben Heighton would be his name engraved on the war memorial outside the church. The news travelled fast around the village, but Reuben was not the first from Dean to lose his life and he would not be the last.

Mary, having been told of Reuben's death in a telegram from William, returned to the butcher's shop the next Friday and went straight to see Reuben's parents to express her condolences. The next morning she was up early to see Jack off with William on the meat round and from there she walked to Covington to see Grace.

Grace's second baby had now arrived and demanded a lot of attention, so it was not until late in the morning that the two of them sat down in the chairs under the big apple tree to talk. Grace brought with her the last letter they had received from George which was dated the end of March. As she started to read out the letter they could hear footsteps on the gravel; Grace rose and looked over the garden hedge.

"Molly dear," she called, "we're here in the garden, come through the gate, there's no need to go through the house."

Molly scurried through the gate, rushing to Mary and hugging her tightly before sitting down next to her on the long bench.

"It's lovely to see you, Molly," said Grace.

Molly smiled politely and fidgeted on the bench; she turned suddenly to Mary.

"I 'eard about Reuben so I 'ad to come. Mrs Hurrell said I could 'ave the weekend off so I come on the train to Rushden."

"You've been quick then, Molly," said Mary, "to walk here in that time."

"I got a lift to Dean in the dray from the station so it weren't too bad," she shrugged. "I went to the butcher's shop and Mrs Dunmore said you were 'ere so I come straight up; I 'ad to see you, Mary."

Amy appeared at the garden door. She looked at Mary and tears came to her eyes and she rushed over. Mary stood up and embraced her and tears rolled down her cheeks as well.

"Don't say anything, Amy, not for a minute," said Mary, and she turned to look at Molly who was now standing close to them. Amy turned to Molly and embraced her and them stood back and wiped her eyes on her pinny.

"I'm sorry, I shouldn't be so upset," Amy said as she turned her head away.

"He was your bruvver, Amy," said Molly, holding her hand and stroking it.

Then Amy looked at Grace.

"Mrs Dunmore, it sounds like your Benjamin's hungry, shall I go and lift him?" she asked.

"Yes, Amy, that's a dear, I'll be in directly," said Grace, turning to the others. "I'll have to go; give me half an hour, you talk to Molly."

She rose from her seat and followed Amy in towards the house.

Molly looked sadly at Mary.

"When I heard about Reuben, I 'ad to come, Mary," she said.

"Yes, Molly," Mary said, reaching for Molly's hand.

"Do you remember, Mary, when we was at Bythorn 'ow 'e came an' 'elped on the farm and lived in the barn?" Molly mused, looking up at the bright blue sky. "I can picture him now; 'e was the loveliest man I ever seen."

Mary pursed her lips, blinking several times as tears started to threaten.

"'E was so 'andsome and strong and tall and 'e were a good man, a real good man, weren't 'e, Mary?"

Mary sniffed, looking away from Molly into the laurel hedge, saying nothing.

"'E din't take no notice of me," Molly went on. "Whatever I did 'e wasn't interested and I know about men, Mary; you know that."

There was silence as Molly continued to reminisce.

"The only person Reuben thought of was you, Mary; 'e was in love wiv you – completely in love and we all knew that, din't we?"

Molly stopped, sighed and frowned up at the sky.

"I were thinkin', Mary, I know you were a lot older than 'im and I know you are still married and all that but you would 'ave made a lovely couple if you tidied him up a bit."

Mary's lip quivered; she bit down on it furiously and continued to stare into the hedge.

"You must 'ave bin a little bit in love with 'im, Mary, you must 'ave," insisted Molly.

"Don't, Molly, don't!" cried Mary, shaking her head. "I can't think about him; I beg you stop! We've got to be brave, haven't we? And I can't if I have to think about him."

She looked at Molly with an expression of abject misery before looking away. A moment or two passed and then Molly said,

"What you got there, then?"

"What?" said Mary looking up.

She nodded to the envelope on Mary's lap.

"That there letter," said Molly.

"That's a letter from George," said Mary, her voice quivering.

"Can I 'ave a look?" Molly asked.

Mary passed her the letter; Molly slid it from the envelope, unfolded it and started to read aloud.

"*Dear William, many thanks for the –*" Molly stopped. "I can't read the next word; 'ere, Mary, you read it, you're much better than me."

She passed Mary the letter.

Mary cleared her throat and started to read:

"*Dear William, many thanks for the sausages.*"

Molly started in surprise and looked to Mary.

"Sausages? You can't send sausages in the post, can you?" she said.

"Well I don't know but they must have, that's what it says here; now let me carry on, Molly."

She looked down at the letter again.

"*We warmed them up on our fire and had them for Saturday morning's breakfast, they were A-One, the best breakfast I've had in the trenches.*"

Mary sniffed and blew her nose on her hankie.

"Go on, Mary," Molly urged.

"*I think we was back having our rest when I wrote last but we are back up the line again now at the old game. We had fine weather last week, it was quite hot in the daytime. We had a little rain the last two days and last night it snowed all night.*'"

Mary's eyes flicked back to the top of the letter.

"When did he send this then?"

"It must 'ave bin a long time ago," Molly said.

"24ᵗʰ March look, it says at the top."

"Go on then, Mary, what else does 'e say?"

"Where were we? Oh yes: *I'm glad to say it seems to be going fast. It was not very nice standing on the parapet in the snow. I don't know if you think the war will soon end, some seem to think it won't last long and others say it will last another year or two. Fritz still seems to carry on the same, there is still some iron flying about. One thing – nights are not near so long and that makes it a bit better for us. I had a letter from Robert the other day, he had not enlisted yet, he said they had got about six feet of snow. I think that this is all this time, with kind regards from Reuben and myself, GW Lowe.*'"

Mary's face contorted and tears flooded her eyes; she closed them tight, her body heaved and she put her hands over her face. Suddenly she threw back her head to let out a terrifying howl before sobbing uncontrollably.

"Mary, Mary, don't cry, don't cry like that," Molly begged, hugging her tight. "Don't cry, Mary; you are always a strong person, come on now, try please, Mary."

Molly picked up the letter from the grass, put it in the envelope and turned to Mary again. As quickly as the sorrow had overtaken her, she regained control; she sat up and wiped her eyes.

"You're right, Molly, I must be strong; that's how I am and that's how I was brought up," she smiled a little. "It's just that I saw Reuben about a week before George wrote this, he must have been sent straight back to the trenches after he reported back."

"Well, 'e's in 'eaven now, ain't 'e, Mary?" said Molly gently.

"Yes, Molly, he is," sighed Mary.

"Ain't we better say a prayer, Mary; that would make you feel better."
Molly looked hard at Mary.

"Yes, we ought, you're right but I can't think of what to say."

"I know," said Molly, "let's say the Lord's Prayer if you can't think of nuffing."

"Close your eyes then, Molly," said Mary as the pair started to recite the words of the prayer.

Having finished, they sat quietly, the tuneful notes of a blackbird punctuating the silence.

"You're right, Molly, Reuben was a really good man, wasn't he? One of the best," she said, patting Molly's hand.

"Do you remember when 'e came in when you were in the barf, Mary? That were funny, weren't it!" They laughed and Mary leant back on the seat.

"We had some good times, Molly, you and me," sighed Mary, smiling at Molly. "Now tell me what's happening at Northampton."

"Well," said Molly slowly, "it ain't all good. Mr 'Arding's 'ad an 'eart attack and 'e's bin in bed for three weeks now. They say it's because they're bin so busy. They got a contract for army boots and they're in workin' day and night, but it's knocked 'im up, I'm afraid."

"Oh dear," Mary said, "I hope he gets better soon; and Rebecca, how's she?"

"She's fine, she misses Mr Hurrell, but she gets lots of letters."

"And Jupp? I mean Vincent," Mary corrected herself.

"Yes," said Molly slowly. "He sends letters as well, he says he don't know 'ow he stays alive, 'e thinks 'e 'as a charmed life."

"And young Arthur, he must be nearly two now, how's he?" Mary asked.

Molly did not answer straight away, instead toying with a loose thread on her dress.

"Well poor Arthur ain't quite right," she said slowly. "But Mrs Hurrell loves 'im with a passion, she does, I'm sure he'll be all right."

Mary looked at Molly with alarm.

"What's wrong with him, Molly?" Mary asked.

"Well he's nearly two, like you said, but 'e don't walk yet and 'e only sits up if you prop 'im up and 'e 'ardly crawls and he don't speak. Never mind, I suppose some of 'em don't, do they?"

"How awful," gasped Mary. "Has she had the doctor to him?"

"Yes, she's had him many times, but 'e says there's no changin' 'im; he was born like it and there's nuffing to be done. He's a lovely boy, mind," Molly said. "I've never 'eard 'im cry, not never and 'e eats all 'is food and 'e's got a lovely smile."

"Molly." Mary's tone had changed, "you've got to tell me the truth. Did the doctor say he had been damaged when he was born?"

Mary put her hands on Molly's shoulders, forcing Molly to look at her.

"Tell me, Molly, tell me! Did they say that I didn't manage the birth properly?"

Molly hesitated.

"Well—"

"Well what?" Mary snapped, still holding Molly's shoulders.

"'E said it was one of the possible causes," shrugged Molly.

Mary groaned.

"Oh no," she said, putting her hand to her forehead.

"It was only one of the possible causes, Mary, and 'e said 'e would 'ave a better idea as he got older, but other than that 'e was in very good health. And Rebecca – I mean Mrs Hurrell – she wouldn't 'ave none of it. She said 'e were born like it and that were that and she said she wouldn't 'ear of any blame on you and the doctor weren't to say any more."

"Oh how awful," said Mary again. "It was a very slow birth, wasn't it, Molly? You told me I should have sent for the doctor earlier, didn't you? What can I do, what can I do? I must go and see her."

Mary looked at Molly.

"No, Mary, you mustn't say anything; she loves that boy so much, she don't care if 'e ain't quite right, and it's funny, I think she loves 'im more 'cos he's like that."

755

"But, Molly, it might have been my fault."

"Yes, but we don't know that, do we? And it's more than likely not your fault and she won't 'ear anyfing of it anyway; so, Mary, you mustn't say, please don't, she will know I told you then and I wouldn't like that," Molly implored. "I'll let you know 'ow 'e's gettin' on. Anyway, I don't think it were your fault either; 'e's too alert, that's what I fink – 'is brain ain't gone, it's just 'is body ain't quite right."

Molly nodded at Mary convincingly – Mary shook her head and looked away.

The doubts about Arthur and his disabilities, together with the death of Reuben, had turned Mary's life upside down. All confidence drained from her and she was overtaken by a mixture of grief and guilt. There was no one to talk to in Dean and the only person with whom she was able to discuss things with was Grace, and even she did not like to talk about Reuben. Lucy was still in France and her letters were few and far between, making Mary feel more isolated than ever. In September, George was injured by a bullet wound in his arm and was sent back to England. After a period of convalescence, he was told that he was unfit for military service anymore and was discharged from the army, returning to Dean and to his job in the butcher's shop.

Mary did not see Rebecca again until the spring of 1917 at her father's funeral. The church was filled with the great and the good of Northampton society, of which Charles Harding had been an important member; like many others in the town he had made a fortune supplying the army with boots. Mary could see Rupert across the church in uniform and after the service she had a brief word with him, before he left to catch a train for France. There was no reception after the funeral; instead Rebecca stood in the churchyard accepting condolences from the congregation as they made their way back home. Mary waited until the majority of the people had gone before she approached Rebecca.

"Mary, how good of you to come," said Rebecca with a smile. "I'm afraid I can't offer you any refreshment. We decided not to; it's the war, you know, and Aubrey's still away. I'm off to the solicitor within the hour to sort things out. I'm going to sell the business; I can't run it and it will sell easily enough. Father had been making a fortune producing army boots. And you, Mary, how are you? There's so much I want to ask, and the children, are they well?"

"They are well. Jack will soon be going into the navy, and Ethil I think will go to boarding school soon."

"And William?" said Rebecca.

"He now has two, you know: two boys and they are well."

Mary hesitated, before asking

"And how is young Arthur, Rebecca?"

Rebecca beamed, a look of joy spreading across her face.

"Mary, he's the love of my life; he's such a joy especially as Aubrey is away fighting. He's not developing so fast in some ways but he's so loving and he's got a wonderful temperament. He's home with Molly at the moment."

They chatted a little more but there was not much more she could learn about Arthur so she said goodbye and made her way to the station.

Mary heard no more from Rebecca until November of that year, when she wrote to say that Vincent Jupp had been killed in action and she was sending Molly back to Dean to her parents to give her a break. She wrote that Molly was somewhat reluctant to go home, only agreeing to go if she knew that Mary would be around. It wasn't until the end of the month that Mary arrived back, setting off early the next morning to call in at Hardwick's and see Molly. She could hear the lowing of the cattle in the yards as she neared the farm and the dog barked at her from its kennel where it was chained. The noise of the dog had alerted Molly, who was standing at the open door as Mary arrived.

"Molly dear, I was so sorry to hear about Vincent; you must have been mortified and after he had been out there for so long."

She gave Molly a hug and followed her into the house. Mary took off her hat and coat and sat at the table on the side nearest the range. Molly said nothing.

"And how are you, Molly?" Mary asked.

"All right I suppose," said Molly with a petulant shrug.

Mary stared at Molly desperately, unsure of how to proceed.

"Where was he killed, Molly?"

"Somewhere called Passiondale or sumfing like that," sniffed Molly.

"So had you heard from him?" Mary asked.

"Not for a couple of mumfs," said Molly, poking angrily through the bars of the fire in the range to make it burn up.

"It ain't fair," she cried suddenly.

"No, Molly," Mary agreed.

Molly turned furiously to Mary.

"We were goin' to get married you know, Mary, and now 'e's gone dead!"

Tears coursed from Molly's eyes.

"'E said 'e 'ad all the luck," she sniffed. "'E 'ad nearly bin there two years you know, and then 'e got killed! It ain't fair! But I ain't 'ad no luck in my life, Mary, 'ave I? It were only a matter of time afore it rubbed off on 'im."

"No, Molly," said Mary gently, "you haven't had much luck, but look—"

"But look what?" interjected Molly crossly. "What am I got? Nuffin' now, just nuffing."

Mary grasped Molly's hand.

"My mum and dad– they ain't no 'elp!" she continued. "And my baby – I 'ad to give 'im away; I couldn't look at 'im – no, not never wiv a chance 'e'd look like 'is farver."

She sniffed sadly.

"And don't tell me, Mary, that I could 'ave brought 'im up, 'cos I never would, I couldn't."

She turned angrily to Mary.

"Any road, you ain't brought up your children, 'ave you?"

"That's a bit unfair, Molly," said Mary quietly.

"No it ain't," Molly snapped back, eyeing Mary aggressively.

"All I'm got is a ring," she sniffed, holding out her hand to look at the small ring on her finger.

"'E were a good man, you know, Mary, 'e really were," she said quietly, putting her hands over her eyes. "I just wish he ain't bin killed; why was 'e killed?"

She sobbed twice and allowed Mary to wrap her arms around her, eventually hugging her back.

"I'm sorry, Mary, I'm so sorry if I said rotten things; I din't mean it, I really din't," she mumbled into Mary's shoulder.

"I know, Molly," soothed Mary, stroking her hair.

"I'll go back tomorra, back to Norfampton," whispered Molly.

"So soon?" said Mary.

"I can't go down to Dean, can I? I might see 'im and then what? And what would all them old bags say when they saw me? They would stick the knife in if they could."

"Now, Molly, you've got lots of friends; Ruby's a good friend," Mary said encouragingly.

"S'pose she is," she said reluctantly.

"And Verity," Mary added. "Your mother's working there, isn't she?"

"Yes," Molly said quietly. "She's bin up already; she's nice, Miss Verity is."

"You know, Mary," said Molly, pulling back to look at Mary, "Mrs Dene's the worst knitter in the world, I'm sure she is. Last Christmas she sent me some gloves to send to Vincent but only one 'ad five fingers."

Mary laughed loudly, Molly grinned.

"She's one of the best, Molly" smiled Mary.

"Yes, she is," said Molly thoughtfully. "She come up yesterday as soon as I got back; don't worry, I weren't rude to 'er like I was to you, Mary."

Molly winked and rose to put the kettle on the hob.

"Cuppa tea?" she asked.

"Thank you," said Mary. "I must call and see Verity on the way back."

"She ain't there, I know that; she's gone to see Colonel Dene, 'e got gassed so Muvver said; 'e's in a recovery 'ospital she said, anyway she's gone to see 'im."

"Poor Colonel Dene, that sounds horrible," Mary gasped.

"It's all horrible, Mary," said Molly simply.

"I suppose it is."

Molly made the tea and poured it out.

"I forgot to ask, Molly, how is Rebecca, and young Arthur, is he improving?"

"She's fine, she sold the factory – it made a fortune, they say, besides all the money it had made afore. Arthur, well there's another thing I don't rightly know. 'E don't speak, you know; 'e makes noises and I sometimes think they are words, she says they are; 'is brain's all there, you know, Mary, I can tell it is, but it's trapped inside his body."

"Does he walk yet?" Mary asked.

"My word no," exclaimed Molly. "Well 'e can a bit if you 'old 'im up, 'e sits up now and 'e just about feeds himself after a fashion but I don't know. Sometimes I don't fink 'e will ever walk proper like – 'e drags 'is foot, poor thing. But 'e's got spirit, Mary; 'e's as brave as brave, never cries, never gives up, 'e don't."

"That's good, Molly; I can't help thinking it's my fault he's like that, I should have—"

Molly turned sharply to Mary.

"Don't, Mary, don't!" reprimanded Molly. "There's no good to be 'ad blamin' yourself now. Not for any of it. You did your best, you know you did; and the best is all as you can do."

Chapter Sixty-One
The Troops Return

The War continued until the summer of 1918. However, the stalemate now seemed to have been broken and on all fronts in France the Allies were advancing on the Germans, with the help of new troops from America. Not many of the soldiers that Mary knew were still fighting; they had either been killed or had been sent home wounded. Only Aubrey was still with his regiment and Rupert was still reporting but he was to an extent out of harm's way. In early September, Mary arrived at Covington Farmhouse to find a letter from Rebecca. She said that she was expecting another baby at Christmas and would Mary attend to the birth. Mary wrote back by return of post that she would be very happy to if Rebecca wanted her.

It was arranged that Mary would arrive at The Covert two weeks before Christmas and would stay into the New Year as the baby was due on Christmas Day. Accordingly, on the day in question Mary made her way to the Hurrell household, walking the mile from the station in the cold morning air. She turned into Amberly Crescent, where The Covert was the first house on the left, and rang the bell. Molly answered the door.

"Mrs Ladds!" she said delightedly. "Do come in, Mrs Hurrell is expecting you; can I take your bag?"

"Molly dear, how are you?" Mary spoke quietly. "It's so good to see you; it's just like old times, isn't it?"

"Nearly," said Molly, raising an eyebrow.

She looked towards the drawing room door but no one had heard Mary arrive, so Molly turned and gave Mary a hug.

"Where is everyone, Molly?" asked Mary, removing her cloak and looking in the mirror of the coat stand, pushing the palms of her hands through her hair to look as tidy as possible,

"I think Mrs Hurrell's 'avin' a snooze and Arthur has gone for his rest; there's only me other than them," Molly said, tiptoeing towards the drawing room.

"Molly, is that you?" Rebecca called from a winged chair by the fire.

"Yes, Mrs Hurrell, it's Mrs Ladds – she's just arrived," said Molly, entering the drawing room.

"Oh, Molly, you should have told me, I wanted to be there to meet her," cried Rebecca, pushing herself up from the chair. Molly stood aside to let Mary in.

"Mary, Mary, how wonderful to see you! I have been so looking forward to you coming, it seems just like old times with you here."

She pulled Mary to her, kissed her on each cheek and stood back to look at her.

"You look just the same as when I first met you, Mary, all those years ago; but I don't like that cap, Mary, it makes you look very official."

Mary laughed and took her cap off, handing it to Molly, who took it to put with her bag.

"Now! Tea, Mary?"

"That would be very welcome," smiled Mary.

"Molly?"

"Yes, Mrs Hurrell, and the cake and sandwiches?"

"Yes please, Molly," said Rebecca, turning to Mary: "I've got so much to tell you, but the best thing is Aubrey should be home for Christmas, I had a letter yesterday. How he managed not to get injured or killed I will never know. I feel so guilty about poor Molly, it was so sad about Jupp, it really was."

She tutted and smiled at Mary again.

"And, Mary, you're well, and Jack and Ethil?"

"Yes," Mary replied, "I am well and they are well, very grown up, you know, both of them! When are we to expect the baby, Rebecca? You don't look as though you have long to go."

"Well if my calculations are right, it should be Christmas Day – wouldn't that be wonderful? But the doctor is coming tomorrow so we can see what he says."

"And Arthur, Rebecca? How is Arthur?"

"You will see him shortly, Mary," said Rebecca. "But he has really kept me going while Aubrey has been in France, he is so good. I know he can't talk well and he does not walk very well either, but somehow he is the most wonderful person."

Molly brought the tea in and poured it out.

"Molly dear, go and fetch Arthur can you, so Mary can meet him for the second time."

Five minutes later Mary could hear feet descending the stairs one deliberate step at a time, the voice of Molly offering encouragement all the time. As Arthur and Molly came through the door, Rebecca's face lit up; she held her arms out as Molly walked the little boy across the room. He was fair-haired; a pretty child with a very serious expression. Molly held one of his hands firmly as Arthur hopped slightly onto one leg, dragging the other forward until he could put some weight on it. Every now and then he shut his eyes and his head twitched to the left. His blond hair was straight and fine and parted very deliberately down the left-hand side. He made no sound although his mouth opened and shut as though he wanted to say something. When he reached Rebecca, Molly let him go and he flung himself forward, burying his face in her skirt. Rebecca picked him up and sat him down beside her, releasing her hold on the boy as she did. Arthur was not ready to support himself and flopped to one side onto a cushion.

"Silly Mummy," said Rebecca, "I let go too soon, didn't I?"

She smiled and sat Arthur up again, holding him for a while until he was steady.

"Now, Arthur, this is Mary; say hello, Mary. She's come to help when the baby comes."

Arthur looked at Mary a little doubtfully, a frown creasing his face, then looked round at Rebecca. Her face invited him to speak, pleaded with him to speak – willing him to say something. Arthur looked from Rebecca to Molly to Mary; his mouth opened a couple of times and shut again. He looked to Mary again and slowly began to smile, before ducking his head and shyly turning back to Rebecca, collapsing back into her lap.

"Whooopsa, darling," giggled Rebecca, lifting him up again.

"Isn't he lovely, Mary? He never cries and he's so brave and he loves his mummy, doesn't he?" Rebecca smiled.

She squeezed Arthur tightly to her side, holding her arm around him, Arthur's head twitched slightly.

"Molly, I think you should show Mrs Ladds to her room and make sure she has everything she wants," instructed Rebecca, not looking up from Arthur.

"Very good, Mrs Hurrell," said Molly leading Mary out of the room.

"Don't you think he's lovely?" Molly said as Mary put her bag on the bed.

"Yes, he's sweet."

"You can't help but love him, Mary, you'll see."

The next day the doctor arrived earlier than expected and Rebecca was still upstairs. When Mary told him this, he bounded up the stairs two or three steps at a time and knocked on the door of Rebecca's room, letting himself in. Mary followed and by the time she arrived he had already started his examination.

"You know Nurse Ladds, don't you, Doctor Pingstone? She came last time," said Rebecca.

"Yes," he said turning and briefly acknowledging Mary.

When he had finished he marched out to the bathroom, washed his hands and came back to collect his bag.

"Well, Mrs Hurrell, all seems very satisfactory; the baby is in the right position and seems to have a strong constitution, so we look forward to its arrival."

"And when do you think that will be, doctor?" Rebecca asked.

"Any time in the next couple of weeks," he replied.

"I'm hoping for Christmas Day, doctor, what a present that would be."

"Yes, quite so," he said with a smile.

"Will you have a cup of coffee, doctor? It won't take a moment." asked Rebecca.

"No," he said. "I must go, I'm so busy: all these cases of Spanish Flu the soldiers are bringing back, it's quite dreadful."

"Oh, I'm sorry," said Rebecca. "But, doctor, before you go I want you to tell Nurse Ladds something."

Mary looked up, surprised, her cheeks coloured a little.

"I know –" said Rebecca firmly, eyeing Mary, "and I know I shouldn't, Mary, but just wait – I got out of Molly that Nurse Ladds feels that Arthur's disabilities are due to the way she handled his birth four years ago. Now, doctor, could you tell her what you told me and I am sure she will believe you."

"Oh, well of course," said the doctor with a small smile. "Arthur's affliction is a neurological condition and nothing to do with his birth. I know his birth was long and at the time I thought there might have been damage, but now it's clear that if it were due to a difficult birth, his brain would have been affected by lack of oxygen. That is clearly not the case; his brain seems extraordinarily good although he can't express himself and is a touch immobile; his intellect is normal, probably above normal."

"Thank you, doctor," Rebecca said, turning to Mary: "Now are you satisfied, Mary?"

"If you are sure, doctor," said Mary quietly.

"I am sure, Nurse Ladds, but my instruction is the same now as it was the last time – to call me if you are at all worried."

"Very good, doctor," Mary said.

"Well I will bid you ladies goodbye," he said, bounding down the stairs as fast as he had come.

"There, Mary, do you feel better now?" said Rebecca when he had gone.

Mary sighed and smiled at her friend.

"Yes, that is a weight off my mind; you can't imagine how I felt when I saw Arthur yesterday."

Rebecca smiled at Mary and reached for her hand.

"And now we can get ready for Christmas and Aubrey's return!"

Over the next few days the house was decorated; a tree was bought, paper chains made and holly placed in the rooms. Molly was sent down to the town to buy various things as Rebecca thought of them and Mary got the delivery room ready, cleaning it thoroughly as the lady who came every day to clean – Mrs Hayes – wasn't very good.

"I don't know why you pay her, Mrs Hurrell, she's worse than useless,"

Molly complained.

"Well there is no one else, Molly," Rebecca retorted. "Everyone else has been in the factories."

"Well, don't expect me to do it; I can't do the shoppin' and the cookin' as well as the cleanin'," grumbled Molly.

Arthur sat and watched the preparations, taking everything in and making his way round the rooms slowly, hanging on to the furniture and goggling up at the decorations. Rebecca ordered the wine, brandy and whisky, and a turkey was delivered.

"Who's going to pluck that, then?" Molly grumbled, looking at the enormous bird. "I can't do everything."

"Now, Molly, don't get like that; I will get Mrs Hayes to pluck it," said Rebecca.

"She can't do it in 'ere," Molly snapped, as she stood in front of the range. "Most big 'ouses like this 'ave a cook, you know, and I'm got to do all that as it is."

"I know, Molly, and we will have a cook now the war's over and a gardener, but just right now, we don't have one so we will have to make do," said Rebecca.

The doorbell rang.

"I'll go," said Mary, who stood at the door of the kitchen.

The postman was at the door with a telegram; Mary handed it to Rebecca who pushed her thumb into the gap at the top and ripped it open to read it. Her face brightened.

"Oh wonderful, look Mary! Molly! It's Aubrey, he's coming back on the 22nd. Oh, I can't wait!"

She kissed the telegram enthusiastically.

"Do you want to send a reply, Rebecca?" asked Mary, looking towards the loitering postman at the door.

"Yes," said Rebecca. "Let's do that, where's my pen?"

She sat down at the table and looked up at the others.

"But where do we send it?"

She looked at the envelope; the telegram had been sent from Boulogne.

"I can't, he's on his way back, there's no point he's probably on a ship now. Well, it doesn't matter – we know when he's coming and we can all get ready; how wonderful, he will be back in time for Christmas."

The turkey was plucked and the cake was iced ready on the morning of Aubrey's return and Rebecca and Mary sat in the drawing room having coffee. Arthur was on the floor, his back to the settee with a cushion each side of him to prop him up.

"When do you think he will get back, Mary? I can't wait, I really can't."

"Well you will *have* to wait, Rebecca," laughed Mary. "I've no idea when he will arrive; it depends on so many things."

Rebecca's hand reached down to her belly, stroking the baby through the fabric of her dress.

"When do you think this one will arrive then, Mary?" Rebecca said, pointing to her bump.

"I don't know, Rebecca but it's going to be soon; it could be any day or any hour come to that, but it will come when it's ready."

"Mary?"

"Yes, Rebecca," Mary said as she watched Arthur goggling up at the Christmas tree.

"I think it would be a good idea if I slept in the delivery room from now on, don't you, just in case it comes in the night?" Rebecca said.

"Yes, I think that would be a very good idea. As I said, we never know when it's going to arrive."

Mary sipped her coffee.

"Shall I go and move your things?" she asked.

"No, I will do it when I take Arthur up for his rest," said Rebecca, smiling down at Arthur.

An hour later, just before they were about to have lunch, there was the sound of wheels on the gravel of the drive.

"Mrs Hurrell, Mrs Ladds!" Molly shouted, running to the door to peer through the stained glass panel.

"It's 'im," she shouted. "It's 'im!"

The front door burst open.

"I'm home," Aubrey shouted. "Where's that wife of mine? Rebecca, where are you?"

Rebecca emerged at the top of the stairs,

"Aubrey darling, I'm coming, I'm coming!" she cried, rushing down the stairs two steps at a time and into Aubrey's arms; they embraced each other.

"That's enough of that, Hurrell, it is only lunchtime you know," a voice said from the doorway.

"Shut up, Rupert," Aubrey retorted, kissing Rebecca again.

"Look who I met on the train," said Aubrey, turning to Rupert. "You know Rupert, don't you, Rebecca?"

"Yes of course, I've known him for years."

"And Nurse Ladds," Aubrey said looking at Mary who was now in her full uniform.

Aubrey shook Mary's hand and kissed it.

"The lovely Nurse Ladds – you know Nurse Ladds, don't you, Rupert?"

Aubrey turned to him.

"Yes, hello Mary," Rupert said with a smile.

"Mary, eh? First name terms! What's going on then, eh? What do you think, Rebecca?" laughed Aubrey, kissing Rebecca again.

"And, Molly," he exclaimed, "my dear, how lovely to see you; you look as lovely as ever."

"Thank you, Mr Hurrell," said Molly, blushing as Aubrey gripped her arms and kissed her cheek.

"Come on then, let's have a drink," he declared, taking Rebecca's hand and leading her into the drawing room.

"Come on, Rupert," he shouted over his shoulder.

Rupert smiled again at Mary and followed Aubrey into the drawing room. Molly looked at Mary with a scowl.

"I wish 'e wouldn't do that," she whispered, wiping her cheek. "'E smells of drink."

Mary shrugged and followed Rupert – he still had his top coat on and carried a bowler hat.

"Do you want me to take those?" Mary asked, prising the coat and hat from his fingers and leaving to hang them up in the hall.

"Now champagne, we must have some champagne, Molly," Aubrey shouted.

"Yes, sir," Molly said from the doorway.

"Champagne, Molly!"

"Yes, sir, I'll fetch it."

She returned moments later with a bottle on a tray; Aubrey took it.

"That's even cold; how did you do that, Molly?"

"We've got a refrigerator, sir."

"My word," said Aubrey, "whatever next!"

He popped open the bottle.

"Rebecca?"

"Oh just a spot, dear, I don't want to upset the baby."

"Nurse Ladds?"

"I won't if you don't mind, Mr Hurrell."

"What? You must! The war's over didn't you know, and I'm home, come on!"

"Well, just a small one then," shrugged Mary, taking the glass.

"The rest for us then, Rupert," laughed Aubrey, pouring out two glasses. "Now, a toast!"

He walked to the fire and leant on the mantelpiece.

"A toast," he announced, "to the end of the bloody war! I know it's been over a month but there we go, to the end of the war!"

He lifted his glass, turning round and kissing Rebecca again.

"Oh blimey," he said, putting his hand on Rebecca's bump. "I nearly forgot – to our new arrival."

He burped and added,

"When it comes!"

They all raised their glasses again.

"Do you want some lunch, Aubrey?" Rebecca asked.

"All in good time, dear, all in good time. We must have another one yet, eh, Rupert?"

"If you say so, Aubrey," said Rupert, watching as Aubrey poured the rest of the bottle out and took a long sip.

"I must get out of this wretched uniform; I've been wearing uniform for three and a half years and I'm just about fed up with it," grumbled Aubrey.

"I've put some clothes out for you on the bed," said Rebecca, as Aubrey left the room, unbuttoning his jacket as he went.

"Have you been back long?" Rebecca asked Rupert.

"Only three days," he said. "But I was back to work yesterday."

"And how did that go?" Mary asked.

"It's so different from being in France," shrugged Rupert. "It's really impossible to tell you how awful it was there."

Ten minutes later Aubrey returned dressed in a blazer and smart trousers, his hair brushed and his face shaven.

"That's better," he said, turning to his wife. "Our room's different, Rebecca; none of your things are in there."

"No, Aubrey, I'm sleeping in the delivery room until the baby comes; Mary thought that would be best."

"Did she then?" Aubrey said looking at Mary. "Quite the 'Lysistrata', aren't we, Nurse Ladds?"

"I don't know what you mean," Mary said, puzzled.

"Come on, Aubrey," Rupert said with some exasperation, "that's unfair."

Aubrey sighed and turned to Mary.

"I'm so sorry, my dear...Nurse Ladds, I mean, no offence meant."

He flopped down into a big armchair and leant back.

"Just one more before lunch, eh Rupert, you are stopping for a bite to eat?"

"If you insist, Aubrey," said Rupert indulgently.

"I do, dear boy, I do," said Aubrey, taking out a cigarette and lighting it.

"Where's the son and heir? Haven't seen him yet," he muttered.

"Shall I fetch him?" Mary said.

"Would you, Mary? That would be kind."

When Mary arrived back with Arthur – half the next bottle of champagne was empty. He clutched her tightly as they entered the room.

"Here he is then," said Aubrey, sitting up in his chair. "Does he say anything yet?"

He turned to Rebecca.

"Not a lot yet, dear," Rebecca replied.

"Can he walk then? Surely, he's over four now," Aubrey said with a hint of exasperation.

"Well, he needs some help but he can walk a little. Come on, Arthur, come and meet your father!"

She smiled down at him; Arthur looked back and smiled faintly, before looking seriously at Aubrey.

"Come on then, Arthur, walk to me, there's a good boy," said Aubrey, holding his arms out.

Mary held him as he took one step and then another.

"Let him go, Nurse Ladds," Aubrey demanded.

Mary loosened her grip, her hands still supporting most of Arthur's weight.

"Let him go; let's see if he can walk – go on, let him go," insisted Aubrey, his voice rising.

Mary reluctantly released her grip, her hands moving tremulously from Arthur's side. Arthur stood motionless; the room was completely silent, all eyes on the small boy. He remained there for a moment, looking at Rebecca and then back to Aubrey. He shifted his weight onto one foot, slowly dragging the other forward – his balance wavered and then, without a sound he toppled sideways with a heart-breaking inevitability onto the soft carpet, rolling onto his back. Mary rushed forward to pick him up.

"Leave him!" shouted Aubrey angrily.

Mary hesitated momentarily, looking at the prone figure with a frown. She shook her head slightly and made her way towards him again.

"Leave him, I said," snarled Aubrey.

Mary stood back and bowed her head, unwilling to watch the small boy struggle. Arthur's head twitched, his arms pushed ineffectually at the carpet and one leg flapped to get purchase on the floor. He tried hard to roll himself onto his stomach, but he did not have enough strength. His head twitched again as he attempted to roll over once more – his eyes widened desperately, his arms outstretched as he lay helpless, unable to shift his weight. Rebecca leapt to her feet, scooped up the boy and sat him on her knee, brushing her fingers through his hair and straightening his sailor's uniform.

Aubrey sat back in his chair.

"Son and heir," he snorted. "More a cripple! *He'll* never handle a rugby ball or pick up a cricket bat." He looked away from Arthur, draining his glass of champagne.

Rebecca said nothing, holding her son to her, a solitary tear rolling down her cheek onto the upturned face of the smiling boy.

Chapter Sixty-Two
A Great Shadow is Cast

The next day Aubrey went to lunch at The County Hotel; he had persuaded Rupert to come with him and he knew that he would find more friends at the bar. After a good lunch and several bottles of wine between them Aubrey ordered a taxi to take them back to The Covert. The cab drew up to the front door and the two men made their way to the house, handing their hats and coats to Molly at the door. Rupert went straight to the drawing room, where Rebecca was reading the paper, greeting Mary –who was walking up and down the hall with Arthur – as he passed. Aubrey followed Rupert in, pausing by Mary at the foot of the stairs. He exhaled and ran a hand slowly down her back; Mary froze as Aubrey's hand continued its progress, lingering on her bottom.

"It's getting cold out there, Nurse Ladds," he whispered, winking and moving into the drawing room. Mary shuddered and continued to walk up and down the hall.

"Mary dear, let me take over, I want to stretch my legs," Rebecca said, emerging from the drawing room several minutes later. "You go and talk to Rupert; Aubrey's already sound asleep."

She took Arthur's hand and beamed down at him as Mary entered the drawing room, sat down awkwardly on a chair opposite Rupert and started twirling her fingers in her lap.

"Have you seen Lucy since she returned?" Rupert asked finally.

"No, not yet," Mary replied. "She has gone straight to help at a convalescent home in Yorkshire, and I don't know when she will get time off."

Aubrey snored loudly – he was very red in the face and his breathing was a little laboured. Rupert smiled and sipped his tea as Mary looked into the flames of the large wood fire, watching the tongues of fire dancing up the chimney. Rebecca led Arthur back into the room, sitting him in the corner of the settee before lowering herself down gently beside him, brushing his hair back with her hand.

Aubrey opened his eyes, sat up and put his hand to his forehead on which

Mary could see small beads of sweat.

"Feel a little under the weather," he said groggily, standing slowly.

As he did so the colour drained from his cheeks, his hands trembling slightly. He took a handkerchief from his jacket and mopped his brow, swaying from side to side. Without warning, he collapsed backwards into the chair, his eyes shut and opened again, rolling hazily around, not focusing on anything.

"Aubrey darling, are you all right?" Rebecca asked worriedly.

Aubrey's eyes focused, moving round until they alighted on her.

"Never felt better," he said hoarsely, passing his hand over his forehead again.

"Come on, old boy," said Rupert. "You don't look too well, what's up?"

Aubrey sat up in the chair, sighed and shivered slightly – his face was now completely grey.

"Don't know," he said in the same hoarse tone. "I must say I don't feel too good, I'll go and take a lie down upstairs, I think."

He made to rise again. As soon as he put weight on his legs, they shook and gave under him; he fell back into the chair shivering.

"Aubrey, what is it?" cried Rebecca, rising and clutching Aubrey's shoulder.

"Now, my dear," said Rupert, "let me take his arm; I'll get him upstairs, you just sit there and rest. I guess he had one or two too many glasses of wine; it has that effect on a chap, you know."

Rupert held Aubrey under the arm, helping him out of the chair and out of the room. Rebecca and Mary watched them go.

"I hope he's all right, Mary; what do you think it is?" Rebecca asked.

"I think Rupert is probably right; the wine has not agreed with him – he will be right as rain in an hour or two, you'll see."

Five minutes later, Rupert returned.

"I've put him in bed," he said. "I would make a good nurse– just like Mary!"

Mary laughed.

"Let him sleep for a few hours, I'm sure he will be fine," Rupert advised, collecting his coat and making for the door.

Later that afternoon, Rebecca came into the drawing room, having checked on her husband. She stood worriedly in the middle of the room, shifting her weight from foot to foot.

"Aubrey's still asleep, Mary; I don't like the look of him, he doesn't look well at all," she said quietly.

"He must have been very tired when he came back," said Mary, looking up from the book she was reading.

"I suppose he was," said Rebecca. "I will wake him in a little while to see if he wants any supper. Molly will have it ready soon."

Twenty minutes later she went back upstairs to ask Aubrey if he could face eating. A piercing scream punctuated the quiet of the house. Mary leapt from her chair, rushing into the hallway. Rebecca was on the landing.

"Mary, Mary! Come quick, come as quick as you can!" she pleaded.

Mary ran up the stairs, followed closely by Molly, and rushed into Aubrey's room. Aubrey lay on the bed; his face was white and a small trickle of blood dripped from one side of his mouth which hung slightly open. The sheets and pillows were covered with spots of blood, which he had coughed up and Mary could see a small amount of blood running from his nose.

"Mary, what is it? Look at him, what is it?" Rebecca shrieked.

"Rebecca dear, you must come away," instructed Mary, pulling her back. "Rebecca, you must come away for the sake of the baby."

"But, Mary, look at him; what's wrong with him?" Rebecca sobbed, turning helplessly to Mary. "What's wrong with him?"

"I think he's got Spanish Flu, Rebecca, and you must keep away; it's very infectious," said Mary firmly, holding Rebecca's hand and leading her from the room. She sat her on one of the chairs on the landing.

"Molly, quickly give me a hand," said Mary, leading Molly back into the room.

"Now, Molly, help me prop him up and get some pillows behind him," she instructed, pulling Aubrey forward.

His breath gurgled in his chest, and he coughed, blood spattering from his mouth and speckling Mary's uniform.

"Molly, put your coat on and go and fetch the doctor; you know where he lives."

"Yes, Mary, what shall I tell him?"

"Tell him you think Mr Hurrell's got Spanish Flu and be quick, Molly."

Molly rushed from the room as Mary busied herself trying to make Aubrey comfortable, and went to change her uniform.

Rebecca was pacing up and down in the drawing room when she made it downstairs, wringing her hands desperately.

"Now, Rebecca, you will have to keep away from him, and let me deal with him; it's most important that you don't catch it."

"But I've been with him; if I'm going to get it, I've got it now surely, Mary."

"No, Rebecca, maybe you have caught it but it's more than likely that you haven't and we can't take the chance. We don't want anything to happen to the baby, do we?"

"I suppose not," Rebecca sighed.

Molly rushed into the room, panting for breath.

"What did he say?" Mary asked.

"'E weren't there but 'is wife said he'll come up as soon as he gets back but she don't know when that will be."

"Very good, Molly, now I will go back upstairs, you look after Mrs Hurrell."

Two hours later the doctor arrived, Mary did not even hear him until he entered the room. He examined Aubrey, took his temperature and listened to his chest.

"How long?" he said to Mary.

"About eight hours; he's bad, isn't he, will he get through it?" Mary asked.

"Yes, he's bad, we will know tomorrow but he doesn't look good."

He shook his head sadly, stood up and turned to Mary.

"Now, Nurse Ladds, you must not let Mrs Hurrell in here and you must be absolutely scrupulous regarding hygiene, you understand?"

"Yes, doctor," Mary said.

"I'm sorry, nurse, I shouldn't lecture you – you know about hygiene."

"Yes, doctor," Mary replied with a small smile.

"I will see Mrs Hurrell and tell her she must not enter this room under any circumstances. It may be that she is already infected so you must pay every attention to her condition; you know the symptoms now, Nurse Ladds."

"Yes, doctor," Mary replied.

There was a light tap on the door and Molly poked her head around the door.

"Don't come in, Molly," Mary said sharply, adjusting a cushion behind Aubrey. "Just wait there."

She moved out of the room, shutting the door behind her.

"Is 'e bad, Mary?" whispered Molly.

"Yes, Molly, he's very bad," said Mary quietly. "But Spanish Flu is very infectious, you will have to look after Mrs Hurrell and I will have to look after Mr Hurrell. Now just wait there while I wash my hands."

She moved to the bathroom door, shook her head angrily and turned.

"No," she said, "I'm stupid."

She looked sternly at Molly.

"Now, Molly, I will wash in the downstairs cloakroom and everyone else in this bathroom, you understand?"

"Yes, Mary."

That night Mary slept in a chair in Aubrey's room and attended to him as the disease took its course; throughout the night she watched as Aubrey grew weaker and weaker and by the morning there was little life left in him. At breakfast, Molly, Rebecca and Arthur waited in the kitchen for Mary to come and report on Aubrey's condition. Mary came into the kitchen, standing well away from the others, a pillow case full of sheets bundled in her arms.

"How is he, Mary?" Rebecca asked tentatively.

"He's very weak, Rebecca," replied Mary. "It's a very aggressive disease and he has it badly."

"He's not going to die, is he, Mary? Tell me he won't die, I couldn't bear it!"

She took a handkerchief from her sleeve and wiped her eye.

"I'm sure he will pull through," Mary said convincingly. "He's very ill but he's a strong man."

She gave Rebecca as broad a smile as she could manage and looked away. Rebecca sighed heavily.

"There, there, Mrs Hurrell," said Molly. "Come on – we've got to be brave, haven't we? We don't want Arthur to see you crying, do we, he won't like that."

She put her arm round Rebecca, who leant into her tiredly.

"You're right, Molly, whatever happens we must think of Arthur."

She looked adoringly at her son and stroked his hair as he struggled to get his toast to his mouth.

"You carry on, Mary," said Rebecca. "I will take Arthur into the drawing room when he has had his breakfast."

Mary offloaded the sheets into an empty chair and looked at Molly.

"Molly dear, don't you touch this, not with you so near to Rebecca; but get Mrs Hayes to take it down the garden and burn it."

"What, them good sheets?" Molly gasped.

"Yes, Molly, they are infected," said Mary firmly. "It's the only way we can be sure of not spreading the infection – they must be burnt. I'm going upstairs to change this uniform."

"If you say so, Mary."

"I say so, Molly," instructed Mary, turning and making for the stairs.

The day crawled by – Mary spent her time rushing up and down the stairs with sheets, towels and cups of warm broth. Aubrey continued to decline; his breathing became slow and shallow, until Mary could hardly hear the air making its progress in and out of his body at all. In the middle of the afternoon the doctor arrived.

"How is he?" he asked as he entered.

"He's hanging on," whispered Mary, "but only just."

The doctor pulled the sheet down from where it was wrapped around Aubrey's shoulders, putting his stethoscope to Aubrey's chest and picking up his wrist. There was a knock at the door; it was Molly.

"Nurse Ladds," Molly said, her face pinched with concern.

"What is it, Molly?" Mary asked.

"It's Mrs Hurrell, she says that the baby has started."

"Very good," said Mary. "Tell her to come upstairs and I will be there in a little while."

"She's come up already, nurse, she's on the bed and 'Arfer is up 'ere as well."

"That's good, Molly," said Mary, turning away from Molly. "You look after them, I will come when I have washed."

Molly stood awkwardly in the doorway, chewing her lip.

"'Er breaving seems a bit funny, Mary," she said finally.

Mary looked at the doctor, who sighed and looked at the ceiling.

"Very good, Molly, we won't be long," said Mary with a slight frown.

The doctor continued to hold Aubrey's wrist.

"He's going, I think," he murmured.

Mary looked down at Aubrey –a small sigh seemed to escape his lips and he lay still. The doctor shook his head and placed Aubrey's hand down on the bed. He lifted the stethoscope into his ears, listened once more at Aubrey's chest and then straightened up. He looked at Mary.

"He's dead," he said quietly.

Mary looked down, gathered herself and pulled the sheet up to cover Aubrey's face.

"What I can't work out is why all of the men dying are his age," said Doctor Pingstone, shaking his head. "It doesn't make sense. Now, Mary – I can call you Mary, can't I?"

"Yes, Doctor Pingstone," she said.

"You won't get an undertaker for a day or two so lock this door and keep the key yourself," said the doctor, curling his stethoscope up and putting it in his bag. "Now where can I wash? I've got to see Rebecca now."

Mary escorted the doctor downstairs to the cloakroom, where he washed and returned to examine Rebecca. Mary met him on the stairs as he was about to leave.

"Mary, we have a problem."

"Yes, doctor."

"Yes," he said, "the baby is fine at the moment but Rebecca is infected with the Flu."

"You are sure, doctor?" Mary gasped.

"I'm sure," he said. "I've seen too many cases in the last month. So, Mary, you will have to manage. I will come back in the morning; I am busy with so many other cases and you must only fetch me if it is an emergency."

"Very good, doctor," said Mary, watching Doctor Pingstone rush down the stairs and out the front door.

"Molly!" Mary shouted, rushing down the stairs.

"Yes, Mary?"

"Go to my room, Molly, and fetch me a clean uniform. I must change quickly; bring it to the cloakroom."

Molly ran upstairs as Mary went and took off her uniform, throwing it on the floor of the cloakroom and washing herself as best she could. Molly arrived and helped her dress, before moving to pick up the uniform from the floor.

"No, Molly!" Mary screamed. "Get Mrs Hayes to do that, and you see to Arthur while I see to Mrs Hurrell."

She straightened her uniform and rushed up the stairs again.

"Molly!" she shouted over the banister. "Ask Mrs Hayes to see me before she goes, we will want her tomorrow."

"You mean Christmas Day?" Molly said incredulously.

"Yes, I mean Christmas Day," shouted Mary, running along the landing to Rebecca's room. She opened the door quietly and crept into the room.

"Mary?" Rebecca said quietly – her voice sounded hoarse and was a little deeper than normal.

"Yes, Rebecca," Mary replied, sitting on the bed.

"The doctor didn't say anything about Aubrey," said Rebecca desperately, looking up at Mary.

Mary looked down and wrung her hands.

"He's dead, isn't he, Mary?" sobbed Rebecca. "He must be or you wouldn't be here; tell me, Mary, tell me the truth; he's dead, isn't he?"

Mary looked at her.

"Yes, he's dead, Rebecca; he died about half an hour ago."

She grasped Rebecca's hand tightly; Rebecca shut her eyes tightly and took a deep breath.

"No, Mary; now's not the time to grieve – the baby's on the way, we have to be strong. Where is Arthur, Mary?" she asked, squeezing Mary's hand.

"He's all right; Molly has him," Mary answered.

"That's all right then," sighed Rebecca, relaxing back onto the pillow.

"Was he in pain, Mary?"

"No, there was no pain, he was very peaceful."

"Mary, I've got the Flu, haven't I?" croaked Rebecca. "The doctor didn't say so but I know, he didn't have to tell me."

"Well I don't know quite what it is," lied Mary. "But let's concentrate on this baby, can we, that's the best thing. Now I must go and see if Mrs Hayes has arrived."

Mary left the room and made her way downstairs to find Mrs Hayes.

"Now, Mrs Hayes, we want you to come tomorrow," Mary said firmly.

"What? It's Christmas Day, din't you know that?" exclaimed Mrs Hayes.

"I know, but we've got a baby coming and Molly can't do everything with Arthur to look after."

Mrs Hayes looked to Molly and back to Mary.

"Well, I don't know about that," she said slowly, before adding aggressively: "It'll 'ave to be extra; I ain't comin' less you pay extra."

"Very good then, Mrs Hayes, but you make sure you are here on time," Mary insisted.

The baby was very slow arriving and had still not come by the next morning. When Mrs Hayes arrived, Molly was in the drawing room helping Arthur open his presents by the overladen tree, several of the presents lying unwrapped. Rebecca's condition had worsened overnight and her breathing now was laboured. Mary sat by her side, mopping her brow with a damp towel and looking down desperately at her friend, who was pale, her breathing shallow. She took one last look at Rebecca and hurried downstairs to the drawing room, where Mrs Hayes was laying the fire.

"Mrs Hayes, I want you to go and fetch the doctor. You know where he lives, don't you?"

"Yes, Nurse Ladds, but what do I tell 'im?"

"Tell him I'm very concerned about Mrs Hurrell and would he attend as quickly as possible?"

"I'll get my 'at and coat then," said Mrs Hayes, rising from the hearth.

"Are things all right, Mary?" Molly asked urgently.

Arthur looked round quizzically at Mary.

"They're not very good, Molly, but you look after Arthur; I must go back to Mrs Hurrell."

It was nearly midday before the doctor came and things had not improved. Rebecca was weaker and appeared to have no strength left. Twenty-five hours after the labour had started, a baby was delivered at three in the afternoon. Doctor Pingstone turned to Mary holding the silent baby in his arms and shook his head; Rebecca was lying back on the pillows – her eyes half closed, semi-conscious. The dead baby was put in the crib and covered up with a sheet and Mary attended to Rebecca while the doctor washed. He came back into the room, looked at Rebecca and motioned at Mary to come out of the room.

"Mary, there's no more I can do here; I have so many more people to see, and it's Christmas Day."

"Will she survive?" Mary asked desperately.

"I don't know, she's very weak; the chances aren't great, I'm afraid."

"Very well," said Mary resignedly.

The doctor reached forward and grasped Mary's hand briefly, before turning to leave.

Mary followed him downstairs, walking slowly into the drawing room.

"Molly, there's something I need to tell you," she said quietly.

"I know what you are going to say, Mary; I can guess what you are going to say – the baby's dead, isn't it? I just know it is."

Molly's lips quivered dangerously.

"Yes, I'm afraid it is," said Mary.

"What about Mrs Hurrell then, Mary, is she all right?"

"She's not good, Molly. I'm going back now, you give Arthur his tea and then put him to bed."

She looked sadly at Arthur.

"Poor little lad, I don't think he knows what has happened," whispered Mary, holding Arthur's chin and smiling down at him – Arthur grinned back.

"'E knows more than you think, Mary; I know he's got a lot of problems but 'e knows what's goin' on, I'm sure 'e does."

Mary nodded and wandered into the kitchen. She made herself a sandwich and a cup of tea and took them back to Rebecca's room, moved the small armchair closer to the bed and watched her friend sleep. Two hours later Molly came to the door, tapping lightly before thrusting her head around the corner.

"Can I come in?" she said quietly.

Mary started – she had been dozing gently.

"Yes," she whispered, "Come on in, it won't matter now."

Molly tiptoed over to the bed and stood behind Mary, looking down at Rebecca.

"She don't look good, Mary."

"No," said Mary. "Have you put Arthur to bed?"

"Yes, an hour ago now."

She looked down at Rebecca again.

"Look, Mary, 'er eyes are open; she wants somefing!" said Molly urgently.

Mary stood up and leant over Rebecca.

"Rebecca, what is it? How do you feel?" Mary said gently.

Rebecca said nothing; her eyes focused on Mary, she looked at Molly and back to Mary again.

"Mary," she said very quietly.

"Yes, Rebecca?"

"The baby."

"Yes, Rebecca."

"Is it dead?"

"Yes, Rebecca," Mary whispered, trying desperately to keep her voice level. "A little girl."

Rebecca sighed heavily, closed her eyes and opened them again. She smiled gently at Molly, her eyes sweeping the room again, alighting finally on Mary.

"Mary?" she croaked.

"Yes, Rebecca," Mary whispered, tears springing to her eyes.

"Mary, I'm dying," she said very slowly.

She squeezed Mary's hand to stop her protesting.

"But I want you to promise me something."

"Yes, Rebecca, anything."

"Mary, I want you to promise me that you will look after Arthur as long as you live."

She closed her eyes and took as deep a breath as she could manage.

"He will always need help, Mary; as long as you live."

"I promise, Rebecca; I promise so help me, God," whispered Mary, her voice cracking.

Rebecca smiled, her grip loosened on Mary's hand and her eyes fell shut.

Mary gazed down at her friend, gently took hold of her wrist and felt for a pulse.

"Molly, give me that mirror," she said quietly, pointing to a mirror on the dressing table.

Molly fetched the small mirror and handed it to Mary, who held it in front of Rebecca's mouth and nose for a moment, pulled it away and looked at it. She sighed heavily and put her ear to Rebecca's chest. After some moments she stood up, took a step backwards and let go of Rebecca's hand.

"She's dead, Molly, she's dead," she stammered, clenching the mirror tightly in her fist.

Molly put her arms around Mary as she sobbed.

"She's dead, they are all dead," wailed Mary.

"No they ain't," said Molly firmly.

Mary sniffed and wiped her eyes; Molly grasped her shoulders and looked straight into Mary's eyes.

"Look, Mary, look over there!"

Mary turned and looked to the door. Arthur was standing in the doorway, one hand on the door handle the other on the doorpost, a small frown lining his innocent face.

"Oh, look at him, poor chap, how did he get here?" sniffed Mary.

"Shall I take 'im back?" asked Molly.

"No, Molly, bring him over there to see his mother, it would be best," said Mary, wiping her eyes.

Molly led Arthur across the room very slowly. He stood by the bed, looking down at Rebecca and then up at Mary.

"Show him the baby, Molly," instructed Mary.

Molly looked up at Mary questioningly – but Mary nodded firmly. Molly led Arthur to the crib, they pulled the sheet back and looked down at the still form.

"Mary, we should say a prayer, shouldn't we?" said Molly quietly.

"Yes, Molly – that is best; come and we will kneel by the bed. Bring Arthur and hold him, he knows how to kneel."

The three of them knelt by Rebecca's bed.

"Say the Lord's Prayer, Mary; I know that one," Molly said quietly.

Mary and Molly closed their eyes and they started the prayer.

A murmuring to their side made both women look up. Arthur, his eyes shut, hands gripping the frame of the bed, was mouthing along with them – a faint noise gurgling from his throat. It was nothing that they could understand, but he was trying to speak with them – with every line he joined in with his own variation.

"Amen," sounded Mary and Molly.

Arthur fell silent, eyes still tightly shut.

"Did you 'ear that, Mary?" Molly whispered.

"Yes, he spoke!" smiled Mary.

"Yes; yes 'e did," said Molly.

Chapter Sixty-Three
A Letter from Toronto

After the funerals had taken place life gradually settled down. It took nearly a year before Mary was appointed Arthur's official guardian and it was not until 1923 that all the financial affairs were settled. Financially there was plenty of money; Arthur had inherited both of his parents' estates, plus the house and some other properties in Northampton. The sale of Rebecca's father's business had made her an extremely wealthy woman so they would all be able to continue to live at The Covert. Molly was kept on as housekeeper with Mrs Hayes as the cleaner, and a gardener was also engaged who doubled up as a chauffeur when needed. Mary had moved all her belongings over from Dean and both Jack and Ethil made The Covert their base. As Arthur continued to grow his disabilities grew with him. His walking did not improve and he continued to twitch his head, always carrying it to one side. His speech manifested itself as grunting and groaning, but after a while both Mary and Molly were able to understand this peculiar language and although Arthur could not carry a conversation as such, he could communicate with them. He was clearly not going to be able to go to school, but Mary decided that when he reached the age of five she would do her best to educate him. In the end, Arthur turned out to be a quick learner, excelling in mathematics, and Mary was able to teach him to read and write quite quickly. Mary was very particular about how he was dressed; the sailor suits were soon replaced with a jacket and waistcoat, or suits which she purchased from Tibbitts. The one thing that Arthur lacked was the company of other young children, which Mary could do little about. The only opportunity they had to meet others was to go and see William and Grace, who now had four boys, the oldest of whom was the same age as Arthur. She would get the chauffeur to drive them over every school holiday and although he was unable to join in the games, the four boys grew to understand Arthur's language. After the war, Lucy returned to nurse in Bedford but after a year or two she also lived mostly at The Covert. Mary herself embraced her life in Northampton – having both the children and Lucy settled at the house gave her life a sensation of fullness with the family all around her, something that had been lacking for so long since circumstances had been the fillip to her existence as a travelling midwife.

One day in late December when all was quiet again after another subdued Christmas, William sent a telegram announcing that he would call the day after next on his way back from Northampton market. It was early afternoon when a knock was heard at the door – Molly, expecting him, answered the door.

"William!" she exclaimed. "Sorry, I mean Mr Dunmore, how are you? Mrs Ladds has been expecting you – please step this way."

"Molly, there's no need to be so formal," William muttered, looking slightly embarrassed.

"I know, William, but Mary likes it like that, you know how it is," she smiled, taking his hat and his coat.

"You know the way, William; I'll go and get the coffee and I've made a cake – you must have a piece."

William went into the drawing room where Arthur sat at the table, a copy of *The Times* newspaper spread in front of him, running his fingers along the lines of type and mouthing as though he were saying the words. Mary was sitting in a chair by the fire, sewing; she rose as William entered.

"William dear, how lovely to see you," she cried. "I didn't hear the door; did Molly see to you?"

She rushed up to him, took his hands and kissed him on the cheek.

"Come and sit down and tell me the news, there must be something to tell."

William sat down on the edge of the chair and smiled gently.

"Well?" said Mary.

"Well," said William, "all is well at Covington and at Dean, but you are right, there is another reason for my visit."

He reached into his jacket pocket and handed Mary a letter.

"This came for you addressed to the butcher's shop two days ago."

"Oh what's this, then?" mused Mary, looking hard at the envelope with her name and address typed on it.

The stamp and postmark were Canadian. She looked back at William; the colour draining from her cheeks. She walked to the mantelpiece, picked up the silver paperknife and slit the envelope open; sitting in her chair again to open the letter. She looked at William once more and over at Arthur who, sensing something was wrong, had stopped reading the paper and was looking at her. She pulled the letter from the envelope and gingerly opened it. Molly entered, put the tray on the table and went back to fetch the teapot.

The letter was from solicitors in Toronto; Brackenbury, Honeybun & Brackenbury and was headed **Noble Thomas William Ladds**. The letter read:

Dear Mrs Ladds,

We the above act for the Algonquin Timber Company and are sorry to inform you of the death of your husband Noble Thomas William Ladds in an accident at the timber mill on 3rd December 1923. We would be grateful if you could forward a copy of your marriage certificate and we will forward his effects and unclaimed pay to the date of his death,

Yours sincerely,

Ernest Brackenbury

Mary put her hand to her mouth and bowed her head. Molly came in with the tea, placing it down before looking searchingly at Mary.

"What is it?" she said sharply.

Mary handed the letter to William, which he read.

"What is it, William?" Molly asked again.

"Noble is dead," William said sombrely.

Molly put a hand to her mouth as William rose, put the letter on the table and moved to comfort Mary. Arthur pulled the letter towards him and read it. After a moment Mary shuddered, rose, eased the letter from Arthur's hand and read it again.

"Did you read it, William?"

"Yes," William replied. "But it doesn't give you much information."

"Dead," Mary said quietly. "It's such a shock, I haven't thought about him for months and now he's dead. It's like a dream; he's been gone for sixteen years and not a word and now he's dead."

"That won't be no loss to the world," Molly said under her breath.

"Molly, that's not very—" started Mary.

"I'm right, Mary," interrupted Molly loudly. "'E weren't no good to no one; ain't I right, William?"

She turned to William for support.

"I suppose you are, Molly, but he was Jack and Ethil's father."

"S'pose 'e was," muttered Molly belligerently. "I'll fetch some more tea, Mrs Ladds."

She bobbed and went out with the silver teapot.

"It's such a shock, William," repeated Mary. "I just don't know what to think. Molly's right, he was no good, but he was my husband. What am I going to tell everyone? I can't just go up to people and say he's dead."

"No," said William, looking up as Molly re-entered with the teapot.

"I know," said William suddenly, "what to do is to put it in the deaths column in *The Times*, enough people will see it and they will tell everyone else and that will save you having to do it."

"Good idea, William," said Mary gratefully, accepting another cup of tea from Molly.

The notice of Noble's death was duly put in *The Times* and Mary received a few letters of condolence. Noble had been buried within days of the accident so there was no funeral to arrange. One of the letters of condolence was from Rupert who suggested that he would visit the coming week.

Molly answered the door to Rupert when he arrived, taking his hat and coat and leading him into the drawing room.

"Mr Nelson to see you, Mrs Ladds," she announced, holding the door open.

Mary was sitting in one of the armchairs and Arthur at the table by the window reading when Rupert entered.

"Rupert, how nice of you to come," Mary said, standing up and shaking Rupert's hand.

"Think nothing of it, Mary, it's the least I could do in the circumstances; it must have been a shock after all these years."

They both sat.

"Yes," Mary said, "it was a shock; it's sixteen years since he left."

"How did it happen?" Rupert asked as Molly appeared with a teapot.

"Do you want me to pour it out, Mrs Ladds?" she asked.

"No, Molly; you go and get Arthur's tea and then come and fetch him when it's ready."

Arthur looked up briefly at the mention of his name and returned to reading his book.

"How is Arthur?" asked Rupert. "Such a sad life for him."

"He's much the same," said Mary. "His disabilities don't improve, but I'm teaching him as much as I can; he's a very good pupil."

"But he can't speak," said Rupert.

"Not that you would understand, Rupert," she admitted with a small laugh.

"Does he understand anything? Can he hear?" asked Rupert.

"Oh yes, he has good hearing," said Mary.

Molly came in, took Arthur by the hand and led him on his hopping progress out across the room. He looked at Rupert seriously as he left, making a little low grunting noise, his head twitching as he left. An hour later Mary collected Rupert's hat and coat as he prepared to leave.

"Can I call again?" said Rupert. "It's so nice to chat to you, Mary, after all these years; we were good friends once, weren't we?"

"I suppose we were," she agreed with a smile.

"So could I call again?" he asked once more.

Mary thought for a moment and then said,

"Yes, that would be nice, Rupert – say the same time next week?"

Rupert smiled broadly and left, a slight spring in his step.

Over the months Rupert's visits became more frequent and after a while they started going to the theatre together. They would catch a train to London and go to a matinee and then return the same evening. Mary enjoyed the trips to the theatre and the company and Rupert seemed devoted to her.

She was now officially a widow and it was not long after she had been sent Noble's effects – a silver cigarette case and his pay to date –that Rupert asked her to marry him. She was naturally pleased by the request and asked for time to think about it. She immediately sent a card to William and Grace to say that she would visit them the next Sunday afternoon.

"You do love him?" asked Grace, when she finally got Mary on her own that Sunday.

The two women were watching the boys playing together at the bottom of the garden.

"I don't know," Mary said frankly. "It's not the same now as it was when I was younger. I made a big mistake with Noble; I know that and everyone told me so, but that's water under the bridge."

She sighed.

"He's a good man and I would like to marry him; I expect I could grow to love him in the end."

She watched one of the boys leading Arthur back towards them across the lawn. She looked at the little blond boy limping across the lawn, a grin all over his face.

"That's who I love the most, Grace," she said quietly, nodding towards Arthur.

A week later Mary accepted Rupert's proposal and they both went together to buy a ring. They decided not to announce their engagement until Noble had been dead for a year, but all the plans for a wedding were to be made and Mary was invited over to the Manor at the end of the week to discuss the details. That morning Mary entered Arthur's bedroom, where Molly was helping Arthur to get ready.

"You're going to marry 'im then?" Molly said glumly.

"Don't say it like that, Molly," laughed Mary. "You could sound a bit more cheerful. Yes, I'm going to marry Rupert."

"Hmm," murmured Molly.

"What's wrong, Molly?" said Mary, looking at her with displeasure. "We're going to get married, aren't you pleased?"

"What's goin' to 'appen to me then?" grumbled Molly.

"Oh, that's what you are worried about," laughed Mary. "Well, you will come as well; of course you will."

"Will I?" said Molly doubtfully. "To that big 'ouse?"

"The Manor you mean, yes of course, it's big enough; I will need you, Molly, to help with Arthur." Molly chewed her lip thoughtfully.

"Well, if you're sure I can come, it would be nice to be out in the country again. You never know, Mary, I might find an 'usband, like you; I don't want to be left on the shelf, you know. You're lucky, you found someone; but there's precious few of them about after that bloody war."

"Molly, don't swear in front of Arthur," Mary hissed.

Arthur looked up at Molly and smiled.

"I'm no spring chicken you know," shrugged Molly. "It ain't so easy to attract 'em as it was."

"Well I'm over forty myself, Molly," sighed Mary.

"I know but 'e waited for you; 'e's bin waitin' twenty years for you, Mary, you know that and I know that, so—"

Mary said nothing, unwilling to rise to Molly's jibe. She adjusted her hat, put the long pin through and turned to Molly.

"How do I look, Molly? Is my hat straight?"

Molly stood back, looked at the hat and surveyed Mary critically.

"Well, you ain't no spring chicken, Mary, but I would say that for someone over forty you look very smart. That Rupert's lucky to 'ave you, that's what I would say."

"Thank you, Molly," smiled Mary. "But I think I'm the lucky one, he's such a lovely man."

"And 'e's got a lot of money, Mary, you mustn't forget that."

Mary said nothing.

"Time to go; are you ready, Arthur?" said Mary.

Arthur nodded, she took his hand and they left for the Manor.

Once there, they were escorted into the drawing room where Rupert and his mother Christiana were waiting. They all shook hands and Mary sat Arthur at a table with a book she had brought for him to read.

Rupert sat next to his mother on the settee, Mary in an armchair opposite. The coffee was served by a thin maid with a pained expression, who handed Mary a cup and saucer and bobbed to her unenthusiastically.

"I'm so pleased that everything has worked out for you both," Christiana said loudly. "It's all so exciting, don't you think, Mary? I'm so pleased that you are going to be my daughter-in-law after all these years."

"That's very kind of you to say, Mrs Nelson, and yes it is exciting."

"Now, Mary, I have decided that you must call me Christiana; that's what I would like, isn't it, Rupert?" She turned to him.

"Yes, Mother," smiled Rupert.

"And a wedding next spring, we thought, wasn't that right, Rupert?"

"Yes, Mother, if it's all right with Mary."

He looked sheepishly at Mary and shrugged slightly.

"That sounds wonderful," said Mary.

Rupert grinned and reached across to squeeze her hand; Mary beamed at him.

"Now, my dears, I have decided that when you get married I will move out into the Lodge; it's only fair to leave you on your own."

"Are you sure?" said Mary, surprised. "It doesn't really seem fair to make you leave."

"Mother and I have talked it over and she is very happy to move, isn't that right, Mother?" interrupted Rupert, turning to his mother.

"Yes, dear," she said. "You can then entertain and go on holiday and do what you like without your old mother-in-law looking on."

"And," said Rupert, "Jack and Ethil could move here. I know they would not be here much but they could have a base, couldn't they?"

"That would really be lovely," sighed Mary, "to have our own home."

"And," continued Rupert, "there is enough room for Lucy as well; she can't spend the rest of her life in nurses' homes, can she?"

"I hadn't really thought about it but that would be wonderful," Mary smiled. She hesitated momentarily before adding,

"But what about Molly? I don't want to let her down."

"Don't worry, there is room for her as well; we have thought about that, haven't we, Mother?"

"Yes, dear, I will take Thisbe with me and Molly can come in her place."

"That's wonderful, Rupert, you really have thought of everything," laughed

Mary.

"Oh there is one other thing—" said Rupert warily.

Mary looked at him sharply, there was a tone to his voice which she didn't like.

"Yes," said Rupert. "It's Arthur. Mother has found him a very nice home for him the other side of Northampton; I'm sure he will be very happy there."

Arthur looked up at the mention of his name.

"What did you say?" said Mary slowly, the colour draining from her face.

There was silence, Rupert looked worriedly at his mother, but before he could think of anything to say Christiana went on,

"Rupert means that Arthur can't live here and we have found this very nice place for him to go," she said firmly.

Mary stood up, looked at Arthur and then back at Rupert and his mother.

"You mean—?" Mary shouted and then stopped.

"We mean that he's not your child. He is a cripple and he would be much better looked after in a home; that's right, Rupert, isn't it?" Christiana said bluntly.

She turned to her son, who hesitated and fiddled with the buttons on his waistcoat.

"Yes," Rupert said finally.

Mary put her hand to her forehead, pursed her lips and looked to the ceiling, anger welling up inside her. She nodded and looked down at Christiana and Rupert.

"I gave my word to that boy's mother," she said tremulously, pointing at Arthur. "That I would look after him for the rest of my life, and look after him I will. If he's not welcome here then neither am I; nothing in the world could separate me from him."

She stopped, trying to contain her hurt, her disappointment. She eyed Rupert angrily.

"I find it incredible that you could even think of sending him away from me."

She looked down at her hands and slid the engagement ring from her finger – laying it deliberately on the coffee table.

"You can keep your damn ring," she hissed. "I won't marry you, not ever."
She moved to Arthur.

"Come on, Arthur, we are going," she announced, closing the book he was reading and leading him across the room – Rupert watching helplessly as she went.

Arthur looked back towards the two dumbstruck figures, tears rolling down his cheeks as he hopped out of the room, his bad leg dragging behind him.

Epilogue – The Covert
March - 1961

Someone is walking down the corridor. I can hear them as I stand waiting next to Grandfather by the solid oak door. The footsteps stop and the door swings open to reveal a grey-haired lady wearing a flour-dusted apron. Grandfather takes his trilby off and holds it to his chest, a smile spreading across his face.

"Molly, my dear, how are you? It's been some time," he beams.

"Yes, William," she says simply, a small smile playing on her lips as Grandfather enters and hands her his hat and coat.

"Oo 'ave we got 'ere then?" she says, peering at me.

"Oh, he's Thomas's eldest," says Grandfather. "He's the driver today"

"Pleased to meet you," says Molly with a smile that promises mischief.

I grin back and follow her and Grandfather to the drawing room.

"Mr Dunmore's arrived, Mrs Ladds," announces Molly as we enter.

The room is large – with a big table one end near the bay windows, the walls are nearly all bookshelved from floor to ceiling. In two armchairs flanking the fire sit two grey-haired ladies and at the table, poring over a newspaper, sits a man in a wheelchair; he has a little fair hair but it is very thin and he wears thick glasses.

"Mary my dear, how lovely to see you," says Grandfather, kissing one of the ladies on the cheek, before turning to the other.

"And, Lucy my dear, I didn't realise you would be here as well," he smiles, bending to kiss her too. "And who do we have here, William?" says the lady called Mary. "I haven't seen him before."

"This is Peter," Grandfather says. "He's Thomas's eldest; just learnt to drive so he's the chauffeur."

I smile at the two women and walk towards them to shake their hands. The chap at the table suddenly sits up from reading his newspaper and makes a sort of a grunt that I can't understand.

"Ah, Mr Hurrell," says Grandfather, moving over to the man who is looking at us both curiously. Grandfather points to the newspaper on the table.

"There's not much good news in there," he says with a laugh.

Mr Hurrell grunts again and starts a strange kind of conversation with my grandfather that I can't understand, much as I try to.

"Come and sit down, Peter and tell us about yourself," Mary says, clutching my wrist and showing me to a small stool at her feet. I smile and sit down and begin to tell her about my week at school.

Grandfather comes back after a couple of minutes, sits himself in a chair and enters the conversation. Molly enters soon after with a tray and coffee pot, which Lucy starts to pour out, sniffing as she does.

Mary throws her a sharp glance and makes to say something before obviously thinking better of it.

"I see Arthur is looking at the financial pages, Mary," Grandfather says as Mary takes Arthur a steaming cup of tea.

"Yes, William, he's very clever with his stocks and shares; he's a wealthy man, you know."

I don't know what stocks and shares are, so I continue to half listen to the conversation until Grandfather finally takes a pocket watch from his waistcoat and flicks it open.

"Well, it's time we went, Peter boy," he announces, standing and bidding goodbye to the assembled company. We move into the hall, where Molly is waiting with Grandfather's hat and coat.

"Thank you, Molly," he says with a grin. "It seems such a long time since we were all at school together."

"That it does," says Molly, and there's a hint of sadness in her voice.

Mary and Lucy have followed us into the hall to say goodbye – I turn to follow Grandfather as Mary lightly touches my shoulder and whispers in my ear,

"Peter boy, do you want to go down the end before you leave?"

THE END

If you have enjoyed this book, please consider leaving a review on Amazon and/or Goodreads. Both will accept reviews even if you did not purchase this book from them. Reviews are there to inform readers and they help a book gain visibility in a highly competitive market.

Thank you

A Note from the Author

I wrote Mary Knighton as a work of fiction set in the period from the end of the nineteenth century until about 1930. I trace the life of the protagonist Mary, from her late school years through a failed marriage until her life is determined by the needs of a disabled boy. All the characters are fictitious; however, there is an element of truth in parts of the plot and some of the individuals bear similarities to those I have known in the past, but who are long since deceased. I have made every attempt to portray country life as accurately as possible, including the isolation which goes along with the idyllic rural scene as well as the brutalities on the one hand which contrast with the passions on the other.

Many of the anecdotal stories I include have been related to me by family or friends and have been used to draw a picture of both rural and urban life at that time. The setting is the junction of the counties of Bedfordshire, Northamptonshire and Huntingdonshire and the place names have been left in the work. I also weave into the plot the effects that national events such as the death of Queen Victoria, and the dreadful carnage of The Great War had on people. I have made every attempt to address the reality of the events, for example the letter read out by Mary from George in the trenches is a copy of a real letter to my grandfather and the description of Victoria's funeral was related by him, as he was there.

Mary's story follows a familiar pattern told many times, but the way in which she uses inner strengths to cope with the desperate situations she finds herself in and the mistakes she makes, gives the narrative an insight into her powerful character. In stark contrast, Molly, whose life is intertwined with Mary's, is a loser of this world, who is unable to turn her misfortune into anything, but more of the same. Many around Mary were seduced by her natural charm and beauty including poor Reuben who was killed on the Somme, but Mary never found real love herself except perhaps in dear Arthur to whom she devoted the rest of her life, after rejecting Rupert.

Acknowledgements

The writing of Mary Knighton, which I started on the 2nd November 2009, has been in many ways the easy part of my project, and if it were not for the help of others it would never have got off the ground. One of my enduring disabilities is chronic and incurable dyslexia. I am also the most inaccurate and pedestrian typist who after many years has never learnt where the letters are on the keyboard, which has meant that all my writing is done long hand. Thus I am very indebted to those who got the script from my readable scrawl into the state it is now.

Sophie Herne did the mammoth task of typing it up and correcting the worst of the spelling and punctuation. Henri Merriam took the scissors to the result, and cut out about 40,000 words of repetition and irrelevant plot line. Antonia Phinnemore then proofread the result and corrected the sequence of events and made the character and place names consistent. She was also very helpful in preparing the submissions to agents, which although unsuccessful gave an insight into the publishing world. The final proofread before publication has been done by Julia Gibbs, and the cover design was by Silverwood Books. Lastly a great thank you to Mary Matthews of Three Shires Publishing, who has guided and encouraged me, and her knowledge and advice has been invaluable in the production of the book.

I have also had unpaid help from many friends and family who have read the book in whole or in part and have made valuable comments. These include Mo Brown (my wife), Mike Hirst, Nannette Brown, Rosemary Hallworth, Kathy Henson, Donna MacKenzie and Harry Franks. The original handwritten script was copied in case of loss and I would like to thank Naomi Groom, of VHS Law, who did this for me. The social media and the business details have been organised by James Brown and thanks to him for that.

There are two others I would like to thank; Caroline Mc Arthur, whose comments on a letter I had written to her, initiated my writing career. Finally, and most importantly, the late Peter Smout who taught me English and got me to just scrape through "O" level. As I left the school after "A" levels were complete he came up to say goodbye and said, "I know you are going to university to study agriculture and you will probably become a farmer, but what you really ought to do is to sit down and write a book.".

Contact Details

If you would like to get in touch, you can find me here.
secondchildltd@hotmail.com
www.twitter.com/covingtonsecond
www.facebook.com/trbrownsecondchild/

Lightning Source UK Ltd.
Milton Keynes UK
UKOW08f2233260417
299938UK00003B/464/P